# The Taken Trilogy

# The Taken Trilogy

◆

## Lost and Found
## The Light-Years Beneath My Feet
## The Candle of Distant Earth

◆

## Alan Dean Foster

# Contents

# Lost and Found

For my niece, Veronica Elizabeth Marshall
A shanghaied dog story.

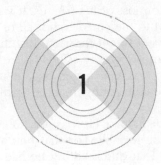

1

Marcus Walker loved Chicago, and Chicago loved him, which is why he was in Bug Jump, California. Well, not in Bug Jump, exactly. As even the locals would admit, one was never actually wholly within Bug Jump. One sort of hovered around its tenuous periphery, much as the peripatetic mosquitoes of midsummer zoned around Cawley Lake, where Marcus had pitched his tent.

One of innumerable splashes of impossible blue that spotted the northern Sierra Nevada like shards of a scattered lapis necklace, Cawley Lake lay at the terminus of a half-hour drive up a road that had been coaxed from reluctant Sierra granite by the judicious application of hard-rock drilling, well-mannered explosives, and much road-crew cursing. The bumps and ruts of the road were hell on Walker's Durango four-wheel drive, but that didn't worry the commodities trader. It wasn't his SUV; it was Hertz's. Slamming up and down the steep grade to and from Bug Jump, the 4X4 accumulated scrapes and dings the way Marcus's forehead collected sunburn.

All in all, he reflected with satisfaction as he heard the SUV complain through another grinding downshift, it had been another very good year for Marcus Walker. Even if he had reached the ripe old age of thirty. Unlike some of his rambunctious yet dismayed colleagues, he did not think it was All Downhill From Here. Having despite several promising opportunities resolutely put off applying for admission to the institution of marriage, he retained certain enviable options that were no longer open to most of his friends. It wasn't, as he repeatedly and patiently explained to the curious, not all of whom were his relatives, that he did not want to get married; just that he was pickier and in less of a hurry than most. Sprung as he was from a home whose parents had split when he was a teenager, he was understandably warier than the average successful young man of committing himself to a similar mistake.

The money he made helped. He was not rich, but given his age and experience, he lived comfortably. For that he could thank hard, hard work and perspicacity. That quick killing he had made in Brazilian OJ concentrate, for example. He gritted his teeth as the SUV was outraged by a pothole, threatening his insurance rider. Among the other traders who worked out of the office, only Estrada had followed the Brazilian weather closely enough to see the possible late frost looming. When it had struck, only the two of them had been properly positioned to deliver the necessary futures at a favorable price to their customers.

Then there was cocoa. Not only had trading in cocoa futures done wonders for his bank account, it had unexpected social benefits as well. Tell a girl who asked what you did for a living that you were a commodities trader and she might shrug, make a beeline for the next bar stool, smile vacuously and change the subject, or tentatively try to find out how well it paid. The usual reaction was for their eyes to glaze over as thickly as the sugar on a Christmas fruitcake.

Telling them you were in *chocolate*, however, fell somewhere between saying that you had just inherited fifty million dollars and that you had a brother who was a wholesale buyer for Tiffany's. Aside from the beguiled expressions such an admission produced, you could smell the concomitant rise in hormone production with one nostril pinched shut.

He chuckled to himself at the various images mention of his vocation engendered among members of both sexes: everything from dashing world-traveling entrepreneur to stultifyingly dull owl-eyed accountant. Nothing he could say ever changed another's perception of his profession.

Though the wooded slopes flanking the narrow, winding road were growing dark, he was not concerned. He'd made the drive from his isolated encampment down into Bug Jump half a dozen times during the past week and felt he knew the sorry excuse for a road pretty well. Returning uphill after dark, he'd travel more slowly. It was just that, while he had enjoyed proving wrong all of his friends who had insisted he wouldn't last more than twenty-four hours in the Sierra Nevada wilderness without running screaming for the nearest Starbucks, he had to admit that he did miss human company. While, based on what he had seen so far, it would be a stretch to so classify some of the local denizens of downtown Bug Jump, there were enough who struck him as being halfway normal for him to look forward to the occasional jaunts into the bucolic mountain village.

Thus far he'd spent five nights of his agreed-upon week in the northern California mountains camping out alone, as promised. With just two more days to go before he drove back to Sacramento to catch his return flight home, he felt he deserved a bit of a break. There was a grocery store in Bug Jump. There was a bank-cum-post office combo. There was a gas station. And so, of course, there was a bar. Bouncing and grinding down the steep slope of half-graded decomposing granite, racing the onset of night, he was not heading for the bank.

The light that appeared in the sky was bright enough to not only draw his attention away from the difficult thoroughfare, but to cause him to stop and temporarily put the big 4X4 in park. It idled at a rumble, pleased at the opportunity to rest, like a male lion contentedly digesting half a dead wildebeest.

Now what the hell is that? he found himself wondering as he rolled down the driver's side window and stuck his head partway out. Could it be a meteorite? Living in Chicago, one didn't see many meteorites. One didn't see many stars, for that matter, and sometimes even the moon was a questionable indistinct splotch behind the clouds. Watching the bright object descend at a steep angle, he was fully aware he had little basis for comparison and small knowledge with which to evaluate what he was seeing.

Within the light, he thought he could make out a slightly oblong shape. That couldn't be right. Falling meteorites were rounded, weren't they? Or cometlike, with a fiery tail? Did they blink in and out like this one as they made their doomed plunge through the atmosphere? It seemed to him that the object was falling too slowly to be a meteorite, but what did he know about representative intra-atmospheric velocities of terminal substellar objects?

Then it was gone, vanished behind the tall trees. He sat there for a long moment, listening. For several minutes there was no sound at all. Then an owl hooted querulously. Burned up completely, whatever it was, he decided. Or hit the ground a long, long ways off. Certainly it hadn't made a sound. Rolling up the window, he put the Durango back in drive and resumed his own less fiery descent. He was thirsty, he was hungry, and if he was real lucky, he mused, he might find someone with whom to strike up a conversation. While he did not think that likely to involve the latest forward projections for pineapple juice concentrate or frozen bacon, he was perfectly willing to talk politics, sports, or anything else. Even in Bug Jump.

Twenty minutes later, the lights of the optimistically self-categorized town appeared below him. Soon he was pulling up outside the single bar-restaurant. A mix of country music and broad-spectrum pop filtered out over the unpaved parking area; the only rap to be found here being on the food. Mother Earth had long since sucked down the original layer of gravel that had once covered the lot. In the absence of rain the uneven, washboarded surface onto which he stepped was as hard as concrete.

It was Friday night, and Bug Jump was jumpin'. Besides his rented Durango, there were more than a dozen other vehicles parked haphazardly around the lot. No cars: only SUVs, pickups, and a couple of sorely used dirt bikes.

Stepping up onto the raised cement sidewalk that flanked the town's only street, he pushed through the outer glass door, walked through the insulated double entryway, and then pushed through the second. His senses were instantly assaulted by a mountain mélange of pumped-up music, loud conversation, raucous laughter, fried food, and pool cues brutalizing orbs of imitation ivory on a felt field of play. Their perfectly round glass eyes as dead and black as those of great white sharks, the cranial components of violently demised ungulates gazed blankly at each other from opposing walls. There was also a bear head, its petrified jaws parted in a rictus of false fury; old metal traps stained with the rust and blood of years and furry critters past; brightly illuminated animated beer advertisements that in a thousand years would no doubt be regarded by awed historians as great works of art; car license plates from other states gnawed through by rust and time; and much other well-traveled detritus.

Though the rapidly falling temperature of the air outside only whispered of approaching autumn, Bunyanesque lengths of amputated oak crackled for attention within the Stygian depths of a corner fireplace fashioned of hand-laid river rock. In a mutually destructive seppuku of air and wood, reflected flames danced off the insides of triple-paned windows that looked out on the parking lot, vehicles, big trees, and mountain slopes beyond.

No one paid him the slightest attention as he sauntered toward the bar. As a trader whose work sometimes took him overseas, he knew how to blend in with the natives. Though he would never be able to pass for a local, after five days up at the lake his flannel shirt, cheap jeans, and hiking boots were suitably soiled.

"Stoli on the rocks," he told the jaded woman behind the bar. She looked, as he had once heard a visiting Texas trader say about another lady, as if she had been rode hard and put up wet. But his drink arrived as fast as one in any fancy drinking establishment in the Loop, and was more honest.

As he sat on his chosen stool and sipped, he contemplated the milling throng with the quiet, self-contained detachment of a visiting anthropologist. There didn't seem to be many other vacationers. Too late in the season, perhaps, what with the local school districts now back in session and the onset of colder weather. It explained why, except for a few locals fishing for end-of-season browns and rainbows, he had much of the lake and the surrounding stolid, slate gray mountains to himself.

Halfway through the Stoli, he started grinning at nothing in particular. Partly it was due to the effects of the iced potato juice, partly to the knowledge that he was going to win the bet with his friends. To a man, and one woman, they had insisted he would be home before the weekend, his tail between his legs—if not gnawed raw by blood-sucking mosquitoes, rabid marmots, and who knew what other horrors the primordial backwoods of California could produce.

Well, they'd underestimated him. Marcus Walker was tougher than any of them suspected. Few knew of his years as an undersized linebacker at the major midwestern university where he had matriculated. Filling holes in the defensive line, he'd sacrificed his body many times. Wildlife didn't frighten him. Isolation didn't psych him. After a couple of days of earnest effort up at the lake, he'd even managed to catch fresh fish for dinner. Without their PDAs, laptops, and cell phones, most of his friends couldn't catch a cold.

And on top of everything else, the woman who materialized next to him filled out her flannel shirt and faded jeans as effectively and impressively as she did the blank space between himself and the next bar stool over. She was his age or a little younger. Having already essentially won his bet with his friends, he promptly made a private bet with himself.

"Jack and water, Jill," she told the bartender. With an effort, Walker forbore from articulating the obvious gambit. Even in backwoods downtown Bug Jump, she'd no doubt heard it before. The opening he did use, when her drink finally arrived, suggested itself as spontaneously as had its inspiration.

Sipping from his short glass while trying his best to ignore the unidentifiable fossilized stain that marred the rim opposite his lips, he opined inquiringly, "Am I the only one who saw the falling star a little while ago?"

She could have frowned, could have eyed him the way locals doubtless did eye atypical bugs in Bug Jump. Having rolled the rhetorical dice, he could not take back the throw; he could only wait to see where and how it would come to rest.

Her eyes widened slightly. "You saw it, too?"

Ah, the Man is still rolling sevens, he thought contentedly. "I'm wondering what it was. When I saw it I thought, maybe a meteor. But it seemed to be coming down awfully slow." He swung toward her on the bar stool.

"I was thinking it was a satellite, or a big piece of one," she replied, showing unexpected sophistication as she picked up her own drink. "If the solar panels didn't burn off right away, they might slow the reentry."

It was not the response he had been expecting. Not that he was disappointed. In his book, when it came to the other gender, education and looks were not necessarily mutually exclusive. He found himself wondering what she did for a living. So he asked.

She smiled responsively enough. Her eyes were the same pale cornflower blue as the shallow parts of Lake Cawley. "Janey Haskell. I work for the satellite TV people. You know: repairs, installs, sales."

That neatly explained the education as well as her knowledge of satellites, falling and otherwise. "Marc Walker. I'm visiting—"

"No kidding," she quipped.

"—from Chicago. I'm in chocolate."

Her eyes lit up. It was expected. Never failed, he mused. Explaining that he was in orange juice concentrates would not have had the same effect.

Despite the fact that he had started on his drink before her, she finished her Jack and water ahead of him. Another seven, he observed happily. He bought her another. When he finished his Stoli, she bought him his next. He was definitely on a roll. They spent the next few hours chatting and laughing and swapping stories and buying each other distilled spirits. When the father of a beard who occupied the bar stool next to him tossed down the remainder of his last shot and lumbered out, she slid onto it with a sensuous squeak of denim against leather. As she did so, her leg bumped up against his. She did not move it away.

If he failed to spend the night in the tent by the lake, he knew, he would lose the bet with his friends. Probing sweet Janey's increasingly moist eyes, he found himself wondering if it might be worth it. His friends wouldn't know, anyway. Early enough in the morning to be convincing, he'd do as he'd done every day since his arrival: switch on his cell phone pickup and send them the usual pictures to prove that he was indeed still where he had promised to be.

Unfortunately, after rolling nothing but consecutive sevens on his pass, snake eyes finally decided to put in an appearance.

The guy's name might even have been Snakeyes. He was short and ugly and looked a lot like something that might have scratched its way out of the dirt behind one of the local ranchettes. In contrast, the two buddies who backed him up were clean-shaven and neatly dressed. At first glance, it escaped Walker as to why such a pair of clean-cut types would even associate with the perambulating lump of soiled goods who seemed to be their leader. Maybe they owed him money, Walker thought. Not that it mattered. The sparks in Shorty Snakeyes's eyes were not reflections of the distant blaze in the corner fireplace.

"You're not from around here, are you, dude?"

Oh, Lord. The slightly inebriated Walker fought down a rising chuckle. Next thing, he'll be asking me to step outside and draw.

He wasn't afraid of the jerk, or his friends. But there were three of them. Not good odds, whether in the city or the country. He wondered if they had just singled him out for entertainment, or if one of them had a specific interest in Janey Haskell.

"The lady and I are having a conversation." While the crowd continued to ignore the looming confrontation, the bartender did not. She was watching them closely. Not closely enough, he knew, to get a cop out here soon enough to put a halt to any real trouble. Besides which, in a violent conflict, any resident gendarme would be more than likely to side with the natives. Even worse than maybe getting beaten up, Walker knew that if he could not get back to his camp in time to make his morning video call, he would lose his bet. And with only two days left to go.

Instead of responding, Snakeyes turned to the increasingly tipsy Haskell. "Beats me, Janey, how you haven't fallen off a roof yet and killed yourself." He indicated one of the two bookending quasi-cowboys. "Rick, how about you drive Janey home?" The big blond nodded.

"Maybe your girlfriend doesn't want to go home just yet." Setting his drink aside, Walker straightened on the bar stool. As always, he was conscious of the fact that his once football-toughened physique continued to give would-be troublemakers pause. Whether that would be sufficient to deter the three intruders remained to be seen.

"She's not my girlfriend," Snakeyes informed him tersely. "She's my sister."

"Even more reason to find out what she wants to do." Walker, sturdily braced by the amount of vodka he had consumed, wasn't about to let himself be intimidated by a brace of mountain bumpkins, even if it meant the possible sacrifice of his nearly won bet with his friends.

"What she wants to do, dude, is keep the doctor's appointment she's got scheduled for tomorrow." He eyed the woman, who by now had to be helped off her bar stool by her erstwhile driver, with unconcealed distaste. "Her test is due back in the morning."

"Doctor's appointment? Test?" Taken aback, Walker struggled for clarification amid the haze that seemed to have settled on his brain. "She sick or something?"

"Or something." Seeing that the visitor was not about to further challenge Haskell's departure, Snakeyes relented a little. "Might be pregnant."

All of the proverbial chips Walker had collected that evening evaporated like the metaphor they were. Neither of the two blonds was the woman's husband. Snakeyes was the woman's brother. Which suggested strongly that the probable daddy of the satellite TV installer's possibly imminent offspring was likely not to be found in the immediate vicinity. Perhaps not even in the great state of California. Clearly, the situation thus implied was not one to make for lasting familial bliss.

Walker found himself longing for the harsh comfort and isolation of the sleeping bag lying in the tent he had set up on the south shore of Cawley Lake.

"Sorrynoharmintended," he blurted hastily as he slid off the stool and whipped out his wallet in one motion. He ended up overtipping the impassive bartender, but there was no way he was going to wait around for his change.

Snakeyes didn't move, but neither did he shift his stance to block

Walker's retreat. He did, however, favor the departing commodities trader with a pithy comment and a withering stare.

"Don't bullshit me, dude. But no harm done—that's for sure."

Out in the chill darkness of the parking lot, the hitherto reliable 4X4 chose that evening to not start. Walker's attention kept shifting frequently back and forth between the glassy rectangle of a door that was the entrance to the bar and the recalcitrant ignition. The entryway remained deserted. When the engine finally turned over, so did his emotions. He backed carefully out of the dirt parking area. All he needed now, he knew, was to back into some local's precious pickup.

Moments later he was safely out on the road. Half a mile up the state highway he swung left onto the gravel track that led up to the lake. After repeated glances into the rearview mirror showed an absence of headlights behind him, he finally relaxed.

Well, it had been a charming if not charmed evening right up until the end. As he put the Durango into four-wheel drive, he realized that he'd actually been lucky. Suppose Snakeyes and the blond brothers hadn't shown up at the bar? Suppose he'd gone home with pretty Janey to check out her installation skills and brother brusque and his buds had come a-knockin' on her front door to remind her of her upcoming date with her favorite OB-GYN dude? Yes, it might easily have been worse.

Instead, he had extricated himself quickly and cleanly from what could have been an exceedingly unpleasant situation. By the time he reached the lake and turned east along its southern shore, he was almost whistling to himself.

As far as he knew, he'd had the whole lake to himself for at least a day. The last campers, a cheerful elderly couple up from Grass Valley, had packed up and trundled out in their aged camper on Tuesday. In contrast to his increasing unease at the lack of human company, after tonight's confrontation he found himself looking forward to a night, and perhaps a following day, of isolation. Just him and the birds, the fish, the flowers, and an occasional grazing deer.

His tent by the lake was undisturbed, the gear stored inside untouched. That was the nice thing about insured rental equipment, he reflected as he braked the 4X4 to a halt, switched off the engine, and hopped out. You could wander off on a hike or a fishing expedition and just leave everything. This wasn't Yosemite or Sequoia. Cawley Lake was pretty out of the way, even for the north-central Sierras. That was why he and his friends had chosen it as the site of their little bet.

The compact propane heater soon had the interior of the dome tent toasty warm while the battery-powered lantern rendered the interior bright enough for him to read from one of the paperbacks he had brought along. Not one to stint when it wasn't necessary, Walker had rented a pop-up shelter large enough to accommodate three adequately and himself in comparative comfort. Having filled up in town on bar snacks, he decided to skip what at that point in time would have been an uncomfortably late supper. After the tension of the near fight, the rented microfiber sleeping bag beckoned enticingly.

He allowed himself an imported chocolate bar (perhaps made with chocolate liquor whose base component he himself had once bid on) and some cold water, then slipped out of his clothes and into the sleeping bag. Reaching up, he switched off the light, then the propane heater. It would get cold in the tent, but not in the bag. Come morning, he would switch the heater on again before emerging. Anyway, the cold didn't really bother him. He was from Chicago.

The territorial night owl began hoo-hooting again, and he wondered at its species. Certainly it was more mellow than the night owls he was used to dealing with back home. Occasionally, something snapped twigs or rustled leaf litter outside the tent. The first couple of nights, the furtive noises had kept him awake. Initial worrisome thoughts of mountain lions and bears gave way to those of coyotes, then beavers, and finally, mice and ground squirrels. Nothing nibbled at his toes. He was not the natural food of the local predators, he reassured himself, and the tent not the kind of burrow they were used to invading in search of prey.

Subsiding adrenaline had kept him alert on the road. Now, as he relaxed, its effects diminished while those of the Russian lemonade grew stronger. Consciousness faded quickly, along with any lingering concerns.

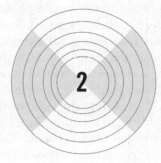

**2**

The crunching woke him. Lying in the sleeping bag, half awake and half asleep, he struggled to revive his muzzy mental faculties. Had he imagined the sound? Had he dreamed it?

*Sss-crunchh*—there it was again. He raised himself up on one elbow, suddenly wide awake. The noise had not been made by a mouse, or by one of the pushy pack rats that haunted his campsite keen on petty theft. It was loud and distinctive and strongly hinted at significant weight being applied to the talkative earth. Bear? he wondered as he sat all the way up inside the tent. Deer?

Or worse—one or more of the transalpine drunken troublemakers who habituated the sole drinking establishment of metropolitan Bug Jump, California?

Parting words of reassurance notwithstanding, maybe just seeing off his besotted gravid sister's temporary gentleman friend hadn't been enough to satisfy Shorty Snakeyes's beleaguered ego. How had they found him? Slipping out of the sleeping bag as noiselessly as possible, Walker dressed in silence, working out of a crouch as he fought with the jeans that kept trying to trip him, staring through the gauzy tent material at every imagined shape and shadow.

It wouldn't have been too hard to track him down. With Cawley Lake as deserted as it was now, close to the end of the season, there were only so many places a visiting camper was likely to pitch a tent. Doubtless a few local fishermen or hikers had seen him up here. In a small town, word about lingering visitors would get around fast.

He felt better when he was fully dressed. Somehow, the thought of getting beaten up while stark naked was far more unsettling. Not that it would matter to his doctor. Or to his friends, who upon his return and reappearance in Chicago would torment him mercilessly for weeks with chorused fusillades of well-meaning "I told you so's."

Fumbling in the dark, he found the fisherman's steel multitool he'd brought with him and unfolded the long blade. Sometimes just a show of resistance would be enough to put off potential assailants. It was one thing to jump some poor tourist caught half asleep in the sack, quite another to confront a fully awake 220-pound opponent holding a knife. If they had guns, however, he would just have to resign himself to taking a beating.

More rustling noises, near the front of the tent this time. Reaching down, Walker picked up the compact high-beam flashlight. Flash them in the eyes, startle 'em, and then stare them down, he thought rapidly. They shouldn't be expecting it.

That the bent-over figure that quickly unzipped the tent flap and thrust its head inside was not expecting to have a bright light shined in its eyes was made immediately clear by its reaction. It let out a startled roar, covered both horizontally flattened eyes with the sucker-studded, flexible flaps that comprised the forward third of its upper appendages, sharply retracted the membranous hearing sensor that protruded from near the top of its conical skull, and jerked back out of the shelter.

Gaping open-mouthed at the unzipped entrance flap, Walker was somehow not reassured by the sudden retreat of the intruder. He did, finally, remember to breathe.

"What in the hell . . . ?"

It was not yet October. Therefore, it was still a while until Halloween. It did not matter. Whatever had pushed the forepart of its outrageous self into his tent had not been in costume. You could tell these things. Yet, it could not be real, either. So, if it was not real, then why was he shaking so badly that the inside of the tent looked as if it was under attack by a flotilla of fireflies?

When his trembling hand finally steadied, so did the flashlight it clutched in a death grip. The firefly armada resolved once again into a single circlet of illumination that waited patiently on the inner lining of the pop-up shelter. Wishing he was at that moment anywhere else, even in Bug Jump's only tavern, Walker extended a tentative hand toward the tent flap, pulled it aside, and peered out through the resultant opening.

The creature whose unprotected eyes had taken the full brunt of his flashlight's LEDs was folded on the ground next to the lakeshore. Standing over it was another of the nocturnal apparitions. This one was holding a device that blinked some sort of dull brown beam rapidly off and on into its companion's face. The standing being was slightly under seven feet tall and, assuming its density was not unlike that of a terrestrial creature, between three and four hundred pounds in weight. Its enormous eyes were perhaps two inches high and six or seven long. Nearly meeting in the center of the sloping face, where a nose ought to have been, they curved almost around to the sides of the tapering head. Moonlight gleaming off the light purple flesh visible outside the creature's attire revealed that its epidermis was pebbled, like a golf ball.

As a partially paralyzed Walker looked on, the creature administering the ophthalmological treatment to its ocularly challenged companion noticed the astounded simian gawking at them from the confines of its small, flexible sanctuary. Raising one boneless arm (or cartilage-stiffened tentacle), it fluttered the end of its sucker flap in Walker's direction and uttered something in a deep, nasal (particularly interesting, given the absence of visible nostrils) voice that sounded like an imploding garbage disposal.

"*Sikrikash galad vume!*"

Having no intention of being vumed, Walker slapped his left front pocket one time to make sure his car keys were still there, burst out of the tent, heart pounding, and raced for the SUV. Despite his mostly sedentary job, as an ex-athlete he had stayed in very good shape, and he covered the intervening gap at impressive speed. The vehicle's comforting bulk beckoned to him like the heated entryway of a downtown shopping mall in mid-January.

*Aliens!* he thought wildly to himself as he ran. Real, honest-to-God, out-of-this-world, from-off-this-planet extraterrestrials. They didn't look like E.T. They weren't slim and short and big-headed, bald, and naked. He was willing to bet, based just on the little he had seen and heard and smelled, that they weren't genital-less, either. They were solid, loud, oversized, and focused. Nothing about them was in the least bit ethereal. And he had (temporarily, he hoped) blinded one.

Confronted with the same situation, he had friends back home who would probably have moseyed over, raised a hand or two, smiled ingenuously, and chirped, "Welcome!" Not Marcus Walker. There were backstreets in Chicago where it would be unwise to do that, too, and instinct told him that it would be unwise to do so now. If these nocturnal visitors wanted company, they could head down the hill to Bug Jump, where their passing resemblance to some of the locals ought to better facilitate any encounter.

Wrenching open the driver's side door, he threw himself into the front seat and behind the wheel, slamming the door shut behind him and thumbing its power lock. Clutching the keys, his right hand stabbed at the ignition as if he were trying to gouge the mechanical life out of the steering column. He cursed silently, having occasionally had a similar problem with women.

A massive shape appeared next to the door and blocked out the moon. Horizontally stretched eyes, like dark rubber bands with pupils, gazed unblinkingly in at him. An actual chill ran down the middle of his back, but he had no energy to spare for shivering.

The key finally found its way into the ignition. As he jammed it forward, the engine roared to life. The lights came on to reveal two more of the flap-armed purplish giants standing directly in front of the vehicle. They wore what looked in the SUV's lights like tight-fitting clothes fashioned of pounded pewter. One raised both upper appendages to shield its ghastly longitudinal eyes against the glare of the headlights. The other pointed something at the 4X4's windshield.

With a groan of protesting metal, the driver's side door was yanked open as if he had never locked it. A long, loose flap of soft, heavy flesh thrust inward—a slick-skinned nightmare. Walker tried to put the SUV in gear. Flap-mounted suckers latched onto his shoulder and left arm. It felt as if he were being simultaneously attacked by a dozen vacuum cleaners. As he fought to put the SUV in reverse, he felt himself being pulled out of the seat. For the first time in his life, he was truly and deeply sorry that he had forgotten to fasten his seat belt. He told himself that there had not been enough time for him to do so, even had he retained the presence of mind to remember to do it.

He did not scream, but he was hyperventilating rapidly, gasping in short, sharp intakes of breath. Uneremoniously, the creature turned and began dragging him across the ground. Staggering to his feet,

Walker gripped the limb that was holding him, using both hands to tug at the part between the sucker-lined flap and the massive body. As if surprised by the resistance, the creature turned. Looking for a vulnerable place to kick and finding nothing recognizable, Walker settled for slamming his right foot into the canyon between the two supportive limbs that likewise terminated in sucker-lined flaps (though unlike the upper appendages, these were sheathed in open-topped plates of what looked like black plastic, as if the owner had been shod rather than shoed). The blow had no effect on his captor.

Should've hung on to the flashlight, he railed at himself.

The creature did, however, respond to this show of physical resistance. The other arm flap swung around and landed hard against the side of Walker's head. It felt as if he'd been hit with a fifty-pound sack of wet oatmeal. A literal sucker punch, it dropped him immediately. Dazed and stunned, he sensed himself being picked up and carried.

The other pair of aliens, including the one he had initially strobed, were waiting by the side of their craft. It was not all that big, Walker reflected through the dull, pounding haze that had fogged his mind. No bigger than an eighteen-wheeler. On the way in, the individual into whose longwise eyes Walker had aimed his flashlight reached out to whack him solidly on the back of his skull, setting his head ringing. So much for the theoretical ethical superiority of star-spanning alien civilizations, he thought weakly.

Then he passed out.

*

When he regained consciousness, the first thing Walker saw was his tent sitting where he had set it up, on a slight rise beside the lake. He was lying on the gravel scree between tent and water. It was midmorning; the mountain air cool and fresh, the pollution-free alpine glow casting every gray boulder and contemplative cloud in sharp relief. The air smelled of pine, spruce, and water clear and clean enough to bottle. In a dark, stunted tree, a raucous Steller's jay was arguing over a nut with a single-minded chipmunk. The rush of white water was a siren call in the distance, where the main feeder stream entered the lake on its far side.

Recollecting aliens, he sat up fast.

It was not a good idea. The action should have been preceded by reasoned thought and a preliminary check of his physical condition. Wincing, he felt gingerly of the side of his face where he had been smacked. It was still sore and probably bruised. Of aliens and alien craft there was no sign, not even depressions in the ground where their vehicle had rested.

Fruit juice would do nothing for his soreness, but it would slake his thirst. Making his way back to the tent, he fumbled with his supplies until he found one of the plastic bottles with the bright label. It was half full of orange liquid. He drained the contents, set the empty neatly aside for transporting down to a recycle bin in Bug Jump, and considered whether or not he had been dreaming. The tenderness in his face and head aside, it was hard to believe that he had imagined everything that had happened to him. It had gone on too long, involved too many elements, was remembered in too much detail to be nothing more than a figment of his imagination. Without straining, he was able to replay the entire encounter in his mind: everything from the initial sounds he had detected outside his tent, to the first alien sticking its god-awful face practically into his own, to his ultimately futile attempts at flight.

What might they have done to him while he had been unconscious? Suddenly frightened, he began checking his body underneath the jeans and shirt, looking for signs of disturbance, entry, exploration. Probing. Isn't that what aliens were supposed to do? He'd never given the slightest credence to such stories when they had been reported in the media. Like the rest of his sensible, sophisticated friends, he'd laughed them off as fit for no more than the front pages of the shock rags that populated the checkout stands at local supermarkets.

Amazing, he thought, how personal experience can bring about such a complete change in one's attitude toward a notorious subject.

Not that anyone would believe him if he ever chose to talk about what had happened to him, here in the California mountains. He had no more intention of relating his incredible encounter to one of his friends than he would of claiming he had suddenly discovered that eating tofu blended with Ben & Jerry's constituted a cure for cancer. The story would have to remain with him, and him alone, forever. Unless he made an attempt to contact others who had experienced similar "contact" with aliens and tried to separate possible truth-tellers from the genuine fruitcakes. He was not sure he wanted to make the effort. He was not sure he wanted to know any more about what had happened to him than he already did.

What had they wanted with him? he wondered as he crawled back out of the tent. If it was just a look, he would have much preferred that they ask first. Offered the choice, he would have been perfectly content to stand still for a painless examination instead of getting whacked around and knocked out. What kind of advanced examination technique was that? At least, he reflected, they hadn't shot him. Not with anything whose consequences he could detect. Emerging from the tent and standing up outside, he felt carefully of his body one more time. Everything seemed to be where it belonged. He was not missing any significant appurtenances. All appeared to be working normally, suggesting that he retained all of his internal organs and their concomitant vital connections.

Had they planted something in him? A transmitter of some kind, perhaps? Or had he simply seen too many bad movies, too much lowest-common-denominator television? How could he begin to impugn motives to aliens, anyway? Whatever they wanted from him, they had obviously obtained to their satisfaction and moved on—to the next camper at the next lake, or to the next wandering sheep herder on the next continent. No doubt they had their aims, their desires, and their own reasons for doing what they did. Doubtless he would never know what those might have been. In this instance, he was more than content to continue to dwell in ignorance.

Raising his arms, he stretched. Despite the violent encounter, he had rested surprisingly well. Having downed the juice, now he was hungry. Initially anxious to pack up and leave, he found that there was no reason to do so. To all outward and inward appearances, it did not appear that he was going to require medical attention. What had happened, had happened. It was over and done with. There was no reason to rush his departure. Besides, another two days at the lake would see him returning to Chicago in triumph, to collect on his bet.

Having survived the astonishing encounter, he found that he felt remarkably well. Exhilarated, even. Such an achievement demanded something of a celebration. In lieu of the usual breakfast bars, he would break out the camp stove and make pancakes. A bit of a project, especially for a city boy like himself, but it was not as if he had to hurry to make a four o'clock appointment. Turning, he prepared to reenter the tent.

The alien that was gazing back at him might have been one of those who had participated in his capture the night before. Or it might have been a completely new individual. In fact, as a stunned Walker gaped, it seemed to him that it must be a different entity because it was noticeably shorter than the three he had confronted previously: no more than six-foot-six or -seven. It had the same wraparound eyes, the same tapering skull, the same sucker-lined upper and lower limb flaps. Its garb was different, however. Looser and paler, as if its owner were clad in affectionate smoke. It stood gazing at him for another moment, then rotated on its two black-shod under-limbs and lumbered away.

Behind it, mountains were missing. So were trees, and his 4X4, and the dirt trail at whose terminus the SUV had been parked. Also blue sky, clouds, and sunlight. In their place was a high, dreary wall of unknown material studded with unrecognizable protuberances and tubes that resembled more than anything else the skin of some dead, bloated, diseased cetacean. Not everything was the same monotonous, dull hue. Some of the projections were dark brown, others a jaundiced yellow. Here and there, hieroglyphs in neon navy blue or carmine floated above specific locations on the wall like photonic barnacles. It looked like a great, hollowed-out, tubular whale.

It was a colorful hell, in a sickly sort of way, a badly shaken Walker decided.

Trembling, he leaned slightly on one of the flexible tent poles for support. It felt real and familiar in his grasp, white and cool and plasticky. He inhaled deeply, desperately. The air was still sweet. When he kicked lightly at the ground underfoot, gravel rattled. In the trees off to his right, the jay and the chipmunk had resolved their differences and gone their separate ways. All seemed well, and healthy, and normal.

Except for one corner of reality that had gone missing.

A window into his world, he thought. They've somehow opened a window into the world that enabled them to look in on him. Unconsciously, he found himself backing up until a cold damp began to chill his ankles. Looking down, he saw that he had retreated all the way into the lake shallows. Stepping out of the water, he turned to look across the glistening expanse to the far shore and the slope of the snow-crowned mountain that towered above it. The longer he looked, the less sure he was of its reality. There was a hint of curious foreshortening, of a fakery of space, that whispered of someone, or something, playing hide-the-slipper with his optic nerves.

Setting out determinedly, he headed for the dirt track where his 4X4 had been parked. If they had removed it, what else of his had they tampered with? No matter. If necessary, he could walk into Bug Jump. It was all downhill from the lake. Let them track and follow him with their window, if that was what they wanted. Maybe they had taken his SUV in order to study its primitive mechanical schematics.

On the other side of the road, he got a shock. One that was literal as well as mental. The slight electric charge caused him to draw back in surprise. Tentatively, he reached out. His nerves were jarred again; slightly more forcefully this time. Beyond the invisible barrier, the road seemed to stretch out tantalizingly toward nearby forest. But no matter how high he reached or how low he crouched, he could not advance beyond the spot marked by the unseen electrical field.

It was the same no matter which direction he, with an increasing sense of panic and urgency, took. North or south, left or right, after traversing forty feet of dirt and gravel, he inevitably encountered a similar restraining electric charge. Despite the cold, he stripped off his clothes and waded out into the lake. Sure enough, after walking, wading, and eventually swimming some forty feet away from shore, he found himself driven back by the all-encircling, invisible field. Lost in mounting fear, he had neglected to consider what might happen to him if he made contact with a strong electrical field while simultaneously immersed in water. But it did not matter. The water did not lethally amplify the effects of the field. Even though he was submerged up to his neck in the little corner of lake, the jolt to his nervous system was no greater than what he had experienced while standing on dry land.

Swimming back, he staggered out of the icy water and returned to the tent to get a towel. Emerging while drying himself, he discovered that where previously there had been one, there were now two of the aliens standing in the corridor and staring at him. He was not sure whether he wanted to scream or cry.

Forgetting his nakedness, still wiping at himself with the towel, he walked around the tent to confront them.

"Goddammit, who are you? What have you done to me? Where is this place?"

The last thing he expected was an answer.

The slightly larger of the pair, who like its companion professed utter disinterest in Walker's nakedness, opened its slit of a mouth. Within, something ghostly white wriggled unpleasantly.

"Long journey," it gargled. "Behave."

Then it turned and clumped away, followed by its companion.

"Wait!" Attempting to follow them, Walker discovered he could see a short distance down the corridor, or tunnel, or whatever it was through which they were striding. It curved darkly to the left, still dense with pseudo-organic protrusions and swellings. To his immediate left and right he had a glimpse of daylight of differing intensity that emanated from unseen sources. Then he came again into contact with something invisible and biting. It was a more powerful shock than any he had felt thus far. Nerves jangling, he staggered back, holding his right wrist as he tried to shake the pins and needles from his hand.

" 'Long journey,' " the creature had said. How he had understood the alien, Walker did not know. Even as he'd heard the sounds, he was aware that the entity was not speaking and he was not hearing English. But he had understood. A journey implied they were all going somewhere together. Journey. His insides went cold and dull, as if he had suddenly become a hollow shell, devoid of any feeling.

The aliens had not opened a window into his reality. They had transplanted a portion of his reality into theirs. Familiar surroundings. It would not do to stick him in a barren cage, or a box. They intended to keep him comfortable—for what purpose he could not imagine and could not envision. Long journey. To where? And with what at its end? It was clear now what had happened to him. He had been abducted— along with his tent, his gear, a minuscule portion of Cawley Lake, and projections or holograms or fake foreshortened representations of everything that surrounded same.

Shaking, he returned to the tent. A check of his cell phone produced nothing—not static, not even a carrier wave. Talk about your long distance. Marcus Walker, phone home. He started to shake.

This won't do you any good, he told himself firmly. Get a hold of yourself—or they're liable to.

He stayed there for a long time, until fake afternoon overtook the fake morning. Only when his legs began to cramp did he feel he had no choice but to step outside.

Nothing had changed except for the position of the sham sun in the fraudulent sky. The corridor beyond his cell, or cage, or whatever it was, was empty. No aliens were to be seen staring back at him, an absence for which he was unaccountably grateful. Not even a little bit of what had happened to him so far could be accounted a hallucination.

He dressed. And having dressed, prepared to make pancakes. Anything to take his mind off what had happened to him. Besides, he doubted that his captors would look kindly, or indifferently, on a hunger strike by a subject they had gone to some trouble to acquire, and he did not want to imagine what methods they might employ to counteract such a demonstration of resistance.

All went well until he tried to fire up the portable propane stove. The self-igniting flame refused to light. Nor would any of the matches he took from his emergency kit work. Snapping them against the striker on the box failed to generate so much as an encouraging spark.

It made sense, he realized when he finally finished cursing and complaining. No matter how advanced, no matter how superior an alien technology, allowing for the presence of uncontrolled open flame was a luxury or a danger that could not be permitted. How the aliens managed to suppress the process of combustion in his stove, let alone a match, he did not know. Finding some satisfaction in private grumbling, he reluctantly put the pancake mix and cooking equipment back inside the tent and settled for opening a box of crackers. This modest nutrition he prepared to supplement with a can of garlic-flavored Cheez Whiz, wondering as he did so if the aliens would permit the can to operate under pressure, or if their life support system would find it as objectionable as it did open flame.

As he prepared to squeeze pasteurized-process cheese food onto a waiting wheat thin, a hole about a yard in diameter appeared in the ground in front of him. Mesmerized, he stared at the dark, perfectly round opening where seconds before there had been solid gravel and grit. As he watched, the missing circle of surface smoothly and soundlessly returned from unseen depths. Atop it was a flat sheet of thin yellow material on which sat two neat piles of paperback-sized bricks; one plain brown, the other white mottled with several shades of green. There was also a two-foot-tall cylinder of blue metal, open at the top. Color-coded, he wondered? Or were the tints just coincidental.

Unsure if he was interpreting the offering correctly, and wondering how and with what they were watching him, he squirted some of the Cheez Whiz onto the cracker. In response, the round platform descended several inches, then rose back up again, a little more rapidly this time. Reluctant to respond, he was also disinclined to get zapped for refusing to do so. Whatever was on the yellow sheet, he decided, it could not be a whole lot worse than Cheez Whiz, especially to a Chicagoan used to real food.

Setting his erstwhile lunch aside, he crawled forward to study the presentation more closely. While none of it looked particularly appetizing, neither did the bricks drip alien mucus or quiver like gelatin. Purely on aesthetics, he decided to try one of the mildly attractive dappled white bricks first. Slipping one end into his mouth, he bit down cautiously. While the consistency was disagreeably rubbery, the taste was not unpleasant: something like congealed beef broth, and not too salty. In contrast, the brown brick was definitely vegan material. If the victuals were color-coded, he reflected, they had been concocted according to a cipher that did not correspond to human analogs. As for the cylinder, insofar as he could determine, it contained nothing more than cold water. It might also be heavily drugged, he realized, but that seemed unlikely. His captors had no need to resort to such subterfuges. They had already shown that they could put him under any time they wished.

We must keep the specimen alive and healthy, he mused gloomily. No matter. He saw no reason not to eat. And there was Cheez Whiz for dessert.

Nothing appeared in the corridor to study the human eating. He was sure they were watching, monitoring him anyway. Given their manifest technological sophistication, it would be silly of them not to. Since there was nothing he could do about it, he decided to try not to think about it.

There were more of the food bricks than he could eat. Not knowing how or when he might be fed again, he did his best to try and finish it all. After a while, the camouflaged delivery platform sank back down out of sight, only to reappear swiftly minus the tray/plate and once more covered with gravel to match its surface surroundings. He wondered where the disappearing alien dumbwaiter went, what lay behind it, how his food was prepared, who or what decided it was edible for him, and finally came to the conclusion it was much too soon to try to figure it all out.

For the rest of the afternoon he wandered around his enclosure (as he had come to think of it), exploring its limits while checking for possible gaps in the system of electrical fields that hemmed him in. After all, just because he was a captive did not necessarily mean he had been taken off Earth. The aliens might still be on the ground somewhere, or have a facility hidden high in the Himalayas, or (less promisingly for one afflicted with thoughts of escape) deep under the sea.

Maybe they just wanted to chat, he told himself as he sat in front of his tent and watched the remarkably realistic counterfeit sun set behind the illusion of distant mountains. Although no one had come to try to talk to him yet. And sociable conversationalists did not go around kidnapping those with whom they wished to converse. He was trying to put the best possible spin on his situation, and it wasn't easy.

Astonishing himself, he managed not only to sleep, but to sleep well. Waking was momentarily disorienting until he remembered where he was and what had happened to him. Emerging from his tent, he saw the same bogus Steller's jay arguing with the same dyspeptic chipmunk over the same illusory nut. That, he decided groggily, was going to get old real fast. He giggled. He would have to have a serious chat with the administrator in charge of prisoner programming.

The giggle made him nervous and uncomfortable, and he broke it off fast. No doubt surrendering his sanity would provide his captors with additional entertainment. It might also make them question the health of their captive. Since the prospect of undergoing a physical checkup by giant, purple, pebble-skinned aliens wielding unfamiliar instruments was less than appealing, he made an effort to appear as normal as possible.

Walking down to the splinter of transplanted lake, he washed his face in the cold, clear water. That helped, a little. As he returned to his tent, he saw two of the aliens watching him from the corridor that formed the fourth side of his more or less square enclosure. He could not tell from looking at them, or at their variable attire, if they were two he had seen before.

Entering the tent, he dressed quickly, perfunctorily. When he reemerged, they were still there—watching, unmoving. After a moment's hesitation, he headed deliberately toward them, halting just short of the restraining electrical field whose location he remembered from his encounter with it the previous day.

The wraparound horizontal eyes that peered back at him were unblinking. He could not plausibly call them cold. He did not know enough about his captors to ascribe emotions to appearances. But neither did those penetrating, unvarying alien stares fill him with warmth.

"Hi." No reaction. Not even a quiet warning to "behave." The solitary hearing organs atop the conical skulls pulsed hypnotically, like small anemones bobbing in a light current. "Who are you? Why have you taken me? Where are we? Are we still on Earth—on my world? Are we moving?"

Since he had been able to understand them yesterday it stood to reason that they should be able to understand him. He had no way of knowing because they did not respond. After another minute of staring, both turned and trundled off silently down the corridor, moving in the same direction that others of their kind had taken yesterday. In place of the black plastic he had noticed previously, the flaps on their feet, he observed, were now encased in what looked like oversized dark socks. These made heavy shush-shushing sounds as their owners lumbered along, their massive bodies swinging slightly from side to side with each step. In the midst of his rising frustration and anger, he noted that he could hear clearly every sound beyond the restraining field. That suggested that air moved freely between his enclosure and the inaccessible corridor. Despite their radically different body types, it also strongly hinted that commodities traders from Chicago and purple aliens from Who Knew Where survived on the same ether juice.

He advanced as far forward as he could without getting shocked. Peering down the gradual curve of the corridor, he jumped up and down while waving both arms wildly over his head. "Hey! Hey, talk to me! At least tell me what's going on! *Say something*, dammit!"

Neither his importuning anger nor the gestures with which he accompanied it sufficed to induce the departing aliens to respond or to return. He was alone again.

Days passed. From time to time, aliens would arrive to observe him. He learned to recognize several. After a while, and their continued refusal to communicate with him, he took to sulking within his tent. That produced a measurable reaction, and not a good one. For twenty-four hours, no food bricks or water emerged from beneath the surface of his fake lakeshore. He was reduced to surviving on his limited stock of energy bars and canned food. Water was no problem, thanks to the ever-replenishing section of lake. But he did not doubt for a second that it could also be taken away as effortlessly as the food bricks had been denied. The lesson was unmistakable. Better to play the game, even though it infuriated him to have to perform like an animal in a zoo.

Animal in a zoo. That was not a pretty thought. Unfortunately, it was not one he could reasonably rule out. Not until and unless one of the aliens chose to speak to him and inform him of their purpose in taking him from his home. No, not his home, he corrected himself. They had removed him from his environment of the moment, which happened to be a tent on the shore of a Sierra Nevada lake. That was the habitat they had reproduced for his living quarters. Ruefully, he regretted that they had not abducted him from, and duplicated the surroundings of, say, a suite at the Four Seasons.

This went on for two weeks and continued into a third, by which time his anger had given way to melancholy and despair. He was alone, his fate unknown, his prospects unpromising. One night, ignoring the fact that he was doubtless subject to round-the-clock observation, he slipped out of the tent and made a mad dash for the corridor. The electrical field that circumscribed his habitat, he discovered, grew more intense the farther one penetrated into it. In addition to momentarily paralyzing him, it slammed him back to the ground inside his enclosure. That was the one and only time he tried to run through the barrier. Careful exploration had already shown it to completely surround him, from the bottom of the piece of lake to the highest point he could reach by jumping or climbing. He could not dig under it, leap over it, or run through it.

And in addition to everything else, the short-lived attempt at flight cost him another day's rations.

Imitation sun shining, bogus birds singing, fake fish jumping, one fine false afternoon found him sitting and sobbing uncontrollably behind the tent. He knew he probably shouldn't be doing it. Observing, taking notes, doing whatever it was that they did in regard to his circumstances, the aliens might decide he was ill and move to try to "cure" him. But all they did was stand in the corridor and watch, as they did several times each day. In fact, there were noticeably fewer daily visits. Were they growing bored with him? Was he proving to be insufficiently entertaining?

"You lousy, rotten, purple bastards!" Eyes red from sobbing, he turned from where he was sitting to rail at the pair who were currently studying him. "Enough already! I'm sick of this! I want to go home!"

He found himself thinking of his friends. Of Charlene, who always had a welcoming smile for him when he arrived at the office. Of Early Hawthorne, who while as somber and staid in appearance as an undertaker, was never without a new risqué joke to tell. Of Tyrone "Ty one on" Davis, with whom he would argue the merits of the current Bears and Bulls rosters during frenetic, hastily gobbled midday meals in one of the three restaurants located on the same block as their offices.

Initially concerned when he failed to return to work, they would then have become fearful, then frantic, and finally resigned. By now they were all probably certain that he was dead. Stumbled off a mountain trail into some impenetrable ravine, his twisted and broken remains devoured by scavengers. That was what they would think, and who could blame them? Thank God he wasn't married. Thank God he had no children. His mother had died of cancer several years ago, but his father was still alive, healthy and remarried. Thoughts of how the old man would react to the news of his only son's disappearance and probable demise set him to sobbing all over again.

When he finally emerged from his extended lament, exhausted and unable to cry any more, he saw that the aliens had departed. Good. Damn good. Futile as he knew the gesture would be, and likely as well to result in the withholding of another day's food bricks, or worse, he had determined to try throwing in their patronizing direction a few of the biggest rocks he could find. Though defense had been his position of choice on the teams he had played on, he had a good throwing arm. Maybe bouncing some fist-sized rocks off a few of those pointy heads would provoke some sort of reaction. Far sooner than expected, he was approaching the point where he no longer much cared what that might consist of.

Straightening from picking up another good throwing stone to add to his growing collection, he happened to look up and off to his right.

What he saw made him drop the couple of rocks he had already accumulated.

The wonderfully convincing lakeshore and distant mountains that had filled that portion of his enclosure had vanished. In their place was, incongruously, a slice of what appeared to be an urban alley. Not a very clean or prosperous one, either. Garbage cans, some vertical and some not, shared space with high dilapidated fences of concrete block and wood slat. Graffiti covered both. Telephone and power poles with lines leading nowhere lined one side of the alley. Like a dead rhino, the rusted and scavenged-out hulk of a thirty-year-old Cadillac dominated the classically urban scene.

Captivated, he rose and moved toward it. Noting the spot on the ground where the restraining field normally flowed, he halted. Extending a cautious hand, he reached out toward the nearest piece of wooden fence that now magically adjoined his own enclosure. Nothing shocked him; nothing stopped him. Here, and for now, the field had been deactivated. The fence felt real beneath his fingers: old, weathered wood, full of splinters and bent nails. There was more graffiti, crude and challenging, far from the spray-paint chic favored by the bored and self-indulgent New York arts intelligentsia. He recognized but could not interpret the gang code.

In the depths of the dead Cadillac, something moved. Walker hesitated, wanting to rush forward, to embrace whomever it was who might also have been abducted along with him. Natural caution held him back. A glance to his right showed that the corridor was still empty. But they had to be watching, or at least recording what was happening. Of one thing he was certain: this section of restraining field had not been deactivated accidentally. Therefore this imminent encounter had been planned. An experiment of some sort, he decided bitterly. Or perhaps, just perhaps, a reaction to his extended crying jag and visible depression.

A shape began to emerge from the rusting skeletal hulk of the decrepit luxury car. Let it be a homeless woman, he entreated silently. Someone with whom to share his isolation and misery. Someone to talk to besides unresponsive aliens. Even a hobo, even a drug addict sleeping it off. Anyone, someone!

Then he saw that the shape was not human.

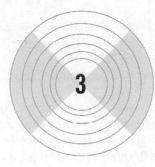

**3**

He did not burst out crying at the apparent disappointment. Neither did he take flight, wide-eyed and afraid. Instead, he just stood and stared as the solitary inhabitant of the car wreck nonchalantly ambled toward him. It had two eyes, like him. It had two ears, like him. It had hair, more than him. It had a tail, not like him, and it advanced at a comfortable trot on all fours.

The dog was a mutt, a forty-pound lump of canine insouciance that looked as if it had been sired by a drunken sea lion who had copulated with an industrial-sized bale of steel wool. Fearless and unafraid, the dog came right up to him, tongue lolling to one side, tail wagging, and sat down.

It wasn't a beautiful eighteen-year-old runaway, he reflected ruefully. It wasn't even a strung-out junkie. But it was alive, and homey-familiar, and of Earth. It was company, though not of the sort he had hoped for. Privately, he found himself envying the mutt. Unencumbered by higher powers of cogitation, it might even be enjoying its new surroundings. Or rather, its transplanted familiar surroundings. Just as he, Walker, had been taken whole and intact along with a copy of his immediate environment, so apparently had the pooch. It might wonder why it could not stray beyond a certain line without being shocked, but doubtless its confusion and bewilderment were mitigated by a steady supply of food and water. Walker wondered what its food bricks looked like, and if they were in fact all that very different from those that were provided to him.

"Well, here we are," he muttered aloud as he bent over to pat the dog on the top of its woolly head. "Two terrestrial mammals cast adrift on a sea of alien indifference."

"Don't mix metaphors with me, bud. This isn't the time or the place for it."

He froze. The words were not an auditory illusion. He had seen the dog's mouth move, had heard the sounds spoken. Which meant the canine shape he was staring down at could not be a real dog. It was an alien invention, perhaps designed and fabricated in some unimaginable alien workshop to ease his loneliness and mitigate his melancholy.

The dog spoke again. "Why did you stop petting me? I haven't had anybody pet me in days." Retracting its tongue and turning, the fuzzy head nodded in the direction of the corridor. "The Vilenjji won't pet me. I've asked them to, but they just give back with that flat, fish-eyed stare of theirs." The tongue reemerged again as its owner panted softly. "Wish they'd take me for a walk once in a while, though. I get tired of hanging around the alley." Peering past Walker, who had suddenly turned into an unmoving poster boy for a life modeling class, the dog chirped excitedly, "Hey, you've got a pond!" Uttering a single, sharp bark, he bounded past the gaping commodities trader.

"Wait—wait a minute!" Awakening from his trance, Walker rushed after the dog.

Not wanting to get wet, or do anything else until he understood better what was happening, he was reduced to standing and calling from the shore while the dog swam and played in the portion of lake. Only when he'd had enough did the mutt dog-paddle out, trot onto shore, and shake himself dry. Absently, Walker wondered if the watching aliens were recording this, too, and whether they were discussing animatedly among themselves the dog's built-in means of shedding water from its fur.

Sitting down, the mutt began cleaning himself. In between methodical, energetic licks, he squinted up at the bewildered human whose enclosure he was presently sharing.

"I'm from Chicago. Illinois." When a dazed Walker still hesitated to reply, the dog prompted, "You?"

"The same. Chi—Chicago."

"Hey, we're neighbors! Whaddya know? Well, a big woof to that. What's your name?"

Walker swallowed hard and sat down on a convenient rock. "Marcus Walker. Everybody calls me Marc. And you—yours?"

Refreshed from its brief swim the dog pushed its forelegs out, stretched, and crossed its paws. " 'Dumb mutt' is one. I often answer to 'Get out of there!' 'Shithead' is probably the most common."

Still tense inside, Walker found himself warming to the animal. Despite its unnatural ability to converse, it did not act like something that was the cold, calculated product of an alien manufactory. Both its sense of humor and its kinked hair reminded him of an old friend he hadn't seen in years, a crazy defensive tackle on his university team. "I can't call you that. How about George?"

" 'George.' " The dog considered the suggestion carefully, the heavy brow crinkling in thought. Then it nodded, ears like kitchen scouring pads flopping against the sides of its head. "Beats 'shithead.' George it is. You're no sweet-smelling bitch, Marc, but it'll be nice to have a companion for a change, someone from home to talk to."

Walker started to grin. "I was thinking the same thing." Then his eyes, and his thoughts, turned again to the still-empty corridor. "You said that the 'Vilenjji' wouldn't pet you. Those are my—our—captors?"

Newly anointed "George" nodded. "Snooty bastards, aren't they? As soon spit on you as talk to you—though I don't know if they have any spit. Leastwise, I've never seen one salivate. Hard enough to get an idea of what all their externals do without trying to visualize the functions of their insides."

Walker nodded knowingly, then asked the question he had to ask. "You're not some kind of alien plant, are you? Something these Vilenjji have cooked up to get me to act differently?"

"Funny," George replied, "I was wondering the same thing about you. No, I'm not some silly stupid alien fabrication." His hindquarters came up. "Want to sniff my butt?"

"Uh, no thanks, George. I'm going to take your word for it that you are what you say you are." He scrunched down a little tighter on his chosen chunk of granite. "And you keep your nose to yourself."

"Will do, Marc. As best as I can. You being human and olfactorily challenged and all, I bet you haven't even noticed what these lumps who snatched us smell like."

"No, not really, I haven't."

Edging closer on its belly, the dog looked around and whispered conspiratorially, "Mothballs. They smell like old, thrown-away mothballs."

Walker shared a smile with the mutt. "Not meaning to insult you or anything, George, but it's been my experience generally that dogs, even those from Chicago, don't talk. Not English, anyway."

"We don't generally speak Vilenj, either," the unoffended George replied. One forefoot rose to dig meaningfully several times at one ear before the dog looked up again. "Implants. One for each internal auricular setup containing, as I understand it, some kind of universal translation node. Soft-wired right into the brain. So you can understand pretty much anything you hear. Every sentient here has them. Even the Vilenjji. Plus, I got a brain boost. Something to do with stimulating and multiplying cerebral folds. All I know is that things that always seemed muddled to me now seem obvious."

"You're very lucky," Walker commented.

Gazing back at him, the dog cocked its head sideways. "Am I? It wasn't a damn Christmas present, you know. They do it so they can talk to you, and so you can talk back. It was done to facilitate communication between captive and captor, between dog and Vilenjji. After it was all done and healed up, given the meager amount of talking they do, I wondered why they bothered. So I asked. They told me they were curious. Not as to why a race of subsentient but semi-intelligent creatures choose to exist in such a subservient relationship with a slightly higher order of being, but as to why we seem to enjoy it so much."

One of the great unanswered questions, Walker mused. "What did you tell them?"

Raising a hind leg, George began to scratch furiously behind his left ear. "I told them that while I couldn't speak for all dogs, in my case it was just because I happen to like humans. Actually, I think that's pretty universal, dogwise. Besides, I told 'em, who says it's a subservient relationship? Not all, but many of us get a free place to live, free food, free medical care, and stuff to play with. Humans have to work their butts off all the time for any of that. All we have to do is lick the occasional face and whine piteously. You tell me who has the better deal."

"What'd they say to that?"

George shrugged, dogwise. "They said a slave isn't a slave unless it possesses the intellectual wherewithal to comprehend the condition of slavery. I told them to stuff it down their masticatory orifices."

Walker shifted on his stone. The corridor remained empty. "If you don't mind my saying so, you have an awfully well-developed vocabulary."

George put one paw to the side of his nose. "Like I said: knowledge boost. I'd give it all back if I could. Talking is hard work. Thinking is harder. I'd rather be chasing cats. Wouldn't you rather be chasing a football?"

The commodities trader looked startled. "How did you know I played football?"

"Didn't. Lucky guess. You're in better shape than most humans your age."

"Thanks." Walker was quietly relieved. It was difficult enough to get used to the idea of a talking dog. He was not sure he could handle one that could also read minds. "You look pretty good yourself."

"Clean living," George replied. "Plenty of cat chasing. Actually, I quite like kitties. But tradition is tradition, you know."

Walker nodded sagely. "Isn't it going to be tough on you when we get out of here? Being so much smarter than the average dog, I mean?" He repressed the urge to pat the woolly head reassuringly.

George snapped idly at an invisible fly. "What makes you think we're going to get out of here?"

That kept Walker quiet for a while. His silence did not seem to trouble George, who was content to rest his head on his forepaws and lie quietly in the artificial sun. Eventually the trader stood, studied their surroundings. The barrier between his mountain lake environment and that of the dog's relocated urban surroundings was still unbarred. The realization that it might be closed off again at any time, at a whim of their captors, and that he might be separated from his garrulous new four-legged friend, left him unexpectedly queasy. He chose not to address the phlegmatic pooch's terse observation directly.

"Didn't I hear you say something about them, these Vilenjji, taking you for walks?"

Lifting his head from his paws, George nodded. "I keep asking them, and I keep getting turned down. Not that they have to worry about it. There's nowhere to run to. Sometimes one or two of them will pay a visit to my cage."

"Enclosure, you mean." Walker had no grounds for correcting the dog, other than psychological. It was easier to think of himself as being kept in an enclosure than a cage. "They come in?"

"Sure. They know I'm not going to hurt them. I mean, I could bite. There's nothing wrong with my teeth. But have you noticed the size of these mutes? What good would it do, ultimately, to take a chunk out of a leg flap?"

"You'd get some honest satisfaction out of it," Walker countered heartily, feeling a lot like taking a bite out of a Vilenjji himself.

George snorted softly. "Then *you* nip one of them. Me, I'd rather keep getting my food bricks."

Walker thought back to the days when he had not been fed, remembering the hollow feeling that by afternoon had developed in the pit of his stomach. The dog was right. If he was somehow going to get through this, he would have to alter his behavior to match his circumstances. This was not a play-off game. No running down an opponent here. He would have to use his brains. Like George.

But he knew he would draw the line at licking a Vilenjji's face, or asking to be petted.

"What else have you seen while you've been here?" He gestured at their immediate surroundings. "This is all I've been allowed to access."

"Well, for one thing, there are a lot more enclosures like yours and mine. Also some that are smaller, some that are substantially larger."

"You mean, like for elephants and things?"

" 'Things' is more like it. I haven't been on the ship for that long, but as near as I can tell, you and I are the only captives from Earth. All the others are from . . . somewhere else." He eyed Walker evenly. "As soon as they think you're ready to handle it, at regular intervals they'll drop the innermost part of your enclosure. The electrical field as well as the hologram, or whatever it is." He nodded in the direction of the corridor. "The rest of the ship is naturally off limits. I suspect that letting you and I get together is a prelude to introducing you to the rest of the gang."

Every time Walker thought he was getting a mental handle on his situation, new circumstances kept cropping up to dump him on his mental butt all over again. " 'Rest of the gang'?"

"All the other oxygen breathers. They're not a bad bunch, I suppose. You meet worse in city alleys. Our laugh-a-minute captors get a kick out of seeing how we all interact, I suppose. Maybe the interactions of different species from different worlds edifies them. Maybe it makes them laugh. I don't know why they do it. If you're that curious, you ask them, when you get the chance. I'm not sure why, but I get the feeling prying into the motivations of the Vilenjji might not be a good idea."

Walker looked around nervously. The enclosure, the cell that he had come to resent so thoroughly, had abruptly taken on all the aspects of a comfortable, familiar home he did not want to lose—even if it was nothing but a carefully crafted illusion.

"How do you know we're on a ship?" he mumbled.

"I asked some of our fellow captives. Must be pretty good size, too, just extrapolating from the enclosures." He lowered his voice. "Listen, Marc. No matter what happens, always stay calm. Keep your head and you'll keep your head, if you know what I mean. Usually, the Vilenjji don't interfere in altercations between captives, no matter what happens. But a couple of days before you got here, a Tripodan from Jerenus IV—"

"What's a Tripodan? Where's Jerenus IV?"

"Shut up and listen to me. The Tripodan, I was told it had caused trouble before. This time, it got into an argument with a Sesu. There are four of them captive here, and they're about as dangerous as pups. But they've got sharp tongues. I mean, sharp verbally. The Tripodan took exception to something one of the Sesu said. Then it took the Sesu apart. The way a human would dismember a fried chicken. I watched, from as far away as I could get, and I know I was whining good and loud the whole time. I was plenty scared, let me tell you, because I had no idea what might happen next.

"What did happen was that a whole squad of Vilenjji showed up and came lurching into the grand enclosure. That's the big central area where all the captives are allowed to mix with one another. I hadn't seen that many of them all in one place before, and I haven't seen that many together again since. They must've been pretty ticked off. The Sesu, I later found out, mate in quartets. Remove any one of the four and you lose breeding capability. No wonder the Vilenjji were upset. They carried these funny-looking, squat little balloonlike guns that spat out some kind of fast-hardening glue. In less than a minute that Tripodan, big and strong as it was, had no more range of motion than the statue I used to piss on in the park back home."

Walker's tone was subdued. "What did they do to it—to the Tripodan?"

"Took it away. Never saw it again." The dog rose, stretched. "Maybe now it's a doorstop in some high-ranking Vilenjji's office. If they have ranks. If they have offices. Me, I've got my standard defense all prepared in case something like that comes after me. I back into a corner and whine my guts out." He eyed the solemn-faced human tellingly. "You ought to try it. Works wonders. Even on aliens."

"I'll keep it in mind." Walker intended nothing of the kind. He hadn't made first string outside linebacker at a major American university by whining in the face of adversity.

Of course, he reminded himself, then he had only been competing against corn-fed 300-pounders from Nebraska and swift tailbacks from the small towns of Texas—not seven-foot-tall aliens who controlled immobilizing electrical fields and paralyzing glue guns. Perhaps under certain circumstances the occasional whine could be countenanced. Like, to preserve his life.

It was getting dark. Walker glanced back at his tent, then toward the invitingly open environment that constituted George's reconstituted urban backstreet. He studied the decaying trash, the torn and tattered cardboard cartons, the rusting ruin of a once-grand automobile, and decided that a change of surroundings could wait. Apparently, the dog had been thinking along the same lines but had come to a different decision.

"Mind if I stay with you tonight, Marc?"

Walker turned toward the corridor. It was still empty, still silent. Still fraught with ominous possibilities better left unconsidered. "Won't you miss your place?"

"My 'place'?" With a twist of his shaggy head, George gestured back the way he had come. "That dump's just where I happened to be hanging out when the Vilenjji picked me up. I'm an orphan, Marc. Lot of us in Chicago." Without waiting for further invitation, he trotted past the commodities trader. "Your place looks clean. I've never been in the mountains. Not much of that in Illinois." Dark, soulful eyes stared up at him. "I can whimper longingly, if it will help, and lick your hand."

Walker had to grin. "I didn't know dogs were capable of sarcasm."

"Are you kidding? We're masters of it. In fact, we're so good at it that you humans don't know when we're having a laugh at your expense. So, what do you say?"

Another glance toward the threatening, dark corridor wherein nightmares dwelled. "What about the Vilenjji? Won't they object to two of their specimens doubling up?"

George shrugged. "Only one way to find out. Nothing we can do about it if they do."

Walker rose from where he had been sitting. With the setting of the "sun," the temperature was starting to cool rapidly. "Actually, I was going to ask you if you'd stay."

The dog spoke while sniffing industriously at the entrance to the tent. "Us terrestrials have to stick together. At least until we find out what the Vilenjji ultimately want with us."

Despite his boredom, his isolation, and his continuing depression, as he walked over to the entrance Walker fervently hoped that day still lay far in the future. "It's a big tent. There's plenty of room. Glad to have the company. Just one thing."

George looked up at him. "I'll go outside to do my thing, if that's what you're wondering. Technically I'm not housebroken, because I've never had a house, but I don't do business where I sleep."

"It's not that." Walker felt slightly uncomfortable, having to put into words a request he had never previously had to articulate. "It's just that, well—do you mind if I pet you once in a while?"

The dog grinned back up at him and replied, in an excellent impersonation of the commodities trader's voice, "Actually, I was going to ask you."

When the hooting of a counterfeit owl woke Walker up in the middle of the night, he found a warm, dark mass pressed tightly up against him. Somehow, the dog had wormed its way into the sleeping bag without waking its principal occupant. Walker's initial reaction was to shove the furry lump out into the tent proper. Instead, he ended up gently raising his left arm and circling it over the warm body, to snug it just a little closer. Deep in sleep, George snuffled once, then lay quiet. The arrangement worked well enough for the rest of the night, except for one time when the dog woke the commodities trader a second time by kicking out with his hind legs. Walker decided to persevere and ignore the kick. He would get used to it.

He'd once had a girlfriend who snored, but never a sleeping partner who kicked.

Perhaps the Vilenjji did not care where George slept, Walker reflected the following morning. More likely, they were pleased to have a new relationship to study. Walker did not care. After weeks of isolation, it was good to have company, and an affable dog was better than nothing. A chatty, talking dog who'd had his IQ boosted was a good deal better.

Their captors must have been pleased. Breakfast brought forth not only the usual food bricks, but a flexible metal bowl full of bite-sized food cubes. Maybe it was the presence of his new compan-ion, but the new food reminded Walker uncomfortably of kibble. It didn't taste like dog food, however. The blue ones tasted like chicken. The pink ones tasted like the blue ones. The yellow, lavender, green, and gold ones all tasted like boiled brussels sprouts, which only proved how little the Vilenjji actually knew about human beings. As if by way of unintentional compensation, two silvery sapphire cubes tasted like fresh banana pudding.

As soon as his palate encountered one of the latter cubes, he made a show of consuming it and its complement as slowly as possible, running his face through the gamut of expressions of ecstasy. Whether his performance would result in more of the silver banana-ish cubes being provided he did not know, but he was determined to try. Although he did not make the connection, what he had done was the human equivalent of George wagging his tail. To top it all off, in addition to the usual cylinder of water, there was a second, smaller one full of some pale gingery liquid. Though it tasted like weak cola, it might as well have been champagne. By the time he had finished eating, Walker felt as if he had consumed the equivalent of a full five-course meal at the best restaurant in New Orleans.

That was when he noticed George looking at him oddly.

"Well, what is it? What's wrong?"

"Nothing's wrong," the dog replied. "Did I say anything was wrong?"

"You've got that grin on your face. I know that expression already."

"How perceptive of you. All right, I'll tell you. But you're not going to like it. I was watching your face while you ate, especially those silver-metallic things. You were begging. You weren't sitting up on your hindquarters holding your paws out in front of you and sticking out your tongue, but you were begging."

Walker looked away. "I was not," he groused.

"Why deny it? As long as you know what you're doing, and why you're doing it, there's no reason to be ashamed. Humans beg all the time. For better jobs, for sexual favors, for the appreciation of their fellows. Is that a higher calling than begging for food? Why do you think you suddenly rated a better spread, anyway?"

Actually, Walker realized, he'd been so busy sampling the new comestibles that he hadn't thought about it. He said as much.

"It's because you're cooperating. You haven't done anything stupid, like try to kill yourself. And you've interacted constructively with me. And vice versa. I got better food, too."

"I did try to break out and jump one of the Vilenjji," he argued, even as he drained the last of the ginger drink from its container.

"That's not stupid: that's expected," George countered unhesitatingly.

"I was going to collect rocks and throw them at the Vilenjji."

The dog's mouth opened and his tongue emerged. He was laughing, Walker saw. "You think any entities smart enough to build something like this ship and travel between the stars a-hunting specimens like me and you aren't bright enough to take steps to protect themselves from the disgruntled? The electrical barriers that restrain us? The deeper you try to penetrate one, the stronger the shock becomes."

"I know that," Walker informed him. "I've tried it."

George nodded. "Everybody does. So did I. We've got one fellow prisoner, doesn't look like much, but she can spit acid. In my book, that trumps throwing rocks as a potential threat. If you could push deep enough into the restraint field, without it first killing you, it would strengthen enough to fry your bones. Same thing would happen to any rocks you threw. Or acid someone spit. The Vilenjji may be big, and ugly, and gruff, but they're not stupid.

"In addition to failing, the attempt would cost you a day's rations, at least. I get the impression that they like their specimens to stay healthy and in one piece. But that doesn't mean they won't mete out punishment if they feel it's deserved. Through withholding food or, in the case of the disappeared Tripodan, something worse."

Seated by the shore of the lake, dangling his bare feet in the cold water, Walker nibbled on the last of the standard food bricks. "So we get rewarded for good behavior, punished for bad. There are no variables?" A twinge of anxious anticipation tickled his mind. "They don't, for example, try to train you? To perform tricks or something?"

George shook his head, rubbed at one eye. "Not so far. Not that I couldn't handle it if they did."

"Of course you could," Walker assured him. "You're a dog."

Eye cleared, George looked up. "And you're a human. Don't try to tell me humans aren't trainable. You have jobs, don't you? Mange, I could train you myself."

"Don't get cocky just because you can talk and reason," Walker advised him. "Humans train dogs. Dogs don't train humans."

"Oh no? What about last night? You were going to kick me out of the sleeping bag, weren't you?"

"I wasn't—I mean, that was my decision to let you stay."

With a woolly shrug, George slid his front legs out in front of him. "Okay. Have it your way."

Nothing else Walker could say or do could induce the mutt to resume the discussion.

**4**

Time passed. Time that Walker was able to track thanks to his watch. Ticking off Central Standard Time, it had no real relevance to his present circumstances. But the mere sight of the digits changing according to what the time was back home helped, in its small chronological way, to mitigate the stress of his captivity.

Then it happened. Without warning, or announcement.

One minute he and George were sitting and watching fake fingerlings swim through the shallows of the transmigrated portion of Cawley Lake. The next, everything beyond the body of water had disappeared. Or rather, had given way.

In place of "distant" mountains and forest there stood an open, rolling meadow. Green sedges fought for space with clusters of what appeared to be rooted macaroni, all dull yellow twists and coils. There were also patches of red weed that was neither true red nor familiar weed, its actual hue shading over significantly into the ultraviolet. Ghost grass. There were trees, some of which entwined to create larger, perfectly geometric forms, while others formed whimsical arches and shelters as they grew.

Roaming over, around, and through the fusion of alien verdure was a Boschian concatenation of beings who looked as if they had stepped whole and entire from the pages of a lost tome by Lewis Carroll. It did not take the edge off their collective consummate weirdness for George to declare that, insofar as he knew, each and every one of the ambulating menagerie was sentient, and at least as intelligent as a dog.

Looking over his shoulder, a momentarily overcome Walker saw his tent standing where he had left it. Beyond lay the empty corridor. To his left were the remnants of the persistent diorama of Sierran mountains and woods. To his right, gravel and lake fragment gave way to George's cozy urban junkyard. Though he knew he ought to be used to it by now, this arbitrary switching on and off of selected quadrants of reality still retained its ability to disconcert.

Leaning over, he whispered to his companion, "Am I correct in assuming that this is the 'grand enclosure' you've been talking about?"

George panted softly. "You would be. Not bad, eh? Of course, I don't know everybody here. Haven't been on board all that long. But I know a few of the guys. And gals. And others." He bounded forward. "Come on: I'll introduce you. No butt sniffing. I learned that right away. Bad protocol."

Walker wanted to tell his friend that he need not worry, because such thoughts had not occurred to him. Even had he been so caninely inclined, he doubted he could have pursued the activity with any exactness, since some of his fellow oxygen breathers were of such outlandish build and construction that it was difficult to know where butt ended and breathing apparatus began.

It seemed equally unlikely that he would be able to converse with any of them, but the individually attuned transplant that Vilenjji manipulators had inserted into his head transmuted virtually all of the intelligently modulated air that was pushed in his direction into words he could understand.

Looking around as the vigorously tail-wagging George led him away from the tent and deep into the far larger enclosure enabled Walker to gain a much better sense of his surroundings. Not only could he see his own personal pen (a term that wasn't much more endearing than cell, he reflected, determining then and there never to use it again) receding behind him, he could make out similarly shaped but far more exotic corrals (that wasn't better either, he decided) nearby. They marched off to the right of his enclosure and to the left of George's. Though he could not quite make out the final boundaries, it appeared as if the smaller enclosures formed a giant ring, with the grand enclosure across which he was presently striding occupying the center. A garland of compartments surrounding a central open area like pearls flattering a diamond. Strain as he might, and certain the every move of every being within the compound was being watched and recorded, he could not pick out a single monitoring lens or similar device. After a few moments, his attention drawn inexorably to the exotic parade of fellow oxygen breathers, he gave up trying.

George had halted before a pair of the most graceful-looking living things Walker had ever seen. Displaying skin that more nearly resembled glazed porcelain, they had flattened heads with large, doelike eyes and downy hearing organs. Disconcertingly, these could retract completely into their platelike central bodies and reemerge elsewhere. Dressed in shimmering sackcloth holed like Swiss cheese, the pliable bodies themselves undulated like peach-colored gelatin. A brace of long cilia fringed the torsos. Like the rest of the creatures' bodies, these too were in constant, hypnotic motion. Only the lower limbs, thicker versions of the raylike cilia, exhibited any kind of stability.

"Greetings of the hour, Pyn and Pryrr. You can call me George now." The dog gestured with his head. "My new companion Marc has gifted me with a new name."

"Geoorrgg—George," the one called Pryrr sang. The tone of voice it employed was natural and unaffected, but it sounded like singing to Walker. "Hello, Maaarrrc—Marc."

"Hello—greetings." Though he excelled at a profession that rewarded the articulate, Walker found himself momentarily tongue-tied. It was not the appearance of the two aliens that challenged his speech: it was their beauty. The splendor of their shimmering skin, of their mesmerizing movements, and their liquid voices.

George was less overawed. "Marc and I are from the same homeworld. So I guess I'm not a solo anymore."

Cilia that caught the light like shards of crystal china rippled rhythmically. "That is a goooddd thing, George." Pyn emphasized pleasure by popping a mutable head through a hole in the front of the flowing garment. "It is good to have the company of another with whooommm one can share memoriess of hooomme." Limpid orbs surveyed the taller human. "You two cannot mate, I thinnnnk."

"Lord, no," Walker blurted. "Different, uh, species. Though George's and mine do have an association that goes back a long way."

"Aaaaahhh," Pryrr sighed—a sound like warm wind rustling tropical palms. "Symbiooootes. Almost as gooooddd."

"Pyn and Pryrr are Aulaanites," George explained helpfully. "They were at sea, in what we would call a cooperating lagoon, rehearsing a presentation for an extended family gathering, when the Vilenjji snatched them. Though they can get around okay on dry land, their compartment is mostly heavy water." Without a farewell, he turned and trotted off. Walker followed. Behind them, the Aulaanites danced in place, cilia describing meaningful streaks of reflective beauty through the accommodating air.

"You told me that the Vilenjji let oxygen breathers interact without constraint. They also let you visit one another's living spaces?"

"So long as nobody makes trouble, yeah." The dog nodded in the direction they were going. "Have a look. More interspecies interactions to study." Slowing, he indicated the small hillock they were approaching. It was covered with something akin to rusted clover that popped and snapped underfoot like fried pork cracklings. "Here's a good place." So saying, he turned a few tight circles before settling himself down in the ground cover.

Wincing at the crunching sounds that resulted, Walker sat down next to him. The single large growth that dominated the hillock resembled a giant multiheaded mushroom with dozens of individual translucent caps. They were delicate enough, Walker saw, that they would have moved up and down in a light breeze. But there was no breeze. Only the distant, unvarying whisper of the unseen recyclers that processed the enclosure's atmosphere.

Spread out before them, several small streams ran downslope to terminate in individual enclosures. In one, Walker thought he could make out harsh light and little growth: some kind of desert environment. In two others, rain appeared to be falling steadily. Highly localized rain.

"You said that the Vilenjji like to study interspecies interactions."

"That's just a guess." Rolling over onto his back, George let his tongue loll lazily out one side of his mouth. With all four paws in the air, he looked almost as relaxed as he did comical. "I haven't been able to find out what the Vilenjji want with us. Of course, I haven't talked to everybody here. There are representatives of dozens of different species, hailing from as many different worlds. If you're interested in asking questions, you can try your luck with any of them." Turning onto his side, he winked at his friend. "Just don't get into any fights. Although from what I've been able to figure out, the Tripodan was the worst of the lot except for one. It's gone, and you don't see much of the other."

Eyeing the perambulating carnival of alien grotesqueries, Walker wondered how to go about approaching even the least off-putting of them.

"Just mosey up and say hi," George advised him. "Nothing ventured, nothing gained. I struck up a conversation with the Aulaanites because I thought they were pretty, and I wanted to tell them so. We've been friends ever since." He sniffed at some bright pink growing thing that was thrusting a spherical head up through the ground cover. "The curiosity turned out to be mutual. Pyn and Pryrr find my appearance, as they put it, 'inconceeeeivably undisciiiiiplined.' "

Leaning back with knees up and palms on the ground, Walker watched something like a miniature elephant crossed with a flock of flamingos amble past in front of them. "I wonder what they thought of me?"

"Ask 'em," George advised. "They're not shy. Very few of the captives are shy. Any that naturally are tend to lose it after spending a few months by themselves alone in their own enclosures."

"Months?" Walker looked down sharply. "Some of these beings have been here for months?"

The dog sneezed, pulled back from the pink pop-up. "That's what I've been told. Among those I've spoken to, a few have been here longer than a year. Divide that by the number of worlds represented by the diversity of abducted individuals you see, and it's clear that our friends the Vilenjji not only know how to cover a lot of ground, but have been very busy."

"But what's it all for?" With a wave of a hand, Walker took in the grand enclosure and its surrounding necklace of smaller, individual living compartments. "Why do they keep picking up individuals from so many different worlds? Just to study them?"

"I told you: I don't know. Maybe some of our fellow inmates do. If so, I haven't met them yet."

"Somebody must know," Walker murmured thoughtfully. "If only from questioning the Vilenjji."

"Ah yeah, the Vilenjji." George snorted. "Our oh-so-talkative hosts."

"You said that you've talked to them." Walker's tone was mildly accusing.

"Couple of times, yeah. Briefly. About all I managed to get out of them, I've already told you. They can be damned close-mouthed."

Over the course of the following weeks Walker met more of his fellow captives. Some were open and friendly, others shy, a few grudgingly antisocial. The latter he tried to avoid, though none of them were really hostile. Not, as a glum and permanently depressed Halorian observed to him, like a Tripodan. In mass they ranged from the single elephantine Zerak he had first seen while seated on the hillock with George, to the trio of turkey-sized Eremot, with their color-changing fur and comical waddling gait. Some were naturally as bright as a human. Others, like George, had been given the Vilenjji brain boost and had learned subsequently how to communicate and learn. It seemed strange that none were demonstrably more intelligent than an increasingly downhearted commodities trader from Chicago, Illinois.

"Maybe they can't catch anyone smarter," George suggested when Walker broached the subject to him. "Or maybe they're afraid to try. Or constrained by other considerations. We don't know. We don't know anything, really, Marc."

"I know that I'm getting out of here," he shot back defiantly. But in his heart he knew better.

His isolation as well as his destiny were brought home to him forcefully one day, as it was to everyone else who happened to be wandering within the grand enclosure at that time. One moment all was as it normally; creatures wandering, conversing, contemplating in silence, some playing interspecies games of their own devising. The next, the artificial sky had vanished, giving way to a shallow-domed transparency. With the sky went the light, so that everyone in the enclosure suddenly found themselves standing or sitting or lying or hovering in darkness. It was not total, however. There was some light. As his surprised eyes adjusted, Walker saw its source.

Stars.

Thousands of them. Probably millions, but all he could see were thousands. That was enough, shining in an unbroken spray through the now transparent ceiling. All the colors of the rainbow, like jewels scattered on black velvet, they shone in all their collective galactic magnificence through the crystal clear ceiling of the grand enclosure. Whether the view had been made available intentionally or by accident, perhaps caused by a glitch in some wiring or computer program, Walker never knew. It lasted for a couple of minutes. Then it was gone. The simulated sky returned, a neutral pale blue. Synthetic clouds drifted, gray and low, hinting at rain that would never fall. Fake sunset loomed inexorably.

For no specific reason, tears welled up in Walker's eyes. Standing there gazing at the alien stars, he had made no sound: simply wept wordlessly. George sat quietly nearby, watching his friend, tail (for a change) not wagging. After a while he said, "I'd join you if I could, Marc, but dogs don't cry. Only on the inside."

Kneeling, still staring at the sky where the stars had been, Walker let his hand fall to the woolly head. As he stroked it gently, George closed his eyes, his expression one of pleasure and transitory contentment.

"That's all right, George. I know you feel the same."

"How else could I feel?" Slipping out from beneath his friend's companionable hand, he rose and started back toward the tent. "Let's get something to eat. You got any of those power bars left? Not the trail granola—that stuff tastes like Styrofoam packing pellets. The ones with the dried fruit."

Straightening, Walker wiped at his eyes and nodded. "I think so. Why? You hungry?"

George looked back over his shoulder. "Not particularly. But food makes me feel better. Any taste of Earth is better than none at all."

Nodding, Walker moved to follow. "I think there are still a couple in my last box. I'll split one with you."

He doubted very much, as they headed back toward the tent together, that they were any longer anywhere near the warm, friendly, ocean-swathed ball of dirt both knew as home.

✳

Days, like gas, continued to pass. Walker knew it was days because his watch, thankfully, continued to function. In addition to telling the time and date in three different (and now utterly irrelevant) time zones, holding a small address book, providing a connection to link to the (now unavailable) Internet, serving as a stopwatch, and offering half a dozen other functions, it contained within its chip brain two different mini video games. Boredom notwithstanding, Walker did not play either of them. He was afraid of sacrificing too much battery power. If nothing else, knowing the time (Pacific, Central, and Eastern) kept him, however tenuously, in touch with home. Peripheral as it was, he was inordinately terrified of losing that contact.

With little else to do to pass the time beyond marking it, he and George tried to make the acquaintance of as many of their fellow captives as possible. There were the reticulated Irelutes from A'ba'prin III, the bounding Mirrindrinons from the system of the same name, the lanky ciliated Tacuts from Domiss V and VI, and many more. Some were friendlier than others, some more talkative, some withdrawn, some barely capable of speech despite having been given cerebral kick starts and verbalizing implants. All shared in a common captivity.

Ultimately, it was the solitary Ghouaba who turned him in.

He was not looking for the blade when he stumbled upon it. Actually, it could not properly be called a blade. It was more like a sliver of sharp ceramic. About a foot long, it lay half buried in the sand that lined one side of the grand enclosure's largest stream. Kneeling, Walker stared at the shiny exposed portion of the fragment, noting how it caught the light. Noting that it held an edge. A quick glance showed no one in his immediate vicinity. George was off somewhere chatting with friends. A brace of Moorooloos slip-slid past, skating on slime-coated foot pads, their attention on one another.

The origin of the ceramic sliver was a mystery. Something left over from the original construction of the enclosure, perhaps. Or even better, some kind of forgotten tool. Either way, it might prove useful. Moving forward so that his body concealed his actions as much as possible from unseen monitors, he reached down and quickly pulled the sliver from its sandy bed. That's when he discovered that it held a sharp edge. It would be good to have a weapon, however primitive. And if the sliver turned out to be a tool of some kind, it would be interesting to experiment with its capabilities. Perhaps it might even be capable of passing through or otherwise disabling a Vilenjji restraining field.

As he rose, he was momentarily startled to see a small alien staring in his direction. He recognized it as a Ghouaba, citizen of a world known as Ayll VI. A male of its species, the Ghouaba was a short, slim biped whose long arms caused its four-fingered hands to drag on the ground when it walked. It had large, owlish eyes; ears that were capable of facing backward or forward; a wide, toothless mouth that seemed to split its flattened, ovoidal skull almost in half; and a small, constantly wiggling proboscis. It looked at him for a moment before turning and walking away with a loose-limbed stride that made it appear virtually boneless, which it was not.

Taking a deep breath, Walker headed back across the grand enclosure, taking as direct a route as possible toward his own personal environment. Once there and safely back inside the tent, he carefully drew the souvenir out from beneath his shirt. No one had challenged his acquiring of the prize.

On closer inspection, he saw to his growing excitement that the fragment was indeed more than just a broken shard of ceramic or other construction material. There were markings in unknown script on one side and several lightly tinted depressions on the other. When he cautiously pushed a finger into one of the large, shallow depressions, it glowed with life. So did the sharp edge of the device. Moving his free hand toward it, he quickly sensed the heat it was generating. Better and better. Was the device some kind of cutting tool? That would not only serve as a weapon, but might even offer a way out of the great circular enclosure. Of course, once outside he had nowhere to go, but it would be nice to have a choice if, say, the Vilenjji started rounding up captives for medical experimentation or some equally disturbing activity. Better to have the option to delay the inevitable rather than to quietly accede to it.

As he was studying the remaining depressions, wondering what they might do, something wrapped tight around his lower right leg and yanked forcefully. He went down hard on his face and chest, the air whooshing out of him as he was dragged backward out of the tent. Furious, he twisted around—to see a pair of Vilenjji towering over him. One had an arm flap wrapped securely around his ankle, the suckers gripping firmly. The other was gazing down at him with that creepy horizontal, wraparound stare. Its sucker flaps held a long, tapering instrument whose point was aimed directly at Walker's chest. He went very still.

He also noted the care with which the Vilenjji who had dragged him out of the tent took the ceramic sliver, pulling it gently free of the human's reluctant fingers. This accomplished, it turned to its companion and hooted softly, like an owl in training for an avian rendition of Handel. Automatically, the implant in Walker's head translated. The Vilenjji was customarily terse.

"Got it."

"How comes a jiab to be in the compound?" the alien wielding the rifle, or whatever it was, responded.

Hairs, or cilia, atop the other's tapering skull fluttered slightly. "Lost. Carelessness. No damage done."

Together, they examined the recumbent human, who was watching them closely and breathing hard. The tip of the weapon device moved slightly. Walker closed his eyes. When he opened them again, the two Vilenjji were departing. Slowly, he sat up. As he did so, he caught a glimpse of a much smaller figure standing just outside the boundary of his private bit of transplanted Sierra.

The Ghouaba was looking straight at him and grinning. At least, Walker thought it was a grin. He might be completely misinterpreting the expression. But he was not misinterpreting the Ghouaba's stance,

nor the ease it exhibited in the company of the two withdrawing Vilenjji. It was instantly clear to Walker how his captors had learned of his
possession of the device. There was no other reason for the Ghouaba to
be there with them.

"You little big-eared bastard!" he growled.

Perhaps the Vilenjji were out of translation range. Perhaps they
chose simply to ignore the biped's angry comment, which was not directed at them in any case. But the Ghouaba heard, and understood, as
its own implant deciphered the human's comment. Despite the fact that
Walker was twice its size and many times its mass, it did not appear intimidated.

"Touch-eh me-eh and Vilenjji see-eh," it countered. "Hurt-eh me-
eh and ugly Earth-thing die-eh. Eh-theht!" Turning away, it confidently
showed the human its back. Possibly also its backside, though Walker
was wholly ignorant of Ghouaban biology.

Rising, ignoring the warning, he started for the grand enclosure,
intending to follow the little betrayer until the Vilenjji had absented
themselves. Then he remembered George's story of the Tripodan, who
had attacked and killed another of the Vilenjji's specimens. "Never saw
it again," the dog had concluded the tale by telling him.

As he stood debating what to do, all but shaking with rage, a vista
of all-too-familiar mountains and forest and sky appeared, replacing his
view of the grand enclosure. No, he thought wildly as he rushed forward. But there was no mistaking the reality of the illusion, if that was
not an oxymoron. Sure enough, as he attempted to push through the
forced perspective of the restored panorama, he came up against the familiar tingling, and then pain, of a reactivated restraining field.

It took only a couple of moments to confirm what he feared. His
access to the grand enclosure—to its rolling terrain, its varied vistas, its
running streams and astonishing assortment of alien verdure, his fellow
captives and their own enclosures—had been cut off. Over the past
weeks the opportunity to converse, to share thoughts and commonalities with other intelligences, had become important not only to his
daily routine but to preserving his sanity.

And George. With the reestablishment of the restraining field on all
four sides, contact with his only real friend, with his fellow abductee
from Earth, was also denied to him. It struck him immediately what
was happening.

He was being disciplined.

For finding the ceramic device and not turning it in, though how
he was supposed to have done the latter he did not know. In that he was

being disingenuous, he knew. He could have waited for a Vilenjji passing down the corridor and waved the device in its direction. That was what a good prisoner would have been expected to do, no doubt. Like that smirking Ghouaba doubtless would have done. Well, Walker wasn't a good prisoner. A stupid one, maybe.

Whatever happened now, the experience had at least taught him something valuable. Whatever it consisted of, his captors' surveillance system was not perfect. He had managed to find, uncover, conceal, and slip back to his tent with the ceramic device. If not for the Ghouaba having informed on him, it was entirely possible the Vilenjji would not have known about it.

They were not omnipotent.

Thus slightly encouraged, all the rest of that day and on into the next he waited for the Sierra panorama to vanish, or for the barrier between his enclosure and George's uprooted urban environment to fall. Neither happened. Nor did it the following day, nor the one after. Bereft of sentient contact, lonelier than he had believed he could ever be, he sat outside his tent or beside the scrap of Cawley Lake and stared morosely at fake sky, false beach, phony forest. So dejected did he become that he forgot to eat his food bricks or cubes, though he did manage to swallow and keep down some water.

He lost track of the days, forgetting to check his still-reliable timepiece. Perhaps, aware of the Ghouaba's role in the betrayal of the human, the Vilenjji were fearful of losing another specimen to internecine fighting. Eventually, his term of punishment was deemed sufficient, his sentence fulfilled. Whatever the reason, on a day he did not mark, the mountainous vista in front of him and the forested one on his right both abruptly and without any warning blinked out of existence, offering unrestricted access once more to the grand enclosure and that of his four-legged canine friend.

As it happened, George was taking it easy outside his crumbling Cadillac condo, gnawing on a grayish blue food brick, when entrée was restored. So happy was Walker to see him that he put aside any thought of marching off in search of the perfidious Ghouaba.

The sight of the mutt jumping into the human's arms and licking his face profusely must be profoundly intriguing to the watching Vilenjji, Walker was convinced. No doubt they were monitoring the release to see how their newly liberated specimen would react to its restored freedom of movement. Silently, he evoked enough seriously bad words and concomitant suggestions for physiological impossibilities to prove conclusively that the Vilenjji were not telepathic and could not monitor his thoughts. Or else they simply didn't care.

Eventually, George got tired of licking him and Walker got tired of being licked. Together, they strolled away from the tent and out into the comparatively spacious confines of the grand enclosure. Espying the disparate pair from Earth, a few other aliens acknowledged Walker's return to their midst. No one rushed over to congratulate him on his release, however, or to question him concerning his activities during the time when he had been kept incommunicado. Curiosity about such matters was not always healthy. It was an attitude Walker, now more than ever, respected.

George could have cared less. He was simply glad to see his friend again.

"I was worried they'd keep you shut away permanently," the dog commented, his tail wagging like a fuzzy metronome. "Then I'd have nobody to talk to about the really important things. Like the taste of hamburger."

"Nice to know I was missed," Walker replied dryly. More seriously he added, "I was beginning to wonder the same thing."

Suddenly, he paused. Shambling slackly across the ground cover not thirty feet in front of him was his betrayer, the oily little specimen from Ayll VI. Preoccupied, it was not looking in his direction. Always a fast sprinter, Walker knew he could be on top of the malicious little being before the Ghouaba realized what had hit him or could react. Without warning, a stinging pain shot through his calf, startling him. His expression transformed by surprise and shock, he looked sharply down at its perpetrator.

"You—you bit my leg."

"Damn straight," George growled as he backed up slightly.

"Why?"

"Because your ass was out of reach." The woolly head jerked in the direction of the sauntering Ghouaba, who was now disappearing out of reach behind a copse of flaring Harakath bushes. "You were thinking of going for it, weren't you?"

"Well, I—how did you know?"

"Everybody knows," George informed him. "I didn't see what happened to you, but others did. You found something. Something the Vilenjji didn't want you to have. The Ghouaba told them about it. They came and took it away from you. Then they sealed you back up in your personal environment. I didn't know if I'd ever see you again. But nobody touched the entity responsible for getting you locked up. Nobody dares. You don't do that here. Remember the—"

"The Tripodan. Yeah, I remember." Walker's fury faded along with the sight of the Ghouaba. "I'll just have to try to restrain myself, keep away from it. But it would be so easy to pick it up and break its neck, just snap it like— Hey, you're not going to bite me again, are you?" He looked alarmed as the mutt came toward him, snarling softly.

"I will if it's the only way I can get your attention."

"Okay, okay." Reluctantly, Walker turned away from the Harakath copse. "I promise. I won't touch the putrid little twerp."

"Better not." George stopped growling.

As they walked off, the human glanced back toward the bushes. "One of these days, though . . ."

"One of these days may never come," George informed him warningly. "Better resign yourself to it."

"All right. I hear what you're saying." Reaching down, he gave the dog a reassuring pat between the ears. "I don't want to get shut away like that again."

Unfortunately, no matter how hard he tried, no matter how great the effort he expended on its behalf, the image of the Ghouaba grinning at him from behind the loglike legs of the retreating Vilenjji simply would not go away.

**5**

t did not help that it was impossible to constantly avoid seeing the being who had betrayed him. Spacious as it was, the boundaries of the
grand enclosure were finite, as were the opportunities to practice
avoidance within. Over the course of the following days and weeks,
during walks and the casual runs he employed to keep his strength (as
well as his spirits) up, he encountered the Ghouaba more than once. On
several occasions, he was convinced that the rubber-limbed little alien
was taunting him.

It was easier when he was running with George. By now he had
come to rely not only on the dog's company, but also on its straight-
forwardness, its utilitarian approach to their adverse circumstances. As
his four-legged friend remarked one time, "The brain boost the Vilenjji
gave me didn't make me a surgeon, or an engineer, or even a meter

reader. All I've got is common sense. But like most dogs, I've got a lot of it."

Keeping that in mind helped prevent Walker from reaching out, snatching up the grinning Ghouaba, and unscrewing its deceitful little head. Aware now that the Vilenjji surveillance system was less than perfect, there was always the chance that he could do the deed and get away with it. The risk, however, was too high for the satisfaction that might be achieved. His captors might not take him away forever, as they had with the Tripodan, but the thought of being locked up in permanent solitary was even worse. As a good commodities trader, he had learned early on when not to overbid on appealing futures. It being his future that was at stake, as opposed to that of a container-ship load of juice concentrate or soybeans, it behooved him to be more cautious than ever.

He was able to take some solace in staring murderously at the Ghouaba whenever their paths happened to cross. How much effect that had on the alien, how much sleep it caused it to lose, Walker did not know. It depended on how the Ghouaba chose to interpret the human's expression. But it made him feel better to favor the creature with a homicidal stare whenever they locked eyes. Being as unfamiliar as the Ghouaba with the meaning of human expressions, he doubted the Vilenjji would lock him away for that.

"I'd pee on it for you," George declared wholeheartedly halfway through their regular morning run, "but there's no telling how our purple hosts would react. Or Ghouaba-boy, either. They might both find it flattering. Or I might get my peter fried by a bolt of lightning. Either way, it's better to give such things a pass. Among dogs, the necessity for revenge fades with time. Why don't you just forget about the incident? It's over and done." Deep brown eyes looked up at him. "What would you have done with that Vilenjji gadget, anyway, if you'd been able to keep it? Threatened to stab one of them unless they turned their ship around and took us home?"

"I don't know." Arms and legs pumping, Walker jogged alongside the dog. "First off, I would've tried to discover what it did, what its various functions were."

George leaped a small growth topped with deep blue bubblelike blossoms. "Maybe it was a suicide device, and activating it would have offed you in a particular messy alien manner. Ever think of that?"

"No." Walker had to admit that he had not. "What we need is more knowledge of this place. How it works, who's in charge, what's waiting for us when this journey is over."

"And then what?" the dog inquired.

"I don't know." Walker sounded more cross than he was, more ir-ritated at himself than at his companion. "Research pluses and minuses first, then make your bid. When you have all the relevant knowledge."

"I'd settle for an extra ration of food cubes," George responded. "But then, I'm a dog. We don't think as far into the future as humans do."

"Lucky you." In tandem, they leaped the next row of ground-hug-ging bushes.

"Maybe you're hurting yourself by thinking too much, Marc." As Walker finally slowed to a halt, breathing hard, bent over with his hands on his knees, the dog trotted around to stand in front of him. He was panting lightly. "Maybe what you need to do is forget the era you evolved from. We're all of us oxygen breathers in and on the same boat here together. Concentrate on what brought your ancestors and mine out of the caves together. Get back to basics. That's all we've got going for us in this place. There's no Internet, no cell phones, no interstellar 911 to call." He pawed at the ground with one foot.

"Like, for example, you dig deep enough here, you find metal. What kind of metal I don't know, but that's something. A piece of knowledge. Digging may not be a real useful skill for a commodities trader in Chicago, but we dogs have never lost the ability, or the incli-nation to pursue it.

"Instead of reacting like you have been to what the Ghouaba did, you need to learn to control your reactions better. Keep your feelings to yourself. In other words, learn how to become a model prisoner. The less trouble you cause, the better you behave, the more rewards you'll get and the less attention the purple-skins will pay to you. I don't care what kind of equipment they're using to keep an eye on our activities. Unless they've got one Vilenjji assigned to each captive, every now and then someone is going to be overlooked. Just like your picking up that gad-get was overlooked." The tail wagged. "We want you and me to melt in with the rest of the overlooked. We want to be counted among the con-tented critters in cages who don't need constant supervision to make sure they don't do something daft."

Walker straightened, took a deep breath. All around them, other captives from other worlds were sleeping, lazing, conversing, eating, exercising, and, in a few cases, engaging in activities that were as utterly unfamiliar to him as they were ultimately unfathomable. Among the as-sembled, who were engaged in pursuits most likely to attract the atten-tion of the Vilenjji? Who were more likely to be ignored, either because they were harmless or better yet, boring?

He nodded in silent agreement with George's wisdom. That was it. That was the answer—for the foreseeable future, anyway. From this moment forward, he would strive to be as boring as boring could be. Boring enough so that the Vilenjji would all but forget about him as their interest turned to other, more unpredictable inhabitants of the enclosure.

And while he was striving to bore, he would make it his task to learn as much as possible about his fellow captives as well as his captors, while drawing as little attention to himself and to George as possible.

※

It was amazing to observe the scruffy mutt in the act of making friends. If dogs were born with an inbred skill, friend-making was it. Tail wagging, tongue lolling, George would saunter up to something that looked as if it had stepped out of a dilettante London writer's opium dream and bark a cheerful greeting. Receiving the modulated sound waves via the appropriate organic mechanism and having them translated by the Vilenjji's internal implant, the apparition thus addressed would bend, kneel, fold, twist, or otherwise respond physically to bring itself more in line with the dog. Within a few minutes, they would invariably be chatting amiably.

Walker tried, but he simply did not have his four-legged friend's knack for ingratiating himself to others. It was a failing that troubled him, because he did not understand it. Back home, he had moved with ease among acquaintances at work and at play. His senior year at university, his teammates had voted him cocaptain. From childhood, he had always gotten along well with people.

Not-people, apparently, were a different matter entirely.

Yet as he trotted from one alien encounter to the next, George was customarily greeted with welcoming cries, squeals, honks, squeaks, whispers, and hoots, whereas Walker's appearance was habitually met by uncertainty, if not outright apathy.

"You have to try harder, Marc," George instructed him one day. "Everyone remembers or has been told of what happened to the Tripodan. By now, everyone also knows what occurred between you and the Ghouaba. What applies among humans and, to a certain extent, among dogs on Earth applies equally here. Set one inmate to spy on another and the job of containment becomes easier for the keepers." Turning, he gestured toward the center of the grand enclosure, where representatives of three species had gathered.

"See how hesitant that group is even though they've been meeting happily together for weeks beneath that tree? Everybody here would like to trust everybody else, with the obvious exception of the Ghouaba. But no one is sure who might inform on them to the Vilenjji and who might not."

Seated on the cushioning ground cover, a discouraged Walker pitched pebbles toward a sculpted depression in the soil covering. "What's to inform about? My finding that Vilenjji device was an exception, wasn't it?"

Tail-wagging slowed, the dog nodded. "As far as I know, it was. But nobody's sure what kind of activity, short of murder, the Vilenjji might not approve of, and nobody wants to risk finding out. So despite the smiles, or the equivalent thereof, everyone here exists in a state of permanent paranoia. Whether that's an intentional consequence on the part of the Vilenjji or just fortuitous for them no one can say. But it's no less real for that. Don't you find yourself constantly looking over your shoulder, toward the nearest corridor, to see if they're watching in person?"

Rising, Walker let the last pebbles fall from his hand. "All the time. You can't help it." He indicated the enclosure in which they stood. "There's nothing else to look at, anyway."

"There is if you have friends." Approaching the human, George pawed at his right leg. "Come on, Marc. I'll help you."

"All right." The commodities trader looked down into the dog's bright, alert eyes. "But I'm not going to lick anyone. Or anything."

George snickered. "Don't say that until you've met the Kitoulli sisters."

It wasn't a question of being subservient, Walker slowly learned. More a matter of showing respect, not only for the representative of another sentient species, but for their particular problems and concerns—even if one didn't understand everything that was being said, or shown. It took a while, but under the dog's tutelage Walker slowly got the hang of it. The results were immediate, and welcome. Inhabitants of the enclosures who had previously shied away from him, or wandered off, or turned their backs (or the equivalent thereof) on him grew gradually more voluble. Having George available to act as an intermediary certainly helped. Nor did a willing Walker take umbrage on those increasingly infrequent occasions when the dog would point out one of the human's faux paws, as George liked to refer to them.

It took weeks. But there came a day when Walker no longer felt it necessary to have George along if he experienced the desire to engage something strange and otherworldly in casual conversation. So far had he come in his social development that he believed he had made the acquaintance of most of his fellow captives. Most, but not all.

One outlying enclosure located on the far side of the grand central mingling area from his own fragment of ship-borne Sierra Nevada particularly intrigued him. Among the astonishing diversity of personal environments, it stood out for several reasons. Where nearly all the individual ecosystems experienced localized fluctuations between day and night, this one was shrouded in perpetual gloom. Though he did not enter it but only strolled on past, it seemed unlikely that temperatures within could vary very much. It appeared to rain frequently, and when it wasn't raining, the interior was typically cloaked in a heavy mist. Wandering close to the very border of this particularly damp transplanted elsewhere, he thought he could hear the sound of water running continuously: not surprising, given the amount of moisture the murky dwelling space received.

"Who lives in there?" he finally asked one morning as he and George enjoyed a counterclockwise hike around the circumference of the grand enclosure. "Have I ever met them?"

Tellingly, the dog kept his friend between himself and this particular slice of alien ecosystem. "I don't know, Marc. I've never met the occupant. All I know for sure is that it has to be an oxygen breather, like the rest of us. Come to think of it, I don't know that I've ever met anyone who *has* met whoever lives in there. That's assuming anything does, and that it's not just an empty cubicle that's been prepped and made ready in expectation of the arrival of some future unfortunate abductee."

Having halted beside the environment in question, Walker leaned forward to squint into the depths of the permanent gloom. "If that's the case, it sure seems like it's been held in readiness for a long time. Leastwise, it has been for as long as I've been here." Looking to his left, he nodded in the direction of the curving arc of individual living areas. "There are more than a dozen unoccupied spaces, and none of them have been given this kind of elaborate prearrival treatment. I bet somebody *is* living in there." He took a step toward the invisible barrier that separated the distinct environment from the grand enclosure.

"Whoa!" George darted around to cut him off. "Where do you think you're going?"

Walker nodded again, this time straight ahead. "If there's nobody living in there, I'll soon find out and there's no harm in looking. If there *is* a sentient at home, maybe it's hurt, or lonely, or otherwise incapacitated, and we can help."

"Maybe it doesn't want to be helped." The dog cast a nervous glance over one shoulder. "Maybe it's solitary and hermetic by nature. Maybe in its society it's considered polite to take a bite out of uninvited visitors. And also, what do you mean 'we'?"

Walker stopped, peered down at his friend. "Who was it who badgered me to be more accommodating, more understanding, of alien needs and customs? Who taught me how to make friends with something that didn't have a hand to shake?"

"I'd met all of those folks previously," the dog pointed out. "It was just a matter of introducing you properly, of helping you learn how to acclimatize yourself to alien customs."

Walker started forward again. "No reason why I can't do that with whoever's tucked away in here. If I get in trouble, thanks to you I now know how to fawn and scrape slavishly to get out of it." He offered his friend a lopsided grin. "If necessary, I can even flop onto my back, stick all four limbs in the air, roll my eyes, and pant with my tongue out."

"Oh what a funny simian you are," George growled. "Listen to me, Marc. If there is something living in there, and it never comes out, and it's not hurt, then it must have good reason for shunning the company of other intelligences. It might not take real kindheartedly to unwarranted intrusion."

"If it's dangerous to others, the Vilenjji will stop me. Wouldn't want one of their trophies to damage another." Trying to peer through to the corridor beyond, he found that he could not penetrate the gently swirling murk to see if any of their captors happened to be present at that moment.

"Don't count on it," the dog warned him. "They didn't arrive in time to keep the Tripodan from dismembering the Sesu. I'd hate to see that happen to you."

"Why, George, what a thoughtful sentiment."

"Sentiment, hell," the dog growled. "Who else is going to feed me their surplus food bricks?" Stepping to one side, he skittered out of the human's path. "Go on, then, if you're so dim-witted that I can't talk you out of it."

Walker stepped past him. "Just say that I'm dogged."

George's tail had stopped wagging, and he made no attempt to hide his unease. "Curiosity doesn't kill cats; only humans. Cats are smarter than that."

With that last observation lingering in his mind, Walker stepped through the unseen divider that separated the grand enclosure from the mist-swept compartment of mystery.

Once inside, the ambient humidity hit him like a wet washcloth across the face. So did something unexpected—the chill. It was cold within the smaller enclosure. Not arctic, but frigid. At least there wasn't much wind. Well, he was from Chicago. He could handle both the damp and the cold. Were the climatic conditions he was experiencing characteristic of this environment the year-round, or were they seasonal and subject to change? If the former, as he advanced slowly he found himself pitying any creature that had evolved in such conditions. And if they were seasonal, he realized, this might be the being's equivalent of summer. Really bad weather on its homeworld might be far worse.

What vegetation he encountered was low-lying and tough, designed to minimize exposure to the constant moisture while maximizing its ability to gather sunlight: a difficult duality for any plant to pull off. Gritty soil had accumulated in the cracks and crevices of otherwise smooth, almost black boulders and stones. Exploring, he nearly stepped off a rocky beach and into a pool of water. Kneeling, he dipped a forefinger into the slowly surging liquid and brought it to his lips. Salty, but with less of a bite than that of a terrestrial ocean, and fresher. Different concentration of dissolved minerals, he told himself as he straightened.

He nearly jumped out of his hiking boots when something howled mournfully behind him. When he recognized the source, he wanted to yell angrily at George to keep it down. He didn't dare. Technically, he was already violating another sentient's private space. If the Vilenjji were watching, their curiosity to see what would happen next apparently outweighed any hesitation they might feel over one of their specimens intruding on another. Or, he told himself, it might be that they couldn't care less, and were not even specifically monitoring the situation.

He was just about ready to give up and subscribe to the theory that the living area was indeed unoccupied when a glint of light in the midst of the mist drew him forward. As he grew nearer, he saw that it emanated from a portion of a particularly large isolated basalt boulder that had gone partly translucent. Pressing his face close to the light-emitting oval, he thought he could make out regular shapes inside. Either what he was seeing was the result of a very elaborate, very clever optical illusion, created for what purpose he could not imagine, or else the boulder was at least partially hollow.

Commencing a cautious circumnavigation of the big rock that towered over him, he arrived eventually on the side that faced the relocated portion of sea. Something scuttled out of his path to disappear beneath the surface of the water. The local equivalent of his spurious blue jay and counterfeit chipmunk, he reasoned.

There was an opening in the front of the boulder. While it was not large, he found that if he got down on hands and knees he could enter easily enough. A soft hum, rising and falling almost rhythmically, drew him onward and inward. As he crawled over the damp rocky surface beneath his hands and feet, it occurred to him that if the boulder was occupied and if anything resident did decide to take exception to his entry, he had put himself in a very poor position to defend himself against attack, or to backtrack in a hurry.

The light ahead grew brighter, allowing him as he progressed to resolve objects of obvious artificial manufacture. Slightly to his right he made out what looked like a very low table. The majority of the ambient light was directed thereon, where what at first glance appeared to be a bright red octopus seemed to be reading a large, self-illuminated picture book. At the same time, espying the intruder, it let out an ear-splitting, high-pitched squeal and, utilizing four of its ten limbs, threw the book-thing at Walker's head. He flinched.

Missing him, it struck the wall to his left, crackled with energy, and went dead. Instantly, the alien slid off the unidentifiable piece of furniture. Standing behind this, simultaneously demonstrating that any or all of its multiple limbs could be used either for digital manipulation or as legs, it gaped at Walker. Its two recessed, silvery, horizontal eyes goggled in his direction. It was about that time that he noticed that the ten limbs, as well as the bulbous body that rode atop them, were lavishly adorned with all manner of tiny cut gems, bits of polished metal, swirls of gaily colored cloth, beads, and less readily identifiable decorations. Visible in the gaps between this extraordinary assemblage of personal ornamentation was smooth, slick flesh tinted maroon, with suggestions of yellow mottling. As for the body, though undeniably cephalopodian in appearance, it was divided into three sections, with a distinct head on top. There was neither neck nor waist, however, and the divisions between the three body sections were not immediately obvious.

In contrast, there was no mistaking the tone of voice that emerged from the pinkish mouth tube that peeped out from among the tangle of limbs at the bottom of the garish apparition. "What by all the Ten Tintinnabulations of Tevoresan are you, and what are you doing in my place of abode?"

Thanks to the technical competence of the Vilenjji implant, Walker was able to immediately discern two things about the creature's rejoinder.

One, it was as shocked by his unexpected appearance as he was by its, and two, it bore a slight but unmistakably feminine lilt.

"Uh, my name's Marcus Walker. I'm a captive here, like you. I'm a human, *Homo sapiens*, from the planet Earth, which is . . ." His response trickled away. Having no idea either where Earth was or where he was in relation to it, he could not be expected to explain it in terms that would make any sense. He took some consolation from the likelihood that the quasi-cephalopodian doubtless languished in a similar situation, astronomically speaking, and suffered from a similar sense of loss and displacement.

True or not, it did not alleviate the other's anger. Moving cautiously on all tens while extending itself to its full height, all four feet of it came scuttling out from behind the table, or bed, or whatever it was. Its gaze, however, never left the intruder.

"Did I invite you into my lodgings, Marcus Walker of Earth?"

"No, but—"

"Did I extend a general invitation to every biped, multiped, and noped that they could encroach on my privacy whenever the whim might strike their atrophied brainpans?"

"I doubt it, but I—"

"Did I let it be known that I would welcome the presence in my residence of any smelly, warmed-over, limb-shorted, flat-faced, calcium-jointed primitives from worlds no one has ever heard of?"

"Now hold on." Having begun by backing down the entranceway that led out of the boulder, Walker found that the stream of insults was beginning to override the initial dismay he had felt at having so visibly upset the inhabitant of the mist-laden ecosystem. "If you'll give me half a chance, I'll apologize."

That finally persuaded the creature to cease its advance. Or maybe it was the dawning realization that not all of the intruder was immediately visible, and that a considerable portion of its very real bulk remained concealed by the tunnel.

"What makes you think," it snapped in a fashion Walker could only categorize as bitchy, "that I would accept an apology from a barely cognizant creature as gross and mannerless as your own dismal, pathetic self?"

By now it had become clear to Walker that the only weapon the creature possessed was a biting tongue. Well, mouth tube, anyway. Startled and outraged as it was, if it had access to any kind of weapon it would surely have made its presence known by now. That in itself was highly unlikely, given the ever-present threat of Vilenjji oversight.

Studying the occupant of the hollowed-out boulder, noting its significantly smaller size, Walker was convinced he could take the acerbic entity every four falls out of five. Whether the same thought had occurred to the creature itself he did not know. If he stopped retreating and advanced in a forceful manner, how much longer would it continue to bluster?

"Listen, I'm sorry, okay? That's my apology, whether you accept it or not." His curiosity about the mist-heavy environment satisfied, more than slightly discouraged by the reception he had received, he resumed backing out.

Once outside again, he grimaced as he straightened up. Mist had given way to rain. Nothing drenching—just a steady drizzle. He'd taken several steps in the direction of the grand enclosure when a voice, this time only tinged instead of dripping with sarcasm, caused him to look back.

"Human Walker."

Turning, he saw the creature standing outside the entrance to its residence. Abode, a boulder, he mused whimsically. Was it representative of the creature's dwellings, or had it, too, been captured along with its kind's equivalent of a tent? Certainly the interior gave little indication as to the cephalopod's true level of technological accomplishment.

"Why did you enter my enclosure?"

He hesitated. He had been gone long enough for George to be in a state of rising panic. But not, he noted, sufficient panic to tempt the dog into coming in after him. "My friend told me that he didn't know if anyone lived in here. As many times as we've passed this opening in the course of our hikes around the grand enclosure, I found myself growing more and more curious about it. So I decided to find out. I thought that if there was anyone living in here, they might be injured and in need of assistance, or too scared to show themselves." He eyed the creature, rock-steady on its ten flexible limbs. "You're not too scared, are you?"

"Scared, scared. Let me see." The creature managed to give the appearance of lapsing into deep thought. "No, I think 'contemptuous' is more probably the descriptive term you are searching for."

Remember what George has told you, Walker thought, forcing himself to remain calm and composed. Be agreeable. Be understanding. Subservient, even. As for provocation—be it verbal, physical, or otherwise—when in doubt, ignore it.

"Then why don't you come out into the large enclosure? Why don't you show yourself?" In the absence of any further demand to leave, he remained. Beading up on his forehead and cheeks, water began to course down his neck and chest. He ignored the damp chill. "Whoever you are."

"Because I . . . ," the creature began sharply, its mouth tube weaving wildly. Then its motion, along with the word-sounds spilling from it, slowed. Moving to a nearby rock, it settled itself down on the slick, damp surface, its limbs splaying out around it in a not-unattractive pattern that reminded Walker of the rays of a setting sun. Muted artificial light glinted off the myriad decorations that adorned its rubbery, supple body.

"Here I am condemning you for the same egregious lack of courtesy I myself continue to display. You, of course, being the lowly primitive biped that you are, have a pretext." Tight-lipped, Walker said nothing. "I can claim no such excuse." It sighed, a remarkable exhibition that consisted of air inflating every bit of its body save the head and limbs. For a brief moment, Walker was afraid that the maroon-hued skin could not fully contain the impressive exhalation and that the creature would actually explode.

"I am Sequi'aranaqua'na'senemu, a female of the K'eremu. I have matriculated to four separate higher levels of erudition, am in my third stage of sexual maturity, and as a fifth-stage Sisthra'andam aspire to that exalted mental and spiritual condition known as Tiuqua'ad'adaquil." Five limbs rose to wave sinuously in Walker's direction. "Since it is visually as well as audibly self-evident that your kind is incapable of mature oral communication, despite the surgical addition of synthetic interlocution supplied by our misbegotten captors, I will tolerate your calling me 'Sque.' " Eyes like pieces of scored steel met his own, outwardly as well as inwardly reflective.

"Now, tell me of you."

Walker swallowed. In a way that he had not been at any time while constricted within the boulder's confines, he found himself well and truly intimidated.

6

He could not, he decided, tell this manifestly highly intelligent creature—this female K'eremu, this fifth-stage Sisthra'andam (he didn't have the slightest idea what that entailed, but it certainly sounded impressive), that his life consisted of trading in bulk food-stuffs, going out on Saturday nights, and watching football on Sundays with his buddies. Somehow that did not seem to stack up meaningfully against someone who had "matriculated to four separate higher levels of erudition." At least, he felt he could not so tell her now.

Anyway, respective accomplishments and number of limbs aside, they were both in the same boat. Same boat—George!

"I'm sorry. I've left my friend behind. Though a representative of a different species, he's also from my world. My absence will have him seriously worried by now." He turned to go.

"Wait!"

Looking back, he saw the K'eremu slide in a single, unbroken motion off her rock and onto all tens. It was a graceful movement, like that of several dancers clinging tightly to one another while all advancing together. Slowly, she started toward him. Decapodal limbs notwithstanding, her manifold stride was short and tentative. He had a feeling that sprinting was not a K'eremu forte.

She halted just out of arm's reach. Tentative hints of conviviality or not, it was clear that she still did not entirely trust him. He could understand her hesitancy. No doubt he more closely resembled a Tripodan, for example, than another K'eremu.

"You wanted to know why you, or any of the others, rarely see me outside my quarters." A softer sigh this time, less suggestive of possible internal organ inflation. "For one thing, I much prefer the climate in here to that which prevails the majority of the time in the inaptly named 'grand enclosure.'"

"So you *have* been outside," Walker remarked.

"Infrequently. Not since you were brought aboard, I believe." A faint hint of a desperate longing shaded her words. "I have been on this ship of the Vilenjji for a long, long time." Limbs stiffened. When they did so, they changed color slightly, shading to a deeper red. "Nevertheless, localized climatic conditions are not what is primarily responsible for my elective solitary." As argent eyes rotated to look up at him again, he sat down, bringing his own orbs more in line with hers. If she appreciated the courtesy, she did not comment on it.

"Then why do you stay holed up in here?" As he posed the query, he found himself wondering if the Vilenjji translator was capable of conveying the full force of an intentional pun.

"I have no one to talk to," she replied tersely.

He frowned and noted that she observed the motion of his eyebrows with casual interest. "From what I've been told, and seen, the translator implants allow any sentient to talk to any other. At least, it does so among oxygen breathers who converse by modulating air."

"No, you do not understand." Ambling close, she sat down next to him. That is, she allowed her flexible limbs to collapse beneath her, causing her upper body to sink vertically until it was once more in contact with supporting stone. "At first, I did try. We K'eremu by nature tend to prefer our own company to that of others, even among our own kind. We are not hermits. Members of a progressive species do not build a civilization by living in isolation from one another. We cooperate when and as necessary. Socially, however, we prefer when possible to keep to ourselves. This is uncommon among space-going species." This declamation she conducted with a waving, dancing pair of limbs.

"Also," she added, "I am more intelligent than any of the other captives. Coupled with the natural impatience that is endemic to my kind, I therefore cannot avoid finding them and their attempts at conversation uninteresting and boring."

Walker nodded slowly. "I see. And how do you find me?"

One limb reached out to rest against his knee. The contact was gentle, almost reassuring, in a feminine sort of way—if the touch of an alien cephalopod could be called feminine.

"Interesting," she told him. Without quite knowing why he should, he swelled slightly with pride. "And boring," she added. Ego deflation was immediate.

"It is not your fault," she hastened to add. "You cannot help what you are. Everyone knows that intelligence exists in direct proportion to the number of a species' manipulative limbs."

Reflexively, Walker found himself regarding his two hands and wondering if his feet would qualify. He could, after all, though with some effort, pick up a pencil with his toes.

"There are many measures of intelligence," he muttered defensively.

"There, there." The rubbery, flexible limb stroked his knee. "Do not take it so hard. Some species are bigger and stronger than others. Some smell better. Others have sharper eyesight, or better hearing. Some run faster. The K'eremu simply happen to be smarter."

"Not too smart to be captured by the Vilenjji," he threw back.

"I was alone. That was typical. Even so, I ordinarily would not have been sufficiently surprised to have been abducted. I had access to means of communication, to ways of calling for help. Naturally, beings that habitually prefer their own society need to have ways of drawing upon the assistance and expertise of others."

Walker was intrigued. "Then why didn't you? Call for help."

"I was, ummm, not my usual self."

Listening, the human wondered if the translator had rendered her speaking accurately. "I'm not sure I understand."

"There are among my kind several easily ingestible herbal blends of particular potency. Among these is one called si'dana, another joqil. I am perhaps to some extent overly enamored of both, and certainly was so at the time of my taking."

His perception of the remarkable alien changed abruptly. "You're an addict!"

The accusation did not appear to sting. "Like any K'eremu, I like what I like."

"How do you cope?" He gestured at their damp surroundings. Thankfully, the light drizzle had once more given way to a heavy, enshrouding mist. "Here, I mean."

"The Vilenjji take care to study each species they intend to sample before settling on the specific individuals they wish to seize. In my case, that apparently extended to a chemical analysis of the food I was eating. Thankfully, a sufficiency of both stimulants is incorporated into my daily rations."

He nodded. "Among my people, addiction to 'stimulants' is not considered a sign of intelligence."

"Would you recognize such a sign if it were waved in front of you? Do not think to criticize your betters!" The limb tip slid off his knee.

His initial reaction was to snap back. But he had learned George's lessons well. He merely nodded, wondering how she would perceive the gesture, and elected to change the subject. No wonder the K'eremu were a race of solitary intellects. If they were all as sarcastic and insulting as this one, it was difficult to see how they could stand one another, let alone anyone else.

"You know how the Vilenjji operate?"

Limbs flexed. He thought he was starting to get the hang of the manifold semaphoring. "Certainly. I talk to them occasionally."

He started. "You talk to them? I've been trying to talk to one of them, any of them, ever since I was brought here. They just stare back and ignore me."

More limb fluttering. "What did I just say about relative intelligence? I can understand why they would want to talk to me. Why would they want to talk to you?"

Walker opened his mouth to reply, thought a moment, closed it. Far worse than the K'eremu's rudeness was the realization that it might have a basis in fact. "Maybe they just find you more, uh, interesting."

"Of course they do. They are very good at recognizing and identifying individual species' characteristics. Unfortunately, they fail to appreciate that I am also far more intelligent than any of them. Where their own abilities are concerned, they are prisoners of a remarkable conceit."

How fortunate that the K'eremu are not. He thought it, but did not say it. George's multiple lessons in tactful humility had been well taken. It was time for another diplomatic change of subject. One that poured out of him in a flood. Not wanting her to think less of him than she already did, he hoped the translator did not convey the fullness of his desperation.

"If you talk to the Vilenjji, then maybe you can help me to understand," he gestured at their surroundings, "all this. Why is this being done? What's going to happen to all of us? Why do the Vilenjji do this? Are they just curious? Are they embarked on some kind of scientific collecting expedition and we're the prize specimens?" He also wanted to ask, "What happens to the specimens when we arrive at the Vilenjji's final destination?" but he could not. Not yet.

Again the swelling sigh. It was remarkable to observe the excessive dilation of her body, which was apparently no more physically damaging to her system than a shrug of his shoulders would be to him.

"Poor biped. You really are ignorant, aren't you?"

Fine. I'm stupid, he thought. Dumb monkey-boy, that's me. But at least I'm not an addict. Go ahead and explain it all; I'm listening. Though he knew George would be frantic by now, the dog would simply have to wait.

Settling herself, her flexible limbs splayed around her lower body like the petals of some great red flower, she proceeded to enlighten him.

"First I need a reference point, somewhere to begin. So that I do not repeat myself." Eyes like deep-set flattened coins regarded him through the drifting, intervening mist. "How much of galactic civilization is your kind familiar with?"

At the risk of seeing not only himself but his entire species knocked down the stupid ladder another couple of rungs, he knew he had no choice but to reply honestly. "None, actually. As far as I know, we're unaware anything like it exists."

It was evident Sque found this hard to accept. "You have no astronomy?"

"We do. I guess our stargazers haven't looked or listened in the right places yet."

"Or with the right methods. Well, I am not going to give you a complete course in galactic history. Suffice to say you would not be able to follow most of it anyway." A pause, during which he did not respond. He was getting good at that.

"Accept that a galactic civilization exists. Your world obviously exists beyond its most distant fringes. Mine lies somewhat closer. So do those inhabited by the great majority of our fellow abductees. It is that isolation from the mainstream of galactic civilization that allows the

Vilenjji to engage in their nefarious activities with some hope of profiting from them."

He nodded reflexively. "Then this is all about profit. This is not some kind of scientific collecting expedition."

She pulsed slightly. K'eremu laughter, he thought. Or maybe just alien flatulence.

"The Vilenjji are no more interested in science than they are in devoting themselves to charitable works. No, I must correct that. One cannot varnish an entire species on the basis of the actions of a few. While I am not intimately familiar with the sociology of Vilenjjian civilization, if that is an appropriate word, I do know that if an evaluation were conducted by an impartial party, they would not rank among the races most noted for their philanthropic attitudes."

"What are they going to do with us?"

"Sell us. Individually if possible, in groups if they feel the need for speed. There are on board this large vessel numerous groups of captives, representing many species: some intelligent, some less so, others simple primitives." The way she looked at him Walker could not be sure into which category she had placed humankind.

" 'Sell us.' " Walker accepted the statement as fact. "Somehow, I always felt that if superior beings existed beyond Earth, they would long ago have dispensed with something like slavery as immoral."

"It is immoral. Did I say it was moral? I did not say that. What I said was that the Vilenjji intend to sell us. Just because a thing is immoral, or against the law, does not mean it cannot exist. Hailing from worlds existing outside the principal ebb and flow of galactic civilization, both socially and galographically, we fall outside the scope of civilized attention. The Vilenjji would not dare abduct and attempt to deal in citizens of known worlds. But because of our comparative isolation, the nature of our intelligence and of our credentials for qualifying for that status are open to general interpretation and remain suspect. That which one species deems civilized, another may regard as unspeakably primeval. You and I, for example."

He considered. "Yet despite your opinion of me, you would not keep and regard me as a piece of property, as something to be owned." There followed a pause, prompting a somewhat louder and slightly belligerent, "Would you?"

"No, of course not," she finally replied. "To do such a thing is contrary to natural law, as well as abhorrent to a higher species. But there are others, less troubled by ethical concerns, who are willing to overlook the moral in their search for novelty. That is how you should now view yourself: as a novelty. A novel commodity, if you prefer."

"I prefer unwilling captive." He wiped at the moisture that had been collecting on his head and shoulders as they talked.

"You have determination. Do not let it lead you to do something you may come to regret. As a general rule, the Vilenjji are indifferent to their captives. Their attention borders on apathy. They are interested only in product. Focus on surviving and they will be content to ignore you. Coming from deep within civilization, they consider themselves far superior to any of their captives."

Walker kept his tone carefully neutral. "That must be hard for you to accept."

A few limbs rose and gestured. "Not at all. My mental capacity is so far beyond theirs that they cannot conceive of so large a gap in intellect. They take my obvious superiority for indifference. Given their lack of interest and their dissolute intent, I see no point in wasting time trying to enlighten them. It would not gain me my release and my return to home anyway. They will simply sell me to a people even less intelligent than themselves."

Could a K'eremu, or at least this particular K'eremu, even be insulted, Walker found himself wondering? He much preferred the company of his own kind. Chicago versus K'eremu. Sooty versus snooty.

"Yet you're stuck in here and they're out there," he could not resist adding.

"A lamentable state of affairs, to be sure," she told him. "Sadly, even advanced intelligence can be surprised and overcome by a sufficient application of brute force. In the use of that the Vilenjji are regrettably proficient. Sophisticated argumentation tends to lose much of its ability to compel when confronted by the business end of a gun."

He was quiet for a while, as they sat together in the mist, each lost in their own thoughts, each contemplating a future devoid of optimism. When he at last spoke again, his tone was subdued.

"Then there's no hope for any of us. To get out of this and get home, I mean."

"Are you being deliberately awkward again?" She scanned his face, and he wondered what she saw there. "Or is it only sincere naïveté? One does not escape from a starship. Even if it were possible, where would one escape to? I do not know how long you have been here, but knowing something as I do of the general speed of this vessel, although speed is not a precisely accurate term when it comes to the physics of interstellar travel, I can tell you that I am many, many dozens of parsecs from my home system. I would seriously doubt that you are much nearer to your own." Limbs shifted. It was starting to drizzle again.

"Best to hope for placement with an understanding buyer, on a world whose ecology is not uncomfortably dissimilar to your own. That, and a remaining life given over to tolerable pursuits. My personal fear is that I will be sold not on the basis of my mental powers but for the attraction of my digital dexterity, and that I will be asked to provide entertainment by juggling with my limbs instead of my mind."

Walker had visions of himself, consigned forever to life on some unknown, unimaginable alien world, collared and chained side by side with George.

"There has to be *something* we can do," he protested. He'd already asked as much of the dog, whose response had been the canine equivalent of "Stick your head between your legs and kiss your ass good-bye." He doubted he would get that kind of response from Sque. For one thing, she had no ass.

But while less colorful, her response was not any more encouraging. "To the Vilenjji you represent an expenditure of time, money, and effort. They will want that returned to them, with a profit. No amount of pleading, of asserting your intelligence, however difficult that might be to prove, of outrage, of appeal to whatever ethical standards the Vilenjji might possess, is going to get you back to your homeworld. I have seen it tried by others; all of that, and more. Nothing works. The Vilenjji are implacable. They are also large, physically powerful, determined, and personally disagreeable. Better to spend your time concentrating on maintaining your health. There is nothing you can do."

He rose. "Maybe there's nothing *you* can do, for all your vaunted intelligence! But I'm getting out of here. Someday, some way, I'm getting out!" Pivoting sharply, he slipped and nearly fell. Recovering as much of his dignity from the near fall as he could, he straightened and stomped out of the K'eremu ecosystem and back toward the grand enclosure.

A lilting, moist voice called after him. "When you do, hold your breath. By doing so, most oxygen breathers can live for another minute or so in the vacuum of space before they either boil or freeze solid, depending on their proximity to the nearest stellar body."

He slowed slightly, turned, and shouted back into the mist that had already swallowed up the K'eremu. "It was very nice to meet you, Sque. Thanks for all the information."

There was no response. He would have been surprised if there had been.

Lying on the ground cover, his head resting on his crossed fore-paws, George perked up immediately when Walker emerged from the mist-shrouded compartment. The dog was livid. While George could not flush, he could certainly make use of his voice.

"What the lost bones happened to you in there? Where have you been? I was almost ready to come in after you!" He paused. "Almost."

Kneeling, Walker reached out to pet the dog. George would have none of it, backing swiftly out of the man's reach. "Don't be angry, George. I learned a lot from the resident."

Anger immediately forgotten, the dog looked past him, toward the rain-swept private enclosure. "Something *does* live in there? What is it? A talking mold?"

Walker shook his head. "Kind of hard to describe to a dog from Chicago. I don't suppose you've ever seen an octopus, or a squid?"

George surprised him. "Sure. Lots of times. Fancy restaurants throw them out all the time. People order them, see what they look like on a plate, then refuse to eat them. I'm perfectly happy to take the throwaways. One being's refusal is another's edible refuse. Not much taste, but filling, and nice and chewy."

"Don't let Sque ever hear you talk like that. She doesn't think much of anything besides her own kind as it is."

"So it's a she. Well, what did 'she' have to say that was so important it kept you in there for hours?"

"I told you I was sorry." Since kneeling was starting to cause the backs of his thighs to ache, he chose a soft-looking spot and sat down. Initial annoyance forgotten, the dog promptly plopped its head onto his lap. Absently, Walker stroked the back of George's head as he repeated everything Sque had told him.

When he had finished, the dog picked its muzzle back up. "Doesn't sound very promising. But then, it's not anything worse than what I expected. We'll just have to take life day to day. She's right about one thing, of course. There's no way out of here. Out of this."

Having refused to acknowledge that verdict from a tentacled K'eremu, Walker was not about to accept it from a dog. Not even one as articulate as George.

*

He was proud of the fact that he never lost control. Even in the midst of tight, last-minute competitive bidding, when the placement of an overoptimistic decimal point could cost clients tens of thousands of dollars, he prided himself on never losing his cool. It was a trademark of his success. He was the ex-football star who knew how to control his emotions, knew how to let that calculator brain of his do all the work. His steadiness under fire, as it were, was a hallmark of his success. His superiors appreciated and rewarded it, his coworkers regarded it with admiration or jealousy, depending on their respective degree of self-confidence and closeness to him, and his rivals feared it. It had always stood him in good stead. It had stood him in good stead for the weeks on board the alien vessel that had now stretched into months.

Uncharacteristically, he forgot to look at his watch on the day that he lost it. His self-control, not the watch. So afterward, he was not sure exactly when it had happened. Or how.

All he knew was that he had awakened as usual, walked with a yawning George down to the transmigrated segment of Cawley Lake to wash his face and hands, and settled down to await the arrival of the morning meal. As always, the neat circle of surface briefly subsided, only to return within a moment piled up with food bricks, food cubes, and the usual liquid trimmings. Maybe it was the water that set him off; a damp fuse to his human explosive. Maybe it was the predictability of it all. He did not know.

All he did know, or rather knew when George told him about it later, was that instead of choosing something to eat from the infuriatingly precise assortment of offerings, he straightened, drew back his right foot, and booted the mixed pyramid of alien nutrients as hard as he could in the general direction of the corridor. Several times during his college career he had been called upon to kick extra points or the occasional short field goal, and he still had a strong leg. His form was admirable, too. Food and water went flying. Impacting on the electrical barrier, a couple of food bricks penetrated nearly a foot before being crisped.

*You learn something every day,* he told himself wildly as the pungent burning smell of carbonized foodstuffs wafted back to him. Vilenjji food bricks, for example, were not improved by further cooking.

"Marc, that wasn't wise."

A slightly crazed look in his eyes, Walker peered down at the dog. "That's okay. Neither am I. Neither are you. Frankly, sanity is beginning to bore me. I'm getting sick and tired of playing the well-mannered little pet." Bending, he began picking up handfuls of dirt, gravel, sand, faux twig and leaf litter, and chucking them methodically at the barrier. Nothing got through. Anything organic got fried.

Visibly worried, George began backing away from his soil-flinging friend. The dog's eyes darted repeatedly from Walker to the grand enclosure. Emerging from mutt jaws as sharp barks, the translator embedded in Walker's head rendered the sounds as, "Please, Marc—stop it. You're making me nervous!"

"Screw that! I'm sick of this, understand? I'm sick of all of it!" Though he began to cry, he did not stop bending, grabbing, and throwing; bending, grabbing, and throwing. "I want out! Let me out! Why don't you take me for a walk, goddammit!"

It took a good five minutes of throwing and screaming, kicking and ranting, before the two Vilenjji showed up. George saw them first, slumping toward the little piece of Sierra Nevada from across the far side of the grand enclosure.

"Marc, stop it now!" he whined worriedly even as he backed around behind the human's tent. "Please!"

Walker did not respond. But, bending to scoop up another double handful of dirt and gravel, he did finally see the visitors. They towered over him, staring down out of blank, mooning eyes, the knot of fringe atop their tapered skulls fluttering eerily in the absence of any breeze. Each held a small device that made double loops around their sucker-lined arm flaps. The instruments appeared to have been drop-forged out of liquid metal. A few dull yellow lights gleamed on their sides.

Now thoroughly unhinged, Walker wanted to scramble up one of those purplish, pebble-skinned backs, grab a handful of that fringe, and rip it out by its roots. Instead, he settled for throwing the debris he had gathered, deliberately and without warning, straight at the head of the nearest alien. Numbed as he was by now to both the Vilenjji's dominance and indifference, he did not expect the action to have any effect. Surely the flung double-handful of gravel and dirt would be stopped by some invisible screen, or shattered to harmless dust by an inexplicable field of force.

The rocks and soil struck the Vilenjji square in the face, whereupon it raised both arms toward the affected area, emitted a high-pitched mewling like a cross between a band saw slicing wood and an untuned piccolo, and staggered backward on its sock-encased leg flaps, one of which showed signs of crumpling beneath the thick, heavy body. Behind the tent, George hunkered down as low as possible and whimpered.

Stumbling into a slight depression in the transplanted surface, the assaulted alien dropped the shiny, smooth-sided, double-looped device it had been holding. Without thinking and without hesitation, Walker made a dive for it. He actually had it in his grasp when his entire body turned to pins and needles. He couldn't move and he couldn't scratch.

The sensation was not especially painful, but the tingling effect threatened to drive him to distraction.

Proof of the seriousness of the encounter took the form of three more Vilenjji—three!—who came lumbering out of the corridor at top speed. They plunged through the deactivated barrier directly into the Sierran compound. Through the agonizing needling sensation that coursed through his body, Walker felt himself being stood upright. Two of them had him, their arm flaps supporting him where his arms met his shoulders. While a pair of newcomers kept their loop weapons trained on his involuntarily twitching body, the lifters proceeded to haul him out of his compartment and back into the grand enclosure. Though all his senses were alert and he was fully aware of what was happening around him, Walker was unable to move. Nervous system frozen in overdrive, he fought to regain control of his uncooperative muscles. Still wiping dirt and grit from its face, the fifth Vilenjji brought up the rear. Other than its initial ululation, it had exhibited no further signs of distress. Though its expression, such as it was, was noticeably contorted from the usual.

Somehow, George managed to find the courage to follow. At a sensible and respectful distance, of course.

Within the grand enclosure, conversation faded. It did not matter if it was a brace of convivial Hexanutes or a bulbous Ovyr locked in soliloquy with itself: all talking ceased as groups and individuals turned to watch the procession traverse the yielding ground cover. In the lead were two stone-faced Vilenjji who between them hauled the unresisting form of a hairless biped from a place called Earth. Behind came two more of the tall, massive-bodied abductors with weapons trained on the human's inert body. Then a single Vilenjji who occasionally dragged its left arm flap across its face and lastly, the small hirsute quadruped who similarly hailed from the third planet circling the ordinary star known to its local residents as Sol.

It was an unprecedented procession. No one among the watchers could remember seeing so many Vilenjji inside the enclosure at any one time. Here were five. What it augured not even the most perspicacious among them could say. Many wanted to query the trailing canine, but despite urgent, whispered appeals, the dog ignored them as it continued to track the quintet of Vilenjji.

The latter were oblivious to the stares and attention of their captives. Their concern was only for the biped. When its fellow oxygen breathers noticed where the Vilenjji were taking it, saw outside which enclosure they stopped, there was what amounted to a collective moan of resignation. When they tossed the human inside, there were multi-voiced expressions of commiseration. Gradually, in twos and threes and groups, they returned to their prior conversations and activities. There was nothing they could do for the biped. There was nothing anyone could do. Not now.

Ducking behind a tree, George waited until the Vilenjji had taken their leave, crossing back over the grand enclosure with their long, slow strides to the exit area on the far side that they always employed for such purposes. Alone, he crept tentatively out from behind the misshapen blue-green growth to stealthily approach the smaller enclosed space where his friend had been dumped. As he feared, the charged barrier that was usually operating there had been reactivated after Walker had been tossed within. Equally as frustrating, it had been opaqued. These two actions would prevent anyone, such as himself, from entering or observing anything taking place on the other side. More critically it would prevent anyone, like Marcus Walker, from exiting. As did many of his fellow captives, George knew what lived, what lay, behind that charged barrier. He had mentioned it to Walker only once before, and then obliquely. If Walker was lucky, he wouldn't remember.

Sitting back on his haunches, the dog threw back his head and began, unashamedly, to howl.

7

As control slowly returned to his muscles and his nerves stopped twanging like violins in a Mahler scherzo, Walker rose to his feet. The Vilenjji had vanished. Where the vista of the grand enclosure ought to have been there now shimmered a pleasant panorama of rolling yellow-green hills covered with ranks of what at first glance appeared to be gigantic cacti, but which on closer inspection revealed themselves to be some sort of strange, dark blue-green, nearly branchless trees. A stream flowed close by his feet. Kneeling, he scooped some up in a cupped hand and tasted of it without swallowing. His expression furrowed. It was water, all right, but so heavily mineralized as to be almost too bitter to swallow. He resolved not to drink from the stream unless he was given no options. Not all trace minerals, he knew, were good for human consumption, and his palate was not sophisticated enough to immediately distinguish between, say, selenium and arsenic.

Turning, he brushed dirt from his pants. To left and right, undulating hills rolled off into false distances. Directly in front of him was another hillside, higher than anything he had seen in the grand enclosure. It was topped by a webwork of blue-green roots that resembled fishermen's nets, a few impenetrably dense bushes from which periodically erupted dark orange bubbles, and some exposed rocks. Slightly to his right, a small portion of the always-present ship corridor was visible. The sky overhead was more yellowish than that of home and his own enclosure, and dominated by a high, thin cloud cover.

It took only a few moments to test the depth of the illusory landscapes. All were clever projections, rich with false perspective, that were in reality manifestations located behind the usual restraining field. He could not get out of the screened-off area into which he had been dumped. Equally clearly, no one could get in. George would have tried by now, Walker knew. Despite the occasional disdain that the dog showed toward his human companion, he and George had become inseparable friends.

What was the point of transferring him to a different environment? he wondered as he explored his new surroundings. Certainly it was less accommodating than his transmigrated piece of Sierra. Here he would have no access to his tent or to his few personal possessions, the latter by now having assumed an importance out of all proportion to their actual functions.

Punishment of some kind. It had to be, he decided. A reprimand for what he had done, throwing the dirt and grit into the unsuspecting Vilenjji's face. Thinking back on the series of events that had led to him being placed in this new ecosystem, replaying them in his mind, he was not in the least regretful. Although slightly deranged at the time, he had struck a small blow for himself and every other captive. He had managed to incapacitate a Vilenjji, however temporarily. He had given back a tiny fraction of the misery and discomfort with which they had burdened him. More than that, he told himself with growing satisfaction, he had succeeded in frightening their supposedly all-powerful captors when he had nearly managed to get hold of one of their weapons. His actions had obliged five of them to alter their daily routine just to deal with him. With one lone, trapped, defiant human.

Yes, he felt good about it as he sat down on a low hillock covered with cushioning ground cover and considered his new surroundings. At least, he did until the hillock moved.

It did not have to shuck him off because he was already withdrawing as fast as he could while it straightened. Slowly, he backed away until he felt the familiar tingle of a restraining field against his spine. He
could retreat no farther in the direction he had chosen. Eyes wide, muscles tense, he watched as the hillock shook itself sleepily and turned
toward him.

What he had taken for soft ground cover was in fact fur; more yellow than green, more bristle than soft. Something over nine feet tall,
the blond monster had bulging, slant-pupiled eyes that emerged from
both sides of its upper body on the end of thick, muscular stalks. Protruding from the center of the upper torso, a similar stalk terminated
in a single fluttering, flexing nostril. Below this a vertical slit ran downward for about a yard. When it parted, like a closet opening, Walker
could see that both sides of the interior were lined with startlingly
white triangular teeth the size of playing cards. The teeth were precisely
offset so that when closed, the vertical jaws would interlock seamlessly.
There was no neck, and because of the length and position of the
mouth, it was difficult to say that there was anything resembling a head.
The body was one hulking, unified mass of muscle.

From within the thick mat of dirty yellow-green quills four cablelike tentacles emerged, two from each side of the barrel-like torso, below the equally long eyestalks. Four more emerged from the underside
to support a body that looked as if it weighed close to a ton. The
beartrap-like jaws flexed, teeth locking and unlocking with raspy clicks,
like ceramic tiles being tapped against one another.

"Mmmrrrgghhh!" the monster rumbled.

As always, Walker's efficient implanted translator did its work automatically. The bellow was speedily interpreted and replayed to Walker as
"Mmmrrrgghhh!"

This was not encouraging.

Searching frantically for a place to hide and espying none, Walker recalled what George had told him about the Vilenjji acquiring captives
of wildly varying degrees of intelligence. Staring silently at the specter
that had risen up before him, he had no doubts as to which particular
species was a likely candidate for occupying the lower end of the sentience scale. Mistaking it for a comfortable resting place, he had disturbed its sleep, or hibernation, or beauty rest, or whatever. Thus far, it
had not reacted to his presence in anything that could be construed as
a positive manner.

No doubt the Vilenjji were watching every minute of it. Another of
their experiments in placing representatives of two highly diverse

species in the same environment in order to be able to observe the consequences of their interaction. Walker wondered if the alien whose eyes had been on the receiving end of the flung double-handful of dirt and grit was among those looking on, and if so, if it was particularly looking forward to the imminent confrontation between human and a very large Something Else. Whatever this daunting creature was, he realized, it was not the missing Tripodan. George's physical description of the latter was proof enough of that.

Would they go so far as to allow one specimen to kill another without intervening when they had the chance to prevent it? Wasn't he equally as valuable on the open market as this thing? For the first time in his life, Walker wished he had a way to loudly trumpet his novelty value.

How intelligent was it? It wore no attire, displayed no artificial covering or adornment of any kind. That suggested an animal, plain and simple. But not all species suffered from the need to clothe themselves. Would one already covered in thick, albeit short, bristles need to do so? Had in capturing this impressive specimen the Vilenjji picked up an alien nudist?

He was speculating wildly. Trapped in the confines of the isolated ecosystem, it was about the only defense he possessed. Searching for a possible vulnerable spot on his potential adversary, he focused on the protruding eyes. As he did so, both suddenly were drawn in until they were peering out at him from the edge of the creature's muscular flanks. The retraction rendered them far less vulnerable to a kick or punch. In contrast, any one of the four massive tentacles protruding from the blocky torso looked thick and strong enough to pull his own arms out of their sockets. Hell, all the alien had to do to finish him off was fall on top of him.

The first time he tried to say something, the words caught in his throat. A wonderful impetus was supplied by the creature itself when, flavescent bristles standing noticeably on end, it took a menacing four-tentacled step toward him.

"Hel—hello," he gargled. Intended to be forceful but not challenging, the stuttered salutation emerged as a frightened croak.

Whether the greeting was understood, or whether the creature decided the sound by itself was sufficient, it halted. In what was possibly the equivalent of a suspicious human raising narrowed eyelids, the two basketball-size eyes slowly extended to left and right on their muscular stalks. Surely, Walker thought anxiously, the gargantuan beast was not afraid of him. It certainly did not act fearful. Suspicious, perhaps. If he was lucky and careful in his reactions, he would do nothing to upset it.

They stood like that, man and monster, regarding each other for long moments. Finally the alien must have realized that the human presented no threat. Or maybe it grew bored. Or decided that the new thing that had been inserted into its realm was not good to eat. Or a combination thereof. For whatever reason, it turned with surprising grace on its walking tentacles and returned to the resting place where Walker had mistaken it for a portion of hill. Despite his fear, observing its movements aroused in the human a degree of admiration. Never in his life had he seen anything so big—not a rhino, not an elephant—move so gracefully. It was a thing of beauty to behold. Or would have been, had he not been scared to death that those self-same movements might at any moment be again directed toward him.

Only when he was certain that the creature had once more entered into a state of repose did Walker edge his way toward the artificial panorama that separated him from the grand enclosure. His heart sank when he discovered that the restraining field remained in place. He was trapped in here with this thing. For how long, only his captors knew. Were they waiting to see how long he could survive in what at best was the temperamental presence of his gigantic new roommate? The prospect only intensified the hatred he felt for his captors. How, he wondered, did this creature feel about the Vilenjji? Did it possess enough awareness, sufficient cognizance, to experience such complex emotions? What would it do when it awoke of its own accord, instead of being startled to wakefulness by an unexpected intrusion? Would it be more amenable to the uninvited such as himself? Or would it awaken hungry? Walker felt like dinner, in both senses of the word.

Nightfall tended to arrive more swiftly in the new enclosure while darkness lingered longer, indicating a different night-day cycle than that of Earth. While the enclosure's denizen slept through it all, Walker found himself being awakened by the slightest sound. Paradoxical that he should be disturbed by the activity of some small alien arthropod or the falling of a root section when the tossings and turnings of the resident he truly feared generated far more disturbance. But when he was asleep, his nerves were unable to distinguish between sounds, and so woke him at the slightest noise. Normally he would have relied on George, who was a naturally much lighter sleeper, to keep watch for him while he rested. But George wasn't here.

Faux morn brought with it a waking chill that found him shivering in his clothing. No tent, no sleeping bag, had been transferred from his own enclosure to enhance his comfort. Given the insult and hurt he had perpetrated on the Vilenjji, he supposed he ought to be grateful that they hadn't killed him outright.

Rising, he advanced experimentally toward the resting place of the enclosure's dominant life-form. Expecting to find it still slumbering, he was surprised to see it squatting down before a flat piece of terrain from which blossomed pitcherlike growths. As Walker looked on, a perfect circle of the flora sank into the ground, to reappear moments later laden with a ceramic cistern full of water and the largest food bricks he had yet seen. There were none of the especially tasty cubes that he and George had come to prize so highly. Only several varieties of food, and the water. He thought he recognized the general appearance of at least one type of brick, though that did not mean he could identify its specific components.

Overnight, the gnawing in his stomach had metamorphosed into a throbbing insistence. He had to eat something, if only to keep his strength up in case he had to run. Given a choice between Vilenjji food bricks and alien greensward, he opted for the former. The problem lay in obtaining one.

Looking around, he searched his immediate surroundings until he found a large piece of wood that was banded like a zebra. Though hollow, the broken branch was still sturdy and intact. It was a poor weapon, but better a poor one than none, he decided as he retraced his steps.

Resting the makeshift club on his right shoulder while gripping it firmly with one hand, he made his approach from the side of the food lift directly opposite the monster, advancing one deliberate but unthreatening step at a time. He had covered half the distance between his starting point and the place where the being squatted when it finally took notice of his approach. Contracted against the side of the massive body while the creature ate, both eyestalks now extended to half their length while the narrow black pupils expanded slightly. It was watching him.

It was also feeding an entire food brick into its vertically aligned jaws. Interlocking teeth, some the size of Walker's open palm, sliced through the dense, compacted loaf of nourishment as if it were made of butter. If his digestive system could tolerate its chemistry, one such brick, Walker suspected, would easily feed him for a week.

He continued his slow, steady approach. Slitted ebony pupils contracted within bulging eyeballs. A low rumbling sound emerged from somewhere deep within the creature. It sounded like the start-up of a piece of heavy machinery in need of lubrication. The food was very close now. Bending forward slightly, his gaze flicking rapidly between bricks and beast, Walker reached for the nearest piece of food.

Two thick tentacles lashed out at him. The speed of the hulking creature's reaction caught Walker off guard. Tentacle tips cracked like whips only inches from his extended hand. Instantly, he drew it back. A check showed that all five fingers were intact. As a warning, the gesture was unmistakable. Next time, he worried, those flailing twin limbs might break his wrist. Or snap his hand off at the joint. Uncertain what to do next, he hesitated, wondering at the same time if any Vilenjji were studying the confrontation. Or if they cared.

He *had* to have food. And water.

Unlimbering the club, he held it as high as he could and advanced again toward the food pile, intending to knock a brick off to one side. In the face of such a determined incursion, surely the beast wouldn't begrudge the harmless biped one brick. Walker's greatest defense lay in the hope that it would not consider him worth killing. And there was always the chance that the Vilenjji, desirous of defending however small and defiant a part of their investment, would intervene to protect him. He would have had more confidence in the latter possibility had it not been the Vilenjji who had placed him in his present circumstances in the first place.

Chewing slowly, the monster continued to watch him as he moved forward. When he tentatively thrust the tip of the branch toward the food, it struck. Ready for it this time, Walker swung the club up, around, and down with both hands, striking at the two tentacles. He did not miss.

The impact reverberated back up his arms. As for the object of his attack, it did not even blink. Instead, both tentacles wrapped around the length of tree branch and ripped it out of his grasp. Had he not let go, he would have found himself lifted into the air along with the club. The creature considered the length of wood for a brief moment. Then the two tentacles snapped it like a toothpick and tossed the fragments casually aside. Meanwhile, both other manipulative appendages continued their steady transfer of food bricks into the seemingly insatiable maw. This feeding was interrupted occasionally as the creature took long drafts of water from the glossy cistern. Standing out of reach, a weary and frustrated Walker could only eye thirstily the rivulets of water that did not vanish down the slit of a mouth.

Only when it had consumed the last of the generous pile of food bricks and drained the cistern dry did the creature rise to its full height, turn, and amble back to its resting place. When he was sure it had lost interest in him, Walker rushed forward. On hands and knees, he made a minute inspection of the place where the food had emerged from belowground. Not a crumb remained, though he did manage to lap up some spilled water that had collected off to one side in a couple of tiny pools.

Thoroughly disheartened, he sat back and stared at the once-more recumbent form of the entity with whom he was being forced to share living space. If nothing else, he could be grateful for the fact that it was not overtly hostile. More than anything, it ignored him. That did not mean he was incapable of irritating it to the point of taking his head off. Yet he had to take that risk. He needed food, fuel. A few more days of this and he would be too feeble to mount a satisfactory attack.

The wooden club had proven less than a failure. What else could he try? His previous assault had been on the Vilenjji. If he succeeded in throwing enough dirt and gravel into one of those protuberant, side-stalked eyes, would it temporarily blind this creature? If so, he could grab a food brick or two and then run like hell. But run where? Though larger than his piece of transplanted Sierra Nevada, the alien's enclosure was not extensive. Unlike Sque's eco-quarters, there were no caves to hide within. Would the creature even bother to come after him, or would it simply wipe its dirtied eye clean and resume eating? He had been unable to come up with a satisfactory approximation of its intelligence level. Clearly, it was aware of him. But in what capacity? As a competitor for food, or as another kind of intelligence?

It didn't matter. None of it. Because in the final analysis, he had to have something to eat.

He could have made the next assault during the midday meal, or at dinnertime. Despite his hunger, he held off. For one thing, his inaction might help to lull the creature into believing that the human had no further interest in trying to partake of the Vilenjji-supplied nourishment. For another, there was always the chance that it might prove sleepier and less alert when breakfast was delivered in the morning. Somehow, Walker managed a decent night's sleep, curled up in a far corner of the environment as far from its monstrous occupant as possible.

False sunrise was followed by both human and monster awakening and moving separately to the place where the food appeared. As before, the creature squatted down expectantly opposite the circular cutout in the ground, its four slightly thicker supportive tentacles compacting beneath it like the folds of an accordion. Halting on the other side, well out of reach, Walker waited. Throughout the silent dance, neither entity made a sound.

The circle subsided, reappeared a moment later piled high with the usual assortment of food bricks and a freshly refilled cistern of water. The creature began to eat. Deliberately doing nothing for a while, a crouching Walker watched and waited. Then he rose and sauntered forward, hands in pockets. Espying his approach, the monster rumbled its familiar warning. Walker halted, his attention apparently drawn elsewhere. The creature resumed eating.

Bringing his clenched right fist out of his pocket, Walker threw the handful of carefully scavenged pebbles hard at the monster's right eye and prepared to dash toward the food as soon as it reacted. It did so—but not as he had hoped.

The two right-side tentacles, which were not engaged in feeding, rose and swatted the flung gravel aside like the harmless grit it was. To see something so massive react to an unforeseen attack with such speed and dexterity was astonishing. The creature barely paused in its chewing. Not one piece of rock got through to strike the bulbous, staring black eye.

A different sound emerged from the beast. Compared to the utterances that had preceded it, the lilting growl was relatively low-key. A grunt, Walker wondered? A belch? A chuckle at his utter and complete ineffectuality?

He fell to his knees, as much from dejection as fatigue. Plainly, there was no way he was going to force this hulking apparition away from the food and water. Unless the Vilenjji reached their fill of the confrontation, or of the punishment they were subjecting him to, or both, he was going to die here: probably of hunger. Another day or two of hopeless attacks against the inarticulate master of this relocated alien veldt would see him rendered too weak to do anything.

Maybe that was what the Vilenjji were after, he thought suddenly. Maybe as soon as he was reduced to near death, as soon as he had learned his lesson, they would appear and return him to his own enclosure. The question was, unfamiliar as they were with human physiology, whether he would have the strength remaining to recover from the experience, and if so, would he suffer any permanent damage as a result of it?

Kneeling there on the yellow ground cover, he contemplated finding as comfortable a corner as possible, lying down, and waiting for whatever might come. There was always the possibility, of course, that the Vilenjji would do nothing. That they would not intervene, but would simply leave him to his own devices. To starve to death.

A thought sparked. Maybe the problem was that he was thinking too much like an ex-football player, or a proactive commodities trader. Maybe he ought to fall back on the advice of others, of friends. Friends like a certain dog.

It was worth a try. At this point, he had very little to lose. And it suited him to be doing something instead of crawling off into a corner like a trapped rat. Maybe that was what the Vilenjji were expecting and waiting for him to do. Well, he would not give the smug purple bastards the satisfaction. He might well die, he might be killed by the creature into whose environment they had deliberately placed him, but he would not surrender without a fight.

Or without a little vigorous cowering.

Falling first to all fours, he then dropped even lower, all the way down onto his belly. The fuzzy yellow alien ground cover tickled his nose and cheeks. He ignored it as he began to squirm guardedly forward.

As the creature continued methodically demolishing food bricks, one dark round eye rotated on its stalk to watch him. Gritting his teeth, he lowered his head until his face was all but in the dirt. Occasionally he would glance up to check his location.

As he neared the monster, he slowed his pace. This required little effort since he was near collapse from lack of nourishment anyway. It took nearly an hour to submissively travel the last forty feet on his belly. By that time, exhausted and filthy, he hardly cared whether he succeeded in snatching a few crumbs of food brick or not.

It struck him that he had made it to within arm's length of the circle that descended into the ground and returned with food. While the bricks themselves were all but odorless, he could swear that he smelled the water in the cistern: cool, sweet, and beckoning. Glancing up, he saw the huge alien looming over him. It continued to eat without pause. There were only three of the big food bricks remaining. Walker hardly dared to breathe. He only needed one. One brick, he thought as he fought to remain focused through an increasing haze of frailty. One brick, and if he was extremely fortunate, maybe a few swallows of water. Timidly, slowly, he extended his right hand as he reached for the nearest unit. Try as he might, he could not still the trembling in his fingers.

Like a rust-colored steel cable, one thick tentacle slammed down inches from his questing fingers, blocking their path.

Walker could have burst out crying. He could have launched into hysterics. He could have risen to his feet and made a mad, doubtless futile dash for the food. But the time spent on board the Vilenjji vessel had changed him. Time, and talking to his fellow captives. Especially to one fellow captive. He neither went mad nor lost control.

Instead, he rolled onto his back, bent his knees up toward his chest, held his open hands palm upward, let his tongue loll loose, and opened his eyes wide in what he hoped was a manner any sentient would interpret as doleful pleading.

The reaction this provoked was not expected.

"Stop that," the creature rumbled softly.

Walker maintained his posture of naked vulnerability. He was sure the creature had spoken. He had seen its ripsaw-lined jaws move at the same time as his implanted translator had brought him the words. Nevertheless, he stayed as he was. For one thing, he was unsure precisely what the monster wanted him to stop.

"I said, stop that," it growled a second time.

Walker retracted his tongue and swallowed. "Stop what?" he whined, as piteously as he could manage.

"Groveling. Begging. It's embarrassing. No intelligent being should have to act like that."

There was no question that it was the creature who was addressing him, Walker realized. It was after all not a mute mountain of bristle-coated alien protoplasm, then, but something more.

Warily, he rolled onto his belly and backed up onto hands and knees. "No intelligent being should let another one starve."

"Why not?" the newly voluble monster grunted. "Supposedly intelligent beings should not try to reduce others to the level of property, yet we are ample evidence such practices exist."

"Then you and I have something in common." Rising slowly to his feet, Walker brushed muck and ground cover from his dirty clothing.

"We have nothing in common except misplaced intellect." Eyestalks rose and dipped. "Sentience and sentenced, adrift among the stars, lost dreaming."

Oh, Lord, Walker thought. Alien haiku. Or something like that. Next thing you knew, the monster would launch into an animated discourse on flower arranging. Was there an opening here he could exploit? And if he tried, would it translate properly, or end up getting him killed? Drunk from lack of nourishment, he felt he had nothing to lose.

"Uh . . . prisoners in arms, trapped among many strangers, sharing pain."

Both eyes turned to look at him as the entire massive body, squatting on its under-tentacles, pivoted in his direction. Walker was un-comfortably aware of the proximity of those clashing jaws and their serrated, interlocking teeth. More significantly, the tentacle that had de-scended like a falling log to block his access to the food was abruptly drawn aside.

"Brothers in singing, forced into small place, empathy tendered."

"Wondering if we two, called to . . . oh hell," Walker concluded, unable to finish the attempt. Then the food brick was in his clutching hands, pieces of it crumbling away beneath the pressure of his desper-ate fingers. He started to turn, to run—only to have the same tentacle that had previously blocked his access to the bricks drop down to cut off his intended escape route. Turning, he saw the vast torso leaning toward him, almost on top of him.

"Stay and converse, fellow singer of rhythms; loneliness taunts. Rather rage than raconteur, would I—'til now."

"Sure. Glad to have a chat." Unable to hold off any longer, Walker opened his mouth and took a huge bite out of the food brick he was holding. At that moment, for all he cared, he might as well have been swallowing alien compost. All he knew was that it went down easily and settled comfortingly into the vacant pit of his stomach. He forced himself to eat more slowly. When later he moved to the cistern and shoved his cupped hands inside, drawing water to his lips, the creature again made no move to stop him.

As his strength slowly returned, he remembered his own loneli-ness, before he had made contact with George. Maybe that was all this thing wanted, too—some like-minded company. Given its overawing size and intimidating appearance, he could understand why the other captives might shy away from any hesitant, clumsy overtures. Perhaps foolishly, he decided to be entirely truthful from the very beginning. Taking a seat opposite the monster, still nibbling on the remnants of the large food brick he clutched as if it was an official Federal Depository ingot, he addressed himself to his unexpectedly lyrical fellow prisoner.

"My name is Marcus Walker. You can call me Marc. All my fellow cargo do. I come from a world called Earth."

"Unknown dwelling place, one among ten thousands, address ab-sent." Tentacles coiled back against furry flanks while eyestalks re-mained fully extended above them. "Call me Broullkoun-uvv-ahd-Hrashkin."

Walker paused in his chewing. His jaws hurt, but he was deter-mined to finish as much of the food brick as he could, as quickly as he could. There was no telling when his fellow captive might revert to growls and blows, or when the Vilenjji might decide to intervene to break up what had turned into an entirely unexpected species-on-species talkfest.

"I don't think I can."

"Honestly said. Be it for you enough to say 'Braouk,' then."

"Okay." To Walker, the way the alien's words reverberated in his head reminded him of a cat hacking up a hairball. But at least it was a phrase, a sound, he could reproduce. And who knew? Perhaps "Marcus Walker" and "Marc" generated similarly unpleasant echoes in the alien's mind. Communication between species need not be pleasant, so long as it was effective.

"Species-wise, I am called human," he added, trying to hold up his end of the conversation.

"Tuuqalian is me. Far from home, longing for deep skies, myself mourns." Lids like curved shades rolled down over both eyes, and the monster—all half a ton of teeth, tentacles, and muscle—shook visibly.

Walker paused, his lower jaw dropping. Was the alien horror crying? No moisture oozed from its bulbous oculars, no sound rose from deep within the hulking body, but it was clearly grieving. For its unseen planet, for hearth and home, for whatever the Tuuqalian equivalent might be. Stunned, Walker did not know what to do. He pondered walking up to the creature and embracing it comfortingly, but did not. Knowing nothing of Tuuqalian ways, he did not know if such a gesture might be misinterpreted. Where a Tuuqalian was concerned, if this specimen was in any way typical of the species, misinterpretation could prove fatal. So he settled for sitting where he was and looking on in respectful silence.

No, he thought. There was one other thing he could do.

"Sorrow is sharing, the abducted are together, many one."

He did not think it would have passed muster in Mrs. Longcarrow's senior English composition class, but the effect on the Tuuqalian was immediate. Both eye coverings slid back.

"You speak comfort and not fear. You seek empathy and not flight."

Walker forbore from pointing out that there was nowhere for him to flee to. However, he was more than willing to take credit where due, and also where not. "It just looked like you could use a kind word or two. Oh, sorry—I'm afraid I'm not really much of a poet."

"All language is music," the Tuuqalian rumbled good-naturedly. "It is only the form, the style of the singing, that varies. The poetry lies in the spirit, not in the words."

His competitors in Chicago would have found that account of one of the Exchange's sharpest operators uproarious, Walker knew. But they would not have expressed their dissenting opinion in the presence of the Tuuqalian. Because the alien would not just have intimidated them; its appearance would have sent them screaming.

Masks, he told himself. Even aliens, it seemed, hid behind masks.

"You really didn't want to hurt me, did you?"

"Yes, I did," Braouk replied, eyes literally wide. "I wanted to smash you, to rip your limbs from your body, to wind your internal organs like thread around my tentacles, to—"

"Okay, okay—I get the idea." Fortunately sated, Walker promptly lost what remained of his appetite. Setting the remnants of the food brick aside, he made a circumspect return to the water cistern. "What about my speaking comfort and seeking empathy?" He drank rapidly, just in case.

"That was then. This is the now. Timing triumphant."

"Glad to hear it. Is that why you've never made friends with any of the other captives?"

"Many reasons clamor for preeminence. That is certainly one of them."

"Speaking of friends," Walker murmured as he used the back of one hand to wipe drops of water from his lips, "there's someone I wish you could meet."

And just like that, the barrier separating the Tuuqalian's environment from the grand enclosure vanished.

**8**

t so happened that when it deactivated, a preoccupied George was pacing back and forth on the other side of the barrier. He had done so several times every day since Walker had been trapped on the other side. The suddenness of the shift caught him by surprise, and he jumped several inches into the air when the familiar opacity was replaced by an unrestricted view of the enclosure's interior.

Keyed up beyond measure, he raced forward—only to dig in all four paws the instant he saw the looming monstrosity that was squatting within arm's reach of his human. He knew what it was. Like a number of the other captives, he had caught a glimpse of the Tuuqalian on the rare occasions when the Vilenjji had let it roam free throughout the grand enclosure. At such times, he and every other oxygen breather had retreated swiftly to their own environments, to leave the ground-shaking creature to itself. Only when it had returned to its own ecosystem and the intervening barrier reestablished itself did the others dare to emerge from their places of concealment. It was the only resident the others had feared more than the now-long-absent Tripodan.

When the Vilenjji had dumped Walker into the Tuuqalian's enclosure, George had immediately lost all hope for his friend. To see Marc now, sitting proximate to and apparently unafraid beside the alien giant, was more than a shock. It was inexplicable. Tentatively, George crept forward in search of explication.

With his stomach full of Vilenjji food brick and water, Walker wanted more than anything to lapse into a deep and relaxing sleep. But he knew he could not. Not yet. Not until he had obtained a few more answers. Not until he could be more sure of the alien he wanted to think of as a friend, but whose mood, poetic declamations notwithstanding, could conceivably undergo a drastic shift at any moment.

Then the barrier had cleared, revealing not only the sweep of the grand enclosure, but the presence of one small inhabitant advancing slowly toward him. Had the Vilenjji heard and responded to his wish? Or was the dropping of the barrier simply coincidence? For that matter, why had the Vilenjji deactivated it at all? He asked as much of the Tuuqalian.

"Who can speak to the motives of the unspeakable?" Braouk declaimed sonorously. "I would like to ask them such things in the goodness of my own time. Alas, I fear I could not keep myself from smashing them, from ripping the limbs from their bodies, from peeling the suckers off their arm and leg flaps one by one, from—"

Much as Walker was enjoying this particular homicidal soliloquy, his attention was drawn to the approach of a singular canine form. "Maybe the Vilenjji got what they wanted out of putting me in here with you," he opined. "Maybe that's why they decided to go ahead and drop the barrier."

Eyestalks inclined toward him. "What could they have wished to obtain from such a confrontation?"

Wiping a few lingering, clinging crumbs from his lips, Walker looked up at the Tuuqalian. "To see how you would react to my presence, and I to yours. To see if you'd kill me."

Massive tentacles writhed ferociously. The sound that emerged from between clashing jaws was as succinct as it was bone-chilling. "Masters of malevolence, silent in their wickedness, parasites upstanding."

Walker nodded somber agreement. "Couldn't have put it better myself. I'm no judge of such things, but I think you have a real way with words."

Eyes turned away from the human. "When the soul speaks, it sings. Alas, these days it sings only of sadness."

An approaching whine drew Walker's attention. "Anyway, that's the friend I wanted you to meet. Same planet, different species." He pointed.

The Tuuqalian turned in the indicated direction. "Smaller, quadrupedal, furred. Two of three sing of familiarity. Which of you is dominant?"

Walker had to smile. "It's an ongoing matter of some disagreement."

Tentacles gestured. "I welcome your friend. I will not eat his parts; I will not dismember him."

Stepping toward the grand enclosure, Walker nodded thoughtfully. "He'll be relieved to hear that."

"Can he also croon lyrical in his speech?" Braouk studied the cautiously approaching shape with evident curiosity and without hunger.

"I don't know," Walker replied honestly. "It never occurred to me to ask him. I *can* say that he's never at a loss for something to say." Cupping his hands to his mouth, he raised his voice. "Hey, George, come on in! It's okay." He indicated the alien. "This is Braouk. He's my friend." Lowering his hands, he glanced over at the towering Tuuqalian. "You are my friend now, aren't you?"

"Now," the giant replied cryptically. Walker decided this was not the time to force the issue. For the nonce, he would settle for not being dismembered and having his parts eaten.

"The barrier's down, Marc!" the dog shouted back. "Run!"

Walker hesitated. For one thing, if it was so inclined, he had no doubt that the Tuuqalian could chase him down if it wanted to. He had already been witness to the speed of its reactions. For another, if he could sustain and nurture their provisional relationship, he might acquire an ally powerful enough to give even the Vilenjji pause. He had little to lose by trying. It was not as if he was going anywhere. At least, anywhere he wanted to go.

"No, I'm staying here, George." He beckoned. "You come on in. I'll introduce you."

Still the dog hesitated. What if the Vilenjji chose to reactivate the barrier—behind him? But he missed Marc. And the human appeared relaxed, confident. A little giddy, maybe, but certainly unharmed. Clearly, there was something to be learned here.

Rising from his crouch, George broke into an easy trot. Moments later he was leaping into Walker's open arms. Comforting pats and tongue licks were exchanged. Looming nearby, the Tuuqalian studied the reunion in contemplative silence.

"It is plain to see that you are good friends," Braouk finally declared. "Fortunate pairing are, two from same world, comforting another. Alas, alas; I have no such."

"Hey," Walker told him encouragingly, "we're here. We'll comfort you."

Bulbous eyes turned back to him. "Can you sarang a turath? Is it within you to morrowmay the tingling ubari?"

"Uh, I'm afraid not, no," Walker was obliged to reply.

"Don't look at me," George added hastily.

"I hear hoping, your tendering is touching, emotive still." The Tuuqalian squatted down on its under-tentacles. "It is good to at least at last have another of understanding and compassion to talk with. I was tired of eating those others who were first placed with me."

"You mean, eating with them?" Walker asked uncertainly.

"No." Saw-toothed dentition made soft clacking sounds against itself. "You sing too much sense not to know of what I speak."

Walker nodded slowly, and a bit unwillingly. "I can see where that would put a damper on casual conversation." Despite the highly unpleasant image his mind insisted on constructing, he settled himself down on a patch of ground cover while George hesitantly sipped from the water cistern. "Tell me something, Braouk: Why do you react like that? Why did you react with hostility toward me when the Vilenjji put me in here with you? You knew nothing about me, either as an individual or as a representative of a different species."

The Tuuqalian did something Walker had not seen before: it sat down. Or rather, it sort of folded up in the middle, ending up not on a nonexistent backside but instead looking like a large lump of yellow-green fur from which four tentacles of varying thickness and length protruded aimlessly. Swaying slowly on the ends of their stalks, the two large eyes assumed even greater prominence, while the menacing maw in the middle was partially concealed from view. If not exactly inoffensive, it rendered the creature's appearance considerably less threatening.

"When I was abducted and brought to this vessel, I lost all sense and reason. Four of the unspeakable ones I injured, despite the quantity of narcoleptic they pumped into me."

Water dripping from his chin, George looked up from his drinking. "Hey, good for you, big guy! No one else I've met here managed to resist with any success."

Both spherical eyes swiveled to meet the dog's admiring gaze. "I am not proud of what I did. The Tuuqalia are a peaceful race. We ask only to be left alone, to sing our songs and compose our verses. Into peace intruding, the hated Vilenjji came, stealing souls. Stealing me." Tentacles powerful enough to rip trees from the ground knotted in barely controlled fury. "I was not happy."

Walker nodded understandingly. "I tried to fight back, too. With little success, I'm afraid. But I tried."

Not wishing to be left out of the pissing contest, George ventured tentatively, "I think I might have nipped one of the ones that picked me up."

"For a long time," Braouk told them, "I was irrational in speech and manner. I raged, and struck out blindly. One time I was so upset that my anger became a shield almost strong enough to allow me to pierce the restraints that were placed upon me." He indicated the invisible electrical barrier that prevented him from reaching the section of corridor immediately outside his enclosure. "But the deeper one drives, the stronger the field becomes, and I was ultimately forced back. After that, I lay for several days recovering from the experience." Eyes moved up and down on their supportive stalks. "While I could not move, I fed on the pain of my anger." His voice rose.

"There are still times occurring when I let the frustration at my condition overtake me. Frenzy of frustration, striking out so blindly, nothing gained!"

"Easy there, big fella, easy." An alarmed Walker scuttled a yard or so backward on the ground cover. "We're friends, remember? Rhyming and reason, talking to each other, exchanging pleasantries?"

Calming down, Braouk looked back at the anxious, seated human. "That's not too bad."

With a start, Walker realized what he had done. He was unconsciously beginning to become comfortable with the manner and pattern of speech the Tuuqalian preferred. In contrast, George eyed him oddly.

"You sure you've never been off the planet before, Marc?"

"Not to my knowledge. Although there were times when my profession seemed pretty otherworldly." Standing, he brushed at the back of his pants, stretched. "You have to learn to contain your temper and manage irritation," he told Braouk. "There are things you can't control. Restraining yourself doesn't mean giving up." He glanced significantly toward the corridor. "As we say in the commodities business, the day may come when the chance presents itself to make a killing, and you have to be mentally ready to take it." Would the watching, monitoring

Vilenjji translate his analogy, or take his words literally? he wondered.

The Tuuqalian was large, loud, and intimidating, but he was not unintelligent. He said nothing, preferring instead to gesture with all four tentacles. Walker hoped it was an indication of understanding.

"Right," George barked in agreement. "That means not eating friends."

"Are you then my friends? I have no friends," Braouk rumbled despondently.

"You do now. Two of 'em." And, showing more courage than Walker had known the dog possessed, the mutt trotted up to the looming wall of the Tuuqalian and deliberately licked the end of one tentacle. Walker held his breath.

Both eyestalks bent to regard the tiny quadruped. Walker knew how fast the Tuuqalian could move if it wanted to. If Braouk was so inclined, if the alien was the least bit irritated by the gesture, the dog would disappear in a single gulp.

Instead, Braouk watched silently as George backed away. "So I have friends, it seems. Stiff of joint, awkward of speaking voice, unusual compassion. I accept your presence, and your offering." Both eyes focused on the dog. "Do not do that again, though."

"Got it," George replied with alacrity. "Among my kind, it's a gesture of liking."

"Among my kind," the Tuuqalian responded, "it is a gesture of tasting."

"Is that why the Vilenjji have kept you isolated so much, and for so long?" Walker wanted to know, anxious to change the subject. "Because you, uh, kept having dinner with anyone you came in contact with?"

"To some extent, I am sure. Certainly each time I made a meal of another of their captives, it cost them future profits." The Tuuqalian looked away. "Partly also, I am sure, they isolated me because I have so often displayed unpredictability in my nature. This prevents them from properly assessing me. My mindless rages they mistake for ignorance, condemning me. Not that, if granted the opportunity, I would in any event wish to squat and communicate pleasantries with them." Tentacles rippled. "What I would like to do is first remove their outermost limbs, then their genitalia, then their eyes, then their—"

"I can't see why they'd shun your presence," George observed perceptively, "or why they wouldn't find you a laugh riot at pack parties." The dog cocked his head to one side. "Do the Vilenjji laugh? You know more about them than Marc or I."

"A stimulating question." Interestingly, when the Tuuqalian turned

thoughtful, his eyes moved toward one another, as if seeking enlightenment in each other's reflection. "I have not observed any behavior
that could be definitively classified as such. But then, those times when
they enter into the presence of the ensnared may not be the ones when
they elect to relax in collective jollity."

"Don't know why they fail to find you amusing," George commented. "Maybe it's your attitude."

Both eyes swerved to gaze down at the dog. "They perceive only my
physicality, and my furies, and do not try to interact with the sensitive
inner part that is my true self."

"Might have something to do with your determination to tear them
limb from limb," Walker pointed out.

"Barbarians. They have technology, are devoid of culture, money-
grubbers!"

"And bulk kidnappers, don't forget," George added helpfully.

"My situation languishes, for want of hope, lachrymose laughing."

Walker pursed his lips. "You're really very good with words."

"Do you think so?" Dark, soulful eyes that were nearly as big as the
human's head extended toward him. Walker held his ground. "How can
you judge? It is not your manner of speaking."

"No, it's not," Walker admitted readily, "but I recognize true sensitivity when I hear it." George stared hard at his friend, but said nothing. The human was only doing as the dog had taught him. "Surely you
must have songs, poems, composed for purely aesthetic reasons, that
have nothing to do with the exchanging of formal communication?"

"Ah, glad I am I did not eviscerate you, and allowed you to eat and
drink." Vertically aligned jaws opened and closed slowly.

"So am I," Walker replied candidly. One globular black eye was so
close that he could see his own mirror image in it.

"Would you like to hear a saga of my people?"

For a second time that morning, Walker settled himself down on
the cushiony ground cover. "I'd like nothing better." As a commodities
trader, he had long ago learned to lie with great facility. Though, he had
to admit, he was more than a little curious to hear how Braouk would
respond. For his part, George winced. The Tuuqalian either did not notice or did not recognize the canine expression.

Walker expected eloquence on the part of the massive alien. What
he did not expect, and perhaps should have, was the length to which
the Tuuqalian would go to express himself. Anticipating a series of
short, choppy poetical phrases, the two captives from Earth were
treated to a seemingly interminable exposition in rhyme, meter, and

deep-throated quavering song on the loneliness felt by their new acquaintance. That they shared its sense of isolation and separation from home failed to mitigate the ennui that inevitably crept into their minds and threatened to shutter their eyes. Neither dog nor man dared to fall asleep, fearing that the inspired declaimer ranting in front of them might look unfavorably upon such a nonverbal disparaging of his efforts.

After another half hour of solid, nonstop singsong lamentation, however, Walker knew he had to do something. How, however, to bring the recitation to an end without the request being misconstrued? George saved him the trouble.

The dog began to howl. It was at once such a familiar and yet unexpected sound, an echo of an absent, atavistic Earth, that Walker found himself choking up. He did not break down because he was far too concerned with how the Tuuqalian might react to such a response.

Braouk stopped reciting and stared at the dog. Head back, eyes closed, lost in the throes of canine abandonment, George failed to notice that the Tuuqalian had gone silent. Walker tried and failed to get his friend's attention. Braouk seemed to lean forward. If the giant chose to strike out, Walker knew there was nothing he could do to stop it.

After listening for a long moment, the big alien appeared to fold slightly in upon itself. Then he resumed rhyming, louder than ever, matching his modulations to the yips and yowls of the small dog seated before him. At once relieved and dumbfounded, Walker could do nothing but sit back and listen—and occasionally, when he believed he was not being observed, try as best he could to cover his ears with his hands.

The improbable duet lasted for a very long while, finally ceasing about the time Walker had determined that if it did not he was going to run screaming into the nearest electrical barrier. Something like mutual congratulations were exchanged between Terran and Tuuqalian as the tip of a massive tentacle gently encircled a proffered paw. More than a little numbed, Walker staggered toward them.

"What was that all about?" he asked George, in reference to the bit of muted conversation he had failed to overhear.

George was looking past him, toward the squatting mass of the Tuuqalian. "We were both decrying your lack of sensitivity." Limpid dog eyes met Walker's own. "You should have joined in. It would have cemented the relationship."

"I'll pick my spots with occasional interjections of poetry, thanks." He hesitated, regarding the now silent alien. "I think our new friend might have something valuable to contribute to our efforts to get out of here."

George shook his head slowly from side to side. "Are you still thinking about that? I keep telling you, man, even if we could get out of the grand enclosure, there's no place to get out to. We're on a ship. In space. You remember space? Cold, dark, lifeless? No air? Get out to where?"

"One small step at a time, poochie."

The dog drew itself up as much as it could manage. "Don't call me that. When we first got together you asked me what you should call me. 'Poochie' was not among the acceptable designations."

"All right." Walker grinned. "I suppose you wouldn't like me to call you 'fuzz-butt,' either."

George eyed him warningly. "Would you like me to pee on your leg?"

More seriously, Walker asked, "I have to at least think about trying to escape, George. Otherwise I'll go crazy just sitting here, waiting until the Vilenjji decide to dispose of us. We may not actually be able to do anything about it, but I'd rather have an impossible goal to focus on than nothing at all."

The dog shrugged. "Suit yourself. Me, I'm happy to roll around in the grass, or whatever they call the stuff that grows in the grand enclosure, gnaw on food bricks, and take long naps. But so long as it doesn't get us killed, I guess I'm willing to give a hearing to the occasional human absurdity."

"No promises," Walker warned him.

The dog sighed. "So what's the first step we take down this long road you've mapped out to eventual futility?"

"We marshal our forces. We take stock of the assets we have at our disposal. That's what my work has taught me to do when faced with a difficult set of circumstances."

"That won't take long." One paw came up. "We have no weapons. I can scratch and bite. You can scratch and bite and be irritating." He looked past Walker to the resting Tuuqalian. "If he's willing to actively participate in whatever insanity you manage to concoct, our friend Braouk might be able to do rather more. What else have we got? Am I overlooking something?"

Walker considered. "Depends on whether she's willing to help or not. To find out about that, everyone really should meet everyone else." Turning, he looked back at the ruminative Tuuqalian. "Braouk, when was the last time you were out in the grand enclosure?"

The huge alien struggled to remember. "I cannot recall. It has been a long while, I think. And it may be that I was so crazed with rage and frustration at the time that I cannot see the history of it in my mind's eye."

"Would you be willing to do so now? To come with me and George? There is another I'd like you to meet. Another sentient who shares our sentiments. Our feelings."

"All do," the Tuuqalian observed. "All here who are captives share in the same aloneness and isolation. What is special about the one of whom you speak?"

Walker smiled knowingly. "She's about as social as you. The two of you share a mutual aversion to company."

Tentacles twisted slowly as Braouk considered. "Is she sensitive, while lost in dreaming, isolation imposed?"

"Actually, she'd as soon eat sand as express compassion. In that way, in spirit, you two are utter opposites. That's why I want you to meet."

Alien bulk leaned forward until Walker and George found themselves in shadow. "I do not understand, Marcus Walker."

"If we're ever going to strike back at our captors, we need allies who complement one another, who bring as many different strengths to the table as possible. That's how a good board of directors operates. Out of conflict arises the best possible solutions." Turning to his left, he looked down. "Don't you agree, George?"

"Uh-huh, sure—if they don't kill each other first. In a pack, it's simple. You stick behind the biggest dog with the biggest teeth."

"Or the smartest one," Walker argued.

A gleam appeared in the mutt's eye. "I see where you're going with this. I'm just not sure I want to go there with you."

"You can always opt out." Rising, Walker started toward the grand enclosure.

"Right, sure." Muttering to himself, the dog trotted along behind the human. "Easy for you to say. If things don't work out, you've got a modicum of mass and muscle going for you. Me, I'm snack food."

Approaching the border between the Tuuqalian's enclosure and the much larger open space beyond, Walker slowed. Hesitantly, he extended an arm. It passed beyond the boundary without encountering any tingling. Stepping through, he turned as George joined him. Behind them, the Tuuqalian wavered.

Walker frowned. "What's wrong, Braouk?"

The alien appeared uncertain. "I like you, human Walker. I like your small expressive companion as well. I would not want to hurt you."

"You won't." Walker beckoned. "Come on. If we hurry, we can begin this before darkness comes."

Still the Tuuqalian demurred. "Nearly every other time I moved beyond my own space, it was to rampage uncontrollably. I do not know if it was something in the atmosphere that changed, or within me, or something the Vilenjji injected into the immediate environment that so affected my soul." Dark eyes regarded Walker indecisively. "If when I step outside this time I again lose control, I might injure you without being aware of doing so."

"You just need to concentrate," Walker advised him. "On what we're doing, on where we're going. I know." He steeled himself. "How about if you spin us another saga of your people as we travel? Wouldn't that help to focus your thoughts?"

"An excellent idea, clever and well propounded, tidily conceived." Advancing on its under-tentacles, the Tuuqalian came toward them—and passed through the inactivated border. It approached very close to Walker, and to George, who had to fight himself to keep from breaking into flight.

It was Braouk who broke, however—into verse. Halfway to their destination, unable to restrain himself, George launched into a series of uninhibited accompanying yips and howls. In response, the Tuuqalian raised the volume of alien baritone to match the canine counterpoint. Walker marched on between them, suffering in silence.

Whether by dog or alien, he dared not be accused of being insensitive.

9

"You can come out. Really, it's okay."

There was a slight echo to the reply; no doubt because it emanated from the very depths of the hollow within the boulder. "I am not coming out. It is not okay. You have in your company the dreadful grotesque enormity. Unlike yourself, I would not benefit from being stepped upon by it."

Walker rose from his crouch before the mouth of the tunnel. Stepping past him, George lowered his head slightly and sniffed at the entrance. "Something in there smells like old, moldy wet towels." His tail wagged briskly. "I like it."

"Disinterest flows freely, fond I am not, bitter talkings." Braouk had both eyes drawn in as close to his body as possible as he strove to shield them from the light rain that was falling. "Also, it is much too wet in here. The Tuuqalia prefer skies that are clear and dry."

*Every cat to its ashcan,* Walker thought. Aloud, he said to the massive alien, "Just give her a couple of minutes. She's . . . shy."

"I am not shy," came the voice from within the boulder. Sque's hearing was sharper than Walker would have expected. "I am selective. I do not engage in conversation with bloodthirsty beings that may also accidentally fall on me."

Walker took a deep breath, smiling to encourage himself more than his companions. "You don't have to worry about that, Sque. Braouk is far more agile than his size would suggest."

"How about his mind?" came the quick response. "Is it also agile?"

An opening. Knowing he was not likely to get a better one, Walker pounced on it. "I'm not qualified to judge such things, Sque. Certainly not to the degree that you are. In fact, I was hoping you'd be able to render an opinion and tell *me*."

"Of course I could. If I would." A pause, then, "What do you call the inquisitive lump of hair with the educated nose that accompanies you?"

The dog inserted itself halfway into the opening. "I'm called George, thank you very much."

"You are welcome, for nothing that I can perceive." The echo receded, and the voice grew slightly more defined. "No doubt the receptivity of your nostrils exceeds that of your intellect. Nevertheless, I am at least not nauseated to meet you."

"Same here," George barked back. To the human standing alongside him he whispered, "You're right, Marc. She just oozes charm."

"I told you: She's shy."

"Uh-huh." The dog nodded. "Like a rottweiler on meth, she's shy."

"Give her a chance." Walker's gaze flicked from canine to Tuuqalian. "She's not used to company."

"Gee, I wonder why?" George kept his voice down. "Could it maybe have something to do with her irresistible personality?"

Walker's mouth tightened. "Try to be civil. If we're going to have a chance of doing anything about you-know-what, we're going to need her."

"Need her?" The dog's expression wrinkled. "Remind me again, why do we need her?"

"Because she's smarter than any of us," Walker whispered back—just loudly enough to feign confidentiality. The result was as he hoped.

Cautiously, several tentacles appeared in the tunnel's opening, to be followed by a tripartite body and yet more tentacles. Sunken eyes like polished silver took in man, dog, Tuuqalian, and man again.

Peering down at the K'eremu, Braouk commented offhandedly, "Hardly worth dismembering."

"Better to be remembered than dismembered," she responded, looking up at him. "You, for example, are rumored to engage in slaughter for the sheer pleasure of it." Six or seven tentacles, Walker noted, firmly gripped the rocky surface beneath and behind her, ready to yank her backward into her granite refuge at the first sign of distress.

Walker spoke up hurriedly. "Any injuries Braouk inflicted on other captives were done out of frustration, or because he was provoked. He's actually very sensitive. Something of a poet, my kind would say."

Horizontal gray eyes flicked sharply in his direction. "Somehow I do not see myself relying on your species' definition of aesthetics. Before I will join you outside the tomb that has become my home, I need verification that I will be treated according to my significance, and not mindlessly subject to some primordial tantrum."

Walker turned to look up at the irritated Tuuqalian. "Braouk would never do that. He's too busy teaching me how to speak expressively, and George how to sing."

"Hey, I don't need any help to—" the dog began, but Walker cut him off.

"You seek lessons in elocution from a stomach that walks?" Sque emerged a little farther. "When I am here?"

"Well," Walker shrugged and turned half away, "I have to make use of what's available. Braouk has already helped me in my efforts to improve myself. As well as any sentient can, I suppose."

"Really? Is that what you think?" The entire rust-hued body was now fully outside the entrance to the hollowed-out boulder. At this point, the fast-moving Braouk could have cut off the K'eremu's retreat whenever he wished. Walker tensed. But for whatever rea-son the Tuuqalian, though clearly annoyed by the K'eremu's attitude, restrained himself from reacting. Walker could only pray that the giant's volcanic temperament stayed under control.

The best way to ensure that, he felt, was to engage Sque in active conversation that preferably ignored the big Tuuqalian. "Of course, if you're willing to help, I can certainly use all the assistance I can get."

"Yes, that is true." Tentacle tips gestured agreement. "I am reassured, human Walker. Your recognition of your own abysmal ignorance is encouraging. It may be that there is yet hope for you and by association, possibly your species. Though a great many doubts manifest themselves in my mind."

"I'm grateful for your forbearance," he told her humbly. George was eyeing him with an interesting mixture of pity and approval.

"Now then." Tentacles spread outward in the shape of a flower as she settled herself down. "You have not returned, I think, to request tutoring in the art of diction. As you honestly say, you can certainly use all the assistance you can get. For what specifically do you come seeking my assistance?"

Walker sat down opposite the splay of limbs, saw a distorted image of himself reflected in silvery eyes. "You told me before that there's no way out of here, no chance of escape. I argued that no matter what, I was going to get out."

"There would seem to exist a bit of a contradiction in our respective opinions," she murmured placidly.

He nodded, conscious of George's eyes on his back. As for Braouk, the Tuuqalian was interested in the byplay in spite of himself. "You may be smarter than me—"

"The term 'may' does not apply here," she interrupted him.

"All right. You *are* smarter than me. You're smarter than anyone. Smarter even than the Vilenjji."

Tentacles gestured. "At last. A modicum of intelligence rears its bone-imprisoned head. I feel a faint hope."

Walker continued. "And since you're smarter than anyone, you're going to help us get out of this." He took a deep breath. "Otherwise, you and all the K'eremu are nothing but big bags of rope-flailing water and hot air, too enamored of their own snobbery and arrogance to admit to the truth."

George tensed. Braouk looked on expectantly. In front of Walker, the middle two-thirds of the K'eremu's body swelled alarmingly, turning in color from a warm maroon to a dull carmine that bordered on bright crimson. The recessed eyes bulged forward so far that the pupils were nearly flush with their sockets. This disquieting demonstration lasted for several seconds. Then the swelling began to subside, the skin to blush a less livid hue.

"Your impertinence exceeds your ignorance—something I would not have thought possible. Do you really believe you can induce me to participate in some as-yet-unquantifiable suicidal scheme by irritating me with infantile name-calling?"

Walker nodded, wondering if the gesture would be properly interpreted. "Yes, I do. Either you're as smart as you say or you're not. Prove it. You talk the talk, now walk the walk. Or squirm the squirm. Pick your own analogy." Inside, he was on edge. Such in-your-face challenges had worked wonders when trading raw materials. Would they have any effect on a sophisticated alien?

"You would not be partial to the one on which I am presently ruminating," she told him curtly. Silence followed. Walker could hear George panting expectantly behind him. A dull rumbling emerged from Braouk, though whether an untranslatable comment or mild intestinal upset Walker could not be sure.

Eventually, damp tentacles gestured through the enveloping mist. "I must be in need of additional joqil. Otherwise, I would react rationally and retire to my abode. In lieu of that, I am made curious as to the unreasonable and unfathomable workings of your primitive mind. How would you propose initiating such an investigation?"

Walker let out a long, slow sigh of relief. "As clearly the most intelligent among us, everything must start with you, Sque. So I tell you by way of beginning that there's an old saying among my people: 'Know thy enemy.' "

Behind him, George muttered softly, "I usually hear 'watch where you're stepping.' "

Walker ignored the dog. "You say that you've spoken with the Vilenjji." He leaned forward eagerly. "Are they always watching? Always listening?" He gestured at their immediate surroundings. "What about when vision is obscured, as it is now by the mist and fog that dominates your enclosure's restricted atmosphere?"

Sque emitted the equivalent of a sigh. "Poor biped. Your consuming ignorance almost draws forth my pity. Do you know nothing of physics? Like any species, the Vilenjji suffer from a range of characteristic physical limitations. Also like any advanced species, they have developed technology that allows them to overcome these. Be assured they are watching us even now. Surely you do not think a little water vapor in the atmosphere can mask our presence here?"

"Uh, no, I guess not," Walker mumbled.

Gray eyes turned toward the empty corridor, barely visible off to his right. "I would be surprised if in addition to simple visuals they did not also have in use the most basic devices for sensing and interpreting heat signatures, for identifying outlines through weather far worse than this, and for keeping track of every one of their captives every moment of every day and night, even in utter darkness. Only a child of a minimal technology could fail to realize this. I do not think they have bothered to place trackable implants in individual bodies. They would regard that, rightly, as an unnecessary expense. One that could additionally be off-putting to a buyer." When Walker did not comment, she added, "As to monitoring sound, that is even easier."

He nodded slowly. "What if two of us happened to whisper to each other while the other two sang, or recited poetry. Loudly. Wouldn't that confuse their auditory pickups?"

Sque considered. At the mention of poetry, Braouk looked more alert than usual. "Quite possibly. However, it does not matter if we manage to agree on a course of action privately. We can only act on a course of action publicly. There is no way we can hide ourselves from the Vilenjji's eyes, may they fester with disease and dry out. Even the most basic surveillance equipment operated by brigands such as our captors should be capable of seeing through rain, fog, snow, and if properly directed, solid stone. There is nowhere we can hide from them." Unexpectedly turning her attention to the watching Tuuqalian, she added, "I am not expecting to encounter elegance of language from one with a reputation for consuming his audience. I am most interested to hear proof of this doubtful claim for myself."

"Yes, Braouk." To his credit, Walker picked up on her meaning immediately, sidling over to be as close to her as possible. Trying to appear enthusiastic without wincing, he added, "Sing us a saga of your people! Sing it bold, sing it clear. Sing it loud."

The Tuuqalian hesitated. Alien or not, Walker's stare was enough to galvanize the giant with purpose. Immediately, he launched into recitation, booming forth verse in clipped yet stentorian tones forceful enough to all but induce ripples in the enveloping mist.

While the towering alien thundered back and forth, tentacles writhing, eyestalks contorting, voice reverberating, Walker and George huddled as close to Sque as they could without sitting on her tentacles.

"Even if this juvenile ploy should succeed in preventing the Vilenjji from overhearing our conversation," she whispered, "it does not matter."

"Are they likely to intervene if they can't?" Walker voiced the question as softly as he could.

"I think not. We appear to be listening to and commenting upon your weighty friend's deafening oration. There is no reason for the Vilenjji to suppose that the subject of our ongoing conversation might include plans for sedition."

"You say that you're smarter than the Vilenjji." While talking, the human kept his attention focused on the boisterous Braouk, who was by now getting fully into the spirit of the moment. *Good*, Walker thought. It would be that much more successful in distracting any observing Vilenjji.

"If I managed to get you out of here, maybe with one other to assist you, do you think you could find a way to deactivate the external barrier that seals off all the enclosures from the rest of this ship?"

She almost—almost, but not quite—turned sharply to look at him. "You speak of doing something impossible and follow it by asking me to do likewise."

His tone tightened. "If I can hold up my end of the bargain, you have to come through with yours. Otherwise, the consequences might reflect poorly on a certain someone's loudly expressed notions of racial superiority."

"I have never turned from a challenge. Certainly not from one posited by an ill-mannered primitive." One tentacle crept sideways until it was resting meaningfully on his thigh. "You spoke of freeing me and perhaps one other to try this thing. I sense that you do not think of yourself as that other. After expending so much effort, you will then remain behind?"

"For the idea I have in mind, it can't be otherwise. I have to stay behind, for reasons that will become clear when I explain it." He nodded toward the rambling, rumbling Tuuqalian. "When Braouk finishes, we'll have George take a turn serenading us and I can explain the details to him. We'll rotate performances so that someone is always making enough noise to garble any auditory pickup the Vilenjji may be employing. If they're as egotistical and overconfident as you say, they probably won't even notice." He leaned so close that he could smell the alien dampness of rubbery flesh.

"Here's my idea. If you can deactivate the barrier and we can prepare a few other residents for what's going to happen, it means that many captives will make a break for temporary freedom all at the same time. That will allow the four of us to rendezvous. If properly surprised by the breakout, the Vilenjji will be busy trying to round up any escapees they can. They'll have no reason to focus on us because our fellow captives will be running every which way, trying to make their short-lived freedom last for as long as they can."

The tentacle moved. "And we four? We will not be running every which way?"

"No. At least, I hope not. That's where you come in. At that point, everything will depend on your knowledge of the Vilenjji and their technology."

"Thus it all comes down to me." The fleshy body pulsed noticeably.

"It would, of course. Very well. I accept the challenge, together with its concomitant responsibility. I do not think whatever you have in mind has a shed sucker's chance of succeeding, but I am willing to try most anything to spike the boredom imposed by this wretched daily existence." Tightening against his leg, the gracile tentacle showed surprising strength.

"Whatever foolishness you have in mind, human Walker, we should commence it soonest. Residents are periodically removed without warning, never to be returned, presumably having been sold. While I expect that to happen to me, as well as to you and to all of us who are being held on this execrable vessel, I do not look forward to the eventuality."

"That's what I like to hear." Walker was aware that Braouk's recitation was beginning to draw to a close. "Unreserved enthusiasm. I believe that you believe the Vilenjji are not omnipotent. That says to me that we can overcome them."

"The Vilenjji, perhaps." From within the splayed mass of tentacles, the pink speaking trunk moved back and forth. "Unfortunately, beyond the Vilenjji lies interstellar space. That cannot be overcome by clever notions and primitive assaults."

Walker nodded slowly, thoughtfully. "Then we'll just have to think of another way to overcome it. But it won't be done if all we do is squat here and cry in our beer."

"That last did not translate," she informed him uncertainly.

"Never mind. I kind of wish I hadn't mentioned it." At that moment, in that place, he would have given a typing finger right down to the bone for a single tall cold one. Licking condensation from the backs of his hands was a pretty piss-poor substitute.

✳

Ensuing days saw the exceedingly odd foursome congregating in one or another's designated enclosure. At such times thunderous poetry, bad song, and enthusiastic howling was seriously indulged in. Only Sque did not participate in these strident vocal exhibitions. Through no fault of her own, the K'eremu did not possess enough lung power to effectively mask the conversations of her companions.

It did not matter. One at a time, a whispering Walker was able to expound on the particulars of his proposal to his fellow sentients. Each time, he was met with doubt and derision. Each time, he explained the details over and over, addressing every complaint, unfailingly pursuing the central proposal with relentless enthusiasm, until he had them half convinced it just might, could just possibly, succeed. He did it so well and so often he even managed to half convince himself.

Anyway, George facetiously commented, if nothing else, making the attempt would provide an interesting morning's diversion. If it failed, they were unlikely to face retribution from their captors. The merchandise might be revolting, but he was counting on the fact that the Vilenjji were too greedy to want to damage it. He chose not to remind himself that they were perfectly capable of meting out punishment without causing lasting injury.

Today they had gathered in Walker and George's transplanted bit of homey Sierra Nevada. While Braouk propagated the requisite camouflaging noise in the form of a loud recitation of the Anaaragi Saga, part twelve, the remaining threesome gathered in the chilly shallows of the fragment of Cawley Lake. Finding the alpine air far too dry for her liking, Sque would only participate in conversation while lying half submerged in the hydrating cold water. Walker sat close to her, George resting in his lap, while the three of them pretended to watch and listen to the animated vocal performance of the flailing, impassioned Tuuqalian.

Contrary to the attitude of general indifference she usually chose to present, Sque had plainly been devoting some time to studying the plan. "For this to have any chance of working, the Vilenjji must be kept as busy as possible as soon as it is put into effect."

George nodded his agreement. "The larger a squabbling pack, the easier it is for a dog with a cool head to slip away with the biggest piece of carrion."

While his eyes were on the stomping, roaring Braouk, Walker's attention was directed at his other two companions. "We can't tell anyone else what we're planning. You never know who might be Ghouabaesque and who might not."

George frowned. "Then how do we motivate our fellow captives to start the diversion?"

"By not telling them, my short and stumpy quadruped," Sque explained carefully, "that they are being asked to engage in such an endeavor. Human Walker is quite correct. Tell but one other the details of our venture, and there is every chance it will soon be known to all. I have no doubt that would be fatal to the enterprise." The cartilage that formed her deep eye sockets would not permit squinting, so she compensated by leaning toward her companions.

"What we can do is spread the story—that did not originate with any of us, of course—that we were told, by one who had heard, from another in a position to know, that there was a rumor that at a certain time, without warning, the barrier that surrounds all the enclosures would have to be momentarily deactivated. For what reasons, this rumormonger did not know. Maintenance, perhaps, or a periodic checking of the structure that delivers power to the system. The reason will not matter to those who are alerted. All they will want to know is when will this happen.

"If it does, when it does, then everyone will be free to react to the resulting state of affairs as each sees fit. Some may elect to do nothing. Some may choose to take a step or two out into a corridor and then retreat to the safety and familiarity of their personal enclosures. But some—hopefully many—may opt to make a break for as much fleeting freedom as they can achieve."

Chilled as Walker's backside was becoming from sitting in the icy water, he was reluctant to stand for fear of having to raise his voice, thus risking that some sensitive, unseen Vilenjji pickup might overhear. So he remained seated, and cold, and continued to whisper in between shivers.

"Even if the Vilenjji are informed of the 'rumor,' or overhear discussions about it, it's still only a rumor. Most likely they'd ignore it. If they try to track it to its source, they'll fail, because everyone including us will say that we heard it from someone else. In the unlikely event that they get really interested, and ultimately manage to isolate one of us as the originator of the story, we can just say that we were trying to boost the spirits of our fellow captives by spreading around an artful fiction."

"What if they do get curious?" George wanted to know. "And start paying extra attention to us?"

Walker found himself gazing at distant sham mountains, wishing so hard they were real that his stomach knotted. "We'll just have to do the best we can. We can't ever be sure when they're increasing surveillance or when they're disinterested, and we can't wait forever because one day, you or I or Sque or Braouk is going to be tranquilized and hauled out of their private enclosure never to be seen again. And this idea won't have a chance of succeeding without all of us working together."

Sque could not keep herself from demurring. "Actually, human Wal . . . Marc, while I see the need for the active participation of the Tuuqalian, and I, and even yourself, I confess that I am at a loss to recognize the necessity of your small companion's involvement." Gleaming horizontal eyes regarded the dog impassively. "Nothing personal."

"On the contrary," Walker quickly shot back before the dog could respond, "George's participation is critical to the success of our undertaking. Among other things, his presence will be vital to looking after your welfare."

"Oh." Dexterous tentacles stroked back and forth, making lazy ripples in the cool, clear water. "I confess that I had not thought of that. Naturally all would be doomed to failure should some harm befall me." Her gaze turned to him. "You are learning, Marc. You show promise. Of course," she added, "when one begins one's ascent from the absolute bottom of the cerebral pit, noticeable advances are easier to make."

Though impressive, Braouk's stamina was finite. The Anaaragi Saga was difficult to sustain in the telling, and part twelve especially so. The Tuuqalian was starting to show signs of slowing down.

"How soon?" While George's excitement was betrayed by the rapid wagging of his tail, any watching Vilenjji should put it down to his apparent enjoyment of the Tuuqalian's resounding recitation.

For an answer, Walker looked to Sque. As long as it was relatively soon, it did not matter to him when they made their move, and she would appreciate being asked to be the one to make the decision. Still, her reply surprised him.

"Tomorrow, at the occasion of the first feeding for those of us who are diurnal. I know the Vilenjji to be light-lovers, as are the majority of their captives. Those who do nocturnal duty will be growing tired and are therefore likely to be less alert and reactive than normal, while those assigned to the daytime period will not yet be fully awake and active enough to participate in the confusion we hope to spawn."

Walker nodded, glanced down at his ready companion. "George?"

"I don't give a cat fart," the dog muttered impatiently. "We've been talking about doing this and planning it for so long I can hardly hold my water from thinking about it." From beneath bushy brows, brown eyes looked up at the human. "Marc, even if we can pull this off, do you really think it will lead to anything?"

"I don't know." Walker looked away. "But I do know that being proactive is better than doing nothing. Maybe something unexpected will present itself. We can't take advantage of an opportunity we don't try to make."

"Blatantly obvious." Like a long, sentient pink worm, Sque's speaking tube swayed slowly back and forth. "There is one small problem that has not, as yet, been discussed. I have been somewhat reluctant to bring it up, lest its import be misconstrued."

Tuuqalian eyestalks were aimed directly at them now, a sure sign that despite his concentration, Braouk's staying power was fading. "What problem?" Walker asked her tersely.

For the first time since he had met her, Sque seemed unsure of herself. "If our gamble should enjoy any degree of success, there is the matter of subsequently securing adequate sustenance to go on."

"We've talked about that," Walker reminded her. "Depending on how circumstances develop, those in need of food will have to scavenge for it as best they can."

She remained visibly perturbed. "It is not so much the basal nourishment that concerns me as it is the potential inability to acquire a sufficiency of certain specific ingredients."

Realization dawned. Walker peered hard into her eyes, not caring if any spying Vilenjji noticed his abrupt shift of attention. "Your daily dose of si'dana and joqil. You're worried about having to go cold turkey on your stimulants."

"The metaphor you choose does not translate well, but the general inference is clear." She drew herself up slightly, her tentacles bunching beneath her. "They are 'herbs.' "

"Oh yeah," George muttered. "Herbs you 'really like.' It's not like you're 'hooked' or anything."

"On the contrary, I admit to the addiction." Silver eyes turned toward the dog. "I am not one to dispute the actuality of a reality. The question is, what can be done about it?"

Walker started to rise. Proceedings had progressed too far to turn back now. If necessary, he was prepared to go ahead without the K'eremu. Better to embark on an ill-prepared effort than none at all.

"You'll just have to eat your fill the night before," he told her. "After that . . . ," he paused. "After that, you'll have an unprecedented opportunity to demonstrate to all of us how a superior intellect can overcome something as trifling as mere physical dependence." Water dripped from his bare legs. "I know you can do it, Sque, because I've seen humans do it.

"One casual friend of mine was a chocolate aficionado. So great was his obsession that he had made a living trading solely in cocoa futures. Whenever anyone would question him about his fondness for chocolate, both professionally and personally, he would go on and on about its hidden health benefits, how it stimulated his libido, and how much of an energy rush he got every time he ate some. Eventually, it killed him." He went silent, wondering if she would buy the edifying fiction.

Sque indicated her understanding. "I will apply the utmost self-control of which I am capable, Marc. I assure you that is quite a considerable amount. But it will still be grueling. An acquired fondness for joqil is not easily forsaken." Though he knew she was not cold, several tentacles quivered. "Surely I can do better than the poor pathetic acquaintance of which you speak."

"I don't doubt it for a moment." It would be a sad day indeed, he mused, if a determined K'eremu could not show more determination than a nonexistent human. Straightening, he used the camp towel that had been draped around his shoulders to begin drying himself. Seeing that the conclave was in the process of breaking up, a grateful (and exhausted) Braouk jumped ahead to the rousing conclusion he had chosen for his oration.

Afterward, they each of them went their separate ways. Sque left with the Tuuqalian, riding (to save time) in the supporting curve of two of his massive appendages. While they walked, she would find an appropriate time and place to inform him that the decision had been made to make their move on the morrow. Walker retired to his tent with George following at his side. While its batteries were beginning to fade, the compact music player he had brought with him could still put out enough decibels to allow man and dog to converse in comparative privacy. He turned it on, and up, as soon as they entered the tent.

George lay down, chin on front paws, watching as Walker finished drying himself and prepared to get dressed. "How about it, Marc? You're convinced we won't get shot, or worse, for trying this. I wish I had your confidence. Not even that squirmy bunch of bitch-slime Sque can really predict how the Vilenjji are going to react."

"I know." Slipping clean feet into dry socks was one of the few earthly pleasures remaining to Walker. It was one that was not going to last much longer, as his limited supply of camp soap had just about run out. At least if he and Sque were wrong and they did get shot, or worse, he wouldn't die in dirty underwear.

His one consolation was that the Vilenjji, faced with a situation they had hopefully never been forced to deal with previously, would also not know how to react. As for the likelihood of dying, he had already given it far too much thought. To his own surprise, the possibility no longer troubled him. There was a time when the thought of a premature death would have sent him rushing for a drink, or set him to silently bawling, or lamenting the loss of all that he had worked so hard to build.

All that was in the past now. Part of a life half forgotten. A life on another world—a real world. Not an artificial one speeding through space subject to the whims and mercies of a taciturn, uncommunicative species of purplish, pointy-headed giants. He was ready to die trying to shake things up.

Trying what? They didn't even have a real goal, except to do something different, something that for a change was not controlled by the vile Vilenjji. Maybe, he thought, that was enough. For now, it would have to suffice.

Given a choice, he would rather have perished, like his imaginary friend, from eating too much chocolate, but on board an alien vessel racing across the cosmos that was sadly not a fate that was open to him.

**10**

It was a damned bright and sunny morning, with the temperature a damned perfect warmth, as it was just about every damned day. Damning the Vilenjji-synchronized repetitiveness of it, Walker and George set off across the grand enclosure to visit Braouk. Along the way, they paused to pick up Sque. The K'eremu emerged from her sodden surroundings in a mood that was unusually subdued even for her. As she was understandably preoccupied, Walker had to spur her to participate in the general conversation.

Finding the hulking Tuuqalian sunk in a dark mood of his own, tentacles and eyestalks entwined in a thick, tight knot, there was some discussion as to whether they should even intrude upon him. After a brief, purposefully loud debate, it was determined that as friends it was their duty to try and rouse him from his proportionately enormous funk. As it was nearly breakfast time, it was either join him in eating or else retrace their steps all the way back to their individual enclosures. It was decided to proceed.

Though they knew the Tuuqalian, none of them knew all the vagaries of his many moods, and so they approached guardedly, keeping close together. As they advanced, a pair of eyes on muscular stalks emerged from the tangle of tentacles to stare down at them intently.

"You three again. I grow sick, dealing with the sight, all obnoxious."

"Take it easy, Braouk." Walker continued to approach, flanked by his friends. "What's the matter? What's wrong?"

Globular orbs turned away from him, toward the expansive circular patch of open surface where nothing grew. "Hungry. Affects it does the Tuuqalian emotional as well as physical state. Did not eat last night, and should have. Emptiness in belly, screaming loudly of deprivation, addles thinking."

"It'll be all right." Smiling, Walker indicated the circle where the bricks and drink always emerged from below. "Food'll be up soon enough."

Limbs like tree trunks trembled. "Hungry now."

George started to back up, muttering urgently, "This isn't good, Marc. I don't like this at all. Let's come back later."

"Foolish four-foot no-hands," Sque admonished him. "We are here now. We came to converse now. I, for one, will not be driven to flight by the anarchic hunger pangs of an overstuffed sentient with only eight serviceable extremities. Far less by one with no head." Disdaining Walker's restraining fingers and moving forward on her own ten limbs, she sidled toward the crouching, markedly unhappy Tuuqalian.

"Here now; stop this nonsense and act your intelligence. Such as it is. We have no time to waste on such puerile indulgences."

Eyestalks swiveled sharply to confront her. The huge, powerful body began to rise on its thick hind limbs. "Always the condescending, disdainful of any other, haughtily patronizing." Menacing black pupils seemed to expand slightly. "Perhaps better stimulating when engaged in another way." Tentacles began to unknot.

Walker's eyes widened. He started to join George in backing up. "Sque—run!"

Perhaps she was too certain of her own unassailability. Perhaps she felt proximity to the mountainous Tuuqalian forestalled any realistic attempt at flight. Or perhaps there was another reason. Regardless, the K'eremu remained rooted to the spot as the angry Tuuqalian loomed over her.

Walker looked around wildly. Sque was caught between Braouk and the corridor. Unexpectedly, a Vilenjji appeared there, sauntering into view rather rapidly from the right. Its linear eyes, not unlike Sque's but much darker and wider, took in the ominous tableau that was being played out within the Tuuqalian enclosure. It stared for a moment, then turned and sloughed off back the way it had come, its pace perceptibly increased.

Maybe their surveillance systems weren't as all-encompassing as everyone imagined, Walker mused.

Then he put the thought aside as the raving, hunger-maddened Braouk reached down with one tentacle, picked up the futilely protesting K'eremu, and popped her into his mouth.

"Oh no, no!" Waving his arms, Walker took a couple of steps toward the giant. In response, the Tuuqalian whirled on him. Dark eyes glared down at the protesting biped.

"Still hungry," the alien growled as it thrust a questing tentacle in the human's direction.

It might have grabbed him, too, except that George interceded. Barking furiously, the dog dashed between his friend and the Tuuqalian. George was not particularly fast, but he was quick. Tentacles flailed impotently, striking at the dog, who danced back and forth between the blows. Visibly torn between taking flight and trying to help his brave friend, Walker ended up standing where he was and yelling desperately at the rampaging alien, trying to shout some sense into him.

"Food!" he finally yelled toward the corridor. "Braouk—the Tuuqalian, needs food! He needs it now! Do something!"

He had no way of knowing if the Vilenjji were listening. Or if they were, whether they were paying serious attention to the drama that was playing out in the enclosure, despite the brief visit from the single visitor in the corridor. Would they react at all? According to the daily, unvarying schedule, regular breakfast/food delivery was still minutes away. Observing what was happening, would they, could they, rush one delivery in time to protect a pair of valuable remaining specimens like himself and the dog?

Whatever their intentions, they were too late. Dodging a pair of descending limbs, George darted to his right—only to run smack into another tentacle that came sweeping around from that direction. It swept up the hairy lump of snapping, snarling canine effortlessly. Heedless of his own safety now, Walker bent and managed to find a couple of fist sized rocks. Using his best baseball throw, he heaved them at the hunger-crazed Tuuqalian. Either one of the stones was big enough to knock a human unconscious. They struck the alien's bristle-covered hide and slid off like spitballs on Teflon.

Barking and biting to the last, George went the way of the over-confident K'eremu, disappearing between vertical jaws into a vast, dark maw. Manifestly too distraught to yell or cry, Walker continued to scavenge and throw whatever he could find: rocks, handfuls of soil, pieces of loose vegetation. None of it had any effect whatsoever on the Tuuqalian. Then it turned to confront him.

With Sque injested and George following, any onlooker aware of the relationship that had developed between man and dog would have found it believable that, his friends consumed, an unhinged Walker would have continued to strike back instead of fleeing. As human and Tuuqalian confronted each other, a soft hissing sound was heard. Turning in its direction, both sentients saw a disc of solid surface begin to sink downward into the ground, exactly as it had done on hundreds of previous occasions. Forgetting his single surviving visitor, the famished Braouk threw himself toward the opening, ignoring the barrage of objects that Walker continued to throw at him.

"Damn you!" Walker yelled at the alien. "How could you do that? Is a little appetite all it takes to make you lose your mind?" Running right up to the massive Tuuqalian, who was now lying prone on the ground, the upper portion of its body jammed partway within the opening as tentacles fished for the food that would be rising within, Walker began hitting and kicking it. His blows had as much effect as the bits and pieces of surrounding terrain that he had hurled at the alien.

Straightening slightly, the single-minded Tuuqalian came up with tentacles full of food. One under-limb snapped forward and casually flicked the howling human aside. Walker was sent flying backward, to land hard on the alien ground cover. He started to get up, recoiled at a pain in his side, and was reduced to sitting and watching helplessly while the alien mindlessly gobbled down oversized food brick after brick, only occasionally pausing to messily slurp gallons of water from the accompanying cistern.

"You senseless cretin!" he cried aloud, not caring who overheard. "You stupid, ignorant, appetite-driven piece of alien crapola. Do you realize what you've just done? Do you even know? When you get hungry, does your brain go completely blank?" Sitting there holding his bruised ribs, he began finally to cry: long, drawn-out sobs of hopelessness. He wondered if the Vilenjji were watching, taking it all in.

Wincing with obvious pain, he struggled to his feet. A rational onlooker would have expected him to stagger out of the Tuuqalian's de-limited ecosystem. Apparently overwhelmed by the catastrophe that had struck him and his friends, he did not. As if wishing to wallow in the extended misery of his loss, Walker instead stumbled over to a far corner of the enclosure. There he sat down, his back against a supportive rock, and began to glare miserably at the still-ravenous alien. Indifferent to the human's presence, Braouk continued to stuff one food brick after another into an apparently insatiable maw. Whenever he would bite one in half with clashing saw edged teeth, Walker would stir himself long enough to hurl another slur, a fresh accusation. These troubled the Tuuqalian about as much as had the kicks, punches, and thrown stones.

Only when there was nothing left and the last crumb of food brick had been devoured did Braouk move away from the place where the food had been delivered. Choosing a comfortable depression, the Tu-uqalian snugged down into it and, without a word to or a glance in his surviving visitor's direction, immediately fell asleep. Walker continued to eye the alien moodily, reduced to muttering the occasional choice insult.

Several minutes passed, following which a pair of Vilenjji appeared in the corridor. Though they kept their voices down, Walker's implant was able to pick up enough of their conversation to suggest that they were discussing the events that had just taken place within the Tu-uqalian enclosure. Any conclusion or determination they reached, however, escaped him. Occasionally one or the other would raise a flap-tipped limb to point or gesture in Braouk's or Walker's direction. When their attention focused on him, he glowered back silently and said nothing. Experience had taught him that they were unlikely to respond in any case.

Eventually they wandered away, disappearing off to the right in the wake of their single predecessor. Within the enclosure, nothing changed. None came to force Walker to move back to his own bit of Sierra. No posse of irritated Vilenjji materialized to take Braouk the way of the Tripodan. Huddled against the rock at his back, knees pulled tightly up against his chest, Walker rested his chin on his hands and scowled silently at the indifferent Tuuqalian. He remained so all that day and on into the night, when at last he managed to fall asleep. Not because he was angry. Not because he was despondent. Not because un-anticipated circumstances had stolen all hope and reduced him to gib-bering despair. No, he had trouble falling asleep because he was excited.

So far, it had worked.

\*

Braouk had snatched up Sque and shoved the K'eremu into his mouth. He had eventually caught George and put the dog into his mouth. But in the midst of his madness there was one thing the ostensibly amok Tuuqalian had not done.

He had not swallowed.

Braouk had dived on the circular food lift the instant it had begun to descend. In addition to digging and scrabbling for the nourishment it was designed to supply to the enclosure, he had momentarily covered the opening with his upper body, and therefore also with his mouth. It had taken only seconds to spit out the two gasping entities who had been concealed within the Tuuqalian's generous oral cavity.

George emerged first, oriented himself as he fell, and bounced lithely off the already ascending lift, scattering the neatly piled food bricks in all directions. Sque followed immediately, her multiple limbs allowing her to secure a better purchase on the lift's surface than any dog could have managed. Even so, given the speed of the ascending elevator, she had just enough time to squeeze her semiflexible body between the piles of rising brick and the underside of the rigid surface that now formed their overhead. Encountering no opposition to their presence, hearing no Vilenjji hisses of surprise, dog and K'eremu scrambled madly for the nearest cover.

Though darkness descended at regular, predetermined intervals within the grand enclosure and most individual holding areas in order to allow their inhabitants to have the benefit of their normal sleep cycles, much of the vast Vilenjji vessel remained at least partly lit at all times. Even those areas where automatics held sway and the owners rarely needed to call in person were graced by a certain minimum illumination.

Still, George and Sque took no chances. Remaining concealed beneath the complex of machinery they had seen, a fair distance from the small lift that provided food to the Tuuqalian cell, they waited for the equivalent of night to fall in the enclosures that now hung heavy over their heads. Meanwhile they used the time to clean themselves, and to study their new surroundings.

Not unexpectedly, the inside of Braouk's mouth had been hot and wet. George had enjoyed the warmth but was now forced to engage in an orgy of licking to try to glean the Tuuqalian equivalent of dried saliva from his fur. In contrast, Sque had actually enjoyed the additional moisture but had reacted poorly to the increased temperature. All that mattered, really, was that both of them had survived the experience.

Minimal maintenance illumination provided just enough light for them to see by. Walker would only have stumbled around blindly in the murky enclosed space, but both the dog and the K'eremu had much more acute night vision than any human. The unlikely pair had the benefit of George's sensitive nose as well.

That was not why they had been chosen to try to make the escape, however. It was because of the four conspirators, only they were small enough to fit inside the Tuuqalian's voluminous orifice, and only he had a mouth large enough to hold someone else. That left Walker out of the oral loop, so to speak. Also, it was vital that Sque, who alone among them knew something of Vilenjjian technology, be among those who attempted the breakout. It was decided that George should go along to provide assistance, and to watch her back, such as it was.

Walker had shrewdly noted that the only possible route out of the enclosures, the only places that were not secured by the electrical barriers put in place by the Vilenjji, were the small circular lifts that three times a day supplied food and water to the captives. These could not be used in escape attempts, had not been used, for the self-evident reason that anyone trying to flee through the short-lived openings, even if they succeeded in squeezing through the temporary gap without getting crushed by the machinery, would easily be spotted by sophisticated surveillance equipment and dealt with appropriately. How to carry out such an attempt while concealing it from watching Vilenjji was a challenge that had occupied his thoughts for some time.

It was only while watching Braouk dine one day that a possible solution as absurd as it was audacious had occurred to him. Assured by the initially unenthusiastic Tuuqalian that he could manage his part of the scheme, there remained the problem of distracting the Vilenjji and somehow persuading them that Braouk had eaten the individuals he had ingested instead of just holding them in his mouth the way a squirrel stores nuts. Eventually, it was the Tuuqalian himself who came up with the idea of going on a hunger rampage.

"After all saying, it is well known, Tuuqalian berserks," was how the big alien had put it. Familiar as they were with his periodic rages, he believed that one more would not arouse any unusual suspicions among the Vilenjji. To further enhance the drama, Walker would react to Braouk's feeding frenzy with as much emotion as he could muster. Anything the human chose to do by way of response, Braouk assured him, the Tuuqalian could and would ignore. And, the dog marveled as he lay on his belly and listened to the ceaseless hum and whir and click of busy machinery all around them, it had worked. So far. He and Sque had made it safely outside the enclosure boundaries, perhaps the first captives of the Vilenjji ever to do so. Assuming the Vilenjji believed the evidence of their own electronic eyes, they could reasonably come to no other conclusion than that the small quadruped and decapod were both demised and in the process of being digested. Which meant no one would come looking for them.

"You've got to hand it to Marc," he whispered, trying to look every which way at once. "For a human, he's pretty damn clever."

From within the rust-red splay of tentacles bunched up next to him, the K'eremu replied, "I confess I was initially dismissive. The audacity of it defies logic. Yet here we are, for the first time since our captivity, free from the caging of the detested Vilenjji. If only for these few moments of freedom, I am grateful for your friend's primal cunning." In the near darkness, watchful eyes glinted. "Given time and sufficient aspiration, I would of course have concocted a similar stratagem myself."

Sure you would, George thought sardonically—but to himself. Having taught Marc how to grovel slavishly, he was not about to disregard his own counsel. If they were going to build on their immediate success, they needed to sustain the full concentration and enthusiasm of the dank cluster of crafty coils resting alongside him.

He wondered how Marc was doing, still trapped up above, still acting the part of the grievously outraged. He had no doubt that his human was at that moment probably wondering precisely the same thing about him.

Lying there in the almost blackness next to the clammy K'eremu, his fur still thickly matted with the sticky residue of Tuuqalian mouth moisture, the dog marveled at what they had already accomplished.

"I'll bet we are the first captives to ever escape from a Vilenjji enclosure."

Nearby, Sque's flexible form was a conical shadow in the dim light. "I cannot say for certain, but we are certainly the first to do so in all the time I have spent on this disagreeable vessel." Eyes shifted. "Odd as it may sound, while reposing within our large companion's capacious mouth and struggling to avoid suffocation therein, it came to me as to how I can adequately deal with my own somewhat quirky tastes."

"You mean your addiction." As he scanned the dark accessway in front of them, the dog was panting softly.

Sque was sufficiently aloof to ignore the recurring aspersion. "Our present position places us just outside the good Braouk's environment and just inside the grand enclosure." One tentacle pointed toward the food lift they had dodged in the course of making their escape. "A similar device for supplying food and water lies beneath every individual ecosystem. As you know, these are in turn arranged in a circle around the circumference of the grand enclosure." The limb continued to gesture. "If we follow these successive food lifts around the curve of the zone where captives are kept, we will eventually reach our own. I will then have access to those food squares that are synthesized specifically for my digestive system, and you for yours."

George considered. "Won't the Vilenjji, or their equipment, notice if food bricks are missing before they're served up top?"

"Nourishment is provided thrice daily," she replied. "A brick or cube here and there ought not to be missed. Even if the absence of one or two prior to delivery are, our captors are far more likely to put it down to an aberration of preparation or delivery rather than theft by individuals they have already presumed dead. In any event," she added as she began to move stealthily forward, "we have to eat."

George could not argue with that. Though still too excited by their success to really be hungry, he saw the wisdom of eating to keep their strength up. Squeezing out from beneath the heavy metal overhang, he followed Sque as she led the way along the deserted accessway.

It did not remain deserted for very long. Though her eyesight was a degree sharper than his, he was the one who heard the slight whispering of air approaching.

"Something's coming!" he muttered anxiously, looking around for a hiding place.

"Here." Sque led the way back into a dark recess between two high metal rectangles. They were warm to the touch, and mewed like kittens trying to hold a high "C."

The device that came trundling toward them down the accessway had no head and not much of a body. It did have a lot of limbs, a number of which terminated in specialized tools. These concerned George considerably more than the machine's lack of a clearly defined cranium.

"What if it looks this way?" he whispered to his companion even as he tried to shrink farther back into the unyielding alcove.

"With what?" Sque shot back. "I discern no obvious visual receptors."

"Maybe it doesn't need eyes. Maybe it uses other mechanical senses."

"Maybe it has big ears," she hissed. George went silent.

Traveling on some sort of air propulsion system, the scooter-sized device approached their place of concealment. Directly opposite, it halted. George wanted to whimper, but held his breath. The machine lingered there for a long moment, hovering less than an inch above the floor, before resuming its programmed itinerary. As it receded down the accessway, both escapees cautiously peered out from within the recess.

"It looked right at us." George hesitated as he watched the machine disappear around a distant curve. "At least, it seemed like it did."

Half a dozen of Sque's tentacles wriggled animatedly. "I do not believe it even saw us, or otherwise detected our presence. I had hoped that would be the case, and logic suggested the possibility. But it is one thing to hypothesize and another to survive."

"You bet your last limb it is." A relieved George trotted out into the corridor to join her.

"It is a characteristic of all but the most advanced automatons that they are designed to carry out only those directives that have been entered into their undeviating neural cortexes. Never having been encoded to look for escapees or intruders, assuming no other captives have ever escaped before, it is rational to presume that they would not recognize one such if they ran right into them."

"So what you're saying is that we ought to be able to move around freely in the presence of everything but the Vilenjji themselves?" The dog's tail was wagging briskly again.

"That is what I am saying." The speaking tube swayed energetically. "What I am going to do, however, is try to avoid contact with automatons wherever possible. I would rather not make the encounter of the one device designed to be the exception. But it appears that we certainly have some flexibility where such encounters are concerned." She resumed scuttling down the accessway.

"It did stop across from us, though." George could not get that nagging little fragment of encounter out of his mind. "It must have detected our presence."

"Detection is nothing. Reaction is everything," Sque declared meditatively. "I theorize it decided we were other devices, not unlike itself. A useful subterfuge that we hopefully will not have to rely upon too frequently."

The truth of the K'eremu's assessment was proven in several successive encounters. Each time they came upon a busy motile device they could not avoid it either ignored them, went around them, or waited for them to pass. Each time, they waited for a posse of armed Vilenjji to come looking for them. And each time, they were left in peace, as before, to continue their progress.

George was starting to feel a little lost. Much of the machine and instrument-filled service area that lay beneath the individual enclosures looked identical to every other part "How do you know how far to go, Sque?"

Her reply was composed, assured. "I routinely memorize every detail of my surroundings. The relevant information was refreshed every time we visited the Tuuqalian's enclosure. Tahst—we are here."

The food bricks and cubes and occasional odd shape that had piled up on and alongside the familiar circular lift looked no different to George than those of any others, but one taste was enough to set the usually reticent Sque to swooning.

"Joqil!" she exclaimed. She seemed to collapse in on herself, only to inflate larger than ever a moment later. "How I have missed it."

"It's been barely a day," George grumbled. "You really do need your fix, don't you?"

"Nothing is broken," she responded immediately. "Or do I miscomprehend your metaphor?"

"Doesn't matter." His own stomach growled. Eloquently. "I could use a snack myself."

"Of course. I will take what I can carry." Silvery eyes met his. "Unless, of course, I can prevail upon you to acknowledge the necessity of providing first and foremost for the most indispensable member of—"

"No," George barked—but quietly.

"I am not troubled, having anticipated such a primitive and benighted reaction." Loading up several tentacles with as many of the food cubes as she could carry, she started back the way they had come.

It did not take long to find the lift that supplied the Sierra section Walker inhabited. The dog's own resettled urban alley environment was right next door. Not wanting to embark on the next move until some time had passed and the riotous occurrence in the Tuuqalian's preserve had faded from the minds of their captors, they settled down to allow George to eat his fill. Nibbling on a food cube, Sque kept watch on the accessway. From time to time preoccupied automatons would pass, busy in both directions. As always, they ignored the watchful K'eremu and the munching dog.

Actively feeding his face, George felt a pang of guilt. Somewhere above their heads and farther around the great carousel of individual enclosures, Marc and Braouk must be consumed with worry, wondering what if anything had happened to their two smaller companions.

Worse, to maintain the illusion of discord they had employed to distract and confuse the Vilenjji, from now on they would have to avoid one another and could not even seek surcease in each other's company or conversation. To do so might raise alarm, or at least suspicion, among perceptive Vilenjji, who might well wonder how one alien who had seen his closest friend eaten by another could remain friends with the perpetrator of such an outrage. That meant Braouk would have to stay in his enclosure while Walker eventually returned to his. As punishment, and precaution, Braouk was sure to be locked down in his environment for the foreseeable future. Not that the big Tuuqalian would mind. He was used to being penned up.

It would be interesting to see how he would react and what he would do, George mused, if he ever got loose. Though their personal acquaintance was not deep, George had acquired the distinct impression that forgiveness was not a particularly Tuuqalian characteristic. The dog hoped to be around at least long enough to behold proof of that.

11

Resisting the urge to creep close to their friends' respective food lifts when these were delivering their regular allotments of food so George could inform their coconspirators of their ongoing success, the two oddly matched but equally determined escapees embarked upon a thorough investigation of the area beneath the captivity enclosures.

"Too chancy," Sque had argued when George had first proposed whispering up proof of their continued survival. "While no visual surveillance devices located aboveground would detect us, there is too much risk of an aural pickup catching your words. Until the right moment, our friends will have to survive without reassurance."

To this George could only nod. The K'eremu was correct. It was not worth risking everything they had achieved thus far just to bark up a word of encouragement to Marc, alone in his enclosure. In his mind, the dog knew that the K'eremu's caution was well considered.

But despite her company, and her illuminating if sometimes caustic conversation, it did nothing to assuage his growing loneliness.

They conducted their observations and study in the form of a widening spiral, commencing their research beneath the approximate center of the grand enclosure and working their way gradually outward. Though not one of the multitude of service mechanicals challenged their presence, or paused long enough to carry out more than the briefest of scrutinies in their direction, the escapees took no chances. Whenever they sensed movement, they stopped whatever they happened to be doing and concealed themselves as best they could from the passing automatons.

It was not difficult to do. The underside of the grand enclosure and its peripheral individual ecozones was a jungle of conduits, servos, conveyance devices, customized life support systems, both optical and hard transmission lines, and much more. Not to mention the elaborate installation that was required to supply individually calibrated food bricks and liquids to captive representatives of dozens of different species. In reference to the latter, Sque went into some detail as to how the sustenance synthesization system worked. George ignored most of the speech. It was not relevant to their immediate situation; his scientific background consisted of rooting through garbage bins to find those bits that were edible; and he was much more interested in finding the critical switch, or circuit breaker, or button, or whatever the appropriate designation was for shutting down the barrier that kept his friends caged up top.

His indifference to her lecture miffed the K'eremu. "Assuming you possess sufficient cerebral folds to be capable of it, how will you ever rise above your present state of scholarly deprivation if you do not make an effort to improve yourself?"

"I'm willing to improve myself." George spoke as the two of them approached an especially well-lit area boasting unusually high ceilings. "Find me a groomer. I'll even stand still for a bath."

Sque made disapproving sounds. "Mere physical modifications mean nothing."

"Is that so?" The dog pointedly eyed the assortment of adornments that decorated the K'eremu's epidermis. "Then why don't you get rid of all that junk jewelry you've got stuck all over yourself? You look like an itinerant garage sale."

Sque stiffened perceptibly. "It is not 'junk.' It is not even properly what you call jewelry. My accumulated qus'ta is an affirmation of my individuality; one that is vital to every K'eremu."

"Uh-huh. Like 'vote for' buttons, except yours all say 'vote for me!' "

"I fail to comprehend any deeper meaning behind your primordial ravings."

"You think that's primordial ravings, you should see me when I find a steak bone somebody's thrown out." Ears suddenly cocked forward. "Getting pretty light up ahead. Think we should turn back?"

The brief acrimony forgotten, Sque turned her attention to the accessway that loomed in front of them. It was much wider and higher than any they had encountered previously, and far more brightly lit.

"By now we should be beneath the outermost edge of the circular enclosed zone. It may be that we have even progressed beyond its limits." She edged sideways until she was under the cover of a swooping mass of metal and ceramic. Following, he found himself envying her ability to change direction without having to turn her body.

As it developed, they had gone to cover just in time.

"I hear something," he whispered to her. A tentacular gesture he had come to recognize showed that she heard it as well.

There were two of them: tall, skin shading from deep purple to lavender on the sucker-lined arm and leg flaps. One wore the same pewter-hued oversuit familiar to George from when he had been abducted. The other was clad in attire that was new to him: a kind of dark orange vestment to which clung via some equivalent of Vilenjjian Velcro an assortment of portable instrumentation.

From their hiding place, the escapees watched as the two Vilenjji continued on down the accessway. Reaching an apparently blank place in the wall at the end of the corridor, they paused for a moment until an opening appeared, allowing them to step through. The doorway closed behind them, leaving in its wake what appeared to be solid metal.

"We will have to proceed with far greater caution here." Sque was carefully edging out from beneath their hiding place. "We have moved from the realm of machines into a part of the vessel that is actually inhabited."

As he emerged, George unconsciously sidled closer to the K'eremu. "Do you still think we have a chance of bringing this off? If we try accessing anyplace sensitive, won't we run into some of them?"

She eyed him tolerantly. "Despite the size of this craft, I do not believe there are so very many Vilenjji on it. The operational details of travel between the stars remains the province of machines that can carry out the steady stream of requisite intricate functions without the well-meaning interference of clumsy organics. Particularly since they are engaged in a highly illegal enterprise, I would think that the complement of this crew is not very large. When faced with an emergency such as we hope to engender, they will be compelled to rely for rectification, at least at first, on their mechanicals. Properly anticipated, that can be to our advantage." She moved out into the light.

George instinctively held back. "Hey, where are you going?"

Continuing to advance on her tentacles, she turned her upper body to look back at him. "Nothing is to be gained by clinging to the shadows. We seek not places to hide, but places to act. In lieu of access to relevant instrumentation, we must find something of significance that we can break—or break into."

Trotting out of the darkness, the dog quickly caught up to her. She was agile, but not very fast. From what he had learned of the K'eremu, boldness was something he had not expected from her. But then, aliens were full of surprises.

It took several days of searching, occasionally ducking back into the maze of machinery to hide from promenading Vilenjji, before Sque let out a cross between a squeal and a hiss that George later learned was the K'eremu equivalent of an expression of surprise.

They were standing before what looked like a three-dimensional representation of a neon sign that had collided with a truckload of pre-decorated Christmas trees. In the course of their cautious explorations they had encountered several similar softly humming fabrications, but without exception they had been much smaller—no larger than mailbox size. This one was big enough for a pair of Vilenjji to enter. It was also the first one to have sparked visible excitement in his companion.

"What is it?" he asked dutifully.

Sque's eyes had expanded slightly in their recesses. "A control box. A significant one. If fortune favors us, the one that we seek." She started forward.

"Wait a minute." The dog looked around nervously. "What if it's protected by an alarm or something?"

"Why should it be?" The K'eremu spoke without looking back at him. "Who would it be alarmed against? Escaped captives? There is no such thing as escaped captives. Keep watch while I work."

Ready to bolt at the first sign of alarm, George followed her progress as she ambled into the lambent control box. There was a slight frisson in the air as she entered, but that was all. Once inside, she began to study the floating, semisolid lights and lines that constituted the actual controls.

She need not have asked George to stand watch. He would have done so automatically, since as soon as she entered the control area her attention became totally focused on the airy instrumentation surrounding her. All around them, vast complexes of machinery labored to provide not only for the health and well-being of the abductees held in the enclosures one level above, but for the Vilenjji as well.

If asked, he could not have estimated how much time passed before Sque turned to call back to him. "I have divined an interesting sequence. I will not explain it to you, since your small mind could not follow the pertinent progressions. You do not need to know or to understand it, anyway. Sufficient to say that I believe I can activate it."

"Then what happens?" George demanded to know.

Those tentacles she did not need to stand upon rose in unison. "If all goes well, chaos." Expanding slightly, then contracting, she exited the control box. "Now we need to find access to the level above."

"What about an air shaft, or something like that?" George asked as he trotted alongside her.

"Use what minimal mental capacity you have." She shuffled forward impatiently, eyes scanning the high-ceilinged corridor ahead, ever alert for signs of approaching Vilenjji. "You and I could possibly pass through such small conduits, but our friends who await us above could not. We must find a route back to this place that is satisfactorily large enough for both of them—the more so for the Tuuqalian than for your biped."

As it happened, a seemingly solid wall at the end of the corridor provided the kind of evaporating door they had observed in use before. As they approached, an opening appeared that was large enough to easily accommodate a Vilenjji. If he bent slightly and turned sideways, it would also allow entry to the hulking Tuuqalian. As soon as they stepped back, the door "closed."

"This will do." A tentacle reached up to rest on George's head. Though it was cooler than a human palm, the dog did not shake it off. "Now it is up to you." Another tentacle gestured. "Once you exit here, turn to your immediate left. A few strides should find you in the inspection corridor that circles the enclosures. Find our friends and bring them back here."

"Nothing to it," George replied boldly. "Then what? We all hide from the Vilenjji together?"

"A beginning," the K'eremu admitted, "that may, with luck, lead to better things."

Following her back to the control box, tongue lolling nervously, the dog nodded. "Right now I'll settle for being out of the cage. How will I know when to start my run? Will you give me a wave, or something?"

"You will know," Sque assured him. "Just do not get caught." She gestured at the underlevel maze of machinery. "The thought of wandering all alone through this vessel for the rest of my days does not appeal to me."

"What?" he said as she reentered the haze of hovering controls. "You mean you'd actually miss the company of mentally deficient individuals like Marc and myself?"

"I did not say that—exactly," she murmured. Then she began thrusting tentacles about, occasionally turning a circle as she worked. To an outsider it appeared as if she was gesticulating aimlessly. Except that when intersected by her weaving appendages, lines of control came alive with different colors, while others shifted position within the box.

When the lights went out, he was ready.

As he charged for the doorway, all four legs pumping furiously, he had a bad moment when it occurred to him that Sque might also have shut down automatic portals. But it opened readily for him as soon as he drew near. A high-pitched shrilling filled his ears. Ignoring the screeching Vilenjji klaxon as he burst through the opening, his paws skidding on the slick floor, he rumbled into the first turn and focused on utilizing the emergency glow that emanated from the floor itself to find his way.

Then it was up the rippling ramp Sque had told him to expect; and before he knew it, he was looking at the enclosures for the first time in many days, only with a significant difference. He was looking at them from the *outside*.

Which way? He thought he had properly oriented himself before starting out. But the combination of screaming alarm, poor visibility, his own excitement, the first sharp turn, and then the ascent up the ramp to a higher level had disoriented him. Skidding to a halt in front of the Jalalik enclosure, he found himself eye to eye with its bemused monocular occupant. Flexible lower jaw nearly touching the ground, the single Jalalik stared back. The implanted translator conveyed its words.

"How there, not here, small pleasant one?" Its bewilderment helped to clarify his own.

Already, the corridor resounded with more than the sounds of the shrill alarm. George knew he could not linger. "Going for a walk!" he shot back as he made a choice and bolted rightward. "Give it a try!"

As the dog disappeared down the corridor, the willowy figure of the bemused Jalalik flowed to the innermost limit of its enclosure. Tentatively, it thrust a bony, almost skeletal finger outward. It passed through the boundary normally delineated by a curtain of nerve-tingling energy. As it thrust forward, the Jalalik followed, until like the dog it, too, was standing in the previously inaccessible corridor. With a quick look in both directions, it began to run, taking the opposite direction from the small quadruped. Very soon it turned up a rampway, its long, slim legs pumping with the sheer inexpressible joy of the gallop.

The more enclosures he passed, the more anxious George became. A few still contained their residents. Shocked and mystified, these confused captives refused to abandon their individually engineered ecosystems, unable to grasp the significance of what had happened, of the fact that the seemingly everlasting electrical barriers that had kept them securely penned up ever since their abductions had ceased to function. But most of the enclosures, and presumably the grand enclosure as well, were empty, as their elated occupants scattered in all directions.

Then he saw Walker. Wearing a harried yet exultant expression, the human stood in the middle of the corridor, striving to avoid being trampled by the stampede of freed captives. When he saw George speeding toward him, his face lit up in a smile the likes of which the dog had never seen before. Without thinking, without hesitation, the mutt bounded into the human's open arms and began licking his face, wetly and noisily.

"All right, all right. I'm glad to see you, too. I was beginning to wonder if I ever would, again." Gently, he set the dog down on the deck and wiped at his face with the back of one forearm. "Couldn't you just shake hands?"

"My style of greeting, take it or leave it. At least I didn't French you." Reunion over, he resumed his run up the corridor. "We can get soppy later. Right now we need to find Braouk!"

Walker hurried after him. "Wait a minute! Where's Sque?"

"Tickling the light proactive!" the dog yelled back to him. "And waiting for us."

"Look out!" George found himself yelling a moment later as the first Vilenjji he had seen since the deactivation burst out of a side corridor and came rushing toward him.

He sounded the warning just in time. The alien flew over him with room to spare, but had he not called out a warning it would have slammed into Walker, who was working hard to keep up, with crushing impact. As it was, the human threw himself to one side just in time to avoid the flying purplish mass. The Vilenjji, however, was not attacking. It was not even in control of itself. This was shown by the force with which it landed on the corridor floor, bounced, and rolled over several times before lying still, its arm and leg flaps splayed loosely around it. On closer inspection, the panting Walker decided that dislocated might be a better description.

Joining back up with George, he resumed running up the curving corridor, until a roar that shook the walls brought them up short. It was thunderous. It was overpowering. It was downright poetical.

*"Perish the foul, to the darkness damning, I send!"* A steady drumming counterpointed the words.

Advancing with instinctive caution, man and dog found their friend. As soon as they saw him, the source of the drumming sound as well as the versing became immediately apparent.

Effortlessly swinging the heavy Vilenjji by one of its under-limbs, the Tuuqalian was repeatedly slamming the alien skull-first against the corridor wall. Or rather, had been, as there was no longer much of the alien's tapering brainpan remaining. That did nothing to reduce the enthusiasm with which the Tuuqalian continued to swing the broken body.

"Braouk!" Walker moved as close as he could without getting himself brained by the very airborne, very dead Vilenjji. "It's me, Marcus Walker! The human." He indicated the eager quadruped at his side. "George has come back. He says we need to go with him!"

*"Now,"* the dog added as sternly as he could.

Slowly, the Tuuqalian stopped swinging the dead Vilenjji, letting the lifeless mass dangle from one pair of cablelike tentacles. "Walker. George. Much pleasure given, it is to me, seeing again." He started toward them.

"You can leave that." Walker nodded in the direction of the mush-headed Vilenjji whose lower limb the Tuuqalian still gripped unbreakably.

"Ah, yes." Letting the flaccid corpse fall limply to the deck, Braouk rejoined his friends.

Sque's prediction had been correct. As human and Tuuqalian joined George in retracing the dog's route, all around them was chaos, the noise and confusion compounded by the unceasing shrieking of the Vilenjji alarm. Vitalized by unexpected freedom, captives ran, crawled, slithered, and in at least one case, glided wherever they could. Their efforts were ultimately futile, of course. Trapped on the ship, with no-where to go, they were each and every one doomed to recapture and reincarceration. So were Walker and his friends, but they were deter-mined to postpone that seeming inevitability for as long as possible. And unlike their fellow captives, they had discovered a prospective means for doing so.

The ramp that led downward lay directly ahead. But instead of fol-lowing George, Walker literally skidded to a halt on the slick floor.

"What are you doing?" With Braouk looming over him, an anxious George paused at the top of the ramp to look back at his friend.

"Just a quick piece of unfinished business." Ignoring the dog's protesting yips, his expression grim and set, Walker disregarded the ramp as he continued past it and on down the corridor.

The Ghouaba never saw the human coming. Wandering aimlessly, marveling at both its unforeseen liberty and new surroundings, its large, slightly protuberant eyes were focused on the far end of the corridor. Old skills unforgotten, Walker tackled the much smaller biped from be-hind, much as he had once brought down opposing quarterbacks.

Since the Ghouaba could not have weighed more than sixty pounds, the impact of a moderately large biped nearly four times its mass hitting it from behind was devastating. As the much lighter alien gasped from the shock of the concussion, Walker felt slender bones snap beneath his weight. The long, slim arms crumpled, fractured in several places. Rising from the writhing jumble of stretched skin and broken bones, Walker began methodically booting the daylights out of the still-living carcass. A firm tug on his drawn-back leg restrained him.

It was George, jaws locked firmly but gently on the human's pants. "Let it go, Marc," the dog instructed his friend as he released his grip on the increasingly ragged jeans. "You want the Vilenjji to find you here?" He nodded at the trashed Ghouaba. "You want the Vilenjji to find you here doing this?"

Walker hesitated. It would only take a moment to break the alien's neck. Then he decided it would be better to leave it the way it was. If the Vilenjji wanted to take the time and trouble to try to fix the damage he had done, the work might keep a few of them busy. Vilenjji occupied with repairing the Ghouaba would be Vilenjji who would not have time to look for him and his friends. Or, he thought, grinning wolfishly, they might decide instead to sell the Ghouaba at a reduced cost and as was: damaged goods. But then, he reflected as he turned to follow George back to the top of the rampway, the malicious little alien had been dam-aged goods from the beginning.

Braouk had not been bored waiting for them. Racing up the ramp to the enclosure level, a pair of Vilenjji armed with restraining glue guns had been caught looking the wrong way. While preoccupied with immobilizing a comparatively harmless, panicky Aa'loupta from Higraa III, they had forgotten to watch behind them. One only noticed the arrival of the rampaging Tuuqalian when Braouk proceeded to separate its companion's head from its upper body. Attempting to bring its own weapon to bear on their attacker, the other Vilenjji ended up eating it, courtesy of Braouk's pistoning tentacles. Walker had to clutch at the Tuuqalian to drag him away from his sport, much as George had been forced to pull Walker off the Ghouaba.

They encountered no further resistance as they raced down the ramp. With those freed captives who had not yet been rounded up now scattering deeper and deeper throughout the ship, the Vilenjji were being forced to split up as well in order to pursue them. And while the other fleeing prisoners, sadly, fled without direction or purpose, the oddly matched trio that came barreling down the ramp knew exactly where they were going.

With an excited George reminding Braouk to duck, they passed through the door the dog was getting to know so well. Partway down the corridor on the other side, a frantic Sque was waiting to greet them. Mounting anxiety had caused her to tie several of her tentacles in knots.

"I was beginning to wonder if your combined paucity of intellect had led you astray," she told them as they slowed to meet her.

"We're glad to see you again, too." Walker was breathing hard, but with the amount of adrenaline that was surging through him at that moment, he felt as if he could run all the way back to Earth. "I don't know how you did it, Sque, but you did it." And leaning over, he planted without hesitation, a loud, echoing kiss smack atop the shiny dome of her head.

She squirmed away from him. "How dare you! After what I have just done for you!"

"That is a sign of endearment among my kind," he informed her. A glance showed an amused George nodding confirmation.

"Oh. I suppose that is all right, then." A tentacle tip brushed self-consciously across the top of her head. "As a superior being, one must learn to tolerate the archaic affectations of primitive peoples, I suppose. At least the gesture was not dehydrating."

As she finished, full illumination returned to the corridor. Four sets of eyes that varied considerably in size and shape scanned their immediate surroundings. They were still alone.

"Seems the Vilenjji have succeeded in restoring their lighting," Walker murmured uneasily.

"Your kind must be famed for its ability to restate the blindingly obvious." Sque immediately headed off to her right, scuttling past the control box. "We need to absent ourselves from this place."

"Drowning in freedom, my hearts are glad, onward advancing," Braouk declaimed as he followed.

"But advancing where?" Walker wanted to know. Having grown used to the K'eremu's innate sarcasm, he was able to largely ignore it.

"I have not just been standing here, tentacles aflutter, waiting for you to put in an appearance." Thanks to her flexible body, Sque was able to look back at him without slowing her forward motion. "In addition to instrumentation, in the time that was available to me I was able to access a selection of schematics of this vessel. It is, as I originally surmised, fairly large. Large enough to hide even one so grossly unwieldy as a Tuuqalian, if we are careful in our movements." They were heading, Walker saw, deep into a rapidly darkening maze of conduits, machinery, and related equipment.

"Won't the pointy-heads have some way of tracking us down as we move through their ship?" George trotted alongside his human, occasionally glancing back over a shoulder. The corridor behind them remained empty as the control box receded around a curve.

"Why should they?" Sque was comfortably, if not justifiably, confident. "No one treks the service ways of a vessel who does not belong there, and anyone encountering difficulty or needing help would carry with them the means to summon it. There is no reason to build in an expensive systemology to follow the movements of those who have with them the means to call for assistance. Exercising care, I think we can extend the period of our freedom for some time."

"They'll be after us," Walker pointed out. An exasperated Sque replied without repeating her previous criticism.

"That the lighting has been fully restored suggests that the electrical barriers that restrain captives within their enclosures have also been reactivated. The Vilenjji will be busy for some time recapturing those of our fellow unfortunates who are racing aimlessly through the same corridors that are utilized by the crew. After that, our captors will be forced to spend some time winkling out the smarter ones among the escapees, who will be busily seeking hiding places from their captors. By that time we should be well away from here, in another part of the vessel, where hopefully they will not think to search for a while."

Both Sque and George seemed to know exactly where they were

going. As such, it did not take long before the escapees found themselves standing (and in Braouk's case, crawling) beneath the particular
enclosure that had been home to Walker from the day he had first awakened to find himself a captive on the alien spacecraft. It felt strange to
be standing there, so close to his simulated piece of California mountains, knowing that familiar objects like his tent, and spare clothing, and
miscellaneous but homey camping gear lay not far above his head, yet
impossibly out of reach. Even if they could somehow manually operate
the small, circular food service lift, he did not dare risk ascending lest
Vilenjji surveillance equipment detect his presence. As far as their current accessibility was concerned, everything from his compact flashlight to his few remaining energy bars might as well have been lying
buried in the dust of Earth's moon.

In place of the latter he and George helped themselves to as many
of the stacked food bricks as they could. Ripping some flexible bits of
what looked like metal fabric from nearby mechanisms, Braouk showed
himself to be as adept a weaver of scavenged materials as of words, fash-
ioning a brace of crude but serviceable carry sacks for all four of them.
The impermeable material was capable of holding water as well as
bricks. Two problems immediately presented themselves.

"I'll carry yours," Walker told his companion when it was apparent
that George's back was too narrow to support even a small sack.

The dog grinned up at him. "I always said humans were good for
something."

The second awkwardness was less easily resolved.

"I do not carry things." Tentacles contracted as Sque refused the
sack proffered by Braouk. "The K'eremu do not indulge in manual labor."

"What do the K'eremu deign to indulge in?" The Tuuqalian's eyestalks extended threateningly toward the much smaller alien.

Walker stepped between them and extended a hand. "It's all right,
Braouk. I'll carry hers."

The big alien hesitated. Then, instead of handing over the pair of
empty sacks he had fashioned for the K'eremu, a powerful tentacle took
the ones the human had been holding out of Walker's hand and slung
them over a fourth limb. They hung there, all four of them, as easily as
an old lady's purse from her shoulder.

"Never mind. I will carry all the food and drink. The sum of it
weighs less on my mind than the complaining of others."

Sque had prepared a riposte, but for once the K'eremu took Walker's cautioning glance to heart, or whatever equivalent internal system she employed to pump critical body fluids through her system.

Retracing their earlier steps, she and George led the way to the locations beneath both her enclosure and that of the Tuuqalian. When they had accumulated all the food bricks, cubes, squares, and liquids they could reasonably carry, the K'eremu led them out from beneath the vast circle of the enclosures and back into the light of the service corridor that encircled them, following, as she informed them, "the map I have made in my mind" based on what information she had been able to glean from her time spent waiting in the manipulative miasma of the Vilenjji control box.

And still they had not encountered or seen a single one of their captors since entering the accessway that encircled the enclosures. Busy the Vilenjji must be, as she had told them, rounding up the more easily recapturable of their fellow abductees. As they emerged from beneath the thick overhang of the enclosures, Walker could not keep from glancing upward. The misery of those being reimprisoned must be beyond measure, he knew. He could imagine how he would feel if, after a few hours of freedom, he suddenly found himself immobilized and dumped back into his own small enclosure.

Maybe before they were retaken, he thought hopefully, a few of the other escapees had managed, like Braouk at the rampway, to sow a little pain and hurt of their own among the arrogant Vilenjji. It gave him considerable pleasure to imagine the latter slumping to and fro, manipulating their capture devices and weapons as they struggled to retrieve every one of their prisoners. If Sque was right, it would take them some time.

Eventually, though, with no destination in mind and no access to weapons, each and every fleeing captive would eventually be returned to its enclosure. No doubt there would ensue the equivalent of a prison lockdown as the Vilenjji repeatedly counted heads. No matter how many times they repeated the count, they would find four of their captives missing. At which point all the resources of the great ship would be mobilized to find them.

Sque seemed to think they could avoid recapture for some time. Walker did not see how that was possible, but was willing to countenance the fact that a K'eremu might be able to envision possibilities he could not. He certainly hoped so. As they turned down the corridor and headed toward what looked like another blank, solid wall, he knew that without her expertise the Vilenjji would probably pick him up inside an hour. Able to squeeze into smaller hiding places, George might last a day or two longer. Braouk they would find right away—perhaps not to their immediate satisfaction. Remembering the fight at the top of the rampway, Walker experienced a surge of bloodthirsty satisfaction that appalled him. Briefly. He did have some regrets, though.

He regretted not being able to participate more actively in the dismemberment of the last two Vilenjji.

At their approach, a doorway materialized in the wall. Why shouldn't it? he mused. Only authorized personnel, only authorized Vilenjji, roamed the manifold corridors of the ship. Their very presence authorized their access. Following Sque, they entered another dimly lit passageway. It was narrow, high enough to accommodate the tall Vilenjji, just barely wide and high enough to admit Braouk. As the Tuuqalian ducked slightly to clear the entrance, the door re-formed behind them.

Ahead lay softly humming machinery that was indifferent to their presence, a passage so extensive that he could not see its terminus, and the mysterious but not necessarily unknowable bowels of the Vilenjji ship.

**12**

His presence not required for the capture at hand, Pret-Klob stood
back and observed thoughtfully as the two desperate zZad skittered backward on the ceiling. Suction pads on the ends of their
feet allowed them to find a purchase on virtually any surface, while
their six multijointed limbs gave them great flexibility. Off to one side,
Arud-Tvet was recording everything for future use.

Not a united company of materialistic individuals inclined to waste
any opportunity that might lead to profit, the Vilenjji had turned the
mass escape from the holding enclosures into an opportunity to learn
a great deal more about their inventory. They were not panicked. The
only urgency that lent itself to the rounding up of those who had taken
flight arose from a desire on the part of their captors to ensure that
none of the escapees came to any harm, lest their asking price have to
be lowered.

There was some concern because the Tuuqalian was still among the unrecovered. Of all the sentients and semi-intelligences the Vilenjji held, they feared it alone. And with good reason, Pret-Klob thought grimly. The lives of four good partholders had already been lost to the rampaging behemoth. He had vowed there would be no more. Despite the high price it might bring he had reluctantly been forced to issue orders to, if it could not be immediately sedated, execute the treacherous entity rather than risk any more deaths. Should that outcome eventuate, they would make up for the loss by boosting the price of the others.

It was fascinating to watch the zZad pair in their struggle to find a way past the Vilenjji who were inexorably herding them to the rear of the storage chamber. If the inventory records were correct, there was one each of a healthy male and female of breeding age. Pret-Klob had no intention of losing them, or of damaging so much as a sensing hair on their underbodies. As stock went, they were not particularly intelligent. In their case, that was a useful feature. Superbly acrobatic as they were, they were just bright enough to accept training. There were worlds whose overlords and merchants would pay many credits to acquire such unique entertainment—not to mention entertainment that could be counted upon to reproduce itself, thereby repaying the original investment many times over.

Ripped from the primitive technology of their home planet, the zZad ought to be grateful that they were going to be given the opportunity to live out the remainder of their lives on a world that was a part of galactic civilization. The suckers on Pret-Klob's arm flaps contracted and expanded reflexively. Regrettably, that was rarely the case with ungrateful inventory. With very few exceptions, if given a hypothetical choice, stock invariably wished to be returned to their homeworlds. Such desires were not Pret-Klob's concern, nor that of his association. Their sole concern was profit. And in a civilization where many wants and needs were easily supplied, profit could be hard to come by. Fortunately, no one had yet found a way to synthesize novelty.

"See how rapidly they can change direction, even when moving upside down." Nearby, Dven-Palt gestured with the device she was holding. It looked like a gun, but it was only one example of the kind of tools the association maintained for manipulating difficult captives. Her task was to back up the trio of crew that was inexorably crowding the pair of desperate zZad into a far corner of the storeroom.

"Yes, their agility is quite impressive," Pret-Klob readily admitted. "See—I think they are about to try to break through."

Raising the device he held in his suckers, one of the approaching crewmembers took aim at the female zZad and fired. The sticket missed as she sprang forward, releasing her grip on the ceiling and bounding off the top of a supply interlock. The male followed behind her, only to run into not one but two stickets launched by the other members of the cornering trio. On contact, the device instantly contracted, collapsing the zZad's multiple limbs tightly against its body. Stricken and immobilized, it whistled for its mate: a series of rapid fretful pipings. From the top of the storage unit on which she had landed, she turned to look back at him. Seeing that the two Vilenjji who had trapped her companion were already finalizing his bindings, she turned away and leaped again.

It was a credit to the creature's nimbleness that the waiting Dven-Palt nearly missed her. That would have resulted in another chase that, while it would have been additionally enlightening as to the evasive skills of the zZad, would have taken still more time away from normal crew duties. Set on low charge to compensate for the zZad's smaller size, Dven-Palt's shocker froze her in midleap. As she crashed to the deck, the two senior Vilenjji rushed to make sure she had suffered no permanent damage.

Passing her pin checker over the elongated, unmoving form, Dven-Palt glanced up at her companion and gestured with her free arm flap. "Internal indications are all in the positive. The creature may suffer some minor bruising, but it did not fall far enough, I think, to break limbs."

The tendrils atop Pret-Klob's tapering cranial cavity squirmed tellingly. "I am pleased to hear you say so. The load of the maintenance physicians is already heavy." Not all of the escapees had been recovered so efficiently, he knew, nor without spoilage. And then there was the need to mend what punishment had been meted out to those who had physically resisted recapture. Still, it could have been worse. Thus far only two of the inventory had died during retrieval. Two, in addition to one who had perished from injuries inflicted by its fellow captives. Pret-Klob particularly regretted the latter loss. The Ghouaba had been clever, and useful.

Well, it should be easy enough to replace. Among the inventory, one or two individuals could always be found who were willing to assist the Vilenjji in return for special food, or entertainment, or other exclusive privileges. With the successful recovery of the zZad, he turned his attention to the communicator attached to his left upper limb and requested an update on the progress of the remaining ongoing recovery.

As he already knew, the ship's automatics confirmed that of one hundred percent of inventory, ninety-two percent had taken advantage of the opportunity to flee their enclosures. Of that, the majority had already been recovered or otherwise located. Of the remainder, not counting the zZad, six were still unaccounted for, including, the ship's automatics now confirmed, two commodities previously thought to be nullified. Pret-Klob scrutinized these indicators without preconception. No matter how well one came to know a commodity, it often exhibited surprising and unexpected behavior as well as unsuspected abilities. The small, physically weak quadruped from the undistinguished third world of a minor sun, for example. Who would have expected it to be among those few escapees still running free? The Tuuqalian's continued autonomy, now, that made sense. But the small furry quadruped had required a cerebral boost just to render it intelligent enough to be capable of basic conversation, and thereby understand the orders that were given to it. Truly, alien species from the rough outer worlds were full of surprises.

He and Dven-Palt watched as the recovered zZad were carefully hauled away. Their injuries and abrasions would be treated, and they would be given appropriate nourishment and medication. Then they would be returned to the enclosure they shared. When they had recuperated sufficiently, they would be allowed to once again join the other recovered inventory in the grand enclosure. By that time, Pret-Klob fully expected all six of the remaining inventory still at large to have been recovered.

If one discounted the deaths of several members of the association at the tentacles of the Tuuqalian, the mass escaping could be considered an instructive diversion. Even those four casualties were not to be entirely mourned, as their shares would now be divided among the surviving crew. Now that a careful tracing and analysis of records made prior to the actual breakout had been completed, it was known that at least one among the escapees was capable of operating Vilenjji instrumentation. Security steps had been instituted to ensure that would not happen again. There would be no more illicit switching of directives, no more unauthorized deactivation of restraining barriers.

He would rest easily tonight. The excitement had been good for the members of the association. But now it was time to ease back into normal routine. Another ship-day at most should see the last of the escapees recovered and returned to their enclosures. Then it would be time to relax again and leave the bulk of the maintenance work to the automatics.

One had to admire whichever species had initiated the breakout. For a primitive sentient or two, they had proven surprisingly creative. Pret-Klob was curious to learn the details of how it had been accomplished. Not only for his own edification, but so that steps could be taken to ensure that it never happened again. It was always interesting when an inferior species managed to rise up long enough to make a blip on the screen of inherent Vilenjji superiority—before they were knocked back down to where they belonged.

Tomorrow, he decided as he and Dven-Palt shuffled down the nearest rampway. Except for the instructive postmortem, it would all be over and done with by tomorrow. He almost regretted that it would be so. The escape and its invigorating aftermath had provided the most enjoyment he had experienced in quite some time.

✴

While Walker kept his eyes on the passageway and George his nose to the deck, Sque led the way through the seemingly interminable maze that was the interior of the Vilenjji ship. Their progress was slowed by the need to avoid, duck beneath, or go around sensors designed to detect the presence of moving, nonmechanical forms. If triggered, these would brighten the lights and increase the flow of fresh air to the affected section. In and of themselves, both consequences were desirable. The problem, Sque pointed out, was that by activating such sensors with their presence they might also send notification of same to some central monitoring facility. This would, in turn, pinpoint their location for the Vilenjji eager to find them.

So for two days now they had tolerated stale atmosphere and dim lighting while they progressed, relying on the word and expertise of the overbearing K'eremu because they had no other choice. For his part, Walker was happy to do so—provided that Sque knew what she was doing. If it all went for naught, he could always strangle her with her own tentacles later.

"Tell me something," he asked after they had just squirmed their way through a particularly difficult and smelly vertical channel. "Are you typical of your kind? I mean, are most K'eremu like you?"

Silvery eyes turned to look up at him. "If by that you are referring to my personality, whose maturity and refinement is beyond your feeble comprehension, I am pleased to say that were you to be fortunate enough to be blessed by a visit to K'erem, you would discover that largely because of my enforced incarceration on this vessel I have become among the most polite and understanding of my kind."

Walker shuddered from head to foot.

"This is interesting." Forced to bend low to avoid striking the conduits that ran along the ceiling, Braouk had stopped beside a brace of

pale translucent pipes. The others gathered around the curious Tuuqalian's bulk.

Standing up on his hind legs and balancing with care, George
sniffed of the spot Braouk was pointing out, where fluid the color and
consistency of spoiled cream was leaking from a tiny crack. The dog's
nose wrinkled in disgust as he settled back down onto all fours.

"Feh. Smells like industrial waste."

"On the contrary," Sque informed him, "I believe this syrupy liquid is a major source of nourishment to our captors." Rotating atop her
tentacles, she studied their immediate surroundings, finally settling her
attention on several panels that lined an isolated post like protective
plates on a dinosaur's back. "I have an idea."

A nervous Walker peered back the way they had come. It had been
some time since they had seen signs of any Vilenjji, or even a mobile
service automaton. "This idea: It's not going to take long to implement,
is it?"

"No." Reaching up, a trio of tentacles lightly caressed his left forearm. "We may do no more than retain our freedom for a few days
longer. Should that sad eventuality be the one to befall us, would it not
be uplifting to return to our enclosures knowing that we have caused
our misbegotten hosts some small discomfort?"

"Oh, yes!" Without even knowing what the devious K'eremu had in
mind, George was enthusiastic.

Braouk was equally willing to assist. "What must do, we who wander shipside, hopefully seeking?"

"First," she told the Tuuqalian, "I need that lower left panel opened.
It appears to be locked."

Approaching the post, Braouk reached out with his left tentacles,
felt tentatively around the edges of the sealed protective plate, and ten-
derly wrenched it aside. Joints groaned in protest as they bent like rubber. Scuttling up alongside him, Sque had the Tuuqalian lift her to Vilenjji working height. While Walker and George kept watch on both ends
of the passageway, she busied herself among the lights within.

Some twenty minutes later, when both man and dog were starting
to get antsy, Braouk lowered her back to the floor. Holding several small
objects in her tentacles, she continued her work. Studying that flat, alien
face when she was finally finished, it was impossible to tell for certain,
but Walker had the distinct impression she was pleased with the results
of her work.

"What did you do?" he asked as they resumed moving down the
corridor.

"Arrogance is its own reward," she told him, without the slightest hint of irony. "The Vilenjji will respond to my efforts, but not until they announce themselves. If I have done my work well, that should be sometime tomorrow, ship-time."

"But what did you *do*?" George reiterated, trotting along between her and Walker.

"Made some improvements to the delivery system, I hope. A pity we cannot linger in the vicinity to observe the results. We shall simply have to imagine them." Horizontal black pupils regarded the human. "Your kind does have imaginations, does it not?"

"Vivid," Walker assured her.

"One doubts . . ." Her voice trailed off momentarily. "I will endeavor to create a mind-picture sufficiently rudimentary so that even you can understand." She proceeded to do so.

\*

Dven-Palt advanced cautiously. From the communicator on her arm, a voice called out to her. It being a restricted linear transmission, only she was able to hear it.

"Anything as yet?" Pret-Klob was asking.

"Not yet," she murmured back. In her other hand she gripped a snadh. Unlike every other device the Vilenjji had employed while recapturing their scattered inventory, the snadh was not intended to net, immobilize, shock, tranquilize, or otherwise render harmless individual life-forms. The dozen small, explosive, hyperkinetic spheres it held under pressure were designed to kill.

The presence of such death-dealing devices was required because the lethal specimen from Tuuqalia was among the four captives still at large within the ship. At least, it was assumed four were still at large. No one was discounting the possibility that the berserker Tuuqalian had killed and quite possibly eaten the other three. So the determined quintet that was tracking them in this particular service corridor had come prepared, if need be, to kill as well as capture.

No one wanted to have to terminate the Tuuqalian. It was an exceedingly valuable specimen and represented high profit to the association. But having already lost several of their colleagues to its fury, they were not prepared to make further sacrifices in the name of revenue.

When the support sensor in Sector Jwidh had initially alerted the monitors to the presence of organic life in Section Thab, there had been some expressions of disbelief. Aside from wondering how the captives, or captive, had succeeded in entering the restricted area in the first place, it was quite a surprise to see how far from the enclosures they had traveled. Not that it mattered. They were only wandering. A little longer and a little farther than the rest of the recovered inventory, perhaps, but still only wandering. There was nowhere for them to go.

And now that their presence had been detected, the recovery team led by Dven-Palt was about to put an end to their undesirable liberty. In the end, the superior species always won out.

Two of the team carried snare boosters. The heaviest recovery equipment in the Vilenjji capture arsenal, it would not only incapacitate a Tuuqalian, but contained within its strands sufficient soporific to simultaneously render two or three of the giants unconscious. The less dangerous escapees, if they still survived, were of minor concern. Virtually any confinement device would serve to restrain them sufficiently for recovery.

They were now very near the location of the sensor that had recently signaled a life presence. The relocation team had gone into action swiftly, and it was likely that whichever of the escapees had activated the sensor was still in the vicinity. The team members advanced with caution because of the possible presence of the unfettered Tuuqalian, but they were not afraid. After all, they were Vilenjji, and this was their business.

On her immediate right, one of the snare wielders balanced his gear carefully in both arm flaps, the multiple suckers gripping it securely. All they needed was a glimpse of the obdurate giant and the tranquilizing mesh would seek its own target. If that failed, there was always the snadh. Nothing could, nothing would, escape the team's attention. Dven-Palt knew that despite the amusing diversion the mass escape had provided, Pret-Klob was keen to bring the last vestiges of it under control so that ship and crew could get back to normal. In a few moments, she hoped, that would come to pass, and this interesting but diverting episode in the life of the association would come to a satisfying conclusion.

"Over here," one of the other team members murmured, gesturing for his companions to join him.

Maintaining their high level of alertness, they gathered around one of the many delivery tubes that supplied sustenance slurry to the Libdh portion of the ship. What had drawn the team member's attention was not the small leak in its side, but the cryptic diagram that had been painted onto the deck nearby using the dried foodstuff itself. When its nature became clear, Dven-Palt felt her orifices tightening. Emboldened by its success at remaining free, the inventory was becoming impertinent. It was evident that in addition to returning them to their respective enclosures, educational measures of a physical nature would need to be applied. Correction was in order. Extending a pod flap, she moved to scuff the diagram of dried foodstuff into oblivion.

Her sock-encased flap struck something immovable. There seemed to be a lump of some more solid material beneath the desiccated brownish-white foodstuff. As the latter was smeared away, a sensor was revealed. There ought not to be a sensor located in that portion of floor, she realized. With realization came unexpected emotion; unexpected emotion led to rapid movement; rapid movement led to the realization that it was not going to be rapid enough.

Triggered by the transplanted sensor, the conduit burst. Milky-white food slurry exploded in all directions, showering the recovery team with thick white fluid that dried quickly to a chalklike consistency. In the resulting alarm and confusion, one of the already stressed booster wielders accidentally fired his device. Seeking the nearest objective within range of the equipment's automatic targeting sensors, the tranquilizer mesh efficiently enveloped one of the other team members. Crumpling onto his pod flaps, that unlucky individual promptly went quiescent and collapsed to the deck, effectively narcotized.

Remaining weapons were raised and swept in all directions. Within the service passageway, nothing moved. Finally assured they were still alone and had been the victims of a deliberate incident, Dven-Palt realized she had no choice but to contact Pret-Klob and inform him of what had happened. In doing so, she was sufficiently preoccupied with what had transpired to forget to mute the visual on her transmitter.

Eyeing her disheveled, food-streaked upper body, the commander of the ship and the head of the association was most definitely not pleased. It was one thing to be outwitted, however transiently, by inferior life-forms. It was quite another to be made a fool of.

*

Two more days passed, ship-time, without any sign of the four remaining escapees. It was as if they had vanished from the vessel. Their continued presence, lurking unseen and undetected somewhere within the ship's service passages, was beginning to affect crew efficiency. Confidence in their own superiority did not keep the individual Vilenjji working at his or her station from occasionally glancing back over their upper limbs to see if something was lurking there. Especially if one was working without help, or in one of the lonelier sections of the vessel that only occasionally required a visit from one of the crew.

It got so bad that, reluctantly, Pret-Klob felt compelled to request an associational consultation. It being unconscionable that such a gathering had been forced by the actions of a quartet of inventory, it was announced that such a meeting was long overdue in any case, and was being called primarily to review and update certain routine procedures. Though the pretense fooled no one, all who attended adhered to it. The alternative was too depressing to countenance.

When all those of rank had signed in, the consultation sphere glowed to life. Since every part of the sphere's interior was equi-distant to every other part, all were equal within its borders, even Pret-Klob. The sphere was not large, but to hold only heads it did not have to be. No Vilenjji was physically present, of course. There was no need to draw crew from stations in order to have a consultation. It was more than sufficient for the avatars of their heads to be there. Nothing more was required. The Vilenjji were not a species who needed to accentuate communication by means of active limb gestures.

A conspicuously reluctant Dven-Palt opened the proceedings with a recapitulation of her hunting team's encounter with the inventory's aromatic affront. It had been, the floating heads of everyone present had to admit, cunningly conceived and executed. A compliment to the abilities of the astray inventory. No one laughed. The mortification that had occurred could have been inflicted on any of them. Anyway, unlike the lesser races, the Vilenjji did not suffer from an overindulgence in high spirits.

When, with relief audible in her final inflection, she finished and returned to silence, Pret-Klob's avatar brightened and opened the consultation to submissions.

"As head of our mutual association, so designated by you all in gratitude for my ability to make decisions, maintain the effective functioning of our enterprise, and consistently deliver a profit, I am ready and willing to consider any and all suggestions and ideas concerning how best to deal with what has developed into a situation unprecedented in our experience. Despite our best efforts (here he deliberately avoided looking in the direction of Dven-Palt's cranial avatar), four of the inventory remain at large somewhere within the ship. While they pose no direct danger to it or to us, and will eventually be found and recaptured, the longer they remain at large the greater is the injury to our self-esteem."

Brid-Nwol's avatar strengthened for attention. "I beg to differ with the associational head when he states that the at-large inventory pose no threat to the ship or to us. Assuming the four are moving about together, they have already demonstrated an ability to pass undetected be-

tween sectors, as well as to physically and adversely affect food distribution facilities. If they can impact upon the latter, what is to stop them
from interfering with more critical components of ship operation?"

"Ignorance," Kvaj-Mwif responded immediately, saving Pret-Klob
the necessity of doing so. "Or fear of damaging equipment and instrumentation that could result in their own deaths. They have by their actions thus far shown themselves to be creatures of logic, albeit inferior
ones. It therefore seems to me unlikely that, having gone to so much
trouble and effort to stay alive, they would suddenly decide to make decisions that could negate all they have striven to achieve."

Brid-Nwol was not to be so quickly put off. "You ascribe to inventory motivation that is rightly the province of higher beings. While we
are well familiar with the physical requirements and responses of inventory in stock, we know little of their primitive psychologies. While
they may resist obstinately one moment, the next could see them re-
signing themselves to suicide—and in so doing, inflicting damage on
the ship, or the association, or both."

Klos-Jlad's brightening silenced them all. Wealthy and knowledgeable, he had been on many voyages of collection and had dealt with innumerable kinds of inventory.

"I personally am of both minds. I do not think the inventory at
large is ignorant. Were that the case, they could not have accomplished
all that they have already. We know from recorded accounts that the enclosure barrier did not fail by accident, but was tampered with. I should
not be surprised if the four for whom we continue to search were responsible. Taken together, these are not the actions of ignorant entities."
Murmurs of concurrence, some reluctant, acknowledged the senior
association member's observations.

"By the same token," Klos-Jlad continued, "I do not think the
absent inventory will initiate any action that could result in harm to
themselves. They have worked too hard to stay alive to go to the trouble of killing themselves. Therefore, they must have some other purpose
in mind."

"Inventory struggles to survive," Dven-Palt pointed out. "The natural desire of any captive upon regaining freedom of movement would
be to retain it for as long as possible. That is their purpose."

"Well appraised," Klos-Jlad agreed. "Still, I cannot keep from wondering if there might be . . ." As his voice trailed away, his avatar faded
commensurately.

Having held her peace for as long as possible, Shib-Kirn now
clamored for attention. "I agree completely with Brid-Nwol. Inventory

cannot be allowed to wander at will through the interstices of the ship. If they do not do something harmful out of malice, they may very well do it out of fatigue, or unawareness, or in the spirit of experimentation." Her gaze encompassed every one of the other attendant avatars.

"I, for one, do not intend to stand quietly by waiting for calamity to strike. A manipulative appendage inserted in the wrong control field can be as damaging as a bomb attached to critical instrumentation. Furthermore, there is the matter of the murderous Tuuqalian. Four dead members is too high a price to pay for preservation of a future sale. It is true that these four remaining unrecovered inventory represent a profit. They also represent a grave threat. I do not believe that the former exceeds the latter. They should be terminated on sight."

The uproar that ensued among the assembled avatars took all of Pret-Klob's skill at soothing to quell. When at last the commotion had died down and the heads had resumed their normal positions and levels of brightness, he addressed the ongoing muttering.

"I agree that we cannot allow inventory, particularly this highly inventive and resourceful quartet of inventory, to run freely through our ship. At the same time it must be conceded that based on events to date, the four have demonstrated skills and talents that render them far more valuable than originally thought. Based on this new information, I have had the ship reappraise their potential value to certain of our regular, best customers."

Mathematics appeared, superimposed on the spherical darkness. In response, comments flew. Like the discussion that had preceded them, they were mightily conflicted.

Silent up to now, Bren-Trad anxiously vouchsafed his opinion. "We cannot just throw away profit like that!" Though some were grudging, the accords that were declaimed in response to Pret-Klob's presentation were largely of similar mind. This was duly noted by all.

"Such is our conundrum, members of the association. The more aptitude and skill the free-roaming inventory demonstrates, the greater their increase in value. The longer they remain at large, the more they validate their enhanced worth."

"By that argument," Brid-Nwol grumbled unrepentantly, "their value will be at its greatest when they have killed us all."

"And so it would be," agreed Pret-Klob without a hint of irony. "However, in order to take advantage of that increased value, we must see to it that it does not quite reach that rarefied level of accomplishment. The astray inventory must be recaptured alive. If for no other reason than that we still do not know how they managed to escape their secured enclosures in the first place."

"One survivor out of four would suffice to provide an explanation." Brid-Nwol was running out of contesting capital, and knew it. "The others could be purged."

"Profit," Klos-Jlad observed sagely, "entails risk. Death is the bottom line. Revenue rises above it. I say the association votes to redouble its efforts to recover the missing inventory—alive. Time enough later, if no other choice remains, to implement termination."

Reluctant in light of the deaths that had been inflicted by the Tuuqalian and the humiliation that had been exacted by all four of the absent inventory, the association decided to proceed as the venerable Klos-Jlad recommended. It was thus agreed: Further attempts would be made to recover the inventory. But at the insistence of Brid-Nwol, Shub-Kirn, and others of similar persuasion, Pret-Klob was compelled to place a time limit on the recovery effort. If the missing inventory had not been recovered in marketable condition within one more ten-day, then the hunting teams would exchange their capture strategy for one of outright extermination.

While Pret Klob was not comfortable with this decision, Bren-Trad and his allies were positively livid. The fervor with which they continued to voice their objections was laudable, but they were outvoted. Profit or no profit, if the inventory had not been restored within the agreed-upon time period, steps would be taken to eliminate it. Pret-Klob sighed internally. No one was satisfied with the final outcome of the consultation. Such was the life of a chosen manager. With luck, and if all went well, the wandering stock would be safely recovered, healthy and in fully saleable condition, and that would be the end of the unruly disputation among members. If not—if the process went wrong, or the specter of something ugly and unforeseen materialized . . .

More than almost anything else, he dreaded the prospect of having to sign off on a write-down of the value of a portion of ship's inventory.

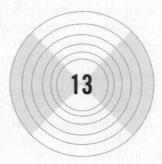

**13**

The view out the port should have been awe-inspiring. Shifted stars and glossy nebulae in far denser concentrations than were visible from anywhere on Earth formed a galactic sky electric with swaths and streaks of color as pure as the elements of which they were composed. Walker could only stare in silence. The sight was mind-numbing, not inspirational. Instead of primal beauty, it only reminded him of how far he was from home, and how unlikely it was that he would ever see it again. Next to him George stood on his hind legs, balancing himself upright with his front paws on the lower edge of the transparency. If the dog's emotions were similarly affected by the sight, he did not show them. Absorbed in examination of a nearby storage bin, Sque ignored both them and the view, while a contemplative Braouk squatted thoughtfully nearby and recited strange verse under his breath.

Forgoing the reality of the breathtaking spectacle's crushing magnificence, Walker turned away. To shift his thoughts from the hopelessness the view incited within him, he speculated on the port's purpose. What was it doing here, away from general access corridors, buried deep within a dark, narrow serviceway? Had it been installed as an afterthought by the ship's designers? Was it placed here on a whim, to provide an unexpected diversion for any Vilenjji who happened to find themselves in this remote and little-visited part of the enormous vessel? Or did it serve some purpose unknown and unimaginable to him, a visitor from a distant world for whom such technology prior to his abduction had never been anything more than a separate section of the daily news? One to which he paid attention only when it affected the stock market.

He didn't know. Neither did Sque, or Braouk. It was simply a port, an unexpected window on the universe located in an unlikely place. To learn the reason for its peculiar placement one would have to inquire of the Vilenjji, or the ship's builders.

Walker wished they had never come across it. Until now, it had been possible for him to entertain thoughts of returning home, however faint the prospect. Cocooned within the vastness of the Vilenjji craft, his mind had been sheltered from the reality of the universe outside. Now that he had looked upon it again, had been forced to contemplate the existence of a cosmos in which Earth was not even visible, the truth of his situation had been driven home with a force no fantasy of repatriation could overcome.

He was lost. Gone, stolen, adrift among the firmament, destined to be treated as nothing more than a piece of walking, talking merchandise intended to fetch a certain price. A commodity to be sold and perhaps traded.

The irony of it did not escape him.

Weighed down by circumstance he sat down on the hard deck, his back to the thick wall pierced only by the port through which the light of unwelcome stars poured relentlessly. Dropping his head into his hands, he lamented his condition. He did not cry. Despondent or not, aimless unhindered wandering through the dark corridors of the alien ship was still better than squirming like a zoo specimen in a cage within the pampering confines of the Vilenjji enclosures.

Walking up to him, George plunked his head down on Walker's right knee. Eyes as soulful as any rendered by Botticelli gazed up at him. "Feeling low, Marc?"

Walker took a deep breath, composed himself, and indicated the softly lambent port above and to the right of where he was sitting. "It's one thing not to be able to see a way home. It's another not to even be able to *see* home."

The dog shifted his head to glance up at the port. "Hey, it's out there, Marc. Somewhere. Kind of like trying to find a bone in a ballpark, maybe, but it's still there."

"So what," he muttered. "Might as well be around the next bend in the proverbial road for all the good it does us." Looking back down at the dog, he ran his fingers through the thick fur atop his friend's head. "Did you know that light bends? I remember hearing about that on the evening news one time. In between the other twenty-four minutes of murder and mayhem."

"Everything bends," George replied somberly, "or it breaks. That's been a big-time dog tenet for thousands of years. It's one reason why we get along so well with you apes."

A smile leaked through Walker's melancholy. Using both hands now, he ruffled the brown curls on the dog's neck. "Another is that you're good medicine for us, George. I have this feeling that if I hadn't met up with you I'd have gone stark raving mad by now. We're not going home, you know. Ever. I think it's time to start getting used to the idea. Either the Vilenjji will recapture us, or we'll die in some unused black back passageway like this one—out of food, out of water, and out of hope."

"Listless biped."

Walker's attention snapped over to the maroon-hued alien who was compacted in the shadows on the other side of the window. "I'm not in the mood for your insults, Sque." Wearily, Walker repeatedly ran a hand through his own hair. "I know you're too full of yourself to suffer from this kind of depression, but you'll just have to put up with the rest of us—those of us who are realists and understand the hopelessness of our situation."

"What makes you think it is hopeless, human?" In the dim light, the flat, silvery eyes of the K'eremu glistened with a metallic sheen that matched the aloofness of her voice.

A glum Walker shifted his backside against the hard material of the deck. "Well, let's see. We're trapped on a hostile vessel in deep space; we're running out of food and drink; we're undoubtedly being pursued around the clock by greedy, contemptuous Vilenjji who can't wait to offload us on some unimaginable world where we'll be treated as no better than property; and the best we can hope for is to keep roaming through the interior of this ship without a destination in mind until they pick us up again. Other than that," he concluded caustically, "I would have to agree that our situation is not hopeless."

"You are correct about nearly everything," Sque replied with unexpected forbearance, "except when you say that we have no destination in mind."

Braouk perked up from where he was leaning against a cylindrical frame nearly as big as himself. "What mean you, small-mouthed in darkness, sputtering mysteries?"

Twisting her body effortlessly, she looked over at the towering Tuuqalian. "Your people are space-going, are they not?" Braouk gestured back affirmatively. "Your people are brave, and committed, and in their simpleminded way sentient, are they not?"

The Tuuqalian's tone sank ominously lower. "How long will you ask of me that which you already know, gray splotch on the shipscape?"

Walker and George hunkered down against the wall beside the port. Though they had come to trust Braouk implicitly, the giant was still utterly alien. The line between his controlled rages and his uncontrolled ones was very slim, and neither man nor dog wished to be caught between them.

Fortunately for Sque, she was too egotistical to be scared. "When bravery pushes up against sentience, common sense comes to the fore. It is to be assumed that your space-traversing vessels are not perfect. Accordingly, it must also be assumed that they have built into them systems and devices designed to cope with emergencies ranging from the simplest to the most extreme. I am referring, self-evidently, to means for evacuation."

She went silent, as if this explained everything. Determined to interpret the implication without having to have it spelled out for him as if to a child, Walker strained to make the correct inference. To his surprise, he actually did so.

"Lifeboats! You're talking about lifeboats. Or at least some kind of secondary vessel that can be detached from the main craft." For some reason, George's look of admiration meant more to him than Sque's diffident gesture of approval.

"The humble biped from a simple world is correct. My too-rapid but still marginally adequate examination of the minutiae of the control box in the corridor tangent to the enclosures revealed to me that this vessel of reasonable size is equipped with as many as four self-contained evacuation craft. It is my intention to seize one, utilize emergency procedures to detach from the main vessel, and flee to the nearest enlightened world that is an affiliate of galactic civilization."

"Are you a pilot, too?" Walker was more than a little overcome by the sudden possibilities the K'eremu had opened up.

The contemptuous tone returned. As was usual with Sque, it did not have very far to travel. " 'Pilot'? Lowly ignorant human, how often must I remind you? Ships intended for use in deep space do not have pilots. Every vessel that is built to travel between the stars is constructed around a central neural cortex whose synthetic life purpose is to guide and maintain the craft of which it comprises such a significant part. No known organic intelligence is capable of performing the necessary permutations with the required speed and accuracy. The K'eremu come close, of course, but choose to devote themselves to higher purposes."

Braouk embellished the explanation. "Any secondary craft designed to preserve organics in an emergency is equipped with a similar cortex. They are built to do only that. Small ship surviving, to the nearest world, automatically goes."

"Then all we have to do is steal one, cut loose, and it'll do the rest." For the first time in days, George's tail was wagging energetically again.

Walker was far less sanguine. "You make it sound so easy."

"Then I have failed to choose my words appropriately, because it will not be so." Confident Sque might be, but she was not naïve. "I have not mentioned this previously because I did not want to raise false hopes among those primitives for whom wishful thinking is such an important component of their mental makeup. But it has been my intention all along to attempt such a venture. It may fail. We may perish in the attempt. But it is a greater goal to aspire to than a limited lifetime of wandering the bowels of this inhospitable craft."

"Suppose we do manage to pull it off?" George wondered aloud. "Won't the Vilenjji just follow and pick us up all over again?" Painful precognitive memories flooded back, of friends being snatched by the remorseless employees and vehicles of City Animal Control, only to escape and be picked up again in a vicious, unending cycle of freedom and imprisonment.

"That is possible," Sque readily conceded. "However, there is a reasonable chance that we may be able to make it to a nearby inhabited world before Vilenjji instrumentation can lock on with sufficient assurance to run us down." Tentacles writhed. "I ask you: Is it not worth trying?"

Walker rose from where he had been sitting. His depression had not left him, but a surge of determination was beginning to push it aside. "Anything's better than stumbling around in the dark waiting for the Vilenjji to pick us up again. Even," he heard himself saying, voicing a phrase he once could never have imagined himself mouthing, "if we die trying."

"That is my nice, single-minded little biped," Sque commented approvingly. "We shall make the effort."

"If you can conceive of doing something like this, won't the Vilenjji?" George observed sagely. "And in that case, won't they have their secondary craft secured, with guards posted to watch over them?"

The K'eremu eyed him pityingly. Which is to say, as usual. "Firstly, to so secure a secondary vessel designed to facilitate swift escape in the event of emergency would be to defeat its purpose. Second, the disregard in which the Vilenjji hold their captives precludes their belief that any of them could attempt something so audacious. To allow the latter would be to admit to an intelligence and abilities on the part of their captives that would raise discomfiting ethical questions about their commerce that the Vilenjji would much prefer not to ponder." Tentacles bobbed and weaved for emphasis as she regarded each of them in turn.

"That is not to say we will be able to stroll right up to a relief craft, saunter through its open accessway, take possession of it, and disengage from this vessel without first having to deal with an impediment or two. But it is not to say that it will be impossible, either. We will know better what obstacles we face when we are in a position to act on them."

"And when might that be?" With every passing moment, now that a glimmer of hope had been raised, Walker was feeling more and more revitalized.

Within their recesses, horizontal eyes went dark. "If the ship schematic I have memorized is accurate, and we encounter no diversions or delays, I should think by the time we have all passed through our next sleep cycle." Silver eyes opened. "Tomorrow, as you would say."

Tomorrow. Walker gazed down at the supercilious, conceited, arrogant alien. "Just when were you going to tell us about this, Sque?"

"Tomorrow," she replied coolly. "Your present wretched emotional condition persuaded me to enlighten you a bit sooner. I realize it may require an unusual effort on your part, but do try to sustain some sense of zeal until we are free or dead, won't you? In support of the endeavor I propose, your purported mind is surplus baggage, but in order to succeed I suspect we will have need of as many limbs as possible."

"Where the hell does that leave me?" George wanted to know.

The K'eremu's eyes dropped to the dog. "Underfoot, most likely. A distraction, at the least. Do not despair. While I can envision numerous possible scenarios, I have no doubt that each will have their part to play in this forthcoming drama."

"Tomorrow, then." Walker found himself gazing once more out the port. All of a sudden, the rainbow incandescence did not seem quite so threateningly vast, quite so terribly intimidating. "What do we do now?"

Sque turned slightly away from him. "We have already enjoyed a small measure of success by employing the tactic known as a strategic diversion. I have in mind another."

"Using the Vilenjji's own technology against them?" George inquired eagerly. "Shutting something else down?"

"Rather more low-tech than that," the K'eremu replied.

Taking a step forward, the hunched-over Braouk loomed over them all. "I find something large, solid, and movable, and flatten several of their pointy crania while the rest of you rush to take control of the chosen craft."

"While the image such murderous exertions call to mind is much to be desired," Sque told him, "it is misplaced and premature. More low-tech even than that."

"More low-tech than hitting someone over the head?" Walker opined uncertainly.

"More basic than you can imagine." Sque sounded pleased with herself: a not uncommon state of affairs. "If fortune holds, more low-tech than our captors can imagine, as well."

"Tomorrow," Walker murmured. It had become a magic word. A destination rather than a description. "What do we do until then? Do we stop and sleep here?"

Like a sentient worm, one tentacle semaphored in his direction. "Do not squander the tiny bit of acumen you have recently displayed, human Walker. We still have some distance to go. It would be disheartening in the extreme to stumble upon stalking Vilenjji on the day before we are destined to risk all."

"Then I'll follow you," he replied readily, "and keep my mouth shut."

Pivoting neatly, the K'eremu resumed scuttling down the long, dim passageway. "Two prudent decisions in one coherent phrase. Despite inherent shortcomings, a glimmer of evolution may be discerned. One can but hope."

Which is what all of them were doing as they silently followed their insufferably egotistical guide onward into the darkness.

＊

Triv-Dwan led the quintet of members forward. Two of them bore an assortment of capture gear. The other three were heavily armed. Bearing with them the decision of the association, as finalized by Pret-Klob and its other senior members, they were operating under a mandate to recapture the still at-large inventory, but not to take chances. It was imperative that the inventory, who had already had the audacity to disgrace a previous search group, not be allowed to escape into the inner regions of the ship a second time. The group's instructions were clear: If the absent inventory could not be recaptured this time, it was to be terminated.

At least, after days of wandering aimlessly, the group now had something definite to track. The sensors they all carried had picked up an unmistakable indicator. At least one large organic signal and possibly more lay directly ahead of them, moving steadily in the opposite direction. Despite the carnage that had been wrought by the free-roaming Tuuqalian, Triv-Dwan felt confident. The two other hunting groups that had also been searching for the missing inventory were closing in on the signal from opposite sides. By coordinating their approach, all three should arrive to confront the source of the signal at the same time. Not even the Tuuqalian, Triv-Dwan felt, could make an escape through three synchronized hunting groups.

Immediately on his right, Sjen-Kloq wrapped her arm flaps tighter around the impressive long weapon she carried. The members of all three groups had been cautioned to attempt capture first and shoot only as a last resort. The warning was superfluous. Everyone knew how much profit was at stake. But they would not put their lives at risk to preserve it. That had been tried immediately subsequent to the initial mass escape of the inventory, and had resulted in the deaths of several members of the association.

It would be good, he knew, to finally see the last of the escapees helpless in clean restraints. Their return would be a lesson to the already recovered inventory: Escape from the enclosures was a futile gesture. Expensive as it had already been, in terms of lives and ship-time, the lesson should not be wasted.

A glance at the sensors that lined his limber right upper appendage indicated that they were closing rapidly on the target. Whatever food and drink the inventory had been able to scavenge should be running low by now, he reflected. Weakness would take its toll on mental as well as physical acuity. With luck, the recapture would go smoothly, with no damage either to inventory or to any members of the three hunting groups. A separate indicator showed that Hvab-Nwod's and Skap-Bwil's teams were closing rapidly. Seeing that all possible avenues of flight were blocked to them, perhaps the inventory would behave rationally and give up without a struggle. If they did so, Triv-Dwan would be among the first to compliment them on having done well to remain at liberty for so long. After all, valuable lessons could be learned even from lowly inventory.

Sjen-Kloq had been forced closer to him by the narrowness of the passageway they were presently negotiating. Triv-Dwan felt the presence of the other members of their group close behind. Having limited space in which to operate did not trouble him. Less room for them to maneuver meant correspondingly less opportunity for the inventory to slip past.

According to the sensor readouts they were very close now. His suckers tightened on the capture device he held. For a change, everything was proceeding flawlessly. Both other groups should be in position within seconds.

"There!" Sjen-Kloq hissed sharply as her own sensors switched from remote to direct visual perception. Simultaneously, Triv-Dwan unleashed his device. From the opposite direction, a member of Hvab-Nwod's team did likewise.

Both shockeshes swiftly enshrouded their target. Enveloped, startled, and stunned, it ceased moving immediately. It did so without protest and without crying out. Weapons and devices at the ready, all three groups rushed forward. What they saw resulted in confusion, bemusement, frustration, anger, and a rapidly dawning realization that this time they had not only been humiliated in the manner of Dven-Palt, but humiliated in a way that was as inimitable as it was ancient.

On Triv-Dwan's limb, as on those of his fellow association members, organic sensors continued to glow with the fullness of detection. Before them, the object of their resolve stood motionless, uncertain how to respond to what had happened to it. It was a repair automaton. A repair automaton that had been methodically and liberally coated with the organic byproducts of not one but four different free-ranging inventory. No wonder the insensate mechanical had given off such a strong and distinctive signal of organic presence. It was emitting other signals as well; ones that Triv-Dwan and his fellow members were at pains to ignore. While distracting, these did not trouble him half so much as the realization that, for a second time, the diligence and technological superiority of the Vilenjji had been systematically deceived.

As he turned away from the sight that was at once unpleasant and taunting, it also left him wondering where, if not here, the unspeakable absent inventory had betaken themselves.

※

The corridor was big. The accessway was big. The final atmosphere lock itself, leading straight into the secondary vessel, was bigger than he had expected. Instead of the small, narrow, easily sealed entrance he had envisioned, Walker found himself sprinting through an arching portal capacious enough to pass a rhino. Scuttling along beside him, listening to his exclamation of surprise, Sque marveled at his lack of common sense.

"These secondary relief craft are designed to accommodate Vilenjji. Vilenjji are large. In an emergency, the intent is to provide for as many individuals as possible. Forcing them to enter a vessel designed to save their lives by making them cross a narrow threshold slowly and one at time would be counter to its purpose."

"A happy coincidence, for which I am grateful, many times." For one of the few times since they had fled the grand enclosure, Braouk did not have to duck or squeeze to fit through a passage. If the Tuuqalian had been relieved by their success before, now he felt positively liberated.

Walker glanced back over a shoulder. There was still no sign of any pursuit. Whether the clever if odious diversion propounded by the inventive Sque had succeeded in drawing the attention of the Vilenjji away from them or because their vain captors had not believed a handful of escapees could conceive of attempting so daring a gambit he did not know. All he did know was that they had successfully gained entrance to one of the subsidiary spacecraft whose location she had memorized from her prior study of the Vilenjji control box.

When the K'eremu, with a boost from Braouk that enabled her to reach the relevant instrumentation, caused the heavy outer and inner doors to spiral shut behind them, Walker felt as if he had just surmounted Everest solo sans supplementary oxygen. If everything went for naught from now on, they had at least in some small way struck back at their abductors. The nature of the triumph was delicious: The abductees were themselves now engaged in the process of stealing from those who had stolen them. Tit for tat, far out among the stars. He wondered if the Vilenjji, when they discovered what was happening right under their olfactory orifices, would feel mortified. He hoped so.

George was running around the interior of the secondary craft, sniffing and exploring. The voluminous central chamber was lined with what looked like giant ice cream scoops: seats or lounges for a couple of dozen Vilenjji forced to abandon ship. With Sque beckoning them onward, they passed through the chamber and into a smaller one beyond. Though it boasted the same customary high ceiling, it overflowed with tiny projection devices and other arcane instrumentation whose purposes Walker did not even attempt to grasp. There were also two more of the archetypical body scoops. As the escapees studied their surroundings, several projection devices winked to life. Bits of dense light, like floating kanji characters mated with exotic flowers, appeared in the air around them. The majority were concentrated forward of the portal through which they had just entered.

"Up," Sque commanded impatiently. For once, an energized Braouk responded without comment, poetical or otherwise. Placing two tentacles next to each other, the Tuuqalian provided a sturdy pedestal for the much smaller K'eremu. Effortlessly, Braouk lifted her up into the web of hovering light-shapes. Gripping his tree-trunklike supportive limbs with half a dozen of her own much smaller ones, she launched into an intense study of the softly glowing, evanescent structures that now surrounded her like so many curious pixies.

That left the two Terrans free to explore the corners of the craft's forward chamber. So elated were both of them at their success in having coming this far that Walker took no offense at Sque's patronizing directive, "Do not touch anything the function of which you do not understand. Which is to say, do not touch anything."

"We're still a long ways from getting free of the Vilenjji," George reminded him, trotting alongside. "We're still a long ways from anywhere."

"But we have a chance," Walker told him. "It might be no more than a minuscule chance, but that's more of one than we had squatting in our enclosures like so many—"

"Dogs in a pound?" George finished for him.

Walker looked down at his friend. "I wasn't going to say that," he replied somberly.

"Doesn't matter. I wanted to. Remember it the next time you find yourself comparing degrees of freedom." The black nose rose and dipped to indicate a nearby patch of luminous alien imagery. "Wonder what that does?"

Walker eyed the cluster of carmine and orange lights that formed an eye-catching basket of floating photons in front of them. Unlike similar luminosities that hovered above their heads at Vilenjji limb-level, this out-of-the-way mass of drifting radiance was practically resting on the deck. Head down, George approached it with his usual caution.

Walker added to it. "Sque said not to touch anything."

"Doesn't smell." The dog raised its head. "It's just light. Why does she get to give all the orders? Why does she get to do everything?"

"Because she knows how," Walker reminded him. "Because she's a representative of the high and mighty all-knowing, all-seeing, all-stuck-up but inarguably ingenious K'eremu. Because if anyone's going to get us out of this, it's her."

"Screw that," George shot back. "It's time I was treated like a dog." So saying, and before a startled Walker could move to stop him, he reached out with his front right leg and gently pawed the bundle of hovering lights.

His claws went right through the drifting shape. They were nothing but lights, after all. Then a rising hum made both of them turn.

"I told you not to touch anything," Sque called down to them from her perch atop the Tuuqalian's extended limbs. Encouragingly, she did not sound any more than usually scornful, much less worried.

The upper half of the front of the chamber was retracting.

As it slid upward into the ceiling, the universe was revealed. Distorted by whatever engine or drive drove the Vilenjji craft, but still stunning in its expanse and glory. It was far more impressive, and more overawing, than had been the view through the modest passageway port they had encountered earlier. Curving halfway around the forward chamber in imitation of a Vilenjji eye, it also allowed them, for the first time, a view of part of the Vilenjji ship itself.

It was immense. Even after days of wandering through its dimly lit passageways, Walker had not really succeeded in acquiring an honest impression of its true size. And they were seeing only a small part of it, he reminded himself. Only that portion that was visible through a corner of the secondary craft's viewport. Certainly it was bigger than your average ocean liner or cruise ship. The sheer scale of it brought home to him in a way nothing else could the magnitude of what they were attempting. The starship was intimidating in ways he had not envisioned. Surely they had no chance of escaping the grasp of beings who could construct, operate, and steer something that was infinitely beyond the collective capability of the entire human species.

"Podal toggle," Sque announced from on high, by way of explanation for what they had done.

So that was what the impudent George had activated. The cluster of dazzling hovering alien luminosity, an incomprehensible mystery, was nothing more than a foot switch. And why not? A wandering spider could short out a massive computer. A skittering rat could interrupt a beam of light, setting off all manner of unforeseen consequences. And a curious, defiant dog could trigger an alien photonic input.

You didn't have to be able to explain the physics of an internal combustion engine to know how to drive a car, he reminded himself. Maybe, just maybe, their chances of actually escaping the clutches of the Vilenjji were a shade more than minuscule.

Turning to study the thousands of silent, alien stars now visible through the sweeping curve of the forward transparency, he came to a solemn conclusion.

He would allow himself at least as much hope as a dog.

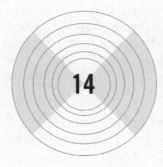

14

Although to all intents and purposes it appeared that they had succeeded in gaining entry to the secondary craft without being observed, it was their activity there that finally alerted the Vilenjji to their presence. As the smaller vessel's internal systems were accessed and brought on line by the busy Sque, notification was passed to relevant instrumentation elsewhere within the main ship. These instruments in turn alerted those whose responsibility it was to monitor such matters.

The fact that every one of the secondary craft's internal monitors had been shut down from inside was in itself instructive. As far as the hastily informed Pret-Klob was concerned, the only question remaining was how many of the still-at-large inventory had managed to gain access to such a sensitive installation. Certainly the missing female K'eremu must be counted among them, since of the four remaining escapees she alone theoretically possessed sufficient skills to control such advanced functions. Perhaps allowing the specimen in question to occasionally accompany selected Vilenjji outside her enclosure had not been a notion that could, in hindsight, be commended for its wisdom.

What of the dangerous giant, the Tuuqalian? Was it still with her? Analysis of the multiple excretory deposits that had been used to deceive Triv-Dwan's hunting group confirmed that it had accompanied the K'eremu at least that far, together with the two oddly matched specimens from the far-distant overheated water world. It seemed likely that all four were now sequestered within the secondary vehicle. At least, he reflected, it was good to know they had finally been located. The task now at hand was to extract them from their final hiding place without damaging either the relief craft itself or the diverse quartet of specimens.

He proceeded to issue the necessary directives.

✳

"Our captors are trying to access the outer lock." From her seat atop the rock-solid Braouk's supportive tentacles, Sque studied the concentrated barrage of flashing lights and drifting colors that filled the air before her. To Walker the condensed light show reminded him of what he saw when he squinted his eyes tight together while driving past a bunch of neon signs at night. He was glad that the coronal hodgepodge made more sense to the K'eremu, because it was nothing but a colorful blur to him.

Braouk's flexible eyestalks allowed him to scan his immediate surroundings without having to put her down. "I see nothing, viewed from my perspective, like weapons. Nothing with which, taking even utmost care, for defense."

"No need to stock weapons in a lifeboat," Walker conceded. A dull thump drew his attention back the way they had entered, through the spherical chamber with its scoop seats, to the now sealed inner lock and beyond. "I wonder if they'd damage their own backup craft just to get at us?"

"Why not, if we've made them mad enough?" George was pacing restlessly back and forth. "Sque said this ship has several others."

"I have sealed the outer lock as best I can," the K'eremu announced from on high. "No doubt they are even now seeking a means to override what I have done. Once they have succeeded at that, they will then need to compute a new sequence to forcibly open the inner portal. We can further seal ourselves in here, but that would only postpone the inevitable."

"Then what do we do?" George asked her.

She spared a glance for the fretful dog. "Remove ourselves from such eventualities—I hope."

The distant thump was not repeated. Standing in the forward chamber with George panting nervously at his side, Walker experienced the kind of helplessness he had not felt since he was the smallest lineman playing for his Pop Warner football team, always facing bigger kids. At such times, he'd gotten run over a lot. Then his growth, both physical and mental, had taken a sustained spurt, and he was the one doing the pancaking.

Now it was like he was ten again, back in kids' league, wondering what kind of stance he ought to assume. Facing the spherical chamber through the open portal of the control room he knew one thing for certain: Die here he might, but he was not going back to the enclosure the Vilenjji had fashioned for him. He'd had enough of Cawley Lake, both the real and the transplanted. Whatever happened next, he was done once and for all with being caged.

Stepping back into the forward chamber, he joined Braouk in searching for something that could be used as a weapon.

The smaller ship rolled slightly to its right. Possessed of an athlete's balance (albeit one who had put on some weight over the previous nine years), he managed to stay upright. Four-footed and with a low center of gravity, George had no problem handling the unexpected jolt, nor did the immovable Braouk. Sque murmured something Walker's implant was unable to translate effectively. Flashing through the air, multiple maroon tentacles conducted light. All the K'eremu needed was a baton and accompanying music, Walker mused, and the illusion would have been complete.

A second jolt followed, stronger than the first. Despite being prepared, this time he was knocked forward, to land on hands and knees. Braouk was hard-pressed to simultaneously maintain his stance while providing a steady perch for Sque from which to operate.

"I cannot proceed effectively if I am to be shaken about like water in a cup," she chided him.

One globular ocular rose upward on its stalk to eye her unblinkingly. The orb, Walker noted, was larger than the K'eremu's head. "Fashion you anything, small master of insults, with results?"

"They're breaking in!" In a panic, George sought out a hiding place beneath a fluted mass of melded plastic and metal forms.

"They are not breaking in," Sque assured him. "Unless I have done everything wrong, it is we who are breaking free!"

At that moment the reason for the jolts and shakes became crystal clear as the secondary ship dynamically disengaged from its primary vessel. As it commenced an automatic slow turn away from the parent craft preparatory to engaging its main drive, there was an instant of complete disorientation accompanied by a rising nausea in the digestive systems of those within. Then the craft's own artificial gravity took hold, the bottoms of Walker's feet once again found the floor, and his stomach settled gratefully back into its customary position. Out the sweeping forward transparency, much more of the Vilenjji vessel hove into view as the relief ship continued its balletic pirouette in the void.

Conditioned by a limited knowledge of spacecraft gleaned almost entirely from watching movies, Walker was expecting something streamlined. It came as a bit of a shock then, to see the gigantic conglomeration of conjoined geometric shapes that constituted the main body of the Vilenjji vessel. The larger craft from which they were escaping was stunning in its disarray. Pyramidal components penetrated battered rectangles and parallelogons. Spheres like bubbles of blown rust adhered to bracing pylons and immense connective cylindrical tubes. Near what he imagined to be the front, or bow, of the hopelessly unruly craft, a succession of grooved cones extended outward into space for what looked like half a mile. Every exposed surface was pockmarked with depressions or festooned with what appeared to be antennae. Here and there, external lights shone steadily or winked in and out of existence.

In place of the grandiose star-spanning vehicle he had envisioned in his mind's eye was a gigantic junk pile of joined-together bits and pieces. While some of the individual components were of impressive size, not one of them would raise appreciative eyebrows in an architectural competition back home. Like the illicit intentions of the Vilenjji themselves, their vehicle was designed with function in mind, not beauty. He found the sheer prosaic ugliness of it consoling.

And they were completely free of it. Free from recapture. Free from their remorselessly coddling, wretched enclosures. Free from—

George made a very rude noise.

About to inquire as to the cause, Walker found that he did not have to. He could not have spoken anyway. All he could do was stare, lips slightly parted. Had he possessed lips, Braouk would have doubtless done likewise. Sque continued to silently manipulate her photic controls—but now to no avail. Having successfully disengaged from the main Vilenjji vessel, the four escapees suddenly found themselves confronted with a new and entirely unexpected predicament.

Another ship. Another really big ship.

It loomed directly in front of them, its prodigious mass slowly blotting out all but small scraps of the visible starfield. Walker had thought the Vilenjji ship sizable, enclosing as it did within its crazy-quilt jumble of linked-together shapes as much usable interior space as several oceangoing supertankers. The vessel that had without warning appeared before them was the size of the port where such supertankers would dock. Furthermore, what he could see of it was far more elegantly put together than the ungainly home of their captors. The newcomer was the color of aged ivory, marred in places by darker rambling slashes on its outer shell that were variously tinted dark green, blue, and several resplendent variants in between.

Hundreds of ports glowed with internal lights sharper and more defined than anything emanating from the Vilenjji ship. If not exactly a space-going city, it certainly expanded Walker's limited scale of alien architectural values. Only Sque, as might be expected, was not overawed. But eventually even she was forced to concede defeat. Turning away from the photic controls, she directed Braouk to lower her to the deck.

"This craft's internal instrumentation is no longer responsive. Either it or the mechanics it commands have been arrested. I can do no more."

"Then that's it." George looked from one companion to another. "Everything we've done has been for nothing. The Vilenjji will open this secondary craft up like a can of old dog food and in a couple of hours we'll be right back where we started. In our cages."

Despite Walker's resolve not to be returned to the enclosures, he did not see that there was anything more they could do to prevent that dismal eventuality from occurring. Braouk might go down fighting, taking a Vilenjji or two with him, but even that seemed unlikely. Surely their captors had learned their lesson by now and would take proper precautions before attempting to repossess the powerful Tuuqalian. As for himself, there was not much he could do against beings seven feet tall who outweighed him by a hundred pounds or more. The last thing he wanted to do, the one thing he had determined not to do, was surrender meekly. Yet without so much as an old razor blade to his name, there was little he could see himself offering in the way of resistance. At least George could take a bite out of a dark leg flap before the Vilenjji wrapped him up in a helpless bundle. He, Walker, could not even do that.

They waited for the end in silence: frustrated man, resigned dog, self-contained K'eremu, pensive Tuuqalian. An odd foursome, cast together by a shared longing for freedom and a mutual hatred of their captors. Walker did his best to reconcile himself to the inevitable. It had been a good run, he told himself. For all they knew, one unprecedented in Vilenjji memory. A few of their captors were dead, a few more humiliated. They had accomplished more than they had any right to expect. As to what the future held for him, he tried not to think about it.

As it developed, he had quite a lot of time not to think about it.

The interior lock of the craft they had commandeered did not cycle open. The outer lock was not blown. They continued to drift between the two larger vessels—one huge, the other immense—like an ant caught between an elephant's forefeet. No attempt was made to communicate with them. Nor was he the only one to be struck by the continuing calm.

"This is very odd." Having been set back down on the floor, Sque roused herself, her body rising upward from the middle of her cluster of tentacles. Silver-gray eyes contemplated the unresponsive instrumentation above her head. A few of the controlling lights were in motion. Though he had noticed the activity, Walker had thought nothing of it, believing it to be part of normal onboard operation. It was plain to see that Sque felt otherwise.

"It would appear that someone is talking to someone else. But no one is talking to us. Yet I should think our presence here would be the focus of any conversational activity."

"Probably deciding thoughtfully, between both of them, what happens." Braouk had settled himself against a wall, his four massive upper limbs crossed across his long gash of a tooth-lined mouth, his eyestalks slumped to where they were nearly level with the deck.

George piped up defiantly. "Well, I wish they'd put their pointy heads together and make up their feeble minds. I'm getting sick of waiting!"

Sque eyed him mordantly. "Freedom wearying you already, little quadruped?"

The dog growled. "How about I see what one of those ropy excuses you've got for appendages tastes like? See if you find that wearying."

A disgruntled Walker spoke up. "We won't gain anything by fighting among ourselves." He tried to find a reason, any reason, to be optimistic. "Maybe they're having trouble forcing their way in. Maybe what Sque did when she sealed us off screwed with their programming or something, and they can't get it sorted out. If they can't, and the locks can only be opened effectively from the inside, maybe we'll have something to bargain with after all."

"Maybe they'll just decide we're not worth it and blow us into our component particles," Braouk muttered disconsolately. "Weepish wailing worries, cautiously composed caring contemplation, emotive endings."

Sque winced visibly. Walker was more tolerant. What George thought of the Tuuqalian's effort was not forthcoming.

"While they might be sufficiently perturbed by our efforts to eliminate us from their inventory," she pointed out, "I seriously doubt they would feel similarly about something as valuable and significant as this craft that we currently occupy. As to the possibility, Marc, that my work may inadvertently have stymied their efforts at recovery, I should not doubt that they served to confuse inferior beings such as our captors. However, I regret to say that any hope this might be anything more than a temporary impediment to their efforts to recapture us is likely to be misplaced. The Vilenjji may be slow, but they are in their own imperfect fashion quite competent."

As if to confirm the K'eremu's analysis of the situation, a groaning sound came from the lock located on the far side of the empty, spherical passenger chamber. The inner lock was being forced. Walker had a bad moment when it occurred to him that the opening of the inner lock did not ensure that the outer lock had been closed. If that was the case, every molecule of atmosphere within the secondary craft would be sucked out into space in a matter of seconds, along with anything else that was not bolted down. Like himself. There was nothing he could do about it now, he knew, except tense up and hold on.

Rising from where he had been resting against the wall, Braouk readied himself for whatever was to come. Unashamedly, his three companions took up positions behind the massive Tuuqalian. Why they did so Walker did not bother to analyze. Certainly they had no chance of fighting their way past any party of well-equipped Vilenjji that had been sent to recapture them. But he was determined to try.

The lock finished cycling. Its inner spiral began to open. As his fingers clenched into fists, he wished for something solid to wrap them around: a rock, a club, something heavy he could swing. Something he could throw. Something he could use to bash purple heads and appendages. Other than sharp invective, there was nothing.

As soon as it had finished cycling, several shapes stepped deliberately through the open lockway. Radiating confidence and alertness, they advanced without hesitation through the spherical passenger chamber in the direction of the forward compartment. One carried instrumentation of a style and type Walker had not seen previously. Of the others,

all were obviously armed except for the one who took the lead. Walker's
fingers unclenched, and his lower jaw dropped slightly. Beside him,
Sque hissed something too sibilant for his implant to translate. In front
of them, Braouk mimed a gesture that was querulous rather than hostile, and whispered something from the Thirty-Fourth Chronicle of Siv-
ina'trou.

The newcomers were not Vilenjji.

⁂

"You will come with us, please." In size, the speaker was little larger
than Sque. The confidence it exhibited far exceeded its physique.

You had to hand it to the Vilenjji, Walker conceded. Brutally indifferent and immoral their actions might be, but they sure knew how to
build translator implants. He understood clearly every word-sound the
alien made. While he was marveling, George was replying.

"Come with you where?"

"To our ship."

"Your ship?" Walker reflexively glanced back toward the sweeping
arc of transparency that was dominated by the imposing exterior of the
newly arrived craft. "That would be your ship there, I suppose?"

Two of the aliens looked at each other. They did not have to turn to
do so. This was fortunate because their heads were fixed to their bodies. Neckless, they would have been forced to pivot their torsos in order to face each other—except for the fact that they had three eyes. In
fact, as near as Walker could tell, they had three of everything.

With their rounded but roughly triangular bodies facing forward,
he could clearly make out the three legs that provided sturdy tripodal
support. Each of three legs terminated in three long, supple digits. A
small, feathery hearing or smelling organ was located above each eye.
One of the latter faced forward while the other two scanned the creature's surroundings to its right and left. There was nothing resembling
nostrils. Below the forward-facing eye, a small, roughly triangular
mouth opened and closed as the alien spoke. Except for being far
smaller, more delicate, and devoid of visible teeth, this alien orifice was
in shape and evolved structure not unlike Braouk's massive clashing
jaws. What epidermis Walker could see sticking out of their attire was a
light beige.

Unlike the Vilenjji, who favored loose, baggy attire, the newcomers
were clad in form-fitting ensembles equipped with a no-nonsense array of supplementary straps, belts, and equipment of jewel-like precision and finish. Every piece of the latter was vibrantly color-coded,

while the triangular suits themselves glowed a slightly brighter shade of white than their vessel. This garb terminated in pallid slippers within which each of the three long toes was clearly delineated.

While the majority of devices on display could be operated by one or two hands, one newcomer neatly balanced an intimidating-looking piece of equipment that wrapped completely around the front of its body and required all three hands to operate. Walker could not imagine what it did, nor did he especially wish to find out.

"You're not going to hand us back to the Vilenjji?" George's hesitant query reflected the same uncertainty that was at that moment being experienced by every one of his friends.

"We find ourselves confronted by a set of circumstances as potentially unsettling as they are peculiar," the unarmed leader replied. Its tone, insofar as the translator implant could reproduce it accurately, struck Walker as determinedly neutral. He decided to regard that as promising. "Nothing will be resolved in haste. Most particularly, nothing will be settled here. We decide nothing imprudently." Stepping to one side, he gestured in unmistakable fashion.

With nothing to be gained by objecting, and failing to see how their situation could be made any worse by complying, the four escapees acceded to the newcomer's demand. As they filed past, Walker noted that while the armed aliens appeared to be impressed by Braouk's size, neither were they visibly intimidated. An impressive people, to be sure.

"Who are 'we'?" he asked the leader as he strode past it. "I mean, you. You don't look anything like Vilenjji."

"I am the facilitator Choralavta of the neuter gender. We are of the Sessrimathe," it added, as if that explained everything.

As they were marched out of the lock and into a waiting chamber that was clearly not part of the Vilenjji ship, Walker leaned over to whisper to Sque, who was scuttling along beside him.

"These are Sessrimathe. Ever hear of 'em?"

"I have not." She glanced up at him from out of the deep recesses of her eye sockets. "As such, I have no notion of how they may think or of what they may intend."

"Returning us to the Vilenjji, probably," George muttered aloud as he trotted along slightly ahead of them both. "Or taking us for themselves, to sell later."

"It's a sad thing," Walker informed the dog irritably, "that all mutts don't have your incurably positive outlook."

The dog looked back over a shoulder at him. "Gee, I can't imagine why I haven't been bubbling over with optimism lately. Maybe you can explain the failing to me—if we live out the day."

In contrast to the colossal craft from which it had been sent, the Sessrimathe transfer vessel was modest enough to be considered compact. With Braouk tucked uncomfortably in the back, there was barely enough room for the aliens and their four—what? What were they now? Walker wondered. Had their status changed? Were they still captives? Or something else? Guests? Future inventory to be logged and appraised by new owners? Time would tell—hopefully in a manner significantly different from George's sour preliminary assessment.

If nothing else, he told himself, they were off the main Vilenjji vessel. No matter what happened next, that had to be considered a plus. At least until something came along to prove otherwise.

Given the comparatively diminutive stature of their new contacts, the corridor they entered into upon exiting the transfer vessel was higher and wider than he expected, a development for which the oft physically put-upon Braouk was especially grateful. Its expansiveness might be explained by the number of tripodal Sessrimathe, who seemed to be everywhere. While many took the time to favor the new arrivals with evident interest, none paused in their activities. An efficient species, Walker decided. Efficient, well dressed, well armed, well equipped. What might their corresponding ethics be like?

For the very first time since he had been abducted, he dared to visualize a glimmer of genuine hope. Hope for what, he could not be sure, but having been deprived of any for so long, he was more than ready to accept whatever might present itself for the taking. Encouragingly, there was still not a single tall, shuffling, condescending Vilenjji to be seen.

They were led into a truck-sized compartment that, like its surroundings, was painted (or stained, or enameled, or poured—Walker could not decide which) white, with silver stripes embedded in the walls that might be decorative, functional, or both. When the stripes began to glow softly, his skin started to tingle. He fought down the urge to scratch, not wanting to do anything that might be misconstrued by their hosts. Though he had no reason to do so, he was beginning to think of them as hosts rather than captors. That old bugaboo hope would not go away.

Though there was no definitive sense of motion, he felt that the compartment must be some kind of internal transport. In order to function efficiently, a vessel this vast would need such, he reasoned. And when they emerged from the compartment's interior, it was to exit into a different, smaller corridor from the one they had traversed before. Here, the curious stares of the far fewer Sessrimathe present lingered longer on the visitors.

Their guards/guides escorted them into another chamber—Braouk barely managed to squeeze through the entryway—and left them there. Enclosed by white walls devoid of ports or windows, the foursome waited for whatever might come. They were restless, but not worried. Whatever the Sessrimathe decided to do with them could be no worse than what they had already fled.

"I could use a drink," George murmured.

A few moments later, a portal opened in one wall, and three metal canisters glided into the room. Opening the simple lids, the captives were treated to glimpses, smells, and the sheen of water, some kind of powerful alcohol, and in the third canister what Walker thought might be blue-tinted hydrogen peroxide. Eagerly, the foursome took turns at the water.

Settling back against a wall and wiping lingering droplets from his chin, Walker found himself mentally racing through every metaphor employing whiteness that he could recall. In the end, he likened his present situation to being trapped inside a tube of toothpaste, wondering whether the Sessrimathe would turn out to be germs or cavity fighters. The allegory displeased him. Aside from its juvenile aspects, he was disappointed he could not do better. The Tuuqalian summed up their situation far more elegantly.

"Could be worse, dallying in this place, sucking atmosphere." The thoughtful Braouk considered testing the doorway to see if it was locked, then decided against doing so. Even if he could manage an exit, there was nowhere to go. Nothing to see but more ivory-hued walls and bustling tripartite Sessrimathe.

Hours later, when the portal through which they had been herded opened anew, they were not surprised to see three of their hosts enter. Two remained by the door. Whether they were guards or observers, Walker could not tell. The third individual approached the curious foursome. It was unusually tall for one of its kind—its immovable, triangular head reached nearly to Walker's chest.

"I am the progenitor Tzharoustatam of the male gender. It has fallen to me to try to make sense out of what has been encountered."

Before Walker or any of her other companions could respond, Sque scuttled forward. "I am Sequi'aranaqua'na'senemu, a female of the K'eremu. These representatives of two other systems and three additional species are my companions in misfortune. Whatever ensues, I ask you not to hold their primitive ways against them. They cannot help what they are."

Two eyes, right and center, regarded her while the left was left to focus on Walker. "What ways are to be held against anyone, or for anyone, are yet to be determined. Contact was made with the other vessel in near space. It is crewed by Vilenjji, a species that is known to us. Not well known, but sufficient for us to be aware that they operate within the parameters of galactic civilization."

As the body pivoted slightly, all three eyes now came to rest on Walker. Once, such an alien, unnatural stare would have made him panicky. After what he had gone through these past many months, he found that now it did not trouble him at all. He had been the focus of too many alien oculars for another one (or three) to unsettle him.

"The secondary vessel from which you were retrieved was encountered in the process of leaving the Vilenjji craft. While we monitored a mix of anger and commotion emanating from the latter, nothing at all was detected from within yours. As we were nearby, Command decided to investigate and to see what if any assistance we might offer in the event there was some problem. The response of the Vilenjji to this courteous inquiry was . . . confused. They insisted that the secondary vessel and its contents be returned to them immediately. When we politely offered to ascertain the condition of the contents of the vessel in question, they responded that this was unnecessary, perhaps even dangerous.

"A solicitous probe of the secondary craft's interior revealed the presence of four active and diverse life-forms—yourselves. This did not strike Command as a revelation of potential danger. Against the ongoing protestations of the Vilenjji, it was determined that we should make an investigation ourselves." All three arms rose and rotated in a gesture that was as alien to Walker as was their owner.

"So—here you are. Have your say." Unexpectedly reverting to silence, the Sessrimathe awaited a response.

"There is much that needs to be said," Sque began without hesitation. "I would begin by commencing an extensive cataloging of—"

"Please." The Sessrimathe cut her off. K'eremu appendages fluttered in frustration as Tzharoustatam refocused his attention on Walker. "You tell me."

"That is a human, from a backward world," Sque persisted, "who is not sufficiently developed to—"

"Please second time." Translated and interpreted, Tzharoustatam's tone was noticeably firm. "I ask the biped." Sque's speaking tube threatened to collapse in on itself, but she had enough sense not to argue further.

The triple stare should have been unnerving. Instead, Walker found it comforting, though he was unsure which eyes to try to meet with his own.

"Can you be brief?" their interrogator requested. "The Sessrimathe are ever busy, and prize time above all else."

"You bet," Walker assured him. Next to him, tail wagging steadily, George offered silent encouragement while the motionless mountain that was Braouk extended his eyestalks as far forward as possible. "We're all four of us prisoners, captives. Abducted from our homeworlds to be sold for profit by the Vilenjji." Not knowing in which direction their captors' ship now lay, he settled for gesturing expansively. "There's at least one other area of enclosures—cages—on the Vilenjji ship that's full of other captives whose sad situation is identical to ours."

Walker could not be certain, but it seemed to him that these disclosures took the Sessrimathe aback. His impression was confirmed by Tzharoustatam's disbelieving reply.

"You are certain of this? You were all of you taken against your will, to be (the revulsion in his voice was unmistakable) sold? Like common property?"

Having not yet been instructed to be silent, George took the opportunity to speak up. "Like old play toys, yes. Sometimes they'd experiment with us, to see who showed what abilities, who was compatible with others, that sort of thing. It was horrible."

"When you stopped us, we were trying to escape," Walker added for good measure.

"Escape? Escape to where?" Tzharoustatam's bewilderment was plain.

"It didn't matter," Walker told him gravely. "Anyplace. We were ready to die rather than return to Vilenjji captivity." He hesitated, but the question that had been festering in his mind ever since they had been brought aboard the Sessrimathe ship had to be asked. "You're—you're not going to return us to them, are you?"

"Return you . . . ?" Interestingly, when the Sessrimathe interrogator flushed, its skin turned not red but the color of burnt umber. "If what you say is true . . ." Pausing again as if to collect himself, Tzharoustatam's left and middle eyes finally turned back to Sque. "Can you, K'eremu, confirm this?"

"Are you saying that you do want to hear my opinions?" Sque's tone was decidedly frosty.

Walker hissed at her, "Sque, for heaven's sake, not now!"

"Oh, very well." Tentacles unclenched. "I confirm everything the backward biped says, as will my other companions. As will those unfortunates who are still held captive within the Vilenjji vessel, if you will take the time to interview them. It is a most monstrous enterprise and nothing less that is responsible for ripping us from our homeworlds." Eyes rife with intelligence met the equally formidable gaze of the Sessrimathe. "Better you should kill us all, here and now, than return us to the Vilenjji and send them contentedly on their way. At least we would perish cleanly. Though," and raising her speaking tube, she sampled the air, "if it comes to that, I personally would prefer to ask the Long Question in a more salubriously humid clime."

"No one is going to kill anyone." Tzharoustatam was clearly horrified that the very notion had been given voice. "Nor is anyone going to be returned to what may be corrupt circumstances. What you have told me demands immediate investigation."

His spirits soaring, Walker forced himself to keep a damper on his hopes. Nothing had been resolved yet, much less anything in their favor. His months on the Vilenjji craft had taught him patience, a quality alien to his chosen profession.

"Meanwhile," the Sessrimathe told them, "you will remain here as our guests. If you have bodily requirements beyond the ingestible fluids that have already been supplied to you, speak them, and they will be forthcoming to the best of our ability."

The dog piped up without hesitation. "I could use a warm, affectionate little—"

"George," Walker said warningly. "Let's not abuse the hospitality of our gracious hosts."

"Oh, all right." At least not right away, the dog decided silently.

"We will need sustenance. Fuel." Sque's lissome appendages danced in the alien air. "I can provide descriptions of necessary proteins, from which additional chemical compounds can be synthesized. That should be adequate for now."

"I am pleased that you think so," replied Tzharoustatam without a hint of sarcasm.

"When—when do you think you'll make a decision? On what to do with us?" Walker asked tentatively.

The triocular gaze turned back to him. "When we have ascertained truth, guest. Until then, you will be given what you need. If there is anything specific beyond what has already been mentioned, speak of it now."

Braouk asked for a certain kind of flavoring to be added to his food. Sque recited in detail the chemical makeup of the drug (or "food additive" as she deftly put it) joqil. A mutt of refined taste as well as enhanced intelligence, George asked if they could synthesize filet mignon, and needed Sque to elucidate the relevant chemistry.

When it came his turn, Walker hesitated. "If you have some kind of universal reader, or translator-equipped device, I'd very much like to learn about your civilization."

Tzharoustatam eyed him approvingly. "Sessrimathe civilization—or galactic civilization."

"Galactic," Walker advised him.

"Nourishment of a different organ. I think an appropriate device can be found. If not, one can be modified. Provided you are willing to allow a brief preparatory study of your central nervous system."

"Like Sque said earlier," Walker told the alien, "nothing you do to us can be any worse than what we've already been forced to experience."

The middle three-fingered hand gestured. "Your requests will be seen to."

George stepped forward to gaze up at the Sessrimathe. "What happens when you've finished your . . . investigation?"

One eye remained fixed on Walker while the other two regarded the apprehensive dog. "You will promptly be informed of the results, and any subsequent decisions." As the alien turned away, Walker marveled at the coordinated movement of its three legs. "Abducted," he thought he heard the Sessrimathe murmur. Then it was gone, followed by its two companions who had not spoken but who had most definitely listened to every word of the encounter. The doorway closed behind them.

Once again, the uneasy foursome were alone in the white room. As promised, Sque was soon contacted for information on ingestible chemical compounds. Not long afterward food was forthcoming, along with a greater variety of consumable liquids. To Walker's astonishment, one shimmering blue canister contained a dark fluid that looked and tasted like several gallons of thick raspberry syrup. His only regret was that he could not drink more than a little of the rich, heavy fluid. It went down even better when drizzled atop something that had the taste and consistency of a venison muffin.

As it had in the course of so many difficult days past, his battered but still reliable watch kept him apprised of the passage of time. Sated with food and drink, they waited amid their sterile surroundings for the next reaction from their hosts.

It came within hours, as Tzharoustatam returned. Once again he was accompanied by two others of his kind. Only this time, both were armed. Within, Walker withered. The presence of weapons was not promising.

It did not immediately occur to him that they might have another purpose.

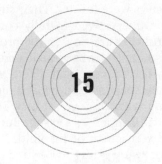

**15**

"**O**utrage! An affront against civilization!"

For a bad moment, Walker thought the Sessrimathe was talking about him and his companions. Then he was able to see that the alien's anger was not directed at him, or at his friends. Tzharoustatam was raving—in the courteous, proper manner of the Sessrimathe, but still raving—about something else. The nature of that something else the three-legged alien was shortly to identify.

"Come with me, all of you." Without waiting to see if they were complying, their host pivoted and strode back toward the portal through which he had just entered.

"Whither we go, relying on new friends, for seeing?" As usual, Braouk lumbered along in the wake of his smaller companions.

"To the Vilenjji," Tzharoustatam informed them.

Sque halted immediately. "Oh, no. You are not turning us back to them. We have already made our sentiments known on that point."

Tzharoustatam turned his body just enough for the left eye to regard her. "Do you think the Sessrimathe as primitive as you do your companions? Our inspection has exposed the truth. It was only a matter of insisting that we be given a tour of the Vilenjji craft. Once aboard, we were able to take ourselves where we wished to go. Observing this and divining our intent, some of the Vilenjji resisted. I regret to say that we were compelled to take countermeasures. There were casualties.

"Your fellow abductees were located. Their situation was as you described it. Enough were interviewed to fully corroborate your earlier statements. These unfortunates are now in the process of being rehabilitated and freed of constraint." Limbs gesticulated animatedly. "A crime against civilization has been committed. There will be repercussions. Reports will be filed. Interspecies relations and interactions being what they are, distances being what they are, it may be that nothing of immediate consequence will happen as a result. But reports will be filed." In the erudite, mature vernacular of his kind, Tzharoustatam's words made it sound as if shots were going to be fired, not reports filed. Perhaps, Walker surmised, what the Sessrimathe was referring to was the civilized equivalent in this part of the galaxy.

"Then why are you taking us to the Vilenjji?" he heard himself asking. Their armed escort, he noticed, did not flank or follow but instead preceded them. As if, he slowly came to realize, their intent was not to watch over them but to protect them.

"So you can be made acquainted with their current status for yourselves. Until all relevant ramifications have been resolved, they have been taken into custody and their ship confiscated. They will be conveyed to the nearest key world where this unpardonable situation can be appropriately discussed and analyzed. Without a doubt, penalties will be incurred. What they have done beggars polite annotation. I myself have heard stories of such things, but never thought them more than rumor or anecdote. I certainly never expected, in the course of my career, to encounter evidence of them in person. To find such unpleasantness verified is most disheartening."

"Then we're free? We're not going to be returned to the Vilenjji's detention?" Having heard it implied, George now wanted to hear it spelled out.

A gracious Tzharoustatam readily complied. "From this moment on, within the recognized limits of galactic civilization, you are not bound by the dictates or whims of any minds other than your own, yes.

As for matters of custody, it is the Vilenjji who now find themselves so classified. They will be turned over to the appropriate authorities for additional processing. Whatever the outcome of any formal investigation into their activities, I believe I can assure you with some confidence that your status cannot possibly be reverted."

Overcome with emotion, George dropped to the floor. Gently, Walker reached down and picked him up, carrying him in his arms as they continued onward.

Once again they found themselves ushered into an intraship conveyance. This time, Walker tingled as much with anticipation as from the effect generated by the transport. When they finally emerged, George had recovered his emotions enough to once more walk unaided.

They were in a large domed chamber. Several dozen Sessrimathe were already there, arranged in double rows. All were armed. They were not what caught his attention, however. Standing out amidst all the familiar whiteness, the bowl of the dome overhead exploded with color. It was a landscape, the likes of which Walker had never encountered. Pinnacles of crystal glistened above rivers the color of antimony. Streams of liquid metal roared and tumbled beneath an angry red-orange sky. The spectacular moving images that filled the bowl depicted a world as alien and inhospitable as it was beautiful. Its purpose might be decorative, or instructive, or intended to awe: He knew not. He was entranced. So much so that Braouk had to prod him with an appendage, the gentle nudge nearly knocking Walker off his feet, when the first Vilenjji were brought in.

They moved with the same side-to-side, shuffling gait he had come to know and loathe so well. As ever, it was impossible to tell just by looking at them what they might be thinking or feeling. The moon eyes in the tapering skulls stared unblinkingly straight ahead, as if their present situation and those responsible for it were of no consequence. Their arms, with their powerful sucker-laden flaps, were fastened to their sides by unseen devices. A taste of their own medicine. Seeing his abductors bound if not exactly shackled filled Walker with quiet glee.

His satisfaction was multiplied by the fact that the once all-powerful Vilenjji had been reduced to such a state by beings far smaller than themselves. As everywhere else on their enormous ship, active, efficient Sessrimathe were everywhere: quietly but firmly directing the detainees toward one of several distant portals, urging the occasional laggard onward, gesturing with Sessrimathe-sized weapons that Walker had no doubt could wreak destructive havoc entirely out of proportion to their unpretentious size. The more he saw of the Sessrimathe, the more he liked and admired them, and not only because they were responsible for liberating him and his friends from the Vilenjji. In contrast to the latter they were, as even Sque might grudgingly be forced to admit, an altogether civilized people.

As they passed in involuntary review, only one or two of the Vilenjji bothered to look up at those who had taken them into custody. Supercilious as ever, it was possible they had not yet fully come to terms with their forcibly altered status. One alien happened to let his glance fall upon the four former inventory. George shrank from that morbidly implacable gaze, while Walker and Braouk were of one mind, eager to respond with violence. Only Sque was unmoved, rendered immune to that unblinking stare by her own incorrigible sense of self-importance.

When the Vilenjji addressed them, it was with an understated confidence that chilled Walker's blood far more thoroughly than any overt display of anger or aggression would have.

"I, Pret-Klob, note a setback that will result in a regrettable downward projection of profits for the forthcoming fiscal period. The association will be forced to modify its most recent fiduciary forecast. A temporary setback only, as are all such for the Vilenjji. It is not unknown for Sessrimathe zeal to be misplaced. This is one such instance. Be assured that in the realness of time, the natural order of things will be restored." The owlish alien eyes seemed almost apologetic. "It is only business."

Emboldened by the alien's restraints, George stepped forward. "Yeah, well, we're free and you're walking around with your forepaws glued to your ribs. Chew on *that* bone for a while!"

Infuriatingly, the Vilenjji did not deign to reply to the small barking creature that was so clearly beneath it both physically and mentally. Escorted by armed Sessrimathe, Pret-Klob was led out of the receiving area in the company of the rest of his intractable association members. When the last of them had vanished through a far portal, Walker turned to Tzharoustatam.

"What's going to happen to them now?"

Patches and stripes of intense blue and pink shimmered against the white background of the Sessrimathe's immaculate attire. "They will be delivered to the nearest world capable of hearing the charges against them. There they will be prosecuted according to the principles of general civilized law. Their vessel has been impounded and is in the process of being thoroughly searched, both to free any additional abductees who may be held elsewhere and to accumulate evidence against your captors. You need no longer fear them."

Leaning forward, Braouk extended all four massive upper appendages in the Sessrimathe's direction. "Hardly we know, how thanks to
give, our liberators."

Tzharoustatam responded with a gesture making use of all three
arms that was as graceful as it was self-effacing. "Civilization stands on
the willingness of those who back up its principles with more than
words. What we did was done not expressly to release you and the others but to uphold those values. You may regard your restored freedom
as an ancillary benefit."

Walker did not give a damn about Sessrimathe motivations. What
mattered were the consequences. The Vilenjji were under arrest, and he
and his friends were free. Free to return home. In the course of his work
as a commodities trader he had encountered and utilized more than his
share of four-letter terminology, but none more appealing than that
one. Home. Never in his life had he ever imagined so small a word capable of encompassing so great a multitude of meanings, so vast a universe of expectation.

Invigorated by the prospect, buoyed by the sight of the arrested
Vilenjji, he did not hesitate to put into words the obvious request—one
that surely needed only to be spoken to be fulfilled, and to set the relevant course of action in motion. If it wasn't already.

"So, Tzharoustatam—I'm assuming your people may want to talk
to us some more, might have some additional questions regarding our
former unhappy situation, but I'm sure you don't mind my asking—
when can we go home?" He felt his companions close around him,
waiting expectantly for the Sessrimathe's answer.

Tzharoustatam considered each of their attentive faces in turn. His
tripartite gaze enabled him to do so quickly. "Yes, there will be additional queries. But they should be perfunctory. After that, you may go
home whenever you wish."

Unable to stand the happiness, a giddy George began running circles around his companions. Struggling to suppress his emotions,
Braouk launched into a murmured recitation of the glorious central
stanza from the Epic of Klavanja. Looking for someone to high-five,
Walker was forced to stay his hand, since there were none to meet
it. Only Sque exhibited no elation, restrained by a natural reticence
and . . . something else.

"It is good to hear you say that." She had to raise her voice in order to be heard above the ongoing celebration. "Naturally, the return of
those so boorishly removed from their homes will start with those adversely impacted individuals who represent the most highly developed

species." Without a trace of embarrassment she added humbly, "That would be me."

Whatever Tzharoustatam thought of this assertive display of alien ego he kept to himself. Before any of the K'eremu's companions could object, voice their outrage, or laugh out loud, the Sessrimathe responded.

"There may be moderating issues of distance and location involved. Astrophysics is not my realm, and I am not qualified to comment on such. However, I am certain the wishes of all will be fulfilled. All you have to do is provide Navigation with the necessary coordinates."

George's woolly brows furrowed sharply. "Coordinates?"

"Of your homeworlds." All three of the kindly Tzharoustatam's oculars inclined toward the dog. "Obviously, we cannot make arrangements for your return home until you show us where your homes lie."

Walker swallowed uneasily. Having been exposed to the immensity of the Sessrimathe ship, having been witness to the efficiency with which they had taken control of the Vilenjji vessel and its crew, he had automatically assumed it would be no problem for such a sophisticated and technologically advanced species to convey him and his friends back to their birth-worlds. To Earth. It was now apparent that there was one small hitch.

They did not know the way.

"Records," Sque was saying. "Implacably efficient, the Vilenjji would have recorded the location of every world they visited, whether they carried out an abduction there or not. The requisite spatial coordinates will be contained within their instrumentalities."

Of course, a relieved Walker realized. Abductees such as himself and his companions constituted the equivalent of stick pins on a map somewhere within the depths of Vilenjji records. It was only a matter of looking them up.

If only.

"Unfortunately," a regretful Tzharoustatam had to tell them, "the Vilenjji are indeed as efficient as you say. They have apparently been meticulous in their wiping of every relevant record relating to their illicit activities. The preliminary search, at least, of their onboard storage facilities has produced nothing but an emptiness as all-embracing as the vacuum outside this ship. Not only are there no coordinates that could point the way to the worlds they have visited, there are no records of even the most basic shipboard activities. Nothing. From the standpoint of available records, the Vilenjji craft gives all the appearance of having been operating in a void." Concerned and compassionate citizen of a wide-ranging civilization that he was, the Sessrimathe tried to offer some hope.

"None of you has any notion of where your world might lie within the galactic plane?"

The group silence that ensued showed that they did not. Not even the erudite K'eremu could be more specific than to suggest that her homeworld lay within the inner half of one galactic arm. The K'eremu name for that arm, of course, meant nothing to the Sessrimathe.

"There are only two main arms." Tzharoustatam was trying to put the best possible light on the increasingly unpromising situation. "It would help considerably if we knew in which one your homeworld resided."

"I am not a spacer," Sque was forced to admit. "Perhaps if I could see an image showing our current location I might be able to recognize whether the arm where we are at present is the same one that holds cherished K'erem."

When Tzharoustatam's three hands came together at the fore point of his body, all nine fingers interlocked in an entwining that was as complex as it was elegant. "I am afraid that our present location is not situated in either of the main galactic arms. Much of civilization, including Seremathenn, lies closer to the galactic center, in the vast mass of stellar systems that wheel around the great gravity well at the center of our star cluster. As the Vilenjji would not dare to commit their outrages in its immediate vicinity, it must be assumed that your homes lie somewhere on the galactic outskirts, relatively speaking. From our present position you would be fortunate indeed to select the correct arm."

"What if we could do that?" Walker found himself wishing he had paid more attention to the fragmentary bit of astronomy to which he had been exposed in school. But he'd had none in college, and in high school had been too busy memorizing defensive assignments for upcoming games to be bothered with trying to remember the locations of stars.

"Why then," Sque informed him dryly, "we could eliminate all those suns that obviously do not correspond to our own, and then among those that do, all scannable systems devoid of planets, thereby leaving us with only a few million star systems to research to find our own."

"Oh." Walker was crestfallen.

Tzharoustatam continued with his encouragement. "It would not be quite so challenging. There exist instrumentalities that can further eliminate those systems containing worlds that are clearly not habitable, and that can seek out and identify communications adrift between the stars. If the correct arm is chosen for exploration and a general idea of location—inner, central, or outer region—is selected, it should be possible to reduce the number of potential locations to a few hundred systems."

"A few hundred. If we are lucky." Braouk was noticeably more depressed than usual. "Even at interstellar velocities, it could take more than several lifetimes to find far distant Tuuqa."

"My people would be even more difficult to locate," Sque commented. "We are not active travelers, or talkers, preferring as we do the company of our own individual selves."

Or maybe nobody else can stand you, a downcast Walker thought unkindly. "Then if we can't go home, what's going to happen to us?"

"Seremathenn!" their host told them cheerfully. "Seremathenn is going to happen to you. It is my home, the home of my kind, and a nexus of civilization for a substantial portion of this part of the galaxy. I must warn you that in arriving there you will all be subject to a certain degree of culture shock—"

"Speak for the others," Sque whistled tersely.

"—to which I am confident you will all adapt. That you have survived in Vilenjji captivity for so long and in such good physical condition is a sign of your ability to accustom yourselves to new and unique circumstances. You will have the benefit of empathetic assistance from private as well as governmental sources. I am sure you will adjust positively."

"But," Walker began plaintively, "while we're grateful in advance for any hospitality that might be extended to us, what we really want is to go home."

"Yes yes." Tzharoustatam was nothing if not understanding. "But there is the small problem of choosing a direction, and securing the means, and affecting the proper timing. Not something, I regret, that falls within my sphere of responsibility. In order to pursue the matter further you must in any event control your impatience and your desires until we reach Seremathenn. At that time you will, I am certain, be put in contact with those authorities who are best positioned to look after your wishes."

These consoling words were all efficiently translated by the Vilenjji implant. No doubt accurately, with careful regard being paid to colloquialisms, slang, and inflection. Walker had only one problem with it. The problem was that he felt he had heard it before, in the course of doing business back home, and on more than one occasion.

Though courteous and even politely affectionate, it felt all too much as if their host was delivering unto them that ominous business benediction widely known back in inconceivably distant Chicago as the brush-off.

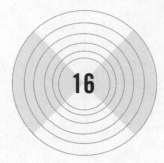

16

Seremathenn was a beautiful world, not unlike Earth, the vision of which in the viewer was dominated by streaks of cloud as white as the Sessrimathe starship and a single large, heartbreakingly symbolic ocean. Walker did not have much time to contemplate the rapidly swelling image because he and his companions were instructed to prepare themselves for landing in a manner as respectful as it was distinctive.

These Sessrimathe, they admire us, he found himself thinking as he struggled to comply with the instructions for arrival. For what we have endured, for what we have survived. For what we tried to do in our attempt to escape from the Vilenjji ship. They just don't admire us enough to get us home.

Maybe he was being unfair, he told himself. Maybe Tzharoustatam had been entirely honest when he had told them there was no practical way of finding their homeworlds. Maybe he, Walker, was refusing to believe it because to accept the facts as stated would be to admit to himself that he would never see anything familiar ever again—not his friends, not his condo, not Mr. and Mrs. Sonderberg's corner deli, not his world. All the things he had followed so closely for so many years—shifts in the market, the Bears and the Bulls (in their sporting as well as financial manifestations), movies, music, television, all the cares and cries and consolations of Earth—meant nothing now. He was being obliged not only to put aside his former life, but his former existence as a human being. Abduction had forcibly transformed him. Deprived of everything he had once known, what was he now? What was to become of Marcus Walker, B.A., M.B.A. University of Michigan, starting outside linebacker his junior and senior years, Phi Beta Delta, late a shining light of the firm of Travis, Hartmann, and Davis, Inc.? They were landing.

He would soon find out.

꙰

They thought they had prepared themselves. Walker was sure their previous months spent in captivity aboard the Vilenjji vessel, coupled with their extended escape attempt and subsequent rescue by the Sessrimathe, had primed him for almost anything. George was of similar mind. Both anticipated Seremathenn to be something like Chicago, only on a . . . well, on a galactic scale.

As ever, the only things shared by imagining and experiencing were their suffixes.

The great conurbation of Autheth had not been built; it had been grown. To Walker and George the description of its manner of fabrication sounded more like magic than science; to Braouk it smacked of ancient alchemy; and to Sque—while acknowledging its beauty and marvels, the K'eremu dismissed the technique with an airy wave of several appendages.

"We amuse ourselves with similar construction modi on K'erem, though admittedly to a lesser degree. Having no need to congregate in such preposterous numbers, our analogous efforts are focused more on aesthetic refinement than vulgarities of scale."

Leaning over quite far, spearpoint-sized teeth very close to the human's shoulder, Braouk whispered tartly, "Unable to handle, each other in kind, self-loathing."

"What'd friend monster say?" a curious George asked his human.

Walker lowered his voice so that Sque, clinging firmly to a forward viewport, could not overhear.

"He said the K'eremu don't build like this because they can't stand each other's company."

Panting as he relaxed comfortably in Walker's lap, the dog nodded knowingly.

Though the towering, arching structures that formed the colorful artificial canyons through which they were presently soaring had been designed to serve practical purposes, that in no way mitigated their beauty or the admiration they extorted from the visitors. In addition to the companionable foursome, the silent transportation vehicle carried another dozen of their fellow abductees. Other craft, Walker and his friends had been assured, were taking equally good care of the remaining captives. Reminiscing fondly about the gentle Sesu and the beautiful Aulaanites, he hoped they were coping adequately.

Since the prospect of having to sex every Sessrimathe they met presented him with an awkward challenge, Walker gladly accepted the testimonial of their recently assigned guide Cheloradabh that she was female. Certainly her attire yielded no clues as to her gender. Physically, she seemed little different from the male Tzharoustatam or the neuter Choralavta. Walker decided that he could survive indefinitely without the need to be made personally conversant with the details of the germane distinctions.

"How do you 'grow' buildings like these?" he inquired as they dipped and wove a path through the soaring structures without so much as threatening any of the other vehicles utilizing nearby airspace.

"Applied biophysics," she informed him. Or at least, that's how the implant in his head interpreted her words. He suspected there were technical refinements that could not easily be translated. "It would take more time and expertise than I possess to explain it to you in detail."

"He would not understand anyway." That was Sque, ever helpful. "I would be interested in hearing some of the specifics myself, at some future date and time. For now it is enough to know that biophysics are involved." She remained fixed to her chosen port. Walker experienced a sudden desire to shove her head down into her body until both were as squashed together as her tentacles. It was an urge he had learned to resist, having had many opportunities during the preceding months to practice such restraint.

"Where are we going?" George asked aloud.

As the transport efficiently piloted itself, Cheloradabh was able to assume a comfortable tripodal stance of relaxation and reply to their questions at leisure. "Novelty is difficult to quantify. On a world such as Seremathenn it is rare, and therefore valuable. You are a story that demands telling, and there are many eager to listen."

Walker understood. "The media. We're going to have our pictures taken."

"I am not certain what you mean by that, but your likenesses were made available to every residence, office, and place of activity on the planet well before your ship arrived here," she explained. "Visuals of you all have long since become familiar to the populace. Actual presence is now requested."

The human was not deterred. "I follow you. We're expected to give interviews, to explain what happened to us. I'm tired, but I can understand the interest. We owe the Sessrimathe at least that much for rescuing us from the Vilenjji, even if it is for novelty's sake."

Sque looked back from where she had attached herself to the window. "We would have managed a successful escape without any outside help."

Though a suitable response occurred to each of them separately, her companions studiously ignored her.

When the transport finally slowed, it came to rest atop a tower of water. Not a water tower, such as could be found even in the heart of Chicago, but a tower of water. While Sque, comfortable on the perimeter of an aqueous environment, exited confidently from the transport, her friends were more tentative.

"None of us breathe liquid," Walker told Cheloradabh. "We'll drown."

"Drown? Oh, I understand." Two of three hands indicated the impossible rippling partition that appeared to bar their way. "That is not water. It is fluid . . . ," she spoke a word the Vilenjji implant could not translate. "You are in no danger. We are all of us oxygen breathers together. Please." She gestured again.

Still uncertain, they crossed the waiting accessway. That in itself took some nerve, since the Sessrimathe-sized bridge linking transport and destination was not wide and spanned a drop of several thousand feet. Only Sque with her ten grasping limbs was not intimidated by the chasm between structure and transport. Of the remaining trio, George managed the crossover best, thanks to his low center of gravity. The taller Walker and Braouk both had to wrestle with vertigo.

The humming, waterfall-like wall parted at their approach. Beyond, they found themselves in a high hallway that appeared to be composed of different-colored liquids. While heights troubled two of them, fortunately none were susceptible to motion sickness. Defying appearance, the dark green floor beneath their feet had the texture of ocean but the consistency of hard rubber.

Fluid hall and liquid floor were no more difficult to accept than the bubble within the not-water to which they were escorted. Instructed to enter, they found themselves floating free within a globe of pale blue radiance. Unable to find a secure purchase, Sque resorted to bunching her appendages tightly beneath her. Though they drifted as if weightless, the presence of gravity was signified by the absence of nausea.

The illumination surrounding them brightened. Curvilinear blue walls faded. Faces appeared where walls had been. The majority were Sessrimathe, but not all.

In these surroundings it was Walker's turn to shine. Favoring privacy, Sque declined to respond to any inquiries unless they were specifically directed her way. Braouk exhibited a shyness heretofore only suspected, while George was content to correct or supplement his human's responses. That left Walker, whose profession required him on any given day to deal with hundreds of questions from dozens of different individuals, to reply to the flurry of queries. While not the floor of the Exchange back home, he found that he slipped easily into the role of spokesman for the foursome.

Yes, they were all right—and grateful for the opportunity to express their appreciation to their benevolent saviors the Sessrimathe. This gratitude appeared to go down as intended. Yes, it was true they had no idea where their respective homeworlds lay in relation to Seremathenn, or any other part of galactic civilization. Did they bear their captors any ill will?

"Careful." Peering out from her wrapping of tentacles, Sque took notice of the question long enough to deliver a discreet warning.

*She doesn't want us to appear uncivilized*, he thought. It made sense. The last thing they wanted to do was show evidence of any traits that could be used to support a distorted Vilenjji version of events.

"We are of course saddened and depressed by what has happened to us. While we are grateful for your hospitality, we would all of us naturally rather be on our way home. As to those who forcibly abducted us, we are confident that they will be treated appropriately by whatever entity is responsible for dealing with such matters."

Something nudged his leg. Glancing down, he saw a floating George bumping up against him. "Nice. Remind me to have you along the next time I run into a certain pair of rogue Dobermans on upper Eighty-second Street."

The questions went on for more than an hour, until Cheloradabh mercifully called a halt.

"More opportunities to converse with the newly arrived ill-starred will follow at specified times. Now you must pardon them, for as the biped pointed out, they are wearied from their experience."

Led out of the bubble, they found themselves once more standing on solid dark water. Walker thought he could see small bits of iridescence moving within it, though whether lightning-quick bursts of energy or equally fleet living things he could not have said. Though he was not conscious of any of the busy Sessrimathe moving to and fro around them staring in his direction, he still looked up guiltily. What opinion would humans form of an alien visitor who spent his time gawking in astonishment at ordinary walls and floors?

Exiting the tower by a different portal than the one through which they had entered, they rode a smaller transport over cityscape that alternated with open woodland and glistening bodies of water. Half an hour later they slowed and began to descend into what appeared to be a forest of gigantic trees. For a second time that day, physical appearances proved deceiving. The impossible forest was as much composed of run-of-the-mill wood as the tower had been of ordinary water. Instead, the colossal "trees" were fashioned of another synthetic, mimicking material that had been employed as much for aesthetic as structural effect.

It felt as if they were entering a huge, hollowed-out tree. The interior smelled like thriving, flower-fraught vegetation. There were even hosts of tree-dwelling creatures skittering about. They reminded him of the individual iridescent flashes he had noticed in the floor and walls of the not-water tower. Such, apparently, was the nature of Sessrimathe construction. Elsewhere on Seremathenn there might be edifices fashioned of faux sand, buildings built of warm ice, structures composed of fake flesh. On a world of incredibly advanced technology, would not ordinary housing make as much use of advanced physics and new materials as starships and weaponry? The Vilenjji had built a better cage. The Sessrimathe built a better habitat.

Leading them into a vein in the "wood," Cheloradabh guided them to a knot in one branch. Having noted earlier the aversion of some of her charges to heights, she had thoughtfully chosen a vertical offshoot of the central structure instead of a horizontal one. A wave of her forward limb caused the apparently solid wall in front of her to shimmer into sparkling sawdust. Once beyond, they found themselves standing in a large room whose perfect oval shape was marred only by bumps and protrusions in the walls and floor. Eyeing these suspiciously, Walker suspected they served some purpose other than mere decoration.

About the far side of the chamber there was no wondering, at least. It consisted of a floor-to-ceiling transparency, lightly tinted to mute the bright sunlight pouring in from outside. Walking to the center of the room while her flanking limbs gestured to left and right, Cheloradabh beckoned with her middle hand for them to follow.

"This is your common area. Private dwelling spaces for each of you are located on opposite sides of the common." She pointed out each individual's entryway. "Anything you need, you may speak for within your personal zones, and it will be provided to the best of the abode's ability." A unified wave utilizing all three arms took in their immediate surroundings and, by implication, much that lay beyond them and out of sight.

"Even for a Sessrimathe, the joy and success of moving into a new residence is the result of an ongoing learning process between dweller and dwelling. Mistakes may—no, will—be made at first. But the building will learn. Sessrimathe buildings are good learners. Be patient with yours, and with your individual dwelling zones, and you will be rewarded with comfort and contentment."

" 'Rewarded.' " George trotted over to the expansive transparency to take in the panoramic view it provided of gigantic tree-buildings and lakes. "I don't recall earning any rewards. Your people are the ones who brought in the Vilenjji, not us."

Cheloradabh hesitated before replying, as if slightly embarrassed. "Funds are made available for such things. Work will not be required of you. The relevant details of this matter have been discussed and approved at higher levels." All three arms gestured reassuringly. "It is felt that this is the least that can be proffered to make up for what you endured at the hands of so-called representatives of civilization."

"So we're wards of the state." Moving forward to stand alongside George, gazing out the transparency at the magnificent, enchanting, and yes, civilized view, Walker had mixed feelings about their new condition. He shouldn't, he knew. It was infinitely better than being wards of the Vilenjji. "Charity cases."

"Survivors." Cheloradabh corrected him as she tripodded backward toward the main entrance. "I leave you to explore your new habitations. For the foreseeable future, I am assigned to you four as adviser. If you experience any difficulties or have any problems that you yourselves cannot solve, please do not hesitate to ask your residences to contact me." The inner wall once more gave way to a flurry of faux sawdust (or maybe it was the technological equivalent of pixie dust, Walker mused), and then she was gone.

Sque had been squirming with impatience ever since they arrived. Now she scurried off in the direction of her private chambers. Walker felt sure her parting words were not a literal translation.

"I hope there is a shower," the K'eremu was heard to mutter.

Walker glanced down at the dog. "What say we check it out, George?"

His four-legged companion shrugged. "Might as well. It's not like I got a heavy date waiting for me." Together, they went their separate ways.

What would a Sessrimathe residence intended for a human be like? Walker wondered as he pushed timidly through the portal that separated his private area from the common room. A cheap hotel room? A French chateau? Where would the Sessrimathe, intelligent and insightful as they were, obtain adequate referents? He found out all too soon.

The tent was as he remembered it. So was the cold, refreshing wedge of Cawley Lake. And the surrounding forest, and distant snow-capped mountains, and the ground, right down to the gravel beach and the sandy soil underfoot. Slightly stunned, he stood just inside the portal and stared. It made perfect sense, of course. Where else would the Sessrimathe gain insight into the living conditions and requirements of a species they had never previously encountered? Only from documentation and examples acquired from the Vilenjji ship, and then only from what the Vilenjji, in their haste to conceal their activities, had not bothered to destroy.

With the best will and the best of intentions, their hosts had perfectly duplicated his cell.

He wanted to scream. Had there been no one to overhear, he would have done exactly that. But the kindly (patronizing?) Cheloradabh had instructed them to address their rooms if there was anything they needed, and he was uncertain how some frustrated screeching would be interpreted by whatever concealed sensors were doubtless even now monitoring his every sound and move.

Calm down, he told himself. This is not a Vilenjji enclosure. Sure, it looks just like it, but so does a small sliver of the real northern Sierra Nevada. It was put here to make you happy, not to incarcerate you. You are not on exhibit.

At least, he assumed he was not. If that was the Sessrimathe intent and they had been lying to him and his friends all along, there would have been no need for the earlier visit to the interview bubble. The more he considered the prospect, the more he thought it should be easy enough to find out the truth.

"Room," he said aloud. After months spent on the Vilenjji ship he felt not in the least foolish about addressing some unseen alien instrumentality. Clearly, this was a civilization rife with such advanced amenities. "Is anyone besides you watching or listening to me now, or otherwise monitoring my activities? Or is my privacy secure and complete?"

"Your privacy is secure." Whether the room was speaking common English or something utterly bizarre that was only rendered comprehensible by the Vilenjji implant he neither knew nor cared. It was enough that it could understand him, and he it.

Might as well accept the reply as truth, he told himself. He had no means of proving otherwise. Besides, if you couldn't trust your own residence, what could you trust? Scrutinizing his surroundings and relying for instruction and explication on the room's voice, he began to experiment with them.

Water he could draw from the fragment of lake. Food would probably prove more problematic. As it turned out, he needn't have worried about that, though he was less than enchanted with the results. In response to his request, a circular hole opened in—he should have expected it—the ground. On a small square platter were three all-too-familiar food bricks and two food cubes. Shaking his head slowly, he walked over, sat down, and took a bite out of one of the cubes. It tasted exactly like its Vilenjji counterpart. Something else the Sessrimathe had gleaned from the surviving records of his former captors. He sighed.

After eating and drinking his fill, he experimented by asking for something sweeter. An hour later, two very small food cubes presented themselves on the platter. One was almost salty, but the other had pleasing overtones of the fynbos honey a well-traveled friend had once sent him from Cape Town. Encouraged, he tried again, this time requesting a different flavor. Thirty minutes later one half-sized food brick offered itself up that tasted of roasted almonds. This time he almost smiled. Steak and lobster might be out of the question, but he felt that with trial and error, the building's synthesizer might eventually be persuaded to manage something that tasted like chicken. Or rather, chicken-flavored food brick. After months surviving on the unvarying diet the Vilenjji had provided for him, he was more than willing to settle for the latter.

Nor, true to Cheloradabh's word, were the building's abilities limited to food modification. He got rid of the tent. In response to the preprogrammed chill of a Sierra night, the ambient temperature was easily stabilized at a comfortable seventy-two degrees. Dividing the fragment of lake, he had one half heated for cozy bathing while leaving the other cool for drinking.

A request for a large bed, however, resulted in the delivery three days later of a king-sized version of his venerable sleeping bag. It was apparent that solid objects required more detailed description on his part, more work (and possibly outsourcing) than simple adjustments to food and water. So it was nearly two weeks before the satisfactory approximation of an air bed arrived. When it finally did, however, he settled down on the first gentle, cushioning surface he had enjoyed in months and slept for ten hours straight. Awakening, he felt more rested than he had since leaving Chicago for the Sierras, all too many months ago.

But he did not necessarily feel more relaxed.

✳

Some days the four of them were left alone, to explore and play with and learn from their new surroundings. Other days (and only after polite requests, never demands), they were taken to visit the discussion bubble, or presented to the curious and often important in person, or escorted on sightseeing tours of Seremathenn that were eye-opening and mind-boggling.

It was a beautiful world, not just one that happened to be home to an immensely advanced society. Adjusted, preserved, modified, sanctified by its enlightened inhabitants, Seremathenn was as cultured an example as one could find of civilization. In the course of their travels over the following weeks and months, Walker and his friends (sometimes including even the recalcitrant Sque) were introduced to marvels of sophisticated technology, innovative art, and curious visitors from other worlds both nearby and distant. Galactic civilization, they learned, was not a monolithic alliance of developed worlds and sentient species, but rather an idea, a notion of mutual civility and respect that precluded the need for rigid governmental ties.

It was, perhaps of necessity, not perfect, as testified to by the activities of individual rascal elements. The professional association of Vilenjji responsible for the abduction of Walker and his friends was one example of the latter. There were, a discomfited (if a dwelling could be discomfited) room informed Walker, others. And beyond those systems that were accounted active members of civilization lay still additional cultures—some powerful, others less so, still others more primitive

than even his Earth. The galaxy was a big place, allowing room for societies at all stages of development.

And yet despite the genuine kindness that was being shown to
them by their hosts, despite his increasing skill at getting his room to
adjust its appearance, contents, and provisions to his needs, as the
weeks slid by he found himself growing more and more uneasy. He
thought he detected some of the same frustration in Sque, and certainly
in Braouk. Only George seemed wholly content, having finally succeeded in inducing his own personal zone to synthesize edible oblong
objects with the flavor and taste, if not the exact appearance and consistency, of prime rib bones.

At least the endless requests to speak with him and his friends, to
meet them in person, to listen to them discourse on their individual
and conjoined ordeals, were growing more and more infrequent. It was
after the conclusion of one such discussion, involving a fascinating yet
disquieting gathering of estimable Sessrimathe and representatives
from at least a dozen other sentient species, that what had really been
bothering Walker hit him hard. Hit him with similar force, though different overtones, as the same words that had been spoken to him by the
K'eremu Sequi'aranaqua'na'senemu in the course of their initial encounter aboard the Vilenjji ship.

"That is how you should now view yourself: as a novelty," she had
told him what seemed like eons ago.

And that was what he was, and his friends, too, he realized with
crushing certainty: novelties. The Vilenjji had intended to market them
as such. The Sessrimathe had saved them from that prospect, only for
them to become . . . exactly the same thing. True, they were guests, not
prisoners. Honored visitors, not chattel. But the end was the same. As
freed captives from exotic, unvisited worlds, they were novelties.

Just as clearly, their novelty value was starting to wear off.

That did not mean they were going to be ignored, or worse still,
thrown out onto what passed for the streets of Autheth. Having dealt
with them for several months now, having met a great many of them
on an individual basis, Walker felt he knew their kindly and civilized
hosts that well at least. They might be three-sided, but they were not
two-faced.

Though they enjoyed their newfound privacy, the four of them had
been through too much together not to occasionally take pleasure in
one another's company. Each had their own interests that their residences could not satisfy. Braouk would ask to be taken to the Jaimoudu

Mountains, there to alternately compose or recite to the winds, as the mood took him. Sque had taken to spending as much time as she could by the shores of Seremathenn's single vast ocean, communing in private with the waves until her escorts despaired of persuading her to return to her assigned dwelling. George spent most of his time exploring the immense pseudo-tree that was their building, relying on his innate ability to make friends with any intelligence, no matter what its shape or species, to find his way around.

All these individual outings provided fodder for conversation when they, by common agreement, gathered together in the common room at least once a week to swap tales of explorations and experiences. It was in the course of one such get-together that Walker finally gave voice to what had begun to trouble him more and more.

"I think our hosts are getting tired of us."

There was immediate objection. "I see no evidence of that," Braouk rumbled in response. "Certainly to me, no one has said, anything untoward."

"I linger by the sea for as long as I wish, lamenting the absence of familiar smells but luxuriating in the sensation of it." Sque lay coiled atop her appendages in front of the opening to the small, comfortable cave she had caused to be installed in the common room. As counterpoint, George had caused to be created something like a shag rug that was anything but, mostly because it was semi-alive and followed him around, while Walker had finally managed to get the dwelling to fabricate a weird piece of furniture that at least nominally resembled a soft chair.

"As the day grows late, my escorts often become anxious," the K'eremu continued, "but they are too respectful of a manifestly superior intelligence to insist on my leaving. I only do so to humor them—and to get back here to get something to eat."

"I guess I'm easy." Lying prone on his rugenstein thing, its cushioning tendrils wriggling unnaturally beneath him as they massaged his belly, George looked up at Walker out of eyes that were presently more curious than soulful. "Something the matter, Marc? Food not to your liking anymore? Temperature not adjusting to your taste? Daily workload of doing nothing and having to find something to occupy your time making mischief with your stressed-out human psyche? Feeling guilty for having been dropped into a swell setup like this?"

Walker shifted uneasily in his chair. Between him and the dog but a good distance from the moisture-loving Sque, a fire burned brightly a few inches above the floor. Its purpose was solely decorative, since a word from any of the residents could instantly adjust the ambient temperature within the room. He had sometimes wondered, but had never gotten around to inquiring, as to the hovering conflagration's source of fuel and combustion. In the end, it was enough that the building provided it on request. It was bright, and cheery, and hinted of home, yet remained somehow . . . cold. An odd condition, to say the least, to ascribe to a fire.

"It's comfortable, George. I wouldn't go so far as to say it was 'swell.' "

"You don't have to go that far," the dog responded. "Whenever the need arises, I'll say it for you. 'This setup is swell.' " Woolly eyebrows narrowed, and his tone grew suddenly serious. "You're unhappy."

"Not unhappy, George. Not unhappy. Homesick."

The dog let out a disgusted snort and sank his snout deeper into the affectionate shag. The rug purred contentedly as it continued to caress him. "I've seen a determined poodle scare off a pair of burglars, I've laid between rails while twenty minutes of freight train clanked past a foot over my head, I've fished a whole, slightly overdone chateaubriand out of a restaurant Dumpster—but I've never yet met a contented human. What is it with you apes, anyway?" Both eyes rolled ceilingward in irritation

"I can't help it, George. I miss home. I miss . . . things." Walker gestured behind his chair, back in the direction of his room. "Don't get me wrong: The Sessrimathe have been great to us. And their technology is—Well, if I could transfer the specifics, any tenth of a percent of what we've been exposed to would make me the wealthiest man on Earth. But it's not everything. I don't think any technology is. I miss the corned beef and Swiss at the corner deli near my condo. I miss Chicago pizza. I miss the tang of the wind off the river, and the sight of crowds shopping downtown at Christmas. I miss dumpy, ordinary, mind-numbing television. God help me, I miss television *commercials*. I miss knowing if the Bears are going to make the playoffs, and if there's another Daley matriculating in the political wings, and what the cocoa crop projections are for the Ivory Coast and the PNG and the Caribbean." He sighed heavily.

"I miss dating, and going home with a date, and even getting rejected by a date. I miss the water cooler at work and the begonia on my little twelfth-floor porch. I miss reading about what's happening in the world and the newest hit singer and the latest movie and the next can't-put-it-down book." He looked down at his friend, his voice (if not his eyes) misty with remembrance. "Don't you ever miss anything, George?"

The dog spoke without lifting his muzzle. Swathed in rug, it made him hard to understand. "Dogs are grateful for whatever they happen to possess at the moment, Marc. Humans are always missing too many things."

Walker looked away. Outside, beyond the wall-to-ceiling transparency, the towering wood-walls of this corner of greater Autheth pulsed with the palest of yellow lights, individual windows such as their own a thousand pinpoints of brilliance against the urbane darkness.

"I can't stay here," he mumbled, a bit surprised to finally hear himself say it.

"Oh, for Lassie's sake!" Standing up, George began walking in circles around the hovering flames. Humping clumsily across the floor, his rug made futile attempts to catch up with him. "What is wrong with you? What were you back home? A movie star? A billionaire? The elephant king? A southeast Asian drug warlord? What did you leave behind that you can't find a substitute for here? This is a terrific setup! All play, pretty much, with no work. And here's another one to chew on: Think you'll live longer under Sessrimathe care, or when poked and cut by pill-prescribing quacks back on Earth? Corned beef sandwiches? Sports results? Give me a break, man!

"So the Sessrimathe and their friends might be growing a little bored with us. So we're becoming yesterday's news. Doesn't everything, and everybody, anywhere? What matters is how they take care of us, and as far as I'm concerned, this is the best anyone has ever taken care of me! I don't give a cat's ass how many arms they've got— or eyes, or other appendages. You remember what Cheloradabh said: 'There's a fund for this sort of thing.' Predicament of the moment or not, exotic alien flavor of the week or not, I don't see why we can't play off being the poor, primitive former captives of the barbaric Vilenjji for the rest of our natural days. The Sessrimathe, for one, are too civilized to let it be otherwise." With that he went grumpily silent, allowed his exhausted rug to catch back up to him, and flumped back down onto its welcoming coils.

Except for the crackle of floating flames, it was quiet in the common room. Outside, the myriad lights of Autheth twinkled through the night. Walker checked his watch: one small, ever-present touch of home, and one for which he was every day thankful. In half an hour's time, the immense and diverse alien metropolis would begin to receive

two hours of precisely calibrated rain. A voice made him look up. It was
as deep as it was tentative, as musical as it was imposing.

"Uhmmgghh, it may seem ungrateful of me to say this, but—I now
experience, from day to day, feelings similar."

Rising and whirling, George gaped at the Tuuqalian. "What? Not
you, too!"

With the two massive tentacles on his left side, Braouk gestured
toward the window. His eyestalks were hanging so low they nearly
touched the floor where he was squatting.

"Sad it is, the refrain bears saying, home calls. I find welcome here,
but not inspiration. And," the giant added touchingly, "there is the matter of unrequited longing for family left behind."

"The mark not necessarily of homesickness," Sque piped up, unlimbering a sufficiency of appendages to emphasize her words, "but of
necessity. While I have applied myself to learning what I can during our
extended sojourn here, it must be admitted that there is only so much
our well-meaning hosts can teach a K'eremu. While their physical science is undeniably impressive, they are plainly lacking when it comes
to the higher facets of philosophy, natural science, and many other areas of advanced cogitation. Only among my own kind can I expand my
mind fully, and properly engage and exercise all its resources, even
though the unique genius that is myself is not always recognized as
such even by my own kindred. For those reasons and not for any primitive sense of 'home illness,' I see an increasingly urgent need to return
to K'erem."

"Well, fine, that's just fine. Fine for all of you." Turning back to
Walker, the dog fixed him with a stare that was suddenly challenging
instead of consoling, penetrating rather than affectionate. "Aside from
the fact that what you're all wishing for is impossible, what about me?"

Walker blinked. "I don't get you, George. What about you? You'd be
able to go home, too, of course."

"Really?" His gaze unbroken, the dog cocked his head to one side.
"What an enticing prospect, Marc. Look, my tongue is hanging out and
I'm salivating at the thought of it." From his chair, Walker stared un-
comprehendingly at his friend and companion. In all their long relationship, including the time spent in captivity aboard the Vilenjji ship,
it was the first time he had ever heard George sound bitter. Sarcastic,
yes; caustic, yes; but never bitter. Until now.

"Go home to what?" the dog continued derisively. "To be the star
of a traveling media circus? A biological freak show? 'See George, the

talking dog, the eighth wonder of the world!' Or in self-defense would I be expected to just shut up, and for the rest of my life not say another word, or have another discussion with another intelligent being. How would you like to have to live like that?"

Walker levered himself forward in his chair. Though assembled of bars and energy clamps and carefully repositioned bubbles of gas, it was utterly noiseless. "You could always talk to me, George," he replied softly.

"Yeah. I could always talk to you." The dog began pacing in swift, tight circles, chasing his own self. "Nothing personal, Marc. We've been through a lot together, and I like you. But that's not enough. You're not enough. Once upon a time that kind of one-on-one relationship would have been fine. But not only has my intellect been boosted, so have my expectations." Halting without catching his tail, or his self, he flicked his ears toward the two aliens who were watching from the other side of the room.

"I've had to learn how to communicate and deal with K'eremu and Tuuqalian, with Vilenjji and Sessrimathe, and with all the other captives I met in the enclosures on board the Vilenjji vessel." The woolly head looked back and up at him. "I can't go back to talking to just one human. Much less barking at him."

"Opportunities for interaction, with many other peoples, awaits beyond." Reaching out and forward, the huge yet philosophically inclined Tuuqalian scooped the dog up in his left pair of cablelike tentacles. Bringing both eyestalks close together, Braouk trained on George orbs that taken in tandem were nearly as big as the dog himself.

"I cannot stay here, George. Sequi'aranaqua'na'senemu, she cannot stay here, either. Your friend Marcus Walker cannot stay here. We must all of us try our best to find our way home again, even though it is likely we will fail. You may remain. The civilized Sessrimathe will be glad to take care of you. By remaining, you can look forward to many years of stimulating interaction with their kind as well as with others who come to visit, to trade, and to learn." Gently, he set George back down on the floor. The pointed tip of one appendage powerful enough to rip the doors off a car lightly scratched the dog between his ears.

George gazed up at the hulking shape. Viewed by an unsuspecting visitor from home in the purposely dimmed light of the room, Braouk had the shadowy silhouette of a perfect nightmare. But to the dog, who by now knew the Tuuqalian well, the alien was a friend: a massive mélange of teeth, tentacles, and bulbous eyes with a heart as big as his body. He turned slightly to his right.

"Sque?"

"You're asking my opinion? I always knew despite the disparity in physical dimensions which of you two was the more gifted." Familiar by now with the K'eremu's casually disparaging speech, Walker said nothing. He had come to find her unbounded egotism almost endearing. From beneath overhanging brows, metal-gray eyes squinted back at the dog. "Loneliness will eventually balance out the initial pleasures to be gained by staying here. I have had time to watch and to learn about you, George. While I could, if forced to, survive in such cocooning surroundings, I do not believe the same to be true of one of your kind. You do not possess sufficient depth of self-importance. You need the company of others."

"In other words, unlike you, I'm not adequately antisocial enough."

"Put it however you prefer." She was too vain to be offended.

"Come with us, George. Something will work itself out." Walker did not exactly plead, but the more it occurred to him that he might actually lose the company of the dog, his one remaining real contact with home, the deeper grew the sudden and surprising ache that he had developed within.

"Right, sure," the dog muttered gloomily. "All we have to do is turn left, hang a right, and we'll find ourselves on the I-55 headed toward the Loop. Provided we can figure out how to parse parsecs. The longer I think about even trying, the more I tend to be of the same opinion as the big guy. As a project, it's doomed from the start. An undertaking in both senses of the word."

Braouk drew up eyestalks as well as tentacles. "Not to try, to concede the inevitable, cowardice becomes."

"Oh, now that's fair." The dog lay down on his rug, which shivered with delight in response. "Work my emotions from both sides." He took a deep breath, his sides heaving. With an expression perfected from years of successful begging on the streets of the Windy City, he eyed Walker dubiously. It was several minutes before he finally replied. "All right, I'll come with you. But only because, like Sque keeps telling me, you need looking after."

Walker blinked. A glance in the direction of the K'eremu produced nothing in the way of a response. "Why you little— How long have you two been dissing me behind my back?"

Lying prone on his belly on the rug, George shrugged slightly. "Like I told you, Marc. I need more than you."

Leaning back in his makeshift chair, Walker was left slowly shaking his head. Before him, the ornamental blaze continued to waltz in midair, fired with the flame of an alien technology. "You know, George, sometimes you're a real son of a bitch."

"I should hope so," the dog replied equably.

The Light-Years Beneath My Feet

For Justin Neal Stumbo

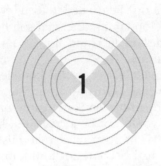

M arcus Walker's khirach-tel soufflé had fallen, and couldn't get up. But it was trying to.

Writhing, peridot-hued filaments of specially sweetened bariile as active as they were tasty twisted and coiled like a nest of worms on speed as they struggled to re-form the compact yet airy loaf Walker had initially marshaled out of ingredients coughed up by the trio of synchronized synthesizers. Adrift in the center of the spherical preparator, suspended within its energized field and shielded from its harmful effects, he strove to maintain a semblance of recipe. All around him, the aromatic components of the special dessert he had engineered emerged from the synths to steadily merge and meld, freeze or bake. If everything came off as planned, the result ought to be a last course spectacular enough to impress the supervising Sessrimathe program that was serving as his mentor and judge.

Unfortunately, everything was not going as planned.

The radiant shower of rainbow-hued geljees that were supposed to execute an iridescent, chromatic englobement of the soufflé were growing impatient. Like bees unable to agree on the location of a hive, they threatened to disperse into individual spheres and shatter themselves against the boundaries of the preparator in a spate of sugary seppuku. Though still coherent, his carefully woven whipped lavender finishing flame, frenetic with edible purple energy, was starting to dance fitfully just beyond his left hand. He could have controlled it better with the cooking wand in his right except that he needed to focus every bit of his attention and newly learned skills on taming the wild soufflé itself. As the anchorpiece of the finished dessert, it could not be ignored, lest it descend swiftly into caloric anarchy.

Matters were not made easier by the knowledge that as he fought to control the culinary chaos swirling around him, his every move was being recorded and judged by the Sessrimathe program. If he failed to control the dessert, it would not be a crisis. But he had made so much progress, had come so far in his studies, that finishing the sweet he had designed from scratch had become for him a matter not just of nourishment, but of personal pride.

He had always given his all and had never quit on the football field. He would not quit in the kitchen—even if it was a kitchen the likes of which had never been imagined on Earth. Within it, automatic perceptors might suspend gravity and spot-control temperature, but it still required a sentient supervisor to direct the process. Doing so was a long way from engaging in the mundane machinations of the Chicago Commodities Exchange. But then, he was a long way from Chicago.

Not to mention Earth.

※

Following his rescue and that of his new friends from their avaricious abductors the Vilenjji, he had found himself untold light-years from home, surrounded and even coddled by the citizens of a highly advanced civilization, exposed to technological wonders any scientist on Earth would have given ten years of life to experience, with ever more promised to come.

No wonder he had speedily grown bored and homesick.

For a while following that rescue, the sophisticated world of their liberators the Sessrimathe had been endlessly fascinating. Months into their new freedom, it merely seemed endless. He came to realize that a good deal of that, and his resultant boredom, was a consequence of his own individual inadequacies. The accuracy of this realization had done nothing to improve his mood.

It seemed as if every one of his companions managed to fare better than the lone human among them. For example, their genial hosts were continually charmed by the contrast between the massive Tuuqalian Braouk's physical power and strength and the delicacy and sensitivity of his poetry and singing. Additionally, the same stentorian recitals of heroic Tuuqalian sagas and rhythmic traditional lamentations that Marc and his friends had begun to find wearisome while they had been imprisoned together aboard the Vilenjji capture vessel proved irresistible to the Sessrimathe. Remarking on this attraction, Sque commented that perhaps their hosts were not so advanced after all.

As for the ever-acerbic K'eremu Sequi'aranaqua'na'senemu, she backed up her interminable boasting with an effortless ability to master an entirely new culture and technology that astonished their hosts. Her companions were less surprised by this achievement. During their time of captivity on board the Vilenjji collecting ship she had demonstrated more than once that her galling claims of intellectual superiority were founded on reality and not empty boasting. There seemed no circumstances, no surroundings, in which she could not, given a modest amount of time in which to make a thorough study of the situation, insinuate herself as if she had been born to them.

As for George, the now casually conversant mutt from the seedy side of the Windy City seemed to have made friends with everyone in their complex. Though the towering, faux-tree living structure was home not only to Sessrimathe but to aliens other than the inhabitants of Seremathenn, it made no difference to George. No matter how outlandish in shape or uncertain of attitude, any independent intelligence was fair game for his probing curiosity. And it was a rare sentient who did not respond favorably to the dog's tail-wagging, soulful-eyed, tongue-lolling queries.

That left Walker, who was neither an intriguingly lumbering aesthete like Braouk, superior adaptive intelligence like Sque, or inherently likeable and manifestly harmless kibbitzer like George. While the four of them argued and debated possible ways and means of attempting to return to their respective homeworlds, what could he possibly do to show them, as well as their polite and courteous hosts the Sessrimathe, that there was something more to him than dead weight?

In Chicago he had been a commodities trader, and a damn good one. Plunged into the superior, sophisticated swirl of a galactic civilization no one had suspected existed, he found to his dismay that here his chosen profession was less than useless. While trade and commerce not only existed but flourished all around him, he did not have a clue how a complete outsider like himself might even begin to participate in its enormously complex and vastly accelerated ebb and flow. Rare was the day when he did not awaken in the quarters that had been assigned to him feeling useless, inadequate, and empty of purpose. If his friends noticed his funk, they were too polite to remark on it. The sensitive Braouk suspected, Marc believed, but the Tuuqalian would never venture to comment on a friend's evident distress without first being approached for consultation.

No, in the absence of readily available help it was up to him to do something about it. Could he do anything else besides engage in the trading of intangible futures? Had his entire existence back home been restricted only to the buying and selling of tanker loads of orange juice and truckloads of coltan? What else could he do? He could play football, and very well. While the games of the Sessrimathe inclined more to the intellectual, in the course of his sojourn on Seremathenn he had observed that other resident and visiting aliens often participated in contests of skill of a physical nature. Not only could he not figure out the objectives of such games, much less the rules, some of the participants were dangerously bigger than he was. While none approached in size and intimidation factor the massive Tuuqalian Braouk, it was clear that if he tried to partake he ran the real risk of permanent injury.

Besides, he wanted to make use of his mind, not brute force, if only to forestall the inevitable comments such participation would have brought forth from the caustic Sque. Her opinion of humankind being already low enough, he saw no need to provide her with additional material for her predictable stream of verbal barbs. Not that she was incapable of inventing plenty by herself.

So—what else could he try? His inadequacy troubled and nagged him for weeks, until it came to him—logically enough—during an evening meal.

George was sharing space with him. The dog was lying on the animate shag rug-thing his own living quarters had manufactured at his request. Outside the single oval window of Walker's room the soaring spires of the artificial tree urb that had become their home glowed slightly in the soft, buttery light of Seremathenn's setting sun.

As always, the small circular aperture in the center of the floor had brought forth food at precisely the time Walker had specified. While he worked his way through the purplish and brown synthesizations, George gnawed enthusiastically on an approximation of a prime rib

bone. It was neither prime rib nor bone, but the dog was content with
the result. One could always close one's eyes at such times, he had
noted on more than one occasion, and imagine being back on Earth.

"George, we're not making much progress at getting home."

Ears cocked toward the human who was his friend, the dog looked
up from his hunk of pseudo-steer. His voice and intelligence the work
off Vilenjji surgeons who were as adept as they were venal, George was
able to make himself perfectly understood.

"How many times do I have to remind you what a great setup
we've got here? Didn't I agree to go home, too—if the rest of you could
figure out how to do it?" He returned to his bone. "It'll happen, or it
won't. If you let it, the worrying will kill you before the chance to try
and get home arrives. Of course, that would alleviate your concerns
too, wouldn't it?"

"I know it's going to take time, George." As he spoke, Walker picked
listlessly at his food. "What I'm getting at is that while all the rest of
you—you, Braouk, and Sque—seem to be adapting to these surroundings, I'm still pretty much at loose ends. It's hard to stay positive when
you don't have anything rewarding to do."

"Yeah," the dog muttered around mouthfuls. "Having everything
done for you, having intelligent machines and helpful hosts respond to
your every need, not having to report for work every day: I can see
where that would get old real quick."

Used to the dog's occasional sarcasm, Walker did not respond to it.
"What I'm saying is that until we can find a way out of here, I need
something to do. Something to occupy my time. Something I can, well,
be proud of. So I'm going to try and build on a favorite hobby I had
back home." He hesitated ever so briefly before concluding, "I'm going
to become a cook."

Jaws parted halfway, the dog looked up at him. Black eyes peered
out from beneath shaggy brows. "A cook. Now that's a useful ambition,
on a world where your room synthesizer burps up a meal whenever
you ask for it."

Having anticipated the dog's objection, Walker was ready with a response. Setting the remnants of his own meal aside and leaning forward, he tried to convey some of the enthusiasm he had felt when the
idea first came to him.

"I know that, George, but I've been doing some research. Certainly
most of the food consumed on Seremathenn and on many other
advanced worlds of this sprawling civilization is provided by highly sophisticated nutritional-synthesization equipment. But not, I've learned,

all of it. A good deal of what is referred to as natural food is still prepared by hand—or whatever type of manipulative limb happens to be involved."

Despite his initial disparagement, the dog was now interested. "You don't say? I never thought about it." One paw gestured in the direction of the room's provider. "When they have synthesization, why would they bother with a primitive activity like cooking?"

"Because," Walker told him with a touch of triumph, "it's considered a form of art."

"Ah!" George looked momentarily wistful. "That makes sense— though not much. I do remember cooking. The thick smells outside certain restaurants. The delicate bouquet of high-class garbage." He glanced again at his friend. "Wait a minute. What makes you think you can do the local kind of cooking any more than you can deal in trading local commodities? Surely the Sessrimathe version of a working kitchen isn't going to be a sink and a stove surrounded by pots and pans?"

"I've been studying the equipment and the techniques needed to operate the relevant mechanisms." He gestured at the nearest wall. "The room has been helping me. It's all new and complicated, sure. But it's not like repairing a ship's interstellar drive, either."

" 'Cooking.' " Forepaws resting on the well-masticated fake bone, George considered briefly, then shrugged. "Go for it, I guess." He returned to his gnawing, a bit more decorously this time. "Just keep one thing in mind." Strong teeth scraped across reconstituted calcium.

"What's that?" Walker pressed him.

"You'd better find somebody else to sample your initial efforts. I'm out."

✳

Even though he'd thought he had some idea of what he was getting into, mastering just the rudiments of Sessrimathe and greater galactic culinary technology, not to mention the essential aesthetic components, had turned out to be far more challenging than Walker had anticipated. There were times, all too many times, when he wanted to quit, to admit defeat and return to a life of depending solely on boring charity. He would not. It was the same determination that had gained him a starting position as outside linebacker on a major university football team, and that had allowed him to keep it through three full seasons. He attacked the multifarious gastronomic trials with the same forcefulness with which he had thrown himself into the path of opposing tailbacks.

The more he learned, the more aware he became of his ignorance.

Only one thing besides raw willpower kept him going. He liked to cook. Always had. When potential lady friends wavered in their desire to go out with him, he could inevitably clinch a date by declaring that he would make dinner, from scratch, all by himself. Presented with such an unexpected avowal from a member of the opposite sex, their curiosity was invariably piqued. They inevitably went out with him if only to see how badly he would fail, and were predictably surprised when the meals he prepared turned out to be not only edible, but excellent.

Surprisingly, it was not the often highly sophisticated utensils and instrumentation that gave him the most trouble and engendered the greatest degree of frustration, but the ingredients themselves. Spices that had minds of their own, sometimes literally. Synthesized tastes whose delicate flavors had to be modified directly at the molecular level. Vegetative bases that refused, on principle, to combine as required with his chosen modifiers or extenders.

Adrift in the center of the preparator, he was more captain than chef, issuing orders to utensils and synths alike, demanding to be obeyed. Food was his symphony, a galaxy of ingredients the notes, and the cooking wand his conductor's baton. Instead of sound there was smell. When things went well, wonderful aromas swirled about him. When they went bad, his work reeked, which unsavory failures the monitoring/instruction program duly and unemotionally noted.

Today was the first time in his life Walker had ever felt personal hatred toward a soufflé.

It was not a true soufflé, of course. It was a khirach-tel, from a recipe derived from a concoction made famous on a legendary world far from Seremathenn. With the aid of the instructor program he had customized its chemical structure, working to tame some of the wilder alkaloids so that the outcome would be something Sessrimathe and human digestive systems could handle. That was difficult enough. Rendering the result tasty was far simpler than making it edible.

Focus, he told himself. Keep it together. The admonition applied to himself as much as to the swirling, balletic elements of the cuisine.

Combining dexterous use of wand and synths, he gradually beat the khirach into submission. The monitoring program proffered grudging admiration. With the khirach-tel itself under control and its more anarchic components restrained, he turned his attention to the geljees. Snapping them into place, he swiftly applied the whipped flame. The end result was spectacular, with the finished khirach-tel floating in the center of its chromatic cloud of orbiting geljees while the whipped lavender flame darted in and out of both, illuminating the khirach from within and sending shivers of light from the hundreds of individual geljees. And it was all, all of it, edible.

He hoped.

There was one way to find out. His friends' quarters, together with his own and the common room they shared, lay elsewhere within the enormous structure.

"Finished," he wearily informed both the preparation chamber and the monitoring program.

The preparator apparatus shut down. As the supportive field surrounding him dissipated, he was lowered gently to the floor. Following his directions, a proper serving tray appeared and took up a supportive position beneath the khirach. Still alive with geljees and flame, it hovered just above the tray's repelling, constraining white surface. When he took possession of his creation, the tray's support field obediently deactivated, leaving him holding it in both hands.

For a long moment he stood admiring his handiwork. Months of long training, of endless study, of frustration and failure and hard work had gone into this moment. During that time he had brought forth numerous other culinary creations, but nothing as elaborate as this. Concerning the aesthetics, there was no issue. The finished khirach-tel was truly beautiful. Part sculpture, part meal, it was indeed a work of art. He could see how it looked. Now all that remained was to find out how it tasted.

He reached out with a hand, hesitated, and pulled it back. Somewhat to his surprise, he couldn't do it. Not the first taste, anyway. He would leave it to his companions to pass judgment. George first, he decided. Despite what the dog had said months ago, George would eat most anything. If the dog rejected it . . .

Preferring not to ponder that awful possibility, he headed for the nearest internal transport. His hopes were boosted by the admiring comments of several Sessrimathe and one Ouralia who glimpsed the khirach-tel in passing.

The floating bonfire that hovered in the center of the common room during the night was replaced during the day, by mutual agreement, with a mist fountain in the shape of some local flowers. The spray filled the air of the room with a cheerful mix of sound and moisture before folding back in upon itself. In response to Walker's question one day, the room had tried to explain to him the mechanism whereby water could be brought forth out of empty air, its shape and direction controlled, kept from falling to the ground, and recycled with no loss to evaporation. He quickly gave up on any thought of understanding what was being explained to him. He did not have the physics for it.

But he did have the physics, and the chemistry, for cooking. So as the transport made its way through the interior of the residential complex, he insisted to his friends that they join him in the common room.

Once there, Braouk eyed the edible fantasy admiringly. "Prepared with skill, the offering awaits eating, brightly dancing." Bulbous eyes extended on the ends of stalks protruding from the upper flanks of his blocky torso, greenish blonde quills quivering, the Tuuqalian reached out toward the tray with the tip of one massive manipulating tentacle.

Walker had to pull it away. "Sorry, Braouk. I have the details of everyone's individual metabolism on file, and while you and I can share many foods, this khirach isn't one of them. I'm afraid you'll have to give it a pass."

Both eyestalks curved forward, bringing the oculars at their tips closer to the human and his tempting creation. "I am not afraid of a small upset to my stomachs. What could happen, if daintily I taste, one lick?"

"You could go blind," Walker told him somberly. "I've subdued most of the alkaloids in the dish, but your system couldn't break down them all. Your body is particularly sensitive to at least two. It's too much of a risk."

The tentacle withdrew. Vertically aligned jaws parted and closed regretfully, serrated teeth interlocking with one another. "Next time please, you will make, something for me?"

Walker smiled. It was a sign of the progress he had made since starting on his training that someone as sensitive as Braouk might actually look forward to the results of the amateur chef's efforts. Walker turned to George.

"You, on the other hand . . ."

"Oh no, not me." The dog backed away slowly. "Remember the last offering you insisted I try? Ended up giving me a touch of the mange."

Walker remembered clearly. "That was a mistake. I should have left out the craadlin seeds. They were oiled on mostly for visual appeal, anyway."

"Yeah, well, mange doesn't have much visual appeal, either." Muttering, the dog gestured with his snout. "If it's so tasty, let her try it first."

Standing half in, half out of the aqueous floral display, a comfortably moistened Sque squinted through silvery eyes as Walker came

toward her. Kneeling, he held out the tray. It was very light, as was the
dish itself.

"I hope you like it, Sque," he offered encouragingly. "It's suitable
for your digestive system, I promise. I know that if you like it, it will
have passed the acid test." As tentacles coiled reflexively and she
flinched back, he added hastily, "I didn't mean that literally. There's no
acid in it."

Droplets of water glistened on bits of the K'eremu's outrageous
personal ornamentation: the strands of iridescent metal, elegant beads,
and other flashy accoutrements that decorated her person. Drawing all
ten limbs beneath her brought her up to her maximum height of four
feet. Horizontal slits of black pupils regarded him from within deep-set
eyes the color of polished steel. Her tone was typically condescending.

"Why should I subject my educated internal constitution to the
misguided flailings of a gastronomic ignoramus such as yourself?"

By now, Walker was so used to the K'eremu's casually insulting
manner of speech that he hardly noticed it. "Because I've been working
at this for many months now. Because I've gotten damn good at it. Because like it or not, you're my friend." When she did not stir he sighed
and added, "And because only your sophisticated palate, or the physiological equivalent thereof, is mature enough to render a fitting opinion
on the result."

She relented. "I must admit that from sharing my company you
have become marginally more adept at recognizing blatant truths." Eyes
inclined toward the tray as one tendril rose from beneath her. Brushing
the tip through the delicate khirach, she swept up a dash of pseudo-
soufflé, a thimbleful of geljees, just a spark of lavender flame, and
brought the blend back to her small mouth. A regretful Braouk and
hopeful George joined the anxious Walker in awaiting the K'eremu's
verdict.

After an interminable pause she blinked both eyes, inflated slightly,
and emitted a pair of bubbles to punctuate her response. "While your
effort founders on the edge of the barely edible and would see you
thrown out of any marginally legal eating establishment on K'erem, it
cannot be denied that the result is tolerable to my system." Knowing
Sque's penchant for giving voice to understatement on a cosmic scale,
Walker was delighted. When she added, "I believe that, in the interests
of fairness to the diligent efforts of a representative of an inferior
species, I should extend myself to the degree of partaking of a second
sampling," and took another bite, his heart leaped.

With the object of his friend's exertions more than validated by the

K'eremu, George promptly dug into the khirach-tel with all the enthusiasm of a cat in a tuna cannery. By the time dog and K'eremu had finished with it, there was barely a flicker of lavender fire and a few desultory geljees left to garnish the scattered remnants of the soufflé itself.

Lying on his right side, belly pooched out from dogged overstuffing, George looked up lazily at where his friend sat supported by a nexus of black and gold wire that passed for a chair.

"I've got to admit, Marc, that you've come a long way since you tried coagulating that jibartle."

Braouk gestured with two of his four upper tentacles. "Remember it well, something hard to forget, that meal."

"It chased us around the room." George belched softly. "It tried to eat Sque." From the vicinity of the fountain, a number of the K'eremu's tendrils gestured by way of punctuation. "Braouk had to kill it."

Walker looked up from his chair. "That was my fault. At that stage I wasn't adequately prepared to tackle such an advanced project. I'd been doing really well, and I got cocky." He shook his head at the memory of it. "Who knew there were dishes that had to be counseled psychologically before they could be served?"

The dog showed his teeth. "That khirach-tel makes up for it. Delicious! What are you going to do now?"

Walker blinked at him. "I don't follow you, George. 'Do'?"

With an effort, the dog heaved himself back onto his feet. Tail wagging, he approached his friend and placed his chin on the man's left knee. The dog's gaze was profound.

"With your new skill. You've put enough effort into it. You should do something with it."

"Actually," Walker admitted, "I hadn't thought about it in that way. Learning local methods of artistic, natural food preparation was just a means to pass the time—and to prove that I could do something more than just exist on Sessrimathe charity."

"Then give back." Sque ambled out from beneath the water blossoms. "Do some demonstrations for our hosts. They will be as amazed as I am. Though we survive nicely thanks to a reservoir of goodwill among our hosts, even a well-fashioned reservoir can leak. Show them that you are more than the underlimbed, ignorant primitive you appear to be."

"Maybe I'll do that," he told her dryly. "I suppose it wouldn't hurt to prepare some demonstration dishes for anyone who might be interested. It would be an easy, and enjoyable, way to show our thanks to our hosts for what they've done for us."

As he slid his head back off Walker's knee, George nodded agree-ably. "Just try not to make anyone sick, okay? And no more dinner that tries to eat the diner."

"I'll be careful," Walker assured him. "I know what I'm doing now." He was not simply boasting. The impossible-to-please Sque's grudging validation of the khirach-tel had been the final approval he had been seeking. He fully expected his subsequent culinary efforts to be even more spectacular. Both George and the K'eremu had the right idea: Whenever possible, he should use his newly won skills to ingrati-ate themselves even further to their hosts. He felt confident he could do that.

What he did not expect was that his exhibition preparations of aes-thetic galactic cuisine would lead to a possible way home.

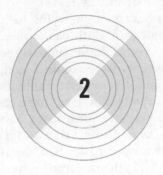

**2**

Walker spun slowly in the center of the demonstration sphere, the ingredients for the sifdd alternately hovering and zipping around him. Beyond the boundaries of the sphere's restraining field he could see the invited guests. The majority were tripodal, three-eyed, triple-armed, beige-tinted Sessrimathe, elegantly and colorfully clad, but here and there other, even more outrageous shapes could be discerned. While his efforts at culinary artistry had not made him famous, they had at least gained him a certain notoriety. If nothing else, he was certainly the best human chef on Seremathenn. He was also the only human on Seremathenn.

This unsought exclusivity did not diminish the satisfaction he felt at what he had accomplished over the course of the preceding months. His unsophisticated species notwithstanding, he knew what he could

do. In the space of a couple of years he had grown more than competent: he had become good.

At his command he was enveloped by a dust storm of different
spices and seasonings. A few onlookers voiced astonishment in the gentle, muted tones of the Sessrimathe while a single loud, sharp whistle
was emitted by an unseen representative of the curious Kyalrand who
were paying their first visit to Seremathenn. His vision momentarily
obscured by the aromatic whirlwind he had called forth, Walker was
not able to identify the individual whistler.

No matter. He was busy enough, trying to control the active components of the incipient sifdd. With dexterous strokes of his cooking
wand and concomitant verbal commands to the ever-alert processing
instrumentation, ingredients were combed, combined, conflated, and
cooked. A ring of ground flowers not unlike flour coalesced around
him. Eddies of puff pastry began to take shape, rising and expanding in
carefully controlled suspension. Spice flares burst in and through the
emerging ring like sharks attacking a strung-out school of bait fish.

When the perfectly crisped pastry had absorbed the last of the fla-
vorings, Walker brought forth miniature waterspouts of liqueur and
fruit juice. Under his guidance, these began to twist and coil about one
another, serpentine shapes already subtle of flavor that he further im-
bued with essence of t'mag and surrun. When all was combined, he
shattered the ring of pastry into a hundred individual shapes, each
slightly different from the next, so that they orbited his waist like so
many miniature moons while a constrained ring of pale pink liquid
swirled lazily about his vertical axis.

He paused there for effect, letting the impressed audience savor the
last moments before final processing. Then, with a flourish of commands and wand, he made the final adjustments to temperature and
individual constraining fields.

The arc of pink fluid splintered, prompting murmurs of appreciation from several in the audience. Attracted to the fields being generated by the individual pastries, independent drifting globules of the
customized liqueur that Walker had lovingly hand-tailored to his own
specifications proceeded to englobe each and every puff. When the last
portion of pastry had been encased, an appropriate collection server
rose from the assemblage of instrumentation behind him. Following a
rising spiral course, the device proceeded to swallow each of his flaky
creations one by one. Once gathering had been completed, the server
returned to its charging base, the demonstration sphere powered down,

and Walker settled gently to the floor. The alien equivalent of applause that ensued was notable for its enthusiasm.

In the course of the reception that followed, he readily elaborated in some detail on the intricacies of his newly honed talent to visiting Sessrimathe who had traveled from many parts of Seremathenn. In between knowledgeable questions and casual conversation, the visitors who filled the greeting chamber in the human's home edifice were treated to samples of the very gastronomic concert they had just seen performed.

Having mastered a modest familiarity with the basics of Sessrimathen conversation, Walker participated in these discussions with verve and ease. By now he was as comfortable around the three-legged Sessrimathe as he had been with fellow boaters out for a Sunday afternoon cruise on Lake Michigan. As was often the case at such moments, he fought hard not to think of home. They were, perhaps permanently he had reluctantly come to realize, a part of his past. Of a different time on a different world—one out of sight, mind, and reach of his present location and lifestyle.

"Not bad." The mild praise arose from somewhere near his ankles. Glancing down, he saw George noshing unashamedly on a sifdd. The dog was lying on his belly, rear legs splayed out behind him, the still-warm pastry balanced between his forelegs. "I can guess how you make the booze ball hold its form instead of turning into an instant puddle, but how do you keep it from soaking into the dough?"

"Same method," Walker told him. "But different coherent charges. One compresses and maintains the liqueur's spherical shape; another repels the fluid away from the pastry. So when you bite into one, you get both a bit of baked dough and a swallow of cooling liqueur. Opposing temperatures, consistencies, tactility, and flavors all in one." He allowed himself a moment of pardonable pride. "Food as physics."

"Not to mention the way your lips and teeth tingle from the lingering charge." Unkempt floppy ears lying against the sides of his head, the dog winked up at his friend. "Maybe sometime you can electrify a bone or two for me."

"Too easy," Walker replied. "I'll show you how to do it yourself." A slight frown creased his features as his companion rose abruptly to all fours. "Something wrong with the food?" He eyed the half-eaten sifdd uncertainly.

"Nope." The dog nodded. "I think you've got company." With that, he gently picked up the remainder of the pastry in his teeth and trotted off into the crowd, exchanging occasional greetings with those

Sessrimathe he recognized. A couple, Walker noted not entirely without envy, reached down with three-fingered hands to pet the dog as he ambled past.

Expecting Sessrimathe, he was mildly startled when upon turning around he found himself confronted not by one of the ubiquitous natives of Seremathenn but by an off-worlder. One of a species he did not recognize. One that was unusually tall, unusually slender, and, it had to be admitted, unusually beautiful.

With a sinuous, graceful gait that bordered on the sensuous, the alien approached on a pair of long legs half hidden, half revealed by a boldly patterned kilt or skirt. The upper portion of the body was equally exposed by a covering of furry straps that crisscrossed the proportionately narrower torso. Protected by smaller straps, both arms ended in dual opposing digits. The head was equally long and slim, equine more than feline but with several features that tended to the piscine. Slender ears a foot long emerged from either side of the hairless skull to extend stiffly upward. Though six foot four or so (notably taller if one included the ears), the creature weighed considerably less than he did. Not one but four tapering tails emerged from a point below the back of the creature's waist. They wove and twisted gracefully in and about one another like a quartet of cobras engaged in animated conversation.

Saucer-sized eyes, big and round as those of a tarsier, with massive golden pupils set against a pale yellow background, focused intently on him. Set below a slightly protruding shelf of sculpted bone that might or might not conceal nostrils, the small mouth was open as if in a perpetual "O" of surprise. He could not discern any teeth. A circular ring of pale muscle that encircled the mouth was stained with several bright colors. The effect was not unlike looking directly down at Saturn's north pole from above.

The creature's skin was smooth as silk. In the ambient light of the room it took on the hue of polished bronze. Walker could not tell if it was leathery, scalelike, or something previously unencountered. All he knew was that the effect was eye-catchingly attractive. And those eyes . . .

Abruptly, the visitor was standing before him. Of all the aliens he and his friends had encountered in their journeying, both on the Vilenjji capture ship and subsequently on Seremathenn, this was so far indisputably the most physically striking. He found himself mesmerized by the multiple switching tails, the shimmering pupils, the achingly elegant upthrust hearing organs, and legs that were as perfectly proportioned as a fractal that had been stretched out straight as a ruler. Apparently, the creature had sought him out and intended to speak to him.

He waited eagerly to see if the visitor's appearance was echoed by its voice, and to learn its gender. Surely it claimed one. No species so stunning could possibly be ignorant of the splendor of sexual reproduction.

"You, human! You pretty damn good cooker, you is."

He winced inwardly. Fingernails dragging across a blackboard. Old-fashioned dentist drills preparing to bite enamel. Metal car parts dragging across a concrete roadbed. A chill ran down his spine that had nothing to do with the moderate temperature in the room.

The sound of the exquisite creature's voice was excruciating to his ears.

Eyelids like translucent lilies momentarily slid down over the spectacular oculars as the creature blinked. As it did so, an iridescent golden frill erected and flexed on the back of the alien's head and neck. "You like cook. You no like talk?"

Unless it was failing for the first time since it had been implanted in him, the Vilenjji translator was providing a faithful rendering of the creature's speech. Swallowing, Walker concentrated on the being's physical beauty while struggling manfully to overlook the sound of its voice. The latter lingered in the air, clinging to his ears like a leech to an open wound. Taking note of the external translator clipped to one slender ear, he felt confident in replying.

"No, I do like—I enjoy conversation. I'm glad you took pleasure from my little demonstration." Desperately, he looked around for someone else he knew, someone he could inform his beautiful but sandpaper-voiced questioner that he absolutely had to speak with—right there and right now. But he recognized no one else in the milling cluster, and George had wandered off somewhere out of sight.

"Enjoy?" One willowy arm reached out to encircle his shoulders, its touch more caress than grasp. "Was overwhelming! Remarkable. Never seen nothing such like it before." The exquisite face bent toward his. "You can prepare many foods suchlike?" The delicate flowerlike fragrance that emanated from the small mouth somewhat mitigated the unrivaled harshness of tone it accompanied.

Holding his ground as well as any cultured Sessrimathe, he forced himself not to turn away. "I've learned how to prepare many specialties, yes, including a few of my own devising based on recipes from my homeworld."

"Earth," the creature snapped. Issuing from that small, ornately painted mouth, the single syllable sounded like a pencil being pushed through a cheese grater. "Home of humans."

"You've been doing some research. On me." His surprise was genuine.

The tips of both ears inclined slightly forward as all four tails came up slightly. "No special research. Perused preparatory materials that accompanied your presentation. Never hear of humans before today. Never hear of Earth before today." She paused thoughtfully. "Self-centered naming. Sessrimathe say you first of your kind they ever encounter."

Walker nodded. While thoroughly entranced by the creature's physical appearance, he could not wait to escape the sound of its voice.

"I am Viyv-pym-parr of the Niyyuu, second daughter of Avur-pym, reigning regent of Kojn-umm Province on the world of Niyu, fourth world of the sun Niy."

Oh, well—royalty, he mused. He forced himself to linger a while longer. Perhaps the alien would hire him to come to her embassy or residence and cook for her and a group of her friends. As his skills had improved, he had been doing more and more of that, fulfilling requests from the curious and those always on the lookout for such novelties. Not for the income, which he and his friends did not need, but to express himself, to have something to do, much as Braouk recited the sagas of his people. Besides, he had not yet tired of looking at those legs, or those eyes, even if they were part and parcel of something that was far from human. Knowing that the Niyyuu was female only added to her attraction—until such times as she opened her mouth.

As to her reasons for seeking him out, his guess turned out to be half-right.

"I needs good cooker in palace. Competent is good. Unique is better even. You human, be both. Only one of you."

He smiled inwardly. Despite all he had accomplished, he was still more highly esteemed for his novelty value than for the skills he had developed. Ah, well. At least he was a sovereign novelty. He responded to her proposal by gesturing in the approved Sessrimathe manner.

"I understand. You'd like me to come and prepare some dishes for you in your residence here on Seremathenn. On which continent is it located, may I ask?" Though not in need of income thanks to the continuing generosity of the charitable Sessrimathe, he would not turn down the chance to supplement it should the opportunity arise. Besides, how demanding could be the desires of a creature so lissome—albeit orally grating.

As it turned out, he had no idea.

"Prepare dishes, yes. Here on Serematheeny no." The arm around his shoulders tightened ever so slightly. The increased pressure was more suggestive than discomfiting. "Need cooker in palace of Kojn-umm. On Niyyuu." When the stunned human failed to respond, Viyv-pym rolled her extraordinary eyes upward and gestured with her other two-fingered hand. "Out there. New audience awaits you."

The offer was as unexpected as it was unprecedented. For the first time since his arrival on Seremathenn, he was being offered a way off world. Offered a chance to travel to a distant elsewhere—and at no cost to himself. Indeed, he would profit economically from the venture. If he accepted, of course. Thinking fast, he knew he could only accept if one condition was met. One condition over which his keen if somewhat crude prospective employer had no control. Looking up, he met wondrous, hopeful eyes and tried not to lose himself in them.

"This may sound strange to you, Viyv-pym-parr . . ."

The eyes came closer. They were not hypnotic—not with that garbage disposal of a voice to accompany them—but they loomed before him like twin cabochons of alien soul. "Okay from now to call me as Viyv-pym. You know me."

Slightly confused by the shift in alien nomenclature but willing to comply, he replied without hesitation. "All right, Viyv-pym." The irregular syllables slid delectably off his tongue. "This may sound strange to you, but before I can give serious consideration to your offer, it's important that I know where Niyu is located in relation to Seremathenn and the rest of the galaxy. I suppose the first thing is to access an appropriate map or schematic and then—"

"Got one right here, human Marc." Both golden-yellow eyes blinked again. Or was it a double wink, he wondered? And if so, what might it signify? Some things, he decided, he was better off not pondering for too long.

From within a hidden pocket concealed beneath the kilt-skirt she withdrew a small stylus with a brushed metallic gray surface. Entwining two long, serpentine fingers around it caused the device to generate several three-dimensional scenes in the space between them. As she cycled rapidly through the available images, he caught fleeting glimpses of life and landscapes that were as foreign to him as life on Seremathenn was to that of Earth. Despite their inherent alienness and the speed of their passing, one or two were more than a little suggestive of something at once familiar and inaccessible.

When the map of the galaxy appeared, she focused on one section and enlarged it. A pinpoint of light brightened. "Seremathenn," she rasped at him. A barely perceptible flexing of one digit caused the light to shift elsewhere. "Niyu."

He caught his breath. While his ignorance of matters astronomic prevented him from even beginning to estimate the actual distances involved, there was no denying that Viyv-pym's homeworld lay an impressive distance from Seremathenn. Furthermore, it was clearly located away from the galactic center and out along one of the galaxy's two main spiral arms. A step of cosmic dimensions toward Earth. Toward home. Although it was apparent that Viyv-pym herself knew nothing of humans or their world, it was conceivable that another of her kind more versed in astronomics or the intelligences that populated the galaxy might have some knowledge of humanity. Or perhaps there were far-ranging sentients with some faint knowledge of Earth who visited distant Niyu but never came as far in as Seremathenn. Possibilities not risked were possibilities that would never exist.

Provided Niyu lay within the right spiral arm—the same spiral arm as Earth. If not, by accepting her offer of employment he would only be taking himself even farther away from the world of his birth, perhaps irrevocably so. His chances of making the right choice in the galactic scheme of things were fifty-fifty. He hesitated—but not for long.

Hell, he'd bought and sold consignments and futures of raw materials worth millions of dollars on odds far worse than that. Of one thing he was 100 percent certain: remaining on Seremathenn certainly brought him no closer to home.

What were his other options? If he declined the Niyyuu's offer he might never come across another half as promising. He might very well live out his life on Seremathenn, the lone representative of his species among millions of creatures whose intrinsic courtesy rendered them no less alien. Or if he bided his time he might encounter other, similar offers—to carry him off in directions even less promising than Niyu. He had not become successful in his chosen profession through indecision. It was time to take a gamble.

"I accept, with one condition."

Eyes like polished pendants of Scythian gold stared back into his own. "You will receive treatment in accordance with you skills. Medium of exchange will be satisfying." The tips of her astonishing ears quivered, and the light of the room shimmered on her bronzed metallic epidermis. "Regency of Kojn-umm treats properly the members of its staff."

"It's not about money, or living conditions. You've researched my background. Do you know how I came to be here, on Seremathenn?"

She turned off and repocketed the compact image generator. As she reached beneath the folds of her kilt-skirt to do so, he found his eyes

wandering. If she noticed the shift in attention or his subsequent confusion and embarrassment, she gave no sign.

"You was Vilenjji captive. A people harboring more than their share
of clods. Is clear violation of all civilized norms to treat any sentients as
goods. Cannot sell sentients." Dark circlet of mystery, the perfect
painted circle of a mouth expanded slightly. "Can only rent them."

Not quite sure that she was making a joke, he held back from
laughing. "During the time I spent on the Vilenjji vessel, I made three
friends. Three very close friends." He took a deep breath. "If I agree to
come and work for you, I would like for them to come along with me."

Again the double blink, twice this time, the lilac eyelids flashing.
"You ask much."

He held his ground, much as he had when confronted by difficult
decisions at his brokerage in Chicago. Trading, doing business, were
skills in which he had full confidence.

"Other captives," she murmured, her voice like steel filings caught
in a car's transmission. "Other uniques. Have these, you's friends, entertaining skills like you?"

Walker proceeded to enumerate the many and varied virtues of his
companions. Fortunately there was no need for embellishment, unless
one counted his bending of the truth when describing Sque's personality as "independent."

For a long moment he was afraid she wouldn't agree to his terms.
He spent the time studying the lithe, limber alien shape while simultaneously wondering what the hell he was doing. The voice, he told himself. Concentrate on that wince-inducing gravel crusher of a voice and
ignore everything else.

*I have been away from Earth for far, far too long,* he reflected to himself uneasily.

"I give you what you want," she finally responded. "Wanting only
one, I deign to accept four." She held up both slender hands. "Count
one unique for each finger." For some reason this observation caused
her to emit a series of short, sharp, and decidedly unfeminine coughs
that he later learned were Niyyuuan indicators of amusement.

The offer was more than he could have hoped for, Walker felt. Now
all he had to do was convince his companions to go along with the
deal. He was certain of only one thing: with friends or without, he was
going with Viyv-pym. He was not going to pass on this, the best chance
that had come along since his arrival on Seremathenn to get him a little nearer home.

But if his friends opted out, it was going to be a long and lonely journey indeed.

"Bargain is striked." One hand reached for him, approaching like an eel swimming underwater. He didn't flinch. He did not *want* to flinch.

The alien hand touched his neck, the two long flexible digits sliding around to the back. Slick, leathery, cool skin brushed the short hair near the top of his spine. He shivered slightly. *Voice*, he reasoned frantically. *Remember that awful voice.* The fingers pressed against him ever so slightly. *Good God*, he thought wildly, *surely she's not going to . . . ?*

The serpentine fingers withdrew. He didn't know whether to feel relieved or disappointed.

"I know you's living details. Transport will be provided you and you's companions. After one ten-day passing, time depart for Niyu. Is doable you?"

He nodded. "Is doable. I will be ready."

The spectacular frill on the back of her head and neck flared, catching the light and splintering it into shards of liquid gold. "Look forward you being on Niyu. I know you will enjoy." A hand and arm gestured at the room packed with the elegant assembled. "In Kojn-umm, not so many always talking. Will be smaller audience for you art, but more appreciative."

With that she turned and strode, or rather flowed, away through the crowd. For some time Walker was able to follow her progress, the slender pointed ears and frilled bronze head rising and falling above the majority of other aliens. Then she was gone. Only then did the full import of his decision hit home. Not only would he be leaving behind the civilized culture of Seremathenn, he would be abandoning, perhaps permanently, the protection and charity that had been afforded him by the compassionate Sessrimathe.

*Real profit only comes from taking real risks*, he reminded himself. He began to make his own way through the crowd, absently acknowledging the compliments that came his way. More important business now pressed heavily on his mind.

He had some serious convincing to do.

※

It was Braouk's turn to choose the ornamentation for the center of their common room. The Tuuqalian had set the room the task of producing a series of small geysers to remind him of a favorite undeveloped region on his homeworld. The result, as installed by the building's AI, was a trio of small, geologically impeccable cones that spouted steadily from the center of the commons. How the building's intelligent response system had managed the plumbing to both deliver and recover the boiling hot water without swathing everything in sight in a sheen of condensation was a mechanical mystery Walker made no effort to try to unravel. He had long since given up marveling at or trying to comprehend the wonders of Sessrimathe science.

The four friends sat around the bubbling, spraying, simulated geysers, but they were not relaxed. Not while faced with the single most momentous decision that had confronted them since their arrival on Seremathenn. To go with Walker or to stay: each of his friends, irrespective of their own individual manner of thinking, could only come to one of two conclusions.

Braouk was uncertain but ready. "Too long here, away from my home, hearts breaking." All four massive upper tentacles curled forward to rest against the sides of his mouth. "I am prepared for whatever may come."

Suspended in his custom-built chair—which he was definitely going to miss, he knew—and with the Tuuqalian on board, Walker turned his attention to the K'eremu. Sequi'aranaqua'na'senemu sat on the floor across from him, her tendrils splayed out around her in familiar floral fashion. She would have reveled in the water from the geysers had it only been many dozens of degrees cooler. As it was, the occasional droplet that escaped the system's recovery field dripped from her maroon skin or glistened on the bits of metal and gemstone and beads that cloaked her person in a small riot of color. Somewhat to his surprise, she concurred with the Tuuqalian.

"There is still much to learn here, both from the Sessrimathe and from those other sentients who visit them. But there is much to learn anywhere that is new, and I tire of the conversation of well-meaning fools, no matter how superficially intelligent they may appear to be." A pair of tendrils rose to wave in Walker's direction. "I too am ready to move on. There is always something to learn, and one may hope, however unreasonably, that such a journey will indeed bring us nearer K'erem, the true center of advanced civilization in this or any other galaxy."

Two aboard. Only one more left to signal his agreement and, truth be told, the one whose acceptance mattered most to Walker. He glanced down at the small figure that was sprawled on the semianimate rug to his immediate left.

"George?"

The dog looked away. "I dunno, Marc. Talk about taking a leap into the unknown . . ."

"You said before that you'd leave here if the right opportunity presented itself. Well, it's presented itself. We don't even have to worry about money. In fact, not only do we get free transportation a parstep closer to home, we're getting paid for going."

Dark brown eyes looked up at him from beneath shaggy brows. "That's just it, Marc. *Are* we getting closer to home? If the other arm of the galaxy is where Earth lies, we'll be heading off down the wrong trail. With a good chance we won't be able to retrace our steps." One paw gestured to take in their surroundings. "We've got everything we could need here, and we don't have to work for it."

Having dealt with it before, Walker had anticipated the dog's reluctance. "We've been over all this, George. Seremathenn is nice, and the Sessrimathe have been very good to us. But this isn't home." He looked up, through the mist being generated by the miniature geysers. "Not for any of us." He indicated the sprawled shape of the K'eremu. "If the odds are acceptable to Sque, they should be for any of us."

"Appropriately astute of you," she observed approvingly. "You continue to exhibit a limited but commendable ability to learn, however slowly."

Wrestling with himself mentally, George held out to the last before yielding. "I said I'd go, yeah. So I'll go." He shook his head slowly. "First I had to give up real alleys. Now I'm giving up artificial ones." Once more the bushy head turned toward the expectant human. "You'd better be guessing right about this, Marc, or I swear I'll end my days chewing on your bones. These Niyyuu who've engaged your services and agreed to take us with you: what are they like?"

"I've only met one of them." Walker leaned back, and his chair leaned with him, careful to maintain his posture and its attitude. "She was very persuasive."

"Obviously," the dog replied impatiently. "I mean, what are they like? You, me, Braouk-boy over there, or"—he shuddered slightly—"the squid?"

Sque took no offense at the implied slight. She was far too aloof to react to insults from so lowly a type as George. Or for that matter, from anyone in the room.

Walker considered. "It's hard to say, having met only one of them. You can't judge an entire species from one individual. But she was . . . nice. Polite. Eager to engage me. Eager enough to agree to take four to get one. I can't say if it's indigenous to her kind, but her voice is a bit on the rough side. No, not rough. Grating. Annoying, even."

"No problem, since you'll be the one talking to her." Rising to his feet, the dog headed off in the direction of his own room. "I'm amenable to this, but that doesn't mean I have to be happy about it."

"Where are you going?" Walker asked concernedly.

The dog didn't look back. "There's a bone I want to commune with. Once we leave Sessrimathe, I don't know if I'll see another one again." He glanced back briefly. "Or if I do, if I'll recognize it as such."

"You worry too much about food!" Walker called after him.

"And you worry too much, period." Ducking his head, George pushed himself through the customized dog door that led to his quarters. "But in this instance, a little worrying just might be justified."

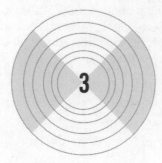

3

Going through the things he had acquired in the years since his arrival on Seremathenn, Walker was surprised at how little there was to pack. Though in possession of a fascinating assortment of devices and objects provided by the Sessrimathe and his room's own synthesizer, on examining them one at a time he found that none of them meant anything to him. They had no connection with a real home, or with the life from which he had been so brutally wrenched. Therefore there seemed little need to take them with him. Doing so would only have meant burdening himself with more to worry about. Surely the Niyyuu, if not as advanced or sophisticated as the Sessrimathe, would provide adequately for his basic needs and for those of his companions.

It developed that his friends felt similarly. Accommodating though it had been to them, Seremathenn was not their home, either. However captivating, the products of its advanced civilization had no connection to their own. Braouk saw no need to take more than the minimal necessities with him, George's kit consisted primarily of his animate rug and a few packaged foodstuffs of which he had grown particularly fond, and Sque disdained nearly everything that was not of K'eremu manufacture anyway.

The winnowing process left Walker with a small carry bag of toiletries, a couple of changes of clothing, and little else. He eyed the modest luggage as he prepared for bed. In a couple of days everything he had worked so hard to assimilate over the past years was going to be put behind him, literally as well as figuratively. There would be a new civilization to adapt to, new marvels to admire, and with luck, access to new intelligences who might at the very least have a clue as to which corner of the cosmos his tiny, out-of-the-way home lay. Directing the room to reduce the internal illumination to minimal, he watched as the walls dimmed until he could just make out shapes and spaces. Among other things, the room was its own night-light. Turning over, he tucked the faux feather pillow beneath his head and closed his eyes.

He was in his rented 4X4 again, sleepy instead of frantic this time, as he stared up at horizontally flattened eyes that flared across the lower portion of a tapering head. A membranous hearing sensor protruded from near the top of the purple conical skull. A single sucker-lined arm flap was reaching for him.

An old dream, he told himself. One that, though he relived it with less and less frequency, never lost its power to unsettle. The alien appendage touched his bare shoulder. It felt very real.

In the dream as well as the reality that had given rise to it, he had been clad in jeans and flannel shirt. His shoulder had not been bare. He blinked. Then his eyes went almost as wide as those of the creature gazing coldly down at him.

Vilenjji. In his room.

As he tried to scream, the heavy arm flap pressed down hard over his mouth. Fortunately, it did not cover his nose. Moving up rapidly behind him, a second Vilenjji easily lifted him up in the bed and despite Walker's frantic, desperate efforts, proceeded to secure his arms behind him. Something was slapped over his mouth. It adhered tightly to the flesh and drew his lips together into a thin, tight line. Eyes goggling, moaning futilely, he was lifted off the bed and found himself being carried ignominiously toward the doorway.

Out in the faintly illuminated common room, his shock was magnified threefold as his abductor set him down on the floor. At least a dozen of his former kidnappers had crowded into the high-ceilinged open space. Arrayed like the specimens they had once been and now threatened to become again, his friends were lined up alongside Braouk's softly gurgling imitation geysers. An outraged Sque had all ten of her limbs secured beneath her while the furious, straining Tuuqalian was cocooned in enough heavy-duty bindings to secure half a dozen elephants. Next to him, a helpless George gazed across at Walker. The dog's dark brown eyes were full of fear.

With the same swaying, side-to-side gait Walker had thought never to see again, a single massive Vilenjji came toward him. With time, the commodities trader had become adept at recognizing individual alien characteristics. A chill as if a glass of ice water had been dumped down his back flowed through him. He recognized the alien.

Bending toward the securely bound human, Pret-Klob peered into much smaller, much rounder eyes that glared back up at him with a mixture of defiance, outrage, and alarm.

"Do you recall my telling you, some time ago, on board the Sessri-mathe vessel that misguidedly chose to interfere in the normal course of commerce, that in the realness of time the natural order of things would be restored?" When a disoriented and increasingly panicky Walker made no move to respond, the Vilenjji commander straightened.

"You wonder at my presence. Know that I regard myself as some-thing of a master of judicial minutiae. It took time, but with work and patience even the overweening Sessrimathe can grow bored with jus-tice. Finally freed from their custody, having 'admitted' to my error and repented most strenuously of my ways, I was eventually able to recon-stitute a small portion of my original association. As primary share-holders, we determined to commence our financial recovery by repos-sessing as much of our original inventory as possible. It is only business." Turning, he hissed orders to his cohorts.

Walker felt himself lifted and bundled into some sort of open, hard-sided container. He was joined by a trembling George and the stolid cephalopodian form of Sque, whereupon the container's lid was moved into place above them. They must have a separate, special con-tainer for Braouk, he thought as the container began to move. A wise decision on the part of the Vilenjji. Given half a chance, the infuriated Tuuqalian would tear every one of the Vilenjji limb from flap. As the flow of adrenaline began to ebb, Walker slumped against the soft inner wall of the container.

They were prisoners again.

Their container admitted sounds as well as voices, though not light.

He could hear the Vilenjji chattering among themselves in their clipped, abrupt manner as the container holding him and his friends was hurried along. Somehow, their captors had succeeded in penetrating the residential complex's admittedly modest security. Breaking the codification that protected the travelers' common room and the individual living quarters beyond had required a higher level of skill. He was not surprised to discover that the Vilenjji were adept at breaking and entering. Antisocial activity in all its many ramifications was a celebrated specialty of theirs.

It felt as if they were moving faster now, probably via one of the complex's numerous internal transports. He struggled ineffectually. At this late hour only the building's few fully nocturnal residents would be about, and they would have no reason beyond individual curiosity to challenge the procession of Vilenjji and their attendant containers. Given the typical level of politeness displayed by the Sessrimathe and the sentients who regularly visited Seremathenn, Walker was not sanguine about anyone choosing to venture such a query. And once outside and beyond the boundaries of the complex . . .

The container came to an abrupt stop. Walker and George looked at one another. Off in a corner of the container, an immensely irritated Sque squatted on her bound tendrils, her silvery horizontal eyes flashing in the near darkness. With her speaking trunk fastened to her head, she was unable to give voice to the outrage she felt.

*Preparing to transfer us to a mobile transport*, Walker thought frantically. From there, a swift journey to the nearest port. Then to a vessel waiting in orbit that would depart as soon as they were aboard for parts beyond the reach of the disapproving Sessrimathe and central galactic civilization. Eventually to be sold.

The way things were going, he and his friends might as well never have been rescued from the Vilenjji ship.

An abrupt leap in the type and frequency of the sounds he could hear outside their prison drew his attention away from increasingly gloomy thoughts. Unexpectedly, the container gave a sharp lurch to the right. It teetered there for a moment before falling over onto its side. Muted yelps came from George as the bound and muffled dog was dumped on top of his friend. Accustomed to never losing her grip, Sque was especially unnerved by the upset.

Loud hisses reached the captives. These were interspersed with coarse, guttural exclamations in a language Walker did not recognize. Muted by distance, the barrier formed by the container, and physical disorientation, his Vilenjji implant was also unable to translate them.

Overturned, the container finally steadied, with George atop Walker and Sque sputtering incoherently behind her bindings somewhere in the vicinity of his feet. With its owner stabilized, Walker's implant was finally able to make some sense of the cacophony outside the container. At the same time, he thought he recognized the second source of shouting.

Though individually distinct, the harsh, rough voices sounded very much like that of the lissome Niyyuu who had recently engaged his services.

Emitting a recalcitrant inorganic screech, the cover of their container was stripped off and pulled back. All three prisoners promptly tumbled out, not onto hard ground or paving, but onto the short blue-green ground cover that wove its way through much of the city. Light appeared, flashed in their faces, and moved considerably away. Tall, slender figures bent to apply small handheld devices to their bindings. Each of the hands that were working on them, Walker noted immediately, had only two opposing digits.

Helped to his feet, he found himself surrounded by a quartet of tall Niyyuu. In the dim light of early morning, with Seremathenn's sun still well below the horizon, he did not try to determine if the concerned Niyyuu who surrounded him exhibited sexual dimorphism. At the moment, there was no sign of the Vilenjji. Only elegant Sessrimathe landscaping, tall trees, and behind them, the flickering lights of their residence tower, itself designed and built to resemble the leafy forest giants it had replaced.

Standing next to his friend, George was licking one paw and using it to clean his mouth and face where the Vilenjji bindings had adhered. "That was close. It was other things, too, but that's the most polite description I can come up with."

"Shameful!" Nearby, Sque had spread herself out and was extending her tendrils one by one, stretching each in turn to relieve the enforced strain that had been placed on the muscles. "Really, the Vilenjji are a species that would benefit from a serious lesson in manners. I would be pleased to deliver such myself, did not circumstances prevent it."

Now provided with a direct line of sight, or rather hearing, Walker's implant effortlessly translated the words of the Niyyuu who appeared before him. "You all right, you and friends?" Walker winced slightly. If anything, this Niyyuu's voice was more of an ear-numbing screech than that of Viyv-pym. He nodded, then realized that the alien probably had no idea of the gesture's significance.

"We're fine. Thanks to you. Another time-part and it would have been too late. We'd have been hustled off world and out of reach."

A second tall, supple figure eased the speaker aside. "Sorry for delay in coming. Takes time analyze data, reach decision, move. Could have alerted Sessrimathe authority, but decided come ourselves."

While George observed the exchange with interest, a grateful Walker bowed slightly to Viyv-pym. In the dim light her huge eyes took on a faint luminosity that was beyond beguiling. Noting his friend's expression, the dog snickered. Or maybe it was just a cough caused by being muffled for so long.

"Why?" Walker stared unabashedly into those eyes, watching as the frill on the back of her head and neck bobbed up and down like a vertical metronome. "Why not call the local authority? Why risk your own lives to help us?"

"Not help you." Though affable as ever, her tone was reminiscent of a steel chisel etching glass. "Protect my asset. Promise already deliver you to Kojn-umm." Smooth metallic skin and gleaming golden eyes leaned closer. "Viyv-pym keeps her promises."

He couldn't determine—certainly not from her abrasive tone—if that last was a pledge or threat. In the end, he decided it didn't matter. Not with half a dozen hulking Vilenjji bodies strewn across the ground and in among the nearby trees. Sessrimathe authority would want to know what had happened here, he knew. Like much else, he decided to leave explanations to the Niyyuu. They were members of this same galactic civilization, while he and his friends were only visitors. Transitory ones, he continued to hope.

"If your new friend is agreeable," Sque declared with a waving of several tendrils, "I believe it would be advisable for us to leave with them now, in the security of their company, lest our barbaric tormentors return in greater strength for another attempt upon our freedom."

"Some did escape." Viyv-pym glanced to her left, her entire upper body swiveling as smoothly as if on gimbals. "As we not know what re serves of personnel or weapons they may have, recommendation of small tentacled one is practical."

"Now?" Walker looked back toward the towering marvel of Sessrimathe engineering that had been his only home for the past two years. "It's very late, and we have personal items we'd like to bring with us."

Sque peered unblinkingly up at him. "You feel in need of sleep, human? This encounter has rendered you sufficiently relaxed to re-retire?"

Walker had to confess that he was not sleepy in the least.

Viyv-pym gestured toward the complex. "Return and gather

belongings. Is enough time, I think. We assist. But leave tonight, now. Scenic Niyu awaits you talents."

Braouk had no head, but the eyes on the ends of their stalks rose to gaze at the night sky. "Standing here talking, time is clearly wasted, departure awaits." Silhouetted against the stars, he was a mountain of stability in the midst of unsettled circumstances.

Was Pret-Klob among the Vilenjji dead? Walker found himself wondering as he and his friends together with a small escort of Niyyuu made their way back to the building. Or had the commander of the avaricious alien association succeeded in escaping into the landscaping? No matter, he tried to assure himself. Where they were going, it was unlikely such as the Vilenjji would follow.

This time, he told himself, he and his friends would finally go down in the ledgers of the Vilenjji as a permanent write-off to inventory.

On the way to the transfer port, their modest baggage tucked neatly in back of the large private transport, Walker tried again to thank their rescuer. In response, Viyv-pym turned in the seat that was too wide and too short for her. It might, he thought, have contributed to the irritation that underlined the words that spilled from the perfectly round mouth, though given the level of apparent prickliness that was the norm for Niyyuu speech it was difficult to tell.

"I tell you already, Marcus, no need for thanking. No one steals from a Niyyuu a contracted employee."

Disdaining the sloping seat, Sque had climbed up onto its back. From there, she could survey the entire interior of the transport, as well as enjoy a better view of the brightening terrain outside.

"While such persistence in pursuit of a mere mercantile end suggests customs aligned with the most primitive, its aptness cannot be denied. In that regard, such diligence can only be commended." Silvergray eyes flashed with intensity. "It does inspire one to wonder at its remarkable timeliness."

Walker looked over to where the K'eremu was perched firmly on the back of the seat. "I don't follow you, Sque."

"An occurrence in habitual accord with the normal state of affairs," she informed him, with no more than the usual condescension. "I am referring to the question of how our self-confessedly unaltruistic liberators managed to conveniently appear in the necessary place at the astonishingly appropriate time to manage our rescue."

George spoke up before Walker could reply, the dog's attention focused on Viyv-pym. "Yeah. How did you know what was going on, and how to find us? The Vilenjji could have bundled us out of our complex via any one of a dozen possible exits."

Silently, Viyv-pym stretched herself across the back of the seat. As the speeding transport rocked silently from side to side, one willowy arm reached toward Walker. This time he didn't flinch at all. Both long, flexible fingers lightly stroked the back of his neck before withdrawing.

"You will remember," she rasped softly. "Our first meeting. After making agreement, I touched you then like so. At that time was conveyed from me an absorptive penetrator."

Walker gaped at her. "You put something inside me?"

"Liquid tracker." Suddenly that round mouth appeared much more alien than inviting. With it she could, he noted, neither smile nor frown. "Harmless, time-delineated insertion. Will be completely gone you system in few more days."

"But why?"

"I should think that intrinsically obvious." If anything, Sque was amused by his discomfiture.

"Keep track you," the Niyyuu told him without embarrassment. "Protect asset. Insure come to no harm. When alerted to unlikely movement of you person at unusual time of day/night, enables I and my staff to respond with caution." She placed the two digits of her left hand over her mouth and spoke between them. He thought he was familiar with Niyyuu laughter. Perhaps this was the species equivalent of a smile. "Good thing do so, too. You not agree?"

"We're very grateful, of course," he assured her as the transport inclined slightly to the right, turning north at high speed. "But you could have told me what you did."

"Not necessary." Radiant yellow-gold eyes enveloped him. "Would have made you feel better to know?" Amidst the aural gravel, a flicker of concern emerged.

"Of course I . . ." He hesitated. Would he have felt better knowing that some kind of alien tracking fluid was coursing through his circulatory system? Did he feel better for knowing it now? It wasn't as if she was somehow taking advantage of him.

As was sometimes the case, George was able to better articulate his friend's feelings than Walker was himself. "Makes you feel a little like property, does it? Remind you somehow of a previous situation?"

Walker glanced over at the dog, who was sitting up now and watching their Niyyuu employer intently. "This is nothing like our previous situation, George. We were prisoners of the Vilenjji: captives. Viyv-pym is hiring us. There's a vast difference in that."

"Difference, okay," the dog conceded as he scratched at one shoulder. " 'Vast,' I'm not so sure."

As soon as she digested the full import of the dog's comments, Viyv-pym grew visibly annoyed. "Captives? Prisoners? What kind insult this? I take yous Kojn-umm because of respect yous' abilities!" One hand pointed at Walker as the tips of her slender ears quivered and her tails lashed the sides of her seat. "Unique being exhibits unique talent. That only reason I extend offer to bring yous all Niyu. You think is nothing for me to do so? Cost involved goes beyond simple hiring. I have personal reputation to maintain!"

She was truly beautiful when she was angry, Walker could not help thinking. If only she wouldn't yell quite so much. The normal Niyyuu tone of voice was discordant enough.

"Okay, okay." Grumbling but far from mollified by her ear-bending outburst, George finished scratching and stretched back out on the seat. "Don't sprain your tongue—if you've got one." He glanced up at the man seated next to him. "Touchy bitch, isn't she?"

Walker held his breath, but evidently the Vilenjji implant translated the dog's comment in a way that was consistent with good manners. At least, Viyv-pym did not respond as a human female might have. Behind them, Braouk was reciting the eighth quatrain of the *Kerelon Soliloquy*. In order to squeeze inside, the Tuuqalian had to lie flat on the empty deck at the rear of the transport. Lost in melancholy reminiscence, he paid little attention to the conversation forward.

Once Viyv-pym had calmed down, Walker was able to reflect more dispassionately on George's comments. Had the dog been out of line, or was he onto something Walker was too excited or blinded to see? Had he advanced their cause of traveling nearer to their homes, or had he simply entered into an agreement that was little different from the one the Vilenjji had intended for them all along? Ostensibly, he and his companions were free agents, able to enter into an employment contract of their own choosing. Could they also exit it if and when they wished? They would be on Niyu—not sophisticated, highly civilized Sessrimathe—dealing with a species that, beyond their obvious physical attractiveness, neither he nor his companions knew anything about. How would Viyv-pym react, for example, if after arriving and performing his demonstrations for a few weeks he announced that he and his friends wished to leave?

Maybe he hadn't made such a smart call after all, he found himself worrying. Worse still, he had inveigled his only friends into going along with it.

Something lightly touched his shoulder. Turning, he found himself staring into black, horizontal pupils set in eyes of silver. A two-foot-long tendril was coiled lightly against his clavicle while the pinkish mouth tube that emerged from the nest of tentacles fluttered in his direction.

"I cannot read thoughts. Evolved as we are, my kind has not yet advanced to that degree. But in the time we have spent forced to endure one another's company I have become somewhat sensitive to your moods and expressions. You fear the consequences of the decision you have made."

There was a time when such close proximity face-to-face with a creature like Sque would have sent Walker reeling in shock. It was a measure of how much he had adapted that he did not even flinch from the rubbery cephalopodian visage.

"Yes, I do." A glance in George's direction showed that the dog had laid his head down on crossed forepaws and was ignoring them both. "George always knows how to stir up my uncertainties."

"A psychological device that should not be cavalierly employed by species unsophisticated in its use. Think a moment, Marcus Walker. If a self-evidently superior being like myself did not believe that there was more to be gained by accepting the offer of these Niyyuu than by declining it, would I have agreed to come along?"

Coming as it did straight from the K'eremu, the realization boosted his spirits. "No. No, you wouldn't have. You would have stayed on Seremathenn no matter how much I urged you to come."

"Precisely. Your oafish pleadings would have had no effect on me whatsoever." The tendril withdrew. "I am here only because I believe it truly does afford me the best opportunity to journey a bit nearer my homeworld that I have been offered since our arrival on Seremathenn, however meager it may eventually turn out to be. My decision has nothing to do with any perceived affection you believe I may hold toward your quaintly primitive individual person."

Walker was more relieved than he would have thought possible. "Thanks, Sque. I needed that reassurance."

"It is unintended," the K'eremu concluded, withdrawing backward to her perch atop the seat behind Walker's own.

Sque's indifference to his situation made her affirmation of his choice of action that much more heartening. Paradoxically, the fact that she could have cared less about how he felt showed how firmly she countenanced what they had done. He settled back into his seat, duly reassured in mind.

Now all he had to do was hope that primitive human and superior K'eremu were not equally misguided in their mutual decision.

※

In its perversely consistent fashion, it was comforting to discover in the course of the long voyage to Niyu that Viyv-pym was no more brusque of manner or grating of voice than any other representative of her kind. In fact, when confronted in close quarters with more than two or three Niyyuu conversing at once, Walker often had to manufacture an excuse to flee the location lest the pain from the sound of their overlapping voices lead to the kind of stabbing migraine he had not suffered since quitting football. He suspected that with time he would get used to the jarring, rasping, scratchy vocalizations. He would have to.

Their new hosts' irritating voices did not trouble the affable George nearly as much, barking being a less than mellifluous method of communication to begin with. As for Braouk, the massive Tuuqalian was not bothered by them at all, while Sque regarded all forms of non-K'eremu modulated communication as unworthy of serious evaluation anyway.

So Walker was left to listen in solitary discomfort to the queries and musings of the crew and the other passengers, struggling as best he was able to avoid cringing every time he was subjected to a particularly screechy turn of Niyyuuan phrase. His Vilenjji implant did its usual excellent job of rendering otherwise unintelligible alien conversation comprehensible, but it could do nothing to mute the actual sound of their speech.

Weeks into the journey saw him gradually becoming inured to the effect, rather like someone who has been bitten numerous times by a poisonous snake and has consequently developed a certain immunity to the toxin. Or maybe, he decided, his outraged ears had been damaged to the point of being unable to discriminate between Niyyuuan vocalizations and any other kind.

Whether by accident or subconscious design, he found himself spending a lot of time in Viyv-pym's company. He did not worry about relaxing too much. For one thing, she never missed an opportunity to remind him that the only relationship they had was that between employer and employee—though she was not engaging him personally. She was only acting as an agent for her government. Additionally, while her appearance and attitude was that of a beauteous alien apparition, her behavior was more akin to that of a crude visitant from some backward region of civilized space. Not that she was in any way boorish or ignorant, he determined. A lot of it had to do with the unfortunate manner of Niyyuu speech.

While he learned much from her about the physical nature of her homeworld, she was oddly reticent to discuss social mores and attitudes. "Yous find out after arriving," she would always tell him. He got the impression she was being tentative rather than deliberately evasive.

George was less convinced. "She's keeping something from us. Not necessarily concealing. Just skipping around certain subjects."

Sitting in the room they shared, dog and Walker exchanged a glance. The Niyyuuan sleeping platform on which he was lying was almost seven feet long but so narrow that he had to be careful not to fall onto the floor whenever he turned over during the chosen sleep period. George had no such difficulty with his platform. It could have easily accommodated a dozen Georges.

"Why would she want to hide anything?" Walker wondered how Braouk was handling the journey. While he could bend low enough to clear the ceilings within the Niyyuuan vessel, the Tuuqalian could only fit through a few exceptionally wide corridors, and then only by turning sideways. As a result, for the duration of the trip he was largely confined to the single storage area that had been converted for his use. While his comparative isolation was unavoidable, Sque's was voluntary. Unless it was obligatory, the K'eremu saw no reason to mix with lower life-forms on a social basis. This was not a problem, as the more they learned about Sque and the more often she was encountered, the more her self-imposed isolation suited the Niyyuu as much as it did the K'eremu.

"If we knew that," the dog was saying in response to Walker's question, "we'd probably have some idea what she was hiding. Maybe I'm way off base here, Marc. I have to keep reminding myself that we're not captives on a Vilenjji collecting craft and that we're here of our own free will."

"It'll be better once we get there. You'll see." Rolling over, he leaned across the narrow divide that separated their respective sleeping platforms and began to scratch the dog's back.

George's eyes half closed, and an expression of pleasure crossed his bushy face. "Farther down. Farther." The dog's eyes shut completely "That's it—both hip bones." Walker continued scratching until his friend settled down on his stomach. "Thanks. Every once in a while it's useful for me to be reminded why I keep you around."

Walker grinned. "Because if we happen to stumble across a pile of dog food, you'll need somebody to operate the can opener?"

"Sque's right. You're learning." More seriously he added, "I may be paranoid, but paranoia's kept me alive more than once. You keep an eye on that Viyv-pym specimen. And not the kind of eye you've been using."

Walker feigned shock. "George, she's an alien. She's not even mammalian, in the scientific sense."

"It's not scientific sense that worries me here." The dog eyed him evenly, cocking his head to one side, ears flopping. "It's another one."

"Look, I won't deny that I find her attractive. But that's all. It's purely a matter of dispassionate aesthetics. The same's true for every Niyyuu. They're just a physically striking species, if verbally irritating." He was very earnest.

The dog nodded tersely. "Let's hope the irritation is confined to the verbal."

"If my spending time trying to learn about her world and her people is worrying you that much," Walker suggested, "why not ask Sque's opinion?"

George snorted softly. "I said I was concerned, not daft. I don't need to go looking for insults. I can find plenty without having to search for them." With that, he rolled over onto his back, thrust his legs into the air, and gave every indication of embarking on a quick nap.

Walker let the matter drop. He was bemused by Viyv-pym, perhaps even beguiled, but he was not worried. She was too direct to be duplicitous. If he hadn't felt that he could trust her, he would never have agreed to undertake the current journey.

Or would he? Had he been blinded by the chance to travel—hopefully—a little closer to home? Was there some aspect of her personality, of Niyyuuan nature, that his enthusiasm for the opportunity had caused him to overlook? He didn't think so. A part of him almost wished his friends had not agreed to come with him, though. Because they had, and because it was his idea, he felt responsible for them. Braouk would have shrugged off the notion with verse, while Sque would have considered it beneath debate. Only the ever-ready George would have dumped a dutiful dollop of guilt on his fellow Chicagoan.

That settled it, Walker decided with a small smile. In some earlier incarnation, George must have been a Jewish or Italian grandmother.

# 4

When word came down from ship command that arrival at Niyu was imminent, Walker's wonderfully durable cheap watch informed him it had been nearly a month since they had left Seremathenn. Knowing nothing of the particulars of transpatial travel except that it was all relative, Walker could not assess if the journey had been swift or slow, or if it would be considered long or short. It was left to Sque to enlighten him as they prepared themselves and their few personal belongings for incipient disembarkation.

"Everything depends on the comparative velocity a container achieves while traversing that singular portion of space-time that makes interstellar travel possible."

She elucidated while clinging to the crest of Braouk's upper body, her tendrils securely entwined in the yellow-green bristles that covered him. One Tuuqalian eyestalk curled up to monitor her position while

the other remained level and drawn in, taking the measure of the path
ahead of them. Though Braouk was only giving her a ride, the incongruous temporary coupling made it appear as if the Tuuqalian had unexpectedly grown a small, rubbery head while the K'eremu had developed a truly enormous lower body.

"I don't need a detailed explanation." Heading down a ramp,
Walker was careful not to bump into George as the dog trotted alongside him.

"That is sensible, since you would not understand it anyway." The
K'eremu considered briefly. "Devoid of the necessary technical input
and basing my remarks, you understand, on the most casual and infrequent observation of the stellar neighborhood through which we have
recently passed, I should say that unless for some unknown and
unimaginable reason our hosts were compelled to take a circuitous
route in returning to their homeworld we have traveled a considerable
distance."

Walker's tone would have done Sque herself proud. "Oh good—
thanks so much for pinning it down for me." He and George turned a
corner, following a male Niyyuuan's lead.

Tendrils fluttered as the K'eremu shifted her position slightly atop
the Tuuqalian's crest. "Do not be impertinent. Do you expect one, even
one such as myself, to be able to accurately estimate the distances involved in interstellar travel by simply eyeballing the view outside an optical port? It is not like pacing off the feluuls on a beach, you know. Besides, the direction we have traveled is far more important than the
distance."

"What direction might that be?" George inquired, glancing back
and up at her.

"The right one, we must hope." The K'eremu went silent. They were
approaching an exit.

Viyv-pym was waiting for them there. The change in her demeanor
was evident even to her non-Niyyuu charges. Her movements were
more erratic, her manner of speaking even sharper than usual, while
neck frill and multiple tails were in constant motion instead of rising
and falling only when necessary to emphasize a point. Walker could not
be sure of his friends' reaction, but to him their hostess looked decidedly nervous. So much so that as she shepherded them through customs checkpoints that were far less elaborate than those they had encountered on Seremathenn, Walker was moved to comment.

"Of course I edge-being," she snapped sharply in response to his
query. "Do you not listen my talking on Seremathenn, on ship? This

very important engaging I have made done with you all." As she spoke, her remarkable eyes were scanning the far end of the hallway.

Wondering as to its purpose, Walker was guided through an archway. Somewhere out of his range of vision, something beeped minutely. It must have been a favorable beep, because he was waved on. One by one, his friends followed—all except Braouk, who was too big to pass through. A trio of gray- and blue-clad Niyyuu armed with portable instruments promptly descended on him and proceeded to pass the business ends of the devices they carried over his body. The Tuuqalian tolerated the intimate inspection for as long as he could stand it. Then he lumbered forward to rejoin his companions. Apparently deciding that their inspection had been sufficient, none of the three Niyyuuan officials chose to challenge his departure, their collective inaction thereby reasserting their species' claim to higher intelligence.

"What's wrong?" Walker finally felt compelled to ask as they continued down the hallway. "Something's wrong, isn't it?" Whatever it was, he prayed it had nothing to do with their presence.

She turned on him so abruptly that he flinched. "Fool of a provisional decision! Is not clear you? I expend much in bringing yous to Niyu. Much more I invest in bringing yous onward to Kojn-umm." When he didn't reply she added, her exasperation unbounded, "Here, home, I am become just like you, pale-skin Marc. I am employee too!"

So that was it, he realized as he strode along beside her. On Seremathenn she might have been dominant and in complete control of her fellow Niyyuu, but here she was subordinate to others. It made sense. In her defense, she had never claimed to be anything more than a posh procurer. But it was still strange to see the one on whom he had come to rely totally frill-flashing with unease at the thought she might have made a mistake.

It would be up to him, he realized, and his friends, to ensure that she did not suffer for making that choice. But mostly up to him.

The group that met them in the middle of an expansive, translucent-ceilinged rotunda was undeniably impressive, standing out from the bustle of other mostly, but not exclusively, Niyyuuan travelers. There were five of the greeters. Like Viyv-pym, each was clad in a variant of the familiar kilt-skirt and upper-body wrappings. Like her, each of the greeters flashed small bits and pieces of personal adornment to which the always-overdressed Sque paid particular attention.

Unlike the K'eremu, they carried forearm-length tubular devices that were strongly suggestive of weapons.

Why would a greeting party sent to welcome a cook and his friends

find it necessary to come armed? Walker found himself wondering. Perhaps the devices served a more ceremonial than practical purpose, and
were carried more for show than out of any fear of necessity. His
thoughts were drawn in that direction because each of the spiral-hol-
stered instruments flaunted one or more types of individual decoration,
from engraving that had been performed on their plasticlike bodies to
distinctive touches that utilized bright metal and polished gemstone.

None of the greeters drew his or her weapon in salute, however. The
leader—a male, to judge by the color and shape of his frill—was almost
stocky for a Niyyuu, though still markedly slimmer than Walker. Striding directly up to Viyv-pym, he briefly inspected each of the alien arrivals in turn before addressing their hostess. Walker's Vilenjji implant
conveyed the meaning of the escort's speech with admirable clarity.

"Sayings tell you hire one. I see four."

She extended one long, sinuous arm in the attentive human's direction. "The one would not come without his friends."

"Friends?" The leader of the escort hesitated visibly. "No two is
alike. All of different species."

"Yet friends they are," Viyv-pym insisted. "Was only matter of additional bringing. Was ample room on ship."

"Perhaps is a problem of adequate room in Kojn-umm." The escort
leader made a gesture Walker did not recognize. He hoped it was more
encouraging that the newcomers' words. "Not for me to say. Not for
you to say." So not saying, he turned to face Walker and his friends directly.

"I am Abrid-lon, scion and accountant of Kinuvu-dih-vrojj, administrator of Kojn-umm."

An accountant. Definitely ceremonial, Walker decided on re-view-
ing the weaponlike devices each member of their escort displayed.

"Nice to meet you." Walker thought about extending a hand, but
decided to hold off. While Viyv-pym was by now familiar with the human gesture, this Niyyuu was not, and it was too soon after their arrival to chance gestures that might be misinterpreted.

Though he wore the same type of external translator Viyv-pym employed, Abrid-lon ignored him. "This is the cook?"

"This indeed him," their hostess replied without hesitation.

Dominating yellow eyes peered down at the shorter but much
bulkier arrival. "I welcome you—and you's friends. All has been made
ready for you. Living quarters to match yous' standards on Seremathenn
close as possible. Working site equipped with latest utensils and tools
for nonsynthesized food preparation. Kinuvu-dih-vrojj and govern-

ment officials look forward to you workings." His frill erected to maximum. "Kojn-umm renowned throughout Niyu for its respect for all arts."

Initially made uneasy by Viyv-pym's unexplained nervousness, Abrid-lon's brusque but heartfelt welcome made Walker feel much better. Behind him, he could sense his companions stirring impatiently.

"I look forward to beginning work," he informed the escort leader truthfully. "How far to our quarters? A time-part or so?"

Abrid-lon gestured apologetically. "Kojn-umm large realm. Some traveling time involved, I say regrettably. With best possible traveling, arrive there late tonight."

Oh, well, Walker mused. He would have the opportunity to view the approach to his new home another time.

He was left to chat with his friends as Abrid-lon engaged Viyv-pym in extended conversation. Distance rendered the Vilenjji implant inoperative, since it was dependent on his own hearing abilities to recover sufficient speech suitable for translation. As they were guided outside the port and toward a waiting transport vehicle, George inhaled deeply alongside Walker.

"Smell that! The air here is even fresher and more oxygen-rich than Seremathenn's. I know it's hopefully just a temporary state of affairs, but I think I'm going to like it here. The locals may be a bit gruff, but they're civilized and friendly enough."

In human and canine terms, anyway, the dog was half-right.

The journey from the port to Kojn-umm's center of government was accomplished by means of small individual transports that traveled above open stretches of land. These cut through fields of waving, short-stemmed corkscrew growths that terminated in flowerlike cerulean and yellow bursts of color. They were more than fungi, less than flowers. A more visually appealing route would have been difficult to imagine. Walker's excitement at finding himself on yet another new world was muted somewhat by the knowledge that it was already late when they had touched down on the surface of Niyu, and that they would not be arriving at their new home until after dark.

Despite the earliness of the hour when they finally reached its outskirts, Ehbahr city was still sufficiently illuminated for the newcomers to be taken aback by its modest size. It would have barely qualified as a small suburb to one of Seremathenn's vast urban concentrations. Among the four fellow travelers, only Sque was not disappointed. The K'eremu preferred isolation and retreat to vast metropolitan concentrations, only joining together to form such when the needs of civilization and

commerce demanded it. Walker, who had been expecting something
like a smaller version of the great aesthetic conurbations that dominated
highly developed Seremathenn, was openly disenchanted.

"Capital Ehbahr is larger than appears, especially at night. Much our
industry built underground," Viyv-pym explained in response to their
queries. "Better to preserve actual landscape for beauty, for living, for
keeping of cultural history."

"Very admirable. We understand." Walker looked over at his closest
companion. "Don't we, George. George?" Head on paws, the dog was
sound asleep. The voyage and subsequent exhilaration attendant upon
landing had thoroughly exhausted him.

"And for war, of course," their guide and hostess added.

Walker blinked. "Excuse me?"

"You heard her." From her position hanging upside down from the
roof of the transport, Sque waved a couple of tendrils. "So much for
trading one 'advanced' culture for another. A fine choice you have made
for us, human."

"Wait, wait." One spoken word, assuming the Vilenjji translator had
correctly conveyed its meaning, had banished all thoughts of sleep from
his mind. "When I agreed to come here, Viyv-pym, you didn't say anything about your realm being at war. Who is Kojn-umm at war with?"
His hopes, so neatly aligned and optimistic, had been shattered like orange juice futures by a frost in Brazil.

It was as if those vast, expressive, yellow and gold orbs had suddenly turned cold. "At moment, with realm of Toroud-eed. Next ten-
day gathering, with somebody else. Then maybe Toroud-eed again, or
possibly Sasajun-aaf. Who else would realm be at war with?" When he
did not respond, she added unhelpfully, "Is nothing worry about. Is
natural state of affairs."

A deep voice, the soul of glumness, rumbled from the back of the
transport. "Here we sit, come all this way, conflict awaiting." Given his
habitual melancholy it was often difficult to tell exactly how Braouk
was feeling. Not now. The Tuuqalian was as disheartened by the unexpected turn of affairs as Sque was scornful. As for George, Walker was
grateful the often-acerbic George was still asleep.

Helplessly, as they slowed and entered the city, he asked, "How can
you be at war with anybody and say it's 'nothing worry about'? Much
less say 'is natural state of affairs'?"

"You not have ongoing or at least periodic war between individual
realms where you's home is?"

He looked away briefly. "Yes, we have such wars, I'm sorry to say. I have been told that Braouk's people do as well. Not Sque's, I believe."

"Only occasionally on a personal level," the K'eremu amended him helpfully. "When two individuals disagree excessively on a point of Melachian philosophy, for example, or concerning the worth of a new piece of siibalon vibrato. On such occasions, fighting usually commences with a vicious exchange of harsh language. On rare instances, blows may be thrown, perhaps even accompanied by a flung rock or two."

"That's not war," Walker muttered crossly. "That's a domestic dispute." He turned back to their hostess. "How long has this kind of episodic fighting been going on?" He trusted his implant to handle the translation of the relevant time frame.

It did. Whatever else one thought about the Vilenjji, their technology was admirably reliable. "About nine thousand years," Viyv-pym informed him without missing a beat. "Ever since Niyyuu become civilized."

"Not a contradiction, in war to engage, called civilization?" Braouk wondered aloud from the back of the transport.

She turned and strained to meet his raised eyes. "On contrary, Niyyuu thoughtfully observe other sentient species and wonder how they maintain civilization without occasional internal warring."

Walker's head began to throb as he tried to make sense of what he was being told. The Niyyuuan's warped logic was occasioning him more pain than the occasional jolt in their ride. "You say sporadic warfare helps you to maintain your civilization, but that it's nothing to worry about. There's a clash of reasoning there I just don't understand. I don't understand it at all."

"You will," she assured him confidently. "You not only do peformancing for Administrator Kinuvu-dih-vrojj and government, you also prepare food for Saluu-hir-lek and his staff."

He frowned. The first name he recognized, but this was the first time that the second one had been made known to him. "I signed on to cook for whoever you wish, but who is Saluu-hir-lek?"

"Commanding general," Abrid-lon called back to him from the front of the transport, "and lord high protector of the conjoined territories of Kojn-umm. Very pleasant person. You will like him."

Curioser and curioser. He was drowning in incomprehension. "I thought Kinuvu-dih-vrojj was the leader of Kojn-umm?"

Viyv-pym exhaled softly in his direction. Her breath washed over him like essence of roses. "Kinuvu-dih-vrojj, she head of government. Saluu-hir-lek, he head of traditional military. One not superior to another. Just different work taxonomy. I procurer. You exotic food preparation demonstrator. You's friends—they receive appropriate classifications in due time." A long, willowy arm reached out toward him.

"You tired, Marc. Long journeying from Seremathenn. Relax, not worry. Kojn-umm pleasant place. Ehbahr city and citizens enlightened, congenial. You will like it here."

Apprehensive and anxious, he slumped back in his seat. "I'm sure I will—unless you lose this war and are overrun by your enemies."

Her painted circlet of a mouth expanded in amusement as she coughed twice. "Perhaps lose. Have lost before. Is no realm that has not. Could not manage world society otherwise. But Kojn-umm not be 'overrun,' in sense you suggest. Cannot happen."

"Why not?" he asked straightforwardly, without wondering if the question might be viewed by his hosts as tactless.

"Because would not be civilized thing to do. You think Niyyuu barbarians? Not as advanced as Sessrimathe, maybe, but plenty civilized and refined are my kind. You will see. Maybe even," she finished considerately, "you like try you's hand at fighting, too, someday."

Walker was quietly aghast. "I agreed to come here to create cuisine, not to kill!"

She gestured placatingly. "Is your choice. Did not mean upset you. Is not necessary participate. Very much competition for spaces in traditional military, anyway."

He sat stunned and silent, unable to believe what he was hearing. It was so at odds with everything he had come to believe about the Niyyuu. Or, he told himself, was it only what he had *wanted* to believe about the Niyyuu? Had he settled hopes and expectations on Viyv-pym and her people that were grounded only in wishful thinking?

"Have *you* fought in this war, in the military?" he finally heard himself asking.

"Oh, most for sure." The eagerness in her voice could not be denied. "Was fortunate enough be awarded two whole full enlistment periods."

"And . . . you killed?"

"Of course." Golden eyes glittered with recollection as her voice quivered with suggestions of thrills remembered. "Not real war without killing."

How could he argue with that? he told himself. For the first time since he had met her, the beauteous and exotic Viyv-pym receded once again into the realm of the utterly alien.

As was often the case, it was left to Sque to emotionlessly evaluate what they had been told. "There are ramifications here we do not understand," she declared quietly from her hanging place in the center of the swaying transport's ceiling. "We must work to acquire the obligatory cultural referents before we can pronounce judgment. Operating in ignorance, we cannot hope to properly assess composite indigenous conditions."

Walker latched onto her uncertainty like an overextended client to a fresh line of credit. What the K'eremu was saying was that there was more here than met the eye, or the ear. Though for the life of him he could not fathom what that might be, he was willing to give it time in the hope that a sensible explanation would present itself.

Traversing parsecs to swap their situation on peaceful, accommodating Seremathenn for a millennia-old ongoing war was not what he'd had in mind when he had signed on hoping to improve their chances of getting home.

Often dimly illuminated, the buildings they passed differed in design, shape, and size from those on Seremathenn. Such was to be expected, since Viyv-pym had informed them that much of Niyu's commerce took place belowground. There was certainly enough nocturnal illumination, however, to guide incoming hostile aircraft, much less anything more sophisticated. Therefore it was abundantly clear the people of Ehbahr city did not fear an assault from the air. That suggested several possibilities, none of which made any more sense to him than what he had already been told. He gave up trying to figure out what was going on and determined to wait for an explanation that did. Hopefully, one would be provided to them.

There was certainly nothing wrong with or Spartan about their quarters. Prepared in advance according to specifications supplied by Viyv-pym, they bordered on the luxurious. Having been provided with particulars by its new employees, the government of Kojn-umm had gone out of its way to make them feel at home.

Walker's personal space on Seremathenn had been accommodating. His quarters in a luxurious section of Ehbahr city consisted of separate, spacious rooms for sitting, sleeping, receiving guests, and performing personal ablutions. Instead of a view of other transformed buildings such as he'd had on Seremathenn, he had transparent barriers that opaqued or vanished at the wave of a hand to allow egress to a porch that overlooked a small stream running through carefully maintained Niyuan forest.

Flashing multihued phosphorescent scales, small creatures of the

night scampered to and fro between foliage and stream. Since the connected rooms did not boast the responsive, all-pervasive synthesized
voice-response system of an advanced Seremathenn dwelling, he was
shown how to request service from a live Niyyuuan attendant. George
would share quarters with Walker, they were informed, while on casual
inspection the easygoing Braouk found his private accommodations to
be more than satisfactory. Upon being shown her own lodgings, which
included a section of the nearby creek to provide constant moisture,
even Sque had less than the normal number of complaints.

Promising to meet with them again in the morning, both Viyv-pym
and Abrid-lon left the newest employees of the government of Kojn-
umm to their own devices. Toying with the receiving room's entertain-
ment/information system, Walker found it to be as highly developed as
anything he had used on Seremathenn. Neither it, nor the peacefully
sleeping city, nor the attitude of the individual Niyyuu he had encountered since arriving squared with the reality of continual, ongoing
combat. For about five minutes, he worried about being killed in his
sleep on the special resting platform that had been provided for him.
Then another kind of reality took over, and he fell into a deep and un-
troubled sleep.

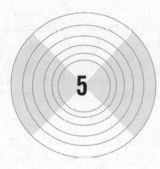

**5**

Walker sat up sharply in the approximation of a bed, awakened by something that sounded like forty chickens being simultaneously strangled. Looking around wildly for the source of the horrible screeching, he searched the entire room twice before he realized it was only the Niyyuuan equivalent of a gentle, mellifluous, pre-programmed wake-up song.

*Have to have that recording changed,* he told himself shakily as he descended from the sleeping platform to manually cancel the persistent wail. No doubt more than a few of the provisions that had been made for his life here would require comparable modifications.

Passing by one of the darkened view-walls, he directed it to vanish. The energizing tingle of fresh air filled the room, accompanied by a flush of bright sunshine. Walking out onto the small porch, he found himself gazing across the nearby stream that had been only a dark sliver

muttering to itself during the night. A quintet of humming furballs he
did not yet have a name for bobbed past, seeking surcease, shade, and
nectar. Rustlings in the underbrush on the other side of the brook
hinted at the presence within of alien ground dwellers. The noises did
not concern him. If any danger existed from native animals, he was certain he would have been informed.

Above and beyond the undulating crest of the carefully maintained
riparian habitat he could see tall buildings rising from the center of the
capital city. The Niyyuu were fond of domes and other bulbous architectural oddities; a partiality that contrasted sharply and perhaps intentionally with their own svelte forms. Beyond the glistening, well-
scrubbed towers of the city, which were modest in size compared to the
structures he had seen on Seremathenn, a line of mountains stretched
across the horizon. No snow capped the visible peaks, an absence that
might have been due to latitude, season, altitude, or a combination
thereof.

"See anything?"

Turning, he saw that George had come up behind him. The dog
yawned mightily, shook from nose to tail, and stretched, his forelegs
extending as far forward as possible.

"Urban structures," Walker informed his height-challenged companion. "Parklike stream and vegetation just below us. In the distance,
mountains—not too high, I think."

"No sign of fighting, uninhibited internecine bloodletting, or rampaging cadres of naturally anorexic soldiers?"

Walker returned his attention to the babbling brook and outlying
buildings. "There's something in the creek that looks agitated, but that's
about it."

"Good. I'm hungry. Let's find something to eat."

Walker waved a windowlike transparency back into place before
turning away from the gap. Where was evidence of the ongoing war of
which Viyv-pym had spoken? "Wait. I have to get dressed."

"I don't." The dog trotted energetically through a portal that
opened obediently in response to his curt bark. "Meet you in the common room, or dining room, or however the appropriate place for taking meals is designated here."

It made no sense, Walker deliberated as he fumbled with his shirt
while doing his best to follow his companion. If the countryside existed in a state of perpetual war, where were the signs of concern, the
hints of resistance? The city had been well lit during their arrival the
previous night. Was it possible to imagine a civilization that possessed

starships but not aircraft? For that matter, bombs could be dropped
from balloons, but there was nothing to indicate that the people of
Kojn-umm feared any attack from the air. Could the confusion he was
experiencing be due to a simple misunderstanding over what he had
been told? But Viyv-pym had said clearly that it was "not real war without killing." He decided to try to set his bemusement aside. Surely clarification would be forthcoming.

George was right about one thing. He was hungry, too. Maybe food
would help to alleviate the headache he was beginning to develop. And
he hadn't even started work yet. Would he need to acquire defensive attire in addition to the appropriate utensils?

The dog located a common room that fronted on a small indoor
garden. None of the plants were known to either of them. Within the
garden, yellow vied with green as the dominant color. One particularly
distinctive growth put forth a single flower that was as long as Walker's
arm. It smelled abominable.

The synthesizer that responded to their requests had been programmed to fulfill their needs, but the equipment, while far in advance
of anything that had been developed on Earth, was no match for the sophisticated instrumentalities of the Sessrimathe. Biting into a disc of
pale pink something, Walker's face screwed into an expression that was
a perfect visual representation of the taste.

"If this is an example of the local cuisine," he observed when he
had choked down enough of the substance to be able to talk again, "I
can see why my services are so eagerly awaited here."

"You're too picky, Marc. You always are." George dug with unreserved gusto into the plate of proteins as colorful as they were unidentifiable that the synthesizer had set before him.

That left Walker to contemplate an unpalatable choice between
looming starvation and distasteful consumption. As he picked at his
food, Sque arrived to join them. Scuttling into the room on half a dozen
of her ten tendrils, bits of polished metal and colorful plastic jangling
around her body, the dripping wet K'eremu left a trail of water behind
her. Preferring to remain as damp as possible for as long as possible, she
had not bothered to dry herself following her most recent immersion.

Though barely four feet tall when erected on all ten tendrils, she
had no difficulty pulling herself up into the chair that was intended for
much taller Niyyuu. In fact, she was arguably more comfortable on the
alien piece of furniture than her human companion was. Designed to
accommodate the far narrower Niyyuuan posterior, Walker's chair

would have made an uncomfortable perch for any human. Constant shifting in search of a more restful position failed to find one.

"Fortunately, I have already eaten. Thank you for asking," she snapped brusquely before anyone could venture so much as a "Good morning." As a sign of further disapproval, several bubbles emerged from the flexible pink tube that was her mouth and rose halfway to the ceiling before bursting.

By now completely used to her moods, Walker ignored her scorn as he picked unhappily at his own food. "I assumed that you had, Sque, or you would have been demanding it as you came in." Slipping a slice of something like slivered eggplant into his mouth, he chewed slowly and experimentally. His palate was less than impressed, but his stomach did not rebel.

*I would kill,* he mused dejectedly, *for a Polish dog. With mustard, and onions, and relish, and sauerkraut.* At the thought, his mouth manufactured saliva in quantity sufficient to impress even Sque. As for barbeque, he dared not even visualize the concept. Instead, he made himself eat another slice of alien eggplant.

To take his mind off historical impossibilities like kielbasa, he engaged the K'eremu in conversation. "How did you sleep? While they're not as stylish as those we had on Seremathenn, I thought my quarters were pretty comfortable."

"I did not ask your opinion," she replied tersely. Two tendrils pulled a conical container toward her and deftly upended a sample of the liquid contents into a smaller container from which she sipped daintily before continuing. "As you observe, these Niyyuu are not as advanced as our former hosts. Neither are they especially primitive. My rooms occupy a level lower than yours. This was done intentionally, I am told, so that I might have regular and unimpeded access to the nearby stream and its refreshing, cooling flow. Such forethought expended on the comfort of a higher being is to be commended. I rested adequately, thank you."

"And how did you find breakfast, Snake-arms?"

As always, she ignored the dog's insult as being beneath her. "Nourishment, though synthesized as expected, was tolerated by my system. It could not compare, of course, to victuals properly prepared." Several slender limbs gestured in Walker's direction. "As they might have been by the primitive but gastronomically talented amateur in our company, to give but one example."

Walker nearly choked on his next mouthful. "Are you paying me a compliment, Sque?"

Silvery eyes looked away, toward the nearest transparency that provided an external view. "Truth compels. You may proffer appropriate obeisance at a later time. I do not wish to interrupt your intake of the dreadful molecular combinations you consider worthy of ingestion."

Walker beamed. A compliment. Sque never gave compliments. The closest the K'eremu came to praising another being was to refrain from insulting it on a regular basis. Walker hardly knew how to respond.

Defying any sense of propriety, local or imported, George hopped up onto the table and began sniffing some of the other offerings. Walker managed to look pained.

"Come on, George. Really."

"Really what?" The dog eyed him impassively. "Really get off the table, or really relax because if I had arms and hands I wouldn't have to do this?" Settling on a chunk of something that smelled like meat even if it looked like cantaloupe, he picked it up in his teeth and returned to his chosen spot on the floor.

They remained like that, in mutual silence, for several minutes— man and dog eating, K'eremu contemplating their primitive activity— when a sudden thought occurred to Walker. Looking up and around, he took in their immediate surroundings before venturing aloud to no one in particular, "Anyone seen Braouk this morning?"

"Not me." George returned to his meat melon.

"I have not yet encountered the ungainly giant." Pulling herself up onto the table, Sque took on the appearance of a kaleidoscopic calamari. Another place, another time, another set of onlookers, Walker knew, and she would be deemed dinner rather than diner. "Maybe he's still resting in whatever warehouse-sized room our lanky hosts have made available for his use."

As breakfast wore on without any sign of the melancholy Tuuqalian, however, Walker found himself beginning to worry. "We'd better go find him, make sure he's okay." He pushed back from the table and stood, glad to be free of the narrow, uncomfortable Niyyuuan chair.

"Worry about that wandering mountain?" George hopped up onto an empty chair to bring himself closer to eye level with his friend. "He worries everybody else, not the other way around."

"I'd feel better knowing for sure that he's okay."

The dog snorted, considered relieving himself on one of the table supports, decided to hold off. Unlike another dog, their hosts would probably frown on such a response. "Might as well, I guess. Nothing else to do here yet anyway."

They found the giant on the roof. In addition to a series of small domes whose function was not immediately apparent, there was a broad deck that had been landscaped with fully grown trees and shrubbery to blend perfectly with the preserved natural environment below. Though it rose to a height of only four or five stories above the ground, the edifice that had become their new home still loomed above the majority of government structures surrounding it. The deck offered a sweeping panorama of the city and the surrounding mountains.

Braouk was standing on the northwest side, careful not to put any weight against the delicate swirl of railing that in addition to being too low for him could never have supported his mass. In contrast, it was almost too high for Walker. Picking up George, he cradled the dog in his arms so his friend could also see clearly. As for Sque, her multiplicity of limbs allowed her to easily scamper up the nearest dome.

"Nice view," George commented approvingly. "Handsome mountains. No mountains where you and I come from."

"Is not mountains, that I stand studying, this direction." The Tuuqalian raised a pair of powerful tentacles and pointed. "There. That outcropping or promontory, that rises just to the left of the main pass. Do you see?"

Walker strained. With his huge oculars mounted on the ends of flexible stalks, Braouk had the best distance vision of any of them. "I do see something. Some kind of building?"

"More than that." This time the Tuuqalian pointed with all four tentacles, the tips touching to form a conical indicator. "Look again, harder."

With a familiarity she would never have dared attempt back aboard the prison ship of the Vilenjji, Sque clambered up Braouk's back, climbing him like a tree, until she stood atop the furry crest with one bulbous Tuuqalian eye raised on either side of her.

"I cannot see anything except these mountains. My eyesight has evolved for precision viewing, not for far-seeing."

George had better luck. "I see smoke, and moving figures. Lots of moving figures. The structure itself is different from anything down here. Looks to be pretty big, and all sharp angles. No tapering towers, no graceful domes."

"I believe it, to be a primitive fortress, without question." As they drew closer together, the better to sharpen the Tuuqalian's view, the muscular eyestalks threatened to squeeze Sque between them. "A castle, or redoubt, of primitive design. Even as we stand here watching, a battle is taking place before its gate and on its ramparts."

"The war!" Now that Braouk had described the scene, Walker found that he was better able to discern individual elements of the distant vista. "Strange. You say that fighting is going on. But I don't see any flashes of light, any explosions."

"Me neither," George added. As an indication of how seriously he took the situation, his tail was virtually motionless.

"That is because there are none," the Tuuqalian informed them. "In keeping with the design and materials of the primitive structure that is under assault, the methods of combat being employed appear to be equally archaic. While it is difficult to tell for certain at such a distance, I think I perceive much tentacle-to-tentacle—excuse me, hand-to-hand—fighting."

Sque gestured with several tendrils. "There is both absurdity and contradiction in what you say. Yet being unable to see clearly for myself, I am unable either to deny or confirm the validity of your observations. I declared upon our arrival here yesterday that there are ramifications to this Niyyuuan war that we do not understand. I confess I am now even more puzzled than I was originally."

Turning, George nodded toward the far portal. "It's time to get un-puzzled. Let's ask her."

Viyv-pym was striding toward them, her slender limbs seeming to float across the floor. She had exchanged her previous attire for a dual casing of gauzy material: half turquoise blue, the other shimmering gold. Here and there, fragments of what looked like frozen methane gave off small wisps of condensation. Twisted tightly around her, the fabric gave her the appearance of someone bound in an oversized strand of DNA. With her high, pointed ears; switching tails; and wide, luminous eyes, she was perfectly breathtaking, Walker decided.

"Yous rested well?" she inquired cheerfully in her familiar grating burr.

Never one to waste words, George raised a paw in the direction of the distant mountain pass. "There's fighting going on up there, just outside your city, right now."

The sparkling Niyyuuan gaze rose briefly. "Yes, at the fortress of Jalar-aad-biidh. Combined forces of Toroud-eed have invested it almost two ten-days now. Under strategy devised by gallant General Saluu-hir-lek our defenders continue hold them off. Is very exciting."

"Exciting?" Once again, Walker found Viyv-pym's reactions in sharp contrast to her appearance. "Aren't your people, citizens of Kojn-umm, dying up there?"

"No doubt are some, yes."

"Well, what is going to be done about it?"

"Take you meet you's staff," she informed him happily. "Begin plan first meal-skill demonstration for government personnel. Important yous make good impression. Very important for you and for me." She eyed his companions. "Must make appearance all of one part. All participate, somehow. Sure you understand necessary justify bringing four not one all way to Niyu."

"Showtime," declared the ever-adaptable George.

"Amateur theatrics, no doubt." Though clearly not pleased, having anticipated something of the sort, Sque kept the bulk of her objections to herself. "Hopefully there will be astronomers in attendance and we can make some contacts useful toward commencing the necessary preliminary studies for continuing on our homeward journey."

Fortunately, their hostess had not overheard the K'eremu's characteristically soft speech. Leaning down, Walker whispered urgently to Sque.

"We just got here. Try to be a little diplomatic, will you? Since we're undoubtedly going to have to ask these people for help, it would be better not to start off by insulting their hospitality."

"What hospitality? We are employees, not guests." Steel-gray eyes looked away from him. "Nevertheless, I shall endeavor to comply. You speak sense."

"Who, me?" Walker responded blithely.

"The universe is ever full of surprises." The K'eremu scuttled off to one side, away from Viyv-pym.

Walker turned back to their patient hostess. "How can anyone be interested in aesthetic food preparation when there's a war going on?"

"Most always a war going on," she told him. "Has nothing to do with living normal life."

"Has nothing to do with . . . ?" Sque was right, he thought. There was much here they did not understand, and it was growing more confusing by the moment.

Viyv-pym turned and beckoned. "Come now, please. Meet staff, explain needs. Have some time prepare properly, but not excessive amount. You interested in course of the fighting, yes?" Both Walker and George nodded. The human wondered if she could perceive the confusion in his expression.

Whether their Niyyuu hostess was that perceptive or not, she removed from within the folds of her garb a rolled-up square of plastic. Unfurled, it sprang to light and to life. Running her fingers over one side, she brought forth image after image until the flexible screen finally settled on one. Satisfied, she passed it toward Walker.

He accepted it without hesitation. It weighed very little, and he was able to examine it without breaking stride. Next to him, George was bouncing up and down curiously, straining to see.

"Let me have a look too, Marc. What is it? Not cartoons, I bet."

"No," Walker responded soberly. Bending over, he lowered the viewer until it was level with his friend's eyes. "See for yourself."

The dog found himself gazing at a scene of relentless and deceptively ruthless Niyyuuan carnage. Clad in armor of varying thickness and elegant but alien design, dozens of Niyyuu were engaged in a brutal clash outside what appeared to be the gate of an ancient stone fortress. While the design differed significantly from its nearest human analog of medieval castles, certain similarities were perhaps inevitable. Projectiles were slung from battlements, though there was no evidence of bows and arrows being put to use. A spear was a spear, though the blueprint might be slightly different.

Edged weapons differed from those that might be wielded by a human in a similar situation. They tended more to the saber than the broadsword—understandable, given the slenderer build of the Niyyuuan. Shields reflected similarly lighter construction. Man and dog saw more than a few that appeared to be composed almost entirely of metal filigree. Or plastic. Despite the clarity and variety of available images, there was still a lot of picture-distorting movement. Speaking of pictures . . .

"I'm afraid I don't get any of this." At once fascinated and horrified, Walker spoke without taking his eyes from the roll-up screen. "How are these images being broadcast?"

"I not technically educated myself in physics of broadcast apparatus," Viyv-pym told him. "Can obtain for you if you like expert in such matters to—"

"No, no," he said, hastily interrupting her. "I mean, some of these images are being sent from right in the middle of the fighting. Isn't that dangerous for the broadcast operator?"

"'Operator'?" She eyed him quizzically. "Images are relayed by advanced instrumentation that operate under all conditions." As she grasped the deeper implications of his question, her ears quivered. "Operators on battlefield are clearly identified. No soldier of any realm dare harm media representative! Accidentally might happen, but that only possible way."

Her sincere shock at the possibility that a live image relayer might be injured in the course of reporting on the conflict did not square with the very real carnage he and George were witnessing on the screen. It appeared that the skirmish was dying down. Fighters on both sides were retreating—the soldiers of Kojn-umm falling back to the fortress, their attackers withdrawing to some unseen bivouac. Both sides took their wounded with them. The rocky slope they abandoned was littered with bodies. Clearly visible were many body parts that had been forcefully divorced from their owners, and a copious amount of blood.

Peering around Walker, Viyv-pym stole a glance at the flexible screen. "Today's fight most substantial. I believe is standoff. For nows, anyway. If fortress can hold several days longer, I think Toroudians will go home. Kojn-umm will move up in preferential trade rankings."

Walker gaped at her. "Trade rankings?" He shook the screen, which flexed easily but did not sacrifice its image. "This hack-and-slash mayhem is about trade rankings?" While he was not exactly sure as to the significance of a Niyyuuan trade ranking, it did not sound like the sort of thing people ought to be dying over.

She indicated in the affirmative, her golden pupils expanding and contracting. "Saluu-hir-lek is fine leader. Sure he pursue dispute to conclusion that favors Kojn-umm."

"Just suppose the military situation is a stalemate, for now," Walker hypothesized. "But what if this enemy, these Toroud-eed, try a flanking movement or something? What if they attack the city itself?"

She inhaled so sharply and drew away from him so abruptly that for a moment he thought she had tripped over some unseen crevice. The Vilenjji implant conveyed her disgust at his words in no uncertain, and highly unflattering, terms. When she realized that his bewilderment, as well as that of his three companions, was genuine, she did her best to try to explain.

"Yous know still so little of Niyyuu society. So I try quick explain yous. Toroud-eed soldiers not never attack anything but Kojn-umm soldiers and recognized, long-established, traditional military targets. What you suggest is not conceivable."

"Just for the sake of argument," George put in, "what if they did?"

As she peered down at him, her tails were entwining in a clear sign of agitation. "Aside from fact such action unthinkable and unprecedented, every other realm on Niyu would gang up on them and raze entire territory of Toroud-eed to bare soil. Committing violence against a nonmilitary target would violate every law of civilized Niyyuuan behavior. General population, civilian population, is never involved in traditional fightings." A soft sighing escaped her round mouth as she resumed walking. Today that orifice was edged in paint the color of sliced limes and granite.

"Was different in primitive times, of course. As Niyyuu become civilized, organize into many thousands small warring states. Resultant general chaos retards development of progressive society. Each state ruled by warlord, military chieftain. People gradually come to recognize problem. Even warlords recognize problem—but not want give up individual privileges, respect, power.

"Decision made between Sixth and Seventh Interregnums to divide functions of state. Civilian peoples form administrations, governments, to deal with everyday livings. Warlords retain small armies to settle differences. But civilian governments never interfere in fightings, and warlord armies never touch civilians. So civilization grows and prospers, but many disputings still settled by combat. Today's armies entirely whole composed of honored volunteers." She straightened proudly. "I tell you before, I earlier participate in such myself."

Walker tried to picture the poised, lissome Viyv-pym tricked out in full body armor, slim bloody sword dangling from one two-fingered hand, jewel-like lightweight helmet steady upon her head. Somewhat to his surprise, it was not difficult to make the imaginary leap. He hurriedly pushed the image out of his mind.

Sque was less forbearing. "This local tradition of constrained violence is nothing more than another take on typical primitive means of avoiding the use of reason."

George was more openly forgiving as he addressed himself to Viyv-pym. "So what you're saying is that the general population isn't involved in these recurring fights at all. That these traditional warlord groups act as proxies for societal disputes while the general population goes merrily about its everyday business, blissfully free of any need to participate in actual combat." The dog eyed her intently. "But what happens when one side's army wins? What happens if you lose?"

"Then dispute that provoke it is considered settled," she told him, as if explaining the obvious to a child.

George still wasn't satisfied. "The victorious army doesn't come marching in? There's no sacking and pillaging and burning?"

Having dealt with previous outrageous statements, this time she was better prepared to respond to more of the same. "I tell you second time: warriors not think of attack civilians, and civilians not think of not supporting warriors. Besides being inviolable custom, is civic and moral duty of all concerned."

Sort of the antipode of Tibetan Buddhism, Walker found himself supposing. In that distant mountain land, people believed themselves obligated to provide food and drink for wandering priests so that the latter could properly perform their duties. Meanwhile, the priests prayed for the people. The lamas didn't try to tell the local electric company how to supply power, and the officials of the local utilities stayed out of the lamaseries. It was all very civilized.

Except that in the Niyyuuan version people died.

"Everyone respect results, of traditional ongoing killing, without argument?" Instead of bending to clear a low archway, Braouk contracted his four treelike walking tentacles and lowered himself by a foot.

"Argument is settled by winning of fight," Viyv-pym told him. "After fighting over, no argument left. Anyone with personal feelings about subject matter of dispute is always given place in army. Ample room then for letting deep feelings be known."

A wonderful way for society's disgruntled to blow off steam, Walker realized. Pick up a sword or spear and hack away at your frustrations.

As they entered one of the building's internal transports and were conveyed swiftly and silently to another linked structure, the juxtaposition of the advanced method of getting from one part of the government complex to another with what he continued to see on the roll-up visual prompted a question of a different sort. He hoped Viyv-pym's translator was capable of handling the same terms and referents as his own.

"I saw plenty of swords and spears, knives and slings, and in the background a few larger devices that looked like catapults and other primitive war machines." He indicated the high-speed, climate-controlled, virtually vibrationless capsule that was presently carrying all of them, including Braouk, in comparative comfort. "Your people have vessels capable of interstellar travel, complex translation devices that function even between species, machines that can synthesize many varieties of food from basic nutritional components, and communications equipment like this." He held up the flexible receiver. "But I didn't see one gun of any size, shape, or style in use during that battle. No explosives of any kind, nothing."

Behind him, Sque commented on his query with a rude bubbling noise. He ignored the K'eremu's snide remark, a typical reference to his manifest stupidity. Maybe the explanation was obvious—but it wasn't to him. At least George had nothing to say. The dog's attentiveness showed that he was as interested in the answer as was his bipedal companion.

"When original concord forged by all warring realms," Viyv-pym explained patiently, "it decided then and there to freeze means of disputation at technological level existing at time of final accord. Has not changed ever since. Permissible weaponry still same as that used during mid Seventh Interregnum."

Walker persisted. "But what's to keep someone on the verge of having their head cut off from pulling out a pistol, just that one time, and blowing their assailant away?"

"Same steadfast compact that keep military from attacking noncombatants." Viyv-pym put a gentle arm around his shoulders. "Must try to see state of affairs from Niyyuu point of view, Marcus." He wasn't sure which was more unsettling: the arm resting on his shoulders and neck, or her use of his first name. "Ancient accord sustains harmony of all Niyu. If one realm breaks tradition, all other realms combine to punish it. If individual breaks with custom, own comrades would provide punishment. Accord has lasted thus for thousands of forty-days." Inclining toward him, she brought her face close to his own. He had to fight not to lose himself in the flaxen depths of her eyes.

"Is not same with you's culture?"

"Not exactly." He swallowed. "We have wars—we do fight—but we're not as . . . polite, about it as the Niyyuu."

A soft barking nearby caused him to glance sharply downward. George was visibly amused. "I can see trying something like this on Earth. Might work with higher beings, like dogs. But humans? You can't even keep from using advanced weapons between mates. There's civilized behavior, and then there's human civilized behavior. Seems like out here there's different degrees and definitions of war, too."

As the transport capsule began to slow, Walker felt moved to defend his species. "At least we're different when it comes to broadcasting the horrors of actual warfare." He handed the roll-up screen back to Viyv-pym. "When it comes to that, the Niyyuu apparently aren't nearly as appalled by it as we are."

"Give me a break, man. You're not appalled at all. I've spent plenty of time on the street. Watched humans at fights. Street gangs versus bikers. Cops against lawbreakers. Always draws a crowd. Maybe their speech is full of horror, but their expressions tell it all. You want to know how your own kind really reacts to combat and violence, study their respiration and pulse and sweat glands, not their language."

"Appalled?" As the transport's door slid aside, Viyv-pym looked from human to canine. "Niyyuu not appalled by fighting. Wars keep the peaces. Combat sustains the concordance." She held up the screen.

"Everyone follow each conflict with much interest. War is politics. Is Niyyuu culture, commerce, entertainment."

"Entertainment?" Walker was aghast.

She confirmed his dismay "Anyone can quote yous history of famous battles, involving many realms. Names of famous soldiers, officers and common. You spend more time on Niyu, you see. Battles broadcast all times. Pick favorite realm, favorite soldiers, favorite fightings. Much to see, much to learn. Much to admire."

Like the gladiators who became media stars in ancient Rome, Walker told himself unhappily. Watch them slice and dice each other, have a few laughs, then go home to the wife and kids. That is, if you didn't bring the wife and kids to the show with you. Today's special: murder and slaughter. Family packages available. All in the name of righteous service and maintaining a widespread, functional peace between competing territories. All without having to resort to the risk of general devastation and the imposition of impoverishing military budgets on a disinclined populace.

Probably the system also worked wonders for the racial psyche. Those who wanted to fight could do so without suffering any social opprobrium. In the absence of advanced weaponry, each individual was guaranteed some chance of surviving combat based purely on the development of individual skills. Those who wanted nothing to do with such old-fashioned violence could not only avoid it, they could participate vicariously through the actions of volunteer armies: others as well as their own. Sure, Walker rooted for the Bears and the Bulls, but back home he and his friends watched other games as well, where they also chose sides. Superficially, the only difference between the sociopolitical situation on Niyu and the National Football League was that the latter involved the spilling of less blood while the former doubtless resulted in more far-reaching eventual consequences than a Super Bowl championship.

Though initially revolted, he had to admit the system had its attractions. Too bad it would never work on or be imported to Earth. For one thing, the necessary cultural background and referents were as different as the two species. War, even limited war, was not a game to be played out on a grassy field. At least not among loutish humans.

As George had so indecorously pointed out, humans were not sufficiently polite.

Eager to initiate the visitors into the intricacies of Niyyuuan society, Viyv-pym kept up a running commentary on the battle as soon as it resumed, pointing out eminent individual warriors and officers, commenting on tactics, remarking knowledgeably on battlefield conditions. Watching and listening to her, a disconcerted Walker found himself wondering if rain would be considered grounds for a bad-weather postponement of the battle. Thus far there had been nothing on the flexible screen to indicate the presence of referees. In their absence, it had to be assumed that the combatants policed themselves. A kind of "call your own fouls" conflict, where intentional tripping was supplanted by maiming and unnecessary roughness was a contradiction in terms. He wondered if there was a Niyyuuan battlefield equivalent of illegal use of the hands, and doubted it.

Then she was rolling up the screen and slipping it back inside her double-wrapped costume. They had arrived at the food preparation area.

The half dozen or so Niyyuu lined up to greet them eyed him eagerly. His reputation having preceded him, Walker did not need to identify himself. More problematic was the matter of what role to assign to his companions. He was disappointed when Viyv-pym drew them off to one side to consult with an elderly local, leaving him to deal with the nutrition technicians alone.

They were enthusiastic enough. His requests for specific equipment were met with a chorus of ready responses, the combined harshness of half a dozen Niyyuuan voices all attempting to answer at once leaving him wishing that his first ingredient was a hearty dose of acetylsalicylic acid. Occasionally putting his hands over his ears he persevered, however, and soon the basic outlines of his demonstration began to take shape. This first performance should be a defining one, he knew. The last thing he wanted to do was disappoint, lest he and his companions find themselves unceremoniously shipped back to Seremathenn. They had come too far to waste time and effort in backtracking.

"This hot-air spinner," one of the younger assistants inquired, "what it be use for?"

"Carelth," Walker informed her. Among the many gourmet Niyyuuan dishes whose constituents he had memorized during the journey from Seremathenn to Niyu, carelth was one basic foodstuff that seemed to offer excellent opportunities for customization.

"But carelth is baked, not hot spun," remarked an older male.

"Not my carelth," Walker told him firmly.

After that surprise, he had them firmly in the grasp of his gastronomic vision. They were not quite sure what he was going to do, but every one of them looked forward keenly to seeing him do it.

**6**

"Where you come from?" the tall, slender, razor-voiced official inquired.

The silvery metallic eyes of the K'eremu gazed out at the assembled, seated governmental elite of Kojn-umm. Like most uncivilized beings, they chose to gather together to eat. Well, she could do nothing about that. Anymore than she could do anything about the mortifying circumstances in which she presently found herself. Thrown together with a primitive if well-meaning biped, his smaller and slightly more developed shaggy companion, and a monstrous contradiction of a representative of another unknown world who was given to speaking in morose poeticisms, she was forced to rely on them for help in getting home. There being some doubt that even someone as gifted as herself would be able to accomplish that feat on her own, she

had resigned herself to an inescapable sequence of successive demean-
ings—such as the one she was being compelled to suffer presently.

As the simple but earnest human Walker had warned her, "Please,
please, try and be polite to these people tonight, Sque. We've got to have
their help if we're going to get any closer to home than Niyu."

So she adjusted her own flashy accoutrements, eyed the lean, exceedingly lavishly dressed male Niyyuu, and replied, "My world, whose
comforting clouds and dampness and isolation I long for more and
more each day, is called K'erem." Two tendrils rose. "It lies some distance farther out in the swarm of stars that is, hopefully, this galactic
arm. My companions and I have come to Niyu in the hope that it has
brought us nearer K'erem and their own homeworlds. Whether that is
the case we do not yet know. In the meantime, we are reliant upon your
good nature and hospitality, twin traits that are the hallmark of the most
basic civilization."

It was a longer reply than the questioner had expected, but it appeared to satisfy him. The other eminent Niyyuu in the room seemed
equally content with the K'eremu's response, though one or two bridled slightly at the implication their civilization might somehow be
classified as "basic."

Still, Walker decided as he and his Niyyuuan assistants continued to
prepare the equipment and ingredients for his effort, for Sque the reply could be counted as exceedingly diplomatic. He tensed slightly
when he heard someone among the assembled follow the first question
with, "I was told you supposedly very smart species. Do something to
impress us with you intelligence."

A silence followed. George muttered, "Uh-oh—I'd better get out
there and start charming the locals," and rushed out to mix with the
crowd of Niyyuuan notables. Off to one side, Braouk prepared to lum-
ber forward and launch into his chosen recitation for the evening, a
personally abridged version of *The Heroic Narrative of Darak-Dun the Third* and
how he crossed the Jaquarianak Range alone in the dead of winter, over
which the Tuuqalian had been laboring for the past several days.

But despite his efforts, he wasn't fast enough to override Sque's
reply.

"Certainly." The K'eremu shifted her tendrils. "I will now discourse
to you upon the relative differences in cognitive aptitude between your
species and mine."

*Omigod*, Walker shouted silently. He was preparing to instruct Braouk
to physically remove Sque from her location in front of the assembled

when the K'eremu began to speak. Listening to her, some of the tension eased out of him.

"It should be clear to even the most casual observer that the tripartite conflation of neuronic axes relate oblately to the peripheral adjudication of hierarchical logic functions in any discussion. We may therefore be safe in assuming that . . ."

Walker had to assume that his implanted translator was functioning properly. If that was the case, then the K'eremu's rambling reply ought to be equally incomprehensible to the attendant Niyyuu. Glancing surreptitiously out at the assembled, he was able despite his unfamiliarity with local expressions to deduce that this was indeed the case. Initially mystified by the K'eremu's response, they quickly returned to more mundane pursuits such as chatting among themselves and sampling the gastronomic treats whose creation Walker had supervised earlier with his staff. While "hors d'oeuvres" had no direct counterpart in the Niyyuuan lexicon, the notion of eating small bits of some food before the rest was straightforward enough.

Sque did not so much conclude her tortuous response as find herself shunted aside by the massive Braouk. Incomprehensibility shaded into uncomplicated recitation as the Tuuqalian launched into his half-spoken, half-sung version of yet another ancient fable of his people. Whatever half-perceivable insults the K'eremu might have delivered were subsumed in the giant's performance.

Upon concluding her own impenetrable discourse, Sque turned to amble past the still-stressed Walker. "That ought to put them in their place," she murmured contentedly. "It is a mark of their own intelligence that no objection was raised to my extensive stating of the obvious." A bubble of satisfaction emerged from the end of her speaking tube.

"Yes, you sure showed them," Walker assured her, forbearing from pointing out that even with the aid of their own translators it was likely that not one Niyyuu on the receiving end of the K'eremu's intricate dissertation had been able to understand more than a word or two of what she had said.

Then it was time for him to go to work. Time to justify the faith Viyv-pym had placed in him and to cement the presence of himself and his friends on this first stepping-stone toward home. As his Niyyuuan assistants moved swiftly to fine-tune equipment, he took a deep breath and stepped out into public view. Wide, penetrating eyes turned to look at him as Braouk concluded the last of his entertaining but interminable recitation with a wave of all four upper tentacles. Surely, Walker mused, this audience could not be any more difficult to please than the many he had entertained on more sophisticated Seremathenn. The proof, as always, would be in how they responded to the products of his labor.

Cooking, he had already decided, was harder than brokering commodities futures, but ultimately far more satisfying.

He needn't have worried. From the time he activated and took control of the stabilizers and manipulators, the previously talkative and occasionally downright rude audience followed his every move with rapt attention.

Who would not? Who would have expected the mass of carefully prepped vegetative and protein components to align themselves not with the cooking apparatus, but in the form of an advancing army, larger ingredients in the rear, smaller scattered to front and sides like so many edible scouts? Who would have expected the various heating and toasting and mixing devices to stack themselves not in a neat, traditional horizontal line, but vertically in the shape of a toy fortress? And with cookery and menu constituents thus confronting one another, like a kid playing with a box of toy soldiers, Walker began to bring them together.

Soulless but determined vegetables assaulted waiting preparation bins, and were consumed. Protein components flung themselves through the air, to be captured by waiting cylinders. Responding only to Walker's directions, the persevering provisions found themselves diced, sliced, toasted, flash fried, waved, sautéed, puréed, and flambéed. Disdaining decorum several minutes into the presentation, someone among the spectators blurted aloud.

"It the fortress! The alien is replaying the battle of Jalar-aad-biidh— with food!"

The swelling tide of verbal appreciation rang in Walker's ears as he fought to concentrate on the work at hand. Initially at a loss as to how to make the presentation of his gastronomic creations properly entertaining, he had hit on the idea of arranging his mobile cooking equipment in the shape of the ancient fortress that guarded the traditional northern approaches to Kojn-umm, and then "attacking" it with the ingredients he had chosen for the evening's meal. At least he no longer had to worry if anyone present would realize what he was doing. Thanks to one enthusiastic spectator, everyone was now aware.

The dark tempest that swept over and brought the edible performance to a dramatic close was the capper, the punch line, to his presentation. The fact that it was composed of a swirling, raging, miniature

storm of carefully selected local spices provoked an outbreak of hooting—the Niyyuuan equivalent, he supposed, of wild applause.

Following the conclusion of his presentation, portions of the finished dishes were distributed by live Niyyuu attendants operating under Walker's instructions. He relaxed only when it became clear that the
guests appreciated the taste of his food as much as they had its highly
visual and dramatic preparation. There were compliments all around.
And when the meal began to draw to a close, he found himself swept
up in a whirl of dignitaries, all eager to thank him by stroking his head
and upper body. The Niyyuu, he already knew, were a very touchy-feely
folk. Fortunately, their complimentary and curious caresses weighed
considerably less on his person than, say, Braouk's did, so he did not
mind.

Viyv-pym also came up to him to praise his effort. Her golden eyes
were even more luminous than usual, he decided. The single piece of
material she wore draped her like chiffon that had been used to strain
flecks of gold from a running stream. Yet again he had to remind himself that, superficial aesthetics notwithstanding, it was an alien body
that stood before him.

"Tonight yous all justify my decision bring you Niyu." Touching
the side of his face, the tips of the two long fingers of her right hand
slid down to his shoulder, then his chest, before retracing their route
and withdrawing. "Already this night I am commended many times for
making that choice. Result is very good for me. Also very good for
you." Frilled head twisting around on its long, slender neck, she indicated the knot of figures that had surrounded Kinuvu-dih-vrojj, the
premier of Kojn-umm. Saluu-hir-lek, the general officer who had been
in charge of the defense of Jalar-aad-biidh, was there as well. Insofar as
Walker could interpret Niyyuuan expressions from a distance, those of
the two important officials appeared animated and content.

Then he saw that they were looking downward instead of at one
another, much less at him. Searching, Walker located the object of their
delighted attention. Between them, a small shaggy dog was standing on
its hind legs, dancing in a circle while pawing the air, tongue lolling.

George didn't need complex equipment or special skills to amuse
and entertain, a knowing Walker reflected. Not that he minded. There
were ample laurels to share this night. Abruptly, a number of insistent
dinner guests crowded close around him, anxious to meet and converse
with this alien master of gastronomy, and he lost sight of his small
friend completely.

Off to one side, Braouk lowered a single tentacle and effortlessly lifted the much smaller Sque up to a level where she could see over the heads of the milling after-dinner crowd. The K'eremu inspected the contented throng with typical condescension.

"Look at them all. A supposedly advanced species making all this fuss over something as simple as a meal."

Braouk leaped to Walker's defense. "It not simple, great skill was involved, in preparation."

"Of a basal physical sort, yes, I suppose. Still, in the final analysis, the result was only nourishment. Our mutual bipedal friend brought forth a meal, not a small sun. However, I do expect his performance will increase our standing among our hosts. That is a certainly good thing, to be desired. Contrarily, it will also increase our standing among our hosts. That is not necessarily a good thing."

Braouk's eyestalks inclined toward the K'eremu, so that one globular orb hovered on either side of her. She was indifferent to the stereo stare. "You say the same thing twice but assign a different conclusion each time. I do not understand."

"Of course you don't," the K'eremu agreed unhelpfully. "In the course of our enforced cohabitation, I have learned that subtle reflection is not a trait characteristic of your species. You are not to be blamed for this, naturally."

A deep rumble rose from the depths of the massive Tuuqalian. "Am I to be blamed if I throw you against the opposite wall?"

"I would stick," she responded, waving several tendrils. "To elaborate on what I said: It is good that friend Walker's skills are appreciated by our hosts. But I worry that he is perhaps too accomplished. It might be better if subsequent explorations into the realm of Niyyuuan food preparation are less awe-inspiring, lest he be declared a national treasure or some similar foolishness, and denied the opportunity to leave."

"Ah. I understand now." Braouk's eyes shifted, literally, away from the K'eremu he was supporting. Peering over the top of the crowd, the Tuuqalian found the human. Walker was still surrounded by admiring Niyyuu. Surely the K'eremu was only being her usual pessimistic self. Surely the Niyyuu would not become so attached to the human Walker's work that they would refuse to let him go.

Did that matter? he found himself wondering. Suppose he and Sque and the quadruped George were given the chance to move on, nearer their homeworlds, but Walker was forced to remain behind? In such circumstances, what would he do? He knew what Sque would do. Of George he was not so certain. He was even less sure of himself. The resulting potential moral dilemma pained his thoughts.

No reason for that, he told himself, since it did not yet exist. Worry about it if and when it presented itself. Meanwhile, best to participate in the evening, share in the contentment of their hosts, and leave pessimistic brooding to the small skeptic with the many limbs.

*

Yet as the days stretched into ten-days, and the ten-days into not one but several multiples, the Tuuqalian found himself reflecting more and more on what the anxious Sque had told him that night.

It was not as if their time passed in misery or boredom. Just as there had been on Seremathenn, there was much to see, do, and learn on Niyu, albeit on a less overawing level of sophistication. But the longer they remained, and the more familiar they became with the sometimes seemingly contradictory but rarely dull culture of the Niyyuu, the farther into the galactic distances the dream of returning to the fields and forests and cities of Tuuqalia seemed to recede.

One morning when feeling particularly lonely he confronted the human directly with his concerns.

Walker was alone at his console, verbally organizing and arranging the components of a custom presentation that had been ordered by a private group centered in Ehbahr. The fact that, largely through his skill and expertise, he and his friends were no longer in any way reliant on the charity of the government of Kojn-umm was a source of considerable pride to him. George was sleeping nearby, curled up on a cushion. While it was not animate in the manner of the custom-made Seremathenn rug the dog had brought with him, its semiorganic contents did rise and fall as well as change temperature automatically according to the needs of his body. Eying the small quadruped, Braouk envied it. George needed very little to satisfy him.

*Perhaps*, the Tuuqalian thought, *if only I did not have, as do so many of my kind, the soul of an artist.* He could not deny, nor did he ever try to, that like many of his people he was inclined to melancholic brooding.

Nevertheless, despite his characteristic glumness, he did his best not to inflict it on the human, who as Sque frequently pointed out, was subject to wildly vacillating and unpredictable bouts of emotion. Having something of value to contribute to their efforts to return home, Braouk had observed, had noticeably improved the human's disposition.

"I offer greetings, on this fine midday, my friend."

Walker nearly jumped out of the narrow Niyyuuan chair, whose rail-thin support he had improved by adding a wide cushion of his own design. "Dammit, Braouk! Do you have to sneak up on people like that?" He eased himself back onto his seat. "I'm always amazed that someone your size can move around with so little noise. I'm afraid you're going to amaze me once too often."

"Apologies." Eyestalks inclining down and forward, one orb peered over each of the human's shoulders. "How go the preparations for your next culinary extravaganza?"

"Pretty good. There are some new fresh fruits just arrived from Dmeruu-eeb, the realm that borders Kojn-umm to the south, and I'm thinking of doing something tropical and sunshiny with them."

Braouk was not certain precisely what the human's explanation signified, but it did not matter. His interest of the moment was not on food. "Marc, I am no less beholden to you for the merit your skills have gained for us among our hosts the Niyyuu than are George or Sque."

"You're welcome." Walker murmured the response without turning away from his intent study of images of food and equipment that floated in the air before him.

"But we have been here for some goodly time now, and we are no closer to continuing on our way homeward than when we arrived."

That made Walker turn away from his work. Behind him, images of foodstuffs and cooking gear hovered patiently in the air, awaiting his attention.

"That's not really true, Braouk." In their time together Walker had learned to focus on one Tuuqalian eye and ignore the other when they were being held far apart, as now. "We've secured the goodwill of our hosts and have successfully established ourselves in their society."

"Our goal though, I must remind you, is leaving. Our aim is to move onward from this place, not to set up a home meadow or become infatuated with the local culture."

Walker glanced to his left. George had raised his head from his pillow. "The hulk is right, Marc. I've been thinking the same thing: that we're getting a little too comfortable here. Maybe that's just what our good friends the Niyyuu want." The dog's eyes narrowed. "Maybe you ought to spend a little more time looking for a way off this ball of dirt instead of drooling over the alien sylph you can't have anyway."

Walker stiffened. "I don't know what you're talking about, George."

The dog let his head flump back down on the cushion. "Uh-huh. And some of my best friends are cats that spray in my face."

Braouk's eyestalks moved uncertainly. "What is George talking about?"

"Nothing," Walker replied irritably. "He considers himself an expert on the behavior of everyone but himself."

"Speaking of butts—" the dog began. Walker cut him off.

"I'm doing all that I can, Braouk. Every time I meet with a government official I mention that we'd like to speak to some astronomics specialists. Appointments are being set up, but nothing's come of them yet. You know how the Niyyuu like their protocol."

"They like your cooking," George interjected curtly. "And they don't want to lose it."

Walker turned on his friend. "Come on, George. You're not implying that the government is deliberately keeping us from meeting with those people?"

The dog stood up on the cushion. His tail was not wagging. "You're right. I'm not implying it. I'm stating it. Think about it, Marc. We've been here how long? You and I and Braouk and Sque have initiated how many formal requests? What is there to keep local astronomics experts so busy? It's not like the stars and nebulae that form the basis of their usual study are going to take a hike any time soon."

Walker looked away, muttering, "I don't believe it. The Niyyuu aren't like that. They've been nothing if not helpful and courteous."

George's dog-logic was relentless. "Except when it comes to that one thing, that one particular request." He glanced up at the looming mass of the Tuuqalian. "What about you, Braouk? Don't you think it's funny that the one kind of Niyyuuan specialists we can't seem to make the acquaintance of are involved in astronomy?"

"It does seem odd." A massive tentacle gently nudged Walker, pushing him back only a step or two. "We are all reasoning beings here, Marcus Walker. Does this avoidance, of one scientific type, seem deliberate?"

"One way to find out." George growled softly at Walker. "Invite a whole slew of 'em to one of your special presentations. That'll put your alien she-lollipop and her friends on the spot. They can't claim *every* astronautics expert in this part of Niyu is swamped with work or out of the realm at the same time."

Walker considered. There was nothing wrong with the dog's idea. And it might settle the argument, one way or the other, once and for all.

"I'll do it." He sat back down at his console. "I'll put the request to Abrid-lon personally."

※

George was initially subdued when that official readily agreed to Walker's request to organize such a meal. The dog further had to eat his words when, one ten-day later, the event actually took place. Prepared for the main scientific society of all Kojn-umm, the event was not overlooked by the avaricious local media, so there could be no claim that researchers and workers in specific specialties failed to be made aware of it.

Among the delighted attendees were more than a dozen specialists in the fields of general astronomy and astronautics. The latter included officers of Niyyuuan starships, prominent among whom were the commander and assistant commander of the very ship that had brought Walker and his friends to Niyu from Seremathenn. Certainly those in attendance were reflective of those Niyyuu with the most wide-ranging knowledge of this corner of the galaxy.

But as George wandered casually through the attentive, seated group of scientists and researchers—Sque being deemed too acerbic and Braouk too intimidating to assure suitably uninhibited responses— he was met by one denial or evasion after another.

"Nobody knows nothing—or will admit to it." The dog's disappointment as he reported to his companions following the conclusion of the performance and meal was plain to see.

"Are you certain you put forth the queries properly?" The continuous movement of Sque's tendrils revealed her agitation.

George eyed her sharply. "I asked them as we rehearsed them. 'Have you ever had contact with any of the following worlds?' I'd say, and then name each of ours in turn. The response was always negative. 'Have you ever had contact with anyone else, of any intelligent species, that might possibly have had contact with any of the three worlds in question?' Same reaction. 'Prior to this evening, have any of you ever encountered representatives of any sentient species matching our descriptions, or encountered others who might have done so?' More of the same. None of them, or at least none of those present here tonight, have ever heard of humans and their Earth, Tuuqalians and their world, K'eremu and K'erem." He shifted his feet, his tail moving slowly.

"I asked if there might be other, more knowledgeable astronomers or galactic travelers elsewhere on Niyu who might be better informed on such matters. I was told that while the independent realms of Niyu engage in healthy intergovernmental conflict where matters of culture and commerce are concerned, when it comes to dealing with the rest of galactic civilization they act as one. Furthermore, science is as advanced here in Kojn-umm as anywhere on Niyu, as evidenced by the expedition to Seremathenn that brought us here."

"A reasonable assertion," the thoughtful Sque declared somberly, "that in lieu of further evidence I see no reason to dispute."

The dog moved closer to the K'eremu—close enough to reach out with a paw and touch the slightly swelling, slick maroon skin. "That's not what disturbs me, though. It was the lack of curiosity." Backing off, he eyed his three companions meaningfully. "You'd think that a bunch of supposedly inquisitive scientific types would be more than casually interested in four previously unencountered intelligences claiming to hail from three utterly unknown worlds. But whenever I found a chance to push the matter with an individual, every one of them without exception seemed more interested in changing the subject, or talking about Marc's food presentation, or the latest fighting at Jalar-aad-biidh, than in wondering about what part of the galactic arm we might have sprung from." He cocked his head slightly to one side. "Strikes me as mighty peculiar."

"Most assuredly unscientific in spirit," an intrigued Sque readily agreed. "As if those to whom you spoke sought to deliberately avoid pursuing the subject."

Braouk was openly bewildered. "But why avoid, a subject of interest, to all?"

"Maybe," George suggested, squinting beneath shaggy brows, "because they were told to."

The Tuuqalian's bemusement only deepened. Both eyes, which together were nearly as large as George himself, inclined downward on their stalks to regard the dog. "Are you suggesting, that such avowed ignorance, was deliberate?"

"All I'm saying," George responded as he turned to leave, "is that for a bunch of sentients whose business it is to ask questions in the pursuit of the furtherance of knowledge, they were a mighty closemouthed bunch."

"Why wouldn't they be interested in trying to find out where we all come from?" Walker wondered aloud.

"Maybe," George added over a shoulder as he trotted away, "because someone is worried that if we find that out, we'll want to go back there."

The three companions were left to stare at the dog's metronomic tail until it vanished out of sight around a corner. It was silent for a long minute before Walker finally spoke up.

"Surely," he murmured uneasily, "I'm not *that* good a cook."

"Novelties," Sque muttered through her slender, weaving speaking tube. "We are all of us novelties." Steel-gray eyes regarded him expres-

THE LIGHT-YEARS BENEATH MY FEET          289

sively. "Possessed of no intrinsic value, such as precious metals or gems, a novelty's worth is determined solely by those for whom it has applied value. It may be that your small smelly friend demonstrates true insight. Certainly it cannot be denied that our constant requests have been met with apathy, if not outright unconcern. Tonight's continuance of that condition suggests nothing less than a deliberate policy."

Walker shook his head slowly. "I can't believe that the Niyyuu intend to keep us from leaving here."

"Nothing is preventing us from leaving here," Sque pointed out as she too turned to retire to her own quarters. "There is simply no help forthcoming in assisting us in determining which way to go when we do leave. And without direction, there is no point in going. One might as well spin on one's appendages until dizzy and scuttle off in any random direction. In deep space, that would be suicidal. The withholding of information is not the same as the withholding of a physicality, but the result is the same."

The departure of the K'eremu left Walker alone with Braouk. After a moment the Tuuqalian too moved to withdraw to his chamber. "It's worth thinking, about what's been said, here tonight. Indifference is not hostility—but not friendship, either."

"What can we do about it?" Walker wondered aloud as he watched the massive Tuuqalian shuffle off toward the exit.

Both eyes curled back on their stalks to look at him. "Why not ask your good friend Viyv-pym?"

Was there a hidden suggestiveness in the Tuuqalian's question? Nonsense, Walker told himself. It was a good idea. The only trouble was, he had on more than one occasion pressed Viyv-pym about the lack of response to their requests, only to receive evasive, noncommittal answers similar to those received by George tonight. That in itself was suggestive.

And not at all reassuring.

✳

"A fraction of you evening-time, might I have?"

His companions having departed, Walker had remained behind to check and ensure that the last of the equipment that had been cleaned by his assistants had been properly deactivated for storage. Thinking himself alone in the empty Niyyuuan durbar hall, he was surprised to find himself confronting a single female.

She was notably shorter than the average Niyyuuan; no taller than himself, and for one of her kind, verging on stout. Her crest was fully erected and flaring a dark blue—taken together with the constant fluttering of her tails, a sure sign of anxiety. In attire she was, again by Niyyuuan standards, conservative, her body wrap consisting of a single yellow- and white-striped satiny material. But her eyes, like those of all Niyyuu, were large and luminous as those of any lemur, and her voice as raspy as that of a lathe shaping wrought iron.

"I am Sobj-oes. I am senior instructor in distant astronautics and vector navigation not only for Kojn-umm, but a consultant for four other realms as well." A two-fingered hand moved to touch his shoulder. By now wholly familiar with the intimate form of greeting, he did not flinch.

"You enjoyed the presentation, I take it?" he asked her, not knowing what else to say.

"Very much so's." She looked around, high, limber ears working. They were alone. "Yous wish go home."

Keeping his voice level, he tried not to look or sound anxious, even assuming she could recognize the meaning of such subtle changes in tone or personal appearance. "That would be a valid assumption, as my friend Sequi'aranaqua'na'senemu would say. But in order to continue our journey from here, from Niyu, we need the assistance of others. To help point the way. Others such as, perhaps, yourself."

Her free hand made a gesture he recognized as an encouraging response. "Yous sentient creatures, not all so very different from Niyyuu. Appearance means nothing." The two fingers of her left hand gently stroked the side of her elongated skull. "What is here is everything.

"I am one of those who was made aware of yous' request, to try locate your homeworlds. This is very difficult business. Even one arm of galaxy is immensity personified. Thousands upon thousands of star systems."

"Astronautics are developed on all of our worlds, so my friends and I are aware of that. All we have is hope, and that others might help. That's all we've been asking of the government of Kojn-umm, and the worldwide organizations that link the Niyyuu together on matters such as science. To date, we have had no response."

Once more his visitor glanced around. With her expansive oculars, it did not require her to turn her head very far to do so. "Yous' query *was* passed along. But with accompanying admonition."

Walker frowned. "What sort of admonition?"

"To conduct search for yous' homeworlds, in line with yous' request. But not to displace other work to do so, also not to make priority."

"I see." He considered carefully. From his years in the business of commodities trading, Walker was intimately familiar with the subtleties of bureaucratic obfuscation—with the ability to seem to say one thing while really meaning another. "Would you say that your 'admonition' might be interpreted to mean an order to go slow in the search for the homeworlds of my friends and I?"

Her right hand lightly touched his chest. "Many interpretations of meaning are possible. That could be one."

"But why?"

She looked away, embarrassed without having any reason to be. "Yous four all unique individuals. No others like you on Niyu, ever. No others like you on Seremathenn, or anywhere else scientific establishment can determine. Your presence here a special thing for Niyu. Extraspecial for Kojn-umm. Pride involved. Pride and logic frequently mutually exclusive occurrences. Besides, you extraordinary food preparator."

He nodded slowly, murmuring to himself, "So George was right. The authorities want to keep us here."

"Not necessarily prevent from leaving," she corrected him. "More akin to not be overly helpful in assisting departure. Difference is political."

"But the result is the same," he muttered. "If the government won't help us, then we're stuck here."

"Not government, no." Her voice softened from the intensely grating to the merely irritating. "Are one or two sympathetic individuals among my colleagues. Must be careful in such work. All afraid, if displease superiors, of losing official position. Few willing take such risking on behalf of strange aliens."

He lowered his own voice. "But you will," he guessed expectantly.

Another gesture he recognized—this one signifying accord. "Is also one other. Famous researcher, much revered by public as well as colleagues. But not untouchable. Must work clandestine, he and I. Have taken what information on yous has been made available by government. In free time, away from official projects, are searching the vastness for transmission samplings of all yous: visuals, language snippets, references by other species not yous but knowing of yous. Maybe, with much lucks, come across something." She eyed him questioningly. "You can suggest preference in area for searching?"

He mulled her query. His companions had long since departed for their own quarters. Alone with the astronomer, it would have been easy for him to instruct her and her distinguished colleague to limit their searching for signs of human life only, to look first for Earth. The sarcastic Sque and the lumbering Braouk could wait their turn.

But what if K'erem or Tuuqalia lay nearby, within easier detection range of Niyyuuan instruments? Could he deny that access, that chance, to people who had gone through the hell of Vilenjji capture and captivity with him? And they were his friends, even if one had a mouth that sometimes seemed bigger than her whole body and the other tended to bore to distraction when he wasn't threatening to accidentally crush anything and anyone who happened to come too close to him. As for George, he knew what the dog would say.

But it wasn't what he chose to say.

"No. No preferences. Whichever of our respective homeworlds whose position you can establish, that will be great. K'erem, Tuuqalia, Earth: locate one and we'll manage a way to get there. Then we'll worry about finding the others."

She indicated her understanding. "I hope we can help yous. Is not right be kept so long and so far from one's own kind when that gap can be spanned. Of course, certain is, the very good chance in attempting search such an immense area that we will not be able locate any of yous' homeworlds."

Extending a hand and keeping his touch as light as possible, he let it stroke her right shoulder in the accepted Niyyuuan manner. "It's enough that someone is trying to help. That you're looking."

She gestured one last time before turning to go. "Niyu not such a bad place. Maybe not Seremathenn, but good air, good food, good people. If search never find anything, yous always have respected life-positions here. Meantimes, keep cheerful." Lengthening her flowing stride, she left him standing among his equipment, watching her distinctive slight sway as she exited the room.

She was right. Despite the constant undercurrent of devious political and cultural machinations, Niyu offered him and his friends a comfortable life and lifestyle.

But no matter how one sliced it, it was a long, long way from Chicago.

7

He was not aware of any outward change in his mood or appearance subsequent to his clandestine meeting with the kindhearted astronomer, but evidently something about either or both struck Viyv-pym forcefully enough to comment on it. It was several ten-days after his surreptitious encounter. Viyv-pym was meeting with him in his quarters to discuss the final details of an elaborate banquet that was being prepared for an interrealm guild of computation engineers, at which his performance was to be the star attraction.

Bending her head slightly to avoid the assembling components that drifted in the air before them both, she tried to meet his gaze. "Something troubles you, friend Marc. It not new. I have been noticing for some time now. Will you not share with me?"

So preoccupied and depressed was he at the moment that her proximity failed to stir within him the usual basket of confused emotions he always felt in her presence. "It's nothing. Forget it." Sighing softly, he looked up at the integrants that patiently awaited his attention and did his best to feign interest in the proceedings. "Let's get back to work."

"No." Reaching out with a long, limber arm, she waved her hand through the hovering holos. They obediently dispersed.

Now he did turn to her. "What did you do that for? It's all saved, but now we'll have to reconstitute before we can finalize."

"Too much works you, maybe, I thinks. You need a change."

He could no longer look at her without wondering how deeply she was involved with or how much she was aware of her government's intention to keep him and his friends restricted to Niyu for as long as possible. He had become very adept at concealing such feelings.

"I'm open to a change," he replied indifferently. Work or a change, it was all the same to him. Both were relentlessly, inescapably Niyyuuan.

Ennui notwithstanding, the comment she offered in response did succeed in surprising him. "There many prominent Niyyuu who admire you work. Prominent among them is Saluu-hir-lek."

Walker shrugged carelessly. "Don't recognize the name." Other than those Niyyuu he worked with, such as Viyv-pym and his own performance assistants, he had not paid much attention to individuals among their hosts. He had met too many to remember them all.

"He attend you first important recital. Saluu-hir-lek is traditional military commander for Kojn-umm, defender of the realm, leader of conventional defense of Jalar-aad-biidh."

"Very nice for him. What has it to do with me?"

"He wants meet you." She was watching him closely, he saw.

"I'm happy to meet with any Niyyuu who appreciates my work," he replied expansively. "When would he like to get together?"

She didn't hesitate. "Tomorrow would work well. I am told is at that time likely to be lull in fighting."

"Tomorrow's fine. Mind if I invite my friends along?"

"They not specifically included in invitation, but should be not problem, I think. I will make certain beforehand. You have experience in combat?"

Whup. Evidently he had missed something. Something important. She now had his full attention. "What has that got to do with me meeting this guy?"

"Battle for fortress of Jalar-aad-biidh is ongoing. Saluu-hir-lek cannot relinquish command merely to facilitate friendly visit. Therefore meeting must take place in fortress. Reaching fortress means crossing line of technological demarcation. Once cross line, any normal Niyyuu

is subsumed in rules of traditional combat. Can be captured or killed."
Seeing his alarm, she hastened to reassure him.

"Line crossing will take place under proper escort, timed for least
likelihood of combat. But when making crossing, must always go prepared. Settle you fears. I will watch over you."

He bridled instinctively at the offer. As an ex All Big Ten linebacker,
no member of the opposite sex, alien or not, was going to "watch over
him." At the same time, he was perfectly aware as the testosterone fizzed
within him that he was being stupid, that his present circumstances
hardly merited comparison with accomplishments on a football field
back home. That did not render the implications inherent in her
thoughtful offer any less potent.

"As a matter of fact," he shot back, "I do have some experience in
hand-to-hand combat, though probably not the kind you're thinking of."

"I pleased hear this. You will be equipped with authorized
weaponry." She studied his build, which was far stockier than that of
the stoutest Niyyuu. "Armor may be a problem. Perhaps by linking
several pieces together . . ." She broke off. "Not to worry. It will be
managed."

"Won't matter," he told her, "with Braouk accompanying us."

But it developed that Braouk was not interested in accompanying
them.

"I say firmly, no interest have I, in fighting," the Tuuqalian replied
when Walker explained the situation to him that night.

"It's highly unlikely you'll have to." Pacing the dining area, unable
to eat, Walker worked to cajole the big alien. "The sight of you in armor alone ought to be enough to send even the most intrepid Niyyuu
fleeing. Hell, it even makes me quake a little, and you're my friend."

Avoiding Walker's gaze, both eyes hovered close together above the
Tuuqalian's massive plate of food, their stalks nearly touching. "But if
they did not flee, I would have to defend myself. You know what, my
temper can be, once roused. I do not want to get involved in the inter-
regional disputes of our hosts, and I most certainly do not want to hurt
anybody. I'm not going with you, Marc."

"Fine. Stay here, then." He turned to Sque.

The K'eremu had swollen to half again her normal size, and her
flexible, tubular mouth was emitting bubbles like crazy. This uncontrolled laughter was sufficient to prevent Walker from even asking her
if she would be willing to accompany him. Thinking he already knew
the answer to his final appeal but nonetheless feeling compelled to

make it, he turned to George, only to be surprised yet again by another of the dog's unpredictable responses.

"Sure, I'll go up with you," his small friend declared around mouthfuls of food. "Be a chance to see something new. If there's an attack on the place while we're up there, it ought to be quite a show."

Walker hardly knew what to say. "I thought you, of all people, wouldn't want to get involved in any fighting."

The dog looked up from his meal. "Who said anything about getting involved in fighting? If your whippet of a girlfriend—"

"She's not my girlfriend," Walker snapped irritably.

"—says they're going to try their best to sneak us in, then I think it's worth a shot. Besides, we'll be crossing part of a battlefield." He smiled, showing small but sharp canines. "There's likely to be bones."

"The Niyyuu might not take kindly to the thought of an alien visitor nibbling on the remains of their kind."

Lips pulled back, the smile remained. "I hope I get the chance to find out." Sticking his face back into the server before him, he returned to his feeding.

Both Sque's laughter and body swelling having settled down, the K'eremu eyed her human companion shrewdly. "I know you too well by now, Marcus Walker. You have not accepted this invitation out of a desire simply to play tourist. Especially not with a chance of real danger, however minimized, involved. You have another rationale in mind."

He turned defensive. "Maybe."

She waved a pair of tendrils at him. "Would you care to share it with us poor unenlightened ones?"

"I'm still considering possibilities," he told her honestly. He took a deep breath. "It just occurred to me that since we're not making any headway in our efforts to engage the Niyyuuan scientific community in our efforts to progress homeward, it might prove useful to make a friend or two among the military."

"Planning to lead a revolt and take over the pound?" George challenged him.

"I don't believe the Niyyuu think like that," Walker replied.

"How do they think about such things, then?" Sque inquired thoughtfully.

Round brown eyes locked with silvery horizontal orbs. "That's one of the things I'm going to try and find out," he told her.

*

The transport that conveyed them through the bustling, modern, smoothly running city and up into the foothills of the surrounding mountain range stopped well short of the line of demarcation.

"From here we walk," Viyv-pym informed Walker and George. "As you been informed, only minor contemporary technology is allowed inside areas designated for traditional combat. Not even communicators. Communication from within is carried out by courier, in old-time manner."

What a polite method of killing one another these people have devised, Walker reflected as he exited the transport. Employing strictly defined rules and limitations, slaughter and slaying could be conducted enthusiastically, with every individual and government firmly bound by the results. Certainly it was a better way than reducing entire territories to ruin and whole populaces to penury. Pity it would never work for humankind.

As George trotted to and fro, sniffing hopefully at the corkscrewing ground cover and bizarrely shaped bushes that clung to the slight slope, Walker decided that their hostess looked even better in sword and armor than she did in her usual daily administrative attire. Tinted a dark golden hue, almost bronze, the armor covered her in linked engraved piecework from neck to feet. Her helmet sported holes to allow her tall ears to protrude easily and a ruler-sized slab to protect the flattened, narrow nasal crest while leaving the rest of her face and her enormous eyes free to scan her surroundings in as many unobstructed directions as possible.

For the ascent, they were accompanied by half a dozen similarly clad soldiers. Though all were well trained in the use of modern wave and projectile weapons, inside the restricted zone none carried anything more lethal than a rapier or throwing blade. A couple hefted loaded weapons that resembled small crossbows. In deference to the Niyyuuan's slender builds, none of the devices weighed very much.

Despite Viyv-pym's earlier assurances, it developed that none of the armor available could be made to fit Walker. He was three times as broad across the chest as the stoutest Niyyuu, and fifty pounds heavier. The "heavy broadsword" they gave him would have been hard-pressed to qualify back home as a saber in a fencing competition. Which did not matter, since what little he knew about swords, fencing, and armor was derived entirely from watching old movies on television. He could only hope that in the event of actual conflict, his natural athleticism would carry him through.

"Should not be any trouble," Viyv-pym reassured him as she adjusted her shoulder braces. "We make access from south. Toroud-eed prefer frontal attack on fortress, also careful to watch access road from west to prevent reinforcements from relieving Jalar-aad-biidh garrison. East and south are open. And forest here will provide cover."

Nodding, he followed her as the small contingent continued to climb.

He was not certain exactly when or where they crossed the line of demarcation. Only that while he struggled uphill, George was having entirely too good a time, dashing from each new growth to the next fresh smell. Walker had always done well in the sprints—but long runs defeated him. And he had never been required to run wind sprints uphill. In college, running the stadium seats was an activity that had thankfully been reserved for backs and receivers, safeties and corners.

Evening was settling in damply around them when the first soldier died. The bolt, or short arrow, caught him in the throat, in the vulnerable opening above the chest armor and below his helmet. Shouts erupted all around Walker as the air was filled with alien exclamations unimaginably harsh in tone. Giving loud and threatening lie to Viyv-pym's earlier assurances, armed Niyyuu burst from the cover of the stunted trees on both sides of the ascending party. The attackers wielded an amazing assortment of weapons, from blades that curled back upon themselves to almost form circles, to pikelike devices that terminated in barbed tips seemingly more suited to catching fish than hand-to-hand combat. They were designed, he realized quickly, for successfully striking at quarry that was nimble and fast but not especially muscular. Though tall, the ultraslim Niyyuu made difficult targets for thrusting spears and swords.

He had just enough time to also note that the attackers' armor was steel-gray instead of golden-bronze before he found himself wildly swinging his own sword in an attempt to ward off a pair of onrushing assailants.

His ferocious but histrionic swings did nothing to slow the attack, but his appearance certainly did. Expecting to confront only others of their kind, the two hard-charging Toroud-eed warriors pulled up short, clearly taken aback at the unexpectedly alien aspect of their intended target. Assailants and quarry stared at one another. One of the Toroud-eed finally took a hesitant step toward the unwieldy apparition, who after all was holding a Kojn-umm sword. A moment later his companion let out a startled yelp and turned to see a small furry alien quadruped hanging by its jaws onto his lower right leg.

A bewildering confrontation with one alien being was unsettling enough. Finding themselves attacked from the rear by a second completely different in size, shape, and appearance from the first, whose teeth for all they knew might contain enough poison to kill a dozen soldiers, the pair turned and fled as fast as their long, lean legs could carry them. Taking note of their retreat, George relaxed his grip, shook his head, spat, and trotted back to rejoin his friend. Sword dangling from one hand, a stunned Walker gaped down at him.

"I didn't know if those two were going to . . . Thanks, George. You made up their minds for them."

The dog looked around warily. Though they were standing off from where most of the fighting was taking place, he was not about to let down his guard. He'd been ambushed and attacked in too many alleys, on too many back city streets, to relax while combat raged around him.

"Too bad Braouk isn't here," he growled conversationally. "If those two were spooked by the sight of you, the appearance of our Tuuqalian friend would probably have dropped them in their tracks." He looked up, tail wagging. "You okay?" His breathing steadying, Walker nodded slowly.

"Good. Hate to lose my human." He indicated the small-scale but intense battle that was playing out nearby. "Our friends the Niyyuu don't look so civilized right now, do they?"

*You'd think an individual on the verge of having their throat cut or their torso run through by a sword would break with tradition and pull out a gun, even a small gun, if only to save their own life,* Walker mused as he watched the fighting. But nothing of the sort happened. Despite the ready presence of advanced weapons in the city and on the ship that had brought him and his companions from Seremathenn to Niyu, not one of the combatants raging through the forest produced so much as a canister of pepper spray in their own desperate defense.

The Kojn-umm did not kill all of the attackers, but they slew or disabled enough of them to compel the survivors to beat a frustrated retreat. A moment later Viyv-pym was at his side, the two fingers of her left hand wrapping around his arm, urging him upward.

"Quickly now, friend Marc! Those who took flight may have others station nearby. Surprise at yous' presence will not stop them kill or capture you if they come back."

Badly winded, he was immensely grateful to discover that they were not all that far from the top of the ridge. The forest had hidden the inward-sloping outer walls of Jalar-aad-biidh from the climbers' sight. Moments later, anxious Kojn-umm fighters from within the fortress were escorting the survivors of the ambush into the safety of the sturdy ramparts.

Though exhausted, Walker had suffered damage only to his pride. Stunned by the swiftness of the unexpected attack, after the first confusing moments he had pretty much stood by while Viyv-pym and her comrades had fought off the assault. Safe and secure now, he had time to reflect more systematically on the events that had taken place and on his reaction to them. Or rather, his nonreaction. Though Viyv-pym and her comrades had expected nothing of him, he peered inward and found himself wanting. Hell, even George had drawn blood.

When he offered apologies for his lack of assistance, neither Viyv-pym nor any of her fellow soldiers appeared upset at his lack of participation. "After all," she told him without a hint of insincerity, "it our job protect you, not other way around. You not trained in our ways of fighting." She caressed his arm. "You cook."

It was the most hurtful thing anyone had said to him since the day he had been abducted by the Vilenjji.

He determined then and there to rectify at the first opportunity his ignorance of swordsmanship and Niyyuuan military training. Such schooling would have to come later, he knew. He had not been escorted to Jalar-aad-biidh to learn swordplay. Also, his own private reason for agreeing to make the dangerous visit in the first place came back to him. He had not made the trip to learn better how to survive on Niyu, but to seek possible assistance in getting off it.

While Walker's escort exchanged excited banter with the defenders of the fortress who had swarmed out to greet them, Viyv-pym escorted him and George deeper into the complex. Though constructed of humble native stone and other simple, natural materials, the rock walls appeared solid and inviolate. As far as he could tell, they did not make use of steel rebars or any high-tech galactic-standard reinforcing materials. To have done so would have constituted a violation of accepted Niyyuu standards for traditional combat, which extended to the construction and maintenance of physical defenses as well as individual weaponry.

"A bit more excitement than I thought we would see." Striding fluidly alongside him, her armor scratched and dented by the blows of the enemy, it was hard for Walker to see Viyv-pym as the same graceful, sophisticated governmental delegate he had first encountered at the elegant reception on Seremathenn. "I glad yous both unharmed."

"We's both glad, too," declared George genially as he trotted along beside Walker. "I only like to play at being dead, thanks."

Negotiating the twists and turns of the inner fortress, it was hard to believe that just outside and beyond the ridgetop redoubt lay a sprawling modern city steeped in technology sufficiently advanced to make any place on Earth look like a mud-wattle village in comparison. The dissimilarity was startling, but not absolute. The inhabitants of the fortress did not stumble about in rags and primitive attire, and the prohibition against the use of modern technology apparently extended only to those elements that could be utilized in warfare. There was ample evidence that modern methods of dealing with hygiene were in use, while the media broadcasters who relayed scenes of the fighting around the planet did so with all the advanced gear that could be put at their disposal. Walker queried Viyv-pym on the seeming latter inconsistency.

"What's to prevent one of these reporters," he asked as a pair of them, draped in the electronic elements of their profession, strode past, "from relaying on-the-spot information to a local commander in the field?"

"Is true such temptation is great," Viyv-pym admitted. "Especially when one side losing badly. But detection not difficult. If what you say attempted and found out, penalties are very severe. Individuals involved sacrifice their position and never find such work again. Are banned for life from such work anywhere on all of Niyu. Also, big communications company responsible lose its right to broadcast all future conflicts. Ratings—" (yet again Walker found himself praising the efficacy of the Vilenjji implant, which could even convey the meaning of local colloquialisms) "—too important to big companies to risk breaking of regulations for temporary gain—even to save lives of soldiers. Everyone on Niyu follows and watches such conflicts. Much in politics is decided by these traditional battles, yet only volunteer military suffers injury. Rest of world goes about daily business in peace and security."

War as politics, and both as entertainment. Was it all so very dissimilar from home? he found himself wondering. Or were the basics the same and only the rules different? He envisioned an imaginary Niyyuuan newspaper, divided into the usual sections: World, Local, Business. The only question was, would you allot war its own section, or file it under Entertainment? Or possibly, Sports? Perhaps the National Hockey League. Rome under the Caesars would have known how to handle and classify it.

He did not remember his previous meeting with General Saluu-hirlek. During that first outrageous, frenetic night when he had performed for local luminaries, he had been introduced to a veritable blizzard of alien faces. George did not remember Kojn-umm's most prominent military personality either. The only faces the dog recalled were those he had been placed in close proximity to, during those moments when he had been picked up and cuddled by enchanted locals. Neither man nor dog knew what to expect.

As it turned out, neither the general nor the room into which they found themselves ushered matched their preconceptions. Despite the alienesque medieval surroundings, there was no throne, and certainly no throne room. Saluu-hir-lek operated out of an office that was quiet, unadorned, and businesslike. Charts and maps, all of them appropriately primitive and two-dimensional, filled the walls and covered several desks. None of the fortress commander's subordinates paused in their work when the trio was admitted, though a few did glance up to steal a quick look. Walker wondered if these were directed at him, George, or their striking female escort.

Rising from behind his desk, Saluu-hir-lek picked up the external translator he had ordered and made sure it was functioning. In response to Walker's question, Viyv-pym explained, "The device has no indigenous military application and is therefore permitted."

"Like flush toilets," George pointed out tactlessly.

Still fiddling with the device, though it was largely automatic, Saluu-hir-lek greeted them effusively, reserving particular acclaim for Walker.

"Ah, the famous small-ear food presenter!" The general glanced downward. "And his irrepressibly cuddly companion." George made a rude noise that was not translatable. "It wonderful see you again. I am pleased to be yous guide and interpreter this aspect of Niyyuuan culture."

The general was much smaller than the average Niyyuu, Walker noted, though far from Napoleonic in stature. Alien and human regarded each other eye to eye. Other than being half a foot shorter than Viyv-pym or the other officers in the strategy room, and noticeably older, Saluu-hir-lek was little different in appearance from the majority of Niyyuu Walker and George had previously encountered. His uniform consisted of a simple brown tunic and the long, wide shoes favored by his kind. Only the three emblems heat-sealed to the center of his shirt indicated his rank. Whether this sartorial simplicity was a reflection of the individual himself or standard-issue attire for general officers Walker did not know.

"I great admirer of you work," the general was saying as Walker studied him. "Never seen such skill. But of course, you learn on Seremathenn." His voice took on the Niyyuuan equivalent of a bittersweet tone, the round mouth contracting. "Someday I like very much visit Seremathenn. But always duty to Kojn-umm calls. Whenever Toroud-eed or Faalaur-oor make trouble, responsible sources come deliver to me their insistence. 'Take command of forces, Saluu-hir-lek! Protect us from evil! Save us from attack!' " One twin-digited hand waved diffidently. "Protect commercial contracts, they mean. Traditional warring is for obtain business advantage, or water port, or favorable trade terms. I understand such local foolishnesses no longer apply on more advanced worlds."

"That's not always the case," Walker told him, thinking of Earth. "Sometimes a culture's technology far outpaces its social development." He indicated their surroundings. "I think the Niyyuu have made an interesting accommodation with their traditional way of settling disputes between neighbors."

"It is kind of you say so. Kind of you think such of Niyu, when you find yourself so far and so lost from your own world."

Sympathy from a general. Well, Walker would take it where he could get it. It boded well for his original rationale in agreeing to this visit. Idly, he wondered how much pull Saluu-hir-lek might wield in the same local corridors of power that wished to keep him and his friends resident on Niyu.

The general gestured toward the doorway through which they had just entered. "Would you like to see some more of fortress of Jalar-aad-biidh? It has served as gateway and protector of capital for many thousand-days."

Why not? Walker thought. "That would be very nice." Near his feet, George nodded assent. The dog was less interested in a tour of traditional alien military fortifications than he was in fresh air. The war room had no windows.

"Excellent!" Saluu-hir-lek moved to lead them. "There small battle for main gate going on right now. Hope is not inconveniencing for you."

Before Walker could raise question or objection, the general was showing them the way out the door, leaving neither time nor discreet opportunity for the human to object.

**8**

B ound together and launched by some unseen and unfamiliar alien mechanism, the three sharpened shafts spun around a central axis as they flew toward him—the spinning, barbed points clearly designed to do maximum damage to anyone they struck. Walker ducked behind shielding stone as they whizzed past to shatter themselves against the wall behind him in a spray of broken metal tips and splintered wooden shafts. All around him was shouting, screaming, and the "nails scraping on blackboards" Niyyuuan equivalent of bloodthirsty cries. Given the inherent raspiness of the native speaking voice, the latter made up in ear-grating harshness what they occasionally lacked in volume.

Huddled at the base of the stone rampart and Walker's feet, George glanced up sullenly. "So much for having a quiet meeting and making polite inquiries."

"Just stay down," Walker advised him. "You'll be fine."

"Sure. Unless the fortress is overrun. Then I'll be fine barbeque."

"What makes you think any local with any sense would try eating something as alien-looking as you?"

The dog turned his face to the wall. "I can't imagine why that thought doesn't make me feel completely secure. Incidentally, you might give it a tumble yourself."

It had not occurred to Walker that the assaulters of Jalar-aad-biidh might regard him as a fit subject for nibbling. As a newly skilled cook, he was not used to regarding himself as a potential cookee. While Saluu-hir-lek—displaying commendable, or foolish, disregard for his own personal safety—rallied his forces, Viyv-pym leaned against Walker to reassure him.

"That arthret that just miss you was an aberration, a lucky launching. See?" She tugged gently on his arm. Not wanting to appear fainthearted in her company, he allowed himself to be pulled forward for a better view.

The panorama spread out before him very much resembled paintings he had seen of ancient medieval battles. The participants were alien, their accoutrements foreign, and the design and layout of the fortress itself different in a number of aspects from what humans would have constructed, but hand-to-hand fighting was fairly similar regardless of body size, shape, and the number of digits on weapons-wielding hands.

He was struck once again by the slenderness of both the combatants and their weapons. The tall, slim Niyyuu swung or stabbed with spears, pikes, and narrow-bladed swords. There was nary a battle-axe or mace in sight. Absent the need to protect barrel-chested warriors, shields were similarly slim and lightweight. Unexpectedly, he almost laughed. In spite of the fact that blood was being spilled in copious quantity, assorted body parts were being carved from torsos, and individuals were dying, the crowded battlefield that spread out in front of the fortress's outer wall appeared populated by clashing armies of heavily armed, heavily armored, high-couture models. Despite the very real death and destruction, a part of him couldn't help thinking *Vogue/Cosmo* rather than *Soldier of Fortune*.

That somewhat risible image vanished instantly when a sling-boosted short spear went right through the neck of a bolt-firing Kojn-umm soldier standing atop an elevated platform off to Walker's left. Dropping her weapon, the female warrior grabbed reflexively at the protruding shaft of the lance as she toppled over and plunged into the swirling throng of fighters below. No more laughter bubbled up in Walker's throat.

Saluu-hir-lek remained in the thick of the fighting: ranging back and forth along the wall, urging on his soldiers, altering defensive strategy in response to shifts in the enemy's plan of attack, shouting commands, all the while doing serious damage with his own sword. Walker could see why the general was lionized by Kojn-umm society. Whether it was tactically wise for him to place himself in such danger was not a matter for visitors to question. Walker hoped the general would survive the battle. While other Niyyuu had been of little help to him and his friends in their quest to get home, dead ones would be of no use whatsoever.

Bobbing up and down in the midst of the ferocious skirmishing like so many electronic imps were representatives of the media from both Kojn-umm and Toroud-eed. They were easily recognizable by their bright orange attire and the fact that they wielded recording and broadcasting equipment, not armor and weapons. Amazingly, they moved with ease among the combatants, who largely ignored their presence.

Walker pointed out the nearest. "Surely the media must suffer the occasional casualty. A stray spear, or short bolt?"

Today painted half blue and half crimson, Viyv-pym's mouth expanded as if she was simultaneously shocked and amused by the notion. "Only rarely. At such times, they become news themselves. No soldier wants injure correspondent. Is bad for career. Soldiers want be interviewed. Good for career. Injured correspondents cannot conduct interviews."

Made sense, Walker knew. A warrior, or an entire army, would not want to be on the receiving end of the unfavorable press the maiming or killing of a correspondent would bring. Mindful of the ramifications, he pressed her further.

"The battlefield reporting—is it honest? I mean, is it straightforward? No picking and choosing of scenes for propaganda purposes?"

"Oh, no," she insisted. "Citizens want, citizens need, to see everything. Good and the bad." She indicated another pair of orange-clad figures moving effortlessly among the combatants. "Communications facilities of Kojn-umm and Toroud-eed share field pickups of both sides. Also others present, reporting back to realms not involved in fighting."

Once again, the sports analogy reared its bloody head. Was there a special global media feed for all of Niyu? The round-the-clock, "all war all the time" channel? Sadly, he realized such an innovation was also possible on Earth.

The fighting was beginning to wind down. "What happens if the Toroudians win? If they were to overrun and take the fortress?" Given what he had already learned about the conventions of Niyyuuan combat, somehow he did not think such a result would result in widespread rapine and looting.

He was right. "Since Jalar-aad-biidh defends capital city," she told him, "Kojn-umm would have to formally surrender to Toroud-eed. In such unlikely happenstances, Kojn-umm would probably pay compensation—indemnity—to victors. Possibly also trade concessions. In extreme case, loss of territory."

"What about a triumphant Toroud-eed taking over your realm completely?"

"It happens, but such a thing is rare in our history." Watching her watching the fighting, Walker could sense that she would rather have been down on the battlefield swinging a sword instead of watching from the comparative safety of the high battlements nursemaiding an alien chef and his small companion.

The latter looked up from where he had squeezed himself into as small and protected a place as possible. "What's to keep a few realms from taking over everybody else and controlling the whole planet?"

Viyv-pym peered down at the dog. "If one realm get too big, too powerful, is inevitably attacked by allied forces of many others and so reduced in size and strength." She spoke with considerable conviction, Walker noted. "That also happens—and is also rare in our history." One long, willowy arm rose to point over the wall. "Not happen here, this day. See!"

The campaign was beginning to slacken as the forces of Toroud-eed, fought to a stalemate if not actually defeated, began to retreat. Their siege engines having failed to breach Jalar-aad-biidh's massive outer stone wall and their swarms of attacking soldiers having been repeatedly forced from its ramparts, they started to pull back. Given the ferocity of the fighting he had witnessed, Walker was surprised as he surveyed the field of battle that it was not littered more profusely with dead bodies. Perhaps, he decided, the Niyyuu cultural dichotomy of war allowed for the application of modern medicine to the wounded. He made a mental note to ask Viyv-pym about it later. Meanwhile, he fought to compose suitable congratulations for the general who was now striding toward them.

Saluu-hir-lek's armor was dented as if he had been run over by a large vehicle, and it was actually cut clear through at one leg. But the general himself appeared to be physically uninjured. His round mouth was expanded to its maximum diameter, while his huge eyes shone with an inner glow. Quadruple tails switched sharply back and forth, and blood stained him from head to toe.

"That should slow them, those effing offspring of Eed!"

Persuaded that the fighting was done with, George rose from where he had been lying. "You mean, they won't attack again?"

Saluu-hir-lek turned to peer over the ramparts and follow the attackers' retreat. "Too soon say for certain. Have better idea tomorrow, when scouts make morning report on enemy disposition. Disposition of forces, disposition of mind!" The general was in a very good mood indeed.

An excellent time, Walker felt, to hit him up for support.

"Come!" Lightly dragging a bloodstained finger down Walker's chest in friendly Niyyuuan fashion, Saluu-hir-lek bade his visitor accompany him. "I must clean up for presentation tonight. Then we talk more." From within the lightweight but sturdy helmet, vast yellow-gold eyes regarded the human. "Maybe I can persuade you cook for me and my staff."

"Kind of short notice, but it might be arranged," a thoughtful Walker told him. "When someone is in a position to provide a special service to a friend, it's always nice to be able to help out."

Any secondary meaning inherent in Walker's response flashed right past the general. Perhaps their respective translators had mangled the verbalization. But from what he had seen of Saluu-hir-lek, Walker was sure the general would remember it.

*

There wasn't much to work with. While the great fortress of Jalar-aad-biidh was amply stocked for war and for the fulfillment of the basic needs of its defenders, there was a decided dearth of advanced, non-essential material. Even its commanding officer had limited access to luxury goods. Walker was relieved to discover that the food preparation equipment, like the medical facilities, was apparently exempt from the cultural restrictions that were placed on any modern technology related to combat requirements.

In concise terms, what that meant was that he had the apparatus with which to exercise his gastronomic skills. Though raw material was lacking, he took its absence as a challenge. The eventual results showed off his innate creativity and talent in ways that swapping raw rubber futures on the Chicago Exchange could not have come close to duplicating.

Certainly Saluu-hir-lek and his staff were more than pleased, if not outright overwhelmed. Following the dramatic culinary presentation and the expansive meal that was its outcome, the general once again invited George and Walker outside. This time they found themselves higher up than before. To the right, the private balcony overlooked the distant, rambling metropolis of Ehbahr, Kojn-umm's wholly contemporary capital city. Straight ahead, a gradually descending slope glittered with splotches of illumination that marked the location of the bivouac of Toroud-eed's troops.

"Wonderful meal, simply wonderful!" the general declaimed to the cool, indifferent night. His round mouth was contracted, sphincterlike, around a transparent tube that dispensed measured quantities of tartly flavored alkaloids. While the slowly dissolving powder produced a pleasant taste and mild rush in the Niyyuu, it would have wreaked serious havoc on Walker's more sensitive digestive system. He had long since learned which local molecular combinations he and George could tolerate and which, harmless though they might be to the natives, man and dog should at all costs avoid. These personal limitations did not hinder his practice of performance gastronomy.

"Glad you enjoyed it." Resting both arms on the high, solid-metal barrier, he let his gaze wander over the ranked lights below. At a distance, they reminded him of so many stars fallen to Earth. Silent soldiers patrolled the walls of the fortress, alert for any inimical nocturnal intrusion. Music, nearly as harsh as Niyyuuan speech, scratched and clawed its way up from the ancient courtyard below. The smaller of Niyu's two moons, irregular of shape but bright of albedo, hung high in the night sky.

"I hope you don't mind my saying," he continued, "that while my friends and I have enjoyed the time we've spent here on your world, like anyone else cut off and long away from their home, we're anxious to be on our way." Nearby and unable to see over the railing, George sniffed meaningfully.

"That only natural," the general responded encouragingly.

"The problem is that we don't have any idea which way, out of an infinity of possible ways, to go from here, and the Kojn-umm government and its allies won't send a ship outward on our behalf until we can choose a reasonable course."

"Also natural, I imagine." Saluu-hir-lek was studying the now-silent field of battle. Distant lights were reflected in his wide eyes.

"It would be helpful," Walker went on, "if someone, someone in a position of real power, could use their influence to persuade the government to initiate on our behalf a real, serious search of the surrounding starfield, with an eye toward locating our homeworlds. We certainly aren't in a position to do it. We've filed repeated requests, only to be told to be patient and that the appropriate resources are being employed on our behalf. But this has been going on for some time now, and so far we've heard nothing."

Saluu-hir-lek did not look at him. That was not encouraging. "I faintly aware of yous' situation. Such searches, I understand, can take long time. Sometimes very long time."

"We understand that." Walker tried not to sound impatient. "It's just that we've heard nothing at all. Possibly if someone like yourself looked into the matter, or used their influence, the relevant government agencies might be more . . . forthcoming."

Their round, muscular mouths did not allow the Niyyuu to smile. Instead, Saluu-hir-lek tried to offer a sympathetic apologia by means of gestures. "Cannot do. Too much responsibility already, being charged with traditionally defend all of Kojn-umm. I sorry, but can do nothing for you." His tone brightened. "I thank yous for staying night. Perhaps following sunbreak, can prepare small morning meal?"

With a heavy sigh, Walker turned away. "Yes, of course I'll conjure breakfast."

"A strange, untranslatable term. Understanding is clear, though. I thank you in advance." He started toward the open portal behind them. "Now is retire time. Soldier needs good sleep as much as sharp sword. Maybe cook as well."

"Whatever." The dog had his head down as he moved to follow the general. The private nocturnal meeting had not produced the results he and Walker had hoped for.

"Is okay yous share habitation? Not much free-spare space in fortress."

Walker glanced down at the dog and mustered a sliver of a smile. "We'll manage. George and I have shared a lot more than a room together."

Tonight they would also, he reflected as he followed their host, share their disappointment.

Their quarters were more comfortable than either had expected, equipped with many of the comforts of modern Niyyuuan technology. As usual, though soft and long enough, the customary sleeping platform was too narrow for Walker to sleep easily on it lest he roll over in

the middle of the night and tumble off. With a second full-size platform at his disposal, George had a much easier time of it—once Walker
helped his small friend up onto the high bed.

"Well, when considered as a summit in search of local allies, that
sucked big-time." Pacing out a circle atop the platform, George
promptly flumped himself down in the middle of the aerogel padding.

Boosting himself up onto the edge of his own platform, Walker regarded his friend glumly. "The general was nice enough, maybe even
understanding, but that was as far as it went."

George sniffed derisively. "Me, I don't even think it went that far. I
think he was being disingenuous the whole time." Rising, the aggra-
vated dog walked to the edge of the platform. "Look, this Saluu-hir-lek
is the top military guy in all Kojn-umm. It's crazy to think that he's not
in on top-level policy decisions. And I have to believe that the employment and disposition of four aliens at government expense counts as a
top-level policy decision."

Walker deliberated. "Then you think he's in on this "go slow in
helping us to return home" policy?"

"Of course he is." George let out a short, sharp growl. "Just like all
the other upper-level local Niyyuu. It's pretty clear to me from the way
he reacted to your low-key request that he's not going to help us any
more than any of the other government officials we've talked to over
the past couple of months." The dog eyed his friend sagely. "You're too
good at your new vocation, Marc. I've been paying attention, listening
to conversations. That's one benefit to being my size. Bigger folk start to
overlook your presence. Not only do the Niyyuu like your cooking presentations, they're basking in the envy of their neighbors. Nobody else
has a human chef. Not to mention a chatty canine, a verse-spouting Tuuqalian, and an encyclopedic, if smart-mouthed, K'eremu. You can be
sure of it: they're going to keep us marooned here as long as they can."
Returning to the center of the platform, he repeated the careful "pacing in a circle" ritual before lying down once more.

"Right now, 'as long as they can' is looking more and more like
forever."

A thoughtful Walker studied the communications ovoid that stood
to the left of his sleeping platform. At a command, it could provide all
manner of services and entertainment. But in accordance with Niyyuuan tradition, it did not permit reciprocal contact with the outside
world. That had to be done by courier, or mirror signals, or some similar old-fashioned method that did not contravene the strict laws governing traditional Niyyuuan combat. Like the rest of the fortress, their

sleeping quarters were an eclectic mix of the antiquated and the completely up-to-date.

While their long journey from Seremathenn to Niyu had hopefully
brought them closer to home, their voyaging had subsequently stalled
due to the lack of cooperation on the part of the Niyyuu of Kojn-umm.
If George was right, and Walker saw little reason to dispute the dog's assertions, an official if unspoken policy of benign neglect had landed
permanently on their repeated requests for help in locating their homeworlds, or even ascertaining in which direction they might lie. In some
ways, outright opposition to their requests would have been simpler to
deal with. But facile prevarication was a tougher opponent: slippery
and hard to pin down.

Take the attitude of their current host. There were moments that
suggested Saluu-hir-lek empathized with their situation. He simply
wouldn't do anything to help them, would not go against governmental dictates. How could Walker and his friends demand action when individuals like the general and his civilian counterparts insisted they
were doing their best?

There was the hope that Sobj-oes, the senior scientist who had confronted him late one evening, would eventually come forth with some
useful information. But suppose she did? he told himself. Then what?
Knowing where Earth—or Tuuqalia, or K'erem—might lie in relation
to Niyu would bring the respective orphans of those three worlds
closer to home only emotionally.

"We need to be more proactive in our cause."

"What?" Half-asleep, George looked up at his friend.

"We need to stop asking for help and do more to help ourselves."

"Uh-huh, sure." The dog's head slumped back down onto his paws.
"When you're ready to hijack a Niyyuuan ship and its crew, let me
know. Sometimes—sometimes I wish we'd recognized reality and
stayed on Seremathenn. Or I wish I had."

Walker had been frustrated. Now he was angry. Slipping off the
platform, he strode over to the other, grabbed the startled dog by his
forepaws, and lifted him up until he was standing on his hind legs. It
brought them nearer to eye level.

"Now you listen to me! We didn't fight our way out of Vilenjji captivity to end up stuck on Niyu or Seremathenn or any other alien world.
Neither did Sque or Braouk. We're going to get home, all of us!"

"Let go of me, or I'll bite the crap out of your fingers," George
warned him.

Walker let the dog drop back down onto all fours. "We need to stick together and to focus on one thing, George—and it's not making our-selves as comfortable as possible in an alien environment. We need to concentrate on ways of getting home."

"Swell." Unable to stay angry at anything for very long, the dog had lain back down and was licking his forepaws where the human had gripped them. "First we have to find it."

"We will. Somehow, someway, whether the Niyyuu help us or not, we will. And once we've done that, we'll damn sure figure out a way to get there!"

"A positive attitude," the dog mumbled sleepily. "That's useful. Since you find Saluu-hir-lek so sympathetic, maybe you can get him to conquer a few neighboring realms for us. Then you can order their sci-entific communities to do what we want."

"Wouldn't work even if we could," a more subdued Walker mur-mured. "Remember what we were told? That if any one realm becomes too powerful, the others gang up on it to put it back in its place?"

George yawned. "Very civilized. Nothing like trading commodities, I bet."

"No," Walker agreed. "This is nothing like that. Nothing at all."

He returned to his sleeping platform and directed the room to darken. But unlike the dog, he did not immediately fall asleep. In fact, he did not fall asleep for some time. His thoughts would not let him. Like the steaming, thick java brewed by his favorite coffee shop on the corner of the office tower back home where he used to work, they were percolating.

9

M orning dawned as so many had since their arrival on Niyu: bright, sunny, cloudless, and depressing. A fine day for fighting, according to the aide who woke them.

As he slipped mechanically into his clothes, Walker noticed that George had not stirred. "Not coming." With a nod of his head, the dog indicated their immediate surroundings.

"There's not much to do here," Walker pointed out. There were entertainment recordings to peruse, but little else.

The dog lifted his head from his paws. "Not much to do until we leave this place, either. We came looking for help. We didn't find any." The furry head dropped back down. "At the risk of appearing impolite, or impolitic, if anybody asks, tell 'em I'm not feeling well. Which is true enough. I've no interest in watching the natives ceremoniously slaughter each other."

"To tell you the truth, neither do I." Walker moved toward the doorway. "But in spite of the general's diplomatic refusal of assistance, you never know when he might let something useful slip."

"If he does, just make sure you don't fall on it."

Walker hesitated, thought to say something else, finally concluded with a familiar "See you later, then," and exited the room. He didn't blame George for staying behind. While adding to their knowledge of Niyyuuan culture, their visit to the fortress had produced nothing in the way of concrete assistance. Not that this was anything less than what they had expected.

Inquiring as to the whereabouts of their host, he was informed that the general was up on the central bulwark. And that was where he found Saluu-hir-lek, intently engaged in a study of the hills and central plain spread out in front of the fortress, organizing tactics for the day's battle. To Walker's disappointment, Viyv-pym was not there. There was no reason for her to be present, of course. Traditional combat was something she had seen before, had experienced on a far more personal level than he ever would.

He did his best to appear cheerful. For his part, Saluu-hir-lek greeted him effusively. The general had as much energy as any Niyyuuan Walker had yet encountered.

Looking past the much broader human, he inquired, "Where you small associate?"

"Not feeling well this morning," Walker told him.

"*Asghik*. I hope it not from eat you's cooking."

Walker blanched, then recognized that his host was making a joke. The general was full of surprises. "Expecting a rough day?" Turning, Walker contemplated the field of battle. All was quiet for now, with no sign of the besieging soldiers of Toroud-eed.

"I think they growing tired. Jalar-aad-biidh has not been breached, much less taken, in long time. This one valiant effort by them. All started because of some trade dispute. Is often the case. One more assault on outer wall fail, I think they go home."

"And what then?" Walker asked curiously. "Will you pursue and try to destroy them so they won't have the strength to attack you again?"

Morning light glinted from polished armor that had been forged in a modern factory and not by two-fingered hands working with hammer and tong. Saluu-hir-lek eyed him from the depths of wide, inquiring eyes. "You interested in military tactics, human?"

"Let's just say that for much of my early life I spent a lot of time dealing with battlefield strategy." He did not add that the object of that strategy had been to advance a small, oblong-shaped, inflated ball down a grassy field. Tactics were still tactics, whether the eventual objective was seven points or seven deaths.

"I am pleased by you interest. Besides cooking, you have perhaps in mind other goals?" Though Walker was mildly boggled by the Niyyu-uan's unintentional pun, the general of course remained utterly un-aware of it.

"I want to go home. My friends want to go home. You know that already, General."

The Niyyuuan gestured acknowledgment. "As I told you yesterday, not my area of influence. Can do nothing. Regrets only I can give you."

They were both silent for a long moment before Walker, simply with an eye toward making polite conversation, thought to ask a question of his own. "What about you, General? What are your goals? Besides the ones your government and your official position have charged you with? Every sentient has personal as well as professional aspirations. Myself, I never thought I would become a professional food preparator. Now I find myself not only cooking, but doing it on different worlds for different species with entirely differing dietary requirements and tastes." Moving a little closer, he lowered his voice conspiratorially. "Given a choice of anything, what would you do? What do you, Saluu-hir-lek, want most?"

A limber, pale hand reached out to him. Starting at Walker's shoulder, two long, flexible, unarmored fingers traced a pattern down his arm.

"Such a thing is not for general speaking." Perhaps this time, Walker mused, the pun was intentional. "But you not Niyyuu, not Kojn-umm. I tell you something, you keep secret. Tell no one. You eyes attest to this?"

Drawn to the alien's unmistakable intensity, Walker did not hesitate. What personal ambition was so dodgy that an individual as powerful and connected as Saluu-hir-lek had to secure assurances of confidentiality before revealing it to an alien visitor?

"Of course," he replied. Then he added formally, "I attest with my eyes that I will repeat to no one of this world what you are about to tell me."

Saluu-hir-lek gestured solemnly. Then, instead of responding immediately, he turned to gaze once more out across the still-peaceful field of battle.

"It an uncommon thing, I know. Other officers, of all ranks, content enough to do their job. To follow orders. But when one is put in position not to follow orders but to give them, sometimes perception of reality, of world itself, can change." He glanced over at Walker. "You have, maybe, some personal understanding of this phenomenon?"

"I'm not sure." Something told Walker to tread with extreme care on this new subject, lest his host drop the matter entirely.

The general gestured enigmatically. "I endeavor explain. I am commander all traditional military forces of realm Kojn-umm. Rise fast within hierarchy. Many promotions." All this was given as fact, Walker noted, for informational purposes only and insofar as he could tell, without boasting. Certainly the speaker did not wait for comment, genuflection, or other approval from his alien audience of one.

"I achieve much already. Defeat forces of Toroud-eed several times. Defeat forces of Biranju-oov twice. Could have taken both guardian fortresses of latter."

"Why didn't you?" Walker asked him.

Saluu-hir-lek's disgust was plain to see, even to a newcomer such as Walker. "Governments make agreements between selves. Civilian control always overrules military, except when actual integrity of realm at stake. Was ordered both times to break off fighting and pull all attacking forces back to Kojn-umm."

"You were disappointed." Walker had quickly lost interest in the silent battlefield beyond the high wall.

Dominating the lean visage, huge dark eyes peered back at him. "You understand—perhaps."

Walker dug in, persistent. "Last night you said that you sympathized with the situation my friends and I find ourselves in. I think I find myself sympathizing with you. You suffer from what my people would call thwarted ambition. Believe me, Saluu-hir-lek, from my previous profession I know many individuals who are afflicted with the same ailment."

The general gestured understandingly. "It good to meet someone who appreciate condition. Even if that someone a great clumsy awkward alien creature like youself."

"Thanks," Walker replied dryly. "I think that, like myself, you also suffer from frustration—though it arises from a different set of circumstances." He moved as close as he could without actually making contact. "You can tell me about it if you like, General—who would I pass the information on to? Given the opportunity, what would you most like to do with your life?"

Saluu-hir-lek paused, as if suddenly aware that he might already have said too much. But the strange, short-earred, lumbering creature was right. Who would it recite the telling to? There was no reason for it to do such a thing. Particularly since it was apparent that the government in power was doing its best to ignore the alien's own requests.

"I tell you something now, human Walker. Confession before morning meal, you may think it. I come this close"—he pressed both fingers of his right hand lightly together—"to taking both traditional defending fortresses of Biranju-oov. Capture both fortresses, means realm suffering the defeat must make major concessions to vanquisher. In commerce, taxation, tariffs, residency matters—everything." His other arm swept forward to encompass the still-tranquil battlefield.

"When finally defeat these attacking forces of Toroud-eed here, I could subsequently muster greater army and chase them back to borders of their own realm. Defeat them also there, I am certain of it! First Toroud-eed, then Biranju-oov. Would become greatest traditional military commander in entire history of modern Kojn-umm." He waited with obvious interest for Walker's reaction.

The human merely replied softly, "And then?"

A great sigh eased out of the general, leaving him for an instant as thin as a reed. "You *do* understand. You have same feeling, I think maybe."

"No," Walker told him firmly. "I'm not interested in what you're interested in, though I would someday like to be head of the company I used to work for. If that can be called all-conquering, then I'm all for it. What I *am* interested in is getting home. Every day that my friends and I are restricted to Niyu is one day more we haven't moved any closer to getting home. It's becoming abundantly clear that in order to get the kind of assistance we need from official Kojn-umm sources, we need more powerful allies among its governing elite." He eyed the general meaningfully. "The greatest military commander in the history of modern Kojn-umm would certainly be one candidate for that list."

Saluu-hir-lek's mouth expanded. "Strategy and tactics. If I were the individual of whom you theorize, is true I might be able to help yous with yous' wishes. But I not that. Cannot be that." He looked away. "You been on Niyu long enough know that one realm grow too powerful, others combine to put it in its place."

"If its power is readily apparent, yes," Walker agreed. "But there are many ways to camouflage intent. To disguise one's true objective. That's something I used to be very good at."

Saluu-hir-lek turned sharply back to face the human. "You have idea? One, or many?"

"One that is many," Walker told him, intentionally cryptic. "Interested?"

The Niyyuuan general remained wary. "This very chancy subject for open discussion. You make morning meal first. Bring you friend along if he feeling better, please. I interested also in his opinion."

"The gist of my idea does not fall within his area of expertise," Walker replied.

"I understand that. But I interested in his opinion all the same. You not object to presence during discussions of you's own friend, do you?"

"No, of course not." Walker had no choice but to concede the point. To have argued it further, he sensed, would have killed the general's interest in such a touchy subject completely.

As it was, Saluu-hir-lek was clearly pleased. "Always better eat first. Not good discuss sedition and duplicity on empty stomach." Putting a long, limber arm around the human, the general escorted him off the rampart and back into the depths of the fortress.

*

"Well, what do you think?"

The waterfall at whose base they had gathered was not high, but it was noisy, which was what Walker was after. As always, their appearance garnered the usual stares from passing Niyyuu. None approached the foreign visitors to the nature park, however. Visiting aliens were accorded the same privileges as locals. That extended to privacy.

And if common courtesy was not sufficient to discourage infringement, Braouk's intimidating presence was sufficient to keep the otherwise intrigued at a distance.

Espying a shallow sandbar, Sque slid gratefully into the water. She remained there with only the upper half of her body breaking the surface, forcing her companions to settle themselves around her. No one minded the proximity to the manicured cataract that over the centuries had undergone a transformation from wild torrent to well-mannered cascade. Though carefully maintained native vegetation, lush and vibrant, flourished throughout the park, Walker would have traded every gaudy frond and twisted fiber of alien exoticism for one glimpse of a solitary daisy.

They had not come to enjoy the scenery, however, but to discuss their immediate future. One that Walker's proposal promised to perturb appreciably.

"Is taking a chance, that could seriously unsettle, existing relationship." Himself larger than many of the surrounding growths, Braouk's initial response to Walker's plan reflected his natural caution. "We have fashioned a comfortable arrangement with the Niyyuu. Involving our-

selves in a scheme such as you propose, Marc, could damage that ir-
reparably."

Walker had anticipated numerous possible objections to his proposal. Braouk's was one of them. "How? All decisions will be made by
Saluu-hir-lek, all orders will be issued by him, and he'll be the one to
execute and follow through on every action." He smiled knowingly.
"That's so he can also claim all the credit. No problem there. We're not
looking to get credit out of this. Our objective is to strengthen one important ally to the point where he'll be able to demand instead of request the kind of assistance we've been asking for."

As a relaxed George dog-paddled nearby, Sque focused her laserlike
attention on the human. "It is apparent you have given this as much
thought of which you are capable. I confess that I am more intrigued
than I expected to be. But our moody Tuuqalian makes a point. Suppose
that events do not proceed in the fashion desired. Our hosts are not so
developed that their base desires have completely atrophied. This society
still understands revenge, for example."

Ignoring the fact that he was soaking his pants, Walker waded into
the water and crouched down close to her. There was a time when such
proximity to a four-foot-high tentacled nightmare like the K'eremu
would have sent him screaming. Time and close acquaintance had long
since altered both his view and his reaction.

"In that case, what's the worst that could happen? The Niyyuu
know we still have friends among the Sessrimathe. They'd probably just
expel us, send us back to Seremathenn. In that case, we'd be no worse
off than we were before we made the decision to come here."

Half a dozen slender tendrils stirred the water lazily. Half in, half
out of the cool stream, Sque was at her most physically comfortable.
Mentally, she was still skeptical.

"It is true that if we do not do something, we condemn ourselves
to remain forever poised on the cusp of inertia: a poor motivator of
proaction." Silver-gray eyes peered intently at him while her pink
speaking trunk weaved back and forth close to his face. Used to its utterly alien presence, he ignored its fluttering.

"In order to have a chance of bringing this off successfully, I'll need
your knowledge and your help, Sque."

"Of course you will," she agreed tellingly. "You would have no
chance whatsoever of succeeding without my active involvement. If
nothing else, you will need the participation of a higher intelligence
merely to keep track of all the possible ramifications of your proposed

machinations. Which, I must admit, show a level of sophisticated multithinking I had not previously associated with you."

"Believe me, I'm just as taken aback as you to find that certain requirements for success in my former profession fit the present situation unexpectedly well. How they'll play out remains to be seen." His legs were beginning to cramp from crouching in the sitting position, and he straightened up, water dripping from his pants. "Saluu-hir-lek is certainly fascinated by the proposal I laid out for him." Turning to his left, he raised his voice to the giant, who remained back in the shade of the trees and well clear of the fast-moving watercourse.

"What about you, Braouk? Will you go along with this? As long as it doesn't violate any accepted tenets of traditional Niyyuuan warfare, I'm sure the general would be delighted to see you in a suit of custom-made Kojn-umm armor."

"More fighting is, not to my liking, right now."

Walker did not try to force the issue. Given time and sufficient motivation, he felt he could inveigle the Tuuqalian into fighting. If not necessarily on behalf of their hosts, then in support of the broader effort to get all of them home. Convinced that was the real goal, Braouk might be willing to set his temperamental recitations aside and pick up a specially forged heavy sword. Four of them. The appearance of an armored Tuuqalian on the battlefield ought to be worth at least a company of regular soldiers to Saluu-hir-lek. The more invaluable they could make themselves to the general, Walker knew, the less likely he was to abandon the visitors' goal once they achieved some measure of success.

That was Walker's ultimate objective: to create an enterprise with a momentum of its own. One that not even Saluu-hir-lek, should he have a change of mind or heart, could halt. All would find themselves swept up in the same risky, mutual challenge.

Could he bring it off? Despite the assurances he had given the general, Walker's confidence wavered. What he had proposed was something rather more demanding than selling pineapple juice futures short. Among his companions, George was a reluctant participant at best, Braouk still remained to be fully convinced, and one could never tell for certain when Sque might change her mind completely about something.

Then he remembered his own argument, and voiced it aloud to his companions. "We'll do this because we can make it work. Because it will ultimately help us in our essential goal, which is to find our way home. But most of all we'll do it because it's the only thing any of us has thought of to get things moving here, since official policy apparently is to politely but firmly ignore our pleas for meaningful help."

"And I shall also participate," Sque added with unexpected passion, "because I am bored—*bored!*" Following this confession, she took on a startled appearance. Limbs flailing fervently, splashing water in all directions, she whirled in the stream to see what had assaulted her from behind. Grinning, George paddled rapidly away.

"I hate to see anyone bored," the retreating dog shouted back as Walker wiped water from his face. "Especially someone with so many loose limbs hanging around just begging to be yanked."

With the perpetrator of the outrage thus self-confessed, an irate Sque went after him. Faster in the water and much bigger than the mutt, it seemed an unequal contest. However, George managed to keep the infuriated K'eremu at bay with the one weapon she did not possess: teeth.

Watching them, Walker marveled at how far he and his friend had come. Not only from Earth, but *of* Earth. He was as comfortable now with K'eremu and Tuuqalian, Niyyuu and Sessrimathe, as he had been with friends and coworkers and girlfriends back home. If it was true what they said, that travel broadens the mind, then his had been broadened beyond the wildest dreams of all but the most mind-expanded travel writers. It had certainly all been fascinating, and enlightening, and awe-inspiring.

But even taken in toto, it was no substitute for a good concert or a night out with friends.

*

Though a bold and forthright fighter, Saluu-hir-lek was capable of subtlety when it was required. Preparations were begun quietly, without shouting or the usual kind of loud, patriotic exhortations to the populace that normally accompanied a significant military buildup. It helped that a major assault on the integrity of Kojn-umm had just been repulsed. The citizenry, not only in the capital but elsewhere throughout the realm, had experienced their fill of local combat. Enthusiasts had turned elsewhere, most notably to the war currently in progress on the other side of Niyu between the powerful realms of Gwalia-uun and Tigrada-eeb.

Largely ignored by the media as well as by the government, Saluu-hir-lek was able to slowly but steadily marshal his forces, increasing the size and strength of his brigades, most importantly those responsible for logistics and support. The latter, Walker knew, would be crucial to the success of his proposal, since if events transpired as hoped the expeditionary army of Kojn-umm would be in the field far longer than was customary.

It took a significant number of ten-days for the army to make ready. As the public became aware that a military campaign of unusual dimensions was being planned, questions about its propriety were raised in the media throughout the realm. Some were doubtful; some were supportive. Used to the respectful excesses of conventional Niyyuuan warfare, the great majority of citizens simply ignored the maneuvers while getting on with their daily lives. Unable to influence the outcomes of battles that nevertheless affected them deeply, they had grown used to trusting the strategic decisions of their military leaders. If it was determined that a punishing invasion of belligerent Toroud-eed was needed as a follow-up to that nation's attack on Ehbahr's traditional fortifications, then so be it. They would provide their support, as always.

And besides, if the assault was to be commanded by Saluu-hir-lek, their finest officer, there was always the chance of achieving a notable triumph, if not a spectacular victory. Commercial advantages could accrue. There was no lack of financial backing for the proposed expedition.

The media duly reported on the extensive planning, which could not be concealed. These reports made for solid, if somewhat monotonous, coverage and were always good for a fill if the day's other news inclined toward the passive. As regular visitors to the main bivouac, Walker and his friends were fascinated by the contrasting combination of high tech and low reality that comprised the preparations.

Advanced air-repulsion vehicles banned from any field of battle delivered supplies that were laboriously transferred to selgeth wagons. The selgeth were hippo-sized bipeds with long trunks and comically floppy ears whose stout bodies ran to an excess of fat. Harnessed to large-wheeled wooden wagons in groups of three, they munched contentedly on whatever plucked vines and cut grasses were laid before them. Blessed with an inherent patience—and a complaisant stupidity—that verged on the somnolent, a troika of selgeth could pull a fully loaded wagon all day long without tiring or complaint. Others were yoked to mobile siege engines whose designs were thousands of ten-days ancient.

Custom allowed barrels and crates, but not their contents, to be made of plastics and other modern materials. Swords and spears and slingbolts could be fashioned by machines in automated factories, but once delivered to the army could only be sharpened and maintained by hand. More out of a desire to be able to defend himself in possible

unforeseen circumstances than from any yearning to participate in actual fighting, at his request Walker was given instruction in their use.
His senior Niyyuuan trainer was fascinated by the profusion of fingers
on each of the human's hands. Though shorter than the two digits that
terminated in a Niyyuuan hand, and less flexible, human fingers were
strong and had the advantage of numbers.

As for the other potential combatant in the group, Braouk needed
no martial instruction. Utilizing all four powerful upper tentacles, all he
had to do was grip whatever weapon was at hand and swing. Whether
wielding sword, club, or stray wagon, the Tuuqalian was bound to do
considerable damage. Especially if, as had happened several times when
they were captives aboard the Vilenjji ship, he lost control of himself. At
such moments, Walker would not want to be a member of a rival army.
Surprisingly—though a rare event—there was nothing in the extensive
official canon of traditional Niyyuuan warfare that prohibited the participation of an alien in local conflict, provided only that it utilized
nothing more lethal than traditional forms of weaponry.

As for George, having nothing to grip a weapon with, he pointedly
removed himself from instruction in their use, while Sque refused absolutely any martial schooling whatsoever. Primal physical hostilities,
she remarked without having to be prompted, were beneath her and
her kind. They had advanced beyond such foolishness. But she was quite
willing to offer her often unsolicited opinion on tactics and strategy.
Just because her kind did not make war among themselves did not
mean they had not studied its format and consequences among other
species.

The day chosen for the departure of the army dawned overcast and
clammy. Walker and George would have preferred more sunshine,
Braouk had expected nothing less, while Sque was delighted with both
the darkness and the damp. As for the soldiers of Kojn-umm themselves, they were so keyed up by many successive ten-days of preparation that they had to be held back by their officers. It had been a long,
long time since the forces of Kojn-umm had made a sortie against those
of Toroud-eed. For years they had been restricted by their cautious
commanders to the defense of ancient fortresses such as Jalar-aad-
biidh. Now they were to be offered a chance to give the Toroudians a
taste of their own medicine.

And then the politicians arrived.

There were four in the delegation who had come up from the capital. They were well dressed, well informed, and well meaning. As they
addressed Saluu-hir-lek and his officers within the somewhat-claustro-

phobic confines of the staff wagon, they cast occasional glances in the direction of the three aliens who were also present.

"What are they do here?" one of the important visitors asked almost immediately.

The general gestured casually in the direction of his guests, as if the presence of outré aliens on a traditional Niyyuuan military exercise were an everyday occurrence. "They bring fresh views and a different perspective on tactics to the grand expedition. I value their advice, though of course I make my own decisions." Saluu-hir-lek leaned toward the leader of the visiting delegation. "What do it matter? Does the government value gastronomic talents of biped so highly it would seek to restrain him from accompanying?"

The inquisitive official was immediately on the defensive. "Nothings, no, General. Was only curious to see them here. Is unexpected."

If they think our presence is unexpected, Walker mused, wait until they see Braouk in full armor. The Tuuqalian was not present at the gathering for one simple reason: even shorn of armor and weapons, if he were to squeeze into the staff wagon there would be no room left for anyone else. No doubt he was even now off somewhere ingratiating himself to the Kojn-umm soldiery with lengthy recitations of venerable Tuuqalian sagas.

"The government has concerns," another of the officials declared doggedly. She was unusually tall and slim, even for a Niyyuu, though the appropriately high-ceilinged interior of the staff wagon meant she did not have to bend to fit within. "It not that they troubled by thought of attacking Toroud-eed. Has been trade and other disagreements between our two realms for many long-times. But to attack an enemy just defeated seems to some an ill-mannered adventure."

Truly, Walker reflected, the Niyyuuan way of war was more than a little different from the brand waged by his own kind.

"You fight force from Toroud-eed at wall of Jalar-aad-biidh for several ten-days," the third member of the visiting party observed. "Beat them back each time. Most commendable victorying." He made a gesture that Walker recognized as a praise flourish. "Why suddenly now the need, at considerable expense to the treasury, to follow so soon to attack that already-defeated force?"

Saluu-hir-lek glanced ever so briefly in Sque's direction. The K'eremu did not react. The attendant politicians would probably not have noticed if she had.

"Toroud-eed expeditionary force seriously weakened by their losses sustained before Jalar-aad-biidh. They barely back in barracks. If

attack them now, good chance they not strong enough to assist much
in protection of Toroud-eed traditional fortifications. Exists for us excellent possibility of overwhelming defenses of the realm. Could bring
momentous, if not necessarily total, defeat on traditional level of
Toroud-eed itself."

The tall female looked at the associate on her left before returning
her attention to the general. "That quite a claim to make, General. Is
also possible by committing so much of military resources of Kojn-
umm to this offensive that we could be as weakened in turn. Assault
will be widely broadcast across all of Niyu. If attack falters, other traditional adversaries of the realm might be tempted attack Kojn-umm
while its main army occupied in front of fortresses of Toroud-eed."

For a civilian politician, Walker decided, the tall representative had
a respectable grasp of military tactics.

Saluu-hir-lek was ready with a response. "Integrity of Jalar-aad-biidh
not seriously compromised by Toroudian assault. Other traditional
walls and citadels not impacted at all. Sufficient forces remain in Kojn-
umm to successfully defend time-honored interests of the realm. If I
not believe this with all my self, I would not propose or plan this expedition against Toroud-eed." His gruff, grating voice ascended until it
filled the interior of the staff wagon with a sound like gravel being
crushed.

"Is long overdue time we teach lesson to Toroud-eed once and for
all. Who here not wish to see such a triumph?"

While impressed by his vision and his commitment, the visitors
were not overawed. "All patriotic citizens would desire to see such an
eventuation, General," the first speaker declared. "What we not wish see
is same thing happen to Kojn-umm while main army of the realm is
occupied with ill-conceived escapade elsewhere."

"We not here to stop you, General," the tall female added. "You
have approval of Council already. We here to inform you that we aware
of all possible consequences." Her wide eyes met his. "For sake you's
excellent career as well as future of realm, we wish you good fortune,
good speed, and caution."

"Yous' constructive tidings welcome and accepted," Saluu-hir-lek
assured them expansively. With a flourish of his own, he escorted them
from the wagon. Once outside, the eldest of the visitors glanced at
the sky.

"No one believe anymore in omens. We a mature species—except
in certain aspects of our culture." He turned to face his host, his eyes
flicking occasionally to the peculiar aliens who always seemed to be

hovering in the background. "I hope you make this happen, General. I have seen many concessions made to Toroud-eed, Biranju-oov, and other adjacent realms. Is time surely for proud people of Kojn-umm to assert themselves more forcefully." He stared at Walker, who remained standing near the rear of the staff wagon. "I hope the strange friends you have acquired help you to victory, and not to ruin."

"Regardless shape or size or origin, I listen open to any who have good advice," Saluu-hir-lek reassured the venerable delegate, "and then I make the decisions that best for Kojn-umm."

Whether this response was sufficient to satisfy the elder, Walker could not tell, but neither the questioner nor any of his companions raised any further objections. They boarded the gleaming, nearly silent vehicle that would whisk them back to the capital in comfort and speed and were out of sight in seconds. But before they departed, one member of the delegation, who had heretofore stayed aboard the now-departed craft and out of sight, emerged to remain behind.

In late evening there was no sunlight to glint off Viyv-pym's traveling armor as she approached the staff wagon, but Walker thought she looked splendid anyway. Next to him, George snorted in disgust, shook his head, and wandered off in search of something to eat.

Halting before him, she stroked his right shoulder and upper arm in greeting. He responded with a light touch of his own. As always, he risked losing himself in those eyes: sunshine and gold.

"Hello, Viyv-pym. Come to wish us good luck?"

"Come to join in great expedition." Her eyes flashed. "Having already served two tour of military duty, had to request special dispensation to participate. Final permission from relevant department received only this morning." She searched his soft, rounded, alien face. "You have objection?"

"Who, me? No, no," he told her, perhaps too quickly. It was a good thing George had already left, Walker realized. Listening to his human friend's near stammer, the disgusted dog might have piddled on his leg. "Glad to have you along. Someone else to talk to."

"I am happy my presence please you." One limber hand dropped to the hilt of her sword. "Opportunity also for small personal glory, and to kill a few rival of Kojn-umm." Together, they started toward the dwelling wagon he had been assigned. "This very bold decision by Saluu-hir-lek. Destination is no secret, of course. Almost impossible conduct any military activity on Niyu in secret. Media are everywhere."

Walker knew that in addition to the expected sizable contingent of media observers from Kojn-umm, broadcast units were also arriving to cover the undertaking from other realms—including Toroud-eed. The presence of enemy media representatives among them did not faze the soldiers of Saluu-hir-lek's army. It was the way traditional warfare had been conducted on Niyu since the beginning of civilized times. "Well-mannered," as one of the departed cautioning politicians had put it. There were ratings to be had, products to be sold, philosophies to be disseminated. A nice, steady, prolonged battle at the ancient gates of Toroud-eed would be good for everyone. Except for the soldiers who died, of course. There was only one glitch in that expected scenario.

Saluu-hir-lek had no intention of engaging in a prolonged conflict.

Unlike troop movements, it *was* possible to keep battlefield tactics reasonably hidden from the enemy. The defenders of Toroud-eed, hopefully still worn out from their failed investiture of Jalar-aad-biidh, would know that the forces of Kojn-umm were coming, but not what they intended to do once they arrived. No military strategist himself, Walker's basic understanding of tactics stemmed from his days on the football field. From what Saluu-hir-lek and Sque had confided in him, he thought the overall plan had a chance of working. How good a chance he did not know.

Like everyone else, he would find out soon enough.

As for Viyv-pym, she was more than a little excited by the chance to go into battle again. Her arrival, at the last minute prior to the army's departure, did arouse a question or two in his mind. He was not quite as smitten as George believed or Sque felt. Was she here for the reason stated, simply because she wanted to participate in the coming fighting? Or had she been sent to keep an eye on him and his fellow aliens, to see if they were engaged in some unsuspected activity inimical to the interests of Kojn-umm? Was she friend, or spy? Or had she been paid to watch over him and ensure that the premier imported culinary attraction of the capital came to no harm and was returned safely to work his gastronomic magic?

All were possibilities, by themselves and in combination. Time, he imagined, would reveal the truth. And if not time, possibly George, who could be positively prescient at times.

Meanwhile, they had a hostile regime to conquer. Walking toward his transportation, Walker found himself and his new companion assaulted, not by swords or pikes, but by media representatives anxious for material. The presence of the famous alien food preparator among the expeditionary force was a useful angle for questions. As Viyv-pym looked on in amusement, he answered all that he could, truthfully and without hesitation. They asked him about cooking, about food, about life on Niyu, about his opinions on the forthcoming campaign. Thankfully, they never asked him about tactics. That was natural enough. Such matters would not be regarded as something with which he would be involved.

Had they asked, he could have told them quite a bit, including some things that would have genuinely surprised, and perhaps even shocked them. Needless to say, he did not volunteer the data.

Because via the planetary media, the military as well as the citizens of Toroud-eed would be watching.

10

Walker had seen a number of movies in his life that depicted or dealt with medieval warfare. Slight variations notwithstanding, it seemed very straightforward. You assaulted the fortress with arrows and rocks and fire. Then troops carrying defensive shields and scaling ladders attempted to surmount and take control of the walls while other siege engines and rams sought to force a way through. Meanwhile, the defenders rained variations of liquid and solid lethality down on the attackers in coordinated attempts to alternately discourage, kill, or drive them off.

There were two notable differences between what he remembered seeing on the large and small screen and the assault on the Toroudian fortress of Herun-uud-taath. First, the combatants had access to destructive technology that far exceeded anything existing on Earth—but were forbidden by custom and ritual from making use of so much as a single-shot pistol. Second, and more importantly, he was not watching a fictionalized representation of some ancient battle: he was part of it.

Or more accurately, he was an active witness. Concerned with the safety of his strategic ally (and superlative chef), Saluu-hir-lek made certain that three of his four alien visitors remained safely away from any fighting. This was not a problem as far as Walker was concerned, since he felt exactly the same way about the carnage that was taking place at the walls of the fortress. The fourth member of their group, however, waded into the fighting with reluctant determination, causing havoc wherever he stomped. The panic generated by Braouk's efforts was more devastating to the opposition than the number of them that he actually slew. It was one thing for a Niyyuu to encounter an alien in the media or even on the street; quite something else to have to deal with it in person, in a battlefield environment. Especially when that alien was a fully armored, four-limbed, one-ton mass of verse-spouting Tuuqalian.

Sque, of course, remained above it all, though not uninterested. After all, she and her friends were participating because they had a personal interest in the eventual outcome, not out of any sense of altruism or deep love for their Kojnian hosts.

"Ruination as entertainment. Devastation as politics. If I do not find my way back to dear K'erem soon, I fear I shall go mad." Tendrils writhed in agitation, visual evidence of her frustration.

"You won't go mad." As they surveyed the distant field of battle, Walker spoke from the other side of the wagon's lookout tower. "You'd end up analyzing the descent into psychosis, and in the process retain your sanity."

Clinging easily to one side of the tower with seven of her ten limbs, she swung silvery eyes toward her human companion. "Do not think that only simple creatures such as your kind can go insane, Marcus. Complexity can also lead to confusion, confusion to angst, and angst to withdrawal. There are many kinds of madness." With a free tendril she gestured at the ongoing battle. "This is only one."

"Madness we can use to our advantage," he countered. In the distance, a gobbet of jellied hydrocarbon exploded in flame somewhere inside the fortress. Exempt from battlefield restrictions and clearly marked as such, a pair of small vehicles hovered low overhead, the shielded advanced recording devices they carried relaying the retrograde mayhem to enthralled viewers on all five continents.

"Time will tell. When surrounded by and dealing only with primitive sentients I must take care to remain hopeful, if not overtly optimistic." Another free tendril curled up and back to scratch at an ear
socket.

Viyv-pym was out there too, somewhere, Walker knew. He hoped
she would be careful, and would return unharmed. Knowing her now
as well as he did, he knew it would have been futile to ask her to refrain from placing herself in harm's way. Slender and light of weight
she was, but so was a stick of dynamite.

At that moment, in fact, Viyv-pym was nowhere near the ferocious
free-for-all that was washing up against the frontal defenses of Herun-
uud-taath in waves of fire and blood. Having joined a select contingent
of carefully picked troops, they had been transferred on tibadun
mounts at high speed to a position in dense woods near the southwest
rear of the Toroudian defensive complex. The greatest threat to the success of such a maneuver lay not in being surprised by defensive forces,
but in being discovered by representatives of the media, who would attack the fast-moving troops with relentless requests for interviews and
their unending search for personal-interest stories.

Having managed to avoid the attentions of both a counterattack and
avid civilian interrogators, and having sent their loping tibaduns back
to the front lines, the would-be infiltrators from Kojn-umm assembled
for a final preassault briefing from their officers. Viyv-pym wondered
how the visitors would react in such a potentially perilous situation.
The giant Braouk would simply have listened in silence, absorbing all
that had to be said. The Tuuqalian was even now occupying much attention at the forefront of the battle. As for the small many-armed dose
of ambulating sarcasm, Viyv-pym knew that she would remain as far
from the scene of combat as she was aloof. The human Walker . . .

Walker was more problematic. Charged with assisting all the aliens
in their interactions with her kind, she found him a continuous bundle
of contradictions. That he could fight she had seen for herself, when he
had been undergoing instruction in the use of hand weaponry. That he
chose not to do so she attributed to a mix of personal and cultural con-
victions. Yet observing him studying combat, those times when he was
unaware that he was being watched, she thought she detected hints of
a repressed desire to throw himself recklessly into the ongoing fight.

Analyzing the motivations of one or more visiting aliens could
wait. At the moment, she and her fellow fighters found themselves
about to embark on a perilous maneuver that would succeed only

through the boldest of actions. Such had been the intent of the risky stratagem from its inception.

Having received their final instructions, the members of the assault force silently spread out and hid themselves among the trees as best they could, waiting for darkness. An hour after the sun fell, following a hasty uncooked meal that made her yearn for Walker's superb cuisine, they began gathering in twos and threes and moving forward. The southwest rear corner of the great fortress of Herun-uud-taath, which guarded the traditional approach through the mountains into Toroud-eed proper, loomed above them. Forbidden from making use of modern sources of illumination, its defenders had lined the multiple ramparts with torches and glow spheres.

The infiltrators from Kojn-umm made no attempt to conceal themselves. They did not approach the complex slowly, by stealth and in shadow. Instead, as they emerged from the forest they formed up neatly into four columns and stepped out smartly onto the paved road that led to the fortress. Pavement soon gave way to the traditionally acceptable dirt and gravel.

Along with many of her comrades, Viyv-pym's mouth shrank to an almost invisible "O" as an inquisitive media scanner passed overhead. It dropped so low she could see the pilot and commentator inside. Marching along, eyes forward, she could almost feel the relay unit's pickup brush the tips of her ears. The uncomfortable sensation made her frill fibrillate and her tails twitch uncontrollably.

Satisfied, the scanner gained altitude without its integrated commentator voicing any queries. Moments later, the first challenge to the contingent's steady approach came from the fortress. A specially trained officer marching in the forefront of the columns replied. As they had been instructed to do, expressions among the approaching troops varied from studiously neutral to intentionally bored.

An enormous metal gate, forged and formed in the ancient manner, groaned inward. Uncontested and unchallenged, the soldiers of Kojn-umm marched in. Viyv-pym smiled inwardly as she passed beneath the gate's arched opening. The ruse, devised by a group that included not only Saluu-hir-lek and his senior officers but the human Walker and the K'eremu Sque, depended on fitting out all of the specially chosen Kojn-umm troops in uniforms not of their home realm, but in those of Toroud eed. They were real uniforms, too. Originals that had been scavenged from the dead left behind by those Toroudians who had many ten-days earlier attacked the fortress of Jalar-aad-biidh. The

special troops had even been instructed in particular Toroudian man-
nerisms.

While marvelously executed, the ruse was not perfect. A few questions were asked. One Toroudian officer, descending a stone stairway,
saw something that did not match his knowledge of What Ought to Be.
Harsh Niyyuuan voices split the night, swiftly giving way to shouts first
of uncertainty, then of alarm.

An officer in the front of the column rasped an order. Weapons
were pulled from scabbards and concealment. Screeching defiance, the
columns broke apart as the soldiers of Kojn-umm, Viyv-pym among
them, clashed with the now-alerted defenders of the fortress.

The attackers had the advantage not only of surprise but also, initially at least, of greater numbers. By the time the alarm had traveled
through the citadel, the invading contingent from Kojn-umm controlled the gate and its immediate vicinity. Despite prodigious efforts by
the fortress's defenders to regain control of the occupied sector, the invading soldiers had solidified their position by taking control of several
guard towers. Unwilling to risk additional casualties in what had clearly
become an internal war of attrition, the commanders of Herun-uud-
taath's defense decided to hold back and wait for dawn. For one thing,
they badly needed to see what, if any, other surprises the invaders from
Kojn-umm might be keeping in reserve.

By the time runners could convey news of the infiltrators' success
to Saluu-hir-lek's headquarters, the general already knew of it from
media reports. It caused quite a sensation. Such successful duplicity
was something of a novelty in military campaigns. Like anything new
on the news, news of it triggered burgeoning interest among millions
of viewers.

Though without reinforcements and heavy equipment the infiltrators could not make further progress, neither could the defenders of
Herun-uud-taath dislodge them from the positions the Kojnians had
taken up inside the rear of the fortress complex. With the strategic
situation thus stalemated but with the forces of Kojn-umm now holding a definite, quantifiable advantage, Saluu-hir-lek rocked his opponents further off balance with his next action.

Instead of seeking immediately to press his tactical advantage, he
requested a conference with his opposite numbers.

Understandably, the general staff of Toroud-eed was at first suspicious. When it was made clear that the request was sincere and contained
no hidden provisions, they found themselves genuinely bemused. Dis-

secting but finding no harm in the proposal, they eventually, if a bit sullenly, agreed.

Preparations were made to meet not far from the base of the fortress's main western gate. The location chosen was just within range of Herun-uud-taath's heavy fire throwers but sufficiently distant so that any contemplated treachery was likely to fail. Since both sides had agreed on the terms of the summit, they were allowed to substitute a modern, portable, prefabricated structure for the more traditional fabric tent. This allowed for a meeting where, among other things, the interior climate could be controlled—a welcome development, since the weather had been unseasonably hot.

To its great regret and vociferous objection, the media that eagerly anticipated covering the elite meeting was banned from attending it. The commanders of both forces had to concur in order for such a ban to be enforced. This they readily did. Neither Saluu-hir-lek nor his Toroudian counterparts wanted flashing scanners recording and transmitting their every mood and word.

No one was more grateful for the declaration that the meeting was to take place than the soldiers on both sides, since all combat would be suspended while talks were ongoing.

The vetted participants arrived early. If the talks went nowhere fast, neither side wanted to lose a day's fighting, lest the other use the time to better position or provision their troops.

Saluu-hir-lek arrived clad in a freshly disinfected and cleaned uniform. Like the members of his staff, he displayed little in the way of adornment. No medals, no ribbons, no intricate epaulets, no serpentine gold braid. On Niyu, members of the military were considered professionals no different from healers or technicians, agronomists or astronomers. Modest insignia identifying their specialties were sufficient to proclaim their status.

His Toroudian counterparts were no different, save that their uniform wrappings were gray and purple in contrast to the Kojn-umm blend of yellow, brown, and silver. They were also an equal mix of male and female. There were no tables—only a sufficiency of the usual narrow-backed, narrow-seated Niyyuuan chairs, arranged in two crescents facing one another. In the absence of modern recording instrumentation, scribes stood ready on both sides to take down everything that was said, so that there could be no chance of confusion later. Though the method was ancient, the materials were not, and could be unceremoniously dumped into any reader and rapidly transmuted into electronic form.

The official Toroudian contingent was impressive. Toroud-eed had fought and defeated several, often larger realms in the perpetual Niyyu-uan search for commercial or political advantage. Its fighters were tough and determined, its government resolute, its traditional defenses well laid-out and maintained. All the more reason Saluu-hir-lek and his soldiers had gained so much acclaim for recently driving them away from Jalar-aad-biidh. It was safe to say that they had been surprised by the Kojnian's decision to counterattack so soon after their recently ter-minated siege.

That did not mean, the general knew, that they were so weakened that their realm could be easily overcome. Hence the need for this con-ference—and for elucidation. Formalities were held to a minimum. There were battles to be fought.

Once the obligatory introductions and stiff pleasantries had been exchanged, Fadye-mur-gos, the commander of Herun-uud-taath's de-fenses, unfolded herself and rose. She was of average height, average breadth, average everything except intelligence and resolve.

"I congratulate yous on deception yous devised to get yous' troops inside the southeastern gate. Unfortunately for yous, they now trapped there, unable to advance any farther into ours defensive complex or to retreat without being cut down both within and outside the walls."

Saluu-hir-lek rose and advanced to meet her. As was usually the case, he was notably shorter than his opposite number. As was also usu-ally the case, he did not seem so.

"It all matter of interpretation. Is Wegenabb half-full or half-de-clining? I would say instead my troops now control southeastern sec-tion of Herun-uud-taath. Use of it is denied yous for any purpose. From present firmly secured position, soldiers of Kojn-umm can harry yous' forces from the rear, cut off any resupply of yous from that main route, and if necessary can fall back in good order with minimal casualties."

No outcries of disagreement rose from her staff, and her eyes did not dilate; but here and there the general saw the occasional half flex-ing of a frill, the tight contraction of a mouth, the stiffening of several tails. The tactical truth, he knew, probably lay somewhere between her assertion and his rebuttal, though he felt confident of his own position. Like any good officer, in conceding her contention a modicum of truth, he was simply being strategically conservative.

Despite their best efforts to conceal it, however, her staff knew who held the plausible advantage.

"In fact," he added for good measure, "we actually do have the means for reinforcing our position inside Herun-uud-taath." He was not certain if they believed that one, but the claim visibly unsettled some of the Toroudian senior staff even more than had his confident rebuttal.

Fadye-mur-gos was not about to let him spew claims unchallenged. "I disagree with everything you assert," she rasped back, shifting her stance so that her upper body and long neck inclined belligerently toward him.

Saluu-hir-lek was not fazed in the least, either by her words or her posture. "I speaking the truth. You may not know it, yous' staff may not know it, but yous' junior officers and soldiers on station know it." After letting that sink in and enjoying their discomfort during the pause, he let loose with something that for the first time genuinely did shock them.

"However, it not matter, because forces of realm of greater Kojnumm ready to stop fighting right now."

At least two of the assembled officers seated behind their commander emitted exhalations of disbelief. She turned on them sharply, silencing any further outbursts of surprise with a warning stare, before returning her attention to her opposite number. She also resumed a fully upright stance.

"I not sure you listened to correctly. You presenting offer of surrender?" Despite her admirable self-control, she could not keep a hint of incredulity from her voice.

"That would be absurd, would it not be? With us holding the strategic advantage?"

"Yous hold no such advantage," she corrected him without hesitation.

He made a coordinated sinuous gesture with both arms. "I not call this meeting for argue merits of current battlefield situation. I making offer to stop fighting, not to surrender. Are very different callings."

"Surely," she responded, recovering some of her momentarily lost poise, "you not asking for ours?"

"No, I not." Head tilted back, huge eyes fully open, he met her gaze evenly.

Clearly, even someone as experienced and knowledgeable as Fadyemur-gos had never dealt with such a situation before, and certainly not on an active battlefield. Despite her partisan bluster, Saluu-hir-lek was confident someone of her martial erudition was well aware that the successful infiltration of a portion of Herun-uud-taath had shifted the balance of power on the battlefield in favor of the invaders. Not deci-

sively, perhaps, but meaningfully. So his offer to call a halt to the fighting, when the forces of Kojn-umm held the advantage, had thrown her
and her staff badly off balance. As she tried to figure out what he
was doing and what he was really after, she was doing her best to stall
for time.

He had no intention of letting her.

"Then I confess I not understand what you really offering, Saluu-
hir-lek."

He allowed his gaze to occasionally travel beyond her so that he
could make eye contact with each and every member of her senior staff.
Some of them were older than she was, he noted, and would find what
he was about to say even more bewildering than what had already transpired.

"What I offering, on behalf of myself, my troops, and the government of greater Kojn-umm, is opportunity for both sides to win."

Fadye-mur-gos thought she had prepared well for this meeting, this
significant confrontation. Even when the conversation with her
renowned counterpart had begun to disintegrate into uncertainty, she
was convinced she remained on top of and aware of all its possible
ramifications, even to the seemingly outrageous. But now, for the first
time in her long and distinguished military career, she found herself at
a loss. It made her very uncomfortable. In the short term, her unease
translated into outrage.

"You trying joke with me, Saluu-hir-lek. I have never hear of such
a thing. This not a game we play in here today. Lives balance on the
blade of our responses."

"All the reason more to listen close, all yous, to what I have to say."

Though still confused, she gestured strongly. "Oh, we all will listen
well. I myself am most very curious hear you attempt clarification of
the blatantly preposterous. Is no war, no battle, where both sides can
win. Always one side win, one lose. Always one side advance to take
control of field of battle, other side retreat."

"Not," Saluu-hir-lek told her, "if both sides advance together."
Turning, he gestured tersely.

Two figures new to the talks entered the meeting area. While one
was only slightly shorter than the typical Niyyuu, the other was a squat,
hirsute quadruped with small bright eyes, a wet nose, and a tongue that
lolled indifferently from the left side of its open jaws. It flumped down
next to the seat of one of Saluu-hir-lek's senior officers as its somewhat
less hairy bipedal companion advanced to stand beside the general.

Along with her own subordinates, Fadye-mur-gos stared at first one new arrival then the other before returning her attention to her counterpart. "These are two of four aliens arrived Kojn-umm some many ten-days ago. I know of them from sightings on general broadcastings. One is entertaining personage; other is celebrated for skill in culinary arts. Neither is soldier. Why they here, at this summiting? What have they to do with action of and on battlefield? You perhaps think to bombard us with expensive food?"

Expecting to encounter no aliens, she wore no translator, but in the long months since they had been on Niyu, both man and dog had managed to acquire a working knowledge of the principal language. Like the Niyyuu themselves, their speech was discordant but straightforward. If his appearance at the conference was something of a shock, his growling knowledge of their language was even more so. Meanwhile Saluu-hir-lek stood back slightly, hugely enjoying himself.

There was a time not so very long ago when Walker would have been completely intimidated by the kind of audience he now faced. No longer. Thanks to the time he had spent in the company of a diversity of aliens while in Vilenjji captivity and encounters subsequent with many more, he had reached the point where he no longer thought of any alien as particularly "alien." They were simply other beings, with elaborate makeup and often impossible forms but with personalities and cultural affectations no stranger than some he had encountered on the streets of downtown Chicago. He faced the bemused, hostile representatives of the defiant military establishment of the realm of Troudeed squarely.

"I am called Marcus Walker. I come from a world that is not a part of what passes for galactic civilization. As such, I am a neutral party to the current conflict." As always when he spoke Niyyuuan, his throat hurt. The nearest earthly analog, he knew from once having seen a documentary on it, was Mongolian throat-singing. But he persevered, and each time he did it, the lining of his throat protested a little less.

"You travel with and support aims and objectives of realm of Kojn-umm," one of the Toroudian officers countered sharply.

Walker met huge, accusing eyes to which he was no longer a stranger. "I travel with the army of Kojn-umm, yes. I can fight but do not. Sometimes I cook for them. That is different from fighting. I would be happy to cook for the valiant soldiers of Toroud-eed as well."

Both his offer and his manner were designed to be disarming. They had the intended effect. The hostility directed toward him lessened perceptibly.

"How could that be?" inquired another senior officer. "Saluu-hir-lek speaks of advancing together. Advancing where, and to what end? You have some knowledge of this or you would not have been brought between the crescents."

"I am beginning think both the general and the alien speak obliquely of possible alliance." As she spoke, Fadye-mur-gos was study-ing Walker closely. "This is impossible thinking. Firsting, were Kojn-umm and Toroud-eed to ally, would create combined traditional military force powerful enough to alarm other neighboring realms, who would join against us. Seconding, who would we ally against, and why?"

"I'm aware of your traditions," Walker told her. "Probably more than I really want to be. However, that's the reality. I know that your two realms can't cement a formal alliance against a third party without in-curring the attention of other realms. So the new kind of relationship that Saluu-hir-lek and the government of Kojn-umm is proposing would not be structured as an alliance, as such a joining together is generally understood. It would simply be your two governments acting in concert for a mutually agreed-upon end."

"Semantics," declared a grizzled veteran of Fadye-mur-gos's staff. "An alliance is an alliance. It is the action that is important, not the naming."

"Not," Saluu-hir-lek put in with satisfaction, "if we appear to act independently of each other."

The veteran was not convinced. His frill, Walker noted, was ragged with age and the scars of many battles. "This talk make my head hurt. A sword is more direct."

"If you break off this fight," Walker continued, "without striking a formal peace agreement, then technically the forces of Kojn-umm and Toroud-eed are still at war, right?"

Fadye-mur-gos turned to her staff, two of whom gestured strongly and without hesitation. "That is so," she hacked at Walker, her tone guarded.

"And if each of you independently and without apparent coordi-nation attack a third entity while still formally at war with each other, perhaps even while continuing to engage in skirmishes against one an-other at the same time, wouldn't it be very difficult for anyone else to prove you were acting together against that third party? As an alliance?"

"I suppose it might so appear," she conceded. Her gaze shifted to the smug-looking Saluu-hir-lek standing nearby. "Of course, even with attempts to control such skirmishes they could easily develop into larger battles. If that happened, and inexplicable fast stopping was put to them, then deception would be exposed."

"Not," the general of Kojn-umm told her, "if they were adjudicated by a third, uninterested party. In such case, would be impossible prove one side colluding with the other."

"What third party could reasonably be expected judge such unprecedented kind of confrontations?" she shot back.

"Your annoying, nosy, ever-present media."

All eyes went to the latest arrival to the conference. Scuttling in on all ten limbs, Sque scrambled onto the back of an empty chair, a position that elevated her to eye level with the others.

"I am called Sequi'aranaqua'na'senemu. I am smarter than anyone in this cheerless fold-up of a building, and I can prove it. I can also prove it to anyone on this benighted world."

Walker winced, but held out hope that as she continued, his companion would moderate her usual contempt.

"If others of your world, including your omnipresent worldwide media, can see that the continuously argumentative forces of Kojn-umm and Toroud-eed continue to battle one another across an ever-widening field of combat, it should make it apparent to all that you are not functioning as true allies. Allies do not go on fighting and killing one another. Seeing this, it is unlikely a devastating coalition of multiple realms will be arrayed against you. At the very least, from my studies of your traditions, it will greatly confuse the matter. Debate will take the form of extended discussion, by which time your objective will be achieved."

"Objective?" Yet again Fadye-mur-gos found herself at a loss. It was not a condition she enjoyed. "What objective?"

"The subjugation of Biranju-oov," Walker told her.

There was a stir among the general staff of the army of Toroud-eed. None of them had any love for that powerful maritime realm. But strong as they were, Toroud-eed had never been powerful enough to contemplate mounting a traditional attack against their larger neighbor. Impossible as the relevant arrangements seemed on the face of it, the offer that was being put forward was too appealing to simply ignore.

Fadye-mur-gos remained doubtful. "This is a ruse, a subterfuge. No matter what ongoing skirmishing between our two armies the media may show, other realms will detect the ghost of an alliance if not the reality of one."

"But they will be uncertain as to its ultimate objective," Walker told her. "And being uncertain, they will delay. By the time they decide to

join and move against you—if they even reach that point of agreement—Biranju-oov's traditional forces will be defeated and its government forced to make the concessions Kojn-umm and Toroud-eed have
long sought from it."

They were tempted, he saw. It was a new idea. Continue fighting
one another while surreptitiously striving toward a common goal. Like
Saluu-hir-lek, they were wondering if it was workable, and if so, if it violated the strict traditions of Niyyuuan combat. To Walker the process
was intimately familiar. It was exactly the kind of ploy traders used on
the floor of the exchange when two or more parties wished to try to
manipulate the market for a particular commodity. They would agree to
bid against one another to drive a price up or down. It was illegal, of
course, and if the respective parties were found out, people could, and
did, get sent to jail.

But this was not Chicago, and the issue at stake was not the price
of cocoa beans.

Fadye-mur-gos and her staff were wavering, he saw. It was time to
push them over the edge. With a nod in Sque's direction and her ac-
quiescent wave of one tendril, he spoke into the pregnant silence.

"There is one more thing." The enemy commander turned to him.
"It is recognized that even with ongoing skirmishes between the forces
of Kojn-umm and Toroud-eed, the appearance of collusion may persist.
Therefore, Saluu-hir-lek has agreed to turn over 'official' command of
the army of Kojn-umm to me and my friends. That would make the appearance of some kind of covert alliance between Kojn-umm and
Toroud-eed appear even less likely."

This time even Fadye-mur-gos could not repress an exhalation of
surprise. She looked immediately at Saluu-hir-lek. When that worthy responded positively, the burst of energetic discussion among her staff
could not be suppressed. Once the import of Walker's statement sank
in, however, she found herself gesturing knowingly.

"Very clever. Perhaps too clever. If little-known aliens appear have
taken control of army of Kojn-umm, outside observers will be distracted by issues that have nothing do with matters of possible alliance.
They be so busy trying analyze ramifications, war may be over before
any kind understanding is reached." Her gaze returned to Walker. "This
only adroit fiction, of course. Kojn-umm would never surrender real
power to off-worlders. No Niyyuuan realm would do so."

"How you know?" Saluu-hir-lek challenged her. "When was last
time such situation transpired?"

It was dead silent in the meeting room. She stared at him for a long moment—and then burst out in the coughing equivalent of robust Niyyuuan laughter, in which she was soon joined by both her staff and that of Saluu-hir-lek. Walker and George both winced. The collective noise sounded like a hundred metal files simultaneously working on one giant piece of rough iron.

When the coughing had died down, she approached her opposite number and drew the two fingers of one hand down the center of Saluu-hir-lek's chest. "On a battlefield, shrewdness sometimes worth more than extra battalions. I readily confess I myself find this distinctive proposal appealing. But not for me decide alone. Proposal must be put to Council of Toroud-eed."

The general indicated his understanding. "Naturally must be. Would be same for me if situation reversed. Meanwhile, fighting between us must continue. But perhaps not unrestrained. Is normal time for customary reassessment of strategic positionings. Troops shift here, catapults and arbalests move there. Now is time for repairing and reprovisioning. Latter is most necessary." Restraining his amusement, he gestured in Walker's direction. "New 'commanders' agree with this assessment." Approaching closer to her, he drew his own hand across her shoulder.

"Best for forces of both Kojn-umm and Toroud-eed to rest and take stock." He performed what Walker now recognized as the Niyyuuan equivalent of a meaningful wink. "Both armies needs be prepared for whatever significant confrontation is to be coming. Not to be suggesting anything, but only by way of illustration, is worth mentioning as example that is goodly marching distance from border of Toroud-eed to ancient walls of Biranju-oov."

**11**

"It is agreed!"

Viyv-pym entered the big dwelling wagon that had been reserved for the use of the aliens. Half of it was occupied by Walker, George, and Sque. The other half was reserved for the use of Braouk. Even so, the Tuuqalian was crowded. Typically, he did not complain—though given his general melancholy it would have been hard to tell the difference from his usual state of mind even had he chosen to do so.

After the excited Viyv-pym had finished delivering her news and withdrawn, George hopped up onto the side sleeping platform that had been added to accommodate him. "Great. Now no matter what happens, we're stuck with it." He turned a jaundiced eye on Walker. "I was a member of a pack once. It's great—unless things don't go well, food runs short, and they decide to turn on and eat the weakest member of the group."

Walker nodded somberly. "Then we'd better keep working to ensure that there's plenty of 'food' to keep the armies of dear old Kojn-umm and Toroud-eed busy."

"Speaking of consumption," Sque ventured, "I presume you have given thought as to how eventually to deal with Biranju-oov, assuming that our initial plans proceed as well as we hope?"

"I'm working on it," Walker assured her touchily. "Let's not get ahead of ourselves."

"I am always ahead of myself." She curled her tendrils around her, forming a platform of tentacles at her base, and blew a contemptuous bubble in his direction. "It is the K'eremu way. It is one reason why we are always ahead of everyone else."

At least he wasn't alone in this, Walker reflected. If things got difficult, he could always turn to Sque and George for advice. For obvious reasons, he hoped he would not have to do that.

At the moment, Viyv-pym's celebratory announcement was a clear indication things were going well. Very soon, word should come that the armies of both Kojn-umm and Toroud-eed had begun moving. Not toward one another, but southwestward, and fighting with one another all the while. From what he had learned about Biranju-oov, it would not be easy to assault, even by the more-or-less combined forces of Kojn-umm and Toroud-eed. If resistance proved as stalwart as expected, the real difficulty would involve keeping the attacking armies of two traditional enemies focused on their new target instead of on each other, while maintaining the fiction of the latter.

Such uncertainty and confusion proved advantageous when the time came to march. Expecting the forces of Kojn-umm to retreat or those of Toroud-eed to surrender, the civilian populations of both realms as well as observing media were flabbergasted when both began marching away from Herun-uud-taath—parallel to one another, and not back toward Kojn-umm. If worldwide media coverage had been extensive before, now it seemed as if every mobile scanner and famous commentator on the planet materialized around, behind, or above the skirmishing columns. As the marching forces continued fighting among themselves, disputing the changing territory that separated them, neutral military analysts found themselves at a loss as to how to describe what was happening.

If the two armies continued to challenge one another, then they could not be prohibited allies. But if they were marching together toward a single, as-yet-undefined goal, then they could be nothing else but. Troops on the ground knew only what they had been told, which was very little and not especially informative. Continue to advance as instructed in good order, and attack and defend against a perfidious nearby enemy that was doing exactly the same. As for the general staffs of both armies, who presumably had some grasp of the mysterious overall strategic picture that must lie behind such unprecedented maneuvers, when they were interviewed each and every senior officer was conspicuously closemouthed.

Something rare and uncommon was happening. Of that, the mystified commentators were certain. When basic geography and some simple extrapolation suggested that both massed forces were stumbling in the general direction of the realm of Biranju-oov, pointed questions as to intentions were put to officers on both sides. All such inquiries were directed up the line of command, at whose terminus the increasingly frustrated inquirers received nothing more informative than pleasant greetings and expressions of regret at the lack of information that was available for general dissemination.

Certainly, it was a march like no other. As soldiers repeatedly attacked and fell back on both sides, their actions were covered in unprecedented depth by the brigade of media observers. Passing to either side of both parallel columns, or above it, casual travelers and commercial transporters added observations of their own. Media and public not only wondered what was going on, but what the ultimate objective was of the unprecedented clash.

By the time the two battling armies swerved away from Biranju-oov's modern capital—with its flexformed buildings, extensive sprawl, and busy spaceports—and headed for the old walled city, savvy observers thought they had finally divined the intent of the unprecedented exercise. There was to be an attack on the maritime realm's traditional defenses, in the traditional manner, by wholly nontraditional elements. For while the forces of Kojn-umm and Toroud-eed began to establish proper bivouacs and bring forward their siege engines, they continued to brawl actively with one another. If the latter was some sort of ruse, the commentators hovering above the incipient battlefield observed, it was being perpetrated with a vengeance: soldiers from both sides continued to die in the seemingly endless series of ongoing clashes.

As if this battlefield situation were not unconventional enough, the military command of Biranju-oov that had settled into the old city found itself presented with not one but two entirely separate sets of articles requesting its surrender: one from each of the attacking armies. Though essentially identical in content, they were put forward by two different delegations. The response of the old city's defenders to this confusion was straightforward.

"Kill them all," Commander in Chief Afyet-din-cil instructed his subordinates, "and we sort out internal arrangements later."

Unlike Kojn-umm and Toroud-eed, whose traditional approaches were defended by fortresses built to control mountain passes, the capital of Biranju-oov was a seaport of notable lineage. While fighting commenced around and before the old walled city and its two fortresses that backed onto a deep cove, the massive modern capital itself had been built up around the greater harbor off to the south. Only tradition preserved the old city's importance. To make war on the capital proper would require modern weapons and tactics whose use was of course forbidden among the Niyyuu. So the defense of the realm was focused on the old city's ramparts. These were stronger facing the sea, from whence assaults had traditionally come in ancient times. For Biranju-oov to be attacked from the land was unusual, but not unprecedented.

Every day, units from the army of Kojn-umm or Toroud-eed would test the strength of the old city's walls and the resolve of their defenders. These attacks were never made in tandem. The two armies made no effort to coordinate their assaults. On a couple of occasions, in fact, these first probes ended in complete confusion when the soldiers involved ignored the city walls and their baffled defenders to turn viciously on each other. At such times the guardians of traditional Biranju-oov would be left gaping in amazement at the fighting taking place on the ancient floodplain below them and wonder what in the name of the Ten Travails of Telek-mun-zad was going on.

No one had ever heard of, nor were there any records of in the long history of Niyu, a three-way war.

Commentators from other realms and other continents exhausted themselves trying to find explanations for what was taking place. Whenever it appeared that the besieging armies were beginning to act in concert, they would fall to fighting among themselves. Just when the defenders of Biranju-oov believed the offensive against their integrity was about to fall apart, the forces of one army or the other would launch a furious individual assault against them. Or a battalion of Toroud-eed would attack and fall back only to have the assault taken up by the opportunistic forces of Kojn-umm.

Scrutinizing all this were powerful realms who had initially worried that a formal alliance had been forged between Kojn-umm and

Toroud-eed. Concerned at first, these interested onlookers now found themselves adrift in a sea of bemusement. What kind of allies consistently attacked one another, even as they were assailing a third party? Was there a real danger to other lands here, a genuine threat, or would the assault on well-defended Biranju-oov collapse under the weight of its own disorientation? Being uncertain of what they were seeing, these outside observers were understandably unsure how to react.

There was some talk of several realms uniting to move against the attacking forces. But which ones? Those of Kojn-umm, of Toroud-eed, or both? No apparent rationale for such a mobilization existed. With confusion deepening among the onlookers, it stood to reason that it might also be deepening among the participants. Accusation of a formal alliance being a serious matter, it was decided to wait, and continue to watch, and see what happened. Besides, intervention in such disputes was always expensive, in terms of both soldiers and public treasure.

Of those involved, happiest of all were the media, who while covering the unprecedented and inexplicable tripartite conflict found themselves enjoying viewer attention that bordered on the historic. His individual impact on the battlefield being unprecedented, Braouk was a particular focus of attention. He submitted to a steady succession of interviews with a mixture of patience and resignation. At least these did not last long. All it took was for some commentator to inquire about the Tuuqalian's passion for recitation, whereupon an obliging Braouk would respond with an example. Ten or fifteen minutes of listening to unbroken moody Tuuqalian saga was invariably sufficient to cause even the most dedicated interviewer to insist that he or she was suddenly needed elsewhere.

The interest in Braouk also served to deflect attention from his less-imposing companions. Sque spent much of her time in solitary moist meditation in the specially hydrated wagon compartment that had been fabricated for her. Though devoid of forbidden modern technology, it was sufficient to keep her happily humid. Though known to food preparation specialists, Walker's fame had not spread quite as far and wide as Biranju-oov, a realm that was sophisticated but not intimate with Kojn-umm. As for George, he was regarded as little more than a talkative novelty, a designation that suited him fine. The time they had spent in Kojn-umm had given him his fill of inane interviews.

So it was that with the military preoccupied with the conduct of the assault and the media focused on its ongoing action and details, no one noticed when a ten-day following the commencement of the siege, one thick-bodied biped and one short quadruped riding a borrowed tibadun slipped out of the Kojn-umm camp in the middle of the night. They headed not for the front lines, or for the parallel encampment of the forces of Toroud-eed, but back along the winding route the advancing armies had taken. After riding a modest distance back the way they had come, they abruptly changed their course and angled sharply to the south.

Reaching their first objective, they abandoned the tibadun. The animal promptly whirled and headed back in the direction of its distant stable mates. Standing on the ground cover of a minor shipping corridor, it was not long before the modern communicator Walker carried was able to hail an empty, automated public transporter. Ascertaining that their interrealm credit was good and notwithstanding their outrageous appearance, the vacant on-duty vehicle descended so that they could board. Having spent time researching their intended destination prior to their arrival outside the old city of Biranju-oov, human and dog relaxed in climate-conditioned comfort as the nearly silent transporter obediently accelerated toward the capital city of the realm.

The modern city.

Far, far from home, the unlikely pair of travelers commented on the size and extent of the Niyuan metropolis with a self-confidence that would have amazed their old friends. Their composure had a basis in experience: after all, they had seen Seremathenn. Traveling at high speed between ceramic-clad towers and forests of brilliantly lit residential complexes, the modern, efficient transport zipped them through the outskirts and deep into the central conurbation proper in less than an hour.

It slowed only when nearing their chosen destination: the seat of Biranju-oov's honored and much-admired government. There, local security took over the transport's internal guidance system. It did not bring them to a stop, nor did it deliver them unwillingly to a waiting station packed with armed guards. Instead, as covertly prearranged, they were efficiently channeled past monumental marbleized office complexes dating from the realm's venerable past, across meticulously maintained parkland speckled with pastel-hued lights and effervescent horizontal fountains, to finally slow as they neared an unspectacular but recently erected structure located on the far side of the complex's center.

Guards did meet them there immediately upon their disembarkation, but the slender, highly trained soldiers were present to serve as the visitors' escort, not as their apprehenders. After many, many ten-days exposed to hand-to-hand combat that utilized only traditional primitive armaments, it was something of a shock for both Walker and

George to find themselves paralleled and guided by Niyyuu armed with sleek, compact energy weapons.

It being the middle of the night and the Niyyuu no less diurnal than the pair of alien visitors, the building was largely deserted. What work was being done was being carried out by individuals in isolated offices. Perhaps the busiest place was the Media Relations Section, but it was located in a different structure entirely. As was customary, all strategic military planning occurred in the delegated war rooms scattered along the length of the old city's walls. As both visitors well knew, the use of advanced computational devices or communications systems was by Niyyuuan convention not permitted.

That did not mean that every defender of Biranju-oov was at that moment posted somewhere within the old city or atop its solid stone walls. Four of the most powerful members of its general staff were at that moment awaiting the arrival of the two aliens. Tired and irritable, frustrated by the lack of progress of the ongoing struggle but unable to significantly alter its evolution, they waited for their visitors in a general state of mind best described as bothered and bewildered, if not actually bewitched.

Predictably, the emotions they felt were largely repressed as Tavel-bir-dom, three-term premier of Biranju-oov, focused his attention on the nocturnal arrivals. The biped was bigger than he had been led to expect: not particularly tall, but very, very broad. In contrast, its companion was smaller than the premier had anticipated.

*I could break its neck with one swift kick*, he mused silently. It was hard to imagine such an oddly matched pair, and from the same planet at that, as the source of so much confusion.

"It late, sleep necessary, and I for one not desire this meeting." Responsible for the command of half the realm's armed forces but finding himself largely sidelined by the current land-based assault, Admiral Jolebb-yun-det had arrived in a fouler mood than any of his contemporaries. His greeting showed it. "Better to have something of worth to say, or I personally tempted disregard articles of agreement sealed by government agency responsible and have you put in national zoo for younglings to throw food bits at."

Taking a couple of steps forward, George hopped up uninvited onto a low empty cabinet and made himself comfortable. "We'll do our best to make sure you haven't lost sleep for nothing." He glanced at his companion. "Offer them the bone, Marc." The dog winked at the admiral, whose small round mouth, painted in war colors of alternating yellow and blue, contracted in bemusement. "It's a really big bone. Big and tasty."

Shadim-hur-lud, representative of the Citizen's Parliament of Biranju-oov, gazed down at the impertinent hairy creature. "I not put off a sound rest to be taunted by alien riddles." Her wide-eyed attention shifted to the patient Walker. "If you have something say, sentient, speak it now."

Taking a step toward them, Walker drew something from a pouch fastened to his belt. No one in the room flinched. The visitors had already been triple-scanned for weapons, sharp objects, and explosive chemical combinations. Had they carried any on or within their persons, it would have been detected by the relevant security equipment that swathed the small meeting room in an aura of complete protection.

Though no bigger than Walker's middle finger, the projection unit generated between himself and the sleepy representatives of the government of Biranju-oov a detailed three-dimensional image of the field of battle. A few flickers of interest showed among the assembled. Not at the use of a technology that was familiar to them all, but at the fact that so strange and unique an alien was making effortless use of it. As Walker spoke, tiny images shifted and moved within the roughly rectangular field.

"Already a ten-day has passed without any of the three sides having gained anything like a strategic advantage over the other."

"That will change soon," declared the fourth member of the group, who was representing the army at the meeting. "We gathering the means push back all attacking forces from old city vicinity and destroy them on open floodplains."

George raised his head briefly from where it was resting on his crossed paws. "Might succeed, might not. Try that kind of massive counterattack and you risk overreaching yourself. Not much chance to second-guess yourselves, if the effort turns out to come up short." The dog showed bright, sharp teeth.

The oversized, dark yellow eyes of Jolebb-yun-det glared down at him. "You very small being to be talking so big."

George shrugged, his fur rippling. "It's got nothing to do with me. My friend and I are just along for the experience."

The premier stared hard at Walker. "How can this be true? You travel with army of Kojn-umm, reports claim you even in command, but now you say you not on their side?"

Official disavowal of modern intelligence-gathering apparatus or no, Walker reflected, it was clear the forces of Biranju-oov were not operating in a vacuum. They knew that he and George hailed from

Kojn-umm and not Toroud-eed. But then, such information would have been readily available from public media reports.

"We travel with that army, yes," Walker told him. "Some say we command it, others that our supposed active participation is a front designed to confuse opponents. Regardless of which is true, it does not mean we necessarily share in all of its goals."

The premier reacted thoughtfully. "So if you not here to betray Kojn-umm, or tell us what its military really want, you must be here to tell us what it is that you want."

*Sharp old polliwog,* Walker thought. *Have to be careful here.*

"All my friends and I want, for ourselves, is to return to our homes. Since we are unable to do that, we've busied ourselves trying to help those Niyyuu we encounter get what they want."

Two fingers splayed, the army's representative slapped a hand hard against a nearby seat back. The sharp *bang* echoed through the room. "It plain to see what Kojn-umm and Toroud-eed want. The capitulation, in traditional terms, of Biranju-oov!"

Walker responded immediately. "Not necessarily. Although it's not widely known," he added as he lowered his voice conspiratorially, "the real quarrel of their respective governments is not with Biranju-oov, but with Charuchal-uul."

Jaws would have dropped had the Niyyuu in the room possessed such facial features. The premier's poise gave way to open bewilderment. "But if Kojn-umm and Toroud-eed not interested in subduing Biranju-oov, then why attack us? If dispute with Charuchal-uul, why not attack them?"

Walker adjusted the tiny handheld projector so that the field of battle was replaced by a detailed portion of Niyu's globe. This focused on that portion of the world everyone in the room was presently occupying.

"By themselves, and especially while continuing to fight each other, Kojn-umm and Toroud-eed could not hope to defeat Charuchal-uul in traditional combat."

"That for a certainty." The army representative made the assertion without hesitation.

Walker took no umbrage at the comment. He had no patriotic capital to gain in rebuttal, and the officer was only stating what everyone in the room knew to be a fact.

"It is too big and too powerful, in the modern as well as the traditional Niyyuuan sense. Furthermore, it has no particular ongoing dispute with either of the realms that are presently attacking you. But," he added softly, "it does with you."

Shadim-hur-lud pressed the tips of all four long, limber fingers together. "You know much about Niyyuuan society, visitor."

George yawned. "We've had plenty of time for study."

"The last formal clash between Biranju-oov and Charuchal-uul was never settled to your satisfaction," Walker continued. "Subsequently, your respective governments have tried their best to paper over the lingering differences. But resentment still simmers on both sides. Especially among certain influential elements of Biranjuan society."

"What, exactly, are you proposing, alien?" The parliamentary representative had one tall ear pointed directly at him, the other at George. "Is it possible we may assume that you can claim speak for forces of Toroud-eed as well as Kojn-umm?"

"You may," Walker lied. Time for elaboration and clarification could come later. Right now it was crucial to secure a commitment from this government. "Despite what information to the contrary you may have acquired from the media, as an entirely neutral party with no personal interest in the outcome of your traditional fighting, my friend and I are authorized to broker an amendment to hostilities between your forces and theirs—provided that all can come to a mutual understanding how certain events should proceed in the immediate future."

The premier, for one, was taken aback by the scope of what was being implied. "Are we to understand that Kojn-umm and Toroud-eed offering to ally with Biranju-oov in battle against the corrupt and fraudulent government of Charuchal-uul?"

"Not exactly," George murmured, further muddying the political waters.

"*Ahskh*," rasped the admiral. "Now truth will appear."

Walker turned to him. "You know that any such formal alliance would be strong enough to alarm every other realm on Niyu. They would immediately combine against it. But if it can be shown that the fighting between yourselves and the forces of Kojn-umm and Toroud-eed are continuing, such a marshaling of planetary forces might well be constrained. Besides which, the forces of Toroud-eed and Kojn-umm would continue to battle among themselves. Everyone would find it perfectly natural that you, of Biranju-oov, would try to make use of that continuing clash and turn it to your tactical advantage."

"A four-way war." By now even the initially mistrustful Jolebb-yun-det was intrigued. More than intrigued, he was becoming excited at the possibilities presented by the alien. "No one has ever heard of such a thing. The Charuchalans will be smothered by their own confusion."

"More than smothered," Walker told him. "Because while Biranju-oov continues to battle in the field with the armies of Kojn-umm and Toroud-eed, your traditional fleet of historic craft, Admiral, will strike the old fortresses of Charuchal-uul from the sea." He went silent—and waited. Nearby, George was unconcernedly chewing his toenails.

"What do yous think?" Tavel-bir-dom regarded his principal advisors. They were all fully awake now and oblivious to the lateness of the hour.

"The traditional navy has not had opportunity to show what it can do for many years," the suddenly energized admiral observed.

"This offers fine chance," the army's representative declared, "to settle historical wrongs of Charuchalans once and for all."

The premier turned to the one member of the group who had not yet spoken. "Shadim-hur, what say you? Will the parliament support, and underwrite, such an unprecedented venture?"

"For a chance to inflict a serious defeat on our old enemy Charuchal-uul, a willingness and a budget can always be found." She turned to regard the pair of expectant aliens waiting in their midst. "I do find myself wonder about one thing, though."

Walker met her stare. "My friend and I are here to respond to your concerns."

"I wonder," she murmured in the archetypal Niyyuuan rasp, "if Charuchal-uul is the end?"

"Not until they are soundly defeated, which occurrence I did not think to see in my lifetime," Tavel-bir-dom remarked before Walker could reply. "Much less during my term of office." Grateful for having been spared the need to respond to the parliamentary representative, Walker smiled at the premier. Like every Niyyuuan, he was fascinated by the degree to which the human's mouth seemed to split his face in half.

"I am sure you comprehend," Tavel-bir-dom went on, "that a decision of such import for all citizens of Biranju-oov must be considered and voted on by full government." A willowy gesture encompassed his colleagues. "We here are only the focus of power, not the power itself."

Walker nodded. "My friend and I won't be missed for a while. With your permission, we'll wait here in Biranju-oov for your decision."

"Should not be long in coming," Tavel-bir-dom assured him. The premier's excitement was now palpable as he contemplated a future that included the defeat of his realm's most persistent and powerful adversary. "Meanwhile, you two will be treated as honored representatives. I ask of you only a little patience. Small enough to request in expectation of very big thing."

As they were ushered out, Walker glanced back to see Shadim-hurlud following him with her eyes. Was she only typically curious about the strange alien who had addressed the gathering, or was her intensity reflective of the preternaturally perspicacious query she had so transiently posed? Walker did not know.

What he did know was that it would be best to take no chances, and for him and his friends to avoid the dangerously perceptive principal representative of the parliament of Biranju-oov as much as possible.

12

Tavel-bir-dom was as good as his ear-grating word. Three days had
passed since the aliens' arrival when the eccentric pair was informed that the government of Biranju-oov had agreed to their
unparalleled plan to move against Charuchal-uul. Despite this welcome
news, Walker and George knew that their work was not done.

Now they had to convince the forces of Kojn-umm and Toroud-eed.

Because despite what man and dog had implied to the leaders of
Biranju-oov, neither of those two commands had agreed to, or indeed
had even been consulted about, such a plan. Neither had any hereditary
dispute with the government or people of distant Charuchal-uul. Their
quarrel was with Biranju-oov. Which was why Walker and George had
been forced to seek the cooperation of that maritime realm at night,
and in secret.

But the Biranjuans didn't know that. If events transpired as Marcus Walker the trader had planned, they never would.

Should the true nature of his Machiavellian machinations be found out, however, there was a good chance all three governments would each vie with one another for the chance to deal with the double-dealing, hypocritical, treacherous aliens in their own way.

Slipping unseen out of modern Biranju-oov, Walker and George went separate ways: Walker to talk to the Kojnians, the dog to inform and persuade the Toroudians. All this taking place, of course, unbeknownst to the eager and already inveigled Biranju-oov. Meanwhile, the three-way hostilities continued on the battlefield before the walls of that maritime realm's old city, with all sides seeking an advantage over the other. As fighting went on, it became apparent this was a strategic impossibility. If the Kojnians appeared to be gaining an advantage, the Biranju-oov would step up their attacks on them. If the reverse was the case, they would concentrate more forces against the Toroudians. And all the while, both Kojnians and Toroudians kept up their assault on the defensive walls of old Biranju-oov while continuing to skirmish among themselves.

Under such circumstances, it was no wonder no one in any camp thought to ponder the same question that so far had occurred only to a certain wary leader of the Biranjuan parliament.

Walker pressed his case to his original Niyyuuan acquaintances with verve. Having already been convinced, Viyv-pym was there in her limited capacity as alien handler to back him up.

"There's really no choice," he was saying as he addressed Saluu-hir-lek's staff. As for the general himself, he struggled to maintain an air of measured solemnity. Of all those gathered in the prefabricated room, he was the only one Walker did not have to convince, having been let in on the plan of action from the beginning. Saluu-hir-lek watched his advisors and officers squirm as the alien laid out what was for them an uncomfortable reality.

"You have to assent to this agreement," Walker told them. "If you decline, the Biranjuans will make a formal agreement with the Toroudians against you. Since Biranju-oov will be seen as defending itself from attack, and not as an aggressor, no objections to such an agreement will be raised in the media or elsewhere. Your army will be soundly defeated, if not wiped out, by the combined forces that will be arrayed against you.

"But if you agree, then this much greater concerted attack against arrogant Charuchal-uul will proceed, to the glory of all."

One of the officers waved a finger in Walker's direction. "You seem much captivated by this possibility, human Walker. What attraction does triumph over distant Charuchal-uul hold for you?"

"None," Walker informed her unhesitatingly. "As it has been from the beginning of this campaign, my only concern is for the welfare of Kojn-umm. Just as it has always been ever since my friends and I first arrived on your world."

"Speaking of yous' friends . . . ," the officer began.

"They are presently occupied with other personal activities," Walker hastened to tell her. "The Tuuqalian in spinning his tales and seeing to his weapons, the K'eremu with her meditating, and the dog George with his usual unpredictable wanderings. Let's not lose sight of why your commander has called this meeting."

A senior advisor spoke up. He looked and sounded unhappy. "I, for one, not like this choice that is presented us. Charuchal-uul is far from Kojn-umm, and we have no historic differences with that vast and powerful realm. If we consent participate in this offensive, and it should fail, we risk incurring their enmity." He looked around at his colleagues. "Charuchal-uul more dangerous to have as long-term adversary than Toroud-eed or even Biranju-oov."

"But if they are defeated," another advisor remarked with barely suppressed excitement clouding his grinding tone, "that will not matter. Could be much to lose, is true. But if expedition ends in triumph, very much to gain."

"I am still troubled," the older advisor husked. "Is no assurance even combined forces of all three armies capable of defeating traditional military of great Charuchal-uul."

"Five armies," Walker corrected him quietly.

There was a perceptible stirring among the assembled. Even Viyv-pym looked at him doubtfully. Only Saluu-hir-lek retained his poise, already aware of what the wily alien was about to say.

It was left to a junior advisor on the general's staff to voice the question that dominated the thoughts of everyone present. "I never good much at mathematics, but last time I check field of battle, only three armies involved in this increasingly untidy conflict." Deep, glistening Niyyuuan eyes locked on Walker. "Would much appreciate it if alien tactician could explain what he is cooking."

Exhalations of amusement issued from her colleagues. As for Walker, no one appreciated the injection of a little levity into what had otherwise been an unremittingly tense situation more than the room's sole human.

Though much shorter than those of the Niyyuu, his fingers had become adept at manipulating their tools. Now he used them to adjust the image that drifted in the air between him and Saluu-hir-lek's staff.

"To the northeast of Charuchal-uul lies the small but energetic realm of Divintt-aap. Their government has already agreed to allow the traditional navy of Biranju-oov to utilize their excellent old harbor. Though modest in number and never a real threat to their far more powerful southern neighbor, their own traditional armed forces are well trained, well equipped, and intimately familiar with the local terrain." Under his direction, the image shifted again.

"Southwest of the Tkak peninsula and the Bay of Ghalaud-pir, the realm of Dereun-oon sprawls over mountains and deserts that flank fertile valleys. These valleys, which constitute the soul of the realm, rely for their lifeblood on the water of great rivers that originate in the even-higher mountains of the Yivinsab Range. Those of you familiar with planetary geography know that the peaks of the Yivinsab lie within the borders of Charuchal-uul." One of the senior advisors uttered a terse exclamation of appreciation. Walker was suitably encouraged.

"Successive governments of Dereun-oon have long coveted full, not just shared, control over the headwaters of these rivers that are so vital to not only the economy of their realm but to its culture. They see in our proposed combined assault on the dominance of Charuchal-uul an opportunity to gain something that has eluded them for a great many years."

Unable to restrain himself any longer, one of the junior officers rose and began probing the interior of the projection with a long finger. "Larger view now becomes clear. Divintt-aap commands northeast while navy of Biranju-oov lands troops and deploys against traditional coastal fortifications. Dereun-oon attacks from southwest." The finger moved: swirling, planning, tracing. "Combined forces of Kojn-umm and Toroud-eed, still fighting with each other, battle way across land bridge between continents of Saadh and Ruunkh to strike traditional Charuchal-uul fortresses from behind." Withdrawing his finger, he looked cynically from the alien to his commander in chief.

"This not all devised by clever food preparator from distant world."

The ground having been prepared for him, Saluu-hir-lek strode forward as Walker stepped back. "Because of profession practiced on his own world, the alien sees opportunities here we, steeped in our own culture, may have overlooked. I have take his conceptualizing and expand upon it." Like any good general, he tried to appear as if he were addressing each of his individual subordinates particularly, to the exclusion of everyone around them.

"For this strategy to work, must continue to maintain fiction of nonalliance. Must continue light fighting with forces of Toroud-eed. As we fall back, not toward home but toward land bridge to nearest coast of Saadh, some forces of Biranju-oov will pursue, supposedly to harry both retreating armies. Media will focus on this strange three-way battle. Cannot be prevented them also noting provisioning and departure of Biranju-oov traditional fleet. But with making skillful effort at dissemination, fleet's true purpose and destination can be suppressed until last minute.

"With luck, cooperative weather, and coordinated timing, all forces will be in position to attack Charuchal-uul simultaneously. Expect fierce resistance then from that dominating realm, and strong counterattacks. But this is traditional Niyyuuan warfare. Charuchalans bound by convention not to utilize modern means of transportation. Will be difficult for them to know where to send reinforcements first. Their internal command and control will be spread thin." He waved an arm fluidly. "We can do this! Will be enough triumph for all to share."

Viyv-pym was not completely convinced. "What if other realms, on other continents, perceive that this is true five-way alliance? Could generate twenty-third world war—using traditional means only, of course. Majority of world and population will be impacted by consequences only when watching media reports."

"There may be efforts at mediation, to keep conflict from spreading even farther," Saluu-hir-lek conceded. "But military intervention unlikely. This is conclusion reached by myself and other advisors. Greater widening of clash would mean great expense to powerful realms not otherwise directly impacted. Is calculated gamble, surely. But this is unprecedented opportunity to acquire significant commercial and political gains. Fortune favors the bold. And as visiting alien has pointed out, for us to refuse to participate means possible strong alliance of Toroudians and Biranjuans against Kojn-umm. Situation for us now is like running on mud. We continue to advance with speed, or we sink in circumstances of our own choosing." He eyed his staff unblinkingly. "Are you all with me?"

The grating exhalations of support that filled the room surpassed even those that had greeted Saluu-hir-lek following his defeat of the attacking Toroud-eed at the walls of Jalar-aad-biidh.

Meanwhile, not all that very far to the south, a small furry quadruped from the same unknown world as the verbally and physically expansive human was outlining the exact same plan to a tentative audience of officers of Toroud-eed, warning them that if they did not agree to participate in the grand adventure, their treacherous quasi-allies from Kojn-umm would surely unite with the defenders of Biranju-oov to destroy them. While some among his listeners questioned the dog's motivation, none could find fault with his logic. Those who were reluctant were swept up in the general enthusiasm for the opportunity to get the better of the traditional defenses of a realm historically too powerful for far-smaller Toroud-eed to ever contemplate attacking.

If anything, the general confusion and conflicting rumors that resulted from the multiple agreements and half assurances usefully served to confuse not only the potential target of so much deliberation, but the mystified media that was struggling to sort it out as well.

*

Among those seeking to make sense of it all, only the government of the ancient and admired realm of Fiearek-iib managed to gain a real inkling of what was happening on the other side of the planet from its peaceful fields and upscale manufacturing communities. As powerful as distant Charuchal-uul, the overseers of that wealthy dominion observed via relayed media and their own operatives the gradual development of the grand strategy put forth by Saluu-hir-lek of Kojn-umm—and his seemingly innocuous non-Niyyuuan advisors.

Premier and vice premier stood together before a force transparency on the sixty-third level of the central administration facility and contemplated the thriving metropolis of Yieranka spread out before them. Midday in Fiearek-iib meant it was midnight in western Saadh. Fighting there would be on hold, as without the assistance of modern means of illumination, the use of traditional implements of warfare rapidly reached a level of diminishing returns.

"What you, really, make of these exceptional developments?" the vice premier asked her only superior. Though they often differed on matters of policy, what was happening half a world away easily superseded any domestic concerns or local politics.

The premier gestured gracefully with one arm. "Remote threats are often the most dangerous, my friend. Believing themselves inoculated by distance, those are ones the comfortable all too often ignore. I been giving the matter more attention than I admit to in official briefings. For the moment, these atypical events half a world away not matter of immediate concern to Fiearek-iib." He turned away from the reassuring panorama of power and accomplishment. "Important thing is to ensure it never will become matter of immediate concern."

"How can we do that without we become directly involved?" the vice premier wanted to know. Though in parliament they waved in opposite on many issues, on this they were agreed. Therefore she flattened her crest and lowered her tails in deference and sought to share the wisdom of one she respected, if often disagreed with.

"Keep close watch on intelligence reportings not only from area of present conflict, but in nearby realms also." His eyes, one whitened and opaqued by an inoperable disease and for which he idiosyncratically refused replacement, inclined toward hers. "If one examine close and dispassionately what has happened in Saadh, an interesting pattern of a kind begin to emerge. Intelligence experts mostly agree it start with Toroudian siege of Jalar-aad-biidh. A few others say it start with arrival in Kojn-umm of four mismatched aliens."

The vice premier's mouth contracted to a point. Despite her advanced age, she was still considered very attractive; almost as famed for the flash of her still-taut frill as for her perceptiveness. "I know almost nothing of these aliens save what little I have encounter in the media. How could they be in any way central to such an upheaval among Niyyuu?"

The premier's expression wrinkled slightly. "Apparently, because they want go home. But nobody in astronomical establishment knows where any of their three homes are. It is reported government of Kojn-umm is very fond of them, and in no hurry see them depart."

"So to pass time they involve themselves in traditional local disputes?" The vice premier was openly dubious. "How that bring them closer to their homeworlds?"

Her superior sighed, air whistling through his perfectly round mouth. "There is much here Intelligence Section do not understand. I myself can claim no revelatory insight. It hard enough determine what drives smaller realms such as Kojn-umm and Toroud-eed without trying also comprehend the motivations of unfamiliar aliens."

"Then what course we set for beloved Fiearek-iib?"

He glanced back toward the peaceful midday setting that glowed beyond the barrier. If one tried hard enough, one could almost smell the newly opened hagril blossoms of the nearby Saralas world-forest.

"I suggest armed forces of Fiearek-iib begin maneuvers of traditional military elements four ten-days early. Will generate early holiday for populace, who will be thankful and not look too deeply into reasoning behind it. Also start initiate conversations on private diplomatic level with all neighbors—not only in continent of Paanh, but across planet. Continue active monitoring of situation in Saadh. Otherwise, unless and until existence of formal alliances against Charuchal-uul can be proven conclusively, Fiearek-iib and neighbors stay out of growing conflict."

The vice premier was silent for a long moment before responding. "Do you really think, my friend, that armies that are fighting among themselves can work together long enough to defeat traditional forces of realm as large and powerful as Charuchal-uul?"

The premier considered. "If this growing confusion of attackers can keep from destroying one another in process, then perhaps. If that happen, and it is end of it, then little will have been changed save for treaties and commercial agreements. But if it continues . . ." His words trailed away.

As always, the vice premier was quick to jump on unspoken implications. "What you mean, 'if it continues'? If Charuchal-uul defeated, there would be nothing to continue. Charuchal-uul dominates Saadh. If it fall to this motley blend of contentious assailants, it will take latter some time just to digest their triumph."

One eye shining, he turned to her anew. "Ambition is a craving that is never sated. Something drive these events that is different from all that have preceded it."

She speculated aloud. "The aliens?"

"Possible. Possibly a combination of factors, a coming together of unique circumstances. We must be ready for anything."

The implications of what he was saying were daunting. "Surely you not think crazy Kojnians and Toroudians could even imagine attacking Fiearek-iib!"

"I not have thought them capable of attacking Biranju-oov, either. Now all three continue appear fight among themselves, yet give every indication of moving against Charuchal-uul: separate but unequal. An outlandish way to run a war."

She gestured deferentially. "In this matter, I and my backers will support you in whatever responses you deem appropriate."

He could not smile, but indicated his satisfaction in typical Niyyu-uan fashion. "I wish I knew of some, beyond what I already have tell you. We must remain aloof, observe carefully, prepare for all possible occurrences no matter how outrageous. And one thing more."

"Speak it, and I will see it carried through," she told him.

When he turned back to the panoramic view for a last time, it was

not to gaze down at it, but beyond. "Have Intelligence find out everything, absolutely everything, that they can about these four visiting
aliens of whom Kojn-umm has become so enamored."

⁕

Coordinated from four different directions, the grand assault on
Charuchal-uul was like nothing seen on Niyu in civilized times. Needless to say, the media swarmed the offensive, in more of a frenzy than
the combatants on the widely spread battlefields. Rendered lax by centuries of confidence in their own power and the knowledge that any alliance strong enough to seriously challenge them would be considered
illicit on the face of it, the Charuchalans hardly knew where to counterattack first. Caught unawares by the need to fight on multiple fronts,
their response was momentarily paralyzed. Defenders of ancient walls
and fortresses fought bravely, even heroically, in the time-honored
Charuchalan manner, but those in the south and east were overwhelmed as the government initially concentrated reinforcements in
the north. When a portion of those were hastily dispatched on forced
marches to help in the south, the northern forts and ports were taken
by contentious battalions of Kojnians, Toroudians, and the marine
forces of Biranju-oov, all simultaneously battling one another for ultimate control of the battlefield.

It was all over so quickly that the proud Charuchalans hardly knew
whom to surrender to first.

News of the startling conquest of Charuchal-uul spread around
Niyu as fast as modern communications could carry it: which was to
say, instantaneously. Much discussion and not a little passionate argument swirled around whether or not the unprecedented cooperation of
the armed forces of not two, not three, but five different realms constituted a formal alliance requiring a coordinated response from the rest
of the planet.

Part of the problem in deciding how to proceed arose from the very
real fact that events had been allowed to progress to the point where
even a coalition of all the powerful realms of the remaining continents
would be hard-pressed to defeat the troublemakers. Especially since rumors abounded that defeated Charuchal-uul, instead of being plundered for commercial concessions, had been offered the chance to
minimize its losses and concessions by becoming the sixth member of
the fractious and unlikely partnership. Making traditional war on
realms of modest power such as Toroud-eed or Divintt-aap was one
thing; marching and sailing by traditional means across half a world to

confront them while they were acting in concert with five other maybe-allies, one of whom was now still-great Charuchal-uul, promised to be costly in both expense and blood.

So extensive realms such as Huoduon-aad and Gobolin-ees held back from issuing direct threats while their governments consulted among one another and tried to figure out the best way to respond to a political-military situation that was without precedent. As they did so, they were quite aware that the rapidly changing situation in Saadh and Ruunkh demanded a response as quickly as possible, lest the perceived controversy continue to escalate.

Intelligence reports were eagerly perused in the corridors of power in Huoduon-aad and elsewhere. Many of these were detailed, some conflicted, others packed with absurdities clearly designed only to justify the expense accounts of their respective perpetrators. But a few stood out in the way they focused on a certain confluence of specifics.

Most notable among these was the observation that nothing out of the ordinary had ensued until an apparently innocuous alien cook and his three equally implausible companions had grown unusually intimate with the military command of the midsized realm of Kojn-umm. That this was a matter of some significance was gradually recognized by the more perceptive among the concerned. As yet, however, they had not the faintest notion of what to do about it.

*

This time the conference was held not in some flimsy portable structure hastily erected on the field of battle, but in the great hall of Sidrahp-syn-sun, in the traditional capital of Charuchal-uul. With its spiraling buttresses and frescoed, bubblelike roof, the ten-story-high vaulted ceiling reminded an awed Walker of a gothic cathedral as it might have been designed by an alien Dali. Even though he had been told that the structure had no religious significance, and its elaborate preserved frescoes depicted alien scenes taken from life on a world other than his own, walking its length still engendered deep and profound emotions in him. For once, Braouk did not have to bend to clear ceiling or overhang.

Subsequent to being stunned by the leniency of their baffling brace of vanquishers, the Charuchalans had been almost painfully eager to accommodate any requests. As opportunistic as any Niyyuu, they sensed in making a willing offer to cooperate the chance to recover their own projected losses at the expense of others. Since tentative agreement had already been reached allowing them to keep all of their territory and

most of their commercial advantages provided they participate in the
peculiar alliance-that-was-not, the present summit had been called to
discuss other matters. Being a conference now of associates, albeit continuously argumentative ones, and not a triumph of conquerors over
the defeated, the mood was markedly more upbeat than its gloomy predecessor.

Representatives of all sides met beneath a vast thousand-year-old
dome that was entirely covered in bas-reliefs of gilded copper alloys in-
set with semiprecious stones. From below, it was like looking up at a
bowl of Heaven, the entire procession of Charuchalan history up to the
time of the building's final construction being depicted on that fabu-
lous curved surface. Walker wanted to lean back, relax, and study each
and every bit of it at leisure, but knew he could not do so. As an important member of the delegation from Kojn-umm, it would not do to
appear too awed.

Speeches echoed as greetings were exchanged. Beneath the dome's
perfect acoustics, Niyyuuan voices grated harsher than ever on other
ears. Disdaining diplomacy, Sque dealt with the din by placing the tips
of no less than three tendrils apiece over each of her aural openings.
Braouk, typically, elected to tough it out. Walker and George had no
choice but to endure, since neither of them possessed the extra limbs
necessary to cover their ears while still allowing them to manipulate
objects in their vicinity.

There were no seats, no tables. It was the Charuchalan fashion to
conduct such gatherings while standing, the theory being that when the
majority began to grow tired of the effort, it was time to terminate the
proceedings. As no one had been allowed into the conference armed,
modern conveniences were permitted in the ancient structure. Anxious
to be consumed, enthusiastic refreshments darted to and fro among the
participants, waiting to be grabbed out of the air. The interior climate
was set at maximum comfort—for Niyyuu, of course. A few select
commentators were allowed to record the proceedings for later broadcast. To Walker, the gathering had more the feel of a sophisticated party
than a formal conference fraught with political and military meaning.

As minor issues were debated and resolved, attentive automatic
recorders faithfully took down everything that was being said. A general atmosphere of good fellowship prevailed. A few senior military figures made bold to discuss which realms should be the subject of the
new association's first expedition even as their soldiers continued to
skirmish among themselves at scattered locations both without and
within Charuchal-uul's extensive borders.

It was left to senior Charuchalan general Deeleng-hab-wiq to move directly beneath the center of the dome, stand in the middle of the mosaic stone floor, and call for attention. Turning a slow circle, he addressed the entire assembly.

"Guests and enemies, honored soldiers of Charuchal-uul and fighters of other realms: unusual times are upon us." Someone made a crude but fitting joke, and the massed exhalations of appreciation ruffled Walker's hair. Unperturbed, Deeleng-hab-wiq continued. "We have seen development of extraordinary tactics that not so much defy tradition as avoid it." Unexpectedly, he halted in his slow turning to stare directly at Walker. "Perhaps significant visitor from unknown world has appropriate definition for it?"

Though used to speaking in front of others—indeed, even shouting in front of them—Walker was caught off guard by the sudden attention. Something was digging at his ankle. Looking down, he saw that George was pawing his leg and staring up at him.

"Say something, stupid. Just don't say something stupid."

It was a potentially pivotal moment in their relationship with Niyyuu other than those from Kojn-umm, Walker recognized. He cleared his throat. "Where I come from, we'd call the strategy that's recently been employed by the forces of Kojn-umm, Toroud-eed, and others an end run. When the forces arrayed against you, both military and cultural, are too strong to break through, you have to find a way around them."

Though the source and inspiration of the analogy was unknown to them, his explanation was clear enough. Murmurs of understanding were exchanged among the assembled.

Senior General Deeleng-hab-wiq was not finished. "Much has been learned from this experience. Though my realm has suffered, it not done so as significantly as would have been case in more ancient, unenlightened times. Instead of penalty, vanquishers of our traditional forces offer us chance to gain back what has been lost, by joining with them." He spared a glance for the ubiquitous hovering recorders. "While we continue forcefully resist their incursion, of course. Fight against, fight together, all at same time. Is unique way of looking at traditional warfare." Stepping away from the center of the intricately inlaid floor, he approached the human, halting less than an arm's length away. The narrow skull inclined slightly to one side, tall ears tilted forward, and moonlike eyes met Walker's own.

"We have learn that this unique perspective originate not with traditional strategic thinkers of any attacking forces, but with foreign visitors from Seremathenn, and beyond. As is natural Charuchalan way, admiration follows."

Walker shuffled nervously. Cheers after a good tackle on the field he was used to. Standing here, in resplendent alien surroundings, subject to the mixed curious and complimentary stares of dozens of ranking Niyyuuan soldiers and politicians, was another matter entirely. He fought to conceal his discomfort. A soft, whispered voice from somewhere near his feet helped to steady him.

"Don't blow this," George hissed warningly.

Walker gathered himself. "My friends and I are thankful for your compliment, but the congratulations deserve to be spread among all the relevant commanders."

The senior general of the armed forces of Charuchal-uul dipped his head briefly in acknowledgment of alien modesty. "Individual accomplishments are inevitably recognized by the discerning. Our research clearly indicates that you and yous' colleagues, though deceptively incompatible, cooperate fully on matters that affect yous all. We of Charuchal-uul, though caught off guard by yous' tactics, learn quickly." One hand reached out to stroke Walker's right shoulder. "Not surprising learn that new ideas come from new minds."

Walker could only mumble thanks on behalf of himself and his companions.

Deeleng-hab-wiq glanced briefly at the attentive crowd. "When seeking the best of new ideas, visitor Walker, we of Charuchal-uul are second to none in our ability to adapt to new conditions. Clearly seeing, if this unprecedented yet not formally allied consortium of realms is to continue to grow and succeed, leadership concurrent with the new ideas that inspire and drive it is required. The thing is decided." Taking two steps back, he gestured ceremoniously.

"The supreme military council of Charuchal-uul, in concert with full parliamentary sanction and approval of the military and governmental representatives of the other relevant realms, have determine to designate you, Marcus Walker of Earth, as chief determiner of strategy and tactics for all future endeavors involving the armed forces of those realms so indicated."

At his feet, George grinned toothily. Feeling a vast presence close behind him, Walker turned to see Braouk looming over him. A massive tentacle came down to rest on his shoulder while an eyestalk curved around either side of Walker's head as the Tuuqalian stared at him in stereo. The big alien rumbled in the human's ear.

"An important development, in our personal seeking, to progress. Thus think I, while observing this honor, so timely."

Conscious of multiple pairs of penetrating Niyyuuan eyes on him, Walker swallowed hard and mumbled, "But I'm just a commodities trader—and a cook!"

13

Stunned and benumbed, Walker was not the only one present to object to the unexpected and startling announcement. Visibly shocked, Saluu-hir-lek stepped out of the circle of dignitaries and into the center. Behind him, Viyv-pym looked more confused than Walker had ever seen her.

"What foolishness is this?" the commander of the forces of Kojn-umm demanded to know. He was so angry his ears were quivering. "I, Saluu-hir-lek, defender of Jalar-aad-biidh, have overseen every military advance since first pursuit of Toroudian attackers! Nomination of alien advisors as heads of Kojn-umm forces was for show only. Any dominant position is rightfully mine." Though utterly alien in appearance, Walker noted, the general made noises like any outraged sentient seeing a life-long dream evaporate before his eyes. The irony was that of all those notables assembled under the great dome, none supported the general's assertion more strongly than did the lone human present.

"It's true what Saluu-hir-lek says. My friends and I were 'made' heads of the army of Kojn-umm for certain reasons that need not be detailed here. The general was the one who was really in charge throughout."

Though he made mollifying gestures, Deeleng-hab-wiq did not back down from his declaration. "All of us, most certainly those whose traditional forces have been defeated, recognize the skill and experience of Saluu-hir-lek of Kojn-umm in directing combat operations. But careful study has shown from whence the original strategy comes that has allowed for the establishment of such unusual combinations of forces. Did not arise from you, Saluu-hir-lek." The representative of Charuchal-uul looked back to Walker. "Is not difficult for the interested to assess that unnatural proposals arise from unnatural sources."

"It not matter!" Saluu-hir-lek was livid. "I the one who directed combined armies. I the one who oversaw movements of forces as well as actual assaults. Besides, is madness to give actual as opposed to sham ability to make operational decisions at such a level to this . . . this . . ."

It was fascinating to watch a Niyyuu sputter, George observed. At such rare moments their round, muscular mouths resembled leaky hose spigots. It reminded him also very much of angry cats, though the Niyyuu were only passingly feline. Standing next to him, Walker was handling it rather well. There was something to be said for being stunned speechless. But if you couldn't talk, you couldn't say something foolish. It was hard for a mute to be imprudent.

"This non-Niyyuu?" the commander of great Charuchal-uul's forces finished for the general. "That precisely the reason why agreement to do so was so swiftly reached among affected governments. Biranju-oov, for example, give every indication of balking if someone like youself named to such a position of power. Same true for commanders of traditional army of Toroud-eed. And I may say with some confidence, of Charuchal-uul as well." His attention fixed on Walker.

"But this creature from who originate distinctive military strategy that lead to unprecedented consequences among the Niyyuu, he not Niyyuu. His advisors not Niyyuu. Not even Sessrimathe. All are complete strangers to our society. Furthermore, have no external interests beyond the immediately personal." Deeleng-hab-wiq did not look at the irate general of Kojn-umm as he said this. He did not have to.

"Alien Walker person not act on behalf of some hidden, unknown power waiting to take advantage of new and confusing situation here.

So he not favor any local faction above another. Not Divintt-aap over
Dereun-oon. Not Biranju-oov over Charuchal-uul." Now he turned and
stared hard at the apoplectic general. "Not Kojn-umm over Toroud-
eed."

Anxious to maintain harmony, Walker stepped forward. "Listen,
nothing I and my friends did or said or advised was for personal gain.
At least, not in the sense your people generally think of such things. We
just want to get home."

Deeleng-hab-wiq gestured understandingly. "All who decide this
matter know that. Such knowledge contribute to our decision appoint
you key position."

Walker spread his hands helplessly. "But I don't *want* it."

The voice of the commander of Charuchal-uul's forces fell slightly,
sounding like two steel screws being rubbed against one another. "You
not consulted," he replied quietly but firmly.

"Actions have consequences, that cannot be foreseen, every time,"
Braouk intoned solemnly behind the anxious human.

At Walker's feet, George whispered upward. "You're stuck with it,
Marc. When a dog's made the leader of the pack, he's got no choice but
to fight to keep it. Otherwise some subordinate will rip him to bits at
the first opportunity, if only to protect his or her own status."

At this, Walker glanced reflexively in Saluu-hir-lek's direction. But
the general of Kojn-umm was not looking at him. He continued to
glare at Deeleng-hab-wiq as if Walker himself was wholly unimportant
to the disagreement at hand.

But not Viyv-pym. She was watching her human charge closely. If
she was seeking evidence of deception on his part, she was looking in
the wrong place.

"This is a thing settled." Deeleng-hab-wiq was not to be moved.

Eying the other assembled dignitaries, Saluu-hir-lek saw that their
resolve was no less strong. Enraged, frustrated, and full of fury at having had his supreme command usurped not only by an alien, but by an
alien who did not even want the honor, he whirled and pushed his way
through the crowd. Viyv-pym hesitated. But she was Kojn-umm. Irrespective of any personal feeling she might hold, she owed her allegiance to her realm. Also her enviable position. Turning, she hurried to
catch up to the rapidly departing Saluu-hir-lek.

The commander of the traditional armies of Charuchal-uul, now a
part of the seething mélange of realms and forces that continued, on a
much lower level, to fight among themselves so as to avoid the stigma
of being considered formal allies, turned back to Walker.

"The soldier from Kojn-umm has ambition. Perhaps too much ambition for a traditional Niyyuuan fighter. Our species has found a way to let us aggressively settle disputes between different traditional territories without adversely impacting overall planetary development. Yous' successful alien tactics have cast new and confusing ideas into ancient cultural mix. This making many uncomfortable. But new ideas, even uncomfortable ones—especially uncomfortable ones—cannot be ignored. They must be dealt with." Taking a step back, he wrapped both long arms around his upper torso.

"We of the assembled traditional fighting forces of Toroud-eed, Biranju-oov, Divintt-aap, Dereun-oon, Charuchal-uul, and perhaps even Kojn-umm await you next advisement."

Having stood openmouthed for so long, Walker became aware that his palate was drying out. He swallowed again, licked his lips. "I—I'll have to consult with my . . . advisors."

"Of course you will. A suitable residency has been prepared for yous here in capital." Dropping his arms, Deeleng-hab-wiq once more approached the human, coming very close. "Is hoped yous will find Charuchalan hospitality as satisfactory as what yous have experienced elsewhere." Lowering his head, he brought it close to Walker's own and whispered.

"Perhaps also you might be persuaded prepare special meal for uppermost level of capital government? Is said that you performances with Niyyuuan cuisine are quite remarkable."

Not knowing what else to say and utterly overwhelmed by the unexpected events that had overtaken him, Walker could only mumble a response. "I'll see what I can do. I don't have my trained assistants here, and I'd be working with unknown instrumentation, and—"

"Whatever is required will be provided," Deeleng-hab-wiq declared importantly as he straightened. He did not elaborate on the request. "Until yous have a proposal for all to consider, yous must relax and regain yous' energy."

Raising one hand, he gestured. A small but well-armed escort appeared. As he and his friends were led away, Walker wondered at the need for it. Was Deeleng-hab-wiq worried that a disgruntled Saluu-hirlek might react violently to the decision that had been made on the aliens' behalf? Or was it simply the Charuchalan way?

Exiting the enormously impressive traditional building, they were bundled into a transport large enough to accommodate them all, including Braouk and their armed escort. Rising above normal traffic, the

huge craft settled into an altitude reserved for travelers on official business and accelerated.

While George kept his nose pressed to the transparent shell of their
craft to better enjoy the passing view of the imposing capital city of
Charuchal-uul, Braouk sprawled his bulk in the back, massive tentacles
pressing up against the sides and floor of the vehicle. That left Walker to
tread in the turbulent pool of his own thoughts until a wandering tendril crept across his shoulder. Turning in his typically too-narrow
Niyyuuan seat, he found the glistening, argent, horizontal eyes of Sequi'aranaqua'na'senemu staring back into his own. As she clung firmly
to the supports of the seat behind him, another of her ten tendrils
snaked forward to join the first.

"So the bumbling, primitive human is given nominal overlordship
over the decisions of a powerful cluster of alien forces. Truly, the universe is replete with wonders."

"I don't want it," he mumbled by way of response. "We weren't
looking for anything like this, and I don't want anything to do with it.
Let Saluu-hir-lek have the control." He grew thoughtful. "I bet I can talk
Deeleng-hab-wiq and the other commanders into reconsidering. I
mean, I understand their line of reasoning, but if I object strenuously
enough, if I show them that I'm really not the individual mentally and
emotionally equipped for the kind of task that they—"

"That does not matter." As was her manner, she did not hesitate to
interrupt before he was finished. "Do not trouble yourself with concern
over everyday decisions involving military matters. What is important is
that these forces that have gathered more or less together regard you as
an honest broker of opinion. What matters is that, despite individual
misgivings, they are likely to respond positively to any request you
might care to make." Glistening a deep red that was almost black, tendrils writhed. Light flashed from the shards of metal and plastic and
thin slivers of gemstone that decorated the sinuous, flexible limbs.

"Regarding specifics, do not worry. As always, I am here to proffer
advice and good counsel. I have some small notions on how best we
should proceed given these most recent developments."

He smiled at the utterly alien shape that clung to the superstructure
of the seat behind him. "I'd be surprised if you didn't, Sque. You're always thinking forward, always one jump ahead of everybody else, so
I'm sure you've been—" His words faded away and his eyes widened
ever so slightly as he gawked at the eternally cool, utterly composed
K'eremu. "My God. You saw this coming, didn't you? All of it. You've
seen this coming right from the beginning, when we pushed Saluu-hir-

lek to pursue the army of Toroud-eed right after their retreat from Jalar-aad-biidh." His voice rose perceptibly. "And all the time, you didn't say anything. You kept it to yourself." His hand moved sharply as he gestured first toward the dog staring at the window, then at the muscular alien mass sprawled in the rear of the transport.

"You've been using us, manipulating us, right from the start of this. Just like you manipulated us to get free of the Vilenjji ship." He slapped his forehead and rolled his eyes. "What could I have been thinking? Or not thinking. I've been so wrapped up in surviving our time here and trying to think of ways to move on that I forgot to pay attention to what you've been doing, to how you operate. You're a scheming little bag of worms, Sque."

The K'eremu bore the human's outpouring of anger and angst in silence. When he finally ran out of steam, her two extended tendrils lightly stroked his shoulder in the Niyyuuan manner.

"I applaud you. Realization of reality never comes to some. Better to achieve enlightenment late than to forever dwell in the darkness. You are correct in your assumptions—but only to a certain extent. Yes, I did foresee certain possibilities and work to bring them about. For them to have the best chance of success it was required that you assume center stage. You are the one who came to Niyu with the lofty reputation, and your body shape and size is far more agreeable and familiar to the natives than is that of the K'eremu. You are also more diplomatic and self-effacing than I. I can recognize the usefulness of such qualities in lesser life-forms even when I do not possess them myself.

"You loudly decry my maneuverings. Let us consider for a time-part how damaging the results have been to you. They freed you from Vilenjji captivity, assured your good treatment on Seremathenn, and most recently have seen you anointed the chief of strategy for a powerful, possibly unprecedented consortium of the natives who are our present hosts." The slender pink speaking tube danced and swayed. "Yes, you surely have done badly from my maneuvering, human Walker. The misery you have suffered as a result must know no bounds."

"Dammit, Sque, it's not that, and you know it!" Taking note of his shouting, George finally turned from the transparent side of the speeding transport. With one hand, Walker removed the pair of caressing tendrils from his shoulder. "It's this not telling us what's going on, what you have in mind, that's so infuriating. If you wanted me to end up as the tactical head of this bad-tempered coalition of traditional Niyyuuan forces, why didn't you just say so? Why didn't you tell me what you were planning?"

"Look inward, Marcus. Take a good look inside your being, if your kind is capable of such candid introspection. If I had apprised you of such intentions back on the old stone walls of Jalar-aad-biidh in Kojn-umm and you had not panicked outright, what would have been your most likely reaction?" Startling him, she proceeded to perfectly mimic his voice. It was yet another ability she had not previously demon-strated. " 'Oh, Sequi'aranaqua'na'senemu, what a clever idea! Oh Sque, I can't wait to put my life on the line in multiple attempts to fool the Niyyuu as to our true purpose! Oh, yes, Sque, I will be able to portray myself as totally uninterested in the outcomes of all subsequent con-flicts!' " Her voice returned to normal.

"It was vital to the success of the enterprise that your innocence as to its ultimate potential objective be at all times preserved. I think you will agree that such has been the case, and that events have developed propitiously. We are now in a position to demand, as opposed to filing polite requests for, assistance from the Niyyuuan astronomic commu-nity in locating our homeworlds. This would not be possible without our successive military triumphs, albeit on the low-grade traditional level. One squad of Niyyuu equipped with modern weapons could dis-perse all the assembled armies of all the six realms we have brought to-gether. But that, fortunately, is not the Niyyuuan way."

He was quiet, trying to digest everything she had said. As usual, no matter how fervently he detested her manipulation of him and his friends, no matter how much he hated being used, he was finally forced to admit that the results just might have been worth all the sneaking and subterfuge. They now found themselves in a position that should greatly enhance their chances of finding a way home. And she was right about something else as well: despite not wanting to admit it, he had to confess to himself that if she had clearly and unambiguously laid out her intentions back in Kojn-umm, he would automatically have rejected them. Not only because he would have believed in their ultimate fail-ure, but because of the potential danger.

At that thought he performed what could only be described as a follow-up double take. "I could have been killed! At any time since we left Kojn-umm, I could have been killed. Or Saluu-hir-lek might have figured out what was going on and had me assassinated. Or the forces of one of the realms we were opposing could have had me killed." Ris-ing slightly, he leaned toward her over the back of his own high Niyyu-uan seat. "That's why you didn't want to put yourself forward as the pro-moter of the eventual strategy that was devised. That's why you've stayed in the background and out of the way. You figured that if anything went wrong with your scheming, as the public face of it I'd be the one who'd get killed." His head snapped sharply to his left. "What are you laughing at?"

Off to one side, George had fallen off his narrow seat and was rolling back and forth on the floor, teeth exposed, his feet pawing at the air. "Slickly snookered by Sister Seafood! And not for the first time, either. Humans never learn. You're so wrapped up in your own vanity and glory, that—" The dog dissolved in laughter.

Having hoped for at least moral support from the canine quarter of the quarrelsome quartet, it was fair to say that Walker was less than pleased with his companion's ebullient response.

"You are of course correct in your assessment." His accusation found Sque as serene and unruffled as ever. "Surely you must admit that for any of us mismatched fellow travelers to have a chance of returning all the way home, it is imperative that I, of all of us, must remain whole and unharmed."

With an effort, Walker controlled his anger. "I do apologize if my desire to go on living conflicts with your overall assessment of how best to deal with our present situation."

The K'eremu was as immune to sarcasm as Braouk was to flung stones. "There is no need to apologize. You are not responsible for responding according to base instincts over which you have no control. It is the same with all the lower orders." Then, perhaps relenting slightly, possibly realizing she might be stepping over a line she could barely perceive, she added, "I am of course directing all my considerable mental energies to seeing that all of us, and not just myself, complete that much-to-be-desired voyage."

Turning away from her and ignoring her gently probing tendrils, he folded his arms over his chest. "Don't knock yourself out," he muttered crossly.

Transparent lids flicked down over silvery eyes. "I am afraid my embedded translator is having difficulty with your last comment."

By way of response, an irate Walker supplied a follow-up whose meaning her translator had no difficulty whatsoever conveying unequivocally. The questing tendrils promptly withdrew. No more was heard from the K'eremu for the remainder of the journey.

From the capacious rear of the transport, verse floated forward borne on the wings of alien melancholy. Braouk was reciting.

"Cast adrift here, fighting and killing daily, empty actions. How I long for the endless fields of Tuuqalia, for its vaulted skies and waving fields of surashh, for its dense forests and cool plains, for its—"

Necessity overcoming the need to visually display his displeasure, Walker uncrossed his arms and pressed his palms tightly against both ears. George used his front paws to press his own ears firmly against the sides of his head. For her part, Sque simply ignored their massive companion's latest interminable recitation. Unequipped to translate it, their Charuchalan hosts remained blissfully ignorant of the content of the alien drone, however much it sounded to them as if the largest of their honored guests must be feeling vaguely unwell.

✳

The most honored commander of the expeditionary army of the traditional forces of the righteous realm of Kojn-umm was in an ill humor. He had been ever since the startling anointment of the ungainly human as the chief strategic planner for the nonalliance of quasi-cooperating military forces of six territories. It was outrageous! It was insupportable!

It was also, however uncomfortable, a fact, and one that he was going to have to deal with. In order to do that, he needed information. Believing he possessed enough of the latter, he had been taken by surprise by the unity of the other realms' decision. He would not make the same mistake again.

Hence his impatience when the citizen he had summoned to his presence finally appeared before him.

While she was not intimidated by the prospect of a private conference with the general, neither did Viyv-pym have any idea what Saluu-hir-lek wanted of her. She found out very quickly, as Saluu-hir-lek addressed her directly and in no-nonsense tones.

"What does this alien Marcus Walker mean to you?"

Her tails twitched involuntarily, a clear sign she did not understand the question. "*Mean* to me? There no meaning attached to relationship. I his appointed guide on and to world and culture of Niyyuu. Same functioning applicable to his three companions. If relationship has any meaning, takes the form of what I am paid by government of Kojn-umm."

His words contradicted his gesture of understanding. "I have had abundant time to observe the alien Walker. Also to observe the alien Walker observing you. Is more there than simple diplomacy."

Initially confident upon being sent for, his guest found herself increasingly bemused. "I confess I not follow the general commander's line of reasoning."

Her unfettered bewilderment was answer enough for his purposes.

"Never mind. I've learned what I need know. You are blameless of participation in this betrayal." Coming close, he lowered his rasping voice. "You must understand, Viyv-pym: I had to find out. Do not carry any concern with you now that clarity in this thing is restored."

Having been accused and then found innocent of something without ever once having been informed of what it was, she was understandably bewildered. Her trial was apparently over without her ever having been brought before a court. Given her initial perceptions, she ought to have felt relieved. Instead, she was more confused than ever.

"You are upset because of the human Walker's elevation," she hazarded.

"Upset!" Once again he had to lower his voice. "Upset, yes. This whole matter is absurd, ridiculous, and unreasonable." His flexible arms snapped in the air of the room like whips. "The alien is a cook, not military strategist. But I not fooled." His large, alert eyes gleamed. "I see what being done. Charuchal-uul, Biranju-oov, and others wish marginalize me and influence of Kojn-umm on future actions. Better they not relax. When time come, I will deal with their deceit."

"And the human?" Viyv-pym was not entirely sure why she should care, or why she asked. She knew only that she did, and she had.

"Eehgh, the human! It strange, but I not mad at him. It clear to me that he being manipulated for the ends of others. What others, I still not certain. No doubt good cook is ignorant of how he being used. No, the alien food preparator is harmless. I more fear the actions of his companions, especially the small rubbery being with many limbs. She says too little, sees too much. I repeatedly reproaching myself for my neglect of her."

Viyv-pym gestured supplely. "I am Kojn-umm. You my superior. I will do whatever you deem necessary to advance best interests of our realm."

"I know that you will, Viyv-pym. For moment, though, nothing can be done. Is better more useful watch and wait."

"For what?" she asked him as she lowered her arms.

He was staring ferociously, but not at her. "For opportunity."

※

Their rooms were admirable, overlooking just one of the great sweeping harbors for which Charuchal-uul was famed throughout Niyu. If the level of technological sophistication was not up to that of highly advanced Seremathenn, it was at least the equal of Kojn-umm. As honored guests, they had no cause for complaint.

At least not against their hosts, whose attitude toward them continued to reflect a mixture of admiration, suspicion, and a curiosity that
bordered on the fawning. Among two of the visitors, there was still
some internal dissension.

Walker was pacing back and forth in front of the floor-to-ceiling
transparency that overlooked the view. If he closed his eyes almost shut
and let his mind drift, he could imagine that he was standing in a sky-
scraper looking out over Lake Michigan. Then he would open them
again, and his sight and mind would be confronted by alien architecture, alien transport, and a sky that was just a shade too greenish.

"You can't keep interfering in local affairs like this. You're going to
make a mistake and get us killed." He halted close to the K'eremu. "Look
how your actions have offended Saluu-hir-lek. I've become familiar
enough with Niyyuuan expressions and reactions to know that this
whole experience has changed him from a friend to someone who
wouldn't be sad to see us disappear."

As she listened to the human, Sque was lolling on one of the narrow padded benches that were the Niyyuuan equivalent of a comfortable couch. While her tendrils sprawled loosely around her, her body
stayed, as always, upright in the center of the ropy mass.

"What I am going to do, Marcus, is get us home. You do still want
to get home, don't you?" He said nothing. "As for offending the ambi-
tious general Saluu-hir-lek, I cannot function effectively if I am forced
to waste time concerning myself with the possible personal disen-
chantments of representatives of the local dominant life-form."

Nearby, George had been running nose patrol over a section of the
peculiarly resilient flooring, absorbing and cataloging smells for future
reference. Now he looked up briefly at Walker. "You sure, Marc, that it's
Saluu-hir-lek you're so concerned about offending?"

Walker's brows drew together as he regarded the busy canine. "I
don't follow you, George."

"It's been a while since we had a visit from our lean and trim original minder, hasn't it? Maybe you're worried our activities might have
offended her?" He bared his teeth. "Maybe you miss her a little?"

"Viyv-pym is our most active and knowledgeable conduit to the
Niyyuu," Walker snapped crossly. "She is our connection to this world
and this culture and has been ever since Seremathenn. I miss her because of that, yes."

"Uh-huh." Cocking his head slightly to the right, the dog sat down
and began scratching himself behind one ear. "Tell me something,

Marc. When you kiss her, is it like sticking your tongue down a vacuum cleaner hose?"

A furious Walker began chasing the dog around the largely unusable Niyyuuan furniture while the agile canine toyed with him, remaining just beyond the human's reach. Sequi'aranaqua'na'senemu did her best to ignore them both as she contemplated their immediate future. Despite a nagging conviction that doing so was a waste of time, she was still determined to do her best to save them both, along with the oversized versifier who was presently sleeping soundly at one end of the large room.

How she missed the reasonableness of K'erem! Of home, of her own kind, each individual secure in the knowledge that he or she was the epitome of evolution. She missed the soothing solitude of her own quiet, carefully landscaped residence, the chance to communicate with others of like mind—over a secure distance, of course—the opportunities for advanced intellectual discourse. None of the latter were to be found here, where she was forced to act always as teacher and never as student.

For all that, for all the inherent physical and mental deficiencies for which they were not responsible, she rather liked her companions. Braouk, with his melancholy manner, ever eager and ready to recount the passionate sagas of his world to any who would listen. If only he would shut up more often. The small quadruped George, whose tail never seemed to stop moving, an appendage as close to achieving perpetual motion as any she had ever seen attached to another intelligent being. Even Walker, forever unsure of himself but unafraid to do whatever was necessary to improve their situation.

She wondered if any of them actually liked her, or if they only pretended to do so in order to keep her superior intellect focused on the business of getting them all home. Not that it mattered. No K'eremu needed to rely on the approval of lesser life-forms to sustain a feeling of self-worth.

On the other tendril, it was doubtful any peaceful, solitary K'eremu had previously found itself in her position. To her discomfiture, she found that she did care if her companions liked her or not. Her tendrils drew in more tightly around the base of her body. No doubt, with time and proper meditation, the unnatural feeling of caring what a motley lot of lower life-forms thought about her would go away.

When the human, out of breath from chasing his smaller but much quicker companion, finally halted, she confronted him. "What difference should it make to you, Marcus, or to any of us, if we intervene in local affairs? Our hosts are barbarians who dwell under the slimmest veneer of civilization." Tendrils rose and fluttered, describing distinct patterns in the air.

"They slaughter one another under the pretext of restraining themselves. The fact that they forbid the use of modern weapons in these bloody ritual exercises between individual tribes shows only that they have an interest in preserving their species, not in improving it. Then there is the obscenely ubiquitous media coverage. No other marginally civilized race of my acquaintance views intraspecies warfare as an excuse for crass entertainment."

His quarrel with George forgotten, Walker looked uncomfortable. "One other does," he muttered uneasily. "Except that it doesn't restrict its use of weapons to the archaic." He did not have to elaborate.

Sque's speaking tube emitted a succession of small bubbles. "I might have suspected as much."

He waited for inevitable indictment, the twist of the verbal knife, the perfectly minted coin of sarcasm. When it was not forthcoming, he blinked and peered down at her. "That's it? You don't have anything else to say?"

Tendrils bobbed and weaved, like an anemone preparing for a prizefight. "What could I add that would embellish the depressing reality of your kind? If your culture is not so unlike that of the Niyyuu, then I should not have to explain why I feel no compunction at manipulating the latter. There is no beauty, no entertainment, no satisfaction to be found in the killing of one's own kind. It is an abomination that all sentient species should have shed. Yet it lingers on in remote, out-of-the-way places."

He found himself nodding slowly. "You're correct, Sque. I have no right to criticize your actions here. The K'eremu, I take it, don't fight among themselves?"

"Only with sharp phrases and pointed words. These cut deeply enough." A knot of maroon-hued coils, she dropped off the couch and slithered past him, stopping at the transparent wall. George trotted over to join her in gazing at the busy metropolitan harbor below. A silence ensued during which the only sounds in the room were the barely audible whisper of the air recycler and the somewhat louder breathing of the dozing Tuuqalian in the back.

"If Fortune is with us, we will not have to concern ourselves with the affairs of this wayward world and its argumentative folk much longer."

Walker looked down at her in surprise. "You've heard something!"

The upper portion of the K'eremu's body arced back, and metallic eyes gazed up at him. "Learning things is as much a matter of listening well as it is of cultivating sources. One picks such bits of possibility out of a society even while its majority is occupied with an activity as wasteful as war. All I am saying is that in the near future there may occur a development or two favorable to that end which is of interest to us all. Should these eventuate, we will need to act together, with one voice." She drew herself up to her full four feet.

"That means my voice, of course, but I am certain you both already understand that."

"I don't understand it," George objected out of principle. "But I'll go along with anything that'll take us a step closer to home."

"Everyone needs to be prepared to fulfill their part." She looked past them both, straining to see past the high, uncomfortable furniture. "Stir that lump of sensitive Tuuqalian flesh from its extended slumber." With several tendrils, she gestured in Braouk's direction. "I will advise you."

"What if these developments you're referring to don't pan out?" Walker asked her.

Glistening eyes turned back to him. "Then your intelligence level will have been raised up an infinitesimal fraction from having paid another time-part's attention to me. Go wake the brute."

Not having anything better to do, Walker did as she requested. Carefully, as always. There were occasions when the Tuuqalian had a disconcerting tendency to wake up swinging.

**14**

Called at Walker's request—but at Sque's direction—the meeting took place a ten-day later. The representatives of half a dozen different realms and their traditional fighting forces gathered in a bubble chamber attached to the end of a pierlike structure that thrust outward from a point of land north of the capital city's main harbor. Though the chamber was not small, the immense transport vessels that skimmed past at high speed, heading for the inner harbor, made it seem so. After many ten-days spent in the field marching with traditional forces, Walker had still not completely reacclimated himself to the trappings of modern galactic technology.

Saluu-hir-lek's accusations made him even more uncomfortable. Unexpectedly reduced in stature to just one more commanding officer among many, Kojn-umm's most famous soldier was spitting mad as he stalked back and forth in front of the transparent, curving wall of the climate-controlled bubble. As was the custom in Charuchal-uul, there was no furniture. Everyone present was forced to stand for the duration of the gathering. Though uncertain as to the specific cultural rationale, Walker observed that it was an excellent way to keep the length of official meetings under control.

The occasional appearance beyond the wall of quartets of leaping segestroth, who resembled a cross between giant goldfish and drowning doves, formed an incongruous background to the general's rant. It seemed that whenever Saluu-hir-lek became particularly wound up, four or eight or twelve of the spectacularly highlighted ocean dwellers would execute a series of their impressive leaps as they traveled back and forth between the harbor and deeper ocean waters beyond.

Walker's discomfort was caused by the fact that he and his companions were the subject of the general's loud complaining. George remained by his side while Braouk stayed as far from the see-through walls as possible. The Tuuqalian, it developed, could not swim. In contrast, Sque hugged the place where the nearest curving wall met the floor, hoping for an early end to the gathering so she could spend some time crawling over the spume-soaked rocks outside.

As Saluu-hir-lek raved on, Walker would look past him to the rest of the official delegation from Kojn-umm. Sometimes Viyv-pym met his stare; other times he found her looking away. He could not tell, as he might have been able to with a human, what she was thinking. With mixed success, he tried to convince himself that it was not important.

Like a pair of dancing snakes, the general's arms kept twitching in Walker's direction. "Look at him! Who this creature to whom you give such power? A visitor from world that not even part of civilization. Such decision run counter to everything in Niyyuuan history." His attention wandered to George, panting softly near the human's feet. "And his companions. What we know of them, of their real motives? Maybe really come here only to make trouble."

"As it has been told to me," the general Afyet-din-cil of Biranju-oov countered, "they originally brought here to make telugrivk. With sweet garnish."

Saluu-hir-lek's furious stare was insufficient to overcome the hacking laughter that the other officer's observation sparked. Telugrivk was a complex dish whose preparation Walker had mastered during his first days on Niyu, and for which he had become widely admired among those Niyyuu fortunate enough to have tasted it.

"It's true we may have acquired some small influence," Walker responded. "But we didn't ask for it, and we certainly didn't go seeking

it." He looked toward Deeleng-hab-wiq. Thus far, the commander of
the traditional forces of Charuchal-uul had remained placidly in the
background. "It was bestowed upon us. And we don't really want it. Not
that kind of power, anyway. What we want is a way to return to our
homes. One that will allow us to do so without having to spend any
more time than is absolutely necessary at stops along the way." Spreading his hands, he moved his arms in as near an approximation of the
relevant Niyyuuan manner as his far stiffer joints would allow.

"I don't see any problem here. We want to leave, and some of
you"—he eyed the silently simmering Saluu-hir-lek—"want us to
leave. Just give us the resources that we need to do so properly and we'll
depart without another word. Any perceived problems caused by our
presence will disappear. We've only done anything we have done up until now because no one would give us the help we need."

Now Deeleng-hab-wiq did step forward. "We would prefer that
you remain among us, Marcus Walker. Having positioned yourself as
you have, you cannot just leave us. Besides"—he eyed his own attending subordinates—"what you request would not only be extremely difficult, but costly."

"The cost can be met."

All eyes turned to the new speaker. Pushing her way to the forefront
of the milling group was a Niyyuu Walker had not seen before. She was
tall even for one of her kind. Clad in a triple wrap of dark blue, crimson, and silver chiffonlike material, she advanced with a flowing grace
unmatched even by Viyv-pym. Even Sque was moved to pause in her
yearning contemplation of the wave-washed rocks outside the chamber
to contemplate the newcomer.

Satisfied with the impression she had made, the new arrival announced herself. "I am Jhanuud-tir-yed, vice premier of the realm of
Fiearek-iib." Murmurs arose from those in attendance who had not recognized the newcomer immediately upon her formal entrance. When
the whispering died down, she continued.

"I have come from halfway around world to attend this meeting. I
represent not only Fiearek-iib, but others as well." She proceeded to coolly
reel off the names of an adequate number of powerful realms to intimidate even the fiery Saluu-hir-lek. That done, she turned her attention to Walker and his now-attentive companions.

"We too wonder at real motivations of strange visitors. You come
among us armed not with weapons or proclaimed ambitions, but with
curious knowledge drawn from elsewhere." One arm rose and described an arc through the air. "Yet now one of you is in position to de-

termine strategy for combined traditional forces of six realms. Six realms that fight among themselves, yet redeploy together. This is a new and atypical thing in Niyyuuan terms. It is worrisome. It concerns government of Fiearek-iib and its friends. Is even talk that should such an anomaly continue to spread, some might have to break with tradition and make use of modern weapons to stop it."

That shocking statement produced little gasps of disbelief as a number of small round mouths contracted involuntarily. What the vice premier was suggesting was nothing less than a dissolution of the compact that had allowed the various realms of Niyu to settle disputes and safely engage in therapeutic warfare for thousands of years. Among the assembled only Saluu-hir-lek, Walker managed to note, did not appear distraught. But then, Walker knew better than most the depth of the general's deepest ambitions.

He became aware that the imposing visitor had once more turned back to him. "To forestall such potential upheaval, has been determined by my government and that of those of our neighbors of like mind to do what we can to remove principal source of much of possible contention."

"That'd be us," George pointed out succinctly from the vicinity of Walker's ankles.

"Yes." She glanced down at the dog. "I am authorized by government of Fiearek-iib and its allies to offer whatever financial and material support is required to help yous return yous' homes. But in return, is something we want."

"Sure," Walker replied without having the slightest idea what he might be letting himself and his friends in for. "If you don't mind my asking, what might that be?"

The voice of vice premier Jhanuud-tir-yed of Fiearek-iib became that of an enthusiastic commoner. "Exclusive rights for representatives of our media concerns to record and later broadcast entire account of yous' attempt to return yous' homeworlds."

The shrill uproar set off in the chamber by this seemingly innocuous request was potentially damaging to ears more sensitive than those of the Niyyuu. Walker knew he shouldn't be surprised. Among certain of their hosts, media rights to a unique narrative were as significant as the conquest of one traditional army by another.

Deeleng-hab-wiq finally managed to restore a semblance of order. The energetic braying and heavy breathing subsided. "What the honored representative from Fiearek-iib demands must be debated. But at first hearing I think is probable suitable mutual agreements can be reached and practical arrangements made." He turned back to Walker. "Is becoming clear that despite wishes of many, yous cannot be held here. Therefore government of Charuchal-uul will also contribute to yous' homeward journey." That said, his tone changed from the officious to the sympathetic.

"But all resources of Niyu insufficient return yous home if is not known coordinates of respective homeworlds."

Not even the commanding figure of Jhanuud-tir-yed had an answer for that. But Sque did.

Scuttling away from the wall, the K'eremu positioned herself between Walker and the vice premier. "One is always grateful for a confluence of favorable circumstances. I requested this meeting through the human Walker to inform all the relevant parties of certain information that has recently come into my possession. I certainly did not expect also to encounter the means by which it might be acted upon. For that I would thank Fate—if I in any way believed in it." Raising her voice, she looked to her left and commandingly waggled several uplifted tendrils. "It is time—come in!"

Yet another new figure came forward from the back of the crowd. Walker reacted with fitting surprise the instant he recognized the newcomer.

It was the Kojnian astronomer Sobj-oes.

She offered greetings in the traditional manner of her realm, with a double-finger caress that stroked him from neck to waist. "Hello, Marcus Walker. It good see you once again."

"But I didn't . . ." He looked sharply down at the K'eremu. "What's this about, Sque? Why didn't you tell me Sobj-oes would be joining us here?"

"Because the justification for her to do so only came to light very recently, Marc." She blew a conciliatory bubble. "There is no reason for anyone, however individually interesting, to interrupt their work and extend themselves for the purpose of delivering non-news."

The implications inherent in the K'eremu's response were as obvious to George as they were to his human companion. Letting out a loud, joyful bark, the dog bounded forward, rose on hind legs, and rested his front paws against the astronomer's slender legs.

"Earth! You've found the coordinates for Earth!"

Walker felt like barking—or at least shouting with happiness—himself. The feeling of utter elation lasted about as long as his friend's shout.

"I afraid not so." The impression of deep regret in the astronomer's voice was profound.

George slumped, dropping his forepaws from the Niyyuuan's lower limbs, his head lowering. Downcast, he turned and walked slowly back to rejoin his friend. But if Walker had been less quick to respond with excitement, he was also less ready to give up hope. Sque had as much as said that Sobj-oes would only come this far if she had something significant to report.

"But you *have* found something?" he pressed her. Though they would not personally be affected by the astronomer's response, the assembled delegates and notables, from Deeleng-hab-wiq to Jhanuud-tiryed and even Saluu-hir-lek, listened with unmistakable interest. So did Viyv-pym, perhaps with feelings more mixed than most.

"As you know, Marcus Walker," Sobj-oes began, "I promise you that night long ago in Kojn-umm that I and a few trusted associates would work in our spare time to try and help yous find yous' way homeward. This work has not been easy. Certain select portions of electromagnetic spectrum very crowded with communicatings of all kinds. Difficult, sometimes impossible, separate unintelligible from understandable, natural from artificial. Search for yous made more challenging by conflicting standards, lack of specifics, other difficulties." One sinuous arm rose to point at the attentive Sque.

"She and I secretly stay in touch these past many ten-days. Exchange information. She make many suggestions. Some very useful."

Walker glanced down at the K'eremu. Her reply was as calm and self-possessed as ever. "You had complex native interrealmic relationships to deal with. I did not want to distract you—certainly not with false hopes."

He would have replied in a suitably acerbic manner, but was too keen to hear what else the astronomer had to say. "What *have* you and your associates managed to find out, Sobj-oes?"

She eyed him warmly. "As I already say, too sadly not coordinates your own home, Marcus Walker. Not actual specific coordinates any of yous' homes. But just possibly, after distilling from very large volume of information by using unambiguous knowledge provided by Sequi'aranaqua'na'senemu as workable sieve, may have found indications of occasional visitation to certain far-reaching region by one of yous' species." She paused to gather herself. "Are unverifiable but highly suggestive signs pointing to intermittent passage through specified area of occasional ships from world called Tuuqalia."

The roar that rose from the rear of the meeting bubble thunder-ously affirmed that the largest individual in attendance had not, after all, been sleeping soundly through it all. As an excited Braouk rose to loom over the assembled delegates, many of whom suddenly found one reason or another to shift their position within the chamber, Sobj-oes the astronomer hastened to calm him.

"I say again: relevant indicators do not provide location of this world. Only that representatives of your kind may have been recorded transiting the fairly extensive region in question."

"It is a beginning." Despite the astronomer's bombshell Sque was, if anything, only a little less composed than usual. "However imprecise it may be, we now have a destination. Our course is clear." Tendrils writhed. "Travel to the place where the outsized saga-singers may have paid a call. In that vast but infinitely reduced section of space, seek ad-ditional clues to the location of their world. Even allowing for the dis-tances the Vilenjji cover in their search for novel species to market, any region visited by the Tuuqalia must necessarily be nearer to K'erem. And to Earth," she added with only the slightest of tactless pauses.

"At least it's a trail to sniff." George was sitting on his haunches, eyes half-closed, contemplating the possibility they might at last actu-ally have secured a line on the first phase of a way home.

A way and a means, if Jhanuud-tir-yed and the other senior repre-sentatives present were to be believed, an elated Walker reflected. In his excitement he barely managed to ask the obvious next question. "Can you show us?" he asked Sobj-oes.

Nodding, she gestured with one sinuous arm. General officers and senior bureaucrats alike made room, forming a compact, curious circle around her. Even Saluu-hir-lek was intrigued.

Removing from her waist pack a small device that would never have been permitted inside a traditional Niyyuuan military encampment, the astronomer coaxed it to generate a three-dimensional map of the galaxy. Rapidly zooming in, she froze the image on a system contain-ing six planets and a pair of asteroid belts.

"Niyu," she explained for the benefit of the nonnatives present. An-other command to the device caused the scale to expand to show hun-dreds of systems, related astronomical features, and a respectable chunk of starfield. "The always-changing, ever-fluctuating area of space those who dwell within its boundaries loosely refer to as galactic civiliza-tion." Once more the image dissolved and re-formed as the scale ex-panded. Expanded until the region affected by civilization had been re-duced in size to a small blotch amidst the blackness. Like the electrified wing of some dark phoenix, several inner bands of one arm of the galaxy filled the refulgent, illustrated space. A minuscule point of light, a microscopic nova, flared approximately halfway out on one arm.

"The region where mention of Tuuqalia has been detected."

Breathy exclamations of surprise mixed with trepidation and concern rose from the assembled. The point of light was located very, very far indeed from the area demarcated by civilization.

"I have traveled to many worlds," Jhanuud-tir-yed declared somberly, "some of which lie far distant from beloved Niyu. But this representation speaks to distances beyond my experience." She looked over at the astronomer. "Your measurements are accurate?"

Sobj-oes gestured unequivocally. "They checked many times, by better scientists than I. At such distances is tolerated some allowance for error. But given distance involved, potential error is not significant."

Stepping forward, Deeleng-hab-wiq let the two fingers of his right hand pierce the projection. Slowly, methodically, they traced the space between civilization and the region highlighted by the point of light. The expanse was daunting.

"I not historian, but I think no ship of Niyu has ever traveled so great a distance. Certainly not in direction indicated." Vast yellow eyes settled on the attentive Walker. "Know, visitor human, that we Niyu not a bold species by nature. We not explorers of the Great Dark. Leave that to far-wandering sentients like the Sessrimathe. The Niyyuu like their world, like being closely linked with civilization. We not the kind to take chances such as this. As you know well, even our chosen manner of internecine warfare is conservative."

With one long, flexible finger, the contemplative Deeleng-hab-wiq stirred stars. "As regarding that, visitors have often forced us to think in new ways. Perhaps now is time to think in new ways regarding bold voyage such as this." Whereupon he added, to show that he had not lost sight of what was really important, "Rights to recording of such an important journey cannot be exclusive. Must be shared. Information must be pooled. This too important an event for one realm, even one such as Fiearek-iib, to control. Related rights should belong to all realms of Niyu."

"That reasonable enough," the vice premier reluctantly conceded, "if all realms contribute to costing."

Interest rapidly gave way to negotiating as the assembled delegates began to argue among themselves over which realm's media representatives were best qualified to accompany and document the unprece-

dented attempt to return the visitors to their homes. Though the de-
baters were utterly alien, Walker noted that their mind-set was not.

After a while, the ear-grating drone gave way to more calculated
discussion as matters of principle were subsumed in debate as to who
should pay what actual costs.

"As initiators of the proposal, the government of Fiearek-iib and its
friends will underwrite a suitable vessel," Jhanuud-tir-yed insisted, "as
well as appropriate crew. Others may participate in proportion to their
fiscal contribution." This pronouncement set off another round of strident discussion, until it was interrupted by a single loud interjection in
a distinctive accent.

"No."

At the declamation, voiced in excellent and suitably grating Niyyuuan, debate faltered as one group of participants after another turned to
stare at the speaker. Viyv-pym especially appeared taken aback.

Walker held his ground. "No," he repeated, more softly this time,
growling out the single Niyyuuan syllable from the back of a throat that
over the past months had grown positively calloused from wrestling
with the local language. At his feet, George looked up at his friend as if
he had suddenly developed a bad case of cat.

"I am afraid I not understand fully what you negating," the digni-
fied but bemused vice premier of Fiearek-iib finally replied.

"You said 'a' ship. One ship won't be sufficient." Pointing, Walker
indicated first Sque and then, gesturing over the heads of the assembled
toward the back part of the chamber, the massive Tuuqalian. "We need
at least three ships. In the event that our respective homeworlds lie great
distances apart and in vastly differing directions, the expedition needs
to leave Niyu prepared to cope with that possibility."

The murmuring that arose from the assembled in response to
the alien's assertion was more sedate and considered than that which
had preceded it, perhaps because this time those involved were not
arguing about one realm or another gaining a financial advantage over
its neighbor.

"There would be other good reasons for proceeding in the suggested manner," the representative from Toroud-eed pointed out. "Embarking on such an unparalleled journey, it would make sense not
everyone have to return if, for example, one ship encounter trouble."

Such thoughts percolated rapidly through the group. "Ships would
be traveling far beyond boundaries of known civilization," the representative continued. "If encounter unexpected hostilities, three properly armed ships much better positioned defend selves than lone one."

A flurry of energetic, thoughtful responses greeted both observations. By the time discussion had begun to die down once again, Walker's rationale for the proposal had been completely submerged in other issues.

George nudged his friend's leg. "Once a trader, always a trader—eh, Marc?"

Bending low, Walker whispered to his friend. "I just thought it would be smarter, and easier, for us to make any demands here instead of dozens of light-years out in unfamiliar space."

"Very sensible." Sque had moved to stand close behind them. "A primitive craving, greed is, but occasionally a useful survival trait. Having three ships at our disposal will certainly do our chances of finding a way home no harm."

Walker looked down at her. "They won't exactly be at our 'disposal,' Sque."

The K'eremu waved a pair of tendrils at him. "Give me one ten-day to finalize details." It was an assertion Walker would not have chosen to bet against. In his short and increasingly implausible life, the K'eremu was as sure a thing as he had ever come across. If only, he thought mildly, he could find a way to convince her to come home with him. For just a little while. So she could study the commodities board for a few weeks, perform a quick analysis or two, and then leave him with just a few negligible recommendations.

It was never to be, he knew. Sque was interested in returning only to K'erem. In the many months they had spent together, she had barely learned to tolerate him. Knowing her as he did now he knew that her impression, and opinions of, his species were unlikely to extend to a desire to remain in their presence any longer than actual survival required.

A pity. He would have loved to have seen what she could do with juice concentrate futures.

Some time later, Jhanuud-tir-yed emerged from a conference that had been winnowed down to only the most important figures present. Walker noted that as chief representative of Kojn-umm, Saluu-hir-lek appeared less than happy at having been excluded from the deliberations of the august group. Waving one arm hypnotically, the vice premier of Fiearek-iib approached the four guests. (Unable to remain quiescent subsequent to the astronomer Sobj-oes's revelations, Braouk had rejoined his companions.)

"It has been decided. Yous will be provided with support in yous' attempt return yous' homeworlds in the form of three of Niyu's finest ships. All three are the most up-to-date and best equipped. Crews will be drawn from vessels operated by all contributing realms. You will have only the best at your service." She gestured significantly at Walker.

"You official position achieved here on Niyu will continue be maintained on board until such time as you voluntarily leave assigned ship. This decision agreed upon by all participating parties out of respect you accomplishments among us—and also as way of settling arguments among representatives of different realms. As you stated in you military strategy, as alien and not citizen of any realm, you able deliver impartial decisions regarding same."

Walker was not so divorced from Niyyuuan society that he was unconscious of the honor. "With my friends' advice and aid, I'll do my best not to betray any trust you place in me."

Both of the vice premier's hands came up. Twinned fingers stroked Walker's chest. "I sorry I not personally have opportunity get know yous better. Yous a most, most interesting fouring of different types. But better yous go than stay." Was that a twinkle in one oversized, golden eye? "Better for yous—and better for us." She stepped back.

"Will take time prepare designated vessels for such unprecedented journey. Until then, a stopping has been called to all traditional fighting. I would personally wish yous return with me to Fiearek-iib to experience hospitality of my realm." She gestured in the direction of the local hosts. "But Charuchalans claim right of eminence. You will stay here until ships are made ready depart this system. Expect by time yous have dealt with several hundred requests for talkings from media, yous be ready leave even for dead, airless moon."

With decisions having been made and harmony more or less achieved, the delegates began to break up into small individual groups. Simultaneously relieved and excited, Walker felt a touch at the back of his pants. Turning and seeing Sque looking up at him, he knelt slightly to be nearer eye level with the K'eremu. He did not try to hide his elation.

"Well, Sque, I'm still not sure how it all happened, but I guess we're finally going home."

The K'eremu was rather more reserved. "Braouk is going home—maybe. You, and I, and the furry thing on four short legs, are going with him. I would say that with much luck and if the Fate I do not for an instant believe in is on our side, we might be fortunate enough in the course of this journey to encounter the tiniest inkling of where your homeworld or mine happens to lie."

Walker's enthusiasm dimmed measurably. "Always the optimist, aren't you, Sque?"

"Always the realist. You still have no true conception of the size of known space, Marcus Walker. Not even of this infinitesimally small portion of it. Yet I will allow that indications of even peripheral Tuuqalian presence in the region where we hope to go is at least a positive indicator. It forms a destination of a sort, however ephemeral."

Nearby, George muttered, "With unrestrained zeal like that I don't see how we can fail to keep our spirits up."

"Not to fear." With enviable deportment, the K'eremu proceeded to adjust several strands of the polished, treated bits of metal that decorated her slick-skinned person. "No matter how disheartening the circumstances may become, you will always have the enlightening presence of myself to uplift your dismal, backward selves. Now you must excuse me, for I have a date with a particularly inviting damp hole in the seawall outside." And without another word, she pivoted on her tendrils and scuttled off through the rapidly dispersing crowd.

15

Though restricted to the use of the facilities intrinsic to the extensive old-time bivouac area that was serving as temporary home to the visiting forces of Toroud-eed, Biranju-oov, and others, Saluu-hir-lek did not complain. As a leader of traditional military, he was used to the kinds of minor privations that simultaneously appalled and fascinated those Niyyuu who preferred to encounter such throwbacks to ancient times only in the media and while surrounded by the comforts of their own dwellings. Since it was his profession, it troubled him only occasionally that while he was restricted to often-primitive amenities, some of which dated to hundreds of years earlier, his alien nemeses were luxuriating in the most modern conveniences the capital city of Charuchal-uul could provide.

He could enjoy them as well, he knew. All he had to do was resign his commission. It raised his spirits to know that the grateful Council of

Kojn-umm would never accept it. Back home, in his own realm, he was a venerated hero. Here, in more cosmopolitan Charuchal-uul, he was but one of several important foreign military commanders. For someone used to being the locus of attention, it was a sobering experience.

With the defeat of the traditional army of Charuchal-uul and the commercial and political advantages thus gained, the combined forces of Toroud-eed, Biranju-oov, Divintt-aap and Dereun-oon had voted to stand back and reflect upon what they had accomplished. All of Saluu-hir-lek's attempts to urge them to build on the triumphs they had already achieved had been met with indecision, if not outright apathy. For one thing, his emissaries had been told, the aliens were leaving. No matter how hard he tried, the general could not convince them that while it might have been the aliens who had developed the initial strategy that had led to their present success, it was he, Saluu-hir-lek of Kojn-umm, who had seen them carried out. And it was he, Saluu-hir-lek, who could lead their combined forces onward, to greater and greater victories. To the total domination, in traditional terms, not of realms, but of this entire continent and perhaps others as well.

They hemmed and hawed. The aliens were leaving. And their troops were tired. No one wanted to march home, or travel by slow, traditional transport. More and more there was a clamor for an end to hostilities. And without the visitors to guide them . . .

The implication was that without the aliens' contribution there was no guarantee of further victories. Nothing an angrily earnest Saluu-hir-lek said could convince the senior officers of the armies of previously defeated realms that they would be able to continue their string of successes without the visitors' participation. In a development that was bitterly ironic, Kojn-umm's greatest traditional military commander found himself a victim of the success of his own subterfuge.

It meant that he would have to go home, too. Carrying with him a considerable degree of accomplishment, to be sure. He had much to be proud of. His successive triumphs had gained much influence for Kojn-umm. He would be hailed in Ehbahr as a greater hero than ever. For most Niyyuu it would have been enough. But not for the frustrated Saluu-hir-lek.

He wanted everything.

There was nothing he could do about it, however. The traditional forces of Kojn-umm could not go on alone, without their quasi-allies. The grand march was finished, done with, over. He would have to take his troops and go home. In triumph, to be sure, but a triumph that would remain personally forever incomplete. What galled him most was that it was clear now that the alien Walker and his duplicitous companions had never had any real interest in the kind of world-girdling conquest that he wanted to pursue. What they had been seeking all along was simply to acquire enough influence to ensure their departure from Niyu, suitably equipped and outfitted to find their way home. Having achieved what they sought, they were prepared to leave him and his greater ambitions in the lurch.

It was not fair. Promises had been broken. Trapped by paradox, he was left stewing in a mixture of triumph and anger.

An orderly entered. No electronics allowed here, in the temporary building that housed his office and that of much of his general staff. Following traditional procedures, information had to be conveyed person to person.

"General, you have a visitor. It claims to know of you by reputation."

Saluu-hir-lek's wide eyes fixed on the equally expansive oculars of the orderly. "'It'?"

The orderly backed out. "You will see for yourself, General."

The being that assumed the orderly's place stood only a little taller than the general himself, but was far more massive. Its skin was a dark purplish hue and as bumpy and uneven as a streambed. Eyes proportionately larger even than those of the Niyyuu nearly met in the center of the tapering skull. Though outrageous in appearance, the origin of the unlikely visitor was not unknown to its educated host. Leaning back in the flexible, narrow seat that flexed obediently under the modest weight of his slender frame, Saluu-hir-lek regarded his visitor. While he was surprised, he was not in the least intimidated. His guest was exotic, but his kind were not strangers to the Niyyuu. Nor to any species that considered itself a member of a widespread and cosmopolitan galactic civilization.

"What matter," the general asked inquiringly, "brings a Vilenjji to traditional combat forces of Niyu?"

Raising one sucker-lined, flap-tipped arm by way of greeting, the thick-bodied visitor sloughed farther into the room. "I am named Pret-Klob, and am here on business, of course. To restore the natural order of things, one might say." Without waiting to be invited, he settled himself as best he could in the center of the floor. "I have come to recover some missing inventory that was formerly the property of my association."

Saluu-hir-lek was unimpressed. "What has that do with traditional forces of Kojn-umm?"

"I have taken steps to do the necessary economic research. While not precisely in your possession, you have apparently recently spent a good deal of time proximate to the property in question. Additional inquiries on my part lead me to believe you might be helpful in its recovery." The flap that comprised the outer half of the creature's right arm flexed meaningfully. "Should that eventuate, there would be an appropriate commission in it for you."

The general was already bored with the conversation. Though he had never previously met a Vilenjji in person, he knew them well by reputation and via the all-pervading Niyyuuan media.

"I not need yous' money."

The thick cilia that topped the Vilenjji's tapering head writhed actively. "Then perhaps another inducement might better encourage you to assist us. I am given to understand that there has of late occurred a lapse in your original fondness for certain other visiting non-Niyyuu with whom you have been working."

What nonsense was this distasteful visitor spouting? "I surmise you speaking of four aliens formerly attached to my staff. What they have to do with the Vilenjji?"

The flap-tipped arm gesticulated again. "They are the property of whom I speak."

That was unexpected. Saluu-hir-lek was not ashamed to admit that he was taken completely by surprise. His mind worked furiously. Who he was clashed violently with who he wanted to be.

"The Niyyuu consider themselves honorable members galactic society. Within that society, holding of sentients as property considered immoral."

"But only illegal on worlds that have specific directives against it." Unperturbed, the Vilenjji gestured afresh. "Otherwise, the relevant business would not be there for such as my association to exploit. The trick is to practice one's trade while staying clear of those meddlesome, do-gooding species who believe it is their moral right to interfere in the honest business of others. The Sessrimathe, for example. Unless my research is seriously flawed, the autonomous realms of Niyu hold no official legal position on this matter. Such isolated instances as might occur are to be adjudicated on an individual basis."

Heedless of the prohibitions against the use of modern devices inside a traditional Niyyuuan military encampment, the Vilenjji proceeded to produce a marvelous little information generator. When he had finished perusing the material this placed before him, Saluu-hir-lek found himself torn between conventional morality and a burning desire for something more basic. Or base.

He had once been very fond of the food preparator Walker. These

days, the emotions he felt toward the scheming human were more than merely conflicted.

"You want me help you recover your 'property?' Property that consist of these four visitors?"

The Vilenjji gestured diffidently. "You may elect to accept the applicable commission for doing so or not. My present resources are limited, but still substantial. I think you would be pleased. There are certain trade goods we can offer you that are not readily available on your world."

Contraband, Saluu-hir-lek mused. There were desirable items that were banned from importation into Niyu. He could not help but wonder what they might be.

"If I assist you in this," he said slowly, "must present image of virtuous soldier only helping scrupulous off-worlders to recover what rightfully theirs. Leave moral implications for others to sort out."

The Vilenjji was perfectly agreeable. "While your reputation is of no concern to us, we of course understand that it is of interest to you. Rest assured we are adept at playing the outraged and offended." His voice, as translated by the device he wore over his speaking organ, grew noticeably edgy. "Recently, we have had much practice."

Saluu-hir-lek pondered the offer while his guest waited patiently. What manner of prohibited goods the dislikeable alien was offering by way of "commission" the general did not know. What he did know was that by reputation the Vilenjji had access to many things that were often as tempting as they were illegal. Then there was the matter of how he had been used, and lied to, by the four visiting aliens. Was he not entitled to some recompense for the insult he had suffered? If he could no longer make use of their singular talents to achieve his personal goals, then there was no reason to champion them or their cause.

They were determined to leave anyway, to embark on an outlandish, unlikely, and probably suicidal quest in search of their unknown and doubtlessly unreachable homeworlds. Dragging three ships of the Niyyuu, their crews, and multiple blinded media recorders with them to oblivion. Was it not his patriotic duty to try to prevent such a disaster? On thoughtful reflection, the government of Fiearek-iib and the others involved in this farce would probably thank him, albeit in private, for saving them the expense of having to provide three ships and their respective complements to try to fulfill the aliens' hopeless and costly request. If the visitors were claimed by and taken away by the Vilenjji, fellow citizens of galactic civilization, could not the governments of the realms rightly claim to be morally guiltless of any consequences? Such was how Saluu-hir-lek rationalized the proceedings.

"I will intercede with pertinent authorities," he responded finally. "Yous have documentation to prove yous' claim, of course?"

"I can supply a surfeit of applicable formulae," Pret-Klob assured him. He rose from his peculiar crouch but did not approach the general's seat. "I will provide the requisite contact information. I understand that our missing property is preparing to depart Niyu. Obviously, this matter of mutual interest must be resolved appropriately and to our mutual satisfaction before then."

With that, the alien turned and departed, lurching away on its foot flaps, leaving behind only promises and a slightly foul smell. As he reflected further on the unexpected visitation, Saluu-hir-lek found himself increasingly troubled by its possible ramifications.

A hastily applied dose of the powerful stimulants he utilized for recreational relaxation whenever combat was not going well was sufficient to cure him of any lingering reservations.

✳

Given how jittery and uneasy he had been those first weeks long ago when he was being held aboard the Vilenjji capture ship, it was amazing how well Walker had adapted to sleeping in alien surroundings. Now, whether on urbanized Seremathenn, in a traditional Niyyuuan military encampment, or aboard a parsec-traversing craft in deep space, he found that he was able to enjoy a deep and relaxing rest anywhere.

Hence the necessity for the hand that had at first touched him lightly on the shoulder to slap, then finally beat on his back before it finally succeeded in waking him up.

"George, dammit," Walker began sleepily as he rolled over. "Haven't you figured out how to let yourself out of a Charuchalan residence yet? If you're bored, you need to—"

A pair of fingers touched themselves to his mouth. They were long, slender, and strong. "No shouting." Admonishing, tense, the voice was familiar, though not in such circumstances. "Cannot tell what capabilities other aliens might have."

He sat up sharply. In the near darkness of the quiet room he could see very little. What light there was came from a distant, pale pink indicator showing that the room's electronics were functioning properly. Hovering above him was the vaguest of outlines; whipcord lean and motionless. But his nostrils detected a certain sweetish fragrance, as of slightly soured roses. It was instantly recognizable. During the preceding months, he had come to know it well.

"Viyv-pym?"

The fingers returned, this time to anxiously stroking his bare left shoulder. "You must rise up, Marcus Walker. Now!" In the feeble light, he saw that while she was touching him, she was looking elsewhere.

As he sat up and slipped off the sleeping frame he found himself, as usual, envying the Niyyuu their superb night vision. The best he could do was stumble and feel around for his clothing. The fact that he was naked did not trouble him and certainly did not interest her.

"What is it? What's wrong?"

"They coming for yous."

Fighting to blink sleep from his eyes and power up the hard drive that was his brain, he struggled to make sense of what was happening. "What are you talking about, Viyv-pym? Who's 'coming' for me?"

"Not just for you. For you and yous' friends. You must all of you leave, now, tonight." Moving away from him, she checked the door readout against the instrumentation that encircled her narrow wrist. "I not know how much time remaining."

While he finished fastening his adapted Niyyuuan attire, she woke George. Growling, the dog snapped upright on his smaller sleeping platform. When he saw who had awakened him, he was just as confused as Walker. She did her best to explain the reason for the nocturnal invasion as they exited the room and hurried to alert Sque and Braouk.

"I have found out that other aliens come look for you."

Hurrying to keep up with her as George trotted alongside, Walker fought to make sense of what she was telling him. The Vilenjji implant functioned efficiently no matter how sleepy he was. "What other aliens?" He thought automatically of the Sessrimathe. Did they want him back? It was flattering, of course, but he had come to Niyu for a reason and had no desire to return to that paragon of civilization and its well-meaning, if sometimes overbearing, inhabitants.

"Big, purple-skinned, with eyes even larger than those of Niyyuu, wider than those of you small many-limbed friend."

George uttered a sound that emerged halfway between yelp and curse. "Do their skulls rise to a point topped with little wavy things, like thick fur?" When she indicated in the affirmative as they turned a corner, there was no ambiguity in the dog's subsequent angry exclamation.

So the persistent Vilenjji had tracked them all the way to Niyu, Walker mused. What of it? Why the worry and near panic on Viyv-

THE LIGHT-YEARS BENEATH MY FEET

pym's part? The Vilenjji had no power here. Or was he, as was all too often the case, overlooking something? Certainly the sense of urgency she had conveyed ever since waking him suggested as much.

The last of the four fellow travelers to be unexpectedly roused from a sound sleep, Sque divined rapidly what had happened.

"The Vilenjji have found an ally among the Niyyuu, or they would not pose a threat to us." Eyes that were slashes of silver set in dark maroon flesh looked up at those of the tall female Niyyuu. "You know who it is."

She indicated in the affirmative. "I am sorry have to say these beings have corrupted the general. He is helping them."

Braouk could not believe it. "Saluu-hir-lek, whom we assisted greatly, now betrays?"

As they exited the structure and hurried toward a silently waiting private transport, the ocean of lights of Charuchal-uul's capital city pulsed around them. Other vehicles slid or soared past on silent repellers. An increasingly apprehensive Walker eyed each and every one of them, wondering which might hold implacable Vilenjji and their newly inveigled Niyyuuan cronies.

"I not sure what they promise him," Viyv-pym told the lumbering Braouk, "but whatever the specifics, they apparently sufficient. Under some galactic law-reasoning, he sending Kojnian soldiers to help 'recover' you." She looked back at Walker, who was following close behind. "This alien say you its property."

"More twisting of the precepts of civilization." Lacking true feet, legs, or massive supporting tentacles on the order of the Tuuqalian, Sque was having a difficult time keeping up. As her kind were not built for walking, running was almost as alien to them as flying. Perceiving her difficulty, Braouk scooped her up and bore her along, carrying the K'eremu as effortlessly as he would have an infant.

"It not matter," Viyv-pym responded. As her breathing grew deeper, her muscular round mouth expanded and contracted like a miniature bellows. "Who wields what guns is what matter now. I make what arrangements I could, but I not Charuchalan and it difficult this time of night to make contact with relevant parties."

"Something both the Vilenjji and our erstwhile comrade Saluu-hir-lek doubtless have taken into consideration." Freed from the debilitating need to drag herself rapidly across the ground, Sque's voice had strengthened.

Thankfully, the transporter Viyv-pym had engaged was large enough to accommodate all of them, including Braouk. Not trusting automatics that could be compromised, she had sensibly arranged for a manually controlled vehicle. In addition to the Charuchalan driver, it contained one other inhabitant.

"Sobj-oes!" As they entered the big transport, George bounded into the astronomer's lap and gave her face a friendly lick. Having no tongue, she could not respond in kind. She had to settle for stroking his head with one hand, a compromise that more than satisfied him. He sat there, head up, eyes alert and forward, tail metronoming. "Where are we going? Someplace to hide out until the local authorities can get a handle on Saluu-hir-lek?"

She hacked up a racking cough of amusement. "Someplace, yes." Leaning to her left to peer around him, she snapped instructions at the vehicle's operator. They were beyond concise.

*He must know where we're going,* Walker thought rapidly. *Viyv-pym and the astronomer must have had enough time to brief him before they got here.*

As the trim but capacious craft accelerated, he found himself seated close to Viyv-pym. "Where are you taking us?" Mindful of George's question, he took a guess. "Local authorities?"

Those bottomless eyes seemed to flow into his. "Not safe. I know that Saluu-hir-lek has been compromised by these aliens. I not know who else. At such times, in such circumstances, all must be considered suspect. Promises of wealth and power render even the most upright susceptible. Also, I have no influence here. This is Charuchal-uul, not Kojn-umm. To ensure yous' safety, must get yous away from here."

"You're sending us back to Biranju-oov?" he wondered.

It was Sobj-oes who replied. Her expression when she looked over at him, or as much of it as he could read, was electric with enthusiasm. "No, Marcus Walker. One hope most fervently that we are sending yous home."

The main port was enormous, as befitted one serving the capital of a powerful dominion. Their transporter hummed right past it. As it did so, Walker could see an impressive ship emerging from the night sky and settling massively to ground. Unexpectedly, George began to laugh, snickering in his suggestive way as he rolled back and forth on the astronomer's narrow, bony lap.

Seeing no humor whatsoever in their increasingly dangerous situation, Walker challenged the dog. "What's so funny? You won't be laughing very long if these Vilenjji catch up with us again."

Composing himself, George scrambled back up into a sitting position. "I'm sorry, Marc. It's just that after all these chronological years and light-years we've traveled, after everything we've been through, here we are being spirited away in the middle of the night again, to be bundled up and rushed off-planet."

"It's not the same," Walker murmured in response. "This isn't Earth."

"Neither is where we're going, remember?"

Angling sharply but smoothly to the left, the transporter entered an access that led to a subsidiary section of the main port. The lights were fewer here, the looming nearby facilities showing ample evidence of age and some neglect. Eying them, Walker had to remind himself that what he was seeing was still hundreds of years in advance of anything on Earth.

Looking like a conjoined cluster of mating white and gold beetles, a transfer craft sat quiescent on its raised service platform. It was not as large as the craft Walker had just seen land at the busy section of the port, but it was far larger than any commercial airliner on his home-world. A loading ramp led at a modest angle up into a dark opening in one of the craft's bulging components. As the transporter slowed to a halt nearby, a squad of energetic, determined Niyyuu emerged from the ship's interior to greet it. All of the tall, slender, big-eyed natives were armed, Walker noted. And not with spears or swords, but with energy weapons and projectors.

Sobj-oes, for one, was clearly relieved to see them. "Some of yous' crew," she informed him. "Most are volunteers. Spirit of adventure not confined to Sessrimathe only."

As he quickly exited the transporter, Walker studied the cluster of assembled Niyyuuan faces. Even in broad daylight and even given the length of time he had by now spent among them, it was sometimes difficult to tell what they were thinking. But it was clear that these were alert and aware. Their two-fingered grips on their weapons were firm. In this group, at least, there seemed to be slightly more females than males.

Without warning, several of them raised and leveled their weapons. Walker tensed, while next to him, George swiftly scampered around behind the human's legs. The guns were not aimed at him and his friends however, but at a point past them. Behind them.

The second transporter that had pulled into the little-used service and loading area was larger than its predecessor. It proceeded to disgorge several dozen armed Niyyuu. Despite the poor light, Walker had no trouble making out the uniforms and insignia of the armed forces of the realm of Kojn-umm. A number of the soldiers appeared disheveled, as if they had been called to duty in haste and forced to dress themselves on the run. In the forefront, he immediately recognized a familiar and atypically undersized figure: Saluu-hir-lek, looking even more uncompromising than usual. Together with that of his companions, however, the bulk of Walker's attention was reserved for the thick-bodied, robed, and sandaled figure that sloughed along beside the Niyyuuan general.

Not only was it a Vilenjji, it was a Vilenjji he and his friends recognized.

"Spawn of sewage, leaver of slime tracks, death sniffer," Braouk rumbled threateningly. As the seething Tuuqalian started forward, Walker hurried to intercept him. There was no need for that—yet.

The Vilenjji was as imperturbable as ever. Businesslike, to another way of thinking. "I see that the special eloquence of the Tuuqalian remains intact. That is gratifying. I am always pleased to find mislaid goods undamaged."

"Sorry we can't say the same for you." An irate George peeped out from behind Walker's ankles.

Implacable, Pret-Klob trained widely curving oculars on the impertinent quadruped. "And the small furred one's intelligence level has not reverted. I always worry about the permanence of complex neural modifications." The tapering skull came up. "I hereby claim property rights of which my association has been illegitimately deprived." One flap-tipped arm rose to point. "That one, and that, and the two behind them. Property of my association."

As the barely restrained Braouk extended a pair of accusatory tentacles, Sque crawled out to the end of one. Her weight did not even cause it to tremble.

"While different worlds adhere to and live by their own individually promulgated legal systemologies, common galactic law forbids the holding of any sentient as chattel. This is not Vilenj. You have no power here."

"On the contrary," Pret-Klob countered her. "All that is required is that means be available for avoiding prolonged deliberation in legal analysis." His eyes bored into Walker's. "Once off this world and in open space, other rulings take effect. I and the surviving, and new, members of my association wish only to recover what is rightfully ours, originally acquired after much hard work and travail. These efforts at recovery have already cost us much." Without changing tone in the slightest he concluded, "Our goods may already have suffered significant depreciation."

"I wish I had bigger teeth," George snarled. "I'd depreciate you right down to that frizzy pinhead of yours, and play kickball with your eyes."

"An unlikelihood," the Vilenjji responded impassively as he turned to peer down at his recently engaged Niyyuuan associate. "Every minute of this disagreeable but necessary enterprise is costly and awkward to expense. General, be so good as to proceed with the recovery of what are rightfully the assets of my association."

At a sign from the grim-faced Saluu-hir-lek, the soldiers behind him started forward. Simultaneously, the remainder of the armed crew of the transfer craft drew and raised their own weapons so that they were in line with those of their comrades. Taken aback by this suggestion of serious resistance, the uncertain Kojnian soldiers held their own weapons at ready. In the distance, another ship thrummed as it lifted toward space.

Across the far too small, intervening strip of plasticized ground, both heavily armed groups regarded each other tensely.

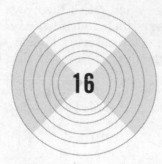

**16**

Heedless of the potent weaponry pointed in her direction, Viyv-pym moved forward until she was standing in front of Walker and George. In a voice that did not shake, she addressed those confronting her. Her words, however, were directed not at a furious, startled Saluu-hir-lek, nor at the hulking alien standing next to the general, but at the troops clustered behind and on either side of them. Despite his nervousness at being confronted by so many lethal devices, as she spoke Walker eyed her with the kind of admiration men in his position usually reserved for females of the species who exceeded their annual sales quotas by six figures.

"Soldiers of Kojn-umm! That yous' commander standing before yous. But this not yous' fight. We do not keep other intelligent beings as property in Kojn-umm. No realm, no commercial concern, no individuals on Niyu keep intelligent beings as property." She paused to let her words sink in. "This foulness of a principle is what yous being asked to support. Not security of beloved home realm in courageous, traditional manner of our kind. Not defense of our homeworld. Nothing but a principle of commerce that as alien to the Niyyuu as is the small-headed creature that presently stand before you.

"By refusing do this dishonest thing yous do not disobey principles of combat for which yous enlisted. Is no proper combat here." One slender arm gestured expansively to take in their surroundings. "This not Kojn-umm. No officer or official of Kojn-umm, no matter how famous or feted at home, have authority here." The arm swung around and down, coming to rest lightly across Walker's shoulders. "These sentients beside me have fought alongside you for many ten-days now. They have helped bring great acclamation to yous and to Kojn-umm. Is not right to betray them for benefit of other alien who has done nothing for either." Her voice lowered.

"Whatever other alien has promised, whatever yous been told, one thing is clear to any soldier who claims Kojn-umm as home: is not right sell honor for profit."

Only the breathy industrial sounds of the nearby main port sifted through the cool night air. Saluu-hir-lek spoke into the darkness. "Kill her."

Long fingers holding weapons tensed on both sides. And—nothing happened. From the back of the force of Kojnian troops someone muttered matter-of-factly, "This Charuchal-uul—not Kojn-umm." Though he whirled around sharply, Saluu-hir-lek was unable to identify the individual who had spoken.

First one, then two more, then every weapon was lowered, on both sides. Crew and indigenous Kojnians regarded one another through the night. An officer of average skill knows when to hold his position and when to attack. A superior one knows when to fall back. Saluu-hir-lek peered up at the Vilenjji.

"I find I without necessary resources to fulfill you request. Therefore it with much regret I say that I must decline you offer." Before Pret-Klob could respond, the general had turned back to the aliens with whom he had shared both the good and the bad for many ten-days.

"If yous go with this Vilenjji, Saluu-hir-lek prevails. If yous leave Niyu, Saluu-hir-lek prevails. Due to financial arrangements, I would prefer first option, but circumstances dictate I recognize second." His eyes came to rest on the unyielding Viyv-pym. "I sorry you attached to political arm of government. You would make fine officer." Pivoting, he gestured to his troops and simultaneously uttered a curt command. In response, they began to holster or shoulder their weapons and shuffle back toward the vehicle that had brought them. The potentially deadly confrontation was over.

Just like that. Only not quite.

Pret-Klob had not moved. If the Vilenjji was armed, he chose not to reveal a weapon. A wise choice, given that the transporter crewmembers who had so forcefully prevented him from recovering his inventory had not shifted their own positions. Instead, he let his stretched oculars scrutinize them one and all.

"Human Marcus Walker, canine George, Tuuqalian Broullkoun-uvv-ahd-Hrashkin, K'eremu Sequi'aranaqua'na'senemu: know for a certainty that this only constitutes yet another expensive delay in the implementation of the inevitable. If you will now come with me willingly, I am authorized, on behalf of my re-formed association, to make a one-time offer and grant you a percentage of the profit of your own individual sales when you are sold."

"That's very generous of you," Walker managed to reply with remarkably little recourse to sarcasm, "but I'm afraid we'll have to decline. We're going home, you see, and letting you sell us someplace would put a serious crimp in those plans." Turning to go, he found himself hesitating.

"Something I don't understand, Pret-Klob. If the Vilenjji are such dedicated businessfolk, and such careful monitors of the bottom line, and these attempts to repossess my friends and I are costing you so much—why do you keep at it? Why don't you just give it up and focus your energies on more immediately profitable activities?"

Pret-Klob gazed back at him. "It is not good to allow inventory to escape. It creates a bad precedent. Most especially, it is not good when the inventory in question, though of variable capacity, is manifestly inferior to the Vilenjji." Efficient translator implant notwithstanding, the other creature's true alienness succeeded in communicating itself to the interested Walker.

"To allow you to go free, after you forcibly excused yourselves from our control, would be to admit your equality with the Vilenjji. This would call into question the very principles on which our trade is founded. That we cannot permit. Hear me clearly, human. There should be no misunderstanding. I and my association will follow you wherever necessary, for as long as is necessary, overcoming whatever difficulties may place themselves in our way, until we have recovered our property. This is an absolute."

Hanging from the end of one of Braouk's powerful tentacles, Sque whispered to Walker, "Do not let his words trouble you, Marc. The Vilenjji are as full of gas as the sixth planet of Asmeriis."

"They don't trouble me, Sque," he lied. Louder, to the Vilenjji, he said, "You do what you have to do according to the principles you live by. We'll do the same. And if we are fated never to meet again, know that I ardently wish you poor sales and inaccurate accounting."

The Vilenjji stared at him a moment longer. Either it was truly impossible to genuinely upset one of his kind, or else they had developed the ability to wholly internalize their irritation to a degree unmatched by any species Walker had yet encountered. Conscious of the fact that the vehicle that had brought him to the port was now almost loaded with its complement of put-out Kojn-umm soldiery, he turned on his sandal-clad foot flaps and lurched heavily in its direction. Insofar as Walker was able to tell, the Vilenjji did not look back.

Not until the big surface transporter had cleared the port perimeter did the armed crewmembers who had put their lives on the line for the sake of the visitors finally secure their own weapons and prepare to enter the transatmospheric transfer craft. A cheerful George was the first one up the ramp, already chatting amiably with and making friends among the delighted crew. Braouk followed, carrying Sque, who avowed to any who would listen that from the very beginning of the confrontation she had known exactly how it was going to turn out. Walking just ahead of them, the astronomer Sobj-oes was unable to escape the K'eremu's unrelenting paean to her own infallibility.

Walker lingered, waiting on Viyv-pym. It was left to her to inform him of something he expected but still did not want to hear.

"I not going with you, Marcus Walker. I not qualified to be of crew."

His head tilted back only slightly, he stared into her wide, brilliant, golden-yellow eyes. "Surely you can't go back to Kojn-umm, Viyv-pym." He gestured with his head in the direction taken by the departed troop transport. "Just because Saluu-hir-lek paid you a backhanded compliment doesn't mean he won't find a way to deal with you once you're both back in your own realm. He may not be human, but I know how guys like that work. We have the same types in my business. They don't forget something like this."

"I need not return Kojn-umm," she assured him. "As someone with off-world diplomatic and commercial experience and expertise, I have been offered a succession of admirable positions by both Biranju-oov and Charuchal-uul. Should I wish take advantage of it, opportunities even in Fiearek-iib are open to me." A long-fingered hand indicated the city that lay just beyond the main port. "Many excellent choices are mine." The hand swept downward, and both long fingers came to rest against his sternum.

"When I first save you from Vilenjji and bring you here from Sere-mathenn to make food presentations for notables of Kojn-umm, I not think it end quite this way." The delicate fingertips brushed his chest. "Good journeying to you, Marcus Walker. I have learn much from you. I hope you have learn some small things, maybe, from me."

"I know that I have, Viyv-pym." Placing the two middle fingers of his left hand against her lower neck, he let them drag gently down her lissome front. Then, impulsively and without thinking about it, he put both arms around her and pulled her close. Though she resisted slightly at first and was taut with lean muscle, he outweighed her by more than a third.

As he put a hand behind her head and drew it down toward his own, a single not-so-subtle thought ran through his mind as he kissed her. *What in the hell do you think you're doing?* For one thing, she had no lips and therefore could not properly kiss him back. He didn't care. He very much wanted to kiss her. If only, he told himself fatuously, in the spirit of scientific experimentation.

Taken completely aback, it took her a moment to respond. When she did, it was perhaps in a similar spirit. Or maybe it was nothing more than an instinctive reaction to what he was doing. In any case, the ring of muscle that encircled her small, round mouth contracted, and she inhaled forcefully.

It was not like his first kiss, nor even like those he had enjoyed on successful outings with members of the opposite sex of his own kind. But his lips were bruised for weeks afterward.

The ironic thing was, if he ever did want to boast of it to his buddies, no one would ever believe him.

※

Jhanuud-tir-yed turned away from the latest multistory media projection that was currently dominating the central atrium of government central in the capital city of Fiearek-iib. Other functionaries, passing around and through the image, were enthralled by the great expedition. As for herself, during the previous ten-days the vice premier had seen and experienced quite enough of the aliens. That they had nearly failed to depart in the intended fashion was a fact known only to a few. With care, it would remain that way, nothing more than an imperceptible bump along the road to what everyone hoped would be a glorious footnote in Niyyuuan history.

Things could have been worse, she knew. They could have been much worse. No one was happier to see the four visitors finally depart Niyu than the venerable vice premier. Given the way the visitors had manipulated the traditional forces of Kojn-umm, Toroud-eed, and several other realms, it was a relief to see them go. While most of the attention had been focused on the bipedal human and the massive Tuuqalian, it was the smaller pair of visitors who had kept Jhanuud-tir-yed awake at night. That seemingly charming four-legged thing—what had it been called? George, yes. A single naming for a singular creature. And that arrogant, pompous jumble of tendrils and glitter who called herself Sque. The vice premier hadn't trusted the K'eremu from the first time she had observed her lurking in the background, letting her more affable companions do the preponderance of the talking.

Now they were gone. Now life on calm, complacent Niyu could get back to normal. And regardless of the eventual outcome of the possibly doomed expedition, of one thing she was certain with regard to the aliens.

It had been worth three ships to get rid of them.

✳

Walker did not know what Sque or Braouk thought of the Niyyuu vessels. Their own species were space-going, sophisticated, and afflicted with their own systems of engineering aesthetics. As for George, the dog volunteered readily, "I don't care what they look like as long as they start up when someone turns the key and go when somebody steps on the accelerator." But Walker thought his first sight of the ships, as they came into view on one of the transfer craft's monitors, was beautiful.

There were three, just as Walker had insisted upon and Jhanuud-tir-yed had promised. Though not nearly as massive as the Sessrimathe ship that had rescued him and his friends from Vilenjji captivity, they were large enough to inspire awe. Burgeoning clusters of conjoined propulsion components and living quarters, illuminated by if not quite ablaze with internal lights, they floated in orbit awaiting the arrival of the transfer craft.

It was half an hour longer before Walker was convinced that their motion relative to that of the three waiting starships had ceased. Concerned, he went in search of Sobj-oes. He found the astronomer forward, chatting with one of the officers who had volunteered to be a part of the expedition. To the human's relief, and somewhat to his consternation, she had a ready explanation for the apparent delay in docking.

"It the media," she informed him. "All those assigned to this voyage clamoring for best position to make first recordings." She indicated the image on the nearest monitor. "This the beginning, an important moment. Each individual desires compose best possible imaging, most dramatic lighting." She inhaled breathily, her red- and-black-painted mouth contracting to a tiny opening. "Is not science. But is necessary."

"My friends and I could do without it," he confessed. "We're pretty tired." He found himself wishing Viyv-pym was aboard, to intercede with the media on his behalf. But Viyv-pym was gone for good, back on Niyu.

*I have been away from home for a very long time,* he reminded himself firmly.

"I'm glad you're coming with us," he told her. Sobj-oes was not Viyv-pym, but she was at least a sympathetic and familiar face.

"I would not miss it." The astronomer was a taut bundle of anticipation and excitement. "We will be visiting a portion of the galaxy far outside familiar boundaries. Opportunities should abound to observe previously unrecorded phenomena, visit new civilizations." Her luminous eyes caught the light as they stared back at him. "What scientist worthy of the designation not leap at the chance to experience such things?"

"This is as much a leap into the unknown for you and the rest of the Niyyuu on this voyage as it is for my friends and I. We're going because we have no choice but to keep going. You have something to return to. Doesn't it bother you that you might not come back?"

A two-fingered hand reached out to stroke his right arm. "Any scientist embarking on long journey knows they might die before end of journey is reached. If no one willing to take that chance, no science ever get done."

A new voice interrupted them. "It is always encouraging to hear a mature understanding of the nature of understanding Nature voiced by one of the lesser orders." Sque arrived in what had become her favored fashion: born aloft on one of Braouk's tentacles, her scorn preceding her. "I myself look forward to the acquiring of new knowledge."

"And I sing," the Tuuqalian rumbled, having to bend low as usual to avoid banging the upper part of his body and his stalk-mounted eyes on the ceiling, "of new spaces encountered, rarely seen."

As well he should, Walker knew, since his homeworld was the one they were heading for, and the only one thus far of the three that the

displaced travelers desperately sought whose location was even feebly
surmised. He steeled himself inwardly. If only one of the four of them
made it home, that would be an impressive accomplishment in itself.
Guided only by a faint perception of distant possibilities, they were
flinging themselves into the unknown.

Three of them were, anyway. Where was George?

He found the dog curled up among piles of last-minute loaded supplies in the transfer craft's storeroom, sound asleep. Kneeling, he gently stroked his friend's back until George awoke. The dog yawned,
stretched, and quivered, pushing out his front legs as he looked up at
Walker.

"What'd you wake me for?" he asked irritably.

"Oh, I don't know." Walker sat down beside his friend. "Maybe because we're about to embark on a journey into deep space that even our
crew has never attempted before. Maybe because we may never see a
civilized world again. Maybe because this is yet another pivotal moment
in our lives. God, what I wouldn't give for a double latte right now.
With nutmeg. And cinnamon."

"You've managed to get hold of three starships. Don't get greedy."

Walker shrugged and smiled. "I'm a commodities broker. It's my
nature to always want to trade up."

George rolled over onto his back and began contorting his spine in
ways few humans could match, scratching his back against the oddly
tactile surface of the package he had chosen for a temporary bed. Walker
looked on with envy.

"Doesn't any of this bother you, George? The fact that we're heading out into a part of the greater galaxy unknown even to the Niyyuu?
That we're going beyond the bounds of what they consider to be
known civilization?"

Ceasing his twisting and scratching, the dog rolled over onto his
belly. Panting contentedly, he looked up at his friend and companion.
"You know what they say, Marc. 'Knick-knack, hyperwack, vector a dog
a zone, this old mutt goes spacing home.' Better wandering infinity
with a full fridge, even if it's an alien one, than stumbling around cold
and starving in the snow in a dirty alley back home."

A glance at one of the transfer craft's omnipresent monitors showed
that they had at last resumed forward motion again and were finally about
to dock with one of the three waiting starships. Walker straightened.

"I wish I had your casual sangfroid, George. I guess no matter what
happens, I'll always be the nervous type." He sighed. "Sobj-oes says

there's no getting away from it: for the duration of the voyage we're going to have to tolerate the Niyyuuan media who've been assigned to
this excursion."

George rose to all fours. "No problem. If they get too pushy, I'll just
start barking at them. Their translators can't handle that."

Walker's smile widened. On the monitors, beyond the starships,
several thousand worlds beckoned. With luck, one of them was small
and blue and gauzily streaked with gossamer white. But first they had
to see home a very large poet.

"I'm glad you've been with me through all this. I don't know how
I could've gotten through it all without your company. You're a good
dog, George."

"And you're a tolerable human, except for the usual odor." Shaking
himself, the dog started for the main hatch. "Let's go deal with the media. They're going to be with us for a long time. Make them no
promises, or I'll pee on your leg."

"Canine eloquence," Walker quipped as he matched the dog's pace.

"I'll believe humans have a better way of communicating," the dog
countered, "when I see the evidence of it in the way they run their civilization."

"Maybe," Walker mused as they exited the storage area and turned
toward the center of the transfer craft, "things will have changed for the
better by the time we get home."

"Don't hold your breath." The dog snorted. "Regarding either possibility."

The Candle of Distant Earth

For Amos Nachoum
Fellow explorer . . .

1

For the eleventh time, Ussakk the Astronomer pored over the most recent collated readouts while trying to decide how best to kill himself. Whichever method he chose, it would be faster and cleaner than what was coming. While the last time the Iollth had ravaged Hyff had been well before his birth, abundant records were available to illustrate in gruesome detail their appetite for destruction. Given the history of their visitations to Hyff, it was remarkable that any of the populace would continue to resist. Yet invariably, outraged at the periodic demands for tribute and treasure, some did. And just as invariably, they died deaths that were as horrible as they were futile.

That much could be tolerated, if not for the disagreeable Iollth habit of slaughtering out of apparent boredom the occasional batch of innocent civilians.

Ussakk felt he would be as fated to be among the latter—that is, if

the authorities did not kill him outright as the bearer of bad news. He
sympathized in advance with their probable reaction. There was always
the hope among his people that the Iollth would tire of their cyclical visits to Hyff, that they would seek to enrich themselves at the expense of
others elsewhere and leave the Hyfft to their peaceful, widespread communities and to the tending of the crops of which they were so proud.

A fool's dream, Ussakk knew. So long as the Hyfft fashioned beautiful objects out of rare materials, so long as their mines produced rare
and unsynthesizable raw materials, the Iollth would return: to plunder,
and not to buy.

The astronomer knew they could not be put off with excuses. A
hundred years ago, the Great Government had decreed that the production of objects of beauty and the mining of gems was to cease. Despite the temporary harm this inflicted on Hyfftian culture, it was
hoped the absence of such things would discourage the Iollth. After all,
one cannot ransack that which does not exist. It was a defensive maneuver predicated on a rational reaction.

Unfortunately, the Iollth did not respond in a rational manner.
In their fury and frustration, their unopposed ships laid waste to a dozen
of Hyff's largest communities. Tens of thousands died. After that, there
were no more attempts to discourage the visitors with clever subterfuges.

Occasionally, there came together bands of Hyfft who were still determined, somehow, to resist. Sadly, having evolved from sedate bands
of farmers who had known nothing but greater and greater cooperation that had eventually resulted in the development of the present state
of high culture, the Hyfft were emotionally and psychologically ill-
equipped for warfare. Even thoughts of acquiring an armed starship
from one of the other space-traversing species who paid the occasional
rare visit to Hyff fell by the wayside when none among the Hyfft could
be found who were bold enough to leave the Nesting World long
enough to travel between the stars to arrange the actual acquisition.

Though technologically advanced, the Hyfft could not find it
within themselves to manufacture weapons. Psychologically crippled,
they could not muster enough individuals to make use of such weapons even if they managed to buy them from elsewhere. Located far from
the fringes of galactic civilization, they did not attract the attention of
those who might have offered them protection.

Besides, it was rationalized, the Iollth did not threaten genocide.
They came only to plunder and ravage, and that only once every hun-
dredth-passing or so. Hardly sufficient reason for distant species with a
surfeit of their own problems to take the time and expense to interfere.

Especially when most of Hyff never even suffered beneath the heavy foot of the visitors, except to witness and weep over their sporadic depredations via relayed images.

That the fast-moving signatures Ussakk had detected emerging from deepspace belonged to the Iollth there was no question. The infrequent and uncommon traders or explorers who occasionally found their way to Hyff always arrived singly. There was one atypical report from three hundred-passings ago of two such vessels arriving simultaneously in orbit around Hyff, but that was only the result of coincidence. They had not been traveling in tandem, and were as surprised by each other's appearance in Hyfftian space as were the Hyfft themselves.

No, without question, a triple signature could signify the imminent arrival of nothing other than the dreaded Iollth.

As the senior astronomer on duty, he had the obligation to deliver the bad news to the local Overwatch, who would then pass it along to all the individual elements of the Great Government. Composed of hundreds of local Overwatches, the Great Government would then dictate an appropriate response. The best that could be hoped for, Ussakk knew, was that the Iollth would take what they wanted, murder for entertainment as few citizens as possible, and be on their way after causing a minimal amount of damage to Hyfftian civilization. It might be, he reflected as he began to make inviolable recordings of the relevant readouts, that with luck he would not be expected to kill himself.

As soon as the necessary recordings had been prepared, he stored them in his body pouch and prepared to leave his post. There was no thought of transmitting such sensitive information electronically. It was his responsibility, his personal *cura*, to deliver it in person. Coworkers were bemused by his nonresponsiveness as he departed. Such glumness was not usually associated with the bright and chipper senior astronomer. But no one pressed the limits of what was culturally acceptable. Though concerned, they left him to his private dejection. That was just as well, since if they had asked what was troubling him, he would have been compelled to answer.

*Let them dwell in happiness and contentment a little while longer*, he decided as he exited the observatory and ambled toward the nearest conveyor. Horror was now in the neighborhood and would arrive on their mental doorsteps soon enough.

The Escarpment of Lann dropped away behind him and his speed increased as the terrain leveled out. Racing toward the city, he was forced to slow repeatedly as his vehicle bunched up behind other conveyors. Each held, at most, no more than a single family. Hyfft did not travel in groups. On a world as heavily populated as theirs, even though that population was evenly dispersed, personal privacy was at a premium. So was courtesy, which was why the anxious Ussakk waited his turn until one by one, those in front of him reached their exit points and left the main conveyor route. Only then did he accelerate again.

There was no road, the conveyor route being only a line on a map that was duplicated in actuality by perfectly spaced sensors buried in the ground. The route Ussakk was following ran through fields of pfale, whose dark green fruit burst from the center of a spray of bright blue-green leaves. Enormous in extent, this particular field was nearly ready for harvesting. For a moment, the color and anticipation took his mind off the dreadful news he was about to deliver. Pfale was famed for its piquant taste, and for the ability of master cooks to turn it into a variety of elegant dishes usually supplemented with a quartet of semell condiments. Descended from wholly herbivorous ancestors, the Hyfft were masters of vegetarian cuisine.

An alien observer might have wondered why the agitated astronomer did not simply accelerate his levitating personal conveyor and pass the slower travelers in front of him. He could easily have done so, to the right or to the left. But such a move would have been an unforgivable breach of manners. On Hyff, one politely waited one's turn. The queue was a way of life, and woe betide any who violated it. Rules such as waiting for those in front to finish whatever they happened to be doing were not merely a matter of unspoken courtesy; they had been officially codified.

Exceptions were tolerated only for extreme emergencies. Unable to see how delivering his bad news a few morning-slices earlier would make things any better, Ussakk preferred to take his time and follow custom. Officialdom might soon berate him as the harbinger of doom, but no one would be able to accuse him of being impolite as part of the process.

The family ahead of him finally turned off, allowing him to accelerate afresh. Once within the outskirts of the city, he was able to take advantage of the much greater multiplicity of available conveyor routes. Like most urban concentrations on Hyff, Therapp was not large. With few exceptions, the majority of structures were built low to the ground in traditional fashion. Such buildings might cover considerable stretches of ground, but that was how the Hyfft preferred it. They did not like heights, and they favored open spaces.

Therapp's administrative center was housed in one such complex, which extended for several midds from the center of the city and across the meandering river that cut through it. Slotting his conveyor in a public receptacle, he quickly swapped it for its much smaller in-house counterpart. Within the vast structure, municipal workers dashed to and fro along clearly designated routings, never so much as nudging any of the pedestrians they passed. Without the internal conveyor, it might take him half a day to walk to the sector he sought.

Like the spokes of a wheel, the adjuncts to the office of Overwatch Delineator fanned out around a central core. As custom dictated, there were twenty-four such offices. Today the office of Delineator was held by number nine. Tomorrow it would be ten, and so on until next-month changeover. In this way the city's administration had twenty-four heads, among whom both responsibility and credit could be divvied up collectively. With only one day in charge each next-month, no one official had time to accumulate power over another. Occasionally, number twelve might swap day-work with the official occupying office twenty-one. Like everything else on Hyff, the system made for an administration that was both civil and efficient.

Today's Delineator was Phomma, of office nine. An unlucky number, Ussakk reflected as he stepped off his conveyor and snapped it into the nearest unoccupied recharger. Unlucky, because she would be the one to have to receive and deal with the dreadful news he carried with him.

When he entered, office nine was occupied by a pair of subordinate administrators engaged in debating the merits of expanding the city's southernmost recreation facility. Both looked up at his entry.

"Devirra li Designer," declared one. "Zubboj vi Procurer," added her companion.

"Ussakk ri Astronomer," he responded. While on business, the Hyfft did not waste time on extended formalities. They were an efficient folk. "To see today's Delineator."

The Designer's reply was prompt and inflexible. "Delineator Phomma qi Administrator sa Nine is not seeing visitors or supplicants until last two afternoon-slices. We respectfully suggest you return to request a meeting at that time." Small, dark, fast-moving pupils regarded him hesitantly. "Unless you already have arranged a meeting time for this morning."

"No, I haven't," he replied, "but I must see the Delineator immediately. It is a matter of global importance."

"Global?" Long, feathery white whiskers twitching to emphasis his amusement, the Procurer eyed his fellow subordinate administrator. "From an astronomer I would expect nothing less than galactic." They shared a casual touch, he clicking his prominent incisors against hers.

Ussakk was as well-mannered as the next person, but today he had no time for sarcasm. "You are more right than you say. The Iollth are returning to Hyff, and will be here within a two-day."

Later, though he could easily justify it, he regretted his bluntness.

A look at his face—eyes staring evenly, whiskers unquivering, short round ears perfectly erect and forward facing—being all that was necessary to convince them that the visitor was not joking, the change in attitude among the pair of subordinate administrators was shocking in its abruptness. The Designer's hairless eyelids fluttered once, twice, before she collapsed. Trembling visibly, the Procurer bent over her and began to tug on her short arms in an attempt to reestablish normal breathing. He was so badly shaken he could not sustain his grip, leaving it to Ussakk to take over and maintain the procedure until the psychologically stunned female finally regained consciousness.

"I apologize," he murmured. "I did not mean to cause shock. That is why I did not use public channels to communicate the information, for fear it might get out before it could be appropriately reviewed. But it must be delivered now, here, so that means of dissemination to the rest of Hyff can be decided upon, and propagated accordingly." His tone, normally relaxed and carefree as that of any of his kind, was unnaturally solemn.

His seriousness seemed to steady the Procurer. "Go on in, quickly," the subordinate administrator told him as he resumed working the Designer's upper arms.

With an acknowledging twitch of the whiskers to the right of his nose, Ussakk hitched up the cross-straps of his formal work attire, turned, and strode toward the inner wall. Sensing his approach, number nine of twenty-four ceremonial panels slid aside to admit him to the circular inner office.

It was beautifully appointed, the citizens of Therapp and the surrounding district being proud of their accomplishments and those of their local artisans. A conical central skylight of synthetic crystal flooded the interior with sunshine lightly tinted gold by the swirling, stained panel attached to it. Directly beneath the skylight, a round desk sat embedded in the mosaic stone floor. There the Delineator of the Day of Therapp sat and worked. Placing the desk slightly below floor level compelled each of them to look up at approaching citizens. In this manner, humility was enforced on the Overwatch's principal public servant.

Delineator Phomma qi Administrator sa Nine looked up and chittered a polite traditional greeting, followed by, "I specifically asked staff to grant me a two day-slice period of privacy. You must have considerable influence to have gained admittance in spite of that." Her long, drooping whiskers inclined toward him as she spoke, the aggressiveness of their posture belying the civility of her words. Unusually, he noted, they were tinted a pale red.

"I am Ussakk the Astronomer, and I have no influence: only bad news."

"Proceed forward." Rising from her seat, she stepped away from the trio of readouts that floated in the air before her. They started to follow obediently until she thought to wave them away. "What news can simultaneously be so bad and so influential?"

He descended the six short ceremonial steps, each corresponding to one of the whiskers that dominated the Hyfftian visage. "This morning I regret to say that I was forced to reconfirm certain previous significant observations made by my facility's instrumentation. Three starships have entered our system from deepspace. Though it has not happened in my lifetime, I know from history that infrequent visitors to our world invariably arrive in only one such vessel. One time, by coincidence, two such marvelous craft arrived at Hyff." He blinked meaningfully. "The presence of more than that can mean only one thing."

As an educated person, the Delineator Phomma knew what it meant, too. To her credit, she neither fainted nor shook. But moisture did begin to appear at the lower edges of both eyes. She wiped it hurriedly away.

"This leaves no time for advance lamenting. That will have to come later." Turning, she moved purposefully back to the seat she had been occupying when he had arrived. Her hovering tripartite readouts had to move fast to hold their positions in front of her eyes. This time she did not dismiss them. "The Great Government must be notified immediately. You will provide all details. Work must be started to minimize the inevitable panic that will greet the official announcement." As her hands moved, the four short fingers on each waving instructions at the readouts, she glanced over at him. "Who else knows?"

Ussakk considered for a moment. "Only the two sub administrators whose permission I had to seek to enter here. Their personal reactions," he added thoughtfully, "were as might have been expected. Otherwise, not even my colleagues at the observatory know. Yet."

She chirruped an acknowledgement. "Then this can be handled appropriately. Or at least, as well as can be hoped." He thought he saw tears begin to rise again, but the Delineator shut them down before they could dampen the neatly trimmed brown fur under her eyes. Leastwise, the formal face paint that streaked and speckled her plump cheeks did not run.

"If you do not require my presence any longer," he murmured, "I should be getting back to my work."

She replied without looking up at him, her hands busy with the readouts. "Your work is here now. As Delineator of the Day for the Overwatch of Therapp, I am requisitioning your services to city administration. When your coworkers have been notified, they can monitor the approach of the . . ." She could not choke the name out, did not want to get the name out. "Of the incoming vessels," she finally finished.

Ussakk was appalled. "I am an astronomer, not a bureaucrat or civil servant. I answer to the Great Science, headquartered in Avvesse. Of what possible use could my extended presence be to the city government of Therapp?"

She paused in her work to study him. His whiskers quivered slightly under her suddenly intense stare, but he held his ground. "It is clear you are not a politician, either. Very well; if you need a reason, I feel that your continued presence in an urbanized area will in itself help to provide some small modicum of reassurance to the general populace."

His small black nose twitched. "How can that be?"

"By showing that you have not run away." She returned to manipulating the readouts. "In the coming days, that may prove critical. I don't suppose you can tell by the angle of approach of the Iollth ships where they intend to put down on Hyff?"

He reminded himself that this was not a fellow scientist he was talking to. "Angle of approach means nothing. They may decide to go into extended orbit around Hyff before choosing a place to—put down. Or they may decide to land at three different places. History shows that—"

"I know what history shows," she barked irritably. He took no offense at the sharpness of her response. Helplessness bred frustration, and frustration bred anger. He felt like doing some yelling and screaming himself. As a scientist, he realized the futility of such reactions better than most.

A tenth of a day-slice later, she waved both hands simultaneously, and the readouts that had been hovering before her vanished. With a weariness not even her elaborate ceremonial makeup could dispel, she turned back to him.

"The appropriate authorities have been advised. The Great Government is now in motion." Eyes as red as her whiskers met his. "All continental representatives are to meet here tomorrow. That is as fast as travel allows. Each of the eight continental Overwatches will determine how best to respond should an Iollth vessel set down in their territory. If all three approaching craft send their landers to one place, a worldwide response will be coordinated." The tearing started again, and this time it did not stop. "As we have throughout our history, we can only hope to minimize the destruction."

Stepping forward, Ussakk took her in his arms. The fact that she was the day's Delineator and he a research astronomer, and that they had never met before this moment, meant nothing. The Hyfft were a species as emotional as they were demonstrative, among whom close physical contact was not only commonplace but expected. Anyway, Ussakk was glad of the opportunity to embrace someone.

He needed the warming physical contact as badly as she did.

✷

They traveled to Therapp from all over the continent of Vinen-Aq, Delineators who under the newly imposed regulations of emergency had found their terms of office extended indefinitely beyond the usual one day. It was not certain that each was the best of their kind to deal with the crisis at hand, but there was no time to process extended evaluations. If you were Delineator on that dire day, you found yourself chosen.

Having come from far and wide, they assembled the following morning in the circular chamber of Therapp's administrative center. Informed of Ussakk's discovery, his scientific colleagues had promptly dropped all other work to devote themselves to the single task of monitoring the approach of the three ships. That left Ussakk free to exhibit himself to the general public. True to Phomma sa Nine's observation, his presence did seem to have a reassuring influence on public opinion.

That did not prevent some panic from spreading as word slipped out. At least by the time it did, the efficient and fast-moving Hyfftian authorities had been given a breathing space in which to prepare. The worst of the panic was quickly contained. But nothing could stop the consequent rush of city dwellers toward the countryside. Every conveyor route out of every conurbation was soon jammed with desperate, would-be refugees. Even so, the lines were orderly. The few seriously unbalanced individuals who actually ignored the designated routes in favor of taking off across private property were quickly apprehended and suitably chastised.

The Hyfft might be prone to panic, but they did so in an orderly fashion.

Within the chamber, designated Delineators from dozens of Vinen-Aq's largest communities milled and conversed. There was no yelling, no piercing echoes of raised voices. Administrators were not allowed that kind of emotional release. But the general conversation was certainly borne along by an uneasy edge.

Nestled in one ear, a communicator kept Ussakk in constant touch with his associates at the observatory. Every similar installation on Hyff had likewise abandoned its regular work schedule to focus on the incoming craft. Thus far there had been no attempt at communication. If history was any guide, Ussakk knew, that would come once the Iollth had settled themselves in orbit and chosen the unfortunate location or locations for their landing. In the past, they had been known to destroy a city center or two from orbit, just as a preliminary object lesson. Or perhaps for entertainment. On that aspect of Iollth psychology, there were few details.

All across peaceful but tense Hyff, ten billion individuals now spoke one thought with one mind, albeit usually in private so as not to offend their neighbors. *Please don't let them land here.* In silently wishing this, Ussakk unashamedly had to admit that he was no different from his less scientifically inclined fellows.

No one thought of mounting an active resistance. Confined to their planet and happy to be so, at peace among themselves for thousands of years, the Hyfft possessed no weapons of advanced destruction: nothing more offensive than nonlethal police gear. Nor did they need any such— except when the Iollth came calling. Discussion of developing such weaponry, which was certainly within the technical ability of Hyfftian science, had come to naught. The one time such a thing had been tried, over a hundred years earlier, an Iollth landing craft had actually been destroyed. Its three companion vessels had escaped to orbit, one badly damaged.

Safe high above the surface of Hyff, their mother ships had proceeded to kill some two hundred thousand Hyfft. After that, their subsequent visitations had met with no further resistance.

Wandering among the dense crowd of visiting, apprehensive Delineators, Ussakk had the opportunity to eavesdrop on numerous ongoing discussions. All he could do was listen, having nothing tangible to contribute. He would much rather have been back at the observatory, even if there was nothing to do there but monitor the rapid progress of the three incoming starships and agonize about possible landing sites.

There was one good thing. Given the speed at which the Iollth vessels were traveling, they should arrive by tomorrow, thus putting an end to all the increasingly nerve-wracking speculation. He felt himself to be as ready as any of his kind for whatever might come. His elderly parents had been sent out of the city, to a (hopefully) safe refuge deep in the agricultural countryside. He was not mated and not courting. He had no offspring. If anyone was suitable for sacrifice at the hands of the Iollth, it was him.

But he didn't want to die.

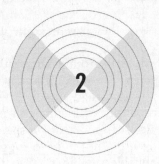

**2**

"It very puzzling." Sobj-oes's neck frill flexed repeatedly as she stared out the port at the beautiful, lush world above which the three Niyyuuan ships had entered orbit. "Is ample evidence here of large population having achieved an advanced level of technology. Seaports, carefully laid out urban cores of modest dimension, atmospheric travel, very advanced and widespread agriculture. Local electromagnetic spectrum is full of noise. But communications specialists say despite repeated attempts, is no response to any of our transmissions."

Relaxing in Marcus Walker's arms so that he could see out the port, George used one paw to dig at a persistent itch, then sneezed effusively. Walker's expression furrowed.

"You could at least cover your mouth."

The dog glanced up at his friend. "Why? Most of it comes out my nose. And paws don't provide much coverage anyway." He looked over at the Niyyuuan astronautics specialist, meeting wide, gold-flecked eyes. "Maybe your people just haven't hit on the right frequency yet."

Using one long, limber arm whose tip terminated in two digits that pinched together forcefully, Sobj-oes responded with a negative gesture that reflected personal as well as professional disappointment. "I assured that everythings have been tried. Most obvious reason for non-communication from surface is that we now well outside boundaries of accepted galactic civilization. Is entirely possible that, despite obvious high level of local technology, has been little or even no contact with any of the civilized species."

"Does that explain why they haven't come up to meet us?" Walker found himself asking.

Straightening her kilt-skirt around long, silk-skinned lower limbs in a manner that reminded him uncomfortably of the distant but not forgotten Viyv-pym, Sobj-oes turned huge, yellow-gold eyes on the human. "Are many communications satellites in multiple orbits around planet, but is no evidences of even a single spaceport. Are large facilities for atmospheric travel, but nothings to suggest locals venture into zone of no air. Not a habitable satellite, no installations on either moon or on outer planets. Nothing."

"Homebodies," George hypothesized thoughtfully. "Found an alley they like and keep to themselves. I can sympathize with that." As Walker set him down, the dog employed a hind foot to scratch at one ear.

"Maybe they have social reasons for not wanting to step off their world." Walker spoke while gazing out the port at the attractive planet below. "Maybe they're shy."

"Spatially speaking," Sobj-oes told them, "this system comparatively isolated. Are no other inhabited or habitable worlds nearby. Indigenous population may think selves isolated, intelligence-wise. This also help to explain why maybe no knowledge of numerous galactic methods of communication."

"We can always communicate with gestures," Walker pointed out.

"If the locals have limbs," George put in, choosing to overlook the fact that his kind were similarly lacking in such useful accoutrements as an opposable thumb.

"*Couhgh,*" the astronomer rasped. Ear-grating Niyyuuan expressions were, if anything, even harsher sounding to the human ear than their wince-inducing language. "We may yet have to resort to something that basic. But to do so means must have face-to-face contact." Her round, muscular, painted mouth expanded and contracted as she coughed slightly to indicate amusement and her foot tall, tapering ears inclined in George's direction as she addressed the dog. "If the locals have faces."

"If you're talking about sending down a landing party, I'd like to come along," Walker told her.

She returned her attention to him. "Is realized that by historic mutual decision of multiple realms of Niyu that you nominally in command of this expedition, Marcus Walker. However, in lieu of specific recommendation from you or science staff regarding this unusual situation, Commander-Captain Gerlla-hyn already think it best you accompany any landing group." Glancing past him, she eyed the sitting dog. "Also yous three friends, if they so wish."

Walker frowned slightly, not understanding. "Why all of us?"

"Perhaps if this world previously visited by Tuuqalian or K'eremu representatives, locals will recognize and be able to make suggestions toward helping find respective homeworlds that we seeking."

Tongue lolling, George shrugged diffidently. "If it's a nice breathable atmosphere full of interesting smells, I'm game."

"Braouk loves open spaces," Walker put in. "After having been cooped up on this ship for so long, I don't think you could prevent him from coming along. But Sque—I don't know." He cast a meaningful glance in the direction of the port and the planet below. "I see oceans. If a landing site could be chosen that's near a shore, it might help me to convince her to participate."

"Unresponsiveness to our arrival being universal," Sobj-oes replied, all four tails twitching slightly, "I see no reason why cannot select local atmospheric craft port near coast for site of first contact."

"Good." Walker nodded approvingly. "I'll talk to her."

George sucked his teeth. "I'd think the scientific contingent would want to put down near the biggest city."

"Is very interesting," the astronomer told him. "Are no urban concentrations over a certain size. Is as if a limit on such expansion proscribed by local custom." She took the opportunity to peer out the port for herself. "All indications point to a most interesting culture, even if it one that has not pursued interstellar travel."

"Maybe they've tried and just couldn't lick the problem of other-than-light speed," George opined.

"When we meet them," Walker commented with a smile, "we'll have to be sure and ask. Wonder what kind of greeting we'll get?"

Not elevated enough to see out the single port now that Walker was no longer holding him, George could only nod in its direction. "If they're indecisive, you can always cook something up for them," he reminded his gastronomically talented human friend. "It's the same among dogs as among humans: when you go visiting, it's always polite to bring food along."

"Like a bottle of wine," Walker reflected, wishing he had one.

George nodded approvingly. "Or a dead rat," he added, wishing he had one.

Sobj-oes indicated confusion as she fiddled with the translator clipped to her right ear. "Not sure I understanding. No matter." She turned to go. "Notification of time of down-going will be forthcoming. Interpretation of preliminary data suggests climatological requirements to be minimal."

Walker nodded knowingly. "I'll change clothes anyway. Want to look my best. First impressions are always important."

✳

Ussakk was compiling statistics when Eromebb the Assistant rushed in and interrupted the work. The face of the younger male bristled with brown and white fur that had not yet begun to curl downward. Whiskers half the length of Ussakk's stuck straight out to the sides of his short muzzle, stiff as needles. He was breathing hard in the short, quick gasps of his kind and his eyes were wide with a fusion of fear and fascination.

"The Iollth are coming!"

Emitting a soft whistle of acknowledgement, Ussakk turned resignedly away from his work. "That is known. It was too much to expect that they would simply arrive in strength, sit in orbit for a while, and then leave. I as well as others told the representatives of the Great Government that failing to respond to their landing requests would not work. You cannot make a threat go away by ignoring it." He whistled again; the equivalent of a soft sigh. "There was no harm in hoping, I suppose. And history teaches us that responding with surface-based weapons only brings immediate reprisal." He gathered himself for the inevitable. "*Where* are they coming?"

"They have signaled their intention to land a small vessel at Pedwath Port. Because of the terrain, much of Pedwath's landing site is constructed atop shallow reclaimed sea bottom. What this signifies, if anything, no one knows."

"It may connote nothing in particular," Ussakk told him. He considered. "Pedwath is on the west coast. I could be there in a couple of hours."

"Less." Eromebb eyed him with the look one reserved for the incu-

THE CANDLE OF DISTANT EARTH

bator of a fatal disease. "The Great Government is putting together a team to meet with the invaders, in the hopes of restricting their depredations as much as possible. A police aircraft is already standing by and waiting for you at Therapp Port to transport you to Pedwath." He puffed out his cheeks, a nervous gesture that inflated the lower half of his face to twice normal size. "That is the message I was sent to deliver to you. I'm sorry, Astronomer Ussakk. I've always liked you personally, as well as working with you, and have been proud to labor in the same work-warren."

Rising from his backless seat, Ussakk leaned forward so that the tips of his whiskers curved toward the younger researcher and lightly brushed his face. "I'm not dead yet, Eromebb."

In reassuring the other male, Ussakk was expressing a confidence he did not feel. As near as he could recall from what relevant history he could remember, few Hyfft survived personal contact with the Iollth. They had a habit of engaging in killing demonstrations, just to remind the local populace of what they were capable.

Well, except for not having formally bred, he had lived a good life, marked by professional achievement and relative contentment. And his lack of a mate meant that he had sired no offspring, so there were no family or warren connections there to be broken. No doubt some sharp eye among the authorities charged with putting together a sacrificial pack to meet the initial wave of Iollth had noticed that and had taken it into consideration. Coupled with the fact that Ussakk had been the first to track the incoming ships, it made him ideal for the purpose.

The farewells of his coworkers at the observatory were marked by strong feelings. Plainly, they did not expect to ever see him again. Not all was emotion and angst, however. Among the tears and touchings and uneasy tail twitchings were hopeful, even desperate requests for him to do his best to try to mollify the Iollth. Perhaps, if the sacrificial greeting pack was inordinately persuasive, the invaders might confine their traditional demonstrative rampaging to the west coast of Vinen-Aq, and depart satisfied with the tribute and plunder they would demand. In that event, the rest of Hyff would be spared all but the cost of cleaning up afterward.

He was understandably distracted as an official conveyor bore him toward the airport. His escort, consisting of two police, said nothing, concentrating their attention on attaining the highest safe speed possible. All other traffic, from commercial to individual, was efficiently shunted aside to allow the law enforcement conveyor to rocket past. He had not even been given time to pack. No doubt the authorities who had consigned him to the greeting party had not bothered to take that into consideration.

After all, a dead Hyfft would have no need of personal paraphernalia that would only be left behind.

As he was rushed through the small terminal reserved for official business, there were few who did not turn to regard him with a mixture of hope and pity. He wanted to speak out, to reassure them, to settle their nerves in the traditional communal Hyfftian manner. Unable to ease himself, there was no way he could reassure them. The best he could do was try to project an aura of calm and not add to the already widespread sense of hopelessness.

Much to his credit, he did not throw up until he was on the aircraft.

Little more than an hour later, he arrived in Pedwath with nothing on his back and little in his belly. Officials were there to meet him and escort him to the terminal that had been chosen as the site of contact. There was no mistaking the sense of growing dread among everyone he passed. Fear permeated the air like farts. Glimpses beyond the corridor down which he was being hustled showed no activity outside.

"Ever since it was determined that the Iollth planned on landing here first," the female on his right informed him in response to his query, "all public facilities were immediately shut down. Historians said they would not put it past the invaders to shoot down any and every aircraft within above-curvature range of their spacecraft. So none have departed Pedwath Port since notification was received." Moving closer, she lowered her voice to a conspiratorial chitter.

"The government is releasing only meager amounts of information. Some reports say there is only one Iollth ship. Others say a dozen." Dark eyes beseeched him. "You are Ussakk the Astronomer. Ussakk the Revealer."

"There are three ships." No one had told him not to speak on the subject, nor did he see any reason to withhold so basic a piece of information. Everyone would know the details soon enough. "Not many."

"Too many," the female officer responded. "Three. I'd hoped it was only one. Are they very big?"

"Big enough," he admitted.

"We are here," she announced, suddenly resuming her official demeanor. But despite her best efforts she could not completely hide her anxiety. No one could.

The assembly-warren he was introduced into was already crowded. A few of those present wore senior police uniforms, the Hyfft having no military. They had no need for one. Nor was it a problem.

Except when the Iollth arrived.

Among those not in uniform Ussakk recognized several prominent scientists. There were also a few community representatives from across Vinen-Aq. Whether they were volunteers or had been ordered to participate by the Great Government he had no way of knowing, though he fully intended to ask.

As he was handed a two-piece translator, one part to drape around his short neck and the other to insert into an ear, a distinctive face jumped out at him. White of fur as well as whisker, bent forward at the upper spine like a cub's mistreated toy, Yoracc the Historian was struggling to insert his translator's receiver into his left ear. Ussakk moved to assist.

"Allow me, honored elder." Carefully, he worked the small, silvery unit into the older Hyfft's hearing organ.

"Thank you." Eyes once replaced regarded him thoughtfully. "You are Ussakk the Astronomer, who first detected the Iollth intrusion."

Ussakk chirruped an affirmative. "I would have preferred it had been someone else."

"We all have our preferences," the historian agreed, "which are now to be ignored. Albeit that it is all secondhand and gleaned from historical records, I am here because of my knowledge of Iollth conduct and behavior." His whiskers trembled slightly but were no longer capable of rising or pointing. "Your presence I find less understandable."

Ussakk whistled softly. "As the bearer of bad news, I suspect that this is my reward. More logically, the authorities must believe I have something to contribute."

Yoracc snorted, both nostrils curling slightly up and backward toward his face. "Sacrificial distraction. You have just arrived?"

The astronomer chirruped an affirmative. "I was rushed out of Therapp without even a chance to settle my personal affairs."

The older male blew empty air. "It was much the same with me, though I am no longer so easily rushed." Raising a short arm, he gestured not at the crowd that milled about within the warren but at the sweeping transparency that revealed the first fringes of urbanization beyond the outer limits of the airport. "It has been bad here. The Overwatch authority has done its best, and is to be commended for doing so, but there was still considerable panic. There were injuries; some serious, all impolite. I would imagine it is ongoing. You did not see evidence of it?" Almost instantly, he answered his own question.

"No, you wouldn't, having arrived directly by aircraft. I am told there is an assortment of some damage within the city itself, but the greatest harm has come from those utilizing conveyors who in their panic have strayed from the designated, marked routes. Without sensors to guide them, they have slammed at high speed into fixed objects as well as one another." His unhappiness showed in his face, in the way in which his ears and whiskers drooped all the way forward. "Already the Iollth have caused many deaths, and they have not yet even arrived."

As fretful, restless chatter rose and fell around them, Ussakk and the historian spent a moment commiserating in silence. "What is it we are expected to do?" the astronomer finally asked. "What does the Great Government want of us?"

"You mean, besides serving ourselves up as an initial sacrifice, in the event the Iollth should arrive in a foul mood?" Plainly, Yoracc the Historian held no illusions about the probable fate that was in store for him. "I imagine we are expected to find out exactly what they want and to try to minimize it. Fortunately, if any part of this can be said to be fortunate, precedence provides us with reasonably clear guidelines. The modern history of Hyff records six separate Iollth incursions. Although serious harm was inflicted each time, it was in direct proportion to the degree of defiance our kind offered." Accepting a drink pipe from a passing automated server, he waved it in the general direction of the eerily deserted airfield beyond the curving transparency.

"Since it has been decided by the present Great Government to offer as little resistance as possible, we may be expected to avoid the worst of Iollth depredations. That there will still be some, history also shows us." With an effort, his whiskers fluttered slightly upward, a sure sign of impending sarcasm. "They have an apparent fondness for reminding the Hyfft what they are capable of inflicting, if our people should be so obstinate as to annoy them."

Ussakk brooded, though not for long. The Hyfft tended not to dwell in moodiness. "How bad will it be, do you think?"

The historian blinked several times in rapid succession; a visual shrug. "That, I am afraid, history does not tell us. The Iollth are not wholly predictable. Certainly some Hyfft will die. Whether the number will eventually be countable on one hand or whether a calculator will be needed to render the final tally, only time, luck, and diplomatic skill will tell."

Having nothing more to ask, and finding the conversation's direction wearing more and more on his spirit, Ussakk bade the senior historian farewell and moved off to a corner of the room that allowed him to press his nose and whiskers up against the curving transparency. Like all such, it was flexible, and allowed him to push his face slightly into it. When he drew back, a slight bas-relief of his visage briefly remained, a rapidly shrinking echo of his appearance. In a little while, it was entirely possible that he would be disappeared just as quickly, and efficiently. He raised his eyes to the clear, blue sky of Hyff.

Most of all, he would miss seeing the stars.

✻

"It all go crazy below."

Sobj-oes strode alongside Walker, her long legs (though not as long as Viyv-pym's, Walker reflected) easily maintaining the pace as they headed for the big cargo shuttle that would carry the landing party down to the surface. George trotted confidently alongside his human. As for Sque and Braouk, they had preceded the two Terrans and were awaiting departure.

"Surface imaging show clear signs of population abandoning not just area of selected landing site, but entire city. Several fires also breaking out." Wide yellow-gold eyes gazed into his much smaller brown ones. "Evidence of widespread panic is compelling."

"Must be us," George commented blithely. "We'll soon straighten them out. They'll relax as soon as they learn that all we want to take away from here is directions."

"Possibly." Walker was trying to make sense of the astronomer's words as they turned into the shuttle bay access corridor. "I wonder if they react like this every time a visiting spacecraft arrives in their system."

"Maybe they don't get many visitors." George effortlessly hopped over a conduit rise in the floor. "They haven't exactly been welcoming. If they don't want company, you'd think somebody down below would at least have the courtesy to ask us to get lost."

"They may not think they're in a position to do so. After all, insofar as Gerlla-hyn's staff has been able to determine, they have no spacegoing capability of their own." When trading commodities, he reflected, those unable to make a purchase sensibly kept the inability to themselves. You didn't advertise weakness.

But weakness was one thing, the kind of regional panic the Niyyuu were observing from orbit another matter entirely. Something else had gripped the denizens of the planet below.

Well, if the locals wouldn't communicate with ships in orbit, perhaps they'd be more inclined to do so in person.

Commander-Captain Gerlla-hyn was taking no chances. As preliminary surveys had shown, the natives were technologically advanced. Just because they had thus far shown themselves to be noncommunicative didn't mean they were helpless, much less friendly. As nominal "commander" of the expedition, Walker had reluctantly agreed that under such confusing circumstances it was always more sensible to deal from a position of strength. So the landing party would disembark armed, in the hope that there would be no shooting but in the realization that anything was possible.

Sque had tried to veto the decision. "There is always the danger our appearance may be misconstrued by the no doubt equally primi-tive locals, and result in a typically primal aggressive reaction." Her silver-gray eyes had squinted even tighter than normal. "There is also the fact that the Niyyuuan warriors who accompany this expedition are overly eager to make use of modern weaponry, having been on their own benighted world restricted to the use of ancient and traditional devices."

But the K'eremu was overruled, both by Gerlla-hyn and Walker. Better for their appearance to be misconstrued than to be subject to a fatal ambush. Despite the signs of apparent panic below, it was possible the city was being cleared of its population to save it from an anticipated battle. George, certainly, understood that the Niyyuuan Commander-Captain could not take chances.

"You don't trot into another dog's territory wearing a muzzle," the mutt had declared firmly.

Commander-Captain Gerlla-hyn was not among those slated for the landing party, Walker noted as he entered the big shuttle. Besides himself and his friends, Sobj-oes was present, as were several Niyyuu who had been to other worlds such as Seremathenn. There was the agreed-upon contingent of warriors, all of whom had volunteered to participate in the great expedition. And the appointed (perhaps anointed would have been a better term) representatives of the worldwide media of Niyu, chattering hoarsely and expectantly among themselves as they prepared to record the encounter for later broadcast to enthralled viewers back home.

Assuming they got back home, Walker found himself thinking. In its scope and expectations, no Niyyuu had ever envisioned anything like this attempt to return himself and his friends to their respective homeworlds. Unlike their heroic hosts, he and George, Sque and Braouk, had nothing to lose by trying.

*Maybe, with luck, we'll all get home,* he mused as he found a too-narrow Niyyuuan seat and tried his best to secure himself firmly for the coming descent. But he had been away for so long now, several years, that that hope grew fainter by the day.

Luck would be needed, he knew, if the seemingly unsettled sentients whose acquaintance they were about to make were going to be of any help at all in that increasingly desperate quest.

Sobj-oes settled herself into the landing seat beside him.

"Still no response from below?" he asked halfheartedly.

Something powerful *whanged* far behind them and the shuttle shuddered slightly. "Nothing," the visibly bemused astronomer told him. "Latest observations confirm locals continue to stream out of city. I am told by military people that it almost as if they expecting an attack. But if not talk to us, how can they find out we only here to ask questions of their astronomers, try some restocking of edible organics, and let Niyyuu who have been confined within ships stretch legs on planetary surface?"

Conversation ceased briefly while the shuttle disengaged and dropped out of the main ship's bay. Artificial gravity faded. There were no ports, but heads-up views of their destination drifted throughout the main cabin, available for anyone to scrutinize.

"You don't think maybe that they're planning to ambush us when we land?" Walker found the awkward possibility unsettling. He was not armed, and unlike on Niyu, any hostile action here would involve weapons embodying more destructive potential than the traditional Niyyuuan swords and arrows.

"In absence of communication, is imperative not begin relationship with miscommunication," she told him. "But must be ready for anything." She waved a twin-digited hand at the image floating in the air before her. "If left up to us, I and fellow scientists would make landing without weapons. As would attached official representatives of media of Niyu. But we not charged with responsibility for protecting and preserving this expedition. Commander-Captain Gerlla-hyn is, and he not send contact force into unknown situation without suitable protection."

Peering around the sizable compartment, Walker noted the presence of two dozen volunteer troops drawn from the many semi-independent realms of Niyu. They had been fitted out with modern arms and body armor—a considerable change from what they were used to using against one another in the traditional realm-against-realm battles that supplied both entertainment and political sway on their homeworld. As only the best had been chosen to accompany the expedition, he had no doubt they were proficient in the use of such arms.

Were their counterparts awaiting their arrival on the planet below? And if so, were they prepared to shoot first and query later? He tried to convince himself that was unlikely. Intelligent species, he had learned, tended not to shoot on sight, but to talk first. To seek commonalities rather than differences. Hostilities were expensive. One had to have sound economic reasons to make war rather than peace.

Besides, unless the survey that had been ongoing ever since the Niyyuuan force had arrived in the system had been badly mismanaged, the inhabitants of the world below had not traveled beyond their own atmosphere, much less between star systems. Surely that put them at a disadvantage in matters military. It was akin to one football team playing another without shoes. Range, mobility, and tactical options were greatly reduced.

The shuttle shuddered as it entered atmosphere, its descent guided by automatics and only monitored by the pilots on board. Chatter among the soldiers that had been almost constant since his arrival began to fade. The Niyyuu were not afraid of fighting, but any sentient was sensible to worry about the unknown.

Hovering before him, the three-dimensional heads-up view of clouds gave way to green rolling terrain tinged here and there with fields of yellow and brown. In places, hills gave way to mountains, none of them daunting. The shuttle passed high over several small cities, none comparable in extent to the larger municipalities of Niyu, far less the extensive modern conurbations of advanced Seremathenn. The shuttle's combat gear was fully activated, but nothing gave chase, nothing tried to bring them down. The nearest anything came to interfering with their descent was a flock of thousands of small winged creatures that appeared on the heads-up as brown-bodied dots. The shuttle flew through and past them far too fast for its external sensors to resolve individual zoological details.

Then they were over ocean and slowing rapidly. A number of watercraft of appealing and functional design flashed by beneath. Once, something large and streamlined burst from the water and glided for an unlikely distance above the surface before sinking once more beneath the waves. Walker saw little evidence of foam. Perhaps the water oceans of this world were less salty than those of home. Thinking of foamless waves made him remember lazy days spent on Lake Michigan. He forced them from his mind.

A voice sounded in the compartment, apprising them of their imminent arrival. The shuttle struck ground, slid some distance on its specially treated skids, and came to a halt. The heads-up showed their immediate surroundings: open tarmac, buildings not far away, a few multi-winged parked aircraft of local design. For a while after that, nothing.

Then the view displayed on the heads-up shifted toward one multi-story structure. Figures were beginning to emerge, approaching the motionless landing craft. As Walker stared at them, intrigued by the short, single-garmented shapes, George nudged his leg. From the seat alongside his human, the strapped in canine nodded at his own heads-up.

"Kind of cuddly-looking, as aliens go," the dog observed. "Except for the guns they're carrying."

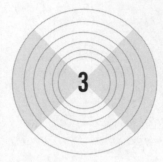

3

Ussakk stared at the alien vessel. Its dimensions loomed all the more impressive when one realized that it was but a fraction of the size of the smallest of the three great starships that were in orbit high overhead. It did not help knowing that had his kind chosen to make the effort, their technological prowess was probably equal to the task of constructing similar vessels.

Something that was unlikely ever to happen, he knew. The Hyfft were too homebound, too attached to their own comfortable, congenial, familiar world to want to cast themselves out into the vast, cold reaches between the stars. There was no need, the authorities declared whenever such proposals were tentatively put forth by the more audacious members of the scientific community. A waste of time and resources. Besides, even if such craft were designed and built, who would use them?

What it all came down to, Ussakk knew, was that when the Hyfft emerged at night from their sophisticated, technologically advanced warrens and looked up at the curving bowl of the universe, they were both awed and afraid. Over the years, he had learned not to judge his kind too harshly. His profession placed him in that exceptional, small group of individuals who felt differently from the majority.

Besides, he reminded himself, the Hyfft had reason to fear the great darkness. When the universe came calling, it was all too often in the form of the Iollth.

A stirring in the crowd of officials and police caused him to tense. He did not have to look far for the source of the unease. A vertical gash had appeared in the side of the landing craft. Like a tongue from the mouth of hungry *dyaou*, a ramp was descending silently from its base.

The figures that emerged were tall, exceedingly so. Well-formed and comfortingly bipedal, they hurried down the freshly extruded rampway in a manner suggestive of disciplined chaos. Those officials standing close around him chittered nervously and shrank back as the big-eyed aliens raised an assortment of unfamiliar tiny devices. The short, stubby fingers of the Hyfftian police tightened grimly on their weapons.

But if the devices the swiftly descending aliens wielded were weapons, they were quickly trained not on the crowd of greeters but on the very same opening from which their manipulators had just emerged. What peculiar manner of Iollth protocol was this? Ussakk found himself wondering. Surely they were not preparing to shoot their own kind? Perhaps the instruments they were so energetically fingering were not weapons after all, but instead served some other as yet unknown purpose. Signs of further movement appeared in the dark recesses of the alien craft. He inhaled sharply. More figures were emerging from within. Shapes that were far more impressive, regimented, and threatening than the group that had preceded them outside.

Unlike the group that had exited first, these newcomers exposed very little bare flesh. They were almost completely encased in form-fitting, nonreflective material of gray and brown. It looked soft, but Ussakk suspected it was designed to repel all manner of hostile intent. While most of the marchers carried long metallic/plastic devices, two advanced slowly under the burden of large backpacks whose contents were a mystery. The astronomer decided he would be quite content if they were to remain so. He cast a glance in the direction of the police. His own escort was already clearly intimidated, and not a shot had been fired.

Not that he blamed them. The shortest of the arrivals was more than twice the height of the average Hyfft. Though slim of build, they had long, no doubt powerful limbs. Surprisingly, each of these terminated in only two digits while the Hyfft could boast four on each hand and three on each foot. He smiled wryly to himself. A small claim to superiority somewhat mitigated by the fact that the newcomers could each boast of four longish tails to the Hyfft's short, stubby one.

The Hyfftian delegation and the new arrivals faced one another uncomfortably across the narrow stretch of flat pavement. One of the few armored invaders who was not carrying one of the ominous-looking long instruments stepped forward. After surveying the half-paralyzed, half-fascinated delegation, each of whom had mentally and emotionally prepared to have his or her life extinguished at any moment, the visitor removed a small, oblong device from its waist and raised it to mouth level. Proceeding to speak into it, visitor and machine delivered a rising and falling stream of incomprehensible gabble to the bewildered crowd.

Without a doubt it was an attempt at communication. It was also a failure, as none of the specialists in the crowd of onlookers recognized so much as a single word. Even the speech patterns were unfamiliar, the cadences jagged and unfathomable.

As the futile effort continued, Ussakk moved to stand close to Yoracc the Historian and dared to essay a whisper. "Tell me, venerable one: Do you have any idea what the creature is saying?"

The historian replied without hesitation. "Not only do I have no idea what the creature is saying, I must confess that I have no idea what the creature is."

To show his confusion, Ussakk blinked speedily several times in succession. He would have accompanied the rapid-fire eye gesture with a sharp chirp-bark of uncertainty, except that it would not be appreciated by those near him and might also be misconstrued by the visitors. "I'm afraid I don't understand. Do you mean you are unsure if it is a male or female Iollth?"

"I mean," replied the historian testily and a bit too loud, "that I don't know if it's an Iollth. In fact, I am fairly certain it is not."

Ussakk eyed the towering, menacing armed and armored figures arrayed before them. "That makes no sense, honored elder."

"I quite agree, querulous youth. In their weapons and bearing they have the general aspect of Iollth, but I am not senile. I remember quite well the imagery that survives from their previous visits, and while there may be some superficial similarities of size and shape, there is much else that does not conform. To begin with, these are tall and slender, while images of the Iollth show them to be shorter and much more thickly built through the lower portion of their bodies, their legs, and especially their feet."

Ussakk's thoughts were crackling like betimp leaves in cooking oil. "Then if they are not Iollth, what can they be?"

"The possibilities are as wide ranging as they are worrying, my young star-gazing friend." The dour historian scratched under his chin, where the hairs had turned as white as his long whiskers. "My first thought, I am afraid, is that they may be something worse than the Iollth."

The astronomer swallowed hard and tried to keep from trembling. "How could that be?"

The older scientist was unrelenting in his speculation. "It could 'be' in many forms. For example, these intimidating visitors could be friends of the Iollth, sent to prepare the way for a later arrival of the Iollth themselves. Or perhaps," he continued morbidly, "the Iollth have informed allies of theirs of the gentle nature of Hyff, have told them what a rich world awaits and how defenseless are its inhabitants."

Accustomed to being surrounded by friends and family, Ussakk found himself being dragged down into the mire of despair by his knowledgeable yet pessimistic companion. Hyfft were by nature buoyant and cheerful. Yoracc was an exception, and not a pleasant one: a grim, brooding, almost bitter store of remembrance. He was also, unfortunately, a realist, Ussakk appreciated. That did not make the elder's listing of possible catastrophes any easier to take.

As if to confirm Yoracc's view of the situation, the lines of heavily armed aliens parted to make way for still more visitors. Though apparently unarmed, they included among their number two creatures who were as different from their predecessors as they were from the Hyfft. One of them was slightly shorter than the alien average, but much, much heavier of build. Other than being bipedal and bisymmetrical, it differed in a bewildering variety of ways from its companions. Interestingly, it displayed five digits on each hand instead of two.

Even more captivating was its companion: a short, quadrupedal, unclothed being covered in ragged fur. Its most notable features were bright black eyes that seemed to miss nothing, and a flat pink appendage that hung loosely over one side of its parted jaws. It too did not appear armed, though its open mouth revealed a set of sharp teeth. Among the Hyfft, intelligence tended to favor slightly smaller individuals. Ussakk wondered if this could be true among the aliens as well.

Then he felt himself being urged forward. Looking to his left, he saw that Yoracc the Historian was also being pushed and shoved in the direction of the alien craft. They were the unhappy recipients of a traditional and concerted community push. In pre-civilized times, such mass compellings were intended to sacrifice those on the outside of a Hyfftian multitude to whatever carnivore happened to be assailing the communal warren. Over time, it had evolved into a time-honored means of thrusting to the forefront those the community felt best qualified to address a particular problem, be it a rampaging untamed carnivore or something more problematical.

In addition to himself and Yoracc, a third individual was being carried forward on the crest of the insistent Hyfftian wave. Fighting to stay on his feet (in ancient times he might have been trampled), Ussakk proffered a hurried introduction.

"I am Mardalm the Linguist," she replied to him over the susurration of shoving and encouraging soft whistling. As she spoke, she fussed with her translator gear, a wearable setup that was far more elaborate than the hastily provided ear-and-chestpiece arrangement that had been given to Ussakk and to the historian. "They expect me to talk to these creatures." With her free hand, she gestured at the aliens they were nearing all too rapidly. "My department was unable to understand their attempts to communicate from orbit. Now they somehow expect me to talk to them in person."

"I know what to do," declared Yoracc blithely from the other side of Ussakk. "Don't make them mad."

Since the historian seemed disinclined to introduce himself to the linguist, Ussakk performed the necessary service. Even in such moments of dire peril, he believed Hyfftian courtesy should remain in force. They might not know who their visitors were, but they should not forget who they were, he felt.

Then they were almost upon the first of the creatures, and there was no time left for comforting thoughts.

Close up, the aliens were even more intimidating than they had been from a distance. Stood on end, the weapons many of the creatures carried would be taller than himself. Visitors and Hyfft stood staring at one another. Clearing her throat with a polite chuff, Mardalm began speaking through the equipment draped around her upper body. A bizarre assortment of sounds came out of an aural projector. None of them made the slightest sense to Ussakk. Nor, apparently, to the aliens, several of whom exchanged glances while commenting in their own incomprehensible and incredibly harsh-sounding language.

Feeling something against his leg, Ussakk looked down and nearly jumped out of his fur. The undersized, four-legged alien was methodically passing its nostrils over his lower body, sniffing with unconcealed

interest. Ignoring the nose, Ussakk remembered the teeth. After analyzing his smell, would this peculiar yet strangely affable creature next decide to sample his taste? And if so, how would, how should, he react?
There was something oddly unthreatening about the activity, though Ussakk knew he could not attribute Hyfftian characteristics to a being so
utterly alien.

The other singular visitor came forward. Unlike the small quadruped, however, this individual was far more menacing. It loomed over
the three resolute if apprehensive Hyfftian scholars, its mass nearly
blocking out the sun. When it knelt, they instinctively retreated several
steps backward. But it was not reaching for them. Instead, it placed a
hand (all five digits were triple-jointed, Ussakk noted) on the spine of
the quadruped and began to stroke. Some form of nonverbal communication, the astronomer quickly decided. Was the kneeling creature
somehow deciphering the quadruped's observations, or urging it to
continue with its examination? A frustrated Ussakk no more knew how
to interpret the aliens' gestures than he did their language.

The second alien rose to its full, intimidating height and looked
back toward the opening in the vessel from which it had come forth.
Ussakk followed its stare, as did his companions. Two more aliens were
emerging.

At the sight of them, a number of the assembled dignitaries cast
aside any and all pretense at dignity and the need to present a united
front in the face of alien challenge. Chittering unashamedly, they broke
and ran for the perceived safety of the nearest terminal. Shaken by the
sight of what was advancing toward them, the rest of the crowd wavered. Mouth agape, Ussakk could only stare in shocked silence.
Mardalm the Linguist reacted similarly. Then, without any warning,
Yoracc the Historian broke from his position and ran, too.

Straight toward the newly emerging aliens.

Had he not been frozen to the spot, Ussakk might have tried to
reach out and grab the crazy old historian. By the time the notion that
he ought to do so bloomed in his brain, the elder was already out of
reach, having scrambled forward past both the quadruped and its massive companion. Expecting Yoracc to be squashed flat on the spot, if for
no other reason than because he had violated some unknown alien protocol, Ussakk and Mardalm looked on in horrified fascination as the
historian came to a halt at the bottom of the access ramp.

Looming above the elder like a monstrous mechanical excavator was
something like a nightmare out of an infant's worst dreamings. Two
nightmares, if one counted the second creature that rode like a hereditary

potentate atop one of the giant's four flexible, tree-like limbs. Both
gazed somberly down at the single elderly, diminutive, bewhiskered native biped who had halted before them. Then, without a sound, they resumed their descent.

If anything, the already diverse gathering of aliens appeared as confused and uncertain by this improbable confrontation as did Yoracc's
fellow Hyfft. There was much stirring on both sides, but neither inter-
vened. The aliens were hardly fearful of anything the lone Hyfft might
do, while the assembled dignitaries and representatives of the collective
Overwatches of Vinen-Aq could only alternately marvel and gape at the
manic boldness of one of their own. The unspoken consensus was that
the historian had gone mad. A consequence, perhaps, of advanced age.
Or possibly by his exhibition of untenable bravado he was sacrificing
himself in a futile attempt to show these allies of the Iollth, or whoever
they were, that his kind could not be easily intimidated. A few hands
within the crowd fingered weapons, but no more. There was no point
in firing until the venerable historian was directly threatened, and by
then it might well be too late.

The two monsters—one immense, the other a mass of squirming
limbs—halted at the bottom of the ramp. If it was so inclined, the gigantic alien could kill the unmoving, staring Yoracc simply by stepping
on him. Instead, it sank down on its four supporting limbs, the better to
bring its frightening tooth-lined vertical jaws closer to the historian. The
better to converse, an edgy Ussakk wondered tensely, or to consume?

Yoracc proceeded to sputter something in a strange singsong voice.
The giant's reaction was immediate. In a far deeper voice, it responded.
At the same time, the bizarre being it held aloft with one upper limb
writhed its own coils. After several dumbfounding moments of this
mystifying vocal byplay, the historian turned and shouted to Mardalm.
Despite Ussakk's hurried attempt to restrain her, she responded by
rushing forward to join the historian. Revealingly, her attitude was one
not of fear but of expectation and even delight.

More impenetrable droning ensued between the two Hyfft and the
two aliens. All of it without, a captivated Ussakk noted, the use of Hyfft
translators. If the aliens possessed similar devices, they were so small as
to not be visible. This went on for some time until the visiting Delineator of the northern city of Andatt spoke up from within the depths of
the thoroughly mesmerized crowd.

"If it would not be too much trouble," she blurted loudly, "could
the honorable historian and noted linguist let the rest of Hyff know
what is going on?"

Yoracc turned while Mardalm continued the animated conversation, for that surely was what was taking place. "Hyfft! Know that this imposing organism standing before you is not Iollth, nor an ally of the Iollth, nor even a passing friend of the Iollth. Neither it nor its associate being nor any of their consorts has ever even heard of the Iollth. Or, for that matter, of Hyff. I myself only finally recognized it from old records. It is a representative of a species that has previously visited our world. Only once, and then many year-days ago. His kind, and it is a he, came this way as explorers and traders. Visitors with whom our ancestors exchanged kind words. That visit took place well before this one's time as well as before yours and mine, so just as we did not immediately recognize him, he did not recognize us." He gestured to his left, where Mardalm hardly paused to look away from her conversation.

"Mardalm the Linguist has the record of their language. But there is only one of these creatures, a Tuuqalian, among the crews of the three vessels that currently orbit Hyff. Those who dominate them are called Niyyuu, a race that until now has been unknown to us. And until recently, I am informed, the Tuuqalia were unknown to them." As he spoke, he was gesturing energetically with both short arms. "Therefore, in all their attempts to contact us from space, the Niyyuu never thought to try the language of Tuuqalia. Never having visited here himself, and not knowing that his own kind had done so long ago, this lone Tuuqalian saw no reason to suggest that the Niyyuu do so."

Pivoting, Yoracc turned away from the intimate conference and back toward the milling crowd. As they slowly digested the historian's knowledgeable and reassuring words, their fear began to give way to curiosity.

"Your translator units are all interleafed with one another as well as with the omnipresent broadcast control. If you will set them so"—and he proceeded to detail the very simple, basic instructions—"the indicators to allow you to receive and speak through your devices in the language of Tuuqalia will be provided." He looked back toward the busy Mardalm. "I am certain that the means to do so in Niyyuuan also will be forthcoming."

Even as he worked to adjust his own equipment, Ussakk was advancing toward the historian, gesturing as he did so. "What then of these other aliens? They are manifestly neither Niyyuu nor Tuuqalia. Nor for that matter is the many-limbed creature the Tuuqalian carries."

Yoracc chirped acknowledgement. "One is called a human; the small quadruped a canine, or dog. They are citizens of still another world that is unknown to us, as is that of the K'eremu that rides high upon the Tuuqalian's limb." Black eyes gleamed. "I am as curious as you to know why there is only one of each of them among this general crewing of Niyyuu. Unless, of course, there are more of them aboard the ships in orbit."

A wave of sound made them both turn. Unlike anything either of them had ever heard, it was at once sonorous and soothing. It boomed and rolled across the tarmac, washing over the assembled luminaries of Vinen-Aq in waves of deep, droning noise. Having set his translator unit according to Yoracc's instructions, Ussakk found he could understand the words contained within the drone. Braouk had chosen that moment to recite part of a saga, and it left his newest audience simultaneously stunned and rapt.

Those who did not cover their ears or disconnect their translators, that is.

✳

It was quite a sight to see Braouk lumbering toward the terminal building, surrounded by locals above whom he towered like Godzilla over Tokyo. Walker had to smile. Several of them chattered concurrently at him as he and George trailed in the wake of the big Tuuqalian and the leaders of the Niyyuuan landing team. Who would have thought, he mused as he strode along, that the one language visitors and locals would stumble upon as a commonality for conversation would be Tuuqalian? If the price of mutual understanding was having to listen to Braouk repeatedly recite, it was one he and his companions would have to pay.

Once the initial contact confusion had been cleared up, he found himself abashed at hearing of the effect he and his friends had had on the locals. Setting down with the intent of only asking a few questions, they had inadvertently terrified the entire population. The reason for this had all been explained by the native called Yoracc the Historian. In turn, researchers among the Niyyuu were able to reconfirm that they knew nothing of the species the locals referred to as the Iollth. From the time the Niyyuuan craft had first entered the Hyff system, it had all been a case of mistaken identity, compounded by the fact that the Hyfft were not space-traversing and knew nothing of sentient species save those that had visited their world.

With everything now clarified, a wave of relief had spread swiftly around the planet. Inquisitiveness had replaced alarm. The immensely relieved Hyfft now wished to learn everything there was to know about their genial visitors. There were to be presentations, feasts, official welcomings. Everyone wanted to greet the travelers, to show them the hospitality of the Hyfft, and to meet them in person. At the very least, Walker realized, they would have no trouble refreshing their ships' stores here. Spared the expected devastation and destruction, their new hosts were almost embarrassingly eager to please.

While expansive by Hyfftian standards, the terminal's interior ceilings were barely high enough to allow Braouk to stand without bending. Even so, he had to watch where he walked. If he grew forgetful, there were always Sque's insults to remind him. The Hyfft were as fascinated by her as by the Tuuqalian who carried her. Choosing to interpret their curiosity as appropriate adoration, the K'eremu was correspondingly content.

As for Walker and George, they found themselves surrounded by chattering Hyfft. So fast did their hosts talk that both sides had to be reminded to wait for their respective translating devices to catch up. It was during one of the brief interludes in these ongoing friendly interrogations that Sobj-oes managed to make her way through the crowd of Niyyuu and now welcoming local dignitaries to confront man and dog. Her great yellow-golden eyes were shining and her neck frill was not only fully erect, but flush with blood. Visibly, she was more than a little excited about something.

She wasted no time in sharing the cause. "Is great news for yous, friends Marcus and George." Turning slightly, she gestured with one limber arm at the milling mob of chattering sentients. "Was long odds to find place where one of yous kind was known. Came this way hoping. Now hopes is confirmed. This indeed region of space where mention of Tuuqalia was sourced. Now we find world where Tuuqalian species has actually visited. I have made acquaintance of local called Ussakk. Is astronomer like myself. He will arrange meeting with others of his kind. With luck, may actually be able generate a vector between this system and that of yous companion Braouk!" Her frill bobbed up and down with her excitement. "Is this not great news?"

"Yeah, great." Somehow, George was unable to muster the same degree of enthusiasm that was being exhibited by the Niyyuuan astronomer. "I don't suppose they've ever heard of Earth?"

All four of Sobj-oes's tails drooped as one. "Are only just beginning to converse with these people. Do not be so quick to give up hope. Must provide what details we have of yous home and yous kinds to local scientific establishment." Looking over the top of the crowd, an effortless task for any tall Niyyuu, she located Braouk and the tentacle-waving

Sque. "Needs to do same for the K'eremu. Relax your frills and . . . hope
that best possible news may yet be forthcoming."

✳

In lieu of an immediate response to their promising inquiries, what *was*
forthcoming was the kind of hospitality Walker and his companions
had not experienced since their sojourn on Seremathenn. As soon as
word spread around the planet that the arriving starships were crewed
not by plundering Iollth but by friendly travelers, one of whom was a
member of a species whose trading ancestors had actually called at Hyff
long ago, the collective sigh of relief was almost strong enough to perturb the atmosphere. What ensued was a battle (a courteous one, of
course, this being the Hyfft) among different regions and Overwatches
to see who would be allowed to play host to the visitors.

In the end, unable to decide among several deserving locales, the
authorities used precedence as an out, and chose to house the visitors
where they had landed, on the outskirts of Therapp. Conscious of the
honor that had been bestowed upon them, the inhabitants of the city
and its surrounding agricultural provinces threw themselves into the
opportunity to show off their region. Not at the expense of others,
however. To have done so would have been distinctly un-Hyfftian.

A goods warehouse was immediately cleared and proper accommodations, insofar as the Hyfft understood them, were thrown together with an efficiency and skill that left the visitors more than a little impressed. It was necessary to adapt the warehouse because, with
the exception of the single K'eremu and one lone dog, none of the visitors could squeeze through the opening of a Hyfftian warren even by
bending.

Nothing seemed to faze their hosts, Walker marveled as he considered the results of their hasty efforts. Not even a need to fashion temporary furniture to accommodate not one but five different body plans.

When their makeshift quarters were ready, it was left to Walker and
his friends to decide, in concert with Commander-Captain Gerlla-hyn
and his staff, if they should actually make use of them.

"The decision whether linger here or not rest with yous," he told
Walker and his friends. "This yous journey. I and my crews charged
with conveying yous where and when yous desire. We will comply with
your decision in this matter."

George was all for continuing on as soon as possible. So was Sque,
who thought no more of the accommodating Hyfft than she did of any
species that had the misfortunate to be not-K'eremu. But Braouk found

himself rather taken by their eager, would-be hosts, not to mention their ability to tolerate and even enjoy his interminable recitations. As for Walker, he confessed to taking pleasure from just walking on solid ground again, beneath a clear and open sky (if one that was a bit more yellow than usual) instead of the hard, cold ceiling of a ship corridor.

Furthermore, it was clear that their hosts were eager for them to stay a while. They were almost painfully grateful that the visitors were something, anything, other than Iollth, and wished to have the chance to express those feelings. From years of trading on the Exchange, Walker was nothing if not sensitive to the need of others to express gratitude. He considered.

There was no rush to be on their way. Earth, K'erem, and certainly Tuuqalia would not change their positions—assuming the Niyyuuan astronomers led by Sobj-oes and her Hyfftian counterparts could actually locate any of them.

The scientists needed time to do their work. Despite Gerlla-hyn's assertions, Walker suspected that if polled, the Niyyuuan crews of the three ships would have voted en mass for the interstellar equivalent of shore leave.

"I think it would be a good thing all around if we stayed here a while," he told the Commander-Captain.

Gerlla-hyn's verbal acknowledgement of Walker's response was terse and formal—but from the way his frill erected and his tails coiled, Walker knew that the Commander-Captain was as pleased as anyone by the human's decision.

It was two days later, after they had been installed in their hastily but stylishly modified temporary quarters, that Walker encountered Sque sitting alone in the rain outside the building. Since even Hyfftian commercial-industrial areas were artfully landscaped, there were tri-trunked tree things and a peculiar reddish-gold brush all around. Woven more than excavated, a small stream caressed the northern edge of the warehouse boundary. That was where he found the K'eremu.

She was sitting in the shallow stream, letting it flow over her ten limbs, her upper body erect and clear of the cooling, moistening water. She did not even care if it carried industrial effluents or agricultural runoff. Under the dark sky, her maroon skin glistened almost black. Closed when he appeared, her recessed, silvery eyes opened at his approach. Even today's selection of the brightly colored bits of metal and ceramic that decorated her person seemed unusually subdued.

Making his way carefully down the slick side of the embankment, he halted just beyond the edge of the lapping water and crouched, the better to bring himself closer to eye level with her.

"What do you want?" Her tone, as conveyed through the Vilenjji implant in his head, struck him as even more bitter than usual. There were overtones, he thought, of depression.

"Just checking on you," he replied. "This is a new world, after all."

"A harmless world," she hissed. "While of moderate intelligence, the inhabitants are inoffensive to the point of banality. I am in no danger here." She did not thank him for his concern. Nor, knowing her as well as he did now, did he expect her to.

Even the rain here was agreeable, he decided. Warm and refreshing; not cold, not stinging. "Enjoying the water?" he asked conversationally.

Since she could not twist her upper body far enough around, she had to turn to face him, her limbs utilizing the purchase they held on the smooth rocks that lined the bottom of the manicured stream.

"I would have preferred to remain by the local sea. But it is best we all stay together. More important for you than for me."

"I agree," he said, hoping to mollify her. One hand gestured at the stream. "What are you doing? Just moistening up?"

She looked away from him. "I am lamenting. Quietly. Or at least, I was until you showed up."

"Sorry," he told her, genuinely apologetic. "What's wrong?"

This time when she looked back over at him, her horizontal pupils had expanded to their fullest extent. "What's wrong? What's wrong?" From her tone, it was apparent that his comment had finally exceeded even her capacity for sardonic reply. Nevertheless, she tried.

"I am alone, lost with and wholly dependent upon inferior beings. I have none to engage in intelligent discourse with, none with whom to debate issues of real importance. Never again will I be enfolded in the soothing, damp embrace of K'erem."

Her manifest misery was so palpable that had it been expressed by anyone other than the redoubtable Sque, Walker would have been moved to tears. As a visual expression of sympathy, they would have been ineffective in the rain anyway.

"This doesn't sound like you, Sque. Well, not entirely like you. You've always shown so much confidence in our chances, even when it seemed we were going to be stuck on Seremathenn for the rest of our lives."

Alien though they were, those metallic gray eyes could still convey the emotion that lay behind them. "And you've thought all along that I believed that. Lesser lifeforms are so easily deceived." Her tentacles stirred sand from the streambed. "Such expressions of sanguinity as I may have declaimed over the past years were for your benefit, and that of your companion and that saga-spinning oaf of a Tuuqalian. Since you have all been necessary to my survival, it was necessary that I keep your own feeble, faltering spirits up." She looked away, down the stream that did not lead to home.

"I have from the beginning never been anything other than realistic about our chances. I believe you yourself, in your simple, uncomplicated way, are equally aware of that reality."

He refused to be disheartened by her despair. He knew nothing of other K'eremu, but this one, at least, he knew was subject to wild mood swings. Rather than go on the defensive, he tried as best he could to raise her spirits.

"Essentially, then, every expression of hope you've put forth has been for our benefit. I'm surprised you'd be so concerned for our mental welfare, even if such efforts were self-centered at heart."

"I am equally surprised," she retorted. "It is a sign of my advancing weakness in the face of utter despondency. I am losing my true K'eremu nature." Tilting back her head and upper body in a single, supple curve, she regarded the benign but leaden sky. Rain fell in her open eyes, but did not affect her. "I will never get home. You will never get home. It is possible, just possible, that the Tuuqalian will get home—if these chittering, chattering, childlike natives with mild pretensions to intelligence can actually coordinate their primitive science with that of the only slightly less primitive Niyyuu. But you and I? We will never see our respective homeworlds again, except in dreams."

They were both silent then, the only sound the tap-patter of gentle rain falling on and around them, plinking out piccolo notes in the mild flow of the stream. After several minutes of mutual contemplation of time, selves, and the alien yet comforting elements, Walker rose from his crouch, scrambled and slid down into the shallow brook, and sat down alongside the startled Sque. When he reached out an arm toward her—a heavy, human, inflexible, bone-supported arm—she started to flinch back. He waited until she was ready. Then he let his arm come down. Since she had no shoulders, and her upper body was one continuous smooth shape from head to lower torso, he let it rest against the place where two of her ropy limbs joined to her body. She did not move it away.

Later, two more of her own appendages writhed around and came to rest atop his wet, hirsute arm. He did not move them away.

With nothing better to do at the moment, George went looking for his friend. It took a while and several exchanges with busy (were they always so busy? the dog wondered) Hyfft before he was directed to a drainage canal outside the converted warehouse.

Through the steady but tranquil drizzle he finally saw them, sitting side by side in the middle of the drainage ditch, Walker's arm around the base of the K'eremu, a couple of Sque's serpentine limbs lying across the man's arm. The dog watched them for a moment, pausing only once to shake accumulated rain from his shaggy coat. Not knowing what was going on but deciding in any case not to interrupt, he turned and trotted back toward the dry shelter of the big warehouse. He would find out what it was all about later. Walker would tell him, whether he wanted to know the details or not.

Meanwhile, if nothing else, at least the acid-tongued, barely tolerable, know-it-all ten-legs had finally discovered the one thing humans were really good for.

4

A rtfully efficient though they were, it still took the Hyfft several days to properly prepare an appropriate greeting for their unexpected but most welcome multi-species visitors. While the initial, hastily adapted warehouse was continuously upgraded to provide better temporary living quarters for the guests, a second structure nearby underwent feverish preparations for use as a center of celebration. Most pleased of all by these developments were the ever-active agents of the Niyyuuan media, who found kindred spirits (if not equivalent fanatics) among those Hyfft charged with relaying the details of the forthcoming gathering to the rest of their utterly engrossed society.

Inexpressibly relieved to learn that the newcomers were neither Iollth nor allies of the anticipated marauders, and in fact had never heard of them, the population of Hyff prepared to put forth the very best of their ancient, extensive, and admirable culture. The best singers and callers were flown in from all across the multiple continents, while specialist chefs made preparations to provide the visitors with the finest local victuals their systems could tolerate. In this Walker found himself, once again, something of a minor celebrity. Nominal leader of the expedition or not, he possessed gustatory expertise that was in constant demand by those seeking to satisfy the appetites of Niyyuu, Tuuqalian, K'eremu, and canine alike. He almost forgot to request certain foods for himself.

The Hyfft being strict vegetarians limited his input somewhat, but he was still able to surprise their hosts with some of the tricks of which the modern culinary technology he had mastered was capable. So it was that he found himself simultaneously enjoying the fruits of Hyfftian cuisine while helping to prepare it. It was more real work than had been required of him since they had left orbit around Niyu.

He enjoyed every bit of it immensely.

For one thing, the Hyfft were not only easy to work with, they were a delight to be around. Averaging a meter in height, with rounded furry bodies and darting black eyes, they reminded him of active bear cubs, though with saturnine faces, complex attire, and dexterous four-fingered hands and three-toed feet. They acceded readily to his suggestions. Nor was the exchange of culinary information exclusively one-way.

The official festivities, which local media broadcast around the globe and contented Niyyuuan monitors recorded with barely restrained glee, began on a worldwide holiday that the current (and much relieved) planetary Delineator had just established by executive fiat. It was to continue for an entire local four-day. Work did not stop entirely, but there was no question the locals were enjoying the unprecedented celebration at least as much as the visitors. Rotating crews by thirds allowed every Niyyuuan technician, soldier, and general crewmember to enjoy a day of it while also participating in basic ground leave. It was something to see one of the slender, graceful, two-meter-tall Niyyuu loping lithely through Therapp surrounded by an aurora of adoring, awestruck locals.

Sated with celebration, Walker and George decided to take some time to trek the city's extensive botanical gardens. These were garlanded with a riot of alien growth that, other than containing a passing affection for the local variety of photosynthesis, were more different from the flora they were familiar with back home than a saguaro was from a sequoia. Taking the tour also allowed them to bring along their own food. After three days of nonstop ingesting of vegetable matter, no matter how superbly prepared, omnivore human and carnivore canine both craved meat. Or at least, meat products. By not attending the day's festivities, they were able to enjoy food from their ship without offering insult to the Hyfftian population at large.

Among their guides (or handlers, as George continued to insist on referring to them) were the astronomer Ussakk, the linguist Mardalm, and a senior, darkly furred government representative who went by the euphonious moniker of Sehblidd.

Trotting alongside the diminutive civil servant made George look bigger than he was. "So tell me, Sehby: What are these Iollth really like and how often do they show up to pick on your kind?"

The bureaucrat's eyes were deeper set than those of the majority of Hyfft, giving him an atypically severe appearance that was belied by his effusive personality. The subject of George's inquiry, however, was enough to dampen his customary enthusiasm. Brushing past a grove of diminutive trees, whose brown trunks were striated with startling streaks of bright orange, he considered how best to respond.

"They are a terrible folk." The delegate's tone was devoid of the usual cheerful chirps that characterized Hyfftian speech. "Of course, I myself have thankfully never actually seen one. The last Iollth raid on Hyff occurred before the time of my birth." Breaking off from a protruding branch what appeared to be a four-petaled flower but was actually more lichen-like, he inhaled its sharp fragrance and passed it along to Walker. Tentatively, the human sniffed the odd-looking growth and was rewarded with a noseful of tingling bouquet not unlike crushed pepper.

"It is very peculiar," Ussakk put in, joining the conversation. "Though we ourselves shy away from interstellar travel, the economics of it are not difficult to assess. As it seems impossible any raid by a few starships on another developed world could justify the expense incurred in doing so, our mental analysts propose that the Iollth must obtain more than just fiscal profit from their wicked enterprise."

Short arms behind his back, Sehblidd let out a terse whistle of revulsion. "It has been suggested that they make these occasional forays for the purpose of plundering and destroying because something in their racial nature compels them to do so."

"In other words," George observed sagely, "because they enjoy it."

The delegate's whiskers rose noticeably, signifying his agreement. "It's difficult to imagine how any species calling itself civilized can embark on such a vile endeavor. But what other reason could there be?"

"Excuse me for saying so," Walker put in, "but this kind of motivation relates pretty closely to what I do—to what I used to do—for a living. It's been my experience that sometimes individuals or groups will go out of their way to get something, even paying more for it than it's worth, that they can't acquire any other way but that they desperately want."

"Yes, yes." Sehblidd gestured absently. "We know that is the case with certain minerals. At least, we assume it is the case. It is almost too much to imagine that the Iollth would rather cross the void between the stars to obtain something they could otherwise acquire by simple mining."

Tail metronoming as he walked, George shrugged expressively. "Hey, I know a couple of dogs just like to fight. They'd rather steal your food than go find their own. To their way of thinking, it's more rewarding." He glanced up at Walker, then away. "I'm not above snitching somebody else's bone myself, if I can get away with it without losing a piece of ear in the process. Humans, of course, never do anything like that."

"Don't insult me until I've admitted to something," Walker chided his friend. He looked back at Sehblidd. "Your people have weapons. Advanced ones, from what little I've seen and learned about such things. You have local and planetary entities that are organized to handle law enforcement. Seems to me you could put together an army pretty quick."

Sehblidd tilted his head back to meet the eyes of the much taller human. "It would be counterproductive. Small arms are little use against weapons that can be launched from space. There have been, in the past, discussions about building armed satellites with which to surprise our tormentors. That technology is not beyond us. But the one time we offered armed resistance, we were badly defeated. The consequences were terrible. If we were to try to employ something like mobile, weaponized satellites and even one Iollth ship were to escape such a counterattack, it could rain incalculable destruction down on Hyff that we would not be able to defend against." His dark eyes glistened. "Or worse, it could flee, and return with a much larger force that would not be surprised a second time, at even greater cost." He looked away, letting his short arms fall to his sides.

"The general consensus is that it is better to allow the Iollth their infrequent incursions, tolerate their brief depredations, and fulfill their demands, than to risk devastation on a far greater scale."

"I'm familiar with that philosophy," Walker murmured softly. "It's part of the history of my kind, too. Sometimes it works, sometimes it doesn't."

"We have adapted to the necessity," Mardalm told him, speaking up for the first time. "That is the situation now. It has been stable, if un-comfortably so, for many thousands of day-slices."

"And you're overdue for a visit from these merry marauders?" George inquired again.

Sehblidd gestured positively once more. "Hence our reaction at your arrival in our system. We are visited so rarely by space-going species, and it has been so long since the last Iollth incursion, that we were certain you were them. Or their friends, or allies."

"What you folks need," George declared as he sniffed intently at an aromatically attractive bush before a frowning Walker nudged him away, "are a couple of big dogs of your own. The techno-military equivalent of a mastiff on one side of you and a rottweiler on the other."

Confused, Sehblidd and Ussakk fiddled with their translating units. It was left to the linguist Mardalm to try to interpret. "I believe the quadruped George is referring to large, powerful creatures from his own domain. The analogy is clear, even if the biology is unreferenceable."

They were approaching the shallow artificial lake that lay in the center of the gardens. Search as he would, Walker was unable to espy a plant or blade of growth that was out of place. Even in their landscap-ing, it seemed, the Hyfft were orderly to a fault.

"Of course," Sehblidd ventured unexpectedly as they continued their stroll, "if we were to have the aid of the aforementioned 'big dogs' in the form of armed space-going craft that had the ability to confront the Iollth on their own terms, resistance might be possible. As you al-ready know, we have no such vessels, nor the ability to construct them, nor the inclination to pilot them." Bright black eyes locked onto Walker's own. "Other species, however, do."

Walker halted and stared down at the diminutive delegate. Ussakk the Astronomer and Mardalm the Linguist were eying him with equal intensity, he noted. So was George, though more out of casual curiosity than with intensity.

"Are you asking for our help?" were the first words out of Marcus's mouth.

Ever the diplomat, Sehblidd kept his whiskers carefully parallel to the ground. "It was your companion who brought up the need for the weak to seek out strong allies."

"My companion has a big mouth." Walker glared down at George with an expression that said clearly, *That's right—put me in the middle.*

"In the first place," he told the trio of suddenly very attentive Hyfft, "we're trying to get home. Involving ourselves in an ongoing armed conflict between two other species wouldn't exactly hasten us on our way."

"Certainly true," agreed the respectful Sehblidd.

"In the second place, this isn't a military expedition."

"But you travel with individual weapons and armor. Surely your ships carry armament as well?" Ussakk asked.

"Yes, they do, but they're for defensive purposes only," Walker countered protectively.

"Understandable," agreed the ever amenable delegate, whiskers locked rigidly in place.

"And lastly," Walker concluded, "that kind of decision isn't up to me. It lies with Commander-Captain Gerlla-hyn and the captains and staff of the three Niyyuuan starships who are trying to help us find our way home."

"Of course," Sehblidd acknowledged without argument.

"Besides which," George added forcefully, intrigued at the direction conversation had taken, "you don't even know when these Iollth are liable to hit you again. Could be next week, could be next century. Even if we and our pack friends had a collective attack of temporary insanity, we can't hang around here waiting for them to put in an appearance. When I suggested you needed strong allies, I meant allies who'd be available to assist you all the time. Not casual passersby like ourselves." He looked up at Walker. "After the celebrations and the exchange of mutual howdy-dos are over, we're out of here. Right, Marc? Marc?"

"What? Oh, sorry, George. I was just thinking."

"Well, don't," the dog instructed him. "It tends to get us into trouble. Unless you're thinking about cooking. And sometimes that gets us into trouble, too."

"Then you won't help us?" Sehblidd murmured. Three pairs of dark eyes continued to gaze mournfully up at the tall human.

"Look," Walker finally told them, after what an increasingly uneasy George felt was far too long a pause, "even if the decision was made to do so, what makes you think we'd have anything to defend? Your own people would have to agree to stand up and fight. You just said that your people had 'adapted to the necessity.'"

"Adapted, yes," Sehblidd told him, and this time the tips of his white whiskers arced noticeably forward. "But that does not mean any of them are happy about it. It is an accommodation that was forced on us because we have not been able to see any other alternative. Offered one . . ." He let the implication hang in the air.

"We're on our way home," Walker informed them decisively. "We've no idea how long it's going to take us to get there, or even if we'll be successful in the attempt. We may have to give up and return to Niyu, the world of our hosts. We can't stay here, waiting to help you defend yourselves against an assault that may not come in any of our lifetimes."

"You could train us," Ussakk declared.

"What?" Walker turned to the astronomer.

"You could train us. Show us how to best organize ourselves for a planetary defense against what is a technologically superior but small attacking force. Perhaps leave us with some advanced weapons, or the schematics for the same that we could try to build ourselves. The Hyfft are not innovators in such things, but we are very good copyists and fabricators." Moving close, he rested one small four-fingered hand on the human's right wrist.

"I am not saying such an effort would make any difference. It may very well be that the Great Government would decide not to employ the results of such training and gifts, and choose to continue appeasing the Iollth. But it would at least provide a possible alternative. We would reward such an effort on your part with everything at our disposal."

"You've been wonderful hosts," Walker told him. "But as I've said, a decision of this magnitude isn't up to me." He glared warningly at George, but this time the dog stayed silent. "Training and the designs for advanced weapons, hmm? Supplying both would still take time. I don't know . . ."

Both Sehblidd and Mardalm came up to him. Echoing the gesture of the astronomer Ussakk, each placed one hand on his left or right wrist. "Please, at least put the matter before those in a position to make such a decision," the bureaucrat implored him. "If you cannot do this, we will of course understand." He stepped back, as did his two companions.

They continued their tour of the gardens. Nothing more was said about the request that had so unexpectedly been put forth. It didn't have to be. Both of Walker's wrists tingled with the memory of those small, clutching fingers.

If only, he thought angrily, the Hyfft weren't so damn selfless.

*

"Madness!" Tentacles fanned out neatly around the base of her body like the spokes of a wheel, Sque focused silvery eyes on Walker and edged closer to the rear of the landscaped pond that had been installed in their quarters solely for her use. "Can it be that your simple mind has so soon forgotten the very reason for our presence here?"

"I agree with the squid." Brusque as always, George promptly plumped himself down on a nearby pillow.

Walker eyed them both. "I'm as anxious to be on our way as both of you are. But if we're going to ask these people for their help in finding Tuuqalia, how can we turn down their request that we help them?"

"Watch me." Rolling over on his pillow, George commenced snoring; loudly, pointedly, and mockingly.

Sque was more fulsome, if less visual, in her objections. "They are not the same thing, Marcus. You know they are not. In nowise is asking for assistance in preparing a vector equivalent to helping an entire species prepare for war."

"For defense," Walker argued. "You've seen some of this world. These are good folk. They don't deserve what these Iollth do to them on a regular basis."

The K'eremu raised four appendages. "None of us deserved to be forcibly abducted from our homeworlds, but we were. None of us deserve to live in a universe that is, save for the occasional pinprick of a partially oxygenated world, harsh, cold, and deadly—but we do. Had we not come along, life here would have proceeded, for better or worse, exactly as it always had. It is not incumbent on us to expend time and effort to change that." Metal gray eyes searched his face.

"Oh, I don't know." Not for the first time, Walker found himself thoroughly irritated by the K'eremu's unrelenting assurance. "Maybe it is because it's the right thing to do."

"Ah, so now the truth comes out." Maroon tentacles waved in the air. "Ethics trump practicality. A noble, but ultimately misplaced gesture."

"Not from the standpoint of the Hyfft," he shot back.

She crawled halfway out of her pond, water dripping from her tentacles and turning her slick skin shiny under the overhead lights. "Might I have the temerity to remind you that we each of us have our own viewpoints regarding this matter, and that they do not necessarily coincide with the needs of the fatuous aliens who happen to be our present hosts?"

"I can't get you to agree to this," he muttered unhappily.

"That's for sure." George had rolled onto his back and was regarding his friend unblinkingly.

"And it's true," a disappointed Walker conceded, "that Gerlla-hyn and his staff would also have to agree. They might balk at a proposal like this no matter what we here decide."

"I think we should help these Hyfft, without question."

All eyes turned to the back of the single, expansive chamber. Braouk reposed there, his massive body squatting on four tree-like lower limbs, his eyestalks fully extended in opposite directions.

"Why?" George demanded to know, sitting up on his haunches. "Because 'it's the right thing to do'?"

"That," the giant Tuuqalian admitted, "and also because it will inspire our hosts to work as hard and as long as possible to discover the information we seek."

The dog snorted. "Easy for you to say, when it's your world they have by far the best chance of locating."

"Find Tuuqalia and it becomes easier to find your Earth," Braouk reminded the dog. "And," he added as one stalk-mounted eye swiveled slightly, "K'erem."

"Perhaps," admitted Sque as she climbed fully out of her pond. Drawing herself up to her full height of a meter and a third, she focused her attention on the lone human. "It might also get us killed. According to our hosts, these near-mythical Iollth are overdue to lavish their inimical attentions on this world, are they not?"

Walker nodded, knowing that the K'eremu was now wholly familiar with the gesture. "That's what the Hyfft have been telling us."

"Then it is not inconceivable that should we linger among them for a while, we might still be here when they arrive, and find ourselves caught in the middle of a resultant conflict that is none of our business and is not in our interests."

George nodded shrewdly. "That might just be what our furry little friends are counting on. That Sehblidd character already as much as asked us to intervene directly. I don't trust him. Too clever by a tail."

"We already declined to do that," Walker reminded him. "Seh-blidd immediately downgraded their request to one for training and the loan of arms or armament schematics. That shouldn't take very long to supply."

"Long enough to get us killed," Sque pointed out, "if these beings arrive while we are still here." Her eyes glittered. "You fail to make your case, friend Marcus. I believe you would fail to make it to Commander-Captain Gerlla-hyn and his staff as well."

They were evenly divided, Walker saw, with himself and Braouk arguing for lending assistance while Sque and George stood against it. It was time to put forth more than words on behalf of his position.

Turning, he extracted a small communicator unit and spoke into it softly. "You can come in now, Ussakk."

"More begging?" Sque hissed derisively as she scuttled unhurriedly back into her pond. "More pleading?"

"No," Walker countered as he watched the Hyfftian astronomer enter from the far side of the refurbished warehouse. "I think, a little history."

Halting before the much larger human, Ussakk had to crane his neck to meet the other biped's eyes. "I thank you for this opportunity. Sehblidd explained to me what was needed, and helped to requisition the pertinent materials." Gesturing with his whiskers toward the other occupants of the high-ceilinged chamber, he began unlimbering the equipment strapped to his back. "This should only take a day-fragment to prepare. Please bear with me."

George sniffed, but this time as much out of curiosity as disdain. "As if we were in a hurry to go somewhere."

True to his word, the astronomer soon had a small device assembled in the center of the spacious compartment. In response to his verbal urgings, it began to project images above and between the small audience. The imagery, Walker noted, was as sharp and three-dimensional as any he had seen generated by Niyyuuan or even Sessrimathe equivalents. Truly, the Hyfft were not backward: they were simply isolated from the mainstream of galactic civilization. Isolated, and pacific.

The historical recordings showed Iollth landing ships hovering low over neatly laid out Hyfftian cities and towns, manipulating physics in assorted inimical ways to rain death and destruction on the helpless communities below. Though sophisticated in their own right, Hyfftian aircraft armed with little more than improvised weaponry were no match for the invaders, who when annoyed by the attention could simply ascend to heights the Hyfft could not reach. From orbit, missiles and energy beams poured down on the helpless defenders. Only faint outlines of the main Iollth vessels were available, taken from ground-based imaging instruments.

When queried about this deficiency, an apologetic Ussakk explained, "My people tried to obtain better images, but whenever an attempt was made to shift a satellite closer to the invaders' starships, it was immediately destroyed. None of our satellites was armed because, as you already know, there is usually no need for them to be. And also because the Iollth would regard such a development as a provocation that would stimulate even harsher response than usual."

The presentation wore on, until everyone was sickened and appalled at the seemingly senseless destruction. Only Sque did not appear touched by emotion.

"If this is an attempt to horrify, it fails. The extent to which many non-K'eremu species pervert their tiny quotient of presumed intelligence is well-known, and constitutes only one more reason why my kind prefer to be left alone. Any half-sentient who travels widely quickly discovers that 'civilization' is a relative term—usually relative to whichever militarily superior species happens to be defining it at the time." Multiple flexible limbs gestured at the waning projection and the last of its disturbing images. "I have seen nothing that surprises me, nor moves me to change my opinion."

"It only mine, reinforces much more strongly, to help," declared Braouk melodiously. A pair of powerful upper appendages moved in the direction of the dire imagery. "To assist those, who help us all, is rightness. Rightness personified." The bulky body swelled with a sudden intake of air, and both eyestalks went vertical above it. "I could not return to the beckoning plains of Tuuqalia knowing I had abandoned such a cry for aid from the very folk who proved responsible for providing me with a direction homeward."

The K'eremu's gray eyes turned to the huge Tuuqalian. "They have as yet provided no such thing."

"Working on it, with all possible speed, they are," her far more massive companion countered. Ussakk added confirmation to the Tuuqalian's claim.

"Theory is not fact, good intentions not conclusions," Sque lectured him.

"I'm still inclined to vote to help," Walker put in.

George looked up at his friend. "Even if it means delaying our journey? And at the risk of imposing on the hospitality and friendship of our friends the Niyyuu?"

Walker nodded. "That's a risk I'm willing to take."

The dog snorted. "Be interesting to see your reaction if the Niyyuu simply decide they've had enough and head home one day without us. That would leave us stuck here permanently." The dog cocked his head sideways. "You've changed, Marc. Time was you'd be a realist, be focused solely on getting back home. What's happened to you?"

Walker watched as Ussakk quietly deactivated his projector and prepared to disassemble it. Despite the mortal danger his people faced, he did not plead for their assistance, was not begging. Physically, the Hyfft was small. But in dignity, he exceeded everyone in the room.

"You're right, George. I have changed. The past several years have changed me." He eyed his friend evenly. "I've learned there are more important things to do with one's existence than trade orange juice futures at a profit." He raised his gaze to the astronomer. "So even if it entails the risk of displeasing the Niyyuu, I'm going to insist that we stay a while and try to help these people."

Sque waved a tentacle. "Two in favor of continuing on, two in favor of wasting time here. We are evenly divided. How shall we fairly decide this matter?"

Walker hesitated. He could have tried to pull rank on his friends, however artificial it might be, but that was something else the past years had taught him. The corporate structure in which he had been immersed for so long and to which he had contentedly adhered notwithstanding, it was clear that consensus was better than command. Each of them had struggled to survive the same trauma, the same strains. Therefore each had an equal voice in their shared future.

"We'll put all arguments, on both sides, to Gerlla-hyn and his staff, and let them decide."

One tentacle fed a local food bar laced with si'dana from her private stock into her extended, pinkish mouth, subsequent to which Sque blew several contented bubbles. "You'll find no comfort there. I hear everything. Already there is dissention among crews. Despite the call of adventure and the opportunity to visit spatial realms new to their species, many among our tall escorts are beginning to express a desire to return to their own homeworld."

Knowing what she said to be true, Walker did not respond. What he did not know was that he and Braouk would find unsuspected allies among the large Niyyuuan contingent who not only would support their desire to aid the fretful Hyfft, but would actively encourage it. In fact, they would fall all over themselves to encourage such a development. Not because they were inherently altruistic, not because they felt any particular sympathy for their diminutive, furry hosts, not even because it was morally the right thing to do.

They would support the time and effort necessary to lend such aid because it would be good for their business.

**5**

Scenes of Niyyuuan warriors training selected Hyfftian police in military tactics made for excellent pictures. So did portraits of Niyyuuan technicians instructing other Hyfft in the use of advanced weapons, some of which could be spared from the arsenals of the three orbiting starships. And images of Niyyuuan engineers working to transfer the design schematics of other armaments to their Hyfftian counterparts for the purpose of hasty manufacture were far more interesting to observe in person than they sounded like they would be at the time the measure was finally acceded to by Gerlla-hyn's staff.

All of them would make for excellent viewing by rapt and image-hungry Niyyuuan audiences when the fortunate media representatives of that world eventually returned home with the recordings they were engaged in making. It was that small but critical and highly vocal contingent of Niyyuu who turned the tide in favor of helping rather than abandoning the Hyfft. Where Walker and his friends were divided as to whether or not to render such assistance, where the Niyyuuan military and technical staff were uncertain, the media representatives who had been given the task of recording the great and unprecedented voyage made the difference.

Helping another sentient species in such a manner would demonstrate the ethical superiority of Niyyuuan principles, the media reps argued. The crews of the three great starships would return home much enhanced in honor. Little actual expense was involved, and not a great deal of time, much of which the ships' crews could expend enjoying the hospitality of the grateful Hyfft and their congenial world.

Above all, this morally commendable exertion would make for great pictures.

Demonstrating admirable, even astonishing energy, the enthusiastic Hyfft proceeded to turn the industrial outskirts of Therapp into the nearest thing to a military base their world had ever seen. Though their domestic police force was characteristically well-organized and extremely efficient, it was rarely called upon to deal with any disturbance more far-reaching than a riot at an arts festival. Preparing for warfare, much less warfare on a planetwide scale, was completely outside their experience. Their racial history was generally devoid of applicable examples, the Hyfft having been an exceedingly cooperative species from the very beginnings of their civilization.

Nevertheless, the police force, at least, possessed weapons in the form of small arms and knew how to use them. Elite units were equipped with what the Niyyuu could spare from their onboard arsenals and trained as rapidly as was feasible in their use. Meanwhile, such devices were scanned and dissected by the Hyfft's own instruments and replicated in factories all across the planet, with the result that within weeks they were being churned out at an impressive rate.

Small arms would be useful only in countering any Iollth who chose to set foot on the surface, however. To deal with invading spacecraft, should the Hyfft prove determined and decisive enough to do so, various commercial satellites had to be converted for offensive use. In this the Niyyuu proved more knowledgeable than Walker had expected. Not that they had used them against their own kind, but like every space-traversing species, the Niyyuu had long ago learned to prepare to defend their homeworld against potential attack from beyond.

Hyfftian satellites proved amenable to the necessary conversions. The sophistication of their technology surprised the Niyyuu who participated in the work. If one excluded their inability to travel beyond the bounds of their own solar system, the Hyfft were quite accomplished. Yet again, it was shown that their lack of the ability to travel in deepspace was due more to failings of culture than of science. Even Ussakk the Astronomer, who might have been expected to jump at the chance to travel beyond the bounds of his local star system, expressed no desire to do so, and was content to carry out his observations with the aid of ground- and satellite-based instrumentation only.

Throughout it all, the attitude toward their visitors of individual as well as groups of Hyfft bordered on the worshipful. Walker and his friends found that they were unable to go anywhere without attracting hordes of locals eager to meet the benign and compassionate travelers from the stars.

Growing bored with Therapp and the surrounding countryside, he and his companions had asked to visit the area around Pedwath, where they had initially set down. Sque all but insisted on it. Gerlla-hyn raised no objection, any security concerns having long since been obviated by their hosts unadulterated hospitality. Since the local passenger conveyors were far too small to accommodate the much larger visitors, cargo vehicles were used to transport them to the coastal city. There the travelers were forced to endure several days of civic feting and thankyous before they were finally able to escape the attentions of a grateful officialdom.

Now Marc and George found themselves strolling down an alien beach of fine pink sand. To their right, the dual-realm inhabitants of Hyff's oceans seemed to spend as much time aloft as they did in the water. On their left, a natural preserve was bordered by hedges of bright orange-green plants that sucked sulfides from volcanic soil and turned them into sugars while respiring oxygen that stank mightily of its unusual origins.

As they walked, their privacy was respected, but only to a certain extent. They found themselves being trailed by half a hundred Hyfft, who were careful to maintain a respectful and polite distance behind the honored visitors. Having learned over the past several months to distinguish among Hyfftian expressions, Walker could only interpret those of their current followers as bordering on the reverential.

When he and George paused to enjoy the ocean view, or to examine the strange arthropods or coelenterate-like creatures that had washed up on or were wandering the beach, their admiring retinue promptly also halted. When the two dissimilar aliens resumed walking, so did their polite yet attentive followers. To be the unwavering subject

of so many intent unhuman eyes was simultaneously flattering and unnerving.

"They think we're going to save them. From the Iollth," Walker
commented as he turned back to the path ahead. From the midst of the
brightly hued bushes off to his left, something erupted into the air with
a squawk like a startled chicken. It had neither feathers nor wings, and
propelled itself slowly upwards into the blue-green sky by means of
several frantically flapping translucent fleshy flaps that sprouted from
its crest.

"They'll have to save themselves." Trotting alongside his friend,
George sampled the seawater through which he was walking. It was noticeably less saline than he expected, though not nearly as tasty as the
familiar waters of Lake Michigan. "This was meant all along to be nothing more than a quick stop on the way home. Pop in, ask directions,
and continue on our way." He looked up at Walker, black eyes gravid
with augmented soul. "I'm tired of this, Marc. It's all been real exciting,
but I'm tired. I want out. I want to move along."

"You're not the only one." As he continued walking, Walker eyed
the first of Hyff's two moons, which was just beginning to show itself
in the northeastern sky. "I'm thinking of getting out of the commodities trading business when we get home, George. Lots of opportunity,
but too much stress." He examined his friend closely. "I'm thinking of
opening a restaurant."

"Oh, now there's a stress-free business," the dog commented sarcas-
tically. Something rippled under his foot and he gave a little jump. Cautiously, he lowered his snout toward the sand to sniff at the ribbon-like,
almost transparent burrowing creature that had startled him.

"Nothing too big." Walker continued to muse on future possibilities. "I wouldn't have access to the tools or ingredients that I do now,
of course. But with what I've learned, I think I could make something of
a name for myself. That would be worth tolerating some start-up stress.
You can't really make a name for yourself trading commodities, you
know. But a good restaurant, especially in Chicago . . ." His voice trailed
off as he fantasized, the dream a small glint in his eyes. Meanwhile, fifty
or so meter-tall Hyfft, black of eye and mottled of fur, continued to trail
behind at a respectful distance.

The two aliens were about to turn back when movement up ahead
caught George's attention. "Something's going on in front of us." He
glanced up at his companion. "Want to check it out?"

Walker glanced at his faithful watch, still keeping time across parsecs and planets. "Getting late."

George's nose was high in the air, sampling. "Smells interesting. Come on—it'll only take a minute."

Letting out a sigh, Walker moved his legs. They couldn't get lost, he knew. All they had to do was follow the beach back to the point where the Hyfftian conveyor had dropped them off. And if they needed help— well, there were half a hundred supplicants following close on their heels who would eagerly provide any assistance needed.

An astonishing sight awaited them on the other side of the next pink dune. Hyfftian soldier-police were making their way ashore, removing compact underwater breathing apparatus as they did so. They were armed, though it was impossible to tell if the weapons they carried were charged. Tight-fitting camouflage suits compressed their fur against their bodies, rendering them not only more hydrodynamically efficient underwater, but nearly invisible. But what really drew the attention of the human and dog were not the dozens of dripping wet, incipient Hyfftian commandos, but the figure in charge of the exercise.

Clutching a wave-worn boulder above the landing beach, Sequi'aranaqua'na'senemu was deep in conversation with a pair of senior Hyfftian officials. As Walker and George approached, it was plain to see that she was not present merely as an observer, but was an active participant in and critic of the proceedings. Within their horizontal recesses, her sharp silvery eyes were alert. Multiple limbs waved and gesticulated as she delivered herself of a steady stream of commentary.

She was also patently surprised to see them.

"Marcus, George: I thought you two would still be aestivating at a more popular location, letting your minds vegetate while our charmingly unpretentious hosts waited on your every biological need."

Walker halted nearby, towering over the two Hyfftian police officials. "And George and I thought you'd be somewhere offshore Pedwath, soaking in the sea." He gestured toward the beach, where nascent Hyfftian fighters emerging from the water began stripping themselves of their new, specially fabricated gear. "What are you doing?"

"Yeah," George added, grinning at the obviously uneasy K'eremu. "You wouldn't, uh, have volunteered to *help* these people in their time of need, would you? Wouldn't that be un-K'eremu? Wouldn't that be engaging in an activity that has nothing to do with getting your supercilious self home?"

Her tentacles contracting defensively around her, she drew herself up to her full height. "What would be un-K'eremu would be refusing to respond when a lesser lifeform appropriately recognizes one that is their superior." In a huff, she turned away from the dog. "My limited activities here are merely designed to confirm that which our hosts already know."

George was not in the least diverted by her protestations. With a nod, he indicated the beach full of budding Hyfftian commandos. "Speaking of knowing, I got the impression that K'eremu tended to keep to themselves. That would seem to rule out a knowledge of military tactics."

"We do indeed prefer our own company," the K'eremu replied sibilantly. "However, circumstances sometimes dictate a need for communal action. Mutual defense is one of these." A tentacle tip brushed clinging water away from one eye. "You should know by now that there is no area of knowledge that is foreign to the K'eremu. While I am not expert in such matters, my understanding of such strategies exceeds that of our hosts by several orders of magnitude. And your own as well, I would suspect."

"Don't bet on it," the dog shot back. "You've never been in a pack fight, whereas I—"

They were interrupted by the arrival of none other than Sobj-oes. While the lanky Niyyuu came loping down the nearest dune, her companion Ussakk the Astronomer paused to chat with the two Hyfftian police officials who had been taking instruction from Sque.

The constant movement of all four tails coupled with the fact that her crest was fully erect indicated that the Niyyuuan astronomer was in a state of great excitement. Indeed, the words spilled so swiftly from her perfectly round, painted mouth that Walker and George's Vilenjji translator implants were unable to keep up, and they had to indicate via gestures that she slow down.

Swallowing, she composed herself and began again. "We have it!" she exclaimed in a voice grating enough to put teeth on edge.

"That's swell," declared George phlegmatically. "*What* do you have?"

"That which we been seeking on yous behalf." Walker had to lean back as one excitedly waving two-fingered hand nearly accidentally smacked him in the face. "Thankings to Guild of Hyfftian Astronomers"—and she turned just long enough to wave in Ussakk's direction—"we have been able to lay out likely vector leading toward homeworld of great storyteller Braouk."

A sudden surge of mixed emotion tore through Walker. "You've actually located Tuuqalia?"

The rapid twitching of her tails slowed and her crest half collapsed. "Well, not world itself. Hyfftian astronomers not know that star's location for certain. But are confident is correct stellar neighborhood. We take yous there, should not be difficult locate Tuuqalian system. More than probable, less than impossible." Reaching out, she rested one hand on Walker's upper right arm and stroked him in the familiar, reassuring Niyyuuan manner. "Is best news have had for you since triangulation of original electromagnetic waves alluding to location of Hyff, yes?"

"I'm happy for Braouk" was all the dog would mutter.

Walker tried to raise both their spirits. "We should be more than happy, George. If we can find Tuuqalia, not only can we return Braouk to his people, but based on the time each of us spent on the Vilenjji capture ship, we can hopefully calculate backward and find indications of Earth. And K'erem," he added hastily. "Also, for all their adherence to ancient traditions, Braouk insists that his kind are a scientifically advanced species. They might know right where to look for Earth and K'erem."

"I know, I know," the dog muttered, rubbing his backside against Walker's right leg. "But there's no guarantee of it, either." Tilting back his head, he looked up at the newly energized Niyyuuan astronomer. "Nothing personal, Sobj-oes. You've been a great friend. But there's no denying we're locked in a race between finding our homeworlds and the inevitable steady increase in homesickness among the crews of your ships. Given eternity, we'd for sure find our way home. But none of us have that luxury. And besides discontent among the crews, there's the matter of finding a way back to Earth within our individual life spans. I don't know if I mentioned it before, but dogs don't live as long as humans." He looked to his left. "Or K'eremu, or Tuuqalians." He dropped to his belly and put his head down on his forepaws. "It's an inequitable universe, Marc."

"Don't I know it," his friend concurred with feeling. "I once placed an advance order for ninety thousand liters of pineapple concentrate at twenty-two cents a liter, only to have the price halve over the weekend before I could dump the stuff."

Raising his head, the dog snapped at something small, hard-shelled, and airborne. "That's terrible, just terrible. How can the threat of being lost forever among the stars possibly compare?"

Walker ignored his friend's sarcasm. "Show some faith, George. We're on our way again, and this time we've got a destination. A real destination."

"Uh-huh, yeah. Somewhere in space probably light-years across, where the homeworld of a race of oversized saga-spinning sometime-berserkers may or may not be waiting to be found. I'm aquiver with anticipation."

Refusing to let himself be baited, Walker let his gaze wander back to the beach below where they were standing. The Hyfftian comman-dos who had emerged from the water were chittering and chirping ex-citedly among themselves, comparing notes and swapping suggestions. Nearby, their two officers continued in animated conversation with Sque. The K'eremu was only too happy to deliver herself of her supe-rior knowledge.

They might not exactly be going home, Walker told himself as he looked on, but for the first time since leaving Niyu, at least they were going *someplace*.

*

Month-slices later, as they prepared to board the shuttlecraft wait-ing on the tarmac of Pedwath Port for their final departure from Hyff, Walker found himself overcome by his surroundings. Given the way the Hyfft had treated them from the beginning of their relationship, he and his friends had expected some kind of formal send-off. But nothing like this. Not on such a scale.

On Earth, a similar formal ceremony of departure might have in-volved a brass band and massed salutes from ranks of smartly uni-formed soldiers. While the Hyfft possessed sophisticated musical in-struments, their tradition favored something closer to a cappella singing. Except that it wasn't singing.

But it surely was enchanting.

Standing shoulder to furry shoulder, two thousand elegantly attired Hyfft brought forth from their small throats a meticulously modulated harmony that sounded like a cross between a gigantic covey of song-birds and an equal number of enthusiastic kittens all clamoring together in chorus. The resultant exquisite sound waves induced delectable vibra-tions in his inner ears. Nearby, the massive Braouk was swaying almost gracefully in time to the lilting tones while Sque's undulating tentacles were nearly as upright and alert as George's ears. Only the Niyyuu, as personified by Sobj-oes and the last of the departing warriors of her kind, seemed variously immune or indifferent to the mesmerizing drone. That was not surprising, Walker realized, if one knew that their "music" tended as much to dissonance as did their language.

A deeper roar began to overwhelm the magical vocalizing. Arising in the east, it drew steadily nearer and more profound, until a hundred Hyfftian aircraft roared by overhead in a formation so precise and tightly packed it would have left a comparable gathering of human aviators openmouthed with awe. As they thundered past, they released something from their internal holds. The drop darkened the sky. It consisted of small objects in every shade, in all colors of the rainbow.

As the components of the release reached the ground, Walker reached up and out with a hand to catch a few of the first flowers. Perhaps the massed aircraft also sprayed the airport area in passing, or possibly the attendant perfume that now filled the air arose only from the flowers themselves. Whatever the source, the mild tang of Hyff's sea air, milder than that of Earth's oceans, was rapidly suffused by a diversity of aromas that bordered on the sensuous. Walker felt himself growing dizzy with the all-pervading fragrance. George had to cover his besieged nostrils, while Sque was largely immune to the effect. Braouk, however, was all but floating on the runway. The sight of the hulking Tuuqalian tipsy with sensory overload brought a broad smile to Walker's face.

Surprisingly, there were few speeches. Some succinct, well-considered words from the local dignitaries they had worked with: the Delineator of the Day for Pedwath, her counterpart from Therapp, the representative of the Great Government itself, and a few more, and then the official farewell finished in a flurry of final refrains from the massed chorus of costumed chanters, visitors and hosts alike drenched in perfume both olfactory and sonic.

Walker had turned and was making his way together with George toward the boarding ramp of the last shuttle when several figures came scurrying toward them out of the crowd of assembled dignitaries. Still sated with pleasure from the effects of the farewell ceremony, he maintained his smile as he identified Yoracc the venerable Historian and Ussakk the Astronomer among them. The other two, whom he did not recognize, wore the practical and readily recognizable garb of officialdom. In contrast to the rest of the crowd, they looked neither happy nor sad. Only oddly unsettled.

Out of breath, they slowed as they approached Walker and his friends. At this point the four Hyfft exchanged glances, as if trying to decide who should be the first to speak. Though in an irrepressibly ebullient mood, Walker was more than ready to depart.

"Come on, then," he chided them fondly. "If this is a last-minute presentation, let's get it over with. Time favors the punctual."

"Time favors no one, least of all the unlucky Hyfft," Ussakk chittered via his translator. Reaching into his pouch, he removed a small piece of equipment. Though its lensor was small, the image it generated filled the space between Hyfft and visitors.

At first, nothing was discernible but stars. Then the resolution improved, the field of view shrank, and a small dot in the upper left-hand region of the projected image resolved itself into a gas giant of modest proportions.

"Avuuna, on the outskirts of the system of Hyff," Ussakk explained.

"Avuuna, we'll be passing you soona," George crooned—but no one was paying any attention to him. The atmosphere around the little knot of Hyfft and visitors had quickly turned solemn.

"This was recorded only a few day-slices ago by the automated scientific station that orbits Avuuna." Ussakk adjusted his equipment one more time.

There were five of the ships. They were sleeker than those of the Niyyuu, and considerably more so than that of the highly advanced Sessrimathe. Their comparative slenderness was only relative, since every starship design Walker had seen, including that of the Vilenjji, involved combining different sized and shaped sections to create the final vessel. In space, there was no functional reason to streamline enormous craft that were never designed to touch down on a world's surface.

Even within the sharp resolution of the three-dimensional projection it was impossible to estimate the relative sizes of the incoming vessels, since there was nothing familiar to measure them against. Walker was assured by Ussakk that readings made by the automatic scientific station indicated they boasted approximately the same dimensions as the starships of the Niyyuu. Though some superficial changes were visible, they were irrefutably the descendents of their predecessors. As to fighting ability, neither Ussakk nor the pair of officials who had accompanied him and Yoracc could say. Never having been able to confront the Iollth in space, the Hyfft had no knowledge of what the invaders' combat capabilities might be in such an environment.

"I not a military person," Sobj-oes observed thoughtfully, "but as yous know, all Niyyuu participate in traditional fighting between realms. From what little I know, it seem unlikely such a force, representing such an aggressive society, would travel unprepared to defend selves against advanced as well as more primitive societies." She gestured in the direction of the attentive Hyfft. "No insult to yous selves is meant by this observation."

"We are aware of our psychological as well as our technological deficiencies," Yoracc snapped back. "The question before us is, what do we do about them?"

"You're sure they are Iollth?" Walker queried the historian.

"No question." Shoving a stubby, four-fingered hand into the projection, the historian stirred starships. "Despite some apparent modifications, the basic designs are unmistakable, and correlate accurately with the pertinent historical records." Retreating slightly so he would not have to crane his neck as sharply, he looked up at Walker. "You've trained many of our people. You have provided us with some weapons. Unfortunately, the designs for more effective devices have yet to be fully implemented."

"What will you, bereft of further assistance, do now?" Braouk rumbled from behind Walker.

The mordant historian snorted and turned away. "Pay. Do what we have always done—give the Iollth what they want. Some Hyfft will die. That is how it has always been. If we had more time, time to build some of the more powerful weapons whose designs your Niyyuu have provided to us, we might be able to give them a surprise." Tired, he rubbed first one ear, flattening it against the top of his head, and then the other. "Either way, I'll be dead before that happens."

While the historian had been replying to the Tuuqalian's question, Sobj-oes had been conferring with an officer of her own kind. Now she leaned apologetically toward Walker.

"Word has come down from the Jhevn-Bha," she explained, referring to the Niyyuuan command ship. "The five incoming vessels now also been detected by instruments on board our own vessels." Her muscular, toothless round mouth paused fully open for a moment before she continued. "If our instruments can sense them, it reasonable at minimum suggest theirs can now also detect us. Gerlla-hyn urges conclusion of this ceremony and return to Jhevn-Bha with all possible speed."

"I'm there," barked George tersely as he started for the beckoning rampway. Having preceded him, Sque was already at the top. Only Braouk and Walker, together with Sobj-oes and a couple of Niyyuuan officers, had yet to board.

As he started to turn, he was struck by a sudden change in the atmosphere. Hitherto politely boisterous, the assembled multitude of Hyfftian performers, delegates, and dignitaries had gone eerily hushed. Plainly, word of the Iollth's arrival in their system had seeped out and worked its way through the crowd. A morning of radiant happiness was dissolving into an afternoon of silent despair.

Dozens, then hundreds of silent faces turned from their neighbors. Not all, but a great many, came to rest on the few figures that were bunched together beside the Niyyuuan landing craft. Walker had to force himself to turn away. They were alien visages, all of them. Unthreatening to be sure, but also unhuman. He was not responsible for them. Ultimately, and especially these past few years, he had come to be responsible only for himself, and perhaps to a certain small extent for George.

"We really must go." Shorter than the average Niyyuu and therefore no taller than the human standing beside her, Sobj-oes was able to reach a flexible arm around his shoulders without having to bend over to do it. "Nothing can do here. Not good be caught on this surface when these Iollth arrive."

"Why not?" Walker muttered even as he let the astronomer lead him toward the waiting shuttle. "We have nothing against the Iollth, and they have nothing against us."

"That true enough," she agreed softly. "But is likely to be some fighting, however short-lived, and munitions not particular about who happen to be standing in their vicinity when they go off."

Reluctantly, he allowed himself to be urged toward the landing ship, up the ramp, and into the portal. Pausing there, he looked back. From the slightly higher vantage point he was able to see better over the heads of the crowd. It was slowly, silently, and efficiently disbanding, each individual Hyfft shuffling toward specified departure points or waiting conveyors. There was no panic; no screaming and wailing, no flailing of limbs or pounding of diminutive chests. The air that had settled over the tarmac and nearby buildings was one of poignant acceptance. Having suffered the same impending, destructive fate multiple times previously, the Hyfft were sadly and stoically preparing to meet it and survive it once more. The attitude of the crowd was heartrending in its resignation. No doubt some among them, like the bitter historian Yoracc, expected to die in the coming day-slices as part of the customary carnage wreaked by the Iollth.

Then he was inside the landing ship. He was still staring out at the civilly dispersing throng as the door cycled closed. A concerned Sobj-oes guided him to his modified thrust chair. Moments later, engines thundered as the shuttlecraft lifted from the surface of doomed Hyff, carrying him and his friends and the last of the visiting Niyyuu toward their waiting starships, and to safety.

**6**

For all its spaciousness and modern galactic comforts, the *Jhevn-Bha* no longer seemed quite so welcoming. It had been home and refuge to Walker and his friends for many months, but after so much time spent on the surface of Hyff, among the congenial inhabitants of that world, the interior of the great starship now seemed cramped and cold. The novelty of both the vessel and its method of travel had become little more than commonplace.

From what little he knew of the motion picture business, Walker found himself comparing travel by such means to the making of movies. With film, he had read, actors spent most of their time standing around waiting for a scene to be set up. Then a minute or even less of filming was followed by more hours of set adjustment, makeup, camera positioning, and so on. It was the same with interstellar travel: long weeks of travel cooped up in a ship, during which nothing happened, until one reached the next destination. There wasn't even a chance of hitting an iceberg.

*How quickly we humans become jaded*, he found himself thinking as he made his way through the access corridor. The Incas were startled and amazed to see men riding on horseback, and thought at first that man and horse were both part of the same outlandish animal. Today their descendants mounted and rode horses without thinking. Later there was the automobile; a shock and wonderment at first, now nothing more than another tool, like a hammer or a screwdriver. Then came air travel; initially restricted to the rich and powerful, today as ordinary a means of transportation as the car. And how had civilization survived without the computer and the internet?

Now here he was, a few years removed from taking taxis and trains to get around Chicago, and already he was bored with interstellar travel. A means of transportation that any scientist on Earth would have given years of their life to experience if only for an hour or so, and he was living it every day. Of course, he didn't have a clue how it worked, and was not even particularly interested in the details. As the old movie said, you turned the key, and it goes.

*I've changed*, he thought as he turned a corridor, and not just because his professional specialty was now food preparation instead of commodities trading. It struck him that he also no longer thought much about the aliens among whom he now lived. Not as species, anyway, but only as individuals. Tuuqalians, K'eremu, Niyyuu. The Hyfft. The vile Vilenjji and the sophisticated Sessrimathe. All the different, diverse, sometimes bizarre races he had been compelled to encounter and deal with. No other human being existed in such circumstances. There was only him, Marcus Walker of Chicago, son of George Walker the retail salesman and Mary Marie Walker the schoolteacher. The closest thing he had to human companionship was his dog, George. Or as George would have put it, the closest thing he had to canine companionship was his human, Marc.

*It's all relative*, he told himself. What mattered was not size or shape or color or number of limbs, or whether one breathed twenty-one percent oxygen, or thirty, or pure methane. What was important in a galaxy full of intelligence was how one related to one's fellow sentients. Discrimination existed, but had nothing to do with appearance. While discouraging to learn that it existed beyond the boundaries of Earth, at least it was based on something other than one's outer shell.

Having been forcibly torn from his homeworld, he wanted only to return there. Since then, circumstances had conspired to place him in a position to have an effect on the destiny of others. It was something he had not sought. At least his former profession had schooled him in dealing with important decisions, even if they had only involved money. How trite that seemed now. How utterly insignificant and unimportant. Nickel prices. Cocoa futures. How severely a lingering drought might affect the soybean harvest in central Brazil. Before his abduction, he had lived a life dominated by inconsequentialities and trivial pursuits. As did the great majority of human beings. But at least he had an excuse.

He hadn't known any better.

Now he had to participate in a discussion that would decide whether or not he and his friends ought to risk their lives to aid a people whose very existence they had been unaware of up until a short while ago. To try to help, or to continue on their course. For better or worse, they now had a destination: a real vector that should lead them to the stellar vicinity of the home of one of his now closest friends: Braouk's homeworld of Tuuqalia. It seemed an easy choice.

Certainly George thought so. The dog spoke up without waiting to be prompted.

"We've come a long way from months lost as captives on the Vilen jji ship," the dog declared to the assembled group. "We lost more time on Seremathenn, pleasant as our stay there might have been. Then there was our little diversion on Niyu." He nodded in the direction of Ger-lla-hyn, the Commander-Captain's first assistant Berred-imr, and the astronomer Sobj-oes. "The flow of time is continuous, don'tcha know. The universe makes no exceptions for individual biological clocks." Turning, he peered up at his human, eyes wide, and rested his front paws on the seated man's knees.

"Don't look at me like that," Walker warned him. "I know that look. It won't work. You're no puppy anymore, and neither am I."

"All right then." With a bound, George jumped up onto the conference table and began to pace purposefully. "Consider this. I'm ten years old. With luck and care, I might have another ten or so in me." Turning, he strode back to Walker, nearly at eye level with him now. "You've probably got half a century, bonobo-bro, maybe more. So excuse me if I seem like I'm in more of a hurry to get home. I know I'll be food for worms one day, but I'd like them to be familiar, homey, terrestrial-type worms. Not some slithering alien glop whose shape is more twisted than its DNA." He smiled thinly. "Call me traditional."

"That something we can all understand." Gerlla-hyn spoke from the far side of the circular, double-topped table. "As you know, tradition is of great importance among my kind." The Commander-Captain's huge yellow-gold eyes focused on the only human in the room. "But sometime, tradition must make space for improvisation. Question before us remains: Is this one of those times? I know what matter to me. But I am, within reason, at disposal of yous." His frill lying perfectly flat against his neck, he leaned forward slightly. "How now wish yous proceed?" Clasped together, the two fingers of one hand indicated George, presently recumbent on the upper table-top. "Already know, I believe, opinion of small quadruped on this matter."

Having already struggled with the question, Walker was ready with an answer. "If we decide to try to help, we first need to determine if it's even feasible. That's a matter for military analysts, not us. Gerlla-hyn, your staff has had a chance to study the accounts compiled by the Hyfft. What do they portend?"

The Commander-Captain turned to the elderly female seated on his left. Berred-imr promptly consulted a portable readout. "Unless unforeseen technological developments present selves, is possible effective defense might be concocted. As in many potential clashes between opposing forces, much depend on intangibles such as tactics. Of these Hyfft know nothing, since historically all fighting take place on surface of Hyff or at least within planetary atmosphere. Hyfft can provide no information on type of Iollth strategies and weapons systems designed for use in free space." She lowered the readout. "Any proposed action on our part must take these unknowns into consideration."

A response that might have been anticipated, Walker realized. Also not an especially encouraging one.

From the far side of the table, Sque emerged from between the two tops to wave a trio of tentacles. "Do you want my opinion, or do you all still remain so low on the intelligence scale that it does not occur to you to ask?"

"Yes, Sque," Walker replied with a measured sigh, "we want your opinion. As always."

Mollified no more or less than usual, the K'eremu clambered up onto the upper tabletop. "Leaving aside for the moment the ethics of this situation and focusing solely on matters military, you are all obsessed with capabilities these Iollth—another inferior species, I have no doubt—may or may not possess. I should like to point out that irrespective of these unknowns, we already have one advantage over them."

"What that be?" a curious Berred-imr demanded to know.

"We know far more about them than they know about us," the K'eremu reminded her matter-of-factly. "Even if they have detected our presence here, they do not know if the technology available to us is superior to theirs or inferior. They do not know if these three ships represent harmless visitors or aggressive warcraft. Their ignorance exceeds ours."

"They'll find out, though," George pointed out from the other end of the table. "The Hyfft will tell them—after we've left."

"That is one possibility." Sque continued to wave several tentacles, apparently under the impression that the constant undulating motion somehow kept her audience in a state of enduring fascination. "Another is that we do not leave, but that we remain to render what assistance we can to our recent hosts."

George lifted his head in surprise. Walker was openly astonished. From the back of the room, hunched low against the ceiling, Braouk thrust both eyestalks toward the table.

"Not like Sque, this sudden unexpected declaration, of help. Is most refreshing, to hear something unselfish, from you."

The K'eremu flashed metallic gray eyes at the hulking Tuuqalian. "I agree. But I have reasons. Perhaps one is that I'm in no hurry to get to your world, which I know from all too much experience is nothing if not aurally polluted." Pivoting on her tentacles, she turned to face Gerlla-hyn and Berred-imr. "Among my kind the ready acceptance of the observably superior, be it collective or individual, is recognized as a sign of high intelligence. As the Hyfft accorded me that status early on in our relationship, I would find it bad-mannered to flee precipitously while they are so grievously threatened."

A slow grin began to spread across Walker's face. "Why, Sque—you like them."

"I do not 'like,' " she corrected him coolly. "I *appreciate* the Hyfft. They demonstrate the kind of courtesy and respect that is all too often lacking among the inferior species." Her stare left the commodities trader in no doubt to whom she was referring.

It didn't bother him. With an effort, he fought back the smile that threatened to spread across his face. "However you wish to define it." He returned his attention to the two Niyyuu. "They've got five ships; we've got three. We know little about them; they know nothing about us."

"Sounds like a good recipe for leaving," an increasingly glum George ventured hopefully. He could tell which way the wind was starting to blow, and it wasn't toward him.

The Commander-Captain and his first assistant conferred. When they had concluded their brief private conversation, Gerlla-hyn looked back at his guests. His frill remained flat and his tails stilled. Not a good sign, Walker felt.

"While we are at yous disposal in yous attempt return home," he informed them, "I still charged with safety of many hundreds of my people. All else being equal, where 'else' remains unknown quantity, three against five not good odds—and we not know if all is being equal. In absence of additional information as to Iollth capabilities, I compelled to urge against remaining here, much less participating in any active defense of this pleasant but unallied, unaligned world."

"Out of the mouths of aliens, sanity." Relieved, George let his head slump back down onto the table.

"That could be taken as an insult by some," an increasingly confrontational Sque shot back.

"Please to understand, friend Sque," the Commander-Captain pointed out, "that in military situation, superior individual intelligence no substitute for lack of same about potential enemy. Cannot risk fighting blind. Not three against five." Respectful of the K'eremu's acumen but in nowise intimidated by it, he thrust all four tail tips in her direction. "Unless can find way change this assessment, I must order departure from this system."

"The Hyfft have survived these incursions before," Berred-imr added. "Will survive again."

"But will Ussakk the Astronomer?" Walker asked pointedly. "Or Mardalm the Linguist? Yoracc the Historian? And all the others with whom we became good friends, who gave of themselves on our behalf without having hardly to be asked?" Turning slightly in his too-narrow chair, he peered across the room at Braouk. "Can we just abandon those who helped find a vector to the vicinity of Tuuqalia?"

The Tuuqalian bestirred himself, and for a moment, the Commander-Captain and his first assistant looked suddenly uneasy. But all Braouk flailed them with was words.

"We are divided, on this contentious issue, between selves. In such situations, is often much better, query others. Put decision making, to those who require, danger chancing. They will insist, that we stay here, to help."

Gerlla-hyn's mouth contracted visibly as his tail tips twitched. Walker frowned while Sque looked on impatiently. Even George, who had already made up his mind, was newly intrigued.

"And who might that be?" the dog asked curtly.

Eyes the size of soccer balls swung around on their flexible stalks to focus on him. "The Niyyuuan media," Braouk reminded them all, this time eschewing verse.

✳

Ki-ru-vad turned from his position at the Gathering station to contemplate the rest of the Dominion chamber. Among the Iollth there was no captain, no commanding individual. Decisions were made communally and rendered by instantaneous collective vote.

"New information has come available regarding the three strange vessels that were detected in orbit around Hyff upon our emergence into this system."

"Show us," chorused his fellow operators from their positions on the inside circumference of the circular chamber.

Obediently, Ki-ru-vad turned back to the ethereal instrumentation hovering before him and swept his tiny hands through it as he sat back on his powerful haunches. Occasionally, the long, flexible toes of one unshod foot would adjust the lower set of controls, their actions coordinating smoothly with the fingers of his much smaller hands. As the Iollth had no need of chairs, there were none in the Dominion chamber.

Dozens of repetitive images formed, one in front of each of the operators present. Each image was identical to the one that hovered in front of Ki-ru-vad, so that each ship's technician could simultaneously evaluate the same information and imagery for him or herself.

The images provided icons for the three ships that had been orbiting Hyff. Had been, because indicators now showed them heading outsystem, packed as close together as drive fields would safely allow. Their identity was a mystery, and would doubtless remain so. They did not originate from Hyff, of course. The Hyfft had no ships.

Everyone in the Dominion chamber was able to follow the progress of the departing vessels until they made the Jump. Once the indicators signifying the locations of the strange craft vanished, in concert with their Jump, speculation abounded as to their origin.

"The Hyfft could have bought ships," one operator pointed out.

"One does not just buy a starship from another species and instantly make use of it," another operator argued. "Much education in its functions and maintenance is required. One certainly does not buy three."

"It does not matter." Ki-ru-vad was already putting the brief appearance of the unexpected vessels out of his mind. "If they were Hyfft, they have fled, as all Hyfft would doubtless wish to do when we arrive.

No matter what they may be carrying away, a whole world awaits us. An amenable world, where we shall relax and sate ourselves, in accordance with ritual." The small, sharp teeth that lined the interior of his wide, flat mouth glistened in the dim light of the Dominion chamber.

"I suspect they were most likely visiting traders, or possibly explorers." Another operator spoke with confidence as she worked at her own instrumentation. Narrow dark eyes reflected back the light from hovering devices. "It may have been time for them to leave. Their departure need not have been sparked by our arrival, and may be wholly coincidental. Or they may have been warned away by the Hyfft. Or, detecting our approach, they may simply have decided against socializing with the unknown." The latter, she knew, would reflect a wise decision on the part of the recently fled. Her kind were not above appropriating the occasional alien vessel and its contents.

"No matter," commented Ki-ru-vad. "Whoever they were and whatever their purpose, they are gone." Leaning back, he used one foot to adjust a readout that was shading toward an unacceptable green. "Dear Hyff lies before us. Its productive and submissive people await our arrival, though not with raised feet."

The soft, sharply modulated whispering that was the Iollth equivalent of laughter passed around the Dominion chamber. Da-ni-wol spoke up. "It is proposed that since it has been longer than usual since our last visit, we should stay longer this time, the better to lavish our attentions upon the sorely neglected Hyfft. It is not meet that they should forget us."

"That is unlikely," responded another operator, without a hint of sarcasm. "Even though additional time has passed, there is not one visit in our history that has been less than memorable." Tiny, thumb-sized ears twitched at the sides of the oval, hairless skull.

Ki-ru-vad indicated agreement. "We should strive to ensure that our forthcoming visit is no less so, and that it lives up to the criterion established by those who have preceded us here in The Work. I myself am looking forward to equaling if not surpassing the labors of my ancestors."

A chorus of approval issued from the circle of operators. Elsewhere within the ship, their contemporaries were preparing for the arrival. All five ships would go into close orbit around Hyff. Advanced weapons activated, landing troops at the ready, they would first contact the authorities, the so-called "Great Government" on the ground, and issue the traditional list of demands. Once the government responded, landing parties would go down, to begin The Work. Any resistance would be met with the customary ruthless and overpowering force.

Though he did not show it outwardly, Ki-ru-vad felt the excitement rising within him. Like all his equals on the five ships, he had already killed and plundered elsewhere. Hyff lay at the farthest limit of their traditional prowling. Once they were finished with The Work here, it would be time to return home. All of them had been away from Ioll for nearly two years now, and were anxious to return, though none begrudged the individual expenditure involved. To do The Work properly required time. Every Iollth knew that.

Only rarely did they encounter any kind of resistance. Their reputation was usually enough to smooth The Work among the lesser species. Personally, he looked forward to such exceptions. The Work was much more stimulating when actual fighting, as opposed to the token ritual slaughter, was involved. He slowed his respiration. They were unlikely to encounter any such from the Hyfft. They were not a warlike people. Even their boring history was largely devoid of actual war. Like the rest of his colleagues, he would have to satisfy his personal desires through the exercise of ritual.

Though with luck, an atypical Hyfft or two might dare to raise an objection to the forthcoming depredations, and that would allow him the pleasure of engaging in formal butchery outside custom.

※

The good feelings he had been experiencing ever since they had arrived in the Hyff system were confirmed when he was among the fortunate ones whose identity was randomly pulled to participate in the initial landing party. Though no resistance other than the usual nonviolent protests was expected, every member of the landing team drew fully powered sidearms from stores. History had shown that crazed and foolhardy individuals, and more rarely, organized groups of rogue citizens, occasionally attempted to extract revenge on the visitors from Ioll. One had to be equipped for the unexpected.

When the last of final preparations was concluded, five landing vessels broke simultaneously from their orbiting mother ships and descended toward the beckoning surface below, each heading separately for one of the five largest Hyfftian communities. As it had in the history texts, Hyff appeared inviting. Not all the worlds visited by the Iollth were so pleasant. Like everyone on board, Ki-ru-vad wore a mask designed to filter out potentially harmful gases and particulate matter, as well as to reduce his oxygen intake. Used to an atmosphere that was six-

teen percent oxygen, any Iollth who breathed Hyff's twenty-three percent for very long would suffer the effects of oxygen poisoning. That
which gives life can also take it away, he mused as the landing ship
made first contact with the outer atmosphere. Just like his own kind.

He had never set foot on Hyff, of course. The last Iollth visit had
taken place prior to his birth. In accordance with Iollth philosophy, visited worlds needed to be given time to recover between incursions. Too
many demands imposed too often would encourage sullenness, nonco-
operation, and even futile resistance among the populace. So each visit
was mounted by a new generation or two. And each, he knew from the
texts, was as successful as those that had preceded them.

Anticipation ran through the assembled troops like free-flowing
hormonal supplements. This battle group had already called on two
other worlds, in two different, far-flung systems. Each visit had been
successful. Hyff lay at the extreme edge of Iollth influence. Once they
had finished their work here, the five ships would at last turn homeward, pausing at two more worlds before returning to Ioll in final triumph. Then there would be a long pause to allow the five unlucky chosen worlds to rest and recover while work on Iollth commenced in
anticipation of the next expedition.

Word that the landing ship was on final approach came to him via
the communicator inside his skullcap. Touchdown followed not long
thereafter. There was no rush to exit the landing ship. Ki-ru-vad and his
dozens of colleagues took their time, marching out in good order.

As always, it was wonderful to breathe something besides ship air,
even if it did have to be filtered through a reduction mask. In line with
the directives that had been broadcast from orbit, the airport was suitably deserted, all native aircraft having been shifted elsewhere. Not that
a disgruntled Hyfftian pilot was likely to try to crash one of the primitive local aircraft into the landing ship, or into the disembarking landing party, he knew. Firstly, it would never succeed. The predictors and
defensive weaponry on board the ship would vaporize any aircraft that
came within a proscribed radius. Secondly, even if by some miracle of
nature a local pilot did succeed in striking such a blow, he would have
to know that it would result in severe repercussions being enforced
against the civilian population. Aware of this, any resistance was defeated before it could get started.

As per historical protocol, a small delegation of local officials was
waiting to acknowledge, if not welcome, the first shuttleload of Iollth.
False pleasantries would be exchanged, whereupon the Iollth would be

conveyed to the lavish temporary quarters they would be inhabiting for the duration of their visit. These would comprise the best the Hyfft could provide, of course. It would not do to displease the delegation. Reprisals were possible for all manner of error, including conscious oversight. Two visits previous, the Hyfft had made such a mistake. By way of showing their displeasure, the Iollth had razed to the ground a small ocean-farming community of several thousand souls. Ever since that incident, the Hyfft had been especially attentive to the demands of their visitors.

As was appropriate, the members of the Hyfftian deputation arrived wearing suitable translators. Between theirs, which Ki-ru-vad had to admit appeared to be of quality manufacture, and those built into the skullcaps and masks of the Iollth, communication proceeded swiftly and without confusion.

"We welcome our guests the Iollth to Hyff," the leader of the delegation intoned as unemotionally as possible. Since there was not a single Hyfft on the planet who would do so willingly, any attempt at false jollity was set aside. This did not trouble the Iollth. They had not returned seeking the hand of friendship, and did not expect their hosts to smile as they were plundered and abused.

A shot split the air. A few members of each species turned to follow the sound. A single neatly attired Hyfft lay prone on the pavement, face-down, a neat hole drilled through the furry skull from front to back. A pair of Iollth stood over the body, peering down. The one holding the activated pistol put a foot on the dead native's head. From heel to toes, the flexible, unshod foot more than covered the motionless head.

Some perceived slight had no doubt drawn the illustrative response, Ki-ru-vad knew. Perhaps the Hyfft had stepped out of line. Perhaps it had looked at the massed Iollth and made an importunate gesture. It did not matter. It was only a Hyfft.

The official welcome had now received a response.

The Iollth were escorted toward the nearest airport building. There conveyors would be waiting to transport these first arrivals from the airport to the special place of residence that had been prepared for them. As soon as the landing area was cleared, the shuttle would lift off and return to its mother ship, there to wait while the next lot of soldiers and the first of property-acquiring technicians boarded for descent. The same scene was being repeated across the planet, in four other major conurbations.

They were nearing the building when thunder behind them signified liftoff of the landing ship. It was only by coincidence that Ki-ru-vad happened to be looking back in time to see the half dozen Hyfftian aircraft come plummeting out of the clouds. His eyes expanded as the ascending landing ship let loose with its full compliment of defensive armament. All around him, startled Iollth were whirling to take in the shocking and wholly unexpected development. Outrage began to boil within the hearts of every soldier present.

First one Hyfftian aircraft went down, trailing smoke and flame. A second, caught head-on by a disrupter, simply shattered into a miniature starburst of splintering particles. A third caught a seeker and blew apart with a satisfying bang. But the other three . . .

The remaining three each launched something. The tiny white trails that materialized from beneath their graceful curving shapes converged on the landing ship. Near-instantaneous defensive weaponry engaged the trails.

The trails dodged.

It was impossible. Ki-ru-vad knew it was impossible even as he watched it happen. The established texts were very clear: the Hyfft possessed nothing in the way of advanced military technology. Nor did even sophisticated species suddenly originate the means for doing so. To defend against something like the landing ship's weapons' integrated systems, you first had to have an understanding of how they functioned. Having had little in the way of exposure to such systems, how could the Hyfft have, in so short a time, developed effective countermeasures?

One trail terminated itself on the exterior of the landing ship. There was a loud explosion. The concussion shook those standing outside the terminal building below, and not just physically. A second trail impacted, then the third. The landing ship seemed to quiver for a moment, its ascent faltering. Then, engines sputtering, it fell backward, picking up speed as it descended. When the crippled, smoking, but still impressive vessel slammed into the runway, the resulting detonation excavated a considerable crater.

The Hyfft were not displeased.

And where were the Hyfft? Ki-ru-vad wondered as, stunned, he turned away from the roaring flames and plume of rising black smoke that marked the spot where the landing ship had crashed and exploded. The official greeting party had disappeared inside the building. Overhead, the three surviving native aircraft circled ominously.

"Inside! Kill them all! Leave none alive!" The orders came rapidly, one after another, relayed to him via the communicator built into his skullcap. Teeth grinding together as jaws flexed, he drew his own weapon and allowed himself to be borne forward by the now livid, furious mass of fellow Iollth.

They poured into the terminal building, dozens of armed invaders looking for something to kill. None of the treacherous Hyfft would survive. And once they had disposed of every member of the official greeting party, Ki-ru-vad knew, they would move on to the city itself. Pedwath would pay for the loss of the landing ship, and pay in such a way and to such a degree that none on Hyff would ever again think to perpetrate such a duplicitous act.

"There!" someone near him shouted, pointing with a small hand. Movement was visible at the far end of the wide hallway that led to the airport's nexus. Immediately, a dozen weapons were raised. A couple of soldiers wielding heavier armament immediately swung around the rifles on their backs and steadied them with one powerful foot as they prepared to aim. Fire poured down the corridor. And for the second time on that inconceivable morning, the utterly unexpected occurred.

The Iollth's fire was returned.

7

I t was all quite impossible, of course. The texts drawn up on the basis of previous visits stated clearly that while Hyfftian civilization maintained a force of police equipped to deal with a broad range of domestic difficulties, they had no military capabilities whatsoever. Nor had they ever, in their modern history, displayed any inclination to pursue them. The fire that Ki-ru-vad and his companions were now taking was not only devastating in its effectiveness, it showed a knowledge of tactics that was as unsettling as the use of advanced firepower itself.

Where had the simple, inoffensive Hyfft acquired such devices? Surely they had not experienced a sudden burst of insight into the methodology of weapons manufacture, much less a desire to pursue it? As the stunned Iollth took cover behind what little protection the terminal interior offered, it was clear they were up against an opponent who understood more than crowd control. Where and how had the

THE CANDLE OF DISTANT EARTH

short, furry denizens of this congenial and wide-open world learned military tactics?

He would have ordered a retreat to the landing ship, except that the landing ship was a smoking ruin outside the building in which they were currently pinned down. The sequence of events implied planning and a good deal of forethought. His thoughts raced even as he tried to aim and fire. Why not destroy the shuttle when it had been on its descent? To lull the visitors into a sense of false security?

Something ionized the air above his head as it thrummed past to punch a hole in the wall well behind him. Whatever had made the sound and drilled the subsequent hole was not something designed for arresting unruly celebrants, nor was it likely to have been derived or modified from such. All around him, soldiers of Iollth were dying. They were trapped. More astonishingly, they were losing; being outshot, outguessed, and outmaneuvered. And this without the locals employing any heavy weaponry. Perhaps they wanted to try to save as much of the Pedwath terminal complex as possible. Possibly they wanted to take prisoners. Ki-ru-vad was unsure whether to be frightened or outraged.

In the end, which came very soon thereafter, he surrendered.

He could see the shock writ large in the faces of those around him as, singly and in small groups, they tossed their weapons into several piles on the attractively mosaicked floor. Only when the last sidearm and rifle had been discarded did their opponents begin to emerge from cover down the corridor and advance toward them. It was mortifying to see the Hyfft, those weak and inoffensive sentients, marching up the passageway to take control of what remained of the landing team. His anger was only partly tempered by his amazement at the sight of the weapons they carried. Fashioned like jewels to fit the small Hyfft's hands, they were like nothing he had ever seen, either in person or in any text.

Then he saw the others.

Tall and slim, they carried themselves like warriors. Their body armor fit their slender forms as if it had been molded onto their lean muscularity. Limber arms and two-fingered hands supported weapons of a design as foreign to him as their bearers. Enormous, curving battlefield lenses covered huge eyes. Backpacks concealed unknown instrumentation and advanced weapons engineering.

As several of the willowy giants moved to stand guard over the growing heaps of surrendered guns, Ki-ru-vad observed several Hyfft (armored Hyfft!) conversing with them. This simple act clarified a great deal. Somehow, from somewhere, and by means unknown, the Hyfft had acquired allies. Aliens who were militarily sophisticated and, again for reasons unknown, willing to put their lives on the line for their much shorter, furry hosts. Professional mercenaries, perhaps. He almost felt sorry for them. They had no idea what they were getting into. And they were about to find out.

Accompanied by a particularly elderly male Hyfft, the female Hyfft turned and came toward him. Instinct, not to mention desire, demanded that Ki-ru-vad kick out with both feet, wrap his powerful legs around her neck, and snap her spine. He did not do so because the two Hyfft were joined by a pair of the tall aliens. Alert and ready, this escort focused on him and his nearby companions. Behind red-tinted transparent battle lenses, their impressive eyes were active and searching. Whoever these tall, interfering strangers were, they were used to the ways of warfare.

Not only that, they had somehow managed to train the formerly innocuous Hyfft in fighting tactics. Being taken by surprise and defeated by tall militaristic aliens was bad enough. Being taken prisoner by armed Hyfft was humiliating. If not from beam weapon or explosive shell, Ki-ru-vad felt he might well die of embarrassment.

Halting before him, the female made some adjustments to the two-piece translator system fastened to one ear and around her neck. Pushing back the battle goggles that protected and concealed her eyes, she looked up at him. He fought the urge to kick her small, flat teeth out through the back of her skull.

"I see by your insignia that you are of a high caste, therefore I address myself to you. I am Delineator Joulabb qi Administrator sa Twelve of Pedwath." She indicated the elder standing next to her. "This is Yoracc ve Historian. He is present to observe, to record, and to comment."

The Iollth muttered something uncomplimentary.

"Make an effort to be civil," Joulabb chided him. "You are defeated. Though we Hyfft are not by nature a vengeful species, there are still those living who are old enough to remember the tales told by their immediate relations of your last visit to our world. It would not take much to convince the populace to dispense with diplomatic niceties and simply kill you all."

Her words burned into him via the translator that was part of the instrumentation banded across the top of his head. Several of Ki-ru-vad's fine, pointed teeth splintered and broke inside his mouth as his jaws clenched. The loss was of no significance, as the lost dentition would soon be replaced by his efficient physiology.

"Those who so reminisce should also remember the consequences of defiance," he growled through his mask. "You are correct about one thing, though: much killing is going to follow this. Once word of what has happened here is digested and confirmed aboard the five ships, there will be such slaughter on Hyff as to make the visits of our predecessors seem like year-end celebrations of birthing."

One of the tall aliens spoke to the Delineator. As Ki-ru-vad's translator was unfamiliar with the creature's language, he was unable to comprehend what passed between them. The female Hyfft helpfully explained.

"Djanu-kun wants to know if I can let him kill you. He doesn't like your attitude."

More curious than afraid, Ki-ru-vad squinted up at the alien. "It understands my speaking?"

Joulabb indicated in the affirmative. "All the Niyyuu were given access to your language, which has been programmed into their own translation apparatus. So he can understand your threats, yes."

Lifting his left foot, the Iollth brought it down hard, smacking the floor with the tough, leathery sole. "Then it understands that it is going to die, along with everyone in this building?"

The alien's reaction was worthy of note. It emitted a series of short, staccato coughs, as did its companion. Unfamiliar as he was with the species standing guard over him, Ki-ru-vad did not learn until much later that this singular respiratory response constituted Niyyuuan laughter. It was just as well. He was already frustrated and infuriated enough to threaten the coordinated pumping of his two hearts.

Again the insolent Hyfft conversed with one of the aliens—the Niyyuu, he told himself. He had never heard of them. It would be interesting to enter that name into the sacred texts and search for a match.

"Djanu-kun begs to disagree. He says that you and your companions fought well, and compliments you on your martial skills."

Ki-ru-vad leaned back slightly and eyed the Niyyuuan warrior anew. If not common sense, at least these creatures were capable of showing proper respect. His opinion of the Hyfft's allies, if not the Hyfft themselves, rose another degree.

"But he and his friends are not going to die," Joulabb continued, "nor is anyone else in Pedwath, or anywhere across the whole expanse of Vinen-Aq. Fighting on this world has ceased." She eyed him evenly and without rancor. "I am in contact with the forces of Hyff across the world. The same fate that has befallen you has overcome the landing parties from your other four ships. All have surrendered." One furry hand adjusted the hearing unit that fit neatly over her other ear as she paused a moment to listen to something.

"No, that is not entirely correct. The landing party of Iollth that set down in the center of Cirelenn refused to lay down their weapons, and had to be completely destroyed." She lowered her hand. "The loss of life is to be regretted."

"It will be regretted far more when devastation such as this generation of Hyfft has not known and cannot imagine begins to rain down from the sky." With one diminutive hand Ki-ru-vad indicated the nearest pile of surrendered armament. "These are toys compared to the weapons that are carried on the five ships themselves. You here may survive. Your proximity to myself and my companions offers you some degree of protection. But other cities, other communities where no Iollth are in danger, will feel the heavy heel of obliteration." He gestured toward the curiously watching Niyyuu. "No contingent, or multiple contingents, of off-world mercenaries is going to save you.

"As for the vessels that brought them here," he added, remembering what had been observed as the Iollth had entered the Hyff system and drawing the most reasonable conclusion, "they have departed. They were observed leaving this system and making the Jump before we entered orbit around your world." He turned his attention to the silently observing Yoracc. "If you know your people's past well, Historian, then you know that no Hyfftian aircraft or surface-based weapons can harm an Iollth spacecraft. As for any small local artificial satellites that may have been modified for military purposes, those are as easily dealt with."

Having listened in silence to all that the unrepentant invader had to say, the elder Hyfft now gestured imperceptibly. Tilting back his head, the fur of which was white with age, he gazed thoughtfully skyward.

"No doubt all that you say is true, soldier of Iollth. We of Hyff and our new friends as well stand before you utterly at your mercy. There is no hope for us."

Oddly, in direct contrast to his words, the historian did not seem especially unsettled. Nor did the Delineator Joulabb. As for the pair of mercenaries, or whatever they were—Niyyuuan warriors—they had not even bothered to follow the elder's lead and look upward.

They just started coughing again.

⁂

On board the orbiting Iollth flagship *Am-Drun-za-div*, one inconceivable report after another passed swiftly before the incredulous eyes of the affiliates of the dominion caste. Sa-ru-vam reacted so sharply to the abrupt flood of disbelief conveyed by the tenuous yet precise instrumentation hovering before her that she nearly lost her skullcap. Large but agile toes worked in tandem with small, delicate fingers in a frantic search for confirmation. The results were undeniable. She knew they had to be so as the chamber came alive with a zephyr of confirming whispers.

"How could this have happened?" she demanded to know of her colleagues. "What of our detectors?"

"All aimed toward the world below," another operator declared, "and aligned to monitor the primitive but efficient artificial satellites of the inhabitants. Nothing directed outward."

And why should there be? she reflected as she stared in dumb-foundment at the increasingly somber readouts. The Hyfft could barely and only occasionally mount even the most feeble opposition from their own world. There was no reason, none whatsoever, to expect an attack from behind, from the reaches of extraplanetary space to which the locals had never aspired, and which they had only cursorily explored with simple automated scientific instruments.

Yet the threat was there, undeniable and immediate. An entire array of self-propelled devices, a potent mix of atomics and kinetics, were poised to close the remaining gap between themselves and all five Iollth craft. Awaiting, no doubt, only a reversion of the command that had halted them just short of their targets. Their origin was clear, now that detection fields had been adjusted to reach out into space and sweep the firmament behind the orbiting vessels.

There were two of the strange ships. Extensive in size, alien in design, and perfectly positioned, they had launched their weaponry immediately after emerging from concealment behind the largest of Hyff's moons. With targets now in range, the Iollth were situated to respond—except that their own weapons would take notably longer to reach the two attacking vessels than the latter's already launched devices would to reach theirs. Assuming the efficiency of the latter matched their stealth, the result would be five Iollth ships and their crews completely annihilated, with no guarantee of destroying their assailants. Electronic predictors repeatedly confirmed what direct observation had already proposed.

Like many battles in space, the end of this one was determined before it could be started.

"The fleeing traders," observed a thoroughly muted Aj-kil-won as he turned around, his feet preceding him. "Or explorers. One is forced to wonder now at their true purpose, their real intent." A small hand gestured at his own floating instrumentation. "Simple traders and explorers do not carry this kind of weaponry. Nor do they deploy it with such tactical skill and efficiency. What interests me at the moment is not how, but why? We have no quarrel with these folk, whoever they may be. Why are they doing this?"

Sa-ru-vam had already given the matter some thought. "Absurd as it may seem, it appears that our Hyfft have somehow, through means unknown and unimaginable to us, acquired powerful allies." Raising one foot, she indicated the lower levels of her own suspended readouts. "Whatever the reason, one thing is unmistakable. We are defeated."

She knew that the soft murmurs of incredulity that echoed through the Dominion chamber were likely being echoed elsewhere throughout the flotilla. There were no records, none, of the inoffensive, harmless, isolated Hyfft ever making use of allies, or attempting to acquire them. This development was unprecedented. Had it not been, it was unlikely the Iollth would have been so swiftly and completely taken by surprise.

Their instruments had shown the three visiting starships fleeing the Hyff system prior to the Iollth's arrival. Developments now revealed this apparent flight to have been a sham, a clever diversion. Somehow, one of the alien craft had managed to simulate three departing drive fields, leaving the other two to conceal their presence behind the bulk of Hyff's largest moon. And in fact, as she contemplated the most likely scenario, her own instruments revealed the presence of a new approaching signal: the absent, and deceiving, third alien craft.

Bitterly, she condemned the certitude and overconfidence that had allowed her kind to be overcome without a fight. The question now was: Why had these mysterious newcomers involved themselves in a confrontation that was none of their business, and what did they intend to do with their victory? She suspected that she and her kind were likely to find out very soon.

Meanwhile, there was nothing for them to do but surrender.

*

"There's nothing for thems to do but surrender." Commander-Captain Gerlla-hyn's observation might have been obvious to Berred-imr and the rest of his staff, but it was far less so to the one anxious human and curious dog who stood in the command room off to one side and out of the way.

"I don't understand. Nobody's fired a shot." Walker looked to his left, to where Sque squatted on her tentacles, as bored with the proceedings as she was with any that did not orbit around her.

"Nobody's even barked." Tail wagging energetically, eyes alert, George stared in fascination at the schematic that floated in the air before them all. It showed clearly the surface of Hyff, the five Iollth ships, the two Niyyuuan vessels, and a scattering of bright pinpoints of light, each one representing a lethal, self-propelled weapon.

It was left to the hulking Braouk, leaning up against one wall as he did his best to avoid stepping on any of the participants, to explain. As he did so, he gestured with both eyestalks as well as all four upper limbs. "No valid reason, to pursue a clash, already won." Both eyes rose at the end of their stalks to study the glowing schematic. "Niyyuuan weapons systems, in excellent position to, finish fight. Whereas the Iollth, have not even commenced, weapons deployment. For them to, do so now would, be suicidal." While one eye remained on high studying the projection, the other dipped down low to regard Walker. "The tactics of advanced armaments, Marcus. Combat in space, between ships, is not like limb-to-limb fighting on a solid surface. Preparation is more important than execution. Outcome is often, foretold before anyone needs, to die."

"Communication is coming in." Everyone turned to where Gerllahyn was speaking aloud. There was a pause, but only verbally. Around the command center, Niyyuuan technicians and crew were actively at work.

"The Iollth have surrendered," the Commander-Captain announced. "The battle is now formally as well as tactically won." Strident whistles of satisfaction filled the room.

*Some battle,* Walker thought. Not even insults had passed between ships. "What now?" he wondered aloud.

"Why now," Sque commented, "we discuss with the Hyfft how they wish to treat with their former tormentors." One tentacle reached up to clean an eye. "Civilized folk would come to some peaceable, mutually satisfactory arrangement for future relations that would not involve the subjugation and exploitation of one species by another. Revenge being a term employed only by the primitive, I would expect the Hyfft to demand it in some measure." Other tentacle tips quivered. "I do not expect, but would be delighted, to be surprised. I am especially glad that our intervention was able to be accomplished with no loss of life on either side."

Walker frowned at her. As was often the case, the K'eremu's words left him with the distinct impression that there was more she could say, that she knew more than she cared to share, if only she would choose to do so. And as was often the case, she remained silent and offered nothing more on the subject at hand. He tried another tack.

"We still don't know what happened to the Iollth landing parties," he pointed out.

"That is so," she admitted. "One can only hope word was received from on high before much violence was committed."

Trotting over to the K'eremu, George sniffed one extended tentacle.

It promptly coiled sharply away from him. It was clear to Walker that his four-legged friend also suspected Sque was holding something back. "What do you care, squid? These Iollth have plagued and mistreated the Hyfft for centuries. Sounds to me like it would do them collectively good to have the crap kicked out of a few of them."

The K'eremu's silvery horizontal eyes withdrew even farther into their sockets. "That is typical of the scatological appraisals that I have come to expect from lower lifeforms such as yourself. Simply because the Iollth are militarily superior to the Hyfft and the latter have been courteous to us does not automatically mean that the Hyfft are superior to their invaders in all other ways. We know nothing of these aggressive visitors other than what the Hyfft have told us. Truly, enough to induce us, or at least you and the Niyyuu, to decide to help them. I maintain that is insufficient grounds for condemning the Iollth unreservedly."

Walker frowned down at the K'eremu. "How can you side with them, Sque? You saw the same horrific historical documentation as the rest of us."

Tilting back her upper body, she looked up at him. "I side with no one who is not K'eremu. I am simply saying that while the Hyfft have grounds for abhorring the Iollth, the rest of us do not." A pair of tentacles gestured at the massive floating image. "It may be that our hosts will wish to execute a sampling of their tormentors. There is no compelling reason why that should be our wish. The Iollth have done nothing to us. It is one thing to intervene to settle a quarrel. It is another to take permanent sides."

She was right, Walker realized. Having been exposed to the historical evidence of the Iollth's depredations, he was pained to admit it, but there was no reason why he and his friends should take an active interest in punishing the invaders.

Or did the K'eremu have something else in mind, as she so often did? If that was the case, she was not volunteering her thoughts. He saw no reason to try to draw them out, as they would only be revealed in her own good time.

Certainly the Niyyuu seemed happy with the outcome. Once the surrender had been recognized and accepted, Gerlla-hyn left the necessary follow-up details in the capable hands of Berred-imr and came over to join them.

"There to be a formal ceremony of surrender on surface." One limber, two-fingered hand indicated the hovering schematic. "All our weapons to remain in position until then, and maybe for some time afterwards, until we certain of Iollth intentions. Knowing nothing about them, cannot trust them so easily." Wide, golden eyes gazed down at them while Braouk in turn regarded the Commander-Captain from on high.

"Should alls be most pleased at success of strategy. Could not work second time since Iollth now aware of our stance, but that is good thing about such tactics. Need only work one time. Is some regretfulness among crews. Not have opportunity in historical times to utilize modern weapons."

Haughtily superior, Sque turned away in disgust, surrounded as she was by inferior minds. Only accident and circumstance had caused her to fall in with these Niyyuu, not to mention a Tuuqalian, a canine, and a human. It could just as easily have been with these Iollth. How she longed for home and intellectual surroundings that, however fractious, were steeped in common sense!

Addressing himself to Walker, Gerlla-hyn continued politely. "As nominal director of forces, is decided you must attend surrender ceremony."

Walker looked startled. "Me? But this is something for the Hyfft to handle, and for your people to oversee." He spread his hands. "I wouldn't know what to do or say."

"That goes without saying," Sque put in, but by now no one was paying attention to her.

"Not need do or say anything," Gerlla-hyn assured him. "Only needs you provide presence." Now that the "battle" was concluded, his frill was completely relaxed, as were his quadruple tails. "Is useful defeated Iollth see that Hyfft have support of not just Niyyuu but four other sentient species as well." His gaze shifted beyond Walker. "Yous all should attend." Both eyes settled on Sque. "Perhaps even K'eremu deign to grace ceremony with presence, so as to demonstrate innate superiority of at least one species among victors."

Sque, who had turned away, now pivoted in place. A few desultory bubbles emerged from her pink speaking tube as she idly jiggled some of the garish metal ornaments that decorated her smooth frame.

"I suppose it is necessary. For purposes of efficiency, if nothing else. These Iollth should cooperate more easily once they see that there is at least one superior mind among their vanquishers. Very well, I will come along. If nothing else, it will provide the opportunity to visit the local ocean once more."

**8**

As Walker hoped, the Hyfftian capacity for tolerance far exceeded any desire for revenge. While there were certainly elements among the population who sought such, especially among those who had directly lost ancestors to incursions by the invaders' predecessors, they were compelled to mute their feelings in favor of the Great Government's decision to conclude a formal and permanent treaty of peace between their species and the Iollth. Whether understanding would follow peace was something only the progress of future relations could decide.

The official ceremony of surrender was more low-key than Walker had anticipated. A comparably important agreement on Earth would have taken place amid a certain pomp. On Hyff, a handful of representatives of the defeated Iollth filed silently into the official gathering chamber of the Overwatch of Pedwath. Accompanied by her daily equivalents, the city's Delineator of the Day was present, as were envoys of the Great Government.

The chamber itself was large but not awe-inspiringly so. Among the Hyfft, representatives of the government felt no need to intimidate those from among whom they had been chosen. The chamber was big enough to accommodate citizens and civil servants engaged in business. Fortunately, the bowl of the slightly curved ceiling was two Hyfftian stories high. This allowed all the participants in the ceremony to enter and file toward the sunken center without having to bend, though Braouk had to do some squirming to make his way inside via the main entrance. Just as Sque pined for the damp and cloudy surroundings of K'erem, the Tuuqalian wished fervently for the wide-open spaces of his own world. Though he was far too polite to say so, he was tired of dwelling among midgets.

Deliberately, he turned his eyestalks away from one of the many Niyyuuan media recorders who sought to document his reaction. They filled the chamber, roving purposefully among Hyfft and Niyyuu alike, their presence and purpose as well as their evident freedom of movement a continuing bafflement to the already disoriented Iollth.

The uniforms of the invader were quite spectacular, Walker observed. Layers of clashing colors clothed their bottom-heavy attire while small stripes of metal adorned their fronts and massive thighs. They did not hop, but rather lifted first one side of their bodies and then the other as they advanced. Under other circumstances their style of personal locomotion would have prompted a smile. Any amusement he and his companions might have felt at the sight was mitigated by their knowledge of the history of Hyfftian-Iollth relations. Given the opportunity, he knew that the funny-striding aliens entering the chamber would happily have slaughtered everyone within.

Instead, badly duped and overcome by Niyyuuan tactics, they had been brought to this moment. There would be no elaborate ceremonial signing of documents, Walker had been told. Such archaisms were unnecessary. Terms had already been agreed upon. The Iollth would cease their raids on Hyff. Any future visits would take place under the aegis of the peace agreement that had been agreed upon by the two species.

Looking askance at the Hyfftian chairs that had been provided for them, the four members of the Iollth delegation finally arranged themselves in a line on the lowest level of the multi-level chamber, settling back on powerful haunches. Overhead lights shone flatteringly on their uniforms. Though it was always difficult to interpret alien expressions,

George voiced the belief that to him the visitors looked uncomfortable but far from beaten.

"Tough bunch of fatties," the dog commented from where he stood atop a seat.

"They're not fat," Walker corrected him. "They just taper toward the top. Big legs and lower bodies; small upper limbs, necks, and heads." He gestured. "Look at the muscles in those legs. You can see them through the clothing."

"Even a Chihuahua could run circles around them." Letting out a derisive snort, the dog settled himself back on his own haunches. "Soon as this is over with, we're out of here."

"Yes," Walker admitted. "The Hyfft helped us; now we've helped them. We're even." Reflexively, he glanced toward the transparent center of the ceiling. "Tomorrow we leave for Tuuqalia." *And hopefully we'll find it,* he added by way of silent prayer. Not only for Braouk's sake, but for their own. He didn't care to think what their next step would be if the Tuuqalian's homeworld could not be located.

Below, Ki-ru-vad's attention drifted from the high-pitched chirping of the Hyfft who was presently speaking, to the upper levels of the chamber. Not one but four non-Hyfft aliens stood or sat there, observing the proceedings. He was at once intrigued and confused by their appearance. None of them bore the slightest resemblance to the Niyyu-uan allies who were responsible for the defeat of his kind. Where had they come from, and what were they doing here, at this significant and degrading moment? Were they simply friends of the Hyfft, or the Niyyuu? Observers? Or something more? It was important to know, because of the Commitment.

Obviously, the Hyfft were unaware of the Commitment. Nor did their ferocious and admirable allies the Niyyuu give any indication of being aware of its reality. Certainly neither representative of either species exhibited any indication of recognition. Ki-ru-vad sighed inwardly. The Commitment could be ignored, of course. But that would be unworthy not only of the dominion caste as a whole and of the many castes that supported it, but of himself personally. Pains would have to be taken to dispel the evident ignorance.

To a certain degree, he was looking forward to it. Whenever the Commitment had been made in the past, it had only led to the elevation of the Iollth. He believed strongly that it would not have to be made to the Hyfft. That in itself was a relief. Bestowing the Commitment was difficult enough. Granting it to the Hyfft, who for hundreds of years had been nothing more than pitiable victims of the noble

Iollth, was almost unthinkable. The Niyyuu, now—that he could see doing. It was likely to be the Niyyuu, he knew. But one could not be certain. Where the kind of unexpected tactics that had been used against his people were concerned, nothing could be taken for granted.

As for himself, personally, he fully expected to be killed, and hoped only that his demise would present itself in a concise and forthright manner. There was nothing in the history of Iollth-Hyfftian interaction to suggest that the victors were inclined to the use of torture. Still, he had steeled himself for whatever might come.

The summit went well. When not being slaughtered and abused, the Hyfft were quite efficient. Aside from having to endure some vociferous chiding for multiple past wrongs committed, nothing was said to the assembled quartet of Iollth about taking revenge. Not even on Ki-ru-vad and his colleagues, who had been chosen by their peers as much for their suitability as sacrifices as for the prestige they conferred on the occasion.

"None of us are to be killed?" he finally felt compelled to ask.

The Delineator of Pedwath regarded her ancient enemy out of small, dark eyes. "What would that gain? An entirely nonproductive response. We prefer that you return, all of you, to your homeworld, to convey the news of what has transpired here." The reaction of the other Hyfft gathered around her was proof that hers was not a response that had been decided individually.

Ki-ru-vad looked over at Sa-ru-vam and the others. They were equally as resolved as he to follow through with tradition. Being of dominion caste, they had no choice.

"We cannot do that," he told the Hyfft.

Confusion engendered animated discussion among the locals until one, whom Ki-ru-vad knew as Mardalm the Linguist, stepped to the fore, fingering her translator gear as she did so.

"There seems to be some confusion in translation. You have agreed to the provisions of treaty. What is it you cannot do? With what element of the surrender terms can you not comply?"

"We cannot return home," Sa-ru-vam told her. Among the Hyfft no one said as much, but it was clear all were thinking, "*Well, you certainly can't stay here.*"

"Why not?" inquired a curious elderly historian from among the pack of suddenly uneasy natives.

Ki-ru-vad explained patiently. "It is a matter of the Commitment. A custom among the Iollth that extends backward for eons, to the time when our ancestors first emerged from the harsh hills of Ioll and set to

fighting among themselves. The Commitment is one of our oldest traditions. On those exceedingly rare occasions when soldiers of Iollth are
overcome, practice demands that the defeated pledge themselves and
their fealty to the one responsible for their defeat." His attitude and
tone showed that he did not believe the individual in question to be
among the multitude of gaping Hyfft.

That was fine with the Delineator. Receiving allegiance from a host
of the Hyfft's ancient enemies was not a condition she was anxious to accept, though she was prepared to do so. All the Hyfft wanted, now that
peace and security had been obtained, was for the Iollth to go away and
never come back. It had never occurred to the Delineator, nor the astronomer Ussakk standing nearby, nor even Yoracc the Historian, that
their erstwhile tormentors might not wish to leave.

No, the Delineator corrected herself. That was not what the horrid,
if overcome, Iollth had said. The bottom-heavy alien invader sought the
one most responsible for the defeat of his kind. To her relief, she knew
that praiseworthy individual was not to be found among the Hyfft.

Uncertainty followed the dissemination of this unexpected development. The commander of the visiting force of Niyyuuan soldiers was
put forth as a logical candidate to receive the resolute Iollth commitment. He promptly declined the honor, and not just because he felt
himself unworthy.

"Was not I who propounded strategy that led to victory," the officer
explained honestly. Lifting a limber, armored arm, he gestured skyward.
"Devising of tactics employed originates with senior command."

Word of the unanticipated conundrum was dutifully passed along
to the ships in orbit. It stimulated energetic debate among Gerlla-hyn
and his staff.

Gazing down at the milling throng of Iollth, Hyfft, and Niyyuu,
George strained for a better look. "Wonder what they're deliberating
down there? I thought this ceremony was supposed to be pretty much
cut-and-dried."

"That's what I thought." From where he had been uncomfortably
seated on a Hyfftian chair alongside his friend, Walker rose and leaned
forward. "My translator doesn't work at this range, but it sure looks like
they're arguing about something."

"Inconsequentialities." Behind them, Sque clung to the back of her
seat and thought fondly of rain. "The lower orders worship mindless
babble for its own sake." Behind her, scrunched down beneath the
curving ceiling and up against the rear wall of the chamber, Braouk

murmured verse under his breath, his vertically aligned jaws opening and closing silently in time to his thoughts.

"I not responsible for this development." Gazing out the port at the world below, his senior officers arrayed behind him, Gerlla-hyn was adamant. "None here can claim credit for such. For elaborating tactics that led to victory in battle, yes. But persuasion to do and therefore ultimate source of causality arose from other source." Neck frill erecting, tails twitching in unison, he gestured at the port. "Credit for initiating alliance with Hyfft lies elsewhere. True responsibility belongs to those who first propounded it." He glanced over at a technician. "Is only proper, I think, to so inform senior Hyfft as to who is nominal commander of expedition, and with whom final decision making on any course of Niyyuuan action ultimately rests."

George frowned as a pair of Hyfft approached. Ussakk the Astronomer was one of them. The other, clad in the finery of a Hyfftian administrator, eyed the canine with the kind of fawning adoration usually attributed to the dog's own kind.

Reaching the level where three of the four aliens reposed, Ussakk made sure his translation gear was fully operational before beginning. Glancing only briefly at George and Sque, the astronomer directed his attention to the lone human, who at the moment was looking more than slightly bemused.

"Your presence is required below," he announced politely.

Walker frowned. "Is there a problem with the surrender?" He looked past the much shorter Hyfft. "I thought the Iollth had already agreed to the terms of the treaty."

"They have," Ussakk informed him. "This is something else. Something in the nature of a post-surrender complication. There is some awkwardness. The Niyyuu have been in touch with their superiors." A small, furry hand gestured cryptically. "It appears only you can resolve the quandary, friend Walker."

"Me?" The commodities trader blinked. "What about the surrender could possibly involve me?"

"Maybe both sides need you to bake surrender cookies," George quipped tartly. With a sigh, he dropped off his seat and started down the ribbed walkway. "Come on. The sooner we find out what they want, the sooner we can head out for Tuuqalia."

The rendering of the Commitment was no small matter. Having been conquered, Ki-ru-vad knew that he and his kind had no choice in the matter. But one could hope for a respectable recipient. Ki-ru-vad studied the human intently. Appearance-wise, the creature was certainly an improvement over the inoffensive Hyfft. While not as tall as the Niyyuu who had done the actual fighting against his kind, the nearly hairless biped was considerably broader and presumably more muscular. Its eyes bespoke a certain intelligence, though less so than the slick-skinned decapod that spread out across the floor behind it. Most promising of all was the tentacled monster that loomed impressively over every other sentient in the room.

But it was the biped that the Hyfft and a Niyyuuan officer had urged forward.

"Wait a minute," Walker protested. What was happening here? "What's going on? What's this all about?" His questions ceased when Ki-ru-vad raised his right side and took a heavy, ceremonial step toward him.

The top of the defeated alien's slim skull came up to the level of the human's chest. Extending its short arms, the Illoth turned them bony side down in a gesture that meant nothing to Walker. One massive foot slid forward, to slide atop the commodities trader's right foot. At that, each of the three members of his caste who accompanied him raised a right foot and placed it behind their neck, balancing easily on their other broad foot. Walker's translator received the alien's words as Niyyuuan speech and efficiently translated them into English.

"Know, all present, that we of the dominion caste, and those of all the lower castes aboard the Five, do thus offer fealty to the architect of our defeat."

Walker swallowed hard. "Excuse me?"

Wide, powerful feet returned to the floor. Ki-ru-vad slipped his own off of Walker's. The alien's foot had not pressed down hard, but neither did it exhibit the disgustingly gracile touch of the Hyfft, either.

"We are yours," the Iollth repeated more succinctly. "All castes, all ships. This is the might of the Commitment. So it has been since the beginnings of Iollth civilization. So it will be until the last of my people breathe their last."

"No. Oh no." Backing up, Walker waved both hands, palms outward, at the alien. Ki-ru-vad strove mightily to grasp the meaning of the energetic but incomprehensible gesture. "We don't want that. I don't want that. There's been some mistake."

Next to him, an amused George was slowly shaking his head from side to side. "You make a decent cook, Marc, but a lousy pack leader." He grinned, showing white teeth. "I guess the Niyyuu don't want the responsibility, either. Gerlla-hyn and his staff must have fingered you once again as the titular leader of the expedition. Carrying that logic to its conclusion, I guess that makes you the ultimate 'architect' of the defeat of the Iollth."

A glance at the small group of Niyyuuan officers confirmed the dog's assessment. Dazed, Walker turned to his other companions. "I can't do this. I can't be expected to do this. I'm already in over my head with the Niyyuu. Braouk, maybe if you . . . ?"

With a shifting of his lower limbs, the huge Tuuqalian turned his dorsal side on the human—though both eyes, on the ends of their stalks, continued to gaze back at him.

"Not for me, the command of others, for fighting. I am a gentle singer of songs, reciter of sagas, lover of the open plains profound. Better for you, manipulator of clever schemes, to lead."

Desperately, Walker tried another approach. "Listen to me, you puerile purveyor of punk poetry! You're the toughest fighter among us, worth more on the battlefield than any fifty humans or Niyyuu. I've seen what you can do, everyone has, and it makes you the master of throwing more than words around! It's your chance to use your true natural abilities, to direct others, to—"

Pivoting on four massive lower tentacles, the Tuuqalian thrust both eyestalks toward Walker so sharply that the human nearly stumbled backward. Even George flinched.

"Not this time, will you incite me, with taunting. We are not now on board the Vilenjji ship, surrounded by captors I was delighted to dismember." A huge tentacle wagged knowingly at Walker. "I am on to you, cunning human." Strong enough to rip off one of Walker's arms, or his head, a second upper tentacle reached toward him—to allow the sensitive tip to stroke the tense commodities trader's right shoulder and drag lightly across his chest.

"You are my friend, Marcus Walker. We have been, through very much together, we two. But in your anxiety you forget that my size and strength does not make me stupid." Withdrawing, the tentacle joined the other on Braouk's right side to wave in the direction of the patiently waiting Iollth.

"These have pledged themselves to you, according to their own custom. Such traditions are no less legitimate than those of my own people. Or those of the Niyyuu, who have done the same." One eye dipped so close that Walker could study his own reflection in the perfectly spherical ocular. "Our objective here, for all of us, is homegoing. If that means that you must show the way for Iollth as well as for Niyyuu, it must be so. Accept this new burden with the grace and skill of which I know you are capable, Marcus Walker." The eye retracted. "And maybe later, you can make dinner, for all."

Rebuffed by the Tuuqalian, a troubled Walker turned to the K'er-emu. Raising several tentacles of her own, Sque forestalled him. From the center of her body, her pinkish speaking tube danced as she spoke.

"I anticipate what you are about to say, friend Marc. That as your intellectual and moral superior, I should be the one to assume this obligation. That, there being no comparison between your level of native intelligence and mine, I should be the one to assume the onus of command of these rapacious but conciliatory folk. That given your inborn obtuseness and ignorance, I should—"

He interrupted dryly. "Granting for a moment the validity of the never-ending comparisons between your species abilities and mine, Sque—how about it?"

Silvery eyes regarded him unblinkingly. "I wouldn't think of challenging you for command, Marc. You are clearly the one best suited to stand in the line of fire and—wait, allow me to rephrase. You are the designated nominal commander of our expedition. It's only right and proper that you ultimately give direction to these simple folk as well as to our humble friends the Niyyuu." A tentacle wiped meaningfully at one eye. "As ever, I shall be available to offer constructive advice, should you have the sagacity to seek it."

As a last hope, Walker turned to George. Except that George was no longer lingering in the vicinity of his feet. The dog had wandered off and was conversing with the astronomer Ussakk. Seeing Walker staring at him, George raised one paw and waved cheerily.

Ki-ru-vad took a step forward—which, given the size of Iollth feet, constituted no small advance. "You must do this thing, Marcus Walker. It has been true throughout the modern history of the Iollth that those who are strong enough to defeat us inevitably lead the defeated on to greater glory and triumph."

"That'd be you, I reckon," observed George, who had trotted back to rejoin his companion. "Or you could offer to lead them to the food synthesizers, though I expect when Ki-ru-vad here speaks of 'greater glory,' he's thinking of something on a somewhat more meaningful scale." Walker glared down at the dog, then turned back to the expectant Iollth officer.

"What if I say no? What if I simply refuse? Won't you go on as you have before—taking your new treaty with the Hyfft into account, of course?"

A small hand executed a gesture Walker could not interpret. The eyes of the Iollth had turned, of all things, limpid.

Surely, an aghast Walker told himself, this leader of murdering invaders, this representative of a species of raiding, killing sentients, was not going to stand before him and cry?

Ki-ru-vad did not. But his reply was undeniably impassioned. "You and your allies have beaten us. We cannot return thus to Ioll. The shame would require that we step, one by one, every member of every caste, naked into the space through which we traveled. Some new victory, however modest, must first accrue to us before we can go home." Though the squat, powerful form straightened, the head of the Iollth still reached no higher than Walker's neck.

"You have to understand, Marcus Walker, that this is how it has always been for the Iollth. You are not of any caste, so your defeat of us carries with it no permanent stain. It is only the weight of the downfall we must remove. This can only be done by replacing loss with triumph, and this must be initiated by the conquerors themselves."

"You again," George reminded his friend helpfully.

"I'm not a conqueror," a frustrated Walker protested firmly. "I'm a cook. And a commodities trader."

"A trader!" The revelation (though Walker felt it to be more of a confession) seemed to please Ki-ru-vad. "Then you must understand what is at stake here, and how it must be resolved. Defeat must be replaced by triumph. You are not in the forefront: you are in the middle. A trader true. An honest broker of downfall and resolution." One foot rose up toward him. Sensing that some sort of response was in order and not knowing what else to do, Walker reached down and grabbed the foot. The material of the slipper-like covering was sandpapery rough. The alien sustained the one-foot-in-the-air pose seemingly without effort.

"You accept."

"No, wait," Walker began again. But Ki-ru-vad had already lowered his right foot.

"It is done. The Commitment has been bestowed." While Walker sought urgently for a way to object further, the Iollth was already speaking into his communicator. Next to him, his three companions had raised their own right feet and were showing the fabric-clad soles to Walker and his friends. A salute, a gesture of fealty, a sign of acquiescence—he had no way of knowing the deeper meaning of the dramatic podal gesture. In fact, he was increasingly certain of only one thing.

He was stuck with it.

Feeling a demand for attention at his left leg, he gazed morosely down at where George was pawing his knee. "Congratulations, Marc."

The trader-chef-conqueror sighed heavily. "What am I going to do? I can't even call in to a radio talk show for ideas."

"Don't panic. You've got us." The dog nodded in the direction of the meditating Braouk and the quietly satisfied Sque. "You've got me. We helped you deal with the Niyyuu. We'll help you deal with these turnip-shaped assassins as well." His ears drooped slightly. "I'm not sure any of this will help us get any closer to home, but I am sure of one thing."

Kneeling, an unhappy but increasingly resigned Walker began stroking George's head, front to back. It was debatable whether the action made the dog or himself feel better. "Nice to know somebody's sure of something. What is it?"

Turning his head, but no so far that it moved out from beneath Walker's massaging hand, the dog indicated the gathering of alien beings that surrounded them: resourceful Hyfft, war-loving Niyyuu, ferocious Iollth.

"Wherever we go from here, we're a lot less likely to be picked on."

✳

Sharing similar martial philosophies, if not predatory behavior, the Niyyuu accepted the presence of the five Iollth ships far more readily than Walker had their overall command. Of course, it was Gerlla-hyn and his staff who were actually in charge of the practicalities of integrating the Iollth force and coordinating their movements with their own. Walker's "command" was a useful fiction. As interaction and exchange increased, the Iollth became aware that the human was at once more and less than he seemed. But if the Niyyuu, whose skill and tactics had actually defeated them, were willing to accept the strangely hesitant biped as their ostensible leader, the Iollth were more than willing to go along.

The Niyyuan ship that had become home to Walker and his friends was once more speeding through the interstellar realm by means he still could not fathom. Or rather, the fleet was. Did eight ships constitute a fleet? What would the enlightened Sessrimathe have thought had they been able to see the four oddly-paired former abductees now? For that matter, he mused, what would his friends and coworkers back home think?

*Don't get carried away, now,* he warned himself. *You're only the "nominal" leader of this escalating force. Gerlla-hyn is really the leader of the Niyyuu, and Ki-ru-vad's caste is in charge of his people. You're no more than a figurehead.*

A figurehead who was listened to, however.

He wasn't worried about losing perspective. To dominate, to rule, one had to want to do so. He wanted exactly the opposite. This invented command had been forced on him. He'd only taken it on, twice now, to mollify others, to satisfy their cultural needs.

After all, as Sobj-oes had explained it to him once she and the rest of the Niyyuu had been informed of the turn events had taken, the Iollth were a space-going species just like the Niyyuu, or the Sessrimathe, or many others. They had traditions deserving of respect, even if the manner in which their traditions were sometimes executed were to be deplored.

Initial requests for Walker and his friends to visit the Iollth ships had been politely declined. At first offended, the Iollth were informed by their former foe and new allies the Niyyuu that as commander of such an extensive force, the human Walker had far too much on his mind to devote any time to such frivolities, pleasant though they might be. This excuse the Iollth understood. At speed, of course, any kind of physical ship-to-ship transfer was impossible. So the Iollth would have to wait until the ships emerged back into normal space-time before they could further venerate their new leader.

Though she was as fully Niyyuu as any warrior of her kind, Sobj-oes, for one, was relieved that the fighting had been resolved with so little loss of life and that all available resources could once more be devoted to trying to carry their four guests homeward—and to the pursuit of science.

"As has been discussed, given what we know about when each of you was taken by the Vilenjji, when we reach world of Tuuqalia we will ask information of their astronomers and try work out vectors for Earth and K'erem from there."

"If we can find Tuuqalia." From his cushion on the other side of the cabin, George spoke without raising his chin from the fabric. "As I recall, you don't have an exact course to the nearest port. Just a line on the general area."

Sobj-oes's neck frill flared. "We confident that once in spatial vicinity of advanced world like Tuuqalia, will be able locate system of singer-warrior Braouk. Work of Hyfftian astronomers correlates well with initial calculations made on Niyu." Towering over the dog, she bent toward him. "You should have more confidence in yous friends, friend George." Straightening, she gestured toward Walker, who lounged nearby trying to unravel the secrets of a Hyfftian play-globe and its concentric spheres of electric color. "You should try be more like your companion Walker."

"You mean, 'dim'?" Unreassured, the dog sank his face even lower into the cushion.

From the far side of the cargo cabin that had been modified for their personal use, Braouk parted vertically aligned jaws and displayed saw-edged teeth. "There is a sub-saga that specifically addresses your apprehension, friend George. If you like, I will recite it, for you."

The dog looked over at the vast hill of flesh that was the Tuuqalian. Braouk had been less melancholy than usual lately. And no wonder, George mused sourly. It was his homeworld they were heading for.

"Thanks, Braouk, but I'm not in the mood."

"Set your mind at rest, sardonic quadruped." From her resting place in a misting fountain that had been installed specifically for her comfort, Sque squinted across at the cynical canine. "So long as you have my enlightening and didactic company to enjoy, you are being well looked after. Probably more so than in your entire life."

Raising his head slightly from the soft artificial material, George gazed thoughtfully at the K'eremu. What would it be like to have a creature like her as a master? he found himself wondering. Of course, Sque doubtless felt she was master of them all already.

Master. Though they had taken him as a captive, the Vilenjji had also given him higher intelligence and the power of speech. In addition to allowing him to communicate with others, these "enhancements" had saddled him with the ability to reflect.

Born a street dog, he'd never had a master. Eking out an existence on the back streets and in the alleys of Chicago, he'd sometimes envied, in his primitive, uncognitive canine fashion, the pampered appearance of dogs on leashes and in cars. They smelled of food, rich and thick. Now he was able to understand why. They lived in houses or apartments with humans. As pets, who had masters. Having been granted intelligence, he knew he now could never suffer such an existence, no matter how cosseting. Not only had he seen too much and experienced too much: he knew too much.

What if, upon some still tenuous and possibly dubious return to Earth, his alien-imparted enhanced intelligence failed, leaving him once more as incapable of advanced cognition as the other mutts with whom he had roamed the rough streets, fighting and breeding, only dimly aware of the greater reality through which they moved? The prospect made him shudder. If it happened, would it occur instantly or as a slow, agonizing diminution of consciousness? When it finally happened, would he even retain enough awareness to be conscious of the loss?

He found himself staring at Walker. Wholly absorbed in trying to puzzle out the workings of the Hyfftian toy, the human ignored him. They had been through much together. Unbelievable experiences. Did that guarantee that in the event of intelligence loss Walker would take him in? As a pet? Would Walker have him fixed?

There were times, he brooded gloomily, when he regretted the involuntary modifications the Vilenjji had made to him. While his enhanced intelligence had opened him to, literally, a universe of experience, it also simultaneously forced him to contemplate the horror of its possible loss. His was no longer a dog's life, simple but content, ignorant but mentally at ease. With a sigh, he rolled onto his side and stretched, all four legs quivering slightly as he did so. In this position he could see one of the many floating readouts that populated the interior of the Niyyuuan ship. At present it was displaying the view outside, precisely adjusted for spatial-temporal distortion. Stars and nebulae shone in the heavens, an unimaginably impressive blaze of ferocious light and dazzling color. Before, they had only been points of light dotting the night sky. Now, he knew what they were. That knowledge simultaneously enhanced and diminished his view of them.

He felt a sudden urge to howl, and caught himself barely in time.

9

Hyperspace, doublespace, inside-out space: the name for the continuum they were passing through translated differently depending not only on whether one was speaking with Niyyuu as opposed to Iollth, but on specific moments in time and transition. Elsewhere, George took to calling it. Whether standing still or traveling at speed by starcraft, it was the place he and his human had been consigned to ever since their abduction from Earth.

"It doesn't matter, Marc," the dog declared as they made their way toward the central command room. "Wherever we are, it's someplace we shouldn't be."

"Not true." Walker nodded to a passing Iollth avatar as the perambulating image of the squat creature floated past them. Similar ancient and traditional martial interests had gone a long way toward relaxing the initial tension between the tormentors of the Hyfft and their

Niyyuuan conquerors, so much so that electronic avatars of both species were now allowed to visit one another's ships.

"We are someplace definite," he told his friend. "We're on our way home."

The dog let out a derisive snort. "Our way home? We're on our way to Tuuqalia, and that if we're lucky. Earth is still nothing more than a word. And if we don't find Tuuqalia, we'll probably have to go all the way back to Hyff and start all over again—or even back to Niyu." He snapped at an imaginary passing fly. "Intellect notwithstanding, what I wouldn't give for the comfort of a sweet bitch and an old bone."

Mentally drifting, Walker nearly murmured, "Me too," before the detailed meaning of his friend's words sank in. "Steak," he mumbled. "Real coffee. No more synthetics."

"We've arrived," George prompted him, breaking into his companion's reverie. "Better pack in useless thoughts. No drooling in the command center."

Gerlla-hyn and Sobj-oes were waiting for them. The Niyyuuan Commander-Captain's frill was taut and his tails were quivering, while the astronomer was clearly straining to contain herself. Above them, multiple levels of Niyyuuan technicians worked at mobile consoles, the design of their workspace reflecting the vertically inclined aesthetic of their kind. A Niyyuuan worker was more comfortable above or below colleagues than beside them.

Though no more unpleasant than that of any other of his kind, Gerlla-hyn's voice still grated on Walker's ears. He was not used to the sound of Niyyuuan voices—and never would be. Such acceptance was beyond the aural tolerance of any human. But he and George had both learned to endure the persistent scraping noises that emerged from the slender Niyyuuan throat to form the terse, brusque speech of their kind.

"Wonderful news!" The Commander-Captain's obvious enthusiasm somewhat allayed the shock to Walker's ears. "We have pick up strong signals that yous large friend Braouk has identified as belonging his people." Twirling gracefully, Gerlla-hyn gestured toward a large floating readout. It responded to his prompting with symbols and ideographs that were as alien as ever to Walker. But there was no mistaking the diagram of a star system upon which all manner of lines devolved.

George sniffed the readout. It had no odor. "Tuuqalia?"

"We hope so. Signalings have been tracked to the fourth world in." Thrusting one of the two long fingers on his left hand into the readout, the Commander-Captain stirred the promising mix. "Am informed by

Braouk signalings could be coincidental, or from visiting Tuuqalian ship, but volume and strength of same suggests plane-tary origin."

"Latest available schematics have been provided yous oversize com-panion," a visibly pleased Sobj-oes informed them. "Distance makes impossible for him to render opinion on surrounding starfield. Is com-plicated by fact that he not astronomically inclined himself."

"A simple soul, our Braouk," Walker murmured as he watched George wander around behind the readout. "I'm sure I couldn't iden-tify my own system from a light-year or two out." He eyed Gerlla-hyn. "So what you're saying is, essentially, we won't know if this is for real until we get there?"

"Ably put, Marcus." Sobj-oes consulted the slim reader that resided in her hands so often Walker would not have been surprised to learn it was surgically affixed to its owner. "Will emerge into normal space soon and initiate formal contact. Friend Braouk says his people a devel-oped, space-going species, though not as avid travelers as Sessrimathe. Must ensure upon emergence that is no confusion as to our intentions."

Walker frowned. "Why would there be? As soon as they learn of our purpose in coming here, they're sure to—"

George interrupted him, his words sage and knowing. "When a strange dog wanders into your neighborhood, Marc, you check him, or her, out. When a strange pack wanders in, you raise your hackles, show your teeth, growl, and prepare to run or stand your ground." One up-raised paw indicated the small sphere that represented their destination. "Not being able to run, the inhabitants of this world, be they Tuuqalian or anything else, are likely to do the latter."

The dog's opinion was supported by Gerlla-hyn. "If one ship is de-tected emerging into normal space of system, would be likely no no-table reaction on part of locals. But are now eight ships escorting you and yous companions. Is number unusual enough to be intimidating." He cast an approving glance down at George. "Would be atypical if lo-cals not show teeth and growl at such an appearance." His tone then changed slightly to indicate mild puzzlement. "What are 'hackles'?"

"Think your frill," the dog suggested.

Three days later, the inhabitants of the fourth world of the system they were entering raised something somewhat more impressive than hackles or frill.

Braouk's joy knew no bounds when the first transmissions aimed at the arriving Niyyuuan and Iollth ships were not only determined to be Tuuqalian in origin, but that they indeed emanated from that long-sought homeworld itself.

"So long away, from my own world, almost forgotten." Braouk did not cry, but both eyestalks and upper tentacles trembled in tandem. It was an astonishing sight. "I can hardly believe we are actually here, nearing the homeworld."

"After all we've been through," George observed perceptively from the far side of the converted cargo area, "I can hardly believe we're near *anybody's* homeworld."

Everyone turned their attention to Sobj-oes. The Niyyuuan astronomer had entered their private quarters to deliver the good news in person. Her frill was flushed maroon, a sure sign of excitement. It made Walker think, even at that joyful moment, of Viyv-pym-parr. An episode in his increasingly improbable past. One best forgotten, yet one he seemed unable to shake. He forced himself to focus his attention on the astronomer.

"You're certain? We've been disappointed before."

Wider even than normal, tarsier-like eyes of yellow and gold turned to him. The round, muscular mouth flexed, the words it emitted mitigating the ear-tormenting timbre of the sound.

"There no mistaking response, Marcus. Utilizing translation facilities, communications staff have already had conversation with inhabitants of fourth world this system. Is without question Tuuqalia." Turning away from the human, she faced Braouk. "Has been explained one of their own is with us and relevant recording has been transmitted to provide credulous with proof."

"Essential that is, to reassure my brethren, of amity." Lowering both tentacles and eyestalks, Braouk rose from his crouch and advanced his tonnage toward the astronomer. "Nevertheless, they will not allow these ships to approach nearer than the orbit of the outer moon Suek. A natural precautionary measure." Though they were nowhere near enough yet to Tuuqalia for the large external readout screen to show anything other than empty space, he turned longingly in its direction.

"My people should be arriving soon. All those on Niyyuuan and Iollth vessels should be forewarned. The coming confrontation is a normal response and not a hostile gesture." While one plate-sized eye remained focused on the hovering readout, the other turned back to Sobj-oes. "It would not do to have the forthcoming greeting misinterpreted. The results could be catastrophic."

The depth of their friend's concern was soon illustrated by the nature of the Tuuqalian greeting to which he was referring. According to Berred-imr of the Niyyuuan command staff, no less than forty ships had risen from the vicinity of Tuuqalia to intercept the incoming force of Niyyuuan and Iollth vessels. It was by far the largest single grouping of starships Walker and his friends, or for that matter the Niyyuu, had ever encountered. Even on their arrival at Seremathenn, they had not seen so many interstellar craft assembled together in one place. What was even more impressive was their first glimpse of one such craft when it arrived and positioned itself fore of the *Jhevn-bha*. Even the intrepid Iollth confessed themselves to be more than a little impressed.

Being big people, the Tuuqalians had constructed big ships.

Taken together, the chain of huge blocky shapes that comprised the three conjoined lines of the Tuuqalian vessel massed more than any three individual Niyyuuan or Iollth craft. Realizing that forty of them now formed an englobement around his own ships was a daunting thought. Almost as daunting as the realization that Walker had come to think of them as "his" ships. The possessive was unintentional, he told himself. He was a nominal leader, not really in charge of anything. Gerlla-hyn was the real commander of the Niyyuuan force, and Ki-ru-vad's dominion caste the controllers of the Iollth quintet.

First, irrepressible thoughts of an inaccessible alien female, and now an absurd mental repositioning of individual importance. He definitely needed to get home. Quickly, before his reasoning splintered any further. More than anything, he needed Tuuqalia to be Earth. But it wasn't, any more than Seremathenn or Niyu had been, and he was going to have to deal with that.

*Concentrate on your happy hulk of a friend Broullkoun-uvv-ahd-Hrashkin*, he told himself. *Be delighted for him that he, at least, has finally found his way home. Share in his joy. Take your mind off ridiculous and improvident thoughts. And worry about what those forty ships are capable of and might do if someone drops a wrong word or makes a wrong move.*

Though the tension generated by the confrontation did not evaporate entirely on board the ships of the Niyyuu and the Iollth, it diminished considerably once the commanders of the Tuuqalian vessels were able to see and communicate directly with one of their own. As Braouk told his story, suitably embellished with the emblematic oratorical flourishes of his kind, Walker and George found themselves growing increasingly weary from the impassioned but interminable recitation. They had heard it all before, not to mention having experienced it for themselves. Eventually even the Niyyuuan staff in the command room turned to other pursuits as the energized Tuuqalian in their midst rambled on and on. Meanwhile the audience of his own kind listened raptly and apparently without boredom to the never-ending transmission.

Once again, Sque had been ahead of her friends. Envisioning the

nature of the initial communication that was likely to take place between Braouk and his kind, the perceptive K'eremu had remained behind in their quarters, happily brooding in her custom-rigged misting
pool. The longer Braouk rambled on, the more Walker wanted to join
her himself.

Feeling a tug at his lower leg, he looked down to see George pulling
at the hem of his pants. As soon as he had the human's attention, the
dog released his grip and whispered urgently.

"At this rate we'll all die of old age before loopy eyes here finishes
his story—let alone before we can start looking for Earth again."

Walker crouched down beside his friend. "We can't just cut him off
in mid-speech," he murmured softly while the Tuuqalian orated on.
"This is his story. His saga." He indicated the main viewer, which
showed several senior Tuuqalians hanging in evident ecstasy on
Braouk's every word. "Interrupting wouldn't only be impolite; it might
damage our relations with his kinsfolk. We need to get off on the right
foot here. We're going to need the help of their astronomers if we're
going to have a chance of locating Earth from here."

"Yeah, yeah, I know," the dog muttered sullenly. His gaze returned
to their oversized companion. As Braouk held forth, his four massive
upper tentacles gestured energetically enough to generate a small
breeze in the command room. When combined with the movement of
his eyestalks, the effect was almost dizzying. "But if he doesn't shut up
pretty soon, I'm going to pee on one of those four lower limbs. Let's
see how he works that into his 'saga.' "

Fortunately, George never had to carry out his threat. After only another two hours of endless declamation, Braouk's floridly embellished
tale of abduction and final return reached the point where he and his
friends and allies had entered the Tuuqalian system and encountered the
wary armada sent forth from his homeworld to meet them. All that remained, Walker supposed, was for them to be escorted into orbit
around Tuuqalia itself, for Braouk to be warmly received by his
brethren, and for the visitors to make application to whatever passed for
a professional association of local astronomers to ask for their help in
locating distant Earth.

Ignorant as he was of Tuuqalian society, he could hardly be blamed
for being so sanguine. Or so wrong.

From orbit, Tuuqalia was an attractive oxygen-infused world.
Though slightly larger than Earth, less area was covered by ocean and
sea. There were mountains, and modest ice caps, but the dominating features were endless stretches of flat plains fractured by enormous

meandering rivers. Unlike Hyff, whose population was evenly dispersed among thousands of towns and small cities, Tuuqalia boasted some extensive urban concentrations. While serving as centers of manufacturing and culture, however, they were not home to the majority of citizens.

Long centuries of the population management that had allowed Tuuqalian society to thrive without having to deal with the threat of overpopulation had also allowed the majority of its people to spread out across its endless plains. Advanced technology made work from a distance possible. Even more than the villatic Hyfft, the inhabitants of Tuuqalia favored a life in the countryside. This was no surprise to Walker and his friends. More hours than they cared to remember had been spent listening to Braouk natter on about the joys of roving his homeworld's vast open spaces, and how he could not wait to indulge once again in that wandering that was so dear to every Tuuqalian's heart. It was understandable, Walker knew. A species as individually outsized as Braouk's needed plenty of room in which to roam.

Well, their hulking friend wouldn't have to wait much longer to enjoy himself in that regard. As soon as they received proper clearance, they would all be able to stand once more on the solid surface of a habitable world, real earth under their feet and open sky above their heads. The difference was that this time, both earth and sky would belong to one of their own. After all they had been through together, it was still difficult to come to grips with the fact that one of them had actually made it home.

Which made the continuing delay in the granting of the necessary clearance all the more puzzling. Almost as puzzling as Braouk's seeming avoidance not only of Walker, but of George and Sque as well—though Sque was just as content to be ignored as not.

Walker wasn't. The same could be said not only for his canine companion, but for everyone else on board the *Jhevn-Bha*. Not to mention the Iollth, whose inherent limited capacity for tolerance and understanding threatened to destabilize an increasingly ambiguous situation. Despite being heavily outgunned by the fleet of massive Tuuqalian vessels that continued to shadow the arrivals while traveling toward their homeworld, Ki-ru-vad's prickly caste of characters threatened to commence landings without permission and dare the locals to react belligerently. The longer they sat in orbit without that permission, the edgier became the Iollth in particular.

Walker could hardly blame them. He wanted down as much as anyone, especially when the citizens of the world below were presumed to be friendly and welcoming. But if that was the case, then why the excessive delay?

At the risk of irritating his friend, he finally felt compelled to directly confront the only Tuuqalian in their midst.

"What's behind the continuing delay in granting us permission to visit, Braouk?" Though he tried to make his manner as forceful as possible, he knew there was no way a hundred humans could intimidate a Tuuqalian.

In spite of that reality Braouk's reaction smacked, if not of intimidation, at least of embarrassment. All four upper tentacles drew in close around his mouth while both eyestalks contracted until the Tuuqalian's eyes were flush against opposite sides of his trunk-like body. In that pose, he looked not only smaller, but far less alien—such a description, Walker knew, being a highly relative term.

"Yeah, what's the holdup?" George demanded to know from somewhere in the vicinity of Walker's knees. "We've had better receptions on worlds where all of us were strangers." The dog made a rude noise. "You offend somebody important before the Vilenjji snatched you?"

Powerful tentacles fluttered in four different directions. To anyone not familiar with the three-meter-tall Braouk, the effect would have been terrifying. Walker and George were merely surprised. Despite all the time they had spent in the Tuuqalian's company, this was a gesture they had not seen before. They did not know it, but their hulking friend was expressing extreme discomfiture.

"Seeking have I, a way to explain, this circumstance." Eyestalks contracted even tighter into the Tuuqalian's sides, the bulging orbs at their tips disappearing partway into matching recesses in his yellow-green, bristle-covered flanks. "It has been tormenting me even before we entered the heliosphere of Tuuq."

"Even before . . ." Walker's voice faded briefly as he digested the implication. Though no match in size for the basketball-sized orbs of the creature before them, his own eyes widened slightly. "You knew this was going to happen! How long have you known, Braouk?"

"And not told us," George added in a huff, using a hind leg to scratch at one ear.

"Since the day we left Seremathenn with thoughts of returning to our homes," the Tuuqalian rumbled apologetically. Seeking to soothe his companions' injured feelings, he added hastily, "No reason needed, to inform you then, of details. A requirement is demanded of all who wish to visit Tuuqalia. None are being singled out here; not inhabitants of Earth, or of Niyu, or of Ioll." Tentacles extended toward them, a reach for understanding. "Though desperate-dying, to touch my home, I re-main. It is why I have stayed with you since our arrival, knowing that I could explain this aspect of my kind's culture better than any who might come to greet you."

"Some greeting." George stopped scratching and flomped disgust-edly down onto the deck.

"I see that I cannot delay any longer, no matter the cultural reper-cussions that may arise."

Walker had been listening intently. He had also been thinking. "Wait a minute. What 'requirement'? What 'cultural repercussions'? Are you saying that unless we fulfill some kind of demand, your people won't let us make touchdown on Tuuqalia?"

One eye, the left one, extended slightly on its stalk, reaching toward him. In the center of the massive body, the fluttering central nostril twitched in agitation. "Not only will you not be allowed to touch down if you do not comply, no Tuuqalian scientist will lift a tentacle tip to help you on your way."

That implied threat was more than discourteous, Walker realized. It represented, potentially, the end of their journey. Without additional as-sistance from the Tuuqalia, he and George and Sque would have no new astronomical leads to follow. They had only managed to find Tuuqalia with the aid of the Hyfft. Without fresh insight from inhabitants of this part of the galactic arm, they would be left to search hundreds of star sys-tems essentially at random—a task that was more than daunting. How long he could rely on the Niyyuu, much less the volatile Iollth, to con-tinue such voyaging on behalf of him and his friends was an imponder-able whose limits he devoutly wished not to have to test. Having a spe-cific stellar destination in mind might make all the difference between being able to continue their search and its complete abandonment.

For that, they needed the help of another sophisticated star-travers-ing species like the Tuuqalia. And to gain that, they had to fulfill some as yet unexpressed requirement.

He took a deep breath, looked down at George, who shrugged re-signedly, and put the question.

"Delaying this won't make implementation any easier, Braouk. What does this requirement consist of? What do George and I have to do to satisfy the appropriate authorities among your people that we're deserving of their hospitality and their help?"

The ton of Tuuqalian hesitated. Despite his size, strength, and daunting appearance, the huge alien looked for all the world like a self-conscious child who had just been caught raiding the cookie jar.

"You have to, to the authority's satisfaction, prove yourselves."

Though George had long ago moved beyond easy intimidation, he was ever suspicious. "Prove ourselves? How? Some kind of contest? Not wrestling, I hope. If that's the case, I'm out." He raised a forepaw. "No opposable thumb. Sorry, Marc."

"Let's not jump to conclusions," a suddenly concerned Walker responded. Addressing himself once more to their reluctant companion, he pushed the question. "Aside from the fact that everyone on these ships wants—no, needs—to feel solid ground under their feet again, we have to have the help and assistance of your people's astronomers. So—what is it that we have to do? To 'prove' ourselves?"

Emboldened by his friends' evident willingness to comply, Braouk was moved to explain. Time had run out anyway. The authorities had granted him more than enough time to put the demand diplomatically.

"The K'eremu are not the only species capable of unsociable behavior. My kind, too, have their pride. They do not accept, far less agree to assist, just any self-declared civilized sentients who come calling. Those who do so must demonstrate beyond doubt that they are capable of more than the construction of interstellar ships and advanced technologies. They must show that they are civilized. And not just civilized. They must demonstrate (Walker's implanted Vilenjji translator struggled with what was unusually complex and Tuuqalian-specific terminology) sensitivity."

Walker was taken aback. It was not what he expected. But whatever this required proof consisted of, he told himself, it had to be more amenable than wrestling.

"I'm sensitive." George rolled onto his back, all four feet in the air, tongue lolling out of the side of his mouth. "See?"

Having at last put the requirement into words, Braouk was visibly as well as verbally more relaxed. "More than physical submission is required. Much more. It has always been so among my people. The Tuuqalia grant their friendship without reservation, but not easily. Furthermore, one cannot satisfy for all. A representative of each species wishing the amity and assistance of the Tuuqalia must reassure individually." Both eyes were once more fully extended on their flexible stalks. One focused on Walker, the other on George.

"You, Marcus Walker, must act on behalf of not just yourself, but all your kind. And you for yours, George." The eyes retracted slightly, glistening. "Scqui'aranaqua'na'scncmu for the K'cremu. Perhaps Gerllahyn, or possibly Sobj-oes, for the Niyyuu, and someone also for the Iollth. One of each."

One time, Walker reminisced, he had been called into the office of the vice president for operations of the firm for which he worked. On arriving, he had been rattled to find not just Steve Holmes, the officer, there, but representatives of several of the firm's major clients. Asked to give his opinion on half a dozen current world situations as they related directly to the firm's business, he'd been subjected to half an hour of intense questioning. Even though no one said so later, he was sure his ability to survive such intense interrogation on such short notice had led directly to his last promotion.

Now he found himself in a similar situation. Only this time, much more than an increase in salary and an office with a slightly better view of the building across the street was at stake. How not only he but how George and Sque and others performed would likely decide whether he would have any chance of ever seeing that office again.

Sque's frequent sardonic comments to the contrary notwithstanding, he felt reasonably confident he could prove that he was civilized. But—how to prove that he, and by inference humankind, was sensitive?

On later reflection, he realized he should have guessed.

"Now that I have finally been able to say these things to your faces," Braouk was telling them, "I will make the necessary arrangements. One each will be conveyed to the surface. One each to represent their own species. One each to prove they are fit to touch Tuuqalian soil." Eyes drew back and tentacles stiffened. "There is no way around this requirement."

"And if we blow it?" George asked.

Both orbs swiveled in the dog's direction. "Then you will have to go on your way, wherever that may be, without impacting Tuuqalian society, and without the aid of its eminent scientists. Companions though we are, companions in adversity though we have been, there will be nothing more I can do for you."

Tuuqalian first, friend second, Walker reflected. Would it have been any different had their situations been reversed? What would wary humans have demanded of someone like Braouk to prove that he was as civilized as they? Or as sensitive?

"I cannot explain, to newcomers in advance, the requirement." Their oversized friend was apologetic but unrelenting. "You will be informed of the details at a suitable time, subsequent to your arrival."

"That doesn't seem very fair," George protested, having regained his feet. "How can we get ready to comply with a requirement when we don't know what it is?"

Having lumbered forward, Braouk now gently rested the end of one tentacle on George's shoulders. The flexible limb was quite capable of reducing the dog's entire skeleton to splinters.

"Your ability to extemporize will comprise a significant portion of the proof," the Tuuqalian explained unhelpfully. "One way the authority will be able to judge both your degree of civilization and species sensitivity will be by observing your reaction to their demand."

"Thanks," the dog replied dryly as the tentacle tip stroked his back, ruffling his fur. "I feel so much better now. Why me?" he muttered under his breath. "Why not a mastiff, or a poodle?" He cast a wan look on his human. "All I want is a bone and a warm bed."

Walker's lips tightened. "We're stuck with this, George. Each of us gets to stand up not just for ourselves but for our entire species. As for me," he drawled, "I'd rather be in Philadelphia."

There was no one present to recognize or understand the reference, but it lightened his mood a little to say it anyway.

There was some hasty discussion among both the Niyyuu and the Iollth as to who among them might best be suited to complying with the still unspecified Tuuqalian demand. Without knowing its nature, it was impossible to determine which of their number would have the best chance of satisfying the enigmatic requirement of their gruff but hopeful hosts. Prove that they were civilized and sensitive, Walker and George had informed them. Who best among the crews of the three Niyyuuan vessels and the five Iollth ships to do that? Who was the most adaptable? Were the chosen representatives going to be expected to fight? Having watched Braouk dismantle tall, muscular Vilenjji as easily as he would a figure fashioned from Popsicle sticks, Walker preferred not even to consider that option. It wouldn't make much sense for them to gain the approval and cooperation of the Tuuqalians if all five of those selected to justify that gain perished in the process of acquiring it.

Though Braouk was not allowed to in any way prepare or coach them for the forthcoming ordeal, it was clear that his old friend desperately wished to do so. If anything, the Tuuqalian who had been their companion during their long journeying seemed more nervous than the human, his canine companion, and the respective Niyyuu and Iollth who were eventually selected to undergo the test.

Each being the sole representative of his kind, Walker and George were spared the discussions among Niyyuu and Iollth that followed the announcement of the Tuuqalian requirement. Of course, Braouk explained, it was not necessary for a representative of either species to participate. But if Sobj-oes and her small but vital contingent of astronomical specialists were to be allowed to consult with their Tuuqalian

counterparts, at least one Niyyuu also had to satisfy the unbending local tradition. Learning that one of the tall, multi-tailed beings who had
defeated them at Hyff was going to make the attempt, the Iollth felt
it imperative that one of their own kind participate and meet the
Tuuqalian criteria as well.

Discussion among both groups led to debate, and debate to open
argument. There being only one of each of them, human and canine
had no choice in the matter of who was to stand for their species. That
was not the case among Iollth and Niyyuu. Internal conflict threatened
to delay the business further, until an exasperated Walker pointed out to
both groups that they were not exactly displaying the kind of sensitivity
the Tuuqalians were looking for, and that if word of the ongoing dissention reached their erstwhile hosts, the original invitation itself
might be withdrawn.

Abashed by an alien whose species had not even mastered the rudiments of interstellar travel, Niyyuu and Iollth settled down to the selection of one individual to represent each of their kind. Neither recognized that Walker's admonition to each had been based on the
possible failure of the other. It was only one in a litany of techniques he
had borrowed for use from his days as a trader of commodities. Tell
one group that their competitors were acting in an acceptable manner
while the other was not, and the first group was likely to comply with
the teller's needs. Then reverse and apply to the other, and so gain the
cooperation of both.

So it was that De-sil-jimd of the communications caste was chosen
to join the group that would descend to the surface with Braouk as their
guide and sponsor, while Sobj-oes's assistant Habr-wec was elected to
represent the Niyyuu. Ignorant of what they were about to face, Walker
thought them both good choices. It would be good to have a communications specialist among the group, as well as a representative of the
astronomical team in the event the occasion arose to ask a pertinent
question or obtain potentially useful information.

And while Iollth and Niyyuu had argued among themselves, and
Gerlla-hyn had been forced to inform the outraged Niyyuuan media
contingent that none of them would be permitted to record the confrontation, Walker strived mightily to convince Sque to participate.

"No, absolutely not." From within the mist cloud of her perpetually damp resting place, the equivalent of a human couch, the K'eremu
adamantly refused to having anything to do with the upcoming challenge. Metallic gray eyes regarded the crouching Walker mordantly.
"Am I wrong in assuming that despite my continued company and

occasional tutelage you have progressed insufficiently far to recognize a negative when it is presented to you?"

Gritting his teeth, Walker held his temper and persisted. "Sque, we don't know what we're facing here. This is as important to you as it is to the rest of us. You know what'll happen if we don't gain the respect and approval of Braouk's people. No help in locating a possible line on Earth. No help in finding a vector for K'erem."

One limb adjusted a strand comprised of bits of colored glass that ran from the smooth crown of the K'eremu's head down her right side. It was beaded with moisture and radiant with reflected light.

"It has all the intimations of a cheap carnival, this 'requirement.' I refuse to debase myself to gain the sanction of a lot of bloated saga-spouting carnivores." Half her ten slender tentacles promptly entwined themselves in a complex knot no doubt fraught with ambiguous significance.

"Technologically advanced bloated saga-spouting carnivores," Walker reminded her coolly. "Astronomically competent bloated saga-spouting carnivores." He straightened, looking down at her. "The bloated saga-spouting carnivores whose help we need if any of the rest of us are going to have a prayer of getting home."

The K'eremu was unmoved. "You may perform for them however you wish and obtain the required assistance."

Walker rolled his eyes and tried to contain his exasperation. "You know that's not going to work. They want to pass on every species, and they already know there's a K'eremu on board because Braouk told them about you."

An unoccupied tentacle splashed water on argent eyes. "Always noise-making, that one." Bubbles formed at the end of her speaking tube, eventually to break free and wander off into the enclosed atmosphere of the room; visual punctuation. Another tentacle swung to the right and picked up a small, tightly sealed square container. An integrated readout on its exterior divulged the contents. It was where Sque kept her stock of si'dana drugs—or rather, stimulants, as she preferred to refer to them.

"It would appear that I have on hand a sufficiency of synthesized chemicals to enable me to tolerate such a degrading ordeal. Even in a fog of my own making I would expect no difficulty in satisfying the stipulations of our garrulous friend Braouk's demanding relations." Her entire body expanded and relaxed, like a momentarily inflated balloon. "I suppose I will have to do this."

Walker smiled. "Braouk will be delighted. He's anxious to show us his world. All of us."

"The lumbering sputterer of interminable singsong may not find my reluctant company quite so vitalizing. In any event, I am glad that one of us, at least, has been returned to their home." She climbed, or rather slithered, out of the misting pool. "His kind had better be able to render unto us the kind of scientific assistance we need, or I am certain I will regret this decision for the rest of my natural days."

"Oh, for heaven's sake," Walker snapped as he turned to leave. "You don't even know what the Tuuqalian requirement for entry consists of. It might require us to do nothing more than swear some kind of mild oath not to harm local interests, or to fill out in person a form or two." Feeling a tentacle questing along the back of his leg, he kicked it gently away. Back home, a rubbery, ropy contact like that might have made him jump a foot straight up. Over the past couple of years, he had grown used to and relaxed with touches that were even more alien.

"And stand off—I'm not Braouk, and I'm not going to carry you."

Slithering out of the cabin and into the first corridor on all ten tentacles, Sque blew a large bubble that, when it popped, disseminated a particularly malodorous aroma. Linguistic sophistication notwithstanding, the K'eremu were perfectly capable of venturing an opinion in a nonverbal manner.

**10**

The Tuuqalian shuttle that carried the representatives of the five visiting species— human, canine, K'eremu, Iollth, and Niyyuu— to the surface was itself larger than some interstellar craft the travelers had seen. A lot of the interior seemed to consist of empty space. No doubt when it was transporting the much bigger Tuuqalians, it was packed full.

Similarly, the interesting high-speed, multi-wheeled ground transport vehicle that transported them from the landing site into the city of Karoceen was plainly not designed for visitors. Everyone except the solicitous Braouk had to be helped to reach the vehicle's high entrance. Everyone, that is, except Sque. Using her suckerless tentacles, the most reluctant among the visitors was able to find sufficient purchase on the exterior of the transport to climb aboard by herself. This achievement had unintended unfortunate consequences, as her four companions

were subsequently forced to listen to a patronizing discourse on the superiority of K'eremu physical as well as mental skills all the way into
the metropolis.

Karoceen was of a size befitting the dimensions of its inhabitants.
Far larger than any urban complex Walker and George had seen on Hyff
or Niyu, it reminded them of the great metropolitan concentrations on
Seremathenn itself. With one notable exception: few of the buildings
were more than five or six stories (albeit they were Tuuqalian stories,
he reminded himself ) high. The Tuuqalia, Braouk explained in response to his question, were not fond of heights. So while Karoceen
and its sister cities were enormous in extent, their skylines failed to impress.

Structures tended to have rounded corners, in keeping with
Tuuqalian aesthetics, and large windows. Many appeared to be composed entirely of reinforced polysilicates or similar transparent materials. When the visitors exited the transport vehicle and were ushered into
one notably tall building of five stories, Walker felt dwarfed by their
native escorts. Being around one Tuuqalian, Braouk, had often been
intimidating enough. Finding oneself on their world, surrounded by
dozens of the multi-limbed, sawtoothed giants, would be enough to
make anyone paranoid. He found himself staying close to the tall young
Niyyuuan astronomer Habr-wec. The normally bold George was also
intimidated to the point where he threatened to walk under Walker's
feet and trip them both.

Only Sque, who had not wanted to come at all, appeared unimpressed, traveling in the manner to which she had become accustomed
atop one of Braouk's powerful upper limbs, her own tentacles providing
her with a grip Walker could only envy. She was spared the anxiety that
afflicted him and the others by her unshakable innate sense of superiority, the knowledge that while all space-traversing species were sentient, the K'eremu were just a little more sentient than anyone else.

Senescent, more likely, Walker grumbled to himself even as he envied her feeling of invincible self-confidence.

Not knowing what to expect, he was taken aback when Braouk and
their escort of four massive armed Tuuqalians finally halted before a
pair of towering doors.

"We are here," their friend informed them, before adding cryptically, "With luck, this will take a long time."

Walker did not have the opportunity to ask what Braouk meant by
that before the doors folded into opposing walls and they were conducted inside.

The chamber was immense, a gilded hall with a floor that sloped upward instead of down as would have been the case in a comparable human facility. There were no chairs. Like the Iollth, the Tuuqalians neither used nor needed such furnishings. Climbing the slight slope that appeared to be paved with a single continuous strip of something like varnished lapis lazuli, they approached a waiting semicircle of Tuuqalians. The distance between doorway and dais being equally Tuuqalian-sized, Walker felt as if he was hiking across the floor of a vast indoor sports arena instead of simply from one side of a meeting room to the other. Silence save for the muted *slap-slap* of their escorts' lower limbs against the floor and a steady cool breeze whose source he could not discern made the distance to be traversed seem all the greater.

Braouk's people had no more use for clothing than they did for chairs, though the dozen or so figures did flaunt various pendants and other identifying devices that encircled their uppermost limbs like massive bracelets. Twenty-four bulbous, unblinking eyes regarded the approaching visitors, bobbing and weaving at the ends of muscular, flexible eyestalks. The sight was as hypnotic as it was unnerving.

The last time Walker had been so intimidated by rank size was when he had been forced to confront the Ohio State offensive line his senior year at his university. There was no basis for actual physical comparison, of course. The smallest of the aliens squatting before him on its four lower tentacles massed as much as the entire State line. The number of writhing, gesturing tentacles arrayed in front of him reminded him of a horde of pythons leisurely contemplating potential prey.

One of the unabashedly curious officials bade the arrivals and their escort halt. Silence ensued while additional stares were exchanged. Standing in a hall that seemed large enough to manufacture its own weather, surrounded by alien giants, some of whom were even bigger than his friend Braouk, Walker waited for whatever might come. There was no backing out now, he realized. No changing one's mind and asking to be returned to the safety of the *Jhevn-bha*. And he didn't think offering to prepare dinner for the dozen officials squatting before him would allow him and his friends to avoid having to satisfy the still mysterious, unstated "requirement." Right now, the only thing available to cut with a knife was the tension.

It was broken by the Tuuqalian squatting at the far left end of the line. Walker's implant had no trouble translating the straightforward local singsong.

"Let the nearer biped begin first!"

With the representatives of the Niyyuu and Iollth standing to his right, it struck Walker that the speaker was referring to him. Dozens of eyestalks immediately coiled in his direction. He could have done without the attention.

Turning to Braouk's familiar, reassuring shape, he whispered, "What are we supposed to do? What am I expected to do? How do we go about satisfying this demand of your people to prove that we're sufficiently civilized and sensitive enough to be allowed to visit your world?"

Each nearly the size of his head, both eyes curved close to him. It was a measure of how far he had come and how much he had changed that their proximity did not unsettle him in the least.

"You must do, the same as I, friend Marcus."

Seeking clarification, he'd hit upon only bafflement. Aware that he was now the focus of the attention of everyone in the vast hall, from Tuuqalian escorts and officials to his own companions, he struggled for understanding.

"Do the same? The same what?" He spread both hands. "You know as well as anyone what I can do, Braouk. I can broker trades, and I can cook."

His massive friend was unrelenting. "You must do one more thing, Marcus. You must do as I." A pair of tentacles swept down the length of the assembled. "Show them the level of your civilization. Show them your sensitive nature. Recite to them, as best you can, a saga. Intonation is important, inspiration is foremost, format is forgiving."

Near Walker's feet and oblivious to the significance of the moment, George was snickering. "Go ahead, Marc. Sing them a saga of humankind. You could use your own original kindly, polite, human profession as a springboard."

"You're not helping," Walker hissed at his canine companion. Furiously, he tried to think of a subject that would satisfy the demands of those assembled to pass judgment not merely on him, but on his entire species. If he failed, it might not mean a crisis: one or more of his companions might proceed to satisfy the Tuuqalian requirement. But it would not be a good way to begin. Besides, now that he was here, he very much wanted to see something of Braouk's homeworld. There was also a matter of pride involved. When faced with a challenge, he had never let his firm down. Could he do no less for his entire species? Fortunately, he didn't have to sing—only to recite. Choosing his words carefully, modifying them to fit the traditional Tuuqalian saga-pattern, he cleared his throat, took a deep breath and began.

"Big blue blot, floating out in space, so far. Very far away, too far for me, to reach. Blue with water, green with growing plants, white clouds. One special city, by a big lake, my home. It miss it, the good and bad, so much. My heart hurts, every time I think, of it. It's your help, that we really need, right now. To find Earth, and my friend Sque's, home-worlds."

He rambled on, sometimes without effort, at other times having to pause as long as he dared to think furiously (did speed count?). The longer he scribed the story, the easier the words came. Having lived alongside Braouk for so long made settling into the proper speech pattern simpler than he would have believed possible.

*Amazing what one could pick up over the years, depending on the company one kept,* he thought even as he continued to churn out words and phrases of parallel pacing. The longer he spun narrative without interruption or objection, the more confident he felt that he was at least being listened to, and the wider the field of acceptable subject matter that occurred to him. Then, with unexpected abruptness, he hit a mental wall. With no more reminiscences to share, no further hopes to declaim, and growing slightly hoarse besides, he just stopped. If the Tuuqalians who had been watching and listening to him had been expecting or waiting for a big finish, it was denied to them. The stress of fulfilling the demand had exhausted him physically as well as mentally.

A wet nose nudged his leg. George looked up at him with as solemn an expression as he had ever seen on the dog's face. "That," his friend informed him somberly, "was as eloquent a collection of words as I've ever heard dribble from your protruding lips, man."

"Thanks, George." Both the Niyyuuan and Iollth representatives also crowded around him to offer muted congratulations, while Braouk threatened to smother his much smaller friend with a complimentary lashing of tentacles. As usual, Sque vouchsafed offering anything like a direct compliment. But neither did she hiss her usual ration of denigration. In fact, when he happened to glance in her direction, the size and shape of the bubbles she was casually burbling from her flexible breathing tube suggested a certain modicum of nonverbal approval.

None of which mattered, of course. Ignoring the continuing congratulations of his friends, he shifted his attention to the line of massive, convened adjudicators. They, too, had been conversing quietly among themselves ever since he had finished. Now the Tuuqalian on the right end of the line, farthest from the one who had instructed Walker to begin, fluttered its single nostril as beartrap-like jaws parted.

"Is good enough, to allow for welcoming, your kind."

Walker's spirits rose as if he had just pulled off a three-way trade involving dollars, euros, and a shipload of raw mahogany. Since at present his kind referred only to him, he assumed he was in.

He was given no time to savor his accomplishment. It was the turn of the young Niyyuuan astronomer to saga-spin on behalf of his people. Having had time to prepare, thanks to Walker's inspired bit of homesick spieling, Habr-wec declaimed in proper Tuuqalian the configuration of stars and planets, of his hopes for learning more about them, of how this journey was the fulfillment of a dream held by every fellow astronomer relegated to observing the heavens only from a planetary surface, and of his hopes that his counterparts on this beautiful world would help him and his friends to realize their goal of returning to their homes the victims of unwarranted abduction presently stranded in their midst. As he spoke, his neck frill flared fully erect, and like a quartet of furry metronomes, his tails kept time to his speaking. Nothing could be done about his Niyyuuan voice, however, the sandpapery nature of which grated even on the recessed hearing organs of the tolerant and attentive row of Tuuqalians.

Despite that unavoidable awkwardness, the concise saga spun by the unexpectedly expressive young scientist also passed muster.

In spite of having been granted far more time to prepare, De-sil-jimd of the Iollth seemed hesitant to begin. Not nervous, Walker thought. Just uncertain. As fidgeting became noticeable among the impatient line of Tuuqalian adjudicators, Walker and his friends gathered around the reluctant communications specialist.

"What's wrong?" Walker whispered. "Can't you think of anything to say?"

"Iollth good fighters, but maybe that all," Habr-wec suggested tactlessly. Walker threw him a dirty look, which did no harm because it was not understood.

De-sil-jimd straightened on his powerful hind legs. "That is not the problem. I can think of much to say, and the form of speaking is not difficult for my kind." Small dark eyes met Walker's. "The problem is that I can only think of one subject to speak strongly about, and it is nothing like the subjects to which you or the skinny Niyyuu have spoken. I am worried it might offend our welcomers."

Walker frowned. "What subject were you thinking of using as a basis for your saga?"

De-sil-jimd turned on his oversized feet to better regard the taller human. "Predation. The Hyfft would understand."

Walker nodded knowingly. It was certainly a contrast with the serene, peaceful subject matter which he and Habr-wec had addressed. But if it was all the Iollth could think of around which to spin the requisite saga . . .

How would the Tuuqalians react? There was only one way to find out.

"Might as well give it a try," he suggested to the bottom-heavy alien. "All they're likely to do is refuse your people landing rights. Habr-wec and I are already in."

The Iollth gestured tersely. Turning slowly, he faced the line of increasingly impatient Tuuqalians and, in a high-pitched voice that was a welcoming contrast to the Niyyuuan discordance that had preceded it, began.

To everyone's relief, the pugnacious nature of the communications specialist's short narrative was in no way off-putting to the attentive jury. If anything, they appreciated its robust nature more than did any of De-sil-jimd's mildly appalled companions. Thinking back to the unrestrained ferocity Braouk had exhibited on board the Vilenjji capture ship, Walker realized he ought not to have been surprised. The Tuuqalians were as open to aggressive saga-spinning as they were to more tranquil reminiscing.

That left only two among the visitors to gain their hosts' tentacle-wave of approval. Her initial reluctance to even participate now appeared in direct contrast to Sque's dynamic verbal invention on behalf of her kind. In fact, after half an hour of tale-telling in perfect Tuuqalian form accompanied by much waving of tentacle tips and blowing of bubbles, those who constituted the imposing array of judges were starting to squirm once again, though this time not from impatience. It was left to Walker to approach the energetically orating K'eremu, crouch down to eye level, and make gentle shushing motions.

Halting in mid-declamation, four tentacles held aloft and preparing to gesture dramatically, she peered over at him. "Something is wrong, Marcus Walker?"

He had long since learned that delicate diplomacy was wasted on a K'eremu. "I think you've sagaed enough, Sque. Time to let our hosts pass judgment. Superb invention, by the way."

"Of course it is," she replied, lowering two of the four uplifted tentacles. "All of my vocalizing is superb. As to letting our hosts pass judgment, their approval of my modest efforts was a foregone conclusion as soon as I began. But I am far from finished." She turned away from him and back to the line of exceedingly tolerant adjudicators. "In point of fact, I have barely concluded the introduction I have composed, and have not yet commenced the body of the recitation."

"And a wonderful recitation it was!" Walker declared loudly, so that all present would be certain to hear him. At the same time, he was gesturing to Braouk. No other Tuuqalian would have understood the significance of that gesture. But to Braouk, who had spent as much time in the company of the K'eremu as had Walker, its meaning and significance were clear.

Stepping forward, he promptly picked up the paused Sque and raised her high. This was her favored mode of travel, carried aloft above everyone else by the prodigiously strong Tuuqalian. She therefore did not object to the unrequested ascension, until a second massive tentacle folded itself gently but firmly around her midsection, collapsing her speaking tube against the slick maroon flesh of her torso. The closest human physical equivalent of Braouk's action would be pinching someone's lips together.

Slitted eyelids expanded. Unable to speak or blow bubbles of protest, she remained elevated above her companions but quite speechless. A necessary interruption, Walker felt certain, lest they find themselves forced to endure her clever but interminable verbal invention for hours on end while trying the patience of the adjudicators.

Despite the surgical delicacy of the intercession, it did not go unnoticed by the assembled panel. Eying the effectively muffled Sque, a Tuuqalian near the middle of the line rumbled inquisitively, "Why is the small many-limbed one now silent, and why is she gesticulating so actively with her appendages?"

Looking back, Walker watched as Braouk promptly passed a second massive tentacle across Sque's body, stilling much of the activity that had drawn the adjudicator's attention.

"It's part of a private ritual of hers," Walker hurriedly improvised. "She likes to be carried. As you've been informed, the four of us who were abducted have been together for some time. Despite being of different species, we've come to an intimate knowledge and appreciation of one another's needs and habits." Gesturing in the direction of the now scrupulously restrained Sque, he lowered his voice slightly. "Our K'eremu's high intelligence is balanced by an unfortunate addiction to certain herbal supplements. Nervousness at the need to satisfy the traditions of Tuuqalia probably led her to . . . well, surely you understand." Repeatedly, he put the fingers of one hand up to his mouth.

Some discussion among the Tuuqalians finally led to the one on the far left announcing, "The presentation of the representative from K'erem is accepted. Only one remains." All eyestalks promptly inclined in the direction of the only quadruped among the visitors.

Walker crouched down beside his friend. "You don't have to do this, George. I know you didn't really want to come." He gestured toward the others. "Everyone else has satisfied the requirement. That means all the crews, from their scientific compliments, to the salivating media representatives, to those who only want to rest and do some sightseeing, have been granted access. You can go back up on the shuttle and relax on board until we're ready to leave this system. You don't have to stay down here."

Cocking his head to one side, the dog looked over at him. "You think I suffered through another atmospheric roller-coaster ride just to turn around and slink back with my tail tucked between my legs? Now that I'm here, I damn sure wouldn't mind a roll in the local grass, or its equivalent." So saying, he took a couple of steps toward the row of expectant Tuuqalians. Walker straightened and, after one more glance to ensure that the irate Sque was still being held firmly in check, waited to see what the dog would do.

It was impossible to tell whether George had been rehearsing while everyone else had been addressing the Tuuqalians, or if his saga was spontaneous. Whichever, he did not hesitate.

"I'm alone here, if I get home, still alone. The only one, of my small kind, who speaks. Gave me intelligence, did our wicked captors, without asking. Gave me speech, not as a gift, or present. To help them, to easier sell me, to others." Lowering his head, his ears falling limp, the dog pawed evocatively at the lapis-blue floor. "I can't decide, if it's a blessing, or curse. I can't decide, if I should return, to Earth. Being a freak, however affecting and admirable, is hard."

As George continued, the immense hall became utterly silent. The small dog-voice bounced off walls so distant the words barely reached, returning as echoes that rarely rose above a whisper. Even Sque, unable to do more than listen and watch, stilled the outraged writhing of her tentacles and paid attention to the small speaker.

When George finally finished and turned to rejoin his friends, it was all Walker could do to repress the tears that had begun to well up at the corners of his eyes. In their place, he did the only thing he was sure would not be misconstrued. Kneeling, he smiled and patted his companion gently on his head.

The Tuuqalian on the far right of the line spoke in a rumble that might have been ever so subtly different from all that had preceded it.

"An exemplar of sensitivity and saga-composing, the small quadruped is accepted, as are any others of his kind."

"I'm the only one," George replied quietly, clearly affected by his own wistful words. "But thanks anyway."

Walker bent over. "That was beautiful, George. I didn't know you had it in you."

"Why not?" Shielded from view of all but his human, one fur-shaded eye winked unexpectedly at the man. "It was only a bit of doggerel."

Grinning, Walker straightened and looked over at Braouk, who as a preventative measure still held the no-longer-struggling Sque in his grasp. "Then we're done here, right? We can let Gerlla-hyn know that it's okay to send his people down, and De-sil-jimd can inform his caste, who'll so notify the rest of the Iollth."

Braouk started to reply. Before he could, a Tuuqalian near the center of the line pistoned erect on his four supportive tentacles and shuffled forward. All four massive upper limbs thrust straight out, the tips coming together to form a pyramidal point. It struck Walker with sudden disquiet that the point was aimed directly at him.

"*Challenge!* I claim challenge!" the Tuuqalian thundered. Unlike George's plaintive opus, the stentorian Tuuqalian phrases boomed repetitively off the high, perfectly curved walls of the hall.

"Challenge?" Walker turned quickly to Braouk. "What is this? I thought we'd all, individually, satisfied your people's requirement for admittance. What's this 'challenge' business?" Though he spoke to Braouk, he found himself staring as if mesmerized at those pointing tentacle tips. There was no question about where they were aimed. When he moved toward Braouk, they followed him.

His hulking companion gently set Sque back down on the floor. Though the body of the livid K'eremu had swelled with fury to the point where her skin threatened to split, she somehow managed to internalize her rage. Only the serious nature of the demanding Tuuqalian who had trundled forward swayed her to contain the flood of vituperation that had been building up within. Her quivering restraint allowed Braouk to respond without having to raise his voice.

"It is a, right reserved to the, first greeters," he rumbled apologetically. "It can only be made one time. A challenge between one representative of Tuuqalia and one visitor. It appears that you are the one to have been so honored."

Walker swallowed, his attention switching rapidly back and forth between the Tuuqalian who was his good friend and the other who was—his challenger?

"Somehow I don't feel especially honored. What does this challenge involve?" His tone was hopeful. "More saga-spinning?"

"I am afraid not." Braouk explained as George, De-sil-jimd, Habr-wec, and even a softly sputtering Sque gathered around to find out what was going on. "By your excellent individual recitations, you have already demonstrated that your respective species are sufficiently civilized and sensitive. To complete the requirement for access, one of you must additionally demonstrate bravery. It is a great honor to be the one so selected to participate in such a demonstration." Though it weighed forty kilos or so, the tentacle that reached out to rest kindly on Walker's left shoulder did not seem half so heavy as the imponderable that continued to hover menacingly in the air.

"How do I do that," he finally muttered uneasily, "if not by spinning a saga?"

"Is not complicated," Braouk assured him, "and not take long, to accomplish." While the one upper appendage still rested on the human's shoulder, another pair indicated the Tuuqalian who had stepped forward and was waiting expectantly. "You and the adjudicator who has issued the challenge will fight."

**11**

I t took only seconds for the full import of Braouk's words to sink in. Walker's response was immediate. "If it's acceptable, I wouldn't mind if someone else received this great honor."

Braouk's eyes rose slightly on their stalks. "That is not possible, friend Marcus. For example, if it was possible to do so, I would gladly accept the challenge on your behalf. But the challenge was made to you. To alter it in any way would be to severely diminish its significance."

"I can live with that," he assured his friend. *Literally*, he thought frantically.

"I understand your concern." Braouk tried to reassure him. "Everything will be all right, friend Marcus. You must trust me."

"I do trust you," Walker told him. With one hand, he indicated the looming mass of his patiently waiting challenger. If anything, the Tuuqalian who had spoken was bigger than Braouk. Like Walker's friend, the challenge-issuer weighed well over a ton. Nor did his size make him slow. Walker had previously seen ample evidence of what a rampaging Tuuqalian could do, when Braouk had finally been freed from captivity on board the Vilenjji capture ship. He had no desire whatsoever to expose himself to similar berserking.

"I just don't trust that one," he finished.

A second tentacle tip fondly stroked Walker's side as both bulging oculars dipped close. "You must do this thing, friend Marcus. It is a requirement."

*How many more requirements do your people expect us to fulfill?* Walker found himself wondering apprehensively. He eyed the huge Tuuqalian who had issued the challenge. Having observed his friend Braouk in action, he knew that the Tuuqalians' size belied their quickness. But they moved around on four thick, stumpy, lower tentacles. Would he have any kind of an advantage there?

Rather than seek an advantage where none presented itself, maybe he would be better off just relying on Braouk's assurances. There seemed no way around it.

"All right. If I have to do this to obtain the aid of your species' scientists, then I'll do it."

Braouk's eyestalks withdrew and he turned toward the line of waiting adjudicators. "The human accepts the challenge!"

*Fight that monster?* Walker mused. How, and with what? Was he expected to contest the challenge with weaponry? There was none in evidence, and no sign of any being brought forth. That, at least, was some small relief. Not that the Tuuqalian would need anything more than its natural ability and strength to reduce him to a pulp, if it was so inclined. Surely he couldn't be expected to go one-on-one with it from a purely physical standpoint? Such a matchup was ludicrous on the face of it. And where was this contest supposed to take place? He quickly found out.

Leaving a hole in the line of adjudicators, the Tuuqalian who had issued the challenge bellowed thunderously and came lumbering off the dais directly toward him.

De-sil-jimd and Habr-wec backed quickly away from the human, the Niyyuun's tails twitching in agitation, the Iollth using its oversized feet to retreat with commendable swiftness. Sque scrambled right back up into the same strong limbs of Braouk whose embrace she had so energetically fought to escape only moments earlier. George rushed to take cover behind their Tuuqalian friend.

"You were a good friend, Marc. Been nice knowing you!"

"Wait, everybody slow down a minute!" Walker protested.

No one paid either his native English words or their respective simultaneous translations the least attention. The rest of the adjudicators had brought forth an array of small instruments and were monitoring the sudden activity with undisguised interest. Was his performance being rated? Walker started to back up and begin a desperate search for someplace that might lie beyond the reach of the advancing Tuuqalian.

The official welcoming examination had taken an unexpected and even irrational turn. Everything had suddenly and without warning been turned upside down. What had happened to the brusque but courteous Tuuqalians who had been so concerned with measuring the level of their visitors' civilizations and their degree of sensitivity? From the lofty intellectual endeavor of creating saga-stories he now found himself thrust into the shiny, polished equivalent of little more than a crude arena. It was as if Virgil had suddenly been ordered to stop composing odes and pick up the armor and weapons of a gladiator.

In his college days, Walker had been something of the modern equivalent of a gladiator. But facing the oncoming Tuuqalian who had challenged him, he did not even have the benefit of helmet and pads. Not that they would have been of much use, anyway.

Needing time, he started running. Shorn of hiding space and bereft of any weapons, he could do nothing else. His friends did their best to cheer him on and uphold his spirits. Hailing as they did from martial societies, both the Niyyuu and the Iollth were more energized by the confrontation than Sque or George, who feared for their companion instead of urging him onward.

Their support was not missed in any case, because there was nowhere to urge him onward to. The walls of the great hall were smooth and gently curved, all lighting and electronics having been fully integrated into the building material itself. Breathing hard, he reached the portal through which they had originally entered. Unsurprisingly, it was locked, but checking it out had been worth a try. With his Tuuqalian challenger looming up fast behind him, Walker bolted to his right, racing around the circumference of the room. In the center of the room, several of the adjudicators were chatting amiably with one another. As he ran, Walker found himself wishing for a couple of small nuclear devices: one for his pursuer, the other for the line of local observers who appeared to be enjoying themselves at his expense. As arriving supplicants, naturally neither he nor any of his companions had been allowed to appear armed before the adjudicators.

At least there was no furniture for him to trip over. Having circled half the oval hall, he found himself nearly back where he had started, close to his friends but at the far right-hand end of the line of adjudicators. He fancied he could feel hot breath on his back and saw-edged teeth clamping down on his skull and spine. He could not linger. Having no time to think, he acted.

He ran straight toward the nearest Tuuqalian.

Busily manipulating a pair of enigmatic devices, it eyed him in surprise, both eyestalks rising upward and as far away as possible from his small but determined onrushing form. The two adjudicators nearest the one Walker was rapidly approaching shifted their position for a better view. Meanwhile, Walker's pursuer had extended all four upper tentacles in an attempt to bring him down.

Darting behind the nearest adjudicator, Walker saw that his risky guess had been correct. Not having challenged him, they did not interfere. They did, however, try to get out of his way. Had there been two or three of them, they might have managed it. But filled with a dozen of the huge creatures, the dais was too crowded. No matter how hard his pursuer tried to envelop the human in its questing tentacles, Walker managed to dart nimbly behind one or two of his hunter's colleagues.

How long could this go on? he wondered wildly. Was there some kind of time limit, or was the contest expected to continue until one or the other combatant fell? Noticing that one of the adjudicators had set its recorder, or whatever the device was, down beside its lower limbs while it worked intently on a second device, Walker nipped in and picked up the instrument before its startled owner could react. The Tuuqalian-sized device was comfortingly heavy in his palm. It was no gun, but it was solid and well-made. Though he'd played linebacker and not quarterback, he'd always had a good arm. Winded now, his expression grim, he turned to face his pursuer.

Tentacles waving, jaws clashing, the challenger came roaring toward him, forcing a path through the milling adjudicators. Evidently it either had not seen Walker pick up the small device, or did not care that the human had done so. Without giving his pursuer a chance to reflect on possibilities, Walker took aim and hurled the apparatus as hard as he could. It struck the oncoming Tuuqalian solidly in its right eye before bouncing off and landing on the floor.

Immediately, the hulking alien halted, its lower limbs scrambling to bring it to a stop. All four grasping tentacles reached up and over to cradle the bruised eye, which had retracted completely into the ocular recess on the same side of the Tuuqalian's body. Several fellow adjudicators rushed to aid their injured colleague.

The others, who heretofore had been milling about indifferently while working with their own individual instrumentation, now proceeded to cluster around Walker. Their massive, menacing forms towered over him.

Well, it had been a good run, he told himself. It wasn't as if he and his friends knew Earth's location and were about to embark on the homeward journey tomorrow. At least George might still make it. He hoped the dog would remember him fondly, and how Walker had sacrificed himself, albeit without having been given a choice, to satisfy the demands of the Tuuqalians and thereby allow his friends to gain access to Tuuqalian scientific knowledge.

It struck him that no one was striking him. The assembly of Tuuqalians who had gathered around him were, in fact, making noises that his implanted translator insisted on deciphering not as threats or curses, but as compliments. The majority of the comments were directed not at him, but to one another.

"Well rendered . . . ," one was saying. "Intelligent decision, to run and not try to stand its ground . . . unusually well-balanced for a creature with only two such spindly limbs and no tail." Walker, who was proud of the effort he had expended in the weight room while in college and who had subsequently worked hard to maintain as much of an aging football player's physique as he could, had never before heard his legs referred to as "spindly." The comments and observations continued.

"Excellent manipulative digit to ocular coordination . . . demonstrated courage by running in among us not knowing what our individual reactions might be . . . clear ability to make use of ordinary objects as weaponry . . ."

It went on in that vein for a while. If nothing else, it gave him time to catch his breath. None of it made any sense. One minute he was being chased around the hall by one of their number whose apparent intent was to do him grievous bodily harm, and the next they were all standing around praising his flight and paltry counterattack. His confusion only deepened when the one who had challenged him approached anew. The eye he had struck was darkened, but Tuuqalian oculars were apparently as tough as the rest of their massive bodies.

"Nothing but sensible and effective reactions. I thank you," it rumbled.

If it hadn't been embedded inside his head, Walker would have tapped his translator to make sure it was still working. "You're thanking me?" he mumbled as an excited George ran up to rejoin him. "For hitting you in the eye?"

The orb in question described a small circle on the end of its strong, flexible stalk. "Admirable inspiration! As was your darting and weaving. You have more than satisfied the final requirement." All four upper tentacles crossed one another in front of the huge, hirsute body to form a precise geometric pattern. "Allow me to be the first to formally welcome you and your companions to Tuuqalia." Having delivered the official welcome that Walker and his friends had been so anxiously seeking, it turned away from him to resume chatting with its fellow adjudicators.

"You all right?" He became aware that George was squinting up at him.

"Yeah, I'm fine. More emotionally exhausted than anything else." Walker gazed at the gathering of huge Tuuqalians. All seemed completely at ease now. No further questions were directed his way, nor was there any indication revenge would be sought for the injury he had inflicted on one of their own. With George at his side, he tottered down the slight slope to rejoin his waiting companions. "Otherwise, just a little a dazed, I guess. What just happened here?"

It was left to Braouk to explain. "Enriching ennobling sagas, since Tuuqalian civilization's beginnings, we create. Reverential tales and inspiring stories. After thousands of years of composition, even the most inventive composers among us have difficulty imagining new themes, new subjects, new visualizations worthy of their efforts. Seeks fresh inspiration, for ideas and composition, every Tuuqalian. New stimulation can, be difficult to obtain, and recognize." Upper tentacles gestured meaningfully. "I am sure you can understand, friend Marcus, that when such presents itself, it is eagerly seized upon."

Walker remained doubtful. "I'm still not sure I understand . . ."

"You," George cut in. "The whole challenge and chase thing—stimuli." The dog nodded in the direction of the milling adjudicators, some of whom had begun to depart but all of whom continued conversing animatedly among themselves. "No wonder the one you hit in the eye thanked you. Not only will he—I think it was a he—get inspired to compose from chasing you, you provided an additional and unexpected incentive when you fought back so effectively."

"Then it was all a sham." Surrounded by his companions, a worn-out Walker stood mumbling to himself. "Just a charade designed to provide new material for saga-spinning."

Braouk eyed his friend gravely, one eye hovering on either side of the human's head. "Your palpable fear, was while being chased, most inspiring. It will no doubt provide the basis for many stirring overtures."

Settling his attention on one eye, Walker regarded the Tuuqalian hesitantly. "Then I was never in any real danger?"

"No."

"What would have happened if I'd just stood still and waited? If I hadn't run or resisted?"

"Nothing," Braouk admitted. "You and the others would have been granted the access to Tuuqalia that you seek. But many here today to pass judgment on you would have gone away disappointed."

"Disappointed, hell!" Walker blurted abruptly. "I was scared to death! I thought that thing, the one who had challenged me, was going to tear me to pieces!"

"Yours was not, the only inspirational source, here today," Braouk replied blithely. "The one who was chosen to challenge you was not only fortunate in being so selected, but played his part well. An eye can heal of its own accord, but the shock of your response provided inspiration that is rare. Ours is a civilized world, wherein the unforeseen is always a delight, because it is so uncommonly encountered."

"You could have told me," Walker grumbled. "You might have warned me."

"Did I not say that everything would be all right?" Both eyes drew back, a gesture that made focusing on the Tuuqalian easier mentally if not physically.

"It's hard to trust anyone's opinion, Braouk, even yours, when you've just been challenged to combat by something ten times your size."

Edging closer, the Tuuqalian placed a comradely tentacle thick as a tree root around Walker's shoulders. "If I had explained fully, and you had been made aware in advance of the purpose of the challenge, would you have reacted similarly? Would you have run as hard and fast as you did? Would you have fought back, to the point of lightly injuring your challenger?"

Braouk had him there, Walker had to admit. "No, of course not. I probably wouldn't have done anything."

"Doing nothing is, a poor foundation for, saga-writing." Like a lazy anaconda, the tentacle slid slowly off his shoulders. "Now, not only will you be able to visit Tuuqalia and confer with our astronomers and other scientists, your name and presence will go down in contemporary saga-telling."

"I'm so pleased," Walker commented dryly.

"Ask him if you're entitled to royalties." George nudged his friend irreverently.

"I'll settle for being alive and in one piece." He took a deep breath, finally at ease.

"I knew it all along."

"What?" He turned in the direction of the familiar mocking voice. Sque scrambled forward. "You are all of you blind as cave-dwelling zithins. The signs were present for anyone to see, and to interpret correctly." She blew a single, disdainful bubble. "If any of you had taken the time to study the body language of the one Tuuqalian in our midst, you would have been able to apply that knowledge to the understated movements of the rank of adjudicators." One tentacle tip cleaned the linear surface of a steel-gray eye. "To anyone who had troubled to do so, interpreting the gestures and tentacle twitches that were rampant among those deigning to pass judgment on us would have been a simple matter."

"I've got a gesture you could try to interpret," Walker groused. "If you had some idea what was going to happen, why didn't you say something? Why didn't you warn me?"

While the one tentacle tip continued with its eye cleaning, a different pair gestured in Braouk's direction. "My rationale for not doing so was similar, if not identical to, that of our overlarge friend. I could see no purpose in intervening in a custom that was so clearly important to those locals whose ultimate opinion would decide whether or not we would find assistance here. Also, even had I expressed my opinion to you, it would not have changed anything. The challenge would still have been issued, and would still have had to be met."

Advancing toward him, she halted at his feet, her eyes and speaking tube at the level of his waist. He felt her grip his sides with first one appendage, then another, and another, until all ten had secured a firm grip. Climbing up his front like a logger ascending toward the top of a tree, she halted only when she was eye to eye with him. Though nowhere near as strong as Braouk, he was still sturdy enough to hold his ground even with her hanging onto him. He was more startled by the unexpected intimacy than by her modest weight. She had never before touched him with anything more than a tentacle tip or two. Now, unexpectedly, she was close enough for him to see the fine gray-pink cilia inside the end of her breath-ing tube. Those strange, horizontal black pupils gazed deeply into his own.

"You are my friend, Marcus Walker. We have been together for a very long time indeed. We have relied on one another to continue living. Despite your unyielding internal skeleton, your stiff and gangly movements, your awkward gestures, your deficiency of limbs, and an intelligence that even after much time spent in my company can still only properly be described as minimal, I would not let anything untoward happen to you that it was in my power to prevent." So saying, she climbed back down off him, leaving only a faint scent of damp mustiness clinging to his clothes.

"You should know by now, if you have learned nothing else, that I do nothing without first considering all possible ramifications. Concerning your recent problematic confrontation, I think you will admit that it has all turned out for the best." Drawing herself up to her full four-foot height, she made a show of adjusting several of the strands of reflective metal and crystal that decorated her body.

He stood staring at her, slightly stunned. In nearly two years of traveling together, it was the closest she had come to expressing anything deeper than wan tolerance for his existence. Sarcasm and the customary jibes about his appearance and mental capabilities aside, what she had just done and said bordered on actual affection. He hardly knew what to say.

Perhaps she sensed his shock, or his discomfiture. "I did not bite you, and even if I had, I suspect there is nothing in my saliva capable of inflicting paralysis on a lifeform so primitively resilient. You may, as soon as you wish, confirm the reality of this observation by moving one or more of your inadequate quartet of appendages, or if the effort of coordinating the requisite muscles and organs is not too much of a strain, by speaking."

"I—thank you, Sque. I won't question your motives again. Either for doing something, or for not doing anything."

Swelling up halfway, she exhaled a stream of aerial froth. "Does a modicum of intelligence begin to show itself? With much continued effort, you may in truth some day achieve an adequate level of common sense. At your current rate of maturation, I should estimate that you might reach that stage in only another two or three hundred of your years." Pivoting on her central axis, she wandered over to ascend Braouk, in order to utilize him as a platform from which to address several of the remaining adjudicators.

George had been no less taken aback by the decapod's unanticipated affirmation. "Whataya know? The squid likes you."

"I never suspected," Walker mumbled, "I never *expected* . . ."

"Not exactly demonstrative, is she?" The dog snorted softly. "No wonder her kind don't mate very often. Aside from conversing via casual insult, if it takes one of them two years to admit to something as low-key as ordinary friendship, think how long it must take two of them to decide to mate."

Ears erect and alert, he nodded in the K'eremu's direction. She was once more comfortably ensconced on one of Braouk's upper limbs, several of her appendages gesticulating in support of whatever edict of the moment she was currently handing down to a pair of attentive Tuuqalian adjudicators.

Everything she had said to him was all very nice, Walker told himself. Welcome, even. But he labored under no illusions. Her admission of friendship notwithstanding, he knew that if the opportunity to return to K'erem presented itself and required that he be sacrificed to make it possible, she would not hesitate to forfeit his hopes and dreams. That was the canny, experienced trader in him talking. He did not mind admitting it to himself.

Of them all, certainly Sque herself would have understood his caution, and no doubt approved.

*

While Sobj-oes, her young colleague Habr-wec, and the rest of the Niyyuuan astronautics team joined with members of the Iollth science caste in compiling a list of formal requests for information to be presented to the Tuuqalian astronomy establishment, a relieved and exuberant Broullkoun-uvv-ahd-Hrashkin reveled not only in the sights and sounds and smells of a homeworld he thought he might never see again, but in the opportunity to share them with the companions of his Vilenjji captivity.

"Come with me, we are going north, this dawning!" he boomed the following morning as he lumbered into the port facilities that had been made available for the visitors' use for the duration of their stay on Tuuqalia.

A sleepy George looked up from his oversized pillow and barked softly before adding, "What's 'north'? If it isn't something unique and special, I'm staying right here 'til it's time to leave again." Mumbling to himself, he rolled onto his other side. "Seen one alien world, seen 'em all."

He let out a sharp bark of surprise as one massive tentacle, its grip gentle as a prehensile feather, picked him up and tossed him playfully into the air. Since Braouk was some nine feet tall, rather high into the air.

"Don't do that!" the dog yelped. Panting hard, he cast a reproachful eye on their hulking friend as Braouk set him carefully back on his pillow. "What do you think I am—a cat?"

As the Vilenjji implants could not translate subjects for which there was no viable counterpart, Braouk admitted that he was at a loss to answer. But his enthusiasm was undimmed.

"To the north, lie the fabled plains, Serelth-idyr."

George refused to be impressed. "What's fabled about them?"

The massive, yellow-green torso bent toward George while both eyestalks dipped closer still. Each vertically pupiled eyeball was nearly as big as the dog. "Therein lies my home, that I have not seen since I was taken by the Vilenjji these all too many planetary revolutions ago. My family, all those I left behind, memories of whom were all that sustained me and kept me from going mad while I was alone in isolation aboard the Vilenjji ship."

"Maybe you wouldn't have been left in isolation," Walker pointed out judiciously, "if you hadn't gotten into the habit of trying to dismember everyone on the ship who made an attempt to talk to you. Remember?"

Both eyes arced in his direction. The multi-limbed giant was visibly abashed. "I was half-mad with despair for my situation and hardly to be held responsible for my actions. You, friend Marcus, should remember that." As he straightened, the buoyant eagerness that had accompanied his arrival returned. "You please come, to meet my friends, in Serelth-idyr. My friends and my family, who when they hear all of the saga of our meeting and our traveling, will welcome each of you as one of their own."

"Okay." Hopping down off his pillow-platform, George trotted over to stand next to Walker. "But only on two conditions. One, we don't have to listen to you recite all of the 'saga of our meeting and our traveling' that I don't doubt you've been slaving over ever since the Sessrimathe rescued us from the Vilenjji, and two, no matter how friendly your friends and family, no backslapping or hugging." By way of emphasis, he arched his shoulders and back. "I have a particular fondness for my spine."

Braouk gestured understandingly. "It is true, that Tuuqalian welcomings sometimes, become physical. I will see to it that you survive." Pivoting on his under-tentacles, he turned to Sque. "Will you come, purveyor of practiced invective, to Serelth-idyr?"

The K'eremu peered out from beneath the small fountain that had been brought in to provide for her comfort. "While the notion of spending time on 'plains' as opposed to a nice beach is not one that I would normally consider inviting, I confess that I am curious to see how oversized beings such as yourself coexist in a social environment. I will come and stay a while, at least until the usual ennui begins to set in."

"Then it is settled." Braouk turned one eye on George and Walker and the other on Sque. "I will keep two of you safe and dry, and the other safe and wet. Prepare yourselves, my friends, for an outpouring of exorbitant good feelings the likes of which you have never experienced and cannot imagine. Because to our very good fortune, on all the plains of the north it is harvest time!"

**12**

Though it seemed the size of a small ocean liner, Walker knew the vehicle that was carrying him and his friends northward from the port where they had been granted entrée to Tuuqalia was nothing more than the local equivalent of a cargo and passenger truck. It was also an impressive example of advanced local technology. Built to accommodate Tuuqalian-sized freight as well as Tuuqalians themselves, it emitted little more than a sonorous hiss as it streaked northward barely thirty meters above the ground at some three hundred kilometers an hour.

Once clear of the city and its port, the craft traveled over terrain that alternated between gently rolling and pancake flat. Though he glimpsed them at speed, Walker was able to see enough of the occasional villages they passed to recognize that they were both larger and more technologically developed than their counterparts on either Hyff or Niyu, though for sophistication they were still surpassed by the stylish, organically integrated municipalities of Seremathenn.

They traveled for several days, stopping occasionally to discharge or take on passengers and cargo. Walker and George looked forward to these pauses, not only because it gave them an opportunity to step outside the confines of the transport, but because they were able to see and experience something of their friend Braouk's homeworld outside a major city. Sque settled for studying through a port the numerous stops that were to her becoming increasingly repetitive. She was anxious to reach their destination, make her observations, return to the port where they had landed, and be about the business of finding her own way home. Xenology, she explained, was all very well and good, but it was no substitute for being among one's own kind. Walker did not disagree. With Sque, it would have been a waste of time to do so anyway.

There finally came a morning when Braouk told them to prepare to disembark. Little in the way of preparation was required, since Walker carried everything he and George needed in a single small satchel of Sessrimathe manufacture. A change of clothing, some hygienic supplies, dried emergency rations, vitamin and mineral supplements, and a remarkable spherical storage device that contained, among other things, not only all the recipes he had pored over and devised himself but three-dimensional recordings of his cooking performances. Together, these comprised the bulk of his "luggage." It made traveling easy, if not homey.

Led by Braouk, they exited the craft onto an unloading platform. It projected outward from two modest structures, a receiving building and a tall, windowless tower of unknown purpose. They were the only passengers to disembark at this stop, though they were joined by several large shipping containers. After a brief conversation among themselves, these split up and went their separate self-propelled ways, scooting along just above the ground on their own integrated propulsion units. When the transport craft finally departed, the four travelers were left alone on the dull bronzed, semicircular metal platform.

It was suddenly very quiet.

How the transport, or anyone else for that matter, could locate such unloading platforms was a matter of some interest to Walker and his friends. No roads led to it, no tracks or markers. It was completely surrounded by flat plains whose only distinguishing features were slightly different varieties of low vegetation. To the south and north, endless fields of something like three-meter-tall purple asparagus marched off toward opposite horizons. To the west, undulating rows of bulbous concave shapes thrust upward from manicured soil like thousands of nut-brown bathtubs balanced precariously on their drainage pipes. As Braouk explained, the bathtub-shaped growths consisted of solid, edible protein while the "pipes" were the stalks and stems from which they blossomed.

Eastward, the flora was neither as tall or as intimidatingly bizarre. The pirulek that dominated that direction was reassuringly green and no more than knee-high. However, the vine-like growths existed in a state of constant motion that was rendered more than a little eerie by the complete absence of any breeze. Despite their garish, unnatural colors and alien shapes, the asparagus trees and bathtub vegetation were less unsettling, Walker decided. At least they had they decency to remain still. Gazing at the twitchy, spasming field of pirulek was enough to unsettle even someone who had already spent time on several alien worlds.

A hum grew audible and suddenly Braouk was pointing excitedly. "My family comes, hardly daring to hope, so long."

The vehicle that slowed to a halt and hovered level with the raised edge of the unloading platform consisted of three flat congruent discs whose alignment formed a triangular shape. Domed on top, flat on the bottom, a large passenger-cargo compartment bulged upward from the point where the three discs intersected. From it emerged a quartet of Tuuqalians who threatened to trample Walker, George, and a sputtering Sque in their rush to wrap powerful tentacles around Braouk. There was much fulsome spouting of poetry. So much so that by the time Tuuqalia's sun had slipped below its horizon and a definite chill had begun to creep into the air, human, dog, and K'eremu had been rendered half-insensible by the interminable outpouring of greetings.

They were roused by Braouk's introductions that, mercifully, were unusually brief for their usually loquacious companion. They were tired, he explained to his family members, and unused to proper recitation. At this explanation, his welcoming relations became by turns apologetic and solicitous.

Bundling the returned abductee (whom none of his thankful family members had ever expected to see again) and his alien companions into the unusual craft, Braouk's relatives conveyed them to the family residence. Being built to Tuuqalian scale, this very modest (as Braouk had described it) center of cultivation struck Walker as no less than a small town. He was assured it was the home of only one family. On Tuuqalia, however, that was a more elastic term than on Earth. Some sixty multi-tentacled souls of varying age and experience lived and worked at the facility, and it seemed that every one of them wanted to personally congratulate not only the returning Braouk but his peculiar friends as well.

In addition to congratulations, much local food was proffered. Some of it his and Sque's personal Sessrimathe analyzers pronounced fit for human, canine, or K'eremu consumption, some the compact units declared inedible, and some the guests themselves rejected for reasons of taste or visual aesthetics. As the Tuuqalian diet was now largely vegetable based, though with significant infusions of synthetic and gathered meat proteins, Walker found there was quite a lot he could eat. George pronounced a good deal of it not only suitable for consumption, but tasty as well, while Sque nattered on about the need to eat to survive regardless of the incontestable insipidness of the nourishment that happened to be available.

When the Tuuqalians were informed that one of Braouk's friends was a professional chef whose talents had been recognized on multiple worlds, there was nothing for it but that Walker had to demonstrate his skills in a food preparation area the size of a small concert hall. By keeping it simple, he was able to prepare a couple of dishes using regional ingredients that did not outrage local palates, whereupon he was promptly anointed a hero as well as a guest. There was little the inhabitants of Tuuqalia enjoyed more than food, a trait Walker had recognized from the first time he had seen a hungry Braouk chomping down food bricks on board the Vilenjji capture ship. Little more, except the composing and reciting of a proper saga, of course.

It was when everyone had finished eating that Braouk was persuaded (without much effort, Walker noted) to tell something of the story of his experiences subsequent to his abduction from a sowing field one night years ago. As his implant translated his oversized friend's reminiscences, Walker was reminded of his own last evening on Earth, when he had been taken from his campsite by those sucker-armed, pebble-skinned, pointy-headed dissolute creatures called the Vilenjji. His and Braouk's experiences, if not the degree of resistance they had put up, were strikingly similar, notwithstanding that Walker's abduction had taken place under one moon, Braouk's beneath three, George's below a flickering neon sign advertising a local beer, and Sque's in relative darkness.

Having heard it all before, more times than any of them cared to count, the guests were excused from Braouk's never-ending ramblings.

Though all were members of one extended family, each individual Tuuqalian had their own dwelling. No two, mated or otherwise, lived under the same roof.

"At last," Sque commented upon learning the details of the local living arrangements, "some small hint of true civilization."

They were given the living quarters of a member of the family who was presently away on business. As the huge resting depression in the floor with its computerized reactive underbase reminded George of a time when he had been caught in deep mud and nearly suffocated, they elected to sleep instead on strands of the self-binding material that was used to fasten bundles of the purple asparagus-like growths for shipment. The cosseting material was pale blue and tough as spun titanium. A pile of it was supple as silk. The trick, Walker told himself as he fluffed up his makeshift bed, would be not to toss and turn too much in his sleep, or he was liable to strangle himself with the stuff.

Perhaps it was the unexpected softness that woke him. More likely it was the noise. Blinking, rubbing his eyes, he observed in the dim light that issued from the floor that both Sque and George continued to sleep soundly. Surely he had heard something?

There it was again. Rising, shaking off several strands of the fluffy binding material, he walked over to the other side of the enormous resting room. As he approached the wall beyond which he thought he heard the noise, the barrier detected his presence and unexpectedly went transparent. Since he was still half-asleep, the effect startled him into taking a nervous jump backward. When he warily retraced his footsteps and extended an arm, the pressure against his open, upraised palm assured him that the wall was still there. He wondered if anyone outside could see in as easily as he could see out.

The resting chamber of the dwelling was located on the top floor of the residence they were occupying. Thus, the now transparent wall provided him with a sweeping view across the nearby plain. Collectively, the family dwellings formed a giant circle, so that each one looked inward to family meeting, working, and dining areas and buildings, and out onto the family's extensive fields.

All three moons were up, with the result that it was quite bright outside. Though the light was wan and more than a little ethereal, he found that he could see clearly. One gibbous satellite was slightly larger than Earth's while the other two were considerably smaller. They cast an otherworldly, tripartite alien glow on the pastoral scene spread out before him. Stretching to the far, unpolluted horizon was an impressive field of the tall, purple-tinged growths he had first seen upon arriving at the disembarkation station.

Lowering his gaze and working it along the interior of the building's now transparent wall, he came to a softly radiant point of blue light that appeared to be fixed in place just above eye level. His eye level, he reminded himself. Fascinated by the steady glow, reasonably confident he was unlikely to encounter anything dangerous in an area designated for sleeping, he extended a finger toward it. A quick glance backward showed that George and Sque were still fast asleep, George nestled deep into a bed of silken wrappings similar to but less voluminous than Walker's own, Sque atop material not unlike an oversized damp sponge that had been improvised for her comfort.

As his finger slid into the blue glow, cool air enveloped his nude form. Large enough to pass a Tuuqalian, the opening that appeared allowed him egress to a small, curved balcony outside the sleeping chamber. Whatever had rendered the wall transparent had done the same for the balcony area, but once he stepped outside, both the flat extension beneath his feet and the wall behind him turned opaque. He could not see back inside the sleeping area. Only the blue glow of the activator, or doorknob, or whatever it was, remained to show him how to get back inside.

While the mellow ruddiness of the three moons casting their magic on the endless field was what had initially drawn his interest, his attention was quickly caught by a rush of motion off to his right. Moving to the edge of the porch, whose spidery plasticized railing was fortunately low enough for him to see over, he stared in awe at the busy nocturnal activity whose distant sounds had teased him awake.

Several streams of tightly baled purple stalks converged on a large, dun-colored structure far enough out in the fields so that the noise of the activity was little more than a distant buzz. Even at a distance and watching by moonlight, he could tell that there were hundreds of stalks in each hefty bundle, and hundreds of bundles in each line. Each self-propelled bundle remained equidistant from the one in front of it and the one behind. Tuuqalians mounted on individual scoop-shaped vehicles soared and darted among and around the parading streams of trussed vegetation. That much he could comprehend. But what unseen mechanism was supporting the truck-sized bales?

Suddenly, one of the vehicles broke off and came toward him, both craft and driver rapidly increasing in size. Other than exposing him to the slight and not unpleasant chill in the air, his utter lack of apparel did not trouble him. Any alien interest that might be shown in his naked anatomy would be purely academic. For that matter, unlike the Niyyuu or the Sessrimathe, the Tuuqalians themselves had dispensed with clothing.

He considered retreating back into the sleeping chamber, or at least waking George. Was it possible he had inadvertently intruded, even at a distance, on some restricted ceremony? As a visitor, he decided to hold his ground and plead ignorance. Besides, he'd already been seen.

Then he recognized the figure riding astride the scoop ship, and relaxed. It was Braouk. Emitting a deep, unwavering hum, the powerful little vehicle pulled up alongside the porch where he was standing. Eyestalks inclined toward him.

"The human night, as I observed it, means sleeping." A pair of huge upper appendages extended toward him. "You are awake and outside. This contradicts your normal activity. Is something the matter?"

"Not at all." Strolling to the edge of the intricate railing, he raised an arm and gestured in the direction of the ongoing activity. "I heard a noise and got up to see what was going on."

Touching controls, Braouk adjusted the scoop ship's position. As it pivoted on its axis, Walker took the opportunity to examine the vehicle more closely. With its smooth ivory-colored surface and lack of external instrumentation or ornamentation, it was simple and straightforward. Even the concave forward portion where Braouk rode was devoid of all but the most basic instrumentation. The local equivalent of a bicycle, Walker mused. Or a motorcycle, or ATV. Working transport.

Like a fast-growing tree branch, a pale yellow tentacle fluttered skyward. "In sky together, Teldk, Melevt, and Melaft, are simultaneously. Here in the northern plains, that means it is harvest time for the mature chimttabt. A special time, for all who live, near here." Descending, the limb gestured toward the ongoing streams of activity off to their right. "Would you like to see better?"

Walker didn't hesitate. Over the past couple of years, he had learned not to hesitate. He who hesitates might miss something. Besides, for a commodities trader, who knew what opportunities might one day present themselves? Perhaps even the chance to trade in bulk chimttabt. He had never been one to pass on an opportunity to learn about a new raw material.

"Sure, let's go," he told his hulking friend.

Braouk made room for the human between his own mass and the upward curving control area that was built directly into the material of the scoop ship itself. Snugging back against the bristle-like yellow-green fur of his friend kept Walker warm and, surprisingly, Braouk's hair was not as itch-inducing against his bare skin as it appeared. To think, he told himself, that at one time he would have fainted in terror if he had been compelled to endure such close proximity to a being like Braouk. Friends with him now for years, he had changed so much that he actually sought the close contact.

I have changed, he thought as the scoop ship accelerated toward the area of greatest activity. Changed in ways that as recently as three or four years ago he could not have imagined. But then, no one could. Three moons gazing down on him from high above, he sped in alien company aboard an alien craft toward a harvest of foodstuffs that more than anything else resembled lavender lightpoles. The food preparer half of him was intrigued by their culinary potential.

As they drew nearer, he saw that attached to the underside of each bale was an individual drive device that both propelled and guided it. Keeping perfect time and interval between one another, one bale after another made its way from distant field to local processing unit under the active supervision of scoop ship-riding Tuuqalians. The system was far more advanced than anything back home, he realized. Why load a truck with tomatoes and further burden it with a driver when you could set the load of vegetables to drive and guide itself to the intended destination?

A new sound reached him. Rising above the hum and whirr of technologically advanced reaping and processing machinery, it was at once familiar and new. New, because of the volume that was involved. Swooping and darting among the gigantic bales of recently harvested *chimttabt*, busy multi-limbed Tuuqalians burst out in boisterous song. No, not singing, he corrected himself. They were collaborating in an a cappella choir of alien saga-spinning. Their strangely pitched, collective voices boomed and echoed like velvet thunder across the unreaped vegetation below, rising and falling almost in concert with their vehicles as they managed the complicated business of *chimttabt* harvesting.

Massive alien muscles swelled against Walker's back as Braouk joined in the joyous chorus. After a few moments, he paused. While the scoop ship hovered, both eyes hooked around in front of Walker to look back at him.

"Will you join, in the communal recitation, my friend? I will provide you with the words. Your system of sound-making is smaller than ours, but the mechanics are not so very different."

"Why not?" After a few tries, listening and repeating, Walker felt he could mimic the Tuuqalian timbre near enough not to embarrass himself.

When next Braouk resumed his work, it was two voices that rose from the scoop ship: one local, the other imported. Human and Tuuqalian. Dipping and darting among the cumbersome bales, they occasionally passed close by other workers. Tentacles waved in their direction and astonished eyes extended fully on stalks as one worker after another goggled at the sight of the small, furless alien not only riding in tandem with one of their own, but joining lustily in the saga-spinning that accompanied the mechanical ballet of scoop ships and bales and multi-limbed operators. And all the while the three moons Teldk, Melevt, and Melaft beamed down from an alien sky on the festive commotion below, in which one lone and lonely human was a most unexpected participant.

The cool air, redolent of growing Tuuqalian things and pungent mechanical smells and the musky body odor of the methodical giant behind him, washed over his face and naked form. Moons and multilimbed monsters, truck-sized bales of plum-hued plants and deep-throated processing devices, danced before his now night-adapted eyes. What was the expression? "Never in your wildest dreams . . ."

It was, he mused as their scoop ship shot close enough past another for him to note with glee the surprised reaction of the other's operator, a long way from motoring boredly through the cornfields south of Chicago to visit friends in Springfield for the weekend.

\*

Tuuqalia's benign sun was just showing itself over the horizon when a jovial Braouk returned an exhausted but exultant Walker to the residence that had been assigned to him and his companions. As he stepped off the powerful little vehicle and back onto the building's upper-level porch, Marc expressed his gratitude by giving the Tuuqalian a punch between upper and lower right-side tentacles, hard enough that he hoped his oversized friend might actually feel it.

"What a great night! I can't thank you enough, Braouk. I've attended some all-night parties in my time, but nothing like this. The diving and swooping, the massed saga-chanting, the colors in the moonlight: it's something I'll remember forever."

"Was just harvest," the alien rumbled diffidently. "But I was, glad you could participate, friend Marcus. At such times, sharing is always best, with friends." One huge appendage curled fondly around Walker's shoulders, then withdrew.

Squinting against the rising alien sun, Walker waved as the scoop ship angled away from the balcony. Turning and walking back to the wall, he casually inserted a couple of fingers into the blue glow of the control and stepped through the opening it produced. As it sealed behind him, a familiar voice barked sharply from the dim depths of the temperate sleeping area.

"Where have you been all night? I've been worried sick."

"Good dog," Walker murmured as he made his tired way toward his crib of silken wrappings. Between the excitement of the nocturnal experience and a complete lack of sleep, he was thoroughly bushed. The makeshift cot with its glistening bale of alien padding called to him.

A fast-moving, small brown shape blocked his path and refused access to the beckoning bed. "Don't 'good dog' me—bad human. Where were you?"

"Carrying out research on local agriculture. And making friends." Lurching to his left, he tried to dodge around his companion. George scampered quickly to cut him off. Behind them, Sque slumbered peacefully on, oblivious to the overwrought confrontation.

"In the middle of the night? On an alien world?" Something caught the dog's eye. Leaning to his right, he tried to peer behind his friend. "What happened to your back?"

"Hmm?" Half-asleep now, Walker tried to look over his shoulder and down at himself. "I don't see anything."

Trotting around behind him, George stood up on his hind legs and rested his forepaws against Walker's thigh. "You look like you've been whipped by a dozen angry pixies."

"What? Oh, that comes from leaning my bare back against Braouk's front all night and being thrown all over the place. You know how bristly his fur is. Almost quill-like. It was to be expected after a night of hard riding." Shrugging George off his thigh, Walker made a beeline for the looming bed and slumped gratefully into the mass of alien wrapping material.

" 'Hard riding'?" George was now able to look his prostrate friend in the eye. "If you tell me you were out rustling alien cattle, I'm going to have to raise serious doubts with Gerlla-hyn's medical staff about the state of your sanity."

"Not cattle," Walker murmured sleepily. "*Chimttabt.* The big, purplish striated stalks we've seen growing in several regions. Self-propelled bales of the stuff." He snuggled deeper into the welcoming mass of soft but strong pale blue strands. "During harvest time, the Tuuqalians of these northern plains work around the clock."

"I see," George observed dangerously. "Really dove into local custom, didn't you? Next time I'd appreciate your letting me know when you're going to do something like that. You might keep in mind that I, at least, have a reasonable phobia where unannounced disappearances are concerned. One you ought to empathize with."

"Sorry." By now almost asleep, it was all Walker could do to mumble a reply.

Standing up and leaning over, George dragged his tongue wetly across Walker's eyes. It was sufficient stimulus to keep his friend awake.

"What were you thinking, Marc? You doing all-night research because you're planning on going native? Thinking about settling down, hiring a few tentacles, and raising some orange and purple outrages of your own? Or have you forgotten that we're supposed to be focusing all our efforts and all our energies on trying to find a way home? Which right now means getting our four-limbed, flex-eyed hosts to dig through their astronomical charts and records in hopes of doing that?"

Raising his head slightly to meet George's gaze, Walker responded irritably. "That's what Sobj-oes and Habr-wec and their Iollth counterparts are doing. Our job is to continue diplomacy by further cementing our relationship with the locals. That's what I was doing. That's essentially what we did on Seremathenn, to a greater extent on Niyu, and to a lesser one on Hyff. Don't fret, George. I'm sorry I made you worry about me. Next time I'll wake you up." He nodded in the direction of the still sleeping Sque. "Take a hint from our decapodal female friend and don't lose sleep."

"Sure," George snapped. "Like she'd care if you went out in the middle of the night and never came back. In contrast, I *do* care."

"I know you do, George, but I was never in any danger, and I know what I'm doing. I like these people, even if they do have twice the appropriate number of limbs, eyes that weave around on stalks like balloons on strings, mouths that run north to south instead of side to side, and enough mass and muscle to out-sumo a grizzly. You need to relax." Lowering his head, he burrowed into the hospitable, cushioning alien material. "And speaking of relaxing, leave me alone. Not to put too fine a point on it, but I'm dog-tired."

"Just don't lose yourself, Marc." George was more worried than he let on. "Just don't let an appreciation for the new and exotic make you lose sight of our real goal." Standing on his hind legs with his forepaws on the edge of the makeshift bed allowed him to poke his snout almost into Walker's upturned left ear. "Steaks and pasta, Marc. Not purple and blue pâté. Ice cream and coffee. Football. The sights and smells of the river. Old friends talking. Making money. Going to the movies (unfinished and discarded popcorn being one of George's own favorite snacks)." Using his snout and neck, he nudged the back of his friend's head.

"Don't forget all these things when you're overcome by some new, alien sight or sound or sensation. Don't forget about home. *Females in heat*," he added as a last resort.

It did no good. His human was fast asleep, wheezing contentedly into the depths of the supportive alien pile.

*Stay here if you want, then*, he thought angrily as he turned and trotted away. Or go back to Niyu and try to establish some kind of relationship with your scrawny alien admirer. Or return to Seremathenn and live off the largesse of the Sessrimathe. I can get home without you.

But he couldn't, he knew. Walker was the titular leader of this voyage, having so been anointed by the Niyyuu and accepted as such by the Iollth and the Hyfft. Without him, if only as a unifying figurehead, it was unlikely even Sque was capable of persuading the Niyyuu, in particular, to continue with the journey.

Probably he was worrying unnecessarily. Hadn't Marc expressed an equally strong desire to find their way back home? The human had just enjoyed an exhilarating nocturnal experience, that was all. George began to feel he was being unduly suspicious. Doubtless it stemmed from all those years of being chased down back alleys by marauding abandoned rottweilers and bastard half pit bulls.

Dog-tired. Come to think of it, all the pacing and worrying about his two-legged friend had left him notably short on sleep himself. Wandering over to his own bed, which was nothing more than a much smaller, less densely upholstered version of Walker's, he stepped into it, paced off three increasingly tight circles, and flumped down into a warm, furry, self-contained pile.

When Sque eventually roused herself, the first thing she did was spend several minutes pondering possible new ways to describe the unremitting laziness of the two semi-comatose specimens from Earth, whose respective consciousnesses she was unable to rouse despite the application of repeated prodding and inventive invective.

*

As Tuuqalians ate their communal meals only twice, once in the morning at sunrise and the other at night during sunset, the vast dining hall was empty save for a few stragglers when Walker and George eventually woke up enough to stumble in and request food. Having by now learned which local victuals were tolerated by their system and which would induce, among other things, uncontrolled vomiting, it did not take long to choose a couple of the smallest of the shallow divided bowls the Tuuqalians utilized. Despite the fact that it was not a recognized mealtime, there was more than enough leftover food to satisfy them both. Together, they ate less than a single Tuuqalian would consume as an appetizer.

Sque accompanied them. Not because she was hungry, which she was not, but out of the usual mixture of boredom and curiosity. One could only slumber for so long in the temporary sleeping quarters that had been assigned to them. Also, thanks to the nature of Tuuqalian cuisine, the interior of the dining hall was just moist enough for her to be comfortable. The cool, dry air of the atmo-sphere outside was much less to her liking.

Climbing up onto the now largely empty curved table, she settled herself down to examine her surroundings. Occasionally she would glance down at her primitive companions, marveling at their ability to consume almost anything with apparent enjoyment. But then, one could not expect even an educated food preparer like the human Walker to possess the educated palate of a K'eremu.

His snout buried in the bowl that had been placed before him, George lay on the floor next to his friend. Walker sat with legs crossed and the food bowl balanced between them. It did not matter that the Tuuqalians did not use chairs because the table was too high for him to reach comfortably anyway. Designed for grasping by massive, powerful tentacles, the single all-purpose Tuuqalian food scoop was equally useless. This deficiency did not trouble George, who had no grasping limbs anyway. As for Walker, he was content to eat with his fingers.

As he did so, he admired the gentle arc of the table edge above him. Its curvature was similar to that of the balcony on which he had stood last night, as well as the fluid lines of the scoop ship he had ridden with Braouk. Tuuqalian design was surprisingly relaxed and sophisticated, all gentle curves and smooth surfaces. It contrasted rather than clashed with the hearty, rough-hewn nature of the Tuuqalians themselves. Like the floor of every local building or room he had entered, that of the extended family dining hall rose gently toward the center. So did the ceiling, giving every Tuuqalian room the aspect of a fried egg.

He realized with a start that local architecture set out in physical reality the same kind of undulating meter that characterized Tuuqalian sagas. All of a unified whole, the subtleness of it had escaped him until this moment. It was something he would never have noticed back on Earth. His travels, his encounters, were sharpening his perception in ways he could never have imagined.

He was no longer the same person he had been when he had been taken, he knew. Whoever had said that travel was broadening could never have envisioned what he had experienced these past couple of years. Not that he had ever been prejudiced, for example, or looked on others who were slightly different from him with anything other than usual jaundiced urban eye. But even any subconscious vestiges of suppressed disapproval of other ethnicities or cultures had vanished due to the company he had been compelled to keep.

Look at the Tuuqalians. The first one he had encountered had struck
him as a ravening monster, best to be avoided if not killed outright.
True, Braouk had been suffering from the effects of his captivity and at
the time had not been quite himself, but that still did not wholly excuse Walker's initial revulsion. He had reacted without trying to understand, like a threatened chimp. Now Braouk and his kind were not only
friends, they were, as the Tuuqalian had recently informed him, family.

Family. He munched on something bulbous and blue that back home
he would instinctively have thrown into the trash. It was sweet and fla-
vorful. What constituted family? Was it only blood? A straightforward ge-
netic linkage? Or could it be expanded to encompass shared ideals, other
intelligences, different desires? Who did he really have more in common
with? His cousin Larry, who thought farting was the epitome of witty
humor and who lived only for inhaling the fumes at Chicago-area race-
tracks? Or Braouk, thoughtful and creative, if characteristically long-
winded? As he chewed, letting alien sugars satiate his system, his attention shifted to where Sque reposed on the table just above him.

Five serpentine limbs dangled lazily off the side of the table while
the other five maintained a grip on its surface. From the center of these
serpentine coilings rose a tapering, maroon-hued mass that gently expanded and contracted with the K'eremu's breathing. Set in slots of silver, her pupils were horizontal instead of round or vertical. Like a
butterfly's siphon, the pinkish speaking tube lay coiled against her body,
just above the round mouth. She was about as far from cousin Larry as
anything animate he could imagine. And yet, for all the sarcasm and inherent condescension of her kind, she was a better friend and companion than his blood relation. On more than one occasion her intelligence and, yes, caring, had gone a long way toward sustaining his life.
All Larry had ever done was borrow money.

How then should one judge intelligence and amity? By the number
of limbs and eyes something possessed, by its manner of speaking, or by
skin color or hair style? The more experiences he endured, the more he
learned, the greater the shallowness of his own kind weighed on him.

*When I get home,* he vowed, *it's going to be different. I'm going to be different.*
He would not have to work hard at it, he knew. Travel was broadening.

They were almost finished when a familiar figure lurched into the
hall, searched with scanning eyes, and found them. Lumbering over,
Broullkoun-uvv-ahd-Hrashkin thrust one eye in George's direction and
the other at Walker.

"Still you enjoy, food of my family, for eating?"

Rummaging around in his bowl, an unsqueamish Walker held up

something that back home he would have consigned to his condo's garbage disposal. "The *poatk* is delicious, and so is everything else."

His muzzle stained dark blue, George looked up from his bowl and burped reflectively. "Not bad, snake-arms. In fact, everything here has been good."

Braouk's fur-quills stiffened slightly with pride. "Everything you are eating is of local manufacture. Fresh food of the northern plains is the best on all Tuuqalia, and that of my family famed as among the finest. It is a shame you will not be able to enjoy it any longer."

Frowning, Walker let his stained fingers drop to rest on the edge of the bowl. "I don't follow you. Is something wrong?"

Flexible, muscular eyestalks brought both eyes so close to him that he could see little else. "On the contrary, everything is very right, for you."

From the curving tabletop above, Sque withdrew from her contemplation of distant automatonic machinery to focus on their host. "You have news." Bubbles of excitement burbled from her speaking tube. "Sobj-oes and the astronomics team have found something."

Setting aside the bowl, Walker rose and wiped his mouth with the back of a sleeve. "They've got a direction! They've plotted a way for us to get home!"

Braouk gestured encouragingly. "I am led, to understand that is, the case. That by working together with the scientific opposite number among my people, our Niyyuuan and Iollth friends have managed to divine a Tuuqalia-K'erem vector." Both eyes retracted. "I insisted on bringing you this wonderful news myself."

On the table, every one of Sque's limbs had contracted up against her body. "I am swollen with excitement. Given the inadequacies of those with whom I had to work, this is a moment I was not sure I would live long enough to see."

"And Earth?" Walker asked eagerly. Sitting attentively by his feet, George was wagging his tail rapidly enough to generate a small breeze.

Both of Braouk's eyes curved around to focus on him once again. Some of the initial keenness had faded from the Tuuqalian's voice. "They have what they believe to be a Tuuqalia-K'erem vector."

The kindly Braouk's lack of a direct response spoke volumes. Walker slumped. The energetic back and forth flailing of the dog's tail slowed. The Tuuqalian did not have to say anything else.

Everything of significance was contained in what he did not say.

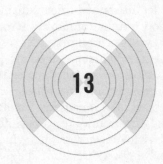

# 13

Returning to their quarters in the company of their companion and guide, they gathered together their few personal belongings prior to departing the northern plains. Walker tried to put a brave face on Braouk's revelation.

"I guess it would've been too much to expect that your people would know where Earth was. We're still isolated, somewhere out on the galactic fringes. It's tough for travelers to find you when you're isolated and alone."

"I think the lyric you're looking for is 'Don't get around much,'" George chimed in. His gaze drifted to Sque, who in her usual fashion was already several steps ahead of them and ready to depart. "I can't see the future." He snorted. "Usually, I can't see beyond the next bone. But one thing I do know: no matter how this ends, I don't see myself spending the rest of my life on K'erem. It's hard enough being around one K'eremu. I can't imagine what living with a whole planetful of them would be like."

" 'Maddening' is the word I think you're looking for," Walker replied understandingly. Though she plainly heard everything that was being said, Sque took no offense at the comments and offered no riposte. She was as used to their sarcasm and occasional jibes as they were to hers. For a K'eremu, it was all part and parcel of a normal conversation.

"You are always, welcome among my family, any time." Discerning the discouragement he knew would greet the deficiencies in his announcement, Braouk did his best to raise the spirits of his two friends. "Or you may choose to return with your friends the Niyyuu to their world, or even all the way back to distant Seremathenn, of which we recall so many good things."

*All the way back,* Walker ruminated. After everything they had undergone, it was a discouraging possibility to have to contemplate. A touch made him turn. Sque had come up silently behind him. She was chewing her morning treat of synthesized joqil, one of the two drugs (herbs, Walker dutifully corrected himself) she needed. Evening time would see her luxuriating in a dose of its complement, the pungent and perversely tempting si'dana. Reluctantly, she had once let the curious human taste the latter. To her disgust, he'd quickly spat it out. The powerful alkaloid tasted like powdered sulfur.

"Do not give up hope, Marcus Walker. How many times these past years would it have been all too easy to do so? I admit to having suffered from intermittent discouragement myself. Who would have not, given the odds arrayed against us?" A triplet of tentacles rose and gestured for emphasis. "Yet here we are on bland, bucolicTuuqalia, having returned friend Braouk to his homeworld. Now it seems that it may be possible for I to do the same." Three more slender, whip-like appendages wrapped encouragingly around his waist.

"By what we have accomplished we have already several times rendered impotent the word 'impossible.' Half of us are to be returned home. I promise, that when we reach K'erem, I will intercede with the relevant authorities on your behalf." The tentacles that had slid consolingly around his waist now withdrew. One arced down to pet George gently on the back of his head, mimicking the gesture she had so often seen Walker perform. The dog flinched, but did not retreat. A pet was a pet.

"Your people have never heard of Earth," a dejected Walker muttered. "We haven't found a single space traversing species that has."

"Just so," she hissed softly through her speaking tube. "But if the Niyyuu can find Hyff, and Niyyuu and Hyfft working together can succeed in locating Tuuqalia, then who is to say what the K'eremu can and cannot find? Would you put the deductive capabilities of all those species up against that of the K'eremu?"

Aware that Braouk was standing right there with them, Walker composed his reply carefully. "I certainly would not be the one to cast doubt on the scientific capabilities of the K'eremu."

"A proper response," she replied in her whispery voice. "My people have achieved many wonderful things. Even finding a primitive, out-of-the-way, backward world such as your own is not necessarily beyond them. I do admit the fact that no one has ever heard of it or visited it tends to complicate the matter, but where my people are concerned, there are no absolutes. Presently, I envision only one problem."

"Why doesn't that overwhelm me with optimism?" George growled softly.

"Finding your world will doubtless require cooperation among the most eminent researchers in several fields," she explained. "As you know, the K'eremu relish their individual solitude. Persuading the germane scientists to work together to try and locate your Earth may prove more difficult than actually doing so." She swelled slightly, increasing her height another centimeter or two. "But as you know, I am not without persuasive skills myself. As a measure of our friendship, I shall exert myself to the utmost on your behalf."

"Thanks, Sque." Walker smiled down at her. "I'm really happy for you, that you're going home. Once we get there, we'll be glad of any help you can give us. We're glad of any help anyone can give us."

"Excellent it is, to hear that said, by you." Looming behind the three of them, Braouk raised all four upper tentacles in a gesture Walker thought he recognized. It seemed inappropriate at that moment, until the Tuuqalian continued. "Because I will still be able to render what aid I can, since I will be accompanying you."

Turning, Walker gaped at the multi-limbed giant. "*What?* But you're home now, Braouk. You're back among your own kind." Raising an arm, he gestured toward the far wall and the distant fertile fields beyond. "Back with your family. Back where you wanted to be." He shook his head wonderingly. "Why would you want to leave all this? George and I aren't asking it of you. We wouldn't expect it of you. We wouldn't expect it of anyone."

"Hell, no," George agreed readily. "I'm not ashamed to say that if our situation was reversed, I'd be staying home in Chicago and waving you a fond farewell. Shoot, I'd settle for staying *anywhere* on Earth." He thought a moment, added, "Well, maybe not Korea. Or Vietnam. But pretty much anywhere else."

"This I do, as much for myself, as you," Braouk informed them solemnly. Walker had shared the giant's company long enough to recognize and interpret certain movements, gestures, and inflections. What he was sensing now, more than anything else, was embarrassment. "I am afraid," Braouk continued, "that I have not been completely forthcoming with you."

Frowning, George trotted up to the base of the Tuuqalian. Though the dog was not much bigger than one of Braouk's eyes, he showed no fear. "That sounds suspiciously like you've been hiding something from us."

Tentacles thick as tree roots swayed a bit aimlessly. "All Tuuqalians dream, of composing a saga, vastly beautiful. But in a mature society such as ours has become, inspiration is often lacking." One eye dipped down to regard the dog while the other gazed at Walker and Sque. "It is said that out of bad things there oftentimes emerges some good. If you had asked it of me when I was a frustrated, introverted prisoner on board the ship of the Vilenjji, I would have replied that such a statement was not only untruthful but heartless." Now all four upper limbs stretched wide to encompass them all.

"But our travels, and the comradeship that has developed between us, has proven the wrongness of that notion and the truth of the ancient adage. From our experiences I have derived much material for, and have been quietly working on, linking together the stanzas and strains of a grand saga that I believe will go down among my kind as one of the better of its recent type. But in order for that to be true, it must have closure. There must be a conclusion that provides sufficient justification for all that has gone before. I thought my returning home would provide that. But since I have been here, I feel it is not so.

"The conclusion to the saga can come only when all of us, when all of you, have also been returned to your homes. That will be my coda. A half-completed saga is no saga worth spinning at all. As for the fulfillment of my personal desires, now that the location of Tuuqalia is known to the ships of the Niyyuu and the Iollth, there will be no problem returning me home. It will always be here for me to enjoy. Whereas true inspiration comes but rarely." The massive torso inclined toward George, teeth like serrated spades locking and unlocking with an audible clicking sound as their owner spoke.

"I hope you will all forgive me this small deception."

With a dismissive grunt, George turned tail on the Tuuqalian. "Why didn't you just tell us that's how you feel? It's no big deal."

"If you had known what I was about," Braouk responded, "it might have altered your behavior. To serve as the basis for such an extended composition, the actions described therein must be entirely natural."

Initially tense, Walker's expression melted into a slight grin. "So that's it. 'Smile—you're on candid saga.' It's all right, Braouk. You can compose about me all you want. I'm just glad we'll be having you along for the rest of the ride."

Stepping forward, he extended a hand. One flexible tentacle tip wrapped around his fingers in the human gesture of friendship Braouk had mastered early in their relationship. There was a time when it would have concerned Walker that the appendage grasping his hand could have effortlessly ripped his arm from its socket. No longer. Braouk might have the look of a nightmare, but he had the heart of a poet.

"Would you like to hear the first quotidian stanzas?" his friend asked eagerly.

Withdrawing his hand, Walker hastily composed a reply of his own. "Still some preparation, we have to do, before leaving. Surely you have arrangements to make, things to see to, as well?"

"Some few," the Tuuqalian admitted. "Also, measures must be finalized for the others who will be accompanying us. It is important, that everything be coordinated, for travel."

That brought Walker up short. " 'Others'?"

Braouk executed the equivalent of a Tuuqalian shrug. "Though your visit has been confined to the territory of my family, the notoriety of your experiences has been widely disseminated and appreciated. I am not the only one who finds inspiration in our history together. Others wish to experience something of it as well and, if possible, gain stimulation from the unique circumstances of our continuing encounter. Also, the government of the conjoined extended families of Tuuqalia is always grateful when one of its citizens is preserved from harm, and now wishes to express its gratitude in tangible terms.

"From both a need to acquire fresh artistic inspiration and a desire to reward you for helping in my salvation, the government has decided to provide four ships to escort and assist you all the rest of the way back to your homeworlds." He straightened proudly. "As you may have observed, Tuuqalians do many things by fours." Again, a single tentacle reached out, to rest its flexible end on Walker's shoulder.

"To avoid confusion and conflict, the four vessels and their crews will participate in and agree to the existing command arrangement. I have spoken with the relevant authorities and explained the particulars to them. The response was amenable. They foresee no difficulty placing the ships under your nominal command."

Walker swallowed. This was getting out of hand. All he had hoped for, when leaving Seremathenn for Niyu, was to find one ship crewed by one sentient species that might be willing to help him and George, Sque and Braouk, find their respective ways home. Now, like some rolling galactic stone, they had gathered to them a very impressive cluster of twelve starships. With him as the ostensible head of operations. He might in truth be little more than a facilitating figurehead, but even that responsibility was growing daunting.

"That's very kind of the extended families." More than a little overwhelmed, it was all he could think of to say.

George was more openly delighted. "One Tuuqalian ship would be enough to scare off any troublemakers. Four of them should be enough to scare anybody. And if that doesn't work, we can always sic the Iollth and the Niyyuu on anything that happens to get in our way. They'd both enjoy the digression."

"We're not siccing anybody on anybody," Walker warned the dog sternly. "This is and will stay a peaceful expedition, no matter how many decide to join in."

"As a show of force," Sque opined from behind them, "the number and diversity of vessels that will now be traveling with us should be more than adequate to stop any confrontation aborning. Even a K'eremu will acknowledge that an overwhelming display of strength is sometimes an adequate substitute for lack of intelligence."

*

There was no impressive ceremony of departure. For all their individual size and strength, and for all the accomplishments of their advanced society, the Tuuqalians were a modest folk. Accompanied by a Braouk reenergized by his return to his homeworld, the travelers were farewelled simply and efficiently and waved on their way. All of it recorded for posterity and with suitably breathless commentary by the ever effervescent representatives of the Niyyuu media, of course.

But there was nothing modest about the four vessels that had moved into orbit proximate to those of the Niyyuu and the Iollth. Even the combative Iollth were impressed, if not actually awed. Each of the arriving Tuuqalian craft was larger than any several Niyyuuan or Iollth ships combined.

Perhaps it was inevitable that a certain tension ensued. It did not last long, as representatives of both of the travelers' allies were immediately invited to tour the newest additions to the expedition. The blocky, multi-cube component designs of the Tuuqalian craft reflected the needs of their oversized crews rather than any military excess. Noting this, Iollth and Niyyuu alike were quickly able to relax and enjoy the educational visits. In turn, crew from the Tuuqalian quartet were invited to visit their counterparts. While this was manageable on the larger Niyyuuan craft, including the Jhevn-Bha, all visits to the five Iollth ships had to be conducted virtually, since none featured internal corridors expansive enough to allow the passage of even a small Tuuqalian.

The exchange of visits and information was followed by a small designated chorus of composers on board the Tuuqalian vessels who commenced creating a special saga to commemorate the unusual coming together. By the end of the first day of continuous and unrelenting recitation, Iollth and Niyyuu alike were more than ready to begin the next stage of the journey.

Navigators provided the necessary equations to ensure that the ships from three different worlds maintained constant speed and contact during the crossing from Tuuqalia to K'erem. When these were executed, the consequences would have been an impressive sight to observe from any other vessel in orbit. Twelve ships featuring the most advanced engineering skills of three different sentient species, all departing simultaneously from the vicinity of Tuuqalia. There would be no noise, of course, but Walker was informed that the synchronized ignition of a dozen interstellar drives should be bright enough to be visible from Tuuqalia's surface.

He was not in a position to witness it, choosing to while away the time in his living quarters on board the Jhevn-Bha until the galactic flotilla was well under way. Though soon cleared to move about, he found that he had no urge to do so. Far more sensitive to his companion's frame of mind than anyone else, George leaped up onto Walker's makeshift bed and settled himself down beside his friend.

"Okay—now what's wrong?" One paw rubbed down an ear. "I swear, it's always been a wonder to me that the whole human species hasn't died out from a surfeit of excessive moodiness."

Walker had to smile. Reaching down, he ruffled the fur on the back of George's neck. In response, the dog rolled over onto his back and presented for attention his far less hirsute belly. Without thinking, Walker obliged, staring at the blank, pale beige ceiling as he caressed the dog's underside. On the far side of the living quarters the Niyyuu had modified to suit the needs of their singular guests, Sque lay flattened out in her makeshift artificial pond with only her head and upper body visible above the dark, brine-infused water.

Though there was room enough for Braouk to join them, their Tuuqalian companion was not present, having understandably chosen to spend time aboard a ship of his own people among his own kind. He would rejoin them again, Walker had been assured, as soon as they entered orbit around K'erem. After all, it would do nothing to advance the work on his ongoing saga if he remained separated from them at such moments.

"I'm just tired, George. Tired of traveling, tired of strange places and peoples. Tired of trying to keep my spirits up when nobody has ever heard of Earth or has any idea where it might be."

"That is not entirely true."

As he turned onto his right side, Walker forced a grumbling George to adjust his own position accordingly. Slinking silently, Sque had emerged from her pond and ambled over to join them. Reaching over the bed, the flexible tip of one tentacle rested against the human's sternum.

"C'mon, Sque," Walker murmured. "You really don't think your people know where Earth is, do you?"

"I admit that there is no reason why they should." The pink speaking tube wove and danced as she spoke, like the wriggling bait of an anglerfish. "Your world has no contact with the civilizations of the galaxy, therefore the civilizations of the galaxy have no contact with it, save for the occasional isolated and highly informal visit by such as the Vilenjji. But you must not underestimate the abilities of the K'eremu. My people are, as you already know, intellectually superior in every way to any species you have thus far encountered."

"Sez you," declared an unapologetic George, unwilling to let the blanket avowal go unchallenged.

As usual, it was left to Walker to maintain the peace. "You've frequently demonstrated your own cerebral gifts to us during the time we've spent together, Sque. And I'm not doubting that there are individuals among your kind who equal and even exceed your own abilities."

"One must not concede to excess," the K'eremu corrected him primly. "However, there are certainly specialists in such fields as astronautics whose experience in those areas is greater than mine. Strive as one might, one cannot claim to be an authority on everything."

As George was about to respond, Walker gently but firmly used his right hand to cover the dog's snout and clamp his jaws together. He continued the conversation, ignoring the claws that pawed irritably at his grip.

"You really think there's a chance that your scientists can find Earth?"

She drew herself up and swelled importantly, bubbles of emphasis spewing intermittently from her speaking tube. "Remember that I remarked a moment ago that it was 'not entirely true' that no one had any idea where your homeworld lies." Several limbs gestured toward the hovering image that supplied the room's only external view. "We know that we are in the right region of the galaxy, because the Vilenjji took the Tuuqalian Braouk, myself, and the two of you from worlds in the same general vicinity. We know that from comparing the relative elapsed time between our abductions."

"A 'vicinity' hundreds, if not thousands, of light-years in extent," George pointed out crustily as he finally succeeded in twisting his jaws free of Walker's constraining grasp.

"That is still something," Sque argued. "Better to have hundreds or thousands of light-years to search than a million. Better to know that such a search is commencing on the correct side of the galaxy. I reiterate: do not underestimate the skills of my people."

"I'm not underestimating them," Walker insisted. "I'm just trying to be realistic about the scope and difficulty of the undertaking." His voice dropped to a murmur. "No matter what happens, it ought to provide more good material for the saga Braouk is composing, anyway."

She gestured with a pair of appendages. "That attitude, at least, is sensible."

"What about you, Sque? I've been watching you ever since we left the Tuuqalian system. You don't seem to be very excited at the thought of finally returning home."

"I am thrilled beyond imagination," she responded in her usual measured tones. "I am eager to the point of self-voiding. Every sentient reveals such feelings in the manner unique to their species. The K'eremu are not what you would call overly demonstrative. But I assure you that I have, since the day of my abduction, not failed to count the moments until I might once again sprawl tranquil and flaccid in the bowels of my own dwelling." Her lengthwise pupils regarded him unblinkingly.

"Having in the course of the time we have spent together learned enough about me and my kind, you will understand, of course, when I do not invite you to share that particular space with me for more than the least amount of time that is considered minimally polite."

Walker nodded understandingly. "The K'eremu passion for individual privacy. We wouldn't think of intruding." He looked down to his left. "Would we, George?"

"Why would anyone want to?" the dog muttered. "I can find damp, dark, stinky, and claustrophobic on my own. I don't need an invitation."

"Then all will be well." Sque slipped backward a body length or so, the end of her limb withdrawing from contact with the human's chest. "Though it may be difficult and time-consuming to assemble together a sufficiency of authority to render the necessary decisions to assist you in your search, I am confident that I can do so. By aiding me in my escape from the Vilenjji . . ."

"Now just a minute," George began angrily, "just who aided who?"

". . . you have caused my society to incur a corresponding debt. As every K'eremu life is unique and irreplaceable, the munificent gesture you have made must be reciprocated. It constitutes a debt that cannot be ignored. Appropriate assistance will be forthcoming. I will see to it." Leaving that assurance hanging in the air, she scurried rather magisterially back to her tank.

Walker rolled over onto his back again. Though Sque was an insufferable egotist, she had more than once proven herself a true friend. He had no doubt she would be as good as her word. The uncertainty that nagged at him revolved not around her, but her kind.

On a world populated entirely by insufferable egotists, how did anyone, including one of their own kind, persuade them to cooperate long enough to help anyone besides themselves?

14

As with all journeys between star systems, that between Tuuqalia and far-flung K'erem was interminable and boring. *How quickly we become jaded to the extraordinary,* Walker thought. It was no different with his own civilization. Each generation came to accept as normal and natural, if not a birthright, the unqualified miracles of its predecessor. As for himself, he was privileged, or cursed, to have come to accept as ordinary such things as interstellar travel, a multitude of sentient nonhuman races, the ability to perform gastronomic wonders with some judicious waving of his hands, and other marvels any one of which would individually have been regarded back home as the discovery of the age.

A real cup of coffee, he mused. Brewed from beans as opposed to being synthesized through advanced alien chemistry. Now that truly would be a miracle he could worship.

Having spent so much time in the company of the redoubtable Se-qui'aranaqua'na'senemu and listening to her never-ending descriptions of her homeworld—the finest and most engaging in the galaxy, of course—he was not surprised by his first sight of it on the internal viewer when the flotilla emerged from deepspace several AUs out. Shrouded in mostly low cloud broken only occasionally by open sky, it was a maze of thousands of small, low-lying landmasses. Not one of them was larger than Greenland, and few appeared, at least from space, much more hospitable.

Sque, on the other hand, was quietly ecstatic. "That I should have survived long enough to see such a sight once again," she murmured as together she, Walker, and George viewed the images that central command caused to be relayed to all operative imagers. In front of them, efficiently mimicking the appearance of solidity, hovered a vision of K'erem about a meter in diameter; all gray terrain, scattered seas, and brooding cloud cover. "Is it not beautiful beyond all others, my home?"

Walker hastened to concur, leaving it to George to add, "Reminds me of a particularly gloomy alley I once had to seek shelter in during a winter storm." Raising a paw, he indicated a lower corner of the image. "There's something that's not a geographical feature. It's moving too fast."

Sque approached as close to the image as she could without actually entering and distorting it. "A ship of my people, I should expect, coming up to meet us."

"Wouldn't there be orbit-to-ground communication first?" Walker queried her, frowning slightly.

She turned toward him. "I am sure the redoubtable Commander-Captain Gerlla-hyn, his contact team, and the committed communications caste of the Iollth have been attempting to do exactly that ever since we arrived within suitable range. They are, however, not as familiar with the customs of my kind as are you. Establishing contact from the surface would imply acceptance of arrival."

"In case you and your aloof kinfolk haven't noticed," George commented dryly, "we've already arrived. It's a fatal accompli."

"You have only arrived physically. Until proper communication is established, you have not arrived in the minds of the K'eremu. Hence the custom of making first greeting an extra-atmospheric one." Pivoting once more to face the suspended planetary image, she studied it anew. "Definitely a ship."

"One ship?" A curious Walker also focused his attention on the lower corner of the image.

This time she replied without looking over at him. "One ship is enough. One ship is always enough."

He was not surprised by her observation. From the years he had spent in her company, Walker knew that irrespective of the situation, Sque was unable to make a distinction between being completely self-assured or unreservedly overconfident. There was no in-between. Evidently, it was the same with all K'eremu.

What did surprise him, not to mention take his breath away, was the appearance of the K'eremu ship. While those of the Tuuqalia, Niyyuu, and Iollth differed in design, all were at heart functional and efficient, the end product of work by mathematicians and engineers. Rising from the cloudy surface of the planet below, the single approaching K'eremu craft was—unexpectedly beautiful.

It was not simply a matter of execution. The attention to external aesthetics was deliberate. Svelte and slippery where the construction of the visiting starships was blocky and rough, the ship looked more like the focal pendant of a gigantic brooch. Multi-hued lights of every color flashed in imaginative patterns from its molded flanks: a detail, he realized, that duplicated stylistically if not functionally the strands of metal and other materials with which Sque daily adorned her own person. Just as they contrasted sharply with her own mottled maroon skin and shape, so the artistic affectations that encrusted the gunmetal gray-black body of the K'eremu starship stood out sharply against its glossy-smooth sides. Compared to the singular sleekness of the new arrival, the space-traversing vessels of the three visiting races looked ungainly and bloated. The sheer beauty of the K'eremu craft was intimidating. He could not help wondering if the effect was intentional.

Despite its gratuitously lustrous appearance, he had no doubt it was fully functional—as would be any weapons it carried. Whether the latter could hold their own against the combined firepower of, say, twelve visiting vessels representing the apex of science as practiced within three different systems he did not know. But if it was all in the last analysis an exhibition of supreme (or foolish) overconfidence, it constituted a bluff of which any trader on the exchange back home would have been unashamedly proud.

He did not bother to inquire of Sque if that was actually the case. That was a matter for Gerlla-hyn and his fellow tacticians among the Iollth and the Tuuqalia to decide.

Perhaps not by themselves, however. Their living quarters' communicator promptly filled the room with a request for the guest traveler

Sequi'aranaqua'na'senemu to please report to ship communications, so that she might aid in furthering formal contact with her people.

"Late," she commented as she turned to comply. "The call for my assistance should have be made the instant the contact craft was detected rising from the surface."

"Maybe sensors didn't pick it up it until just now," Walker pointed out as he slipped off his bed and moved to join her.

Turning to look up at him, she continued scuttling on her way. When one is equipped with ten limbs spaced equidistantly around one's body, every point of the compass is equally easy to access.

"The contact vessel would have made its presence known immediately after liftoff, so that there would be no confusion among visitors as to its nature. That there has been no panicky shooting speaks well of our escort." She expanded to twice normal size, then contracted. "Even at this point in time, when contact is imminent, I find it hard to countenance that I will soon be again conversing with my own kind."

"Bet you can't wait for it," George declared, muting his usual cynicism.

"I anticipate it with boundless glee," she confessed as they moved out into the corridor and started toward the section of the *Jhevn-bha* where Command was located. "A day or two of unbridled conversation and contact. Then travel to my own residence, that I can only hope has been preserved, followed by thorough immersion in a period of blissful extended solitude."

Walker shook his head. Their obvious intelligence notwithstanding, it never ceased to amaze him how a species as ferociously introverted as the K'eremu had managed to build a viable civilization, much less one capable of interstellar travel. Strikingly attractive interstellar travel, if the ship that had now joined the visiting flotilla was not a deliberate aberration. Wondering if the interior was as extravagantly decorated as the outside, he hoped they might be offered the opportunity to visit.

They were not. Permission to board was explicitly refused. Indeed, Sque appeared somewhat put out by the Niyyuuan officer who ventured to make the request. The denial was not reflective, she explained, of any kind of overt hostility. As her human, canine, and Tuuqalian companions could attest, the K'eremu simply were not fond of company, under any circumstances.

Though on the face of it that observation seemed to portend difficulty in expanding further contact, the contrary proved to be the case. In fact, it was much easier to obtain permission to land on K'erem than it had been to visit Tuuqalia. While the precise nature of the permission

granted was the exact opposite of effusive, the necessary formalities
were executed swiftly and efficiently. Anyone who wanted to visit the
surface would be allowed to do so—although in the absence of a local
guide such as Sque, their movements would be severely circumscribed.

As representatives not only of the visiting vessels but of their own
adverse situation, Walker and George were included in the first landing
party. So was Braouk, who eagerly anticipated adding whole stanzas to
his ongoing saga. Sobj-oes and her assistant Habr-wec were added
along with representatives of the Iollth and Tuuqalian scientific staffs, in
the hope that work could begin immediately utilizing the knowledge
of their K'eremu counterparts in the search for the unknown world
called Earth.

Descending to the surface via shuttle, Walker was struck by the
dearth of lights on the nightside. While not actually surprised by the
lack of any visible proof for the existence of urban concentrations,
familiar as he was thanks to Sque with the K'eremu dislike of crowds,
the complete nonexistence of any such suggested a primitive and backward society, which he knew for a fact the K'eremu were not. The
construction of complex apparatus such as starships, for example, required extensive manufacturing facilities incorporating functioning
high technology.

"Like our dwellings, we prefer to sequester such things below the
surface," she informed him when he inquired about the apparent ambiguity. "Also, a great deal of our industrial complex is highly mecha-
nized. More so even than what you saw on Seremathenn." Silver-gray
eyes only slightly more vibrant than the clouds they were preparing to
penetrate looked up at him. "Surely you did not envision my kind toil-
ing away in the heat and repetition of a common industrial plant?"

Secured in a nearby landing seat that had been specially adapted to
accommodate his diminutive form, George glanced over. "Yeah, Marc,
what were you thinking? Imagine a K'eremu deigning to get its tentacles dirty with manual labor!"

As usual, the dog's sarcasm was lost on Sque, who simply accepted
the canine observation as a statement of fact. "Precisely the point. All
such activities on K'erem have been automated for a very long time indeed. They are appropriately supervised, and provide adequately for the
needs of the population."

It certainly explained the absence of lights, Walker reflected as the
rapidly descending Niyyuuan shuttle simultaneously entered atmosphere and daylight. Also the scarcity of any aboveground structures of
consequence. Instead of cities, they passed low over rocky, heavily

weathered islands and a few larger landmasses. Vegetation was abundant, but tended to be twisted and low to the ground. There were no jungles, no tall forests—at least, none that were visible to the shuttle's sensors. Here and there a single, unexpectedly tall tree or analogous local growth shot skyward like a solitary spire, a dark green landmark isolated in an otherwise endless heath- and moor-like landscape.

Reflecting the want of urbanization, there did not even appear to be a designated landing facility. That only revealed itself when, in response to their arrival and patient hovering, a portion of rocky terrain irised open to divulge a dry and expansive subterranean port. Descending in response to lackluster but adequate instruction from below, the shuttle settled gently to touchdown. Engines died. After years in Vilenjji captivity and additional ones spent in sometimes hopeful, sometimes despairing wandering, Sque had come home.

Almost, Walker decided. No doubt there were still formalities to be concluded. Hopefully, they would not involve anything as intimidating as those they had been forced to deal with on Tuuqalia, or as complex as those they had adapted to on Niyu.

First impressions certainly hinted at a different approach. As they emerged from the shuttle, their formal arrival on K'erem being thoroughly documented by the ever present Niyyuuan media, Walker and his friends were greeted by—nothing. Not only was no crowd or group present to welcome one of their own back to the communal fold, there was not even a single official present to direct them to the proper office. Bemused, Walker glanced upward. Though an unseen, unsensed field of some kind kept the fine mist that was falling from entering the landing facility, the air within was still noticeably cool and damp. Optimum climate for a K'eremu, he knew, drawing his lightweight clothing a little tighter around him. Of his friends, only he felt a chill. Braouk and George both came equipped with their own built-in insulation. Still, he was not alone in his climatic sensitivity. Both the hairless Niyyuu and short-furred Iollth were similarly affected.

Scuttling to the fore, Sque called back to him and, by inference, to the rest of the landing party as well. "Please wait here a moment. It is necessary that I deal with the formalities."

Halting halfway between the shuttle and a vitreous gray bulge in the nearest wall, she generated from her speaking tube a sequence of perfectly tuned whistles accompanied by a stream of bubbles. A portal appeared in the bulge. Slowly radiating concentric rings of force rippled through the material as the gap widened, reminding Walker of the effect he used to produce as a child by dropping a slice of apple into a

bowl of hot cereal. As a first indication of the stature of K'eremu science, the expanding doorway was pretty impressive.

Another K'eremu, only the second he had ever seen, scurried
through the opening and moseyed forward to halt directly in front of
Sque. Multiple appendages rose and touched, stroked and gripped, executing an intricate pantomime that would have put the most complex
human handshake to shame. After several minutes of this, while Walker
and the other visitors watched with interest, the newly arrived K'eremu
pivoted and retreated back the way it had come. Sque returned to her
companions.

"We can move along now."

Walker gaped at her. Behind him, Sobj-oes and the rest of the waiting Niyyuu and Iollth looked uncertain.

"That's it?" he mumbled. "What about formal immigration procedures? Registration? Signifying that we're here only for peaceful purposes?"

"Everything has been taken care of," she assured him genially. Leaning the upper portion of her body slightly to her right, she directed her
attention to Sobj-oes and the rest of the scientific compliment. "I will
initiate proceedings to place you in touch with your superiors here.
Meanwhile facilities, of a sort, will be made ready to accommodate
you." Her eyes shifted back to Walker, George, and Braouk. "Amenities
for travelers are limited. K'erem knows many visitors, but for some reason they do not choose to linger."

Walker let his gaze rove over the unadorned landing area, defunct
of life, much less any kind of formal greeting. Overhead, the gray and
cloudy sky continued to weep cold damp on a barren surface landscape.
"Maybe it's the enthusiastic welcome they get."

"Or maybe it's the balmy weather," George added distaste-fully.
"This I can get at home in March. If it's like this here all year round . . ."

"The climate today is most salubrious," Sque countered, slightly
miffed. A pair of tentacles beckoned. "If you will all follow me, your
immediate needs will be seen to."

They shuffled across the flat white landing surface. There was little
of the excited conversation that normally accompanied touchdown on
a new world. Something about the surroundings served to mute casual
chatter. The atmosphere in the landing area was not morbid, just
gloomy. As gloomy as the perpetually dank weather, Walker decided. He
was happy for Sque, who had been returned to her home, but under
the circumstances and that leaden sky above, it was hard to be happy
for anyone else.

While contact between Sobj-oes's team of astronomers and their K'eremu counterparts (not "superiors," as Sque had so casually claimed) was initiated, their many-limbed companion of the past years invited them to accompany her on her return to her own personal dwelling. Having nothing else to do, and loathe to be left alone at the glum port facility, Walker and his friends agreed.

There was none of the excitement and anticipation that had accompanied their similar recent visit to the home province on Tuuqalia of Braouk's extended family. Though the interior of the cargo vehicle that was provided for the journey was sparse and thoroughly utilitarian, they had no choice in the matter of transportation. It was the only mover that could accommodate someone of Walker's size—never mind Braouk. As they accelerated outward from the port, following one of the guidance signals that passed for a major transport vector, the Tuuqalian consoled himself by transforming the sights into saga. Needless to say, the stanzas he composed in the course of their journey were notable for their somberness, though they did no more than accurately reflect the dim and overcast terrain through which they were traveling.

Sque, at least, finally showed some signs of excitement. Her abode, she had learned, had not been disturbed during her absence, nor had it been given over to another. It should be, she told them, just as she had left it on the night when she had been abducted by the Vilenjji. Soon they would have the opportunity to experience real K'eremu hospitality.

"Isn't that a contradiction in terms?" George ventured—but only loud enough for Walker to overhear.

His friend hushed him. "It's not Sque's fault that she is the way she is. The K'eremu, her people—they're just not an outgoing type. Not like the Tuuqalia, or the Niyyuu."

"What," the dog countered, "just because they're conceited, arrogant, self-centered, balled-up bunches of slime?"

Leaning over, Walker put a cautioning hand on his friend's snout. "They're the conceited, arrogant, self-centered, balled-up bunches of slime we're going to have to rely on to help us find a way home. Don't forget that."

Shaking off the human's hand, George let out a resigned snort. "Much as I'd like to, I guess I can't." Standing up on his hind legs, he rested his forepaws on the transparent inner wall of the transport. "What a depressing chunk of rock. I bet there isn't a decent place to bury a bone within a dozen parsecs of this place."

At least they weren't confined to the cargo carrier for very long. Sque's habitat lay little more than half a day's travel from the port where they had set down. As they approached the shadowed, churning sea, cool lights began to emerge from the surrounding landscape, shining from within the depths of homes built into the raw rock, or constructed of material that matched their surroundings so closely it was impossible to tell excavation from artifice. As their vehicle started to slow it also began to descend a gentle grade leading toward a small cove and the water beyond. Eventually, it halted not far from the shoreline itself. A visibly energized Sque bade them disembark. As they did so, everything suddenly changed.

The sun came out. And lit an amethyst sky.

Lips parted, Walker gaped at his abruptly transformed surroundings. So did George and Braouk, when the Tuuqalian finally succeeded in squeezing his bulk out of the transport. Sque had advanced a short distance down an artistically winding path before she noticed that her companions were lingering behind as if stunned senseless.

"What is the matter with you all?" Impatient and perplexed, she scuttled back to rejoin them. "What are you all staring at like a bunch of paralyzed *dreepses*?"

Head tilted back, Walker simply nodded slowly without lowering his gaze to look at her. "The sky here. The color—it's not blue. It's—lavender."

"Lilac-like," agreed Braouk euphoniously. For once, he and the human were equally in tune with what they were looking at.

Silvery-metallic eyes glanced upward from beneath protective ridges of cartilage, eying the appearance of the first gaps between clouds. "Ah—I understand now. What is normal for me is apparently quite new to you. I will endeavor to explain in a manner sufficiently simple for your rustic minds to comprehend."

She proceeded to do so, but while the Vilenjji implants performed effectively with ordinary speech, and coped adequately with the occasional colloquialism, their programming for any language was not heavy with scientific terminology. Still, Walker managed to grasp the basic concepts. Something to do with K'erem's sun being different than those of their own homeworlds. As a consequence, more violet light entered the atmosphere of K'erem than that of Earth or Tuuqalia. She proceeded to add something about shorter wavelengths and higher frequencies, and violet light scattering more than blue, after which the lecture descended into details of optics and physics that were not only beyond the ability of his implant to translate smoothly and effectively, but beyond his capability to understand in any case.

It did not matter. He had understood enough. And no special

knowledge was required to appreciate the beauty of a sky that was tinted amethyst instead of turquoise.

Naturally, it affected the appearance of everything through which they resumed walking: the rocky, uneven landscape, the hardscrabble native vegetation, even the paved path that worked its winding way down toward the sea. Only when they reached the terminus of the walkway did his attention turn from lavender sky to the purple-hued foam that crested the occasional wave, and to the strange creatures that frolicked along the shore.

More than anything else, the majority of them resembled half-drowned bats. But they were not mammals, and the wing-like projections that extended from their backs had not evolved with flight in mind. Fist-sized and highly active, they scurried back and forth, plowing the dark sand with flexing undershot scoops that were more like tapering shovels than beaks. Bipedal, their muscular little legs drove them forward through and across the sand. Their communal hissing as they plowed the narrow beach sounded more like a swarm of bees than a flock of birds.

"Tepejk," Sque pointed out almost affectionately. "Nice to see them again. Young K'eremu are often told to approach life like the tepejk." A trio of tentacles rose and pointed. "Notice the pitch and design of their limbs. They cannot back up; they can only drive, drive forward. To reverse course they must turn completely around. Their legs are designed to enable them to scour the sand that hides their food, tiny silicaceous lifeforms." Turning to her left, she beckoned for them to follow. "Come. Home awaits."

A smaller side path led along the beachfront, past several lights shining from the interior of what appeared to be a low bluff. Sque's abode lay at the end of the winding route. Despite the ease and expertise with which it blended perfectly into the surrounding terrain, she did not have to tell her friends where to stop. All three of them recognized it. Walker sucked in his breath sharply.

The entrance was an exact duplicate of her living quarters on board the Vilenjji capture ship.

"I can see what you are all thinking," she told them, studying the diversity of faces. "You may already have noted that my home lies at the very end of this larger community space." Turning, she gestured up the beach. "Unable to sleep one night, I was out wandering. The Vilenjji abduction took place far enough away from my home to preclude detection. As all of you know, our former captors were quite skilled at their nefarious activities."

Walker gestured back the way they had come. "That must have been quite a walk. It looks like there are multiple residences scattered all through this section of coast."

"Too distant to overhear, or to notice." Her limbs lowered to her base. "Then too, as you should know by now, K'eremu tend to keep to themselves, and to mind their own business. Needless to say, there was no crowd present to witness my abduction."

Flowing easily over the wave-worn rocks that lined both sides of the access path, she worked her way down to the beach, scattering feeding tepejk from her path. Her companions followed without effort. George began to trot up the shoreline, holding his nose close to the ground, sniffing out the details of yet another alien world. Braouk settled himself among the larger boulders, not wanting to coat his bristle-like fur with sand. Only Walker felt comfortable sitting down and letting his backside sink slightly into the cool, moist surface. Walker, and his ten-limbed female friend.

"Home." The way even the perpetually acerbic K'eremu hissed the word brought a lump to Walker's throat. How many times had he uttered the English equivalent silently, to himself? At last, and against seemingly impossible odds, Sequi'aranaqua'na'senemu had come home. Squatting nearby, the Tuuqalian Broullkoun-uvv-ahd-Hrashkin composed with silent ferocity, adding to the extension of his monumental ongoing saga that was intended to describe their travels and adventures. Up the beach, George was now digging at the dark, faintly mauve sand in an attempt to expose something small and vigorous that was frantically burrowing in the opposite direction.

Home, Walker mused. Would he and George ever see it? Or were they doomed to be travelers forever, visitors to worlds wondrous but alien, welcoming but unfamiliar? Could Sque's people really do as she claimed? Much K'eremu oratory was backed by accomplishment, he knew. But not all. The K'eremu were arrogant but brilliant—Sque was proof enough of that. Yet, they did not know everything. They were not omniscient. He did not really care whether they were or not.

He cared only if they could find Earth.

Having stopped digging, George had backed slightly away from the excavation he had made and was barking challengingly at the hole. Walker squinted in the dog's direction. A pair of weaving feelers had emerged from the cavity and were fluttering at the dog's face. Sensibly, George kept his distance, but continued to bark. His four-legged friend wanted to get home as badly as he did, Walker felt, but the dog's one-day-at-a-time approach to their situation allowed him to avoid much of the stress that plagued Walker daily.

*That's the secret,* he told himself. *Dig holes, and don't worry so much about what tomorrow may or may not bring.* But hard as he tried, he couldn't do it. Unfortunately for him, he was a human, and not a dog.

Nearby, Sque lolled in the metronomic wash of the sea, more at ease than he had ever seen her. It began to rain, a heavy mist that aspired to drizzle. Bubbles formed and drifted free from the tip of her speaking tube.

"Excellent. All that was needed to complete my homecoming was for the weather to turn good again."

Walker blinked up at the clammy precipitation, wiping moisture from his eyes. Like hands coming together, the clouds had closed in again, shutting out what had been a briefly glorious purple sky.

"I'm happy for you, Sque," he told her, "but as you know, the rest of us prefer to be out of this kind of weather instead of out in it."

A stream of small bubbles burst from her speaking organ. "I know, yes, I know. Bright sunshine and enervating dryness, that's what you three crave. Desiccation and dehydration." She heaved herself out of the centimeter-deep water. "Let it not be said that I was a poor host. We will retire within."

Sque's dwelling was thankfully larger inside than had been her makeshift abode on board the Vilenjji vessel, though Walker still had to enter on hands and knees and once inside sit on the floor with his head bent to avoid hitting it on the ceiling. George experienced no such difficulty, but there was no way Braouk could be accommodated. Supplied by Sque with a remarkably thin and light but thoroughly waterproof sheet of some glossy fabric, the Tuuqalian sat outside and contentedly compiled stanzas. The chill and dark that would have bothered Walker, and to a lesser extent George, did not affect him.

While the Vilenjji had successfully duplicated the exterior of Sque's home, they had never been inside. The interior was far different from the minimalist décor Walker remembered from the capture ship. In sharp contrast to the rough-hewn, natural coastal setting outside, the interior was lined with instrumentation and devices whose surfaces betrayed a silken texture. Soft light emanated from several locations within the dwelling, their purposes unknown. There were also what appeared to be works of art. All were multi-dimensional. There was nothing resembling a painting or sketch.

There were only two rooms, she informed them. A central, ovoidal living area, and a smaller storage chamber beyond. Everything she—

a sophisticated, highly intelligent K'eremu—needed was in this one room and could be accessed by touch or voice command. To prove it, she brought forth several slick-sided mechanical shapes that emerged like gold-hued polyps from the lower portion of one wall.

"What do those do?" George sniffed cautiously of one of the metallic blobs.

"Kitchen," she told them brusquely. She could not smile, of course, but in an unmistakable gesture of the kind of affection she could not quite voice, one tendril snaked out to gently caress Walker's leg. "Don't you think, after all we have been through together, that it is about time that I cooked something for you?"

Consigned to Sque's care until some notification of progress came from Sobj-oes's busy scientific team, Walker found himself worrying about Braouk. He need not have bothered. As it developed, the big Tuuqalian did not mind spending all his days and nights outside the residence that was too small to admit him. With the bolt of glossy material provided by Sque to help shield him from the rain, he was quite at home beneath a large rocky overhang nearby. As for the temperature, it was often much colder during wintertime on the plains that were his natural home. He passed the days composing. When it was time to eat the food the synthesizer in Sque's home churned out for her guests, the Tuuqalian would hunch low near the entrance to receive his own massive portion, and also to chat with his friends.

Since Sque herself showed no inclination whatsoever to entertain her visitors, and in fact kept to herself as much as possible, and Braouk was preoccupied with his saga-spinning, Walker and George were left to themselves to wander the stony slopes that surrounded Sque's abode, and to explore the narrow beach of dark sand that fronted the cove like a necklace of unpolished hematite.

Occasionally when they were out strolling along the beach, they would encounter another K'eremu. Apprised of the return of the prodigal cephalopod Sequi'aranaqua'na'senemu and of the presence of visiting aliens in their midst, these locals would hurry to scurry away from oncoming human and dog. When surprised, or hailed, sometimes they would reply with a gruff hiss and an emitted bubble or two before vanishing along the nearest escape route.

"They really don't like company, do they?" George commented one afternoon when not one but two local residents utilized all ten limbs to the max to avoid having to confront him and his tall friend.

Walker watched the second K'eremu disappear over a slight hillock fragrant with what looked like acres of rosebushes that had been stomped flat. "They don't even like each other, remember? That's why we've never seen more than two of them together at any one time."

The fur on his feet slick with seawater and bearing clumps of black sand, George trotted along easily beside his human. "Despite what Sque told us about how automated their society is, wouldn't they have to congregate together to build things? Like a house, or a path, or maybe civilization?"

Walker shrugged and tugged his shirt collar closer around him. An intermittent breeze was blowing in off the gunmetal gray sea, and he was cold. "I wouldn't wager against anything the K'eremu try to do, or the way they choose to do it. I guess it's easier for them to deal with automatons than with each other."

George paused to sniff something hard-shelled and dead, snorted, and resumed his walk. "It's their innate sense of superiority. Individual as much as racial. Collectively, they're convinced the K'eremu are the sharpest, smartest species around. And each K'eremu is sharper and smarter than its neighbor. It's a wonder they've cooperated enough to advance as far as they have."

"Yeah, cooperated."

The dog frowned up at his friend. "You said that funny. What're you thinking, biped?"

"Oh, nothing, nothing really." He looked out to sea. A great bluish-green bulk was heaving itself slowly above the waves, as if the accumulated wastes of a million years had suddenly acquired sentience and decided to belch themselves surfaceward. The misshapen mass was festooned with scraggly lengths of scabrous brown growths that writhed and twitched with shocking, independent life. At a distance, it was impossible to tell if they were appendages, parasites, or something unidentifiable.

"You'd think at least one or two of her old neighbors would've dropped by to congratulate Sque on surviving her abduction, and to welcome her home."

George grunted knowingly. "She wouldn't have let them in. I'm telling you, Marc, it's one thing to label somebody as antisocial; it's another to see it applied to an entire species. When a strange dog wanders into your territory, you have to at least make initial contact before you can decide whether it's friend or foe." With his snout he indicated the widespread, artfully concealed dwellings that inhabited the coast they were passing. "There's sure no equivalent of sociable butt-sniffing here."

"No butts, either." Idly, Walker kicked at something half-buried in the sand, jumped back as it shot into the air, spun several times on its longitudinal axis while spraying water in all directions, and landed hard on the sand. Whereupon it promptly scurried on a dozen or more cilia down to the water's edge. There it crouched, looking like an ambulatory rubber glove, and spat at them as it glared up out of a single flattened red eye.

The clouds broke, revealing K'erem's spectacular alien sky. The planet's strange sun beamed down, warming Walker with its eerie violet glow while electrifying the normally dark and clammy landscape with shocking wine-colored highlights. As always, it had a profound effect on Walker, though much less so on the largely color-blind George.

"This isn't such a bad world," the commodities trader observed. "At least, not when the sun is out."

"No, it's not," George agreed without hesitation.

It was enough to halt Walker in his tracks. "What did you say?"

The dog sat back on his haunches and stared out at the alien, lavender-tinted waves. "It's not such a bad place. Reminds me of the city on a late autumn afternoon."

Walker knelt beside him. "Those are about the first kind words I've heard you say about any place we've been. What's changed?"

The light wind racing in off the ocean rippled the dog's fur. He shrugged diffidently. "I dunno. Maybe I'm adapting. Maybe I'm resigned. Maybe I'm losing my mind. They say travel is broadening."

Grinning, Walker reached over to scratch his friend's neck. "The first space-dog. Harbinger of a new species."

"Hairbinger, you mean."

They stayed like that for a long while, man and dog, the former with his horizons broadened, the latter with his intelligence elevated, contemplating a sheet of water that was farther from the familiar wavelets of Lake Michigan than either of them could have imagined as recently as four years ago. Then they rose and, each lost in his own thoughts, made their way back to the compact, low-ceilinged home of their inherently irascible, intrinsically reluctant, many-limbed hostess.

15

Sque was waiting for them when they returned. That is to say, she was in her domicile when they got back. As to whether or not she cared if they returned or if they happened to drown in the merlot-shaded sea was a matter for conjecture.

They were greeted first by Braouk, who was sitting beneath his usual stony overhang letting the occasional burst of purple sunshine warm his fur. Noting their approach, he bestirred himself, rose up on all four supportive limbs, and lumbered toward them.

"The charming Sque, I have been advised, has information. Of what nature she would not tell me, but insisted on waiting until you returned and all could hear it together."

Walker's heart thumped. He glanced excitedly down at his companion. "Finally! Some news regarding the hunt for Earth, I bet."

"Some news, anyway," conceded George, his reaction more guarded than that of his friend.

Wanting all three of her companions and visitors to simultaneously learn the details of what she had to tell them, as Braouk had said, she exited her dwelling as soon as Walker and George alerted her to their return. She carried nothing with her, unless one counted the usual ribbons of personal adornment. Walker was unable to restrain himself from prompting her.

"News of the search for our homeworld?" he asked eagerly.

Metallic gray eyes turned to regard him. Having lived with her for so long, he had learned to recognize certain subtle movements. A swelling here, a tentacle twitch there. At the moment, she seemed ill at ease. That was unusual in and of itself. It did not bode well.

He was right. "No news of the search for your homeworld, Marcus. And I am very much afraid there will not be any news of the search for your homeworld." Her body expanded slightly, contracted more slowly as she punctuated her response with an exhalation signifying resignation. "Because there will not be any search for your homeworld." Reaching up with one appendage, she used it to delicately clean one aural opening. "At least, none that involve the K'eremu."

Walker swallowed. He felt as if someone had kicked him in the throat. "I don't understand, Sque. Why not? What's wrong?"

"Nothing is 'wrong,' Marcus." Though the tone of her voice did not change, the intensity of her feeling was underlined by the fact that she had used his personal name twice in as many responses. "The K'eremu are simply being the K'eremu."

"Slimy bastards." George made no attempt to hide his bitterness.

"I assure you that neither epidermal viscosity nor the composition of individual ancestry has anything to do with the decision."

Walker suddenly felt sorry for her. As much as was possible for one of her kind, she clearly felt disturbed at having to deliver such bad news. She was K'eremu, but she was also their friend.

Putting aside his resentment and frustration, he made himself inquire patiently, "Why won't your people help us? What do you mean when you say that 'the K'eremu are simply being the K'eremu'?"

She gesticulated with three limbs, and this time it was a gesture whose meaning he could not divine. "There is no hostility involved, Marcus. Only characteristic indifference. If the average K'eremu, and those are two terms I assure you are not often used in tandem, is not concerned with his or her neighbor, how can they be expected to involve themselves in the far more alien and complex troubles of others? Especially those of insignificant non-K'eremu primitives?"

"Is that what you told your authorities we are?" George snarled. It had been a long time since he had heard the dog growl like that, Walker reflected.

Sque reacted immediately, and in a manner sufficiently unexpected to startle both man and dog. One flexible appendage whipped out and smacked the dog across his snout. So startled was George that he did not even respond with an instinctive bite. Instead, he was knocked back onto his haunches, where he sat, stunned, staring at their hostess.

"Do you think so little of me, after all this time we have spent in one another's company?" She swelled up so prodigiously Walker thought she might burst, the expression "bust a gut" having a more literal application among the K'eremu than any other species he had yet encountered. To his relief, the furious bloat rapidly subsided.

"That may indeed be what you are," she went on, having brought herself under control once more, "but it is not how I presented you and your case to the relevant segment of K'erem's scientific establishment. Plainly, my account made no difference to those in a position to act upon it."

"What about our part in helping to rescue you," Walker ventured, "in helping a K'eremu to return home? Did you mention that? You said it would be worth something."

"I did indeed allude at length to your humble and unassuming assistance," she assured him. "It seems to have swayed no opinion. Without a compelling reason to do so, no astronomer of K'erem will expend the time or effort to assist your Niyyuuan and Iollth friends in their attempt to locate your homeworld. That if they wished they could do so I have no doubt. The problem is not execution, but motivation." A pair of tentacles reached out to wrap around his right leg and squeeze gently. Apologetically, even.

"I am sorry, Marcus Walker and George. There is nothing more I can do. Rare is the individual K'eremu who can persuade another."

"Because each one feels superior to every other one," a disconsolate George muttered. "A standoff of superciliousness." He looked up at Walker. "That means there's no higher court we can appeal to, because none of these squids recognizes another of their kind as having a superior grasp of any situation. How do you convince a pod of conceited egotists to change their minds?"

"I don't know," a dejected Walker muttered. Wind nipped at his ears. "I don't know."

"I sorrow also, for my good friends, at this." Braouk rested one massive upper tentacle across Walker's shoulders, lightly stroking George's back with another. "The K'eremu are not Tuuqalian."

"Observations of the obvious don't help us much." Shrugging off the caress, George jogged off toward the low alien scrub that dominated the landscape in the vicinity of Sque's residence. Walker didn't try to stop him. Let his friend and companion brood in privacy. They'd had little enough of that during these past years traveling.

He looked back down at Sque. "Is there anything else we can do? Anything that might change the minds of the K'eremu who could help us?"

Half a dozen appendages waved fluidly in a gesture of substantial import. "You can try putting your case to some of them directly; possibly one at a time, certainly not many, since as you know we are not especially fond of one another's company."

Her suggestion wasn't exactly encouraging, he decided, but it was a beginning. Certainly it was better than sitting around helplessly bemoaning the fate to which an unkind, uncaring universe had consigned them. From the time he had been introduced to the Vilenjji capture ship, he had taken a proactive role in his own survival. That was how he had conducted his trading of commodities; that was how he had conducted his life. He would not change that now, not even in the face of seemingly indomitable K'eremu obduracy.

"All right then: we'll start with one. Can you at least line up an initial interview with an appropriate entity? We'll try putting our case to the scientific authorities that way, like you say. One at a time."

She hesitated, but only briefly. "It may take a little while to make the necessary arrangements, but I think it might be possible."

Bending down, he leaned so close to her that she could have touched his face with her speaking tube. "And will you continue to speak on our behalf?"

"Having only recently returned to it, I dislike the idea of being away from my residence again so soon. But"—and she reached up with an appendage to flick him gently on one cheek—"if nothing else it may prove entertaining. A relief from the tedium of everyday existence is always welcome."

"Oh, it won't be dull, I promise you that." Straightening, he cupped both hands to his mouth and raised his voice. "George! Get back here! We're going traveling—again."

✳

The route they took several days later was as familiar as their intended destination. There being no facility on all of K'erem dedicated to the (according to the K'eremu way of thinking) unnatural and downright repulsive enterprise of mass assembly, it was decided to hold the meeting Sque had arranged as well as any subsequent ones at the port where they had first set down. The port, at least, was equipped with facilities for the handling and distribution not only of cargo, which was almost entirely dealt with by servicing automatons, but also the occasional odd guest. Such uncommon visitors had to be very odd indeed, Walker reflected as he and his companions disembarked from their transport and entered once more into the facility, given that the K'eremu were not exactly a warm, wildly welcoming folk.

As he had during the course of his initial arrival at K'erem, he once more had the opportunity to admire and marvel at the smoothly supple bronzed and silvered shapes that comprised his surroundings. Devices and mechanisms extruded silently from or retracted almost sensuously into walls, ceilings, and floor, pulsing with oozing mechanical life. From time to time K'eremu automatons slid, scurried, or shushed past the travelers as they followed Sque deeper into the complex. Walker likened it to strolling through a set of alien internal organs that had been fashioned from several different consistencies and colors of liquid metal.

Infrequently, they encountered another K'eremu. Espying the visitors, these locals would every so often offer a greeting to Sque. Just as frequently, they ignored her. Argent eyes flicked over human and dog and Tuuqalian. They did not precisely drip contempt. They did not have to. If you were not K'eremu, you barely qualified as sentient. And if you were K'eremu, regardless of profession or specialty or age or education, you were superior to everything and everyone else, including your neighbors. Recalling the arrogant attitudes of certain human teenagers he had met, Walker was thankful he had not been forced to deal with any juvenile K'eremu. Doubtless they raised the description "insufferable" to new heights. Or maybe, he thought, adolescence progressed differently among his hosts. When traveling among alien cultures, anthropomorphism was the first casualty.

There were three K'eremu waiting for them in an immigration holding chamber just beyond the point where arrivals officially disembarked from or reboarded visiting ships. All three were bedecked with the kind of trashy, glittering individual bodily adornments Walker and his friends were familiar with from time spent in Sque's similarly gaudy company: K'eremu bling. The slick, shiny skin of two of the aliens was the same yellow-mottled maroon hue as Sque's, though the patterns differed. The third's epidermis was a darker red, almost carmine, and marked with mildly eye-catching splotches of yellow that shaded to gold. Sexual dimorphism being readily recognizable among the K'eremu, and Walker having been enlightened as to the details by Sque, he duly noted that the trio waiting before them consisted of two females and one male.

"You should feel honored," Sque hissed softly up at him. "Rarely do more than two K'eremu come together in person for any purpose."

"Then why aren't there only two?" Walker whispered back at her.

"Two might never come to a decision. When K'eremu desire to reach a consensus, the number involved in the discussion must always be odd, never even."

The trio did not look happy. Dozens of tentacles writhed in annoyance. Introductions were perfunctory and delivered with the same kind of generic irritation Walker and his friends had been subjected to ever since they had made Sque's acquaintance back on the Vilenjji ship. Accustomed to it, he was able to largely ignore it. Adhering to usual K'eremu practice, formalities were, well, brief.

"Speak," snapped the larger of the two females, whose name (greatly shortened like Sque's for the convenience of inarticulate alien visitors) was Alet. "My time passes, and I can think of at least a hundred things that would be better done with it."

Walker looked down at George; George promptly settled his belly down on the shimmering bronzed floor and crossed his front legs. Walker looked at Braouk; the Tuuqalian giant squatted down on his four under-limbs, and Walker realized that yet again it was being left to him to make their case. Clearing his throat, which caused the male member of the impatiently waiting trio to wince visibly, he took a step forward. After a moment's thought he crouched down, the better to put himself eye level to eye level with the three already visibly indifferent K'eremu.

"I am—" he began. It was as far as he was allowed to get before he was brusquely interrupted by the female called Mhez.

"We know who you are. We know all there is to know about you that is knowable by K'eremu." A pair of appendages waved briskly. "I am of the personal opinion that is more than enough. We know where you came from, how you came to be here, and what you want. Your request has already been denied." A couple of desultory bubbles wandered aloft from the end of her speaking tube. "Our astronomers have a higher calling, and better things to do, than waste their time seeking the location of remote worlds inhabited by boorish primitives."

George sprang to his feet, only to visibly control himself in response to a cautionary wave from Walker. "We're aware of your opinion of us."

"Do you dispute it?" challenged the male, whose abridged name was Rehj.

"I think you underestimate us." Walker composed his reply carefully. He was acutely conscious of the fragile nature of the confrontation, and that the trio of scarcely attentive K'eremu might decide at any moment to bring it to an abrupt and unproductive end. "For one thing, as our friend and companion Sque can attest, George and I are intelligent enough to recognize the innate and unarguable superiority of the K'eremu." Behind him, a rude canine noise sounded. Unfamiliar with the nature of the auditory discharge or its possible import, the K'eremu ignored it.

As a result of Walker's comment, some shuffling ensued among the judgmental trio. "That shows wisdom, if not intelligence," declared Alet. "It also conforms to the opinion of another who has exhibited an interest in this situation."

A frowning Walker immediately glanced over at Sque. Their K'eremu companion raised a pair of appendages.

"I have done nothing more than comment honestly on what I have observed these past several years. You should know that I can be nothing but honest."

"That kind of honesty doesn't seem to be helping us much," George observed tartly.

"The other to whom I refer," Alet continued irritably, "is not the K'eremu Sequi'aranaqua'na'senemu, who has been forced to associate with you in the course of your wandering." Pivoting slightly, she gestured in the direction of the fluid wall to her left. Like chrome jelly stirred by an active hand, a portal appeared in the undulating surface and a figure stepped through to join them.

Walker lost a breath. George growled softly as the hackles rose on his shoulders. Braouk started forward, only to be restrained by Sque.

"There can be no fighting here," she warned their hulking companion. Tentacles gestured simultaneously in several directions. "There are dynamic devices present that will restrain even such an oversized sentient as yourself, and not always gently." At her words of warning the Tuuqalian paused, vertically aligned jaws opening and clashing in frustration.

Advancing on thickened, flap-padded feet, the Vilenjji Pret-Klob came toward them, halting well out of reach of any of his former captives. Huge eyes that nearly met in the center of the tapering, cilia-crowned skull regarded them impassively.

"Greetings to inventory," their former captor murmured with utter lack of emotion. "Tracking you has been one of the most psychologically rewarding if fiscally unproductive experiences of my lifetime."

"How did you find us?" a stunned Walker blurted. "How *did* you track us?"

Cold, calculating eyes met his own. "On every world you visited, you stood out, human investment. By virtue of your uniqueness, you drew attention. The media of Niyu, where you traveled upon entering the service of one minor official there, was constantly full of your exploits: political, military, and culinary. That is how we initially located you there. You will recall that unfortunate confrontation, when this increasingly costly recovery operation would have ended but for the misguided interference of some of the natives. By the way, I congratulate you on your mastery of a new skill. I am always pleased when an item of inventory takes the time and trouble to enhance its own value without the need of additional financial input from my association. You are to be commended on your initiative."

"Keep it," Walker growled, no less gutturally than the snarling dog now standing at his feet.

"As you were journeying in the company of three well-armed vessels, we could hardly attempt to recover you through the use of force. Subsequent to your illicit flight from that world, the Niyyuuan media very usefully indicated in detail and at length the next destination to which you hoped to travel. As you know, the nature of our business requires my association to travel quite extensively. We had no difficulty locating Hyff. Though we arrived there in the wake of your enterprising engagement with the Iollth, by presenting ourselves to the locals as your friends, and making ourselves useful in other ways, we succeeded in learning that you were going to try to reach Tuuqalia." Vast flattened eyes shifted to the barely restrained Braouk. "That being a world whose location in the stellar firmament we already knew, we then traveled there."

Mindful of Sque's warning, Walker was also keeping a watchful eye on the silently seething Braouk. "I hope you had enough brains not to try to abduct another Tuuqalian."

The Vilenjji's response suggested common sense, if not morality. "Actually, as we were already there, and had successfully carried out such an appropriation previously, the possibility was discussed. It was decided, however, that despite the potential profit, since the prior acquisition from that world had proven untenable, not to mention lethal,

THE CANDLE OF DISTANT EARTH

it fell on the downside of cost-effectiveness. Hence, no: no further acquisition was attempted on that world."

"How fortunate for you," Braouk rumbled.

"We only just missed you there," Pret-Klob continued serenely, "but by the same means that have so greatly facilitated our commerce in the past, we did learn that you next intended to visit K'erem. We were most impressed to learn that you had acquired the assistance and company not only of the original three craft that had accompanied you from Niyu, but by now of Iollth and Tuuqalian help as well." Eyes appraisingly traveled the length and breadth of the enraged Braouk. "You are well and intact, I see. That is good. Throughout the term of our following you my associates and I were much concerned for the state of our long-lost inventory."

"Not your inventory, this particular saga spinner, or friends." Reaching out with the two massive appendages on his left side, Braouk extended them protectively out over Walker and George. Probably correctly, the Tuuqalian was assuming that Sque was in no danger here on her homeworld. Though where the capricious K'eremu were concerned, Walker cautioned himself, nothing could be taken for granted.

"I'd like to know," he pressed their tormentor, "why you continue to bother. In my trade, when a business deal goes sour and costs you money, you don't pursue it." He indicated his friends. "We'd call it 'throwing good money after bad.' "

"For one thing," the Vilenjji told him easily, "in the course of your traveling, you have accumulated knowledge and skills that have greatly enhanced your value beyond that of simply being interesting uneducated specimens from unvisited worlds. More importantly"—and as he spoke, the tendrils atop his tapered head writhed and twisted vigorously—"there is principle involved. The Vilenjji do not willingly surrender inventory without making as aggressive an attempt as possible to recover it. Also, as I may have explained previously, it sets a precedent that is very bad for business if it is learned that inventory has been able to disengage from us without any compensation. That is damaging for customers to know, and damaging for inventory still in retention to know."

"All right," Walker shot back, his tone an uneasy mix of disquiet and defiance, "so you've managed to follow us this far." He jerked his head sharply in the direction of the three inquisitive K'eremu. "Alet says you have an 'interest in the situation.' I can tell you right now that's as far as it's going to go."

"On the contrary," Pret-Klob replied, unperturbed as ever, "I hope, and expect, that 'it' will continue onward to what I consider to be the most desirable and logical conclusion. Unable to recover our absent inventory by force, the members of the association have consistently sought a way to bring other means to bear on this odious and ongoing dilemma. It may be that those means that would not be practical on, say, Niyu or Tuuqalia may have more efficacious application here." The Vilenjji appeared to gather himself.

"In connection with that I have lodged a formal claim for the return of our absent property with the amorphous entity that passes for local authority on this world." A sucker-lined upper arm flap indicated the unblinking Sque. "With the exception of one among you, the rights to whom my association must for obvious practical reasons abjure any claim."

Feeling slightly faint, Walker struggled to hang on to his wits. Turning away from the poised and expectant Vilenjji, he directed his attention to the trio of silently watching K'eremu.

"This is insane. Surely you can't give any credence to this contemptible creature's outrageous claims!" Behind him, Braouk was already searching for an escape route, calculating whether it would be better to try to flee the port complex or take one or more of the three monitoring K'eremu hostage. Though mindful, and respective, of Sque's warning, he would readily die without seeing Tuuqalia again and with his grand saga unfinished before he would submit to Vilenjji captivity a second time.

George took a couple of steps toward the trio, nodding in the direction of the ever watchful Pret-Klob. "No matter what this ambulatory vegetable claims, we're all of us here independent intelligences. Capturing and selling a sentient is against the laws and customs of galactic civilization."

It was Rehj who responded coolly. "What galactic civilization would that be? Whichever, it is not one to which the K'eremu belong, nor to whose laws we subscribe."

That was right, Walker thought furiously. K'erem lay far, far outside the boundaries of the culture and society inhabited by the Sessrimathe and the Niyyuu, among others. Undoubtedly Pret-Klob and his loathsome association were counting on that.

"Though no decision has been rendered in this matter," Mehz informed him, "it would behoove you to offer a better argument."

"I have an argument." The Vilenjji waved the flattened, sucker-lined extremity of one limb. "At this moment, there are in orbit around K'erem twelve warships crewed by representatives of three different warlike species, with delegates from a fourth." In what was not quite a bow, his cloaked, purple-tinged upper body inclined in the direction of the three. "While I do not doubt the ability of such superior beings as the K'eremu to defend themselves and their world from any imprudent demonstrations of bellicosity, twelve ships is an impressive number. One that, directed and designed by other intelligent races, might conceivably pose a threat even to K'erem itself."

Standing for a moment on his hind legs, George whispered up at his human. "What's the moldy old eggplant getting at?"

"I don't know," Walker replied honestly, plenty worried in spite of his ignorance.

Both travelers quickly found out, as Pret-Klob continued. "By coincidence and good fortune, the commander of this entire force stands now before you. Neutralize him and his companions while still keeping them alive and well, and you eliminate any motivation for those on board the twelve armed ships to cause trouble. And in doing so, you also make permanent allies and friends of myself and my kind."

Rehj could not frown, but conveyed the impression of doing so. "What 'commander'?"

The arm flap that had been deferring to the three K'eremu now swung around to point directly at the startled Walker.

16

Not only was it a clever ploy, an apprehensively admiring Walker had to admit, it gave evidence of the veneer, if not the spirit, of intelligent thought. But while he was striving not to panic as he sought wildly for a suitable rebuttal, it became evident that the K'eremu, neutral in the dispute though they might be, were not to be easily persuaded to support either side.

"We could accomplish the same thing by simply keeping them here on K'erem and preventing them from returning to their ships. Realizing the hopelessness of recovering these three alive, those vessels would eventually depart." Alet focused silver-gray eyes on the much bigger Vilenjji. "Such a course of action, however, would do nothing to satisfy the claim you have made."

Mehz spoke up beside her, the ambient light of the chamber gleaming brightly on his more reflective epidermis. "While not subject to the laws of this distant galactic civilization of which everyone speaks, and indifferent to them, I admit to being personally uncomfortable at the idea that one intelligent species might profit through the buying and selling of representatives of another."

"Keep in mind," Pret-Klob responded greasily, "that by many standards they do not qualify as intelligent. Certainly not by K'eremu standards." He gestured with both arms. "Do they come here in ships of their own people? No. Do they exhibit advanced technology of their own design? No. Have they, since they have been on your world, demonstrated any special insight or ability that would lead you to countenance such higher sentience? I think not." One sucker-lined arm flap stabbed suddenly in George's direction. "As for that specimen, before it underwent an extensive internal adjustment by us, its intelligence was of such a low order it could neither think nor speak properly."

Growling, head down, George started forward. "How about if I think I'll speak about taking a bite out of—"

Whispering urgently, Walker grabbed the dog by the nape of his neck to hold him back. "Don't do it, George. I'd like to take a bite out of him myself, but that's just what he wants: to upset us enough to get proof of what he's claiming." Ignoring the Vilenjji, he turned his attention back to the watchful, contemplative threesome.

"I don't pretend to lay claim to any special intelligence. I'm only a trader in basic commodities—and a chef. If I'm not as smart as the average K'eremu, I'm still intelligent enough to do those simple things, and do them well. Surely that qualifies as sufficient sentience." Releasing his grip on George's neck, he patted the still softly snarling dog on the head. "My friend here can't cook, and he can't arrange complex trades, but he can observe, and analyze, and comment intelligently on what he sees." Jerking a thumb back over his shoulder, he concluded by observing, "And our large friend here is a composer of sagas and sonnets, whose people designed and built the four largest of the visiting vessels that are currently in orbit around your world. I think without a doubt, that even if our level of intelligence doesn't approach that of the K'eremu, it's enough to qualify each of us as intelligent." He glowered at Pret-Klob, who was as usual unaffected by the glare. "Too intelligent by half to be returned to the tender mercies of a third party that intends to treat us as nothing more than a commodity."

Distasteful as they found mutual proximity, the three K'eremu moved close together to consult. They said nothing Walker could overhear, but a prodigious volume of bubbles issued from the trio of nearly entwined speaking tubes. After several moments had passed, it was finally left to Alet to explain.

"Clearly, you are at least minimally intelligent." Walker's spirits rose. "By your own standards." They promptly fell anew. "We are not sure that is adequate to allow us to render proper judgment in this matter."

A stalemate? Walker reflected. What did that mean, if the K'eremu charged with dealing with this business could not come to a resolution? The stated ambiguity did nothing to reassure him.

Just when it seemed that the final determination might as easily go one way as the other, Sque stepped, or rather scuttled, forward. Walker glanced over at her in surprise, while George, for once, sensibly kept his mouth firmly closed.

"While the simple nature of the three primitives whose company I was compelled to share these past several years is undeniable, I believe they have demonstrated intelligence sufficient to warrant their continued existence as independent entities."

Walker immediately looked to Pret-Klob. While obviously upset at Sque's intercession on behalf of the remainder of his fugitive inventory, the Vilenjji wisely did not comment. Not with the current speaker having been among the former unwilling detainees held in captivity by his association.

"On what do you base that conclusion?" Alet asked her. Encouragingly, all three of the arbitrators appeared more than usually interested in what the fourth member of their number present had to say.

Sque was now gesturing with nearly every one of her appendages, executing a succession of complex gestures that were as much dance as exclamation. There was far too much for Walker or his friends to follow. But the combination of words and waves was having an effect on the trio who were to decide their fate.

"On their continued recognition of myself as the prevailing intelligence among them and, more critically, on the aid they rendered," Sque declared in response to the question. Functioning with marvelous independence of one another, her gesticulating limbs individually pointed out Walker, George, and Braouk. "Without their assistance, primitive as it may have been, I would not be here now, faced with the need to confront you physically in a manner I am certain you find as unpleasant as do I. That effort on my behalf alone justifies their claim to retention of individual autonomy: the undeniable fact that they assisted a K'eremu."

With that, she retreated from uncomfortable nearness to the three others of her kind. Walker badly wanted to add a comment of his own, but dared not. Instead, he knelt to let his right hand methodically stroke George's back. Recognizing the import of the moment, the dog continued to remain silent. Behind them, Braouk withheld the saga stanza he had just completed, conscious of the fact that it would be better to wait for a more propitious moment in which to deliver himself of his latest lines.

A second consultation among the three K'eremu went on longer than its predecessor. At its conclusion, the trio gratefully separated. Mehz waved three appendages at them, one for each supplicant.

"In the absence of compelling evidence to the contrary, it has been decided that no better way exists to resolve this apparent dilemma than to rely on the word of that paragon of sentient evolution, another K'eremu." Other limbs gestured in Sque's direction. "We accept your reflection. Your primitive acquaintances are free to return to their waiting craft."

Walker wanted to jump up and shout, to fling his clenched fist into the enclosed, perpetually damp air of the port. He restrained himself lest the reaction be thought overtly primal. Certainly it was impossible to envision a K'eremu reacting the same way in a similar situation. He settled instead for giving George a last firm pat on the head, straightening, and letting Braouk wrap the tip of one massive tentacle around his five human digits.

It was only by chance that he happened to notice the weapon gripped firmly in the suckers of Pret-Klob's right arm flap.

"I and the other members of my association have not traveled this long and this far to be denied that which we seek. The inventory is coming with me."

The oddly circular hand weapon, Walker noted without moving a muscle, was aimed at the lone male among the three watchful K'eremu. They did not appear overly concerned by the Vilenjji's unexpected show of force. But then, a K'eremu never did. Feeling Braouk's mass shift subtly behind him, he slowly raised a forestalling hand. His arm could not stop the Tuuqalian if he wanted to make a rush at the Vilenjji. A tank would be necessary. But the gesture was enough. Respecting Walker's insight, Braouk held his ground.

"Interesting aggressive device," Rehj commented thoughtfully, eying the weapon. "By way of contrast, our far more sophisticated equivalents are notably less injurious."

None of the three K'eremu reached for a control, or made an unusual gesture, or took out a concealed device. None spoke a command or called for help. One moment, a large and very determined Vilenjji was standing nearby, his weapon trained on the trio. The next, Pret-Klob went stiff as purple pine, his body unmoving as a flash-frozen crab spat out by the quick-freezer of a Bering Sea trawler. Pulsing softly, a pale aura now enveloped his body, or perhaps emanated from it. Walker couldn't tell.

*There are devices active here that will restrain,* he remember Sque warning him earlier. For once, their K'eremu companion had resorted to understatement.

"There is one other matter that should be attended to." As if nothing untoward had happened, Alet advanced a few body lengths in Walker's direction. "Now that you know the location of K'erem, if we allow you to depart, what guarantee do we have that we will not be troubled by your annoying presence again?"

"We promise." Walker responded reflexively, just as he would have if he been in the midst of an important business meeting with any client. "We won't come back. Honestly. Not that your world doesn't have its undeniable charms," he added hastily, the trader in him contriving the necessary tact, "but for us K'erem has always been just a way station, not a destination."

"Just one more hydrant on the highway of life." Fortunately, the K'eremu's translators could not quite manage a seamless interpretation of the dog's comment.

"It be same, with me and mine, forever," Braouk hastened to assure the watchful trio.

"What better way to be rid of them," Sque added conclusively, "than to send them on their way back to the homeworlds they seek?"

A voice issued from the partially immobilized Pret-Klob. "Only the association knows the location of the human and canine world. The Niyyuu do not know it, nor do the Iollth, or the Hyfft, or the Tuuqalia. It is so isolated and distant that none are aware of its location but us. It will not be divulged; not even for a price." While the Vilenjji could move neither head nor eyes, Walker became convinced his former captor was staring directly at him, and him alone. "There is principle involved."

Though Pret-Klob could not have known it, it was exactly the wrong thing to say. If only he had not said "only." Because in doing so, he had unwittingly laid down a challenge to the K'eremu.

This time it was Mehz who stepped forward to confront the visitors—still maintaining a suitable distance, of course. "Sequi'-aranaqua'na'senemu speaks sensibly. In the interests of ridding K'erem's vicinity of you as quickly and expeditiously as possible, it will be recommended that our astronomical facilities be encouraged to cooperate with your own meager equivalents." Silvery eyes glanced indifferently in the direction of the immobilized Vilenjji. "So many of the lesser species suffer from an appalling conviction of their own supremacy."

George could not restrain himself. "A failing that fortunately escapes the K'eremu."

"Yes," agreed Mehz without a hint of irony. "I suspect you will all be on your way sooner than you think."

Walker gestured at the powerless, silently fuming Pret-Klob. "What about him?"

Alet spoke up. "The unpleasant creature will be returned to its own orbiting vessel. Hopefully suitably chastened. Neither he nor any other from his craft will be permitted to return to the surface of K'erem. They have violated our generous hospitality."

Walker wanted to say, "What hospitality?" He did not, and this time George held his peace. Possibly because Braouk had, as he had once done with Sque on his own world, thoughtfully wrapped the tapered end of a very large and very strong tentacle around the dog's mouth.

✳

Sque's condescending brethren were as good as their supercilious word. Working in conjunction with, if not alongside, Sobj-oes and her team of Niyyuuan, Iollth, and Tuuqalian professionals, the K'eremu did indeed locate Earth.

Several of them.

As proof of intelligence could not be detected over such vast distances, the grudgingly helpful K'eremu had been reduced to searching for systems that matched Walker's layman's description. Only their astounding scientific resources and expertise allowed them to winnow down worlds abounding from thousands of potential stellar candidates, to hundreds, to—finally—four. By terrestrial standards the four lay unreachable distances apart. In the advanced ships of the Niyyuu, Iollth, and Tuuqalians, the prospective journey was not an unfeasible one.

As they made ready to depart from the vicinity of K'erem's sun, a last surprise awaited the travelers. It arrived in the form of a communication that materialized within Walker and George's living quarters, and took the form of the avatar of a certain very familiar K'eremu.

"A last farewell, Sque?" Walker faced the projection while George dozed on his pillow-bed nearby. "I know we didn't have much time for leave-taking below." He did not add that the K'eremu had neglected to

see them off. While disappointed, he had not been surprised. If nothing else, her nonappearance was characteristically K'eremu. Now, it appeared, she might have had second thoughts, and had decided to project a formal goodbye before the orbiting ships headed outsystem.

"As usual, your perception is inaccurate." The three-dimensional
image hovered before him. "This communication represents nothing of
the kind. I continue to accompany you, though of course I cannot be
expected to tolerate your physical proximity any more than is minimally necessary."

That brought George's head up off his bed. "The squid's coming
with us?"

"Not with you specifically," the projection replied, choosing to ignore the dog's impertinence. "It has been decided that there is useful
data to be acquired from accompanying you on your return. Just as the
ungainly Tuuqalian Braouk has continued to accompany you to acquire
material for his pitiable saga, so I and others of my kind have determined to do so in the everlasting pursuit of knowledge." She abruptly
vanished, to be replaced by a new image: of one of the sleek, breath-
takingly beautiful ships of her kind. The substitution was brief, and she
quickly returned.

"There are twenty of us on board," she informed Walker and
George, in reference to the newly arrived craft whose image they had
just viewed. "The minimum necessary to supervise the operation of a
long-range vessel. Also near the maximum number of K'eremu who
can stand to be in one another's company."

"We're glad to have you along," Walker told her feelingly. "I was
afraid I wasn't going to get the chance to say a real goodbye."

"Uneconomical frivolities," she replied. "Sometimes to be favored,
nonetheless. While we cannot of course greet one another in person
while we are in transit between star systems, there will doubtless be opportunities to do so during those times when we are not."

"Wonderful," George groused from the vicinity of his pillow. "I do
so miss the comforting caress of wet, slimy tentacles."

As always, Sque did not react to the sarcasm inherent in the dog's
response, because to her it was only natural to take his words at face
value.

*

The excitement Walker and George felt as the ships returned to normal
space turned to disappointment when it became clear that the system
they had entered was not home to Earth. The outer portion was home

to the essential number of gas giants, their existence necessary so that their gravity might sweep up planetary dust and debris and allow the formation of habitable inner worlds. The third of these looked very much like Earth, even to the swathes of fleecy white clouds that streaked its very breathable oxynitro atmosphere. There were water oceans, and dry continents, and evidence of life. But it was not Earth. A quick scan revealed that it harbored no intelligence. At least, none that had developed so much as rudimentary electronic communications.

It was an empty, uninhabited paradise. News of its existence would cause a sensation on Earth, where any working astronomer would part with years of his or her life for the chance to be the herald of such a discovery. Instead, it was left to Walker and George to admire it, have Sobj-oes and her colleagues methodically note its coordinates, and watch via the communications system in their quarters as it receded behind them.

"Could have had a world to ourselves," George commented as the blue and white image shrank in the view space that occupied the center of the room. "No one to tell you where to pee, no one to yell at you to stop barking."

"No one to talk to," Walker added. "I'm sure we'll have better luck at the next star."

How far had he come, he reflected. How much had he changed, that he could make a statement like that sound as casual and natural as if he was discussing the next stop on the commuter train that served the Big Windy's suburbs.

But they did not have better luck. While the second system's sun was a near twin of Sol, and the fourth world out was indeed habitable, it was not welcoming. Some unknown disaster or plague had reduced all life on its surface and in its roiling seas to a fraction of what it once must have been. Not even the K'eremu desired to risk encountering what unspeakable virulence might linger on the devastated surface. Their ship and every other departed without penetrating the unnamed world's atmosphere, leaving it untouched, uncontacted, and unknown. Whatever terrible secret it harbored remained inviolate in the wake of their hasty departure.

Having been twice disillusioned, neither man nor dog expected much when the third system of the four identified by the K'eremu was reached. So it was with a mix of shock and delight that they reacted to the news that not only had electromagnetic means of communication been detected emanating from the third planet out from the sun, but that a portion of it matched perfectly the language employed by Walker and his canine friend. Allowed to sample it for himself, a misty-eyed Walker found himself listening to the evening news on the BBC. While not exactly the same language he and George spoke, it was more than close enough to provide the necessary confirmation.

They were home.

After so many years away, he found he did not know how to react. As the ships emerged into normal space somewhere in the vicinity of the orbit of Neptune, he retreated to quarters, leaving George to further query Sobj-oes and her team in their research facility elsewhere on the ship. As he was trying to decide how next to instruct Gerlla-hyn to proceed, indeed, trying to decide how to proceed himself, a Niyyuu announced himself at the portal.

"A moment of you time, human Marcus Walker. I am Qeld-wos. With me is also colleague Nabn-dix. We not formally met. Are members of much respected communicators public of Niyu."

The Niyyuuan media, Walker realized. Ever present, ever alert for a new angle on the return of the peculiar aliens to their homeworlds, and occasionally irritating. Especially at this singular moment, when he wanted, when he *needed*, to be left alone to try to figure out what to do next. Which, he reflected, was probably precisely why they wanted to see him now. Oh well. It would be impolite to deny them a minute or two. He directed the portal to open.

Two had announced themselves. Three entered. The third was not a representative of the energetic Niyyuuan media. Walker's eyes widened, and then he opened his mouth to shout in the direction of the room's communicator.

A flash from the circular weapon clasped in the powerful suckers of the third visitor's right arm flap knocked Walker to the floor. As the pair of obviously surprised Niyyuu turned in his direction, Pret-Klob fired at each of them in turn. The tall, slender forms crumpled. Perhaps they had received a stronger charge from the Vilenjji's weapon. Or possibly Walker's constitution was tougher. Regardless of the reason, while both human and Niyyuu lay stunned, only he remained conscious.

Advancing with the peculiar side-to-side lurching motion that was so distinctive of his kind, Pret-Klob entered farther into the room until he was standing almost directly over the recumbent human. Walker felt as if every part of his body had gone to sleep. The tingling sensation was intense. As he struggled to speak and to move arms and legs, he watched helplessly as the Vilenjji adjusted something on the side of his weapon.

Where was George? he found himself thinking frantically. Paralyzed, he could not call to the communicator for help. Slowly, he felt some feeling, some muscular control, returning. The pinprick, stabbing sensation of returning neurological normality was excruciating.

"Umg . . . unk . . ." He still couldn't form words. Not quite. But soon . . .

"Soon" soon became irrelevant. The Vilenjji was not stupid. His very presence here, on board the *Jhevn-bha*, attested to that. It should not have been. But it was. As soon as he had regained sufficient control of his larynx and tongue, lips and lungs, Walker wondered at it aloud.

By way of response, the calm and composed Vilenjji pointed to the still unconscious bodies of the two Niyyuuan media representatives. "After the unmentionable K'eremu returned me to my own vessel, following my regrettably unsuccessful attempt to repossess property rightfully belonging to my association, I subsequently made contact with the pair who presently occupy the floor across from you. A proper entrepreneur is always alert to potentially useful contacts. Familiar as I was from the time I had been compelled to spend on Niyu with the characteristic excesses of their kind, I devised a procedure that, with luck, I believed might allow me to make contact with my absent inventory yet one more time." The arm flap that held the circular weapon gestured absently. "As you can observe, that possibility has been fulfilled."

Breathing hard, still unable to move his arms or legs, Walker looked up at his tormentor, his relentless pursuer, his primary abductor, and wished he had enough muscular control to spit.

"You bribed them," he managed to whisper accusingly, in reference to the two inert Niyyuu.

"Not at all." It was difficult to tell if the Vilenjji's tone was reflecting as abstract a quality as pride. "They were traveling on a different vessel, one of their own kind. Less than fully versed in the details of the relationship between myself and wandering inventory, they proved amenable when my representatives suggested that there was an acquaintance of yours who very much wished to see and offer you congratulations before your final return to your world.

"Captivated by the visual and aural possibilities inherent in such a confrontation and knowing that I would be alone and isolated as the only one of my kind to participate in the further progress of this expedition, it was agreed that I could arrange to pay for transport and accommodation on their ship, and that when the opportunity presented itself, they would arrange for me to join them so that they could record the proposed meeting between us. After which, having no other choice, I would return with them to their vessel, thence to be reunited with my

own people at some undetermined future date." This time it was the
unarmed limb that gestured.

"On board their vessel I kept largely to myself, both from choice
and need. With Niyyuu, Iollth, Hyfft, and the occasional Tuuqalian mixing freely during the visits to previous systems, my presence went
largely unremarked upon. Each group assumed the other had authorized it. The only risk was that knowledge of my presence might be
conveyed to this particular vessel, and thence to you or to someone familiar with our less than genial mutual history." Now there was no mistaking the conceit in his tone. "Thankfully, that did not occur."

The tingling pain coursing through Walker's body was diminishing, but was still prevalent enough to make him clench his teeth.
"You're right. You're all alone here. Your association can't help you.
There's no way you can—recover your wandering inventory. So—what
do you want?"

An answer appeared in the form of the muzzle, or business end, of
the Vilenjji's circular weapon, as it inclined downward until it was
pointing directly between Walker's eyes. As much as it was possible for
his muscles to freeze up again, they did so. He gaped at the purple-
skinned, big-eyed alien.

"You're going to kill me?"

"I am going to kill you," Pret-Klob replied calmly.

Walker struggled for a response. His initial reaction was to say
something dramatic, along the lines of "If you kill me, you'll never get
off the Jhevn-bha alive!" He did not say it because it was patently clear
that Pret-Klob had already considered and accepted that inevitability.
Walker realized he was neither going to reach or affect the Vilenjji that
way. So instead, he retorted, "You're going to destroy valuable stock?
Without any possibility of recompense? That doesn't sound like prudent Vilenjji business practice to me."

"It is not. However, more than plain profit is at stake in this now.
That is your fault. Your continued existence, and in particular your
ability not only to successfully remove yourself and your companions
from the association's original vessel, but to somehow orchestrate a return here, to your home system, stands as an ongoing affront to every
principle that the association and all related Vilenjji enterprises hold
most dear. It is unnatural. It cannot be permitted to eventuate." The
muzzle of the weapon descended slightly toward Walker. Instinct told
him to close his eyes. Experience and determination told him not to.

Pret-Klob was not finished. "Do you remember what I said to you
when last we saw one another on board the ship of the interfering

Sessrimathe? 'Be assured that in the realness of time, the natural order of things will be restored.'"

"Yeah," Walker mumbled softly. "I remember that. I also remember you saying 'It's only business.'"

The tendrils atop the Vilenjji's tapering skull writhed forcefully as the huge eyes continued to focus unblinkingly on the human at its feet. "Only business. Part of that is to restore the natural order of things. That demands that an incontestably more primitive creature not be allowed to humiliate one demonstrably more superior."

"What," Walker told him, realizing he did not have much time left and thinking furiously, "if I could prove to you that I'm not your inferior, and that we're equals? Would that satisfy you? Would that fit into your 'natural order' of things enough to satisfy you and preserve this principle you're so concerned about that you're ready to die for it?"

It seemed to him that the Vilenjji hesitated. "You cannot prove such an assertion. To do so would oblige me to admit that it was wrong to take you in the first place."

"That's what I'm thinking, too." Making a supreme effort, Walker found that he could sit up. While he was once more fully in control of his faculties, he knew that to yell at the communicator for help would be futile: the fatalistic Vilenjji could kill him long before any help could arrive. All that was left to him by way of a defense was logic and reason.

It was time, he knew, to attempt to make the trade of his life.

"I can't go home," he said simply.

The Vilenjji stared at him, unblinking as ever. "Of course you cannot. I am going to kill you."

"Even if you don't kill me, even if you weren't here, I can't go home."

The muzzle of the alien weapon wavered ever so slightly. "I do not understand. Do not take my noncomprehension as an admission of equality," he added quickly.

"I won't." Walker found it was surprisingly easy to warm to his task. It was something he'd been ruminating on, had been forced to ponder, for a long, long time. "Finally, actually getting here makes me realize something that's been nagging at me and troubling me for some time now. I've changed too much." Finding he could once more control his arms, he made use of them to emphasize his conversion. "I can't go home anymore."

The Vilenjji stared at him.

"After everything that's happened, after all I've been through, I just don't think I can do it. I'm not a citizen of one world anymore. Not of any world. I've been exposed to too many wonders, seen too much, to go back to living on one small, out-of-the-way, backward world, however familiar. I thought that's what I've wanted ever since my friends and I were rescued from your captivity by the Sessrimathe." He shook his head in wonder at his own words. "The Sessrimathe. I'd like to see Seremathenn again. Spectacular place, wonderful people. And Niyu, and Hyff, and Tuuqalia. Maybe visit Ioll, and a dozen or so other worlds." He met the Vilenjji's much broader gaze challengingly. "I'd even be curious to see what Vilenj is like.

"But I can't go back. Sure, I can long for a piece of chocolate cake, or a Sunday football game. And I probably will. But would I trade a visit to the mountains of Niyu or a performance of the silica-dancers of Seremathenn for them?" He shook his head. "Not anymore. I've changed too much. I've *learned* too much." He smiled. Not for the effect it might have on the Vilenjji, but for himself. "I've learned how to cook. I can do things no chef back home can even imagine. I might even manage a reasonable facsimile of a chocolate cake. Or trade for one." With difficulty, he struggled erect and met the Vilenjji's alien gaze without blinking.

"I've become as much a civilized resident of this galaxy as the Niyyuu, or the Hyfft, or even the K'eremu. Or you, or any Vilenjji." That said, with finality, he did close his eyes, and waited for the fatal shot.

Seconds passed. The seconds stretched into a minute, then two. A weight descended on his left shoulder and he flinched. But there was no pain, and none of the agonizing tingling that had coursed through him earlier. He opened his eyes.

Under-flaps splayed out to both sides, Pret-Klob had squatted down in front of him. The circular weapon had been put away. The weight Walker felt came from one wide arm flap resting on his shoulder. The last time he had felt such a weight, it had been dragging him forcibly out of his rented SUV beside Cawley Lake high in the Sierra Nevada of northern California. Whatever the Vilenjji had decided to do, he suspected that was a place he would never see again.

Because he had told the truth.

As much as he might want to see the lake, or revisit certain haunts and certain friends, he couldn't go back to the life he had known on Earth. Or any life on Earth. For him, Earth had become—what was a suitable term?

Small. That was it. In a galaxy of wonderments, the majority of which he had yet to experience and could not even envisage, Earth was small.

He was aware that Pret-Klob continued to stare at him. " 'The natural order of things.' It is not a fixed immutable. Everything can change. One who is adept at commerce learns to recognize such shifts. In abandoning your primitive world, you abandon your primitive self. I cannot countenance this change as being one applicable to every member of your species—but I must acknowledge that with which I am personally confronted." Dragging itself heavily down Walker's arm, the end of the powerful appendage attached itself to his hand. Suckers took hold—but not hurtfully.

"While I continue to remain tentative as to the specifics of this unexpected revelation, I am persuaded to acknowledge at least one of your kind as an equal. Or at least, a near equal. Therefore, I will not kill you, Marcus Walker."

Walker managed to remain as composed as possible under the circumstances. "Much obliged." It was another measure of how much he had changed that he was able to add, "No hard feelings. I understand when you say it was only business. I'm—I was, in business myself. I was a trader in commodities. You know—raw materials?"

Releasing the human's hand, Pret-Klob glanced thoughtfully over at the pair of Niyyuuan media representatives. They were beginning to moan and stir, their brightly colored frills flexing spasmodically, their quadruple tails twitching reflexively. He had not intended to kill them, and he had not. Satisfied that they would recover fully, he turned his attention back to his graduated inventory.

"That is most interesting. Perhaps we might even do some business together ourselves one day. My association is always ready to learn from others."

Walker squinted up at the Vilenjji. "Even from former assets?"

A thick appendage gestured meaningfully. "It is the substance of knowledge that matters, not its source. One seeks profit wherever and however one can find it."

"Couldn't have put it better myself. You know, there was this one time I was offered three containership-loads of processed cocoa and I had to—"

He broke off. Pret-Klob was being polite. The Vilenjji would have no knowledge of or interest in cocoa, cocoa futures, or how the fluctuating political situation in Ivory Coast versus that in Venezuela might affect that particular market. If they were going to do anything together, a prospect that remained questionable, it would have to involve matters of mutual understanding. Could he somehow work his newly acquired culinary expertise into any such problematic equation?

"First thing: no trading in sentients," he told the alien assertively. "Even if they're not as intelligent as Vilenjji—or humans, or Tuuqalians, or K'eremu. Not only does it go against civilized galactic behavior, it's not—nice."

"I respect your self-elevated status," Pret-Klob replied evenly, "but it is not for you to render judgment on the commercial traditions of another species."

They sat and argued for some time. All the while Walker wondered at how far he had come, from being a captive of the Vilenjji to sitting peacefully across from one while discussing the nature and ethics of Vilenjji business.

Displaying the noteworthy resilience that defined their craft, as soon as they had recovered from the muted effects of Pret-Klob's weapon, both Niyyuuan media representatives set aside their distress at having been deceived and mistreated by the Vilenjji in favor of recording the fascinating discussion taking place between it and the solitary human.

While they were not shocked, their feisty aplomb was not matched by that of the four-legged terrestrial who walked in on them. It was difficult to say which George found more shocking: the presence of their former captor Pret-Klob in his and Walker's private quarters, or the fact that man and Vilenjji appeared to be engaged in nothing more confrontational than polite and animated conversation.

"Shouldn't be any abducting of dogs, either," Walker declared, adding a cryptic comment to the conversational brew into which his canine companion had just wandered.

Dazed, George entered farther into his quarters, sparing nary a glance for the two Niyyuuan media representatives who were busy recording everything within range of their pickups.

"Captivating reaction," declared one.

"Very attractive, yes," agreed the other as she adjusted the myriad devices that spotted her slender front like so many electronic boils. "It will be well received when played for audience back home."

"What's going on here?" Sidling up alongside his friend, George continued to keep a wary eye on the looming bulk of the Vilenjji. "What's he doing here?"

Reaching down, Walker stroked the dog's head and back, reassuring him. "Pret-Klob arranged to accompany us here in order to kill me. Probably you, too." He returned his gaze to the big alien. "Instead, we had a chat, and we've come to an understanding. Nobody's going to kill anybody, and his association will quit its claim to us. We might even end up doing some business together." He winked at the bewildered dog.

"No kidnapping and abducting of close relations, though. Oh, and one other thing. I'm not going back to Earth." His voice was steady now, confident. As assured as his words. "It's not home anymore, and I've decided I can't do it. I don't *want* to do it. I want to see, and experience"—he took a deep breath, let it out slowly—"everything else. But I'm sure Gerlla-hyn can find a way to drop you off. Back in Chicago, or anywhere else you might prefer."

Recovering his composure, George stared evenly up at his human. Then he stepped forward—and nipped him on the leg. Letting out a yelp of mixed pain and surprise (more the latter than the former), Marcus gaped at his companion. Pret-Klob looked on with quiet interest, while the two Niyyuuan media representatives could hardly contain their delight at the action they were recording.

"George, what . . . ?"

"You stupid, stupid man. You stupefied hairless ape. Don't you remember anything? Don't you *see* anything?" He paused, then added, "Evidently not, because all you can do is sit there with your mouth open and nothing but seeohtwo coming out." The dog began to pace in an agitated, tight circle. "How many times did I mention that on Earth I'd be a talking freak, or have to live an existence as an enforced mute? How many times did I point out that out here I'm just one alien among hundreds? That not going back would be by far the most sensible and rational end for me?"

Walker found his voice. "But every time we talked about returning, every time it was brought up, you were as steadfast about it as I was."

The dog lunged forward again, and Walker jerked his leg back just in time. "There's intelligence, and then there's smarts. You may be intelligent, Marc." He nodded in the direction of the interested Vilenjji. "Intelligent enough to satisfy our walking eggplant, here. But when it comes to smarts, you come up shorter than an addled Chihuahua.

"Of course I talked like I wanted to return home. I did that for *you*. I was supporting *you*. Because your need to do so was so obviously desperate. Because it was all you talked about. Because—you're my friend, Marc." The furry head dropped, then came up again. "Me—I don't care if I ever see a cold, friendless, empty alley again. As far as I'm concerned, the whole mutt-catching, puppy-abusing, neuter-happy place can go to the dogs!" He glanced over at the delighted media representatives. "You get all that? Good! You can add that because of the changes

I've undergone, because of the way I've changed, I know that I'd be better off on Niyu than on my homeworld—though Seremathenn would be better still. Dog-breath, I'd even prefer K'erem. At least the smells are interesting, and I wouldn't have to spend the rest of my life being prodded and poked in the service of advancing 'science.' "

It was quiet in the room, the ship silent around them, the hum of the Niyyu's equipment barely audible.

"Well," Walker finally murmured.

Standing up, George put his front paws in his friend's lap and stared earnestly into his face. "I don't have anything worthwhile to go back to, Marc. But what about you? Are you sure about this? Are you really sure?"

Walker smiled. "I'm sure, George." He reached out to stroke the dog's back, running his fingers down the dense fur. "I've hopped the train I want to be on. I got on board some time ago, I think. It just took a while to admit it to myself." He shrugged meaningfully. "After persisting and fighting and struggling so long and so hard to get back here, it turns out there's no here here for me anymore."

By now at least partly convinced that their former Vilenjji tormentor really did no longer mean them any harm, the dog allowed himself to relax. "How you gonna keep 'em down on the farm once they've seen galactic civilization? I'm glad, Marc. More than glad. I'm happy. I can live out my life without having to hide my ability to talk. Or my intelligence." His gaze narrowed as he eyed the watchful Vilenjji sharply. "You're sure about this 'understanding' Marc says you and he have reached?"

The Vilenjji reached toward George, who flinched instinctively. But the gesture ended in a stroke, albeit one that was rough and suckerlined. "I am not ready for, nor am I in a position to suggest wholesale changes in the structure and purpose of the association. But if better means of making a profit can be devised . . ." He left the thought hanging, along with a steady look at the human.

Walker found himself thinking back, all the way back to his original abduction that crazy night at his camp in the Sierras. This had all begun with a group of aliens who had abducted him with the intention of putting him up for sale. Of making use of him. For some time now, he had been making use of aliens. Sessrimathe and Niyyuu, Hyfft and Iollth, Tuuqalia and K'eremu and others; all had been caught up and put upon and cajoled in the service of him and his three friends. It was not unlike the ways and means he had employed to great success during his work with the Chicago Commodities Exchange.

He found that he was looking forward to the future with high expectations indeed. As to Earth, he would always have his memories to
tide him over any unforeseen bouts of homesickness. Memories, and
George. He would forgo visits to Starbucks for adventures in star systems. Instead of keeping tabs on football, he could watch the well-mannered, carefully structured internal wars of Niyu.

Niyu. There was someone there, as thoroughly and truly an alien as
any he had yet encountered, whose acquaintance he very much wanted
to renew. What would Viyv-pym-parr think if he returned? Of one thing
he was certain: the rabid and active Niyyuuan media would have a field
day with such a reunion, however biologically platonic.

Could there be anything more? In the spirit of scientific inquiry
that had become one of his new motivations, he fully intended to
find out.

But not right away. The Tuuqalians would want to go home, but the
Iollth had pledged themselves to him—for a while, at least. As for the
K'eremu, Sque had said that they had accompanied him in hopes of
adding to their immense store of universal knowledge. As he was their
nominal leader, the Niyyuu might go along with any decision he chose
to render—for a while, at least. Especially if their avid and ever ambi-
tious media had anything to say about it.

There was plenty of time yet before his extraordinary diversity of
friends had to return to Niyu, and to their respective other homeworlds. Plenty of time for him to further cement relations with, and try
to dissuade from the abduction and selling of sentients, the Vilenjji
Pret-Klob. Time to travel, to explore, to *see*.

Rising, he turned and addressed the pair of contented (and now
fully recovered) Niyyuu. "We're not going on to my homeworld. My
companion and I"—he indicated George, whose tail was metronoming
briskly—"have decided that locating it was return enough. We'll be going back to Niyu, I expect."

All four of the female's tails swayed back and forth in a vigorous visual expression of professional contentment. "That wonderful news to
hear, Marcus Walker! The longer expedition journeys, the more opportunities we have for making fine and memorable recordings."

Walker nodded encouragingly. "That's what George and I were
thinking. As official representatives of the Niyyuuan media, you two
might as well be the ones to so inform Gerlla-hyn." He grinned, as
much to himself as for the benefit of aliens unfamiliar with the mean-ing
behind the expression. "Tell the Commander-Captain that the fleet (*the
fleet!* he thought wonderingly) will be taking the scenic route home."

They did not quite comprehend his words, their own translators functioning shy of the comprehensiveness needed to fully interpret the human's comment, but they would understand soon enough.

"Did you then have particular routing in mind?" the male inquired tentatively.

Walker considered. Untutored and undereducated in astronomy, he would have been forced to confess an ignorance of his own homeworld's immediate galactic neighborhood. That there was much to experience in its vicinity he had no doubt. The galaxy, as he had already involuntarily seen, was replete with endless wonders. A tug at his leg made him look down. As he did so, George released the grip his jaws had taken on a pants' leg.

"I don't know about you, man, but as for myself, I've always had a serious urge to see the Dog Star."

Walker smiled. Not too many years ago, and regardless of source, such a request would have been no more than a mild joke. Not, he reflected as he contemplated his astounding and astoundingly familiar starship surroundings and the three aliens who waited on his reply, anymore.

Nor for him and his small and inordinately loquacious furry friend, ever again.

# EPILOGUE

Jeron was very proud of the telescope his parents had given him two birthdays ago. In the time since then, he had mastered its use and added one accessory after another to the basic unit. He'd spent hours and days photographing the moons of Saturn and Jupiter, working his way out to those of Uranus and Neptune as well as distant nebulae and star clusters.

But this morning he was confused. The tiny section of night sky he had set his scope to automatically scan had come back with an anomaly. It was one of those distant areas of the solar system where nothing was supposed to exist. Which was precisely why he had been scanning it. Amateur astronomers tended to find the most interesting things where nothing was supposed to be, and thus where the professionals did not bother to look.

The sequence of photographs showed a mass of incredibly small objects where none ought to be. Furthermore, they appeared and disappeared over an all too brief series of sequential images. Present and gone, far too rapidly to be wandering asteroids, or cometary fragments, or anything else for which he could think of a reasonable, rational explanation. Despite checking and rechecking his scope and its attendant devices and finding them in perfect working order, he knew that the objects' appearance had to be the result of a functional irregularity. Had to be, because they could not be anything else. He could just see himself forwarding and reporting to one of the professional organizations that vetted the thousands of reports turned in by dedicated amateurs such as himself a sighting of a tightly packed cluster of baffling, inexplicable objects located somewhere in the vicinity of Neptune's giant moon Triton.

Especially when the number of them totaled thirteen.

## ABOUT THE AUTHOR

ALAN DEAN FOSTER has written in a variety of genres, including hard science fiction, fantasy, horror, detective, western, historical, and contemporary fiction. He is the author of the New York Times bestseller Star Wars: The Approaching Storm and the popular Pip and Flinx novels, as well as novelizations of several films including Star Wars, the first three Alien films, and Alien Nation. His novel Cyber Way won the Southwest Book Award for Fiction in 1990, the first science fiction work ever to do so. Foster and his wife, JoAnn Oxley, live in Prescott, Arizona, in a house built of brick that was salvaged from an early-twentieth-century miners' brothel. He is currently at work on several new novels and media projects.

## ABOUT THE TYPE

This book was set in Joanna, a typeface designed by Eric Gill in 1930. Named for his daughter, it is based on designs originally cut by the sixteenth century typefounder Robert Granjon. With small, straight serifs and its simple elegance, this face is notably distinguished and versatile.